**BEAUTIFUL AND BOLD
THE TEXAN WOMEN—
AND THE MEN
THEY LOVED AND
FOUGHT FOR**

**Serena Williams Varga**—the beautiful half–Indian, born in a Comanche village, the "outsider" who thought she didn't need love . . .

**Thorne Stewart**—the bold intruder who claimed both land and sensual pleasure with rough abandon . . . and who lusted for *everything* Serena had . . .

**Todd Stewart**—Thorne's uncle, a gentle man determined to make a new life grow with his crops from the fertile Texas soil . . .

**Rebecca White**—the woman Todd loved for her quiet courage . . . and the wife of Todd's best friend . . .

**Felipe Varga**—Serena's son, fiercely proud of his American, Indian, and Spanish blood, prepared to fight Thorne Stewart to the bitter end for the land and the love he knew were his . . .

**Cassie Stewart**—child of the frontier, whose love for Felipe was cruelly interrupted by war.

# THE TEXAN WOMEN

*Corinne Johnston*

A JOVE/HBJ BOOK

First Jove/HBJ edition published December 1977

Library of Congress Catalog Card Number: 77-80708

Printed in the United States of America

---

Jove/HBJ books are published by Jove Publications, Inc.
(Harcourt Brace Jovanovich)
757 Third Avenue, New York, N.Y. 10017

*To Ollie, without whom I would never have won the battle of San Jacinto*

# Contents

Part One—Serena

Chapter I     Hayden Edwards's Colony—
          Early 1826       11
Chapter II    Hayden Edwards's Colony—
          Summer 1826       43
Chapter III   Hayden Edwards's Colony—
          August 1826       73
Chapter IV   Hayden Edwards's Colony—
          November 1826       99

Part Two—Todd

Chapter I     Savannah, Georgia—
          Winter 1811-1812       121
Chapter II    New Orleans, Louisiana—Fall 1821       143
Chapter III   Austin's Colony—September 1825       177
Chapter IV   Texas—Winter 1825-1826       205

Part Three—Felipe

Chapter I     Hayden Edwards's Colony—1826       241
Chapter II    On the Bexar Road—
          December 1826       261
Chapter III   Austin's Colony—May 1827       289
Chapter IV   The Bexar Road—1831       317
Chapter V    The Bexar Road—January 1832       341

Part Four—Cassie

Chapter I     Austin's Colony—Spring 1832       385
Chapter II    Austin's Colony—December 1832       409

| | | |
|---|---|---|
| Chapter III | The Bexar Road—August 1833 | 433 |
| Chapter IV | The Bexar Road—February 1834 | 457 |
| Chapter V | San Antonio de Bexar—Fall 1835 | 483 |
| Chapter VI | San Antonio de Bexar— | |
| | Mid-January 1836 | 509 |
| Chapter VII | Gonzales—February 29, 1836 | 535 |
| Chapter VIII | Groce's—April 11, 1836 | 575 |
| Chapter IX | East of the Brazos—April 20, 1836 | 601 |
| | Epilogue | 623 |

# Part One—Serena

# Chapter I

## HAYDEN EDWARDS'S COLONY—
## Early 1826

The first time Thorne Stewart and I saw each other, something caught fire between us. Intangible though that something was, it was enough to make me catch my breath sharply. As our eyes met and locked, I knew that he had felt it, too.

Ever since my fourteen-year-old son, Felipe, had come home and told me about meeting a little girl of twelve not far from our cabin, I knew we could expect a visit from her father. She had told Felipe that we were on his land, although I knew the reverse to be true. The land—twenty-five million *varas*—had been in my husband's family for three generations. The fact that the parchment on which our grant was written had been destroyed—by the same fire that had cost my husband his life seven years earlier—in no way affected the validity of our ownership. I had hoped that this man, who laid claim to a sizeable portion of what was Felipe's, would, once he knew about the grant, bow out politely and seek some undisputed land elsewhere. After all, he had only arrived a few weeks earlier, and he and the man with him had only begun to cut down some trees and clear a cabin site, and that was nothing compared with the work that had been done by three generations of Vargas. Since Esteban's death, I had let most of the fields return to a natural state, but this neglect reflected my limitations, and in no way affected Felipe's right to every square *vara*. We kept only a few fields in corn, enough for our own needs.

11

My sole aim was to nurture Felipe, his brain as well as his body, see that he grew up intelligent and strong, so that one day he could take over as the *hacendado* he was destined to be.

I insisted Felipe continue learning his letters. "An important landowner must know how to read and write," I said firmly. Esteban had been a learned man, and our cabin had been lined with bookshelves. The books, like everything else we owned, had been destroyed in the fire. Felipe and I were left with little besides the clothes on our backs, three rifles, and the crops already in the ground that year. I felt certain that Esteban had kept a hoard of silver and gold coins in some hiding place in or near our cabin, but though Felipe and I had combed through the ashes, we could find nothing. I think the reason Esteban had never told me where he kept his coins was because of a superstitious feeling that, as long as he alone knew where they were, he could not die. It is possible that one of the peons found the money before Felipe and I recovered from our shock and started to search for it, but it was more likely that it was just too well hidden.

Until the fire, the peons had remained with us in the lawless void which Texas had become following the Battle of the Medina in 1813. At that time, most of the residents in and around Nacogdoches fled to the east, into the United States, and the Spanish soldiers withdrew to the interior of Mexico. Only Esteban's strength had kept our peons with us during those years, and it did not surprise me that they disappeared a few days after his death. A woman and a child of seven offered them scant protection in Texas at that time, for all sorts of criminals and drifters and schemers had come into the state, and honest people feared to stay.

It was not because I was particularly brave that I decided Felipe and I would remain on our property. It seemed wrong to abandon the land that was to belong to my son, and we really had no other place to go. Many of the exresidents of Nacogdoches had fled to Natchitoches, but I had had my fill of living there years ago, after my

12

mother and I had been "rescued" from the Comanches. I had no desire to return.

I had been six years old when we were taken from the Comanche village, and I had known no other life. My mother was a white woman who had been taken as a wife by the brave who had captured her in a raid; her white husband and children had been killed in that raid. In spite of my mother's unhappiness, I had known only content-ment there. I had my Indian playmates, I loved my mother, and I revered my Comanche father. Though he was gone much of the time and never showed me affection in the way of white fathers, he was kind to me.

Somehow, white men had heard that my mother and several other white captives lived among us and, one day when most of our warriors were away, they scooped us up and took us away with them, back to where white people lived.

I still remember my mother crying tears of happiness in those first few days, as we were being hurriedly packed off to "civilization" before the braves could find us. She said she was crying because she was happy, that she was return-ing to her people at last, to the life for which she was fitted. She said I would be raised as a proper lady. In the trusting way of children, I accepted what she said, though it seemed strange to me when she said, "From this day forth, you must forget your Indian name. You will be called Serena, after my mother, and you will share my surname, Wil-liams."

As Serena Williams I had been led, wide-eyed, into Natchitoches. I remember seeing a little girl about my own age watching as we came into town. She was standing si-lently along the side of the street, watching us, as were many of the townspeople. I let go of my mother's hand and walked toward her, thinking how much she resembled a favorite playmate I had left behind. But as I approached her, hoping with all my heart to win her for my friend, her eyes grew wide with terror and she ran and hid behind her mother's skirts, sobbing wildly. Puzzled, I returned to my

13

mother and asked her what was the matter with the little girl. "It is your clothes," she said. "She thinks you are an Indian, and she is afraid of you. It will be different when you have changed into the clothes of a white child."

But new clothes didn't help. No longer did my approach elicit screams, of terror from my peers, but their disdain was even more hurtful to my pride as a six-year-old. I didn't cry. I had been taught at an early age that tears displeased my elders and that feelings of pain or hurt were to be hidden behind a silent mask. This seemed to spur my white tormentors on. They would spit upon me, or as I walked by, a foot would suddenly reach out and trip me. Cruel fingers would reach out and pinch with malicious delight whatever part of my body they could easily grab.

My mother had expected to find her sister in Natchitoches, but she learned that her sister had died and her brother-in-law had remarried. It was to his house that we were taken. It was plain he didn't want us.

"It's not as if she was a real blood relation to me," I overheard him say to one of our rescuers. "And she's been a squaw for seven, eight years now. No telling what filthy habits she's picked up, or what diseases, living among them savages. And the child, half Comanche—"

The man had interrupted his protests. "But you must take her! You're the only people she has!" Then he added, in exasperation, "We risked our lives to get the two of them back, and this is the thanks we get! What else am I going to do with them?"

I eased out of the partially opened door and looked down at the clothes they had given me to wear. Suddenly I hated the strange garments, hated the men who had rescued me from a life I had loved. I hadn't asked to be rescued. They had brought me to an uncle who wasn't really an uncle and who didn't want me or my mother, who had children whose only interest in me seemed to be in how much they could torment me.

As I looked around at the unfamiliar walls, I felt a surge of homesickness for my tepee, my father, and my playmates, and I yearned for the openness of the prairie. I went to the room they had given my mother and me to use for sleeping, and started looking for my buckskin dress. There were curious things in the room, and I walked to the large cabinet and opened it to look for my dress. It was nowhere about.

I went in search of my mother and found her preparing food with the woman I had been told to call Aunt Sophie, though she was no more a relation to me than the man I had been instructed to call Uncle. The only ones who were really related to us were the three older children, my cousins. I asked my mother where she had put my buckskin dress, and before she could answer, Aunt Sophie said, "We burned it, of course. Such a filthy verminous old thing! Why would you be looking for it when we have given you such nice clothes to wear?" She shuddered, as though the very thought of the garment repelled her.

"I want to put it on," I said, looking at her squarely, wondering how she had dared to burn what was mine, or why my mother had permitted her to do such a thing.

She looked at my mother, her eyebrows raised in an odd manner, and my mother told me I had no need of an Indian dress any more.

"But I do need it. I want to go back to our village."

My aunt murmured something under her breath, and my mother came and knelt in front of me and put her arms around me and said that we were home now, among our own people, where we belonged. There would never be any going back.

We stayed for nine years, but I never felt we were among our own people, and though my mother never complained, I knew she was no more at ease there than I was. We remained in the house with the man and woman I continued to address as Aunt and Uncle, though after a few days we were moved from the large room we had been given at first to a shed at the back of the house, which was barely big enough to hold the bed we shared. My mother's status became that of a servant. I was thought to need the civilizing effect school would have on me, so I was allowed to attend, but outside of that I was treated by all adults except my mother as if I simply didn't exist.

Such was my welcome into the white man's world, and it was no wonder that I recalled nostalgically the happier moments of my early years. I longed for the freedom I had known, for the place where people spoke to me willingly. I yearned for acceptance, an acceptance that was denied me in the world to which my mother insisted I belonged.

My Indian training had been ingrained into my very soul and the way I carried myself, the manner in which I put my feet down, the quietness of my ways were alien to the others. I was often accused of sneaking up behind other children when in fact I had been walking in a perfectly normal manner. My mother soon despaired of trying to get me to wear the kind of slippers worn by other little girls. As soon as she put them on me, I removed them. To keep me from walking around barefoot, she capitulated and kept me supplied with the moccasins I preferred. As I grew older, I helped her prepare the hides and cut and stitch the pieces. Sometimes she managed to get a few colored beads, and I added these to the moccasins.

My mother died when I was fifteen, and I had not realized until her death how much she had placed herself as a buffer between me and the world that refused to either accept me or let me go. I overheard Aunt and Uncle talking about me the day after my mother's death, asking each other what they were going to do about me.

"No respectable man would marry a breed," Aunt Sophie pointed out, "and I'll not have her on my hands for the rest of my life! She's a good worker, I must admit. But it's an embarrassment to have her around."

I heard the discouragement in Uncle's voice as he agreed with her. "I don't know how we'll ever get shed of her. She won't likely ever get any honorable proposals. Like you say, a man don't look to a half-breed when he's choosing a wife. The best we can hope for is that she might run off with a mountain man when she gets a little older. She's

16

comely enough to catch a man's eye, and she don't look all that Indian."

As he finished, Aunt Sophie looked up and saw me. Exasperated, she said, "Serena, I wish you wouldn't sneak into a room all the time." She didn't even seem embarrassed by the knowledge that I had heard what they were saying.

The problem was solved for all of us soon afterward by a Mexican-born Spaniard named Esteban Varga. He came into Natchitoches one day several months later to get some supplies. He saw me, and inquired about me, and called on Uncle. I was called into the parlor, then they introduced me to Esteban.

Uncle said incredulously, "*Señor* Varga here wants to marry you."

I looked at the stranger, and remembered having passed him on the street earlier that day. I remembered, too, that I had been aware of his stare for a long time. I was used to that and accustomed to pretending I didn't notice. Usually the stares were frankly contemptuous or, more recently, openly lascivious. His stare had held neither contempt nor lasciviousness.

"*Señor* Varga," I asked, "do you know I am a half-breed?" I was compelled to use the derogatory term I had so often heard, to see if it shocked him.

Aunt gasped at the bluntness of my question, and I knew that she hoped he didn't know.

But Esteban merely nodded and said, in his highly accented English, "Yes, I know. The Comanches are a much respected tribe." He was seated in a chair that was too small for him, and the knees of his long lanky legs seemed to stick up uncomfortably. Though he was lean, his shoulders were broad, and his arms muscular, his hands workworn. I judged him to be quite old, well over forty, for his hair was beginning to gray. Except around the temples, his hair was dark, almost as dark as mine. But it was his eyes that caught my attention, and I liked what I saw there. I heard it said once that the eyes are the windows of the soul, and I had always felt this to be true. Often, people smiled with their mouths but their eyes remained unsmiling, and I knew that their smiles were not to be trusted. Esteban's eyes were kind, and to my surprise, he was smiling his approval of the frankness that had so shocked Aunt Sophie.

"I did not realize you were so young," Esteban said. "Your Uncle tells me you are not yet sixteen. If you feel you are too young to leave your home. . . ."

I returned his smile, knowing I had found a friend. This was perhaps even more important to me than finding a husband. "I will be happy to marry you, *Señor* Varga, as soon as you'd like."

Three days later, we were married by a Catholic priest. Aunt Sophie, a staunch Calvinist, was appalled. It made no difference at all to me. When Esteban said it would please him to have me become a Catholic before the priest married us, I agreed at once, and Aunt Sophie thought it scandalous that I would overthrow Calvinism for what she called heathen idol worship. She did not know that it really made no difference to me one way or the other, that I found switching faiths as easy as walking from one room to the next. Right after the ceremony, Esteban and I rode to Nacogdoches and, beyond it another half-day's ride to the three-room cabin he had built on his property.

I had supposed I was merely exchanging my mistress and master, Aunt Sophie and Uncle, for a different—and I hoped a kinder—master. I soon found out otherwise. Esteban wanted not another worker for his house and his land but a lady-wife, a mistress for his estate and a mother for his sons. He did not expect me to do any work, did not want me to. He had two of the peons' wives come to the cabin to do what he called heavy labor. And so I was left to the pleasure of preparing special dishes for him, and making for him the buckskin clothing he preferred and trimming it with beadwork, which delighted him. He had friends among the officers at the Spanish garrison in Nacogdoches, and occasionally we entertained some of these men in our home or went into Nacogdoches to visit with them. I applied myself to learning Spanish and even to learning to read it, which pleased Esteban enormously.

It is hard to describe my relationship with him. I was very young and often felt more like a beloved daughter than a wife. He was kind and seemed to derive happiness from being good to me. I, in turn, welcomed this kindness, basking in a devotion I had never hoped for when I agreed to marry him. I tried in every way I could to make him happy in return. I truly loved him, if not in a passionate man-woman fashion, with a sincere devotion and respect. I did not object to the sexual aspects of being married to him, for in that, true to his nature, he was gentle and considerate. It seemed important to him to make my body respond to his with a quiet sort of pleasure before he sought his own release. I sometimes pretended to a pleasure I didn't feel just to give him a feeling of satisfaction.

"Ah, Serena, what children we will have!" he said one day. We lay in bed and he rested his hand on my stomach in order to feel the stirrings of life within. I was carrying Felipe. "They will have the heritage of three great nations: the glory and pride of Spain, the strength and bravery of the Comanche, and the indomitable spirit of those who live on the American frontier. All this is ours to give them. What children they will be!"

I smiled at his happiness. I was well content in the knowledge that he took pride in my Comanche blood. This approval did much to bolster my self-esteem and erase the bad memory of Natchitoches.

There was never a more affectionate and loving father than Esteban. He took pleasure in performing the smallest task for Felipe, and their devotion to each other was a constant source of contentment to me. I wanted to give him other children, to fill the cabin with them, as he would have liked. But this was not to be, and four tiny graves nearby attested to my failure to fulfill this wish. Three of the babies survived only a few hours, a few days, one a bit longer.

"Never mind, my dear," he said when we lost the last

19

one. "You have a fine son in Felipe, a healthy boy, and for this you must be thankful." It was typical of him that his concern was not for his own loss, but for mine.

As Felipe grew, it was apparent he had taken his appearance from both of us. He had Esteban's bone structure and showed every indication of growing tall and lean. His eyes were Esteban's, and his forehead was high like his. But the rest of his face—his cheekbones, his jaw, his mouth—were somewhat like mine and like a face I remembered dimly as belonging to one of the Comanche warriors, probably my father, perhaps one of his brothers. I searched deep into the reaches of my memory for the positive identity of that face, but the warriors had been away for long periods, and time had erased too much and dimmed what remained. As soon as Felipe was able to toddle, I made buckskins for him, miniature copies exact in every detail to those I made for Esteban. One of my fondest memories was of watching them ride off together, dressed alike, with Felipe tucked in the front of his father's saddle. Esteban frequently took him along when he went to supervise the work on our *hacienda*.

Until things changed so abruptly in 1813, when an attempt to wrest control of the country from the remaining Spaniards failed, Esteban had had contracts to furnish the Spanish soldiers with corn and cotton. After that, there were no longer any contracts. The residents in and around Nacogdoches fled and the soldiers left, and it seemed we were the only ones remaining. Unperturbed, Esteban calmed the fears of our peons, and we continued to grow cotton and corn, but only for our own needs. It was not a bad life, and I was well satisfied with it, and with the kind and loving man who had chosen to make me his wife. And then, suddenly, I was widowed.

The three of us had been out hunting not too far away when the fire started, and we had seen the smoke and run home as fast as we could. Felipe was seven, and it was one of his first hunting forays, for Esteban had decided six months earlier that the boy was responsible enough to have his own rifle and learn to shoot it. He had ridden all the way to Natchitoches to buy one for him, and had worked with him as patiently as he had previously worked with me when he had taught me to shoot.

Esteban reached the cabin ahead of us, and by the time Felipe and I arrived, I heard him shout, "The parchment!" over the thundering roar of the flames. Before I could cry out to stop him, he disappeared into the fire. The cabin was destroyed in minutes, and a spark flew to the roof of the nearby barn. It, too, burned to the ground. So quickly was the pleasant and pampered life I had led for eight years reduced to ashes. The good and loving husband who had worked so hard to ensure my happiness perished in the flames.

Felipe had tried to break away from me to save his father. Had I not known the futility of going in there after Esteban, I would have rushed into the inferno myself. It took every bit of my strength to restrain Felipe, but finally, through his grief, he realized there was nothing to be done.

Esteban had insisted Felipe begin learning his letters when he was five, in both Spanish and English simultaneously. He wanted me to teach him the few Comanche words I still remembered. "All of it is part of his heritage— all of it, and the land. Some day, the land will be very valuable." And so, after Esteban's death, I continued with Felipe's education. We rode into the empty town of Nacogdoches, to the house of a friend of Esteban's who had had a habit of not returning borrowed books. I found the door to his small house unlocked; robbers had undoubtedly been there—and probably more than once—for it had been stripped of anything of value. But they had apparently considered books worthless, and except for the ones they had torn up to start their fires, the volumes had been flung about on the floor and left there. Most of them were intact, though dust and mildew lay heavily upon them. I was particularly pleased to find an English Bible among the Spanish books, for with it I could teach Felipe to read English as well. We gathered up the books and took them to the small cabin we had made for our home. I was pleased with what our foray had yielded.

It was as well that the peons left right after Esteban's death, for we were forced to move into one of their tiny cabins. And so began our unending struggle for survival. From that day forward, my unswerving purpose in life was to see that Felipe grew up strong and healthy and alert, ready to fulfill the bright heritage Esteban had foreseen for him. Some day, I thought, our world would right itself, and again there would be peons to work our land and buyers for our crops, and we would build once more a comfortable life for ourselves. It was toward that day that I worked, and for that day that I was determined Felipe and I would survive.

For a while, late in 1821, it seemed that things were finally about to get back to normal. When news of the signing of the Treaty of Córdoba became known, some of those who had fled Nacogdoches so hastily in 1813 began to return, to pick up the threads of their lives in Texas. Nacogdoches didn't grow to its former size, for there were no longer Spanish soldiers billeted there. Nor would there ever be again. Before the 1813 exodus, there had been as many as six hundred people living in the town. But in the Treaty of Córdoba, the Spaniards agreed to leave Mexico. Still, the town grew to about a hundred residents, and it was heartening to see again some signs of life in the once-deserted houses and empty streets.

At about the same time, the first American colonists came into Texas. The first of them were only passing through on their way to join a man by the name of Stephen F. Austin, who had been given a grant of land south of us for the purpose of bringing in settlers. But later, some of the Americans making their way to Austin's colony changed their minds, and they stopped and settled instead around Nacogdoches. Some of them applied to the government for approval of their claims on an individual basis, but many made no application at all, and this certainly added to the later confusion over titles.

It was not until late in 1825 that the settlers came to our area in any number. At that time, Hayden Edwards received a grant of land in and around Nacogdoches, and he came with his first group of settlers and began to dole out the land, much of which already belonged to others. The land-hungry Americans grasped it greedily, as though there weren't vast unclaimed reaches of land elsewhere to the west.

And then came Thorne Stewart, who dared to claim for his own a portion of the very land I was holding for my son. When Felipe came home all upset from his chance encounter with Cassie Stewart and told me what he had learned, I thought of all we had endured for the previous eight years: the days we had gone to bed hungry, the times we had sat up all night, rifles loaded, not knowing but what at any moment we might be attacked by a band of ruthless white men we knew to be in the vicinity. Was it all to be for nothing if the Americans could come and steal our land before Felipe was old enough to look after it himself?

During those eight years between Esteban's death and the arrival of Edwards and the people he brought, Felipe and I made four trips to San Antonio de Bexar, trying in vain to get some proof of Esteban's ownership of the land. Twice we went when we were still under the deteriorating Spanish rule, and the last two times after the Treaty of Córdoba had established Mexico's independence. But after the Spanish were ousted, all records of anything done by them seemed to have been pushed into some forgotten corner with deliberate carelessness, and it was hopeless to try to find somebody who might know what had become of them. I had even written a letter to Spain asking for some confirmation of our ownership, but no answer had ever come back.

For several years, an old Comanche lived with us. He had been cast out by his own people when he became too old and useless for them to want to care for him any more, and somehow he had found his way to me. I thought he might have been a man I remembered from my childhood, but I was not certain, and he never volunteered any information about his past. His face was etched with the wrinkles of his great age, and his movements were slow. But his mind remained sharp, and his coming was good for Felipe. He taught him the Comanche tongue even as he evoked long-forgotten words from my own memory, so that it was not long before we could converse fairly freely. He also taught Felipe many of the things a Comanche youth would learn. Under his tutelage, Felipe became adept at mounting and riding an unsaddled horse, at making and using a bow and arrows. The two of them spent whole days away from the cabin as he taught Felipe how to track game, how to read signs. I remembered how Esteban had felt about the richness of Felipe's mixed heritage, and I knew that he would have liked the way Felipe and I welcomed the old Comanche into our home. Once or twice each year, we went out in search of buffalo, and it was an odd-looking hunting party we formed: a wizened old man, a woman, and a boy. But we found buffalo, killed them, skinned them, and dried the meat in the age-old manner of the Plains Indians, and each time we returned laden with buffalo robes and jerky.

Before Thorne appeared on our land that day in January of 1826, Felipe and I were again alone, for the man he called his Comanche grandfather had finally succumbed to the weight of his years the previous winter. He had seen his end coming, and told Felipe exactly how he must bury him in a tree, had even picked out the tree he thought best. We both missed the old man, for he had enriched our lives immeasurably.

I heard the three horses approaching that day, heard them pause at the old cabin, and took advantage of the delay to change quickly to my only cloth dress, the one I had been wearing on the day of the fire. It was old and had been patched often, was undoubtedly out of fashion, but I knew I must not greet them in a buckskin dress. It would not do at all for them to think they were dealing with a squaw. As I heard them move into the clearing, I stepped

24

into the doorway, waited for them. Instinctively, unthinkingly, I had picked up my rifle.

I awaited their coming with mixed emotions, feeling much as I knew the war leader of a tribe must feel when he knows a battle is imminent. For eight years, I had been defending my son's rights against unknown forces, against phantom enemies. Now the enemy had materialized, had become a specific person. And he was approaching at that moment. It was not without a certain exhilaration that I looked forward to doing battle against a tangible opponent, at last. Felipe had told me the younger of the two men was the one who had staked his claim to part of the Varga grant, and my eyes quickly slid over the child and the older man and lingered on the one I knew to be our enemy. He was impatient, I could tell that from the way he urged his horse ahead of the others, then brought him up sharply. Too, there was a certain pride—excessive, so that it amounted to arrogance—in the way he held his head. When he dismounted and started toward the cabin, I noted that he took long solid strides, putting his feet down firmly at each step.

*He is very sure of himself,* I thought, and for a moment I felt a twinge of fear. *But I am equally sure,* I reminded myself, pulling myself up to my full height, *and I have right on my side.* I had been girding myself for just such a battle for eight years; I knew I must not show any signs of faltering now that the battle was about to be joined.

"Mr. Stewart?" I said as he approached the cabin. Our eyes met and held, and I was determined that I would not be the first to look away. But in spite of myself, I caught my breath, for far from wanting to look away, I felt an unexpected reluctance to break our gaze, and I was not at all sure it had to do with trying to best him in the battle we both knew was to come. "I have been expecting you," I continued. "Won't you come in, please?" I remained in the doorway till he was a few feet from me, and I was forced to tilt my head back and look up in order to continue looking at him.

25

He was a large man, even taller than Esteban had been, and of a heavier build. Finally, when our eyes could hold no longer, I lowered my head and motioned him into the cabin. As he started to walk past me, my body flushed warmly with awareness. I had never known any man but Esteban, and he had been gone eight years. I had not concerned myself about occasional sexual yearnings, for I had learned to live with them and knew they would soon pass. But as Thorne Stewart brushed by me and his arm accidentally contacted mine momentarily, my body ignited at his touch, and desire, sparked so suddenly and unexpectedly, roared through me like a hidden flame.

*A foolish time for such absurd thoughts,* I reprimanded myself angrily, and I was glad he could not know what I was thinking.

The older man and the girl followed him inside, and I motioned them all to a seat. The child was pretty in a vivacious sort of way, with lovely bright eyes and a large expressive mouth—too large, perhaps, for a child, but she would soon grow to it and would be even prettier in a few more years. The other man was of the same size and build as the younger one, though a little heavier and a bit thicker about the middle, and as he removed his hat, I saw his hair was white, shocking for its abundance as well as the purity of its color.

But it was not these two with whom I must concern myself, I knew, so I returned my attention to the man who was my adversary. With such a man as I had judged him to be, I must jump to the attack at once, not allow him the opportunity to fire the first shot in the verbal warfare that would be an inevitable part of our opening battle. I had dared to hope that my unknown opponent might be a man with whom I could reason; I was certain from Thorne Stewart's arrogant manner as he had approached and entered the cabin that he was not.

As soon as he had seated himself, I began by telling him that he would have to move, that he was on our land. He

26

countered by calling us squatters, which I assured him we were not.

"We hold the land by virtue of the Varga grant," I informed him, "which was issued by King Carlos III of Spain to my husband's grandfather."

"Your husband?" He lifted one eyebrow slightly in a subtle effort to insult me.

"Esteban Varga." I said his name slowly, clearly. "He died eight years ago, when our large cabin burned. I am his widow, and I am holding the land for his only heir, our son, Felipe."

"I scarcely see how it can belong to you and your son when I have been allowed by the duly authorized *empresario* assigned to the area by the Mexican government to claim it in my name." His words were spoken almost too calmly, too slowly, and I saw his jaw clench when he finished, knew it had been an effort for him to keep his temper in check.

"Perhaps the man you mentioned was not properly informed."

"Perhaps you were misinformed by your—" the slight hesitation that was meant to imply doubt "—husband."

"I was not misinformed, Mr. Stewart. I saw the parchment every day for eight years. It hung on the wall of our cabin."

"The parchment—" again, the slightly raised eyebrow, the hesitation, the implication of doubt "—was destroyed when the cabin burned, of course."

"My husband lost his life trying to save it." I refused to blink, to look away. I would not let him think his insults even touched me.

"Then admittedly, you have no proof."

"Not right now. At the time it was issued, it was properly recorded with the authorities. Many old registries were misplaced when the Spanish left. Somewhere, there is a record of it."

A look of triumph swept over his face. "Somewhere," he repeated, and I thought that the word, the tone in which it was uttered, was intended as the final intimidation, the final statement of disbelief.

But he had more to say before he left: more slurs, more attempts at intimidation. As he started to leave, he even threatened to use force to move us, and I scoffed openly at his words.

The girl and the older man, neither of whom had said one word, started to follow him out of the cabin. The poor child was almost in tears, and it was all I could do to keep from putting my hand sympathetically on her shining brown hair and telling her not to worry, that there was plenty of vacant land elsewhere her father could claim easily enough. But I knew that would be construed by my opponent as a sign of weakness, so I did nothing of the sort. As the older man walked past me, our eyes met, and I was pleasantly surprised to read the understanding there. He had been introduced as Thorne Stewart's uncle. I thought it a shame his nephew did not share some of his compassion.

Oddly enough, I had the feeling that in some way Thorne had enjoyed our encounter, that he was excited by challenge, liked a chance to prove himself, and had derived a good deal of satisfaction from feeling that he had emerged from our meeting the victor. *But he has gained nothing,* I reminded myself.

Just as they were leaving, Felipe came around the side of the cabin, carrying a rabbit he had caught. He glared at the Stewart men, and shouted after them angrily. I could never imagine where he got his impulsive temperament, for Esteban had been calm and soft-spoken, and all my life I had been accustomed to masking my feelings. But Felipe was quick to anger and as quick to forgive; he could be frowning one minute and smiling the next. At that moment, his face was darkened by a scowl. The two men were already riding away, but the girl, taken aback by Felipe's sudden appearance and his angry shouts, had hesitated a moment before she mounted. She yelled back at him and took something out of her pocket, threw it ineffectually at him. It fell

28

short of its mark, and Felipe moved to pick it up as she rode off. I saw then that it was a piece of hardtack she had thrown, and he bit into it defiantly as he continued to shout after the three riders long after they were lost to sight.

I sighed, waiting for his fury to spend itself. I had not even tried to call to him, to calm him, for I knew it would be useless.

"Come, Felipe," I said when he had quieted, noting suddenly how much he had grown since the previous fall when I had made him a new buckskin outfit, "I have made us some good soup today. We will save the rabbit for tonight."

Thorne Stewart came again a month later, alone. Felipe was cleaning his rifle just outside the cabin, and he dropped what he was doing and strode in purposefully behind Thorne, as though he would protect me from him.

As soon as Thorne was in the door, he announced with smug assurance, "I have spoken with Hayden Edwards, and he has said that you must leave."

I almost laughed aloud at his solemn pronouncement, but I merely answered quietly, "I am not concerned with what Mr. Edwards says."

"Well, madam, you had better begin to concern yourself, for this land is included in the grant he received from the Mexican government, with the power to dispense it to settlers as he sees fit." He took a few more steps into the cabin, but when I motioned him to a stool he made no move to sit down, and I wondered if he chose to remain standing on purpose, knowing his size seemed to make the cabin shrink, make me well aware of my smallness. I, too, remained standing, wishing heartily I had not inherited my mother's petite stature.

Thorne reached inside his shirt, drew out a paper, waved it at me threateningly. "This notice orders you to leave, and it is signed by Hayden Edwards himself," he said confidently. Then he added with, I was sure, a deliberate desire to insult me, "Can you read, or shall I read it to you?"

Before I could answer, Felipe snatched the paper from

his hand with a lightning-quick motion and threw it on the fire.

"That is what we think of your notice!" he said defiantly, smiling with satisfaction as he watched the flames shoot upward and quickly reduce the paper to ashes. Then he turned to face Thorne. "So much for your Mr. Edwards," he said triumphantly.

"Why, you ill-bred young pup—!" He glared at Felipe, and for a moment I was afraid he was about to strike him. I placed myself between them.

"Mr. Stewart," I said, "I have no desire to read anything Mr. Edwards has written. Felipe merely did exactly what I would have done."

"You can't destroy his order just by burning the paper." His eyes were directed over my head at Felipe, at whom he continued to glare angrily.

"Nor is a land grant from the Spanish crown any less valid just because a parchment has been burned," I countered, looking up at him defiantly. We were close, too close. When I had jumped between him and Felipe, there had been little room separating them. Again, as had happened when he had accidentally brushed by me the first time we met, I was acutely aware of him as a man. It was no part of my conscious thoughts, but I could not deny it, for something seemed to spark between us each time we met, something beyond our conscious control, as though flint had accidentally rubbed itself against steel. And as surely as I knew that I could not deny the knowledge of this, I knew that he must be aware of it, too.

I stepped back, determined to put more space between us, to move my body, which seemed no longer completely in my control, farther away from his. Never had every part of me yearned with such abandon for sexual gratification. My flesh longed for his touch, even as my mind, knowing him for my enemy, rebelled at the thought.

"If you have come here only for the purpose of threatening me, I don't think we have anything further to say to each other." I hoped the abruptness of my dismissal would

30

make him go, get away from me at once, leave me again in peace, and in control of my rebellious flesh.

But, to my discomfiture, he seemed in no hurry to leave. He remained where he was, looking at me with a deliberate slowness. His eyes traveled leisurely, insolently the full length of my body before he began to move toward the door. I felt my cheeks flush, wondered if he had guessed my thoughts.

"No, I suppose we haven't anything else to say to each other, not today. But I warn you, I still intend to see you removed from my property. Since you refuse to honor Mr. Edwards's edict, I'm afraid I must resort to force."

As he turned to leave, it occurred to me that he had always refrained from addressing me as *Señora*—or Mrs.— Varga. Obviously, from his behavior the first time we met, he doubted that there had been a marriage. I suddenly wondered if proof of my marriage would be difficult to find in Natchitoches, if there would be a problem in proving beyond a doubt that Felipe was Esteban's legal heir. There was so much to prove, and the burden of obtaining that proof seemed to rest on me.

"You cannot force us off our land," I said as I followed him toward the door, feeling the need to utter the bold brave words as forcefully as I could. I did not want him to guess that I had begun to feel inadequate against the enormity of the problems facing me, against the inexplicable yearning of my flesh for the body of a man I hated, a man who was the embodiment of the threat I had lived only to defeat for the past eight years.

"We'll see." In a few quick strides, he reached the door, started out it.

Felipe was right behind him, didn't wait for him to get all the way through the doorway before he flung the door shut upon him. When it bounced back off Thorne's heels, Felipe thrust it forward again, this time slamming it resoundingly. Then he turned to me, his eyes as bright with rage as the orange flames that had devoured the paper. "How dared he look at you like that?" he sputtered. "Did

31

you see him? Did you see, Mother, the way he looked at you? It is the way we saw men look at the *putas* in San Antonio de Bexar!"

"Hush, Felipe." I urged, forcing my voice to remain calm in order to hide the tumultuousness of my thoughts, the guilty knowledge that I had deserved just such a look as Thorne had given me. "I discovered long ago that looks cannot harm anyone. I am much more concerned about his refusal to admit our right to be here on our land than I am about the way you think he looked at me."

But Felipe's fury was not spent, and he would not be soothed by my words. "He called me ill-bred! Just because I snatched that lying paper from his hand. I wish I had looked at it before I burned it. It probably had nothing written on it at all. I wish—I wish I had let Cassie Stewart get lost that day I found her in the woods. Then maybe they all would have gone away and left us in peace!"

"I'm afraid there would only have been others," I said, silently deciding to go to Nacogdoches myself and talk to this man Edwards. If what Thorne had said about him being given all this land to dispense as he saw fit were true, then he must certainly be told of our claim and have its extent outlined for him.

"I wish it had been anybody but him! I hate him! I hope I never see him again!"

"So do I," I agreed. "But I'm afraid we haven't seen the last of him." After I had spoken, I wondered if I had not lied, if I was not, in a strange way, looking forward to our next meeting with an inexplicable feeling of anticipation.

When Felipe had calmed somewhat, I had told him I was going to Nacogdoches, and he had protested indignantly. "But Edwards is the very man who has come in here and tried to steal our land!" he objected. "How can you deal with such a man?"

"We may have no choice. If what Mr. Stewart said is true, that Edwards has been given all this area to dispense as he sees fit, then I must let him know of the Varga grant. Unless he knows of it, he will make the same mistake again

32

that he did with Thorne Stewart, and give away more of your land. You can see the logic of that, can't you?"

"What if he doesn't listen?"

"Perhaps he's a very fair-minded man," I suggested, wanting desperately to believe that the unknown Mr. Edwards would listen to me, honor the Varga grant. Yet I knew he would demand to see proof of it, and of course I had none.

We set out for Nacogdoches several days later, where my fears were realized. Hayden Edwards listened politely enough to me as I outlined the extent of Felipe's land, but when I had finished he said, "A grant from the Spanish crown? Twenty-five million square *varas*? That is quite extensive, a full league. What proof do you have?" When I told him of the fire and the parchment that was destroyed and the records that had been misplaced, I could see the growing impatience in his eyes. "Why didn't you register your claim with me in November? Everyone with a previous claim was told to do so."

"I knew nothing of any such order," I answered, knowing it would not have made any difference if I had come sooner. If he did not believe me now, he would not have believed me then.

"You come to me with such an extensive claim, and you have not the smallest shred of evidence to support it? Do you honestly expect me to honor such a sizable grant as you outline, on only your word?" He stood up in a gesture of dismissal.

"But somewhere there is proof. There must be. I thought perhaps you had access to the old records and would know—"

He shook his head wearily. "I'm sorry," he said abruptly, but his eyes told me he was not. "Now if you will excuse me—" He left the sentence unfinished, moved to show me out of his office.

"But you mustn't give away the Varga land," I insisted desperately. "It has been in the family for three genera-

33

tions. My son will be the fourth. You must give me a chance to find proof—"

He sighed. "Madam, I have had the misfortune to have been given a grant in an area once occupied by settlers, and I have quite enough troubles trying to separate false claims from those that are bona fide, without concerning myself about a claim that has no documentary backing whatsoever. Please, I am a busy man." He opened the door and motioned for me to leave.

Felipe was waiting outside, and as the door closed behind me he asked anxiously, "What happened?" When I didn't answer, he urged impatiently, "Tell me."

"Nothing," I said. "Nothing happened. He listened to my story, but when he asked for proof and I said I had none, he dismissed me."

"I knew it would be a waste of time to come here!" Felipe's jaw jutted out angrily.

I shrugged. "I thought it worthwhile to try. I hoped he might have the records, but apparently he doesn't."

"I guess we aren't the only ones who have problems," he said as we made our way out into the busy, dirty street. "While you were inside, another man came in and said he owned some land that somebody else was on, too."

"Oh, really? And did he have proof?"

Felipe's face dropped. "Yes, he said he had a title."

I remembered Edwards's words, his statement about separating false claims from those that were bona fide. Ours was bona fide, but where, where was the proof we needed?

"Let's go home. We have nothing further to accomplish here. You were right, Felipe. It was a waste of our time to come."

"Maybe not completely," he said as we started to mount. "While I was tying up our horses, a man came up and asked if I'd be willing to sell them. I thought he was joking at first, but he said he wasn't. He offered me ten dollars apiece for them."

"Ten American dollars?" I had never considered mustangs as having any monetary value. They roamed the prairies, free for the taking, and had ever since I could remember. "Perhaps we could spare a few."

"That's what I thought. I told the man I might come in tomorrow with a couple he could buy, and he said he'd be looking for me." He grinned. "I thought I could give him that black stallion that rides so rough and the stubborn pinto mare."

Felipe had gone into Nacogdoches leading the two mustangs the next day, and he had not yet returned when Thorne came by. Again, he came alone. And again, he began his conversation by insisting we must leave.

"I'll send my coachman, Daniel, here tomorrow to help you collect your things." He looked around the cabin and his eyes indicated that they had seen little worth collecting. "He will take you any place within reason that you choose to go. Bexar, even, or perhaps one of the other colonies—"

Puzzled, I looked at him. I didn't believe he really expected me to agree so readily to his demands, and I wondered that he had chosen to waste his time coming to issue them. "We're going nowhere," I said resolutely, feeling that I was acting out a part, knowing I must say that or something similar in order for him to continue.

"I'll even give you some money to help you settle elsewhere," he said, ignoring my words, as though he hadn't even heard them. We were inside the cabin, and he had seated himself on one of the beds.

I remained standing, feeling that it gave me a rare opportunity to keep my eyes above his, so that at last it was he who must look up to me. It is odd how being forced to raise one's eyes to someone will put a person at a distinct disadvantage. This time, I was determined to use this unexpected advantage to gain dominance of our conversation.

"You're willing to bribe me to leave?" I made no effort to suppress the smile that came to my lips at the thought. "How much, Mr. Stewart? How badly do you want me to remove myself and my son from your path?" He certainly knew as well as I that I had no intention of accepting any

35

such bribe, yet I could see my taunts made him uncomfortable.

For some reason, he was unwilling to chance discounting the possibility that I might be seriously considering his offer, and he answered, "I would give you fifty dollars." When my expression didn't change, he quickly amended, "A hundred, maybe—"

"A hundred dollars!" If he mistook my derision for pleasure at the thought of his unexpected generosity, he soon learned otherwise. "For that, you expect me to relinquish my son's claim to twenty-five million square *varas*? Why, that's only the price of ten mustangs. That would be quite a bargain, to pay so little for so much land, wouldn't it, Mr. Stewart?"

He ignored my jibe and went on. "My means are limited. I couldn't give you much more. You would have to sign a disclaimer. . . ."

There was something bothering him, something that had suddenly made him particularly anxious to have us gone quickly, something important enough to him to make him take a chance on such an absurd offer. I didn't know what it was, but that didn't matter. I sensed my advantage, pressed it. "You seem less sure of yourself and your rights today, Mr. Stewart. Why? Why have you come to offer me money, even a wagon and driver, if we will leave? What has made you suddenly so anxious to see us gone quickly?"

I could see my question had made him uncomfortable, and for a moment he could think of no answer. But he quickly recovered, tried to hide his discomfiture behind more brash words. "I could have you thrown off, you know. Edwards has given me the right. I was only trying to help you, give you a chance to decide where you would like to go, assist you in getting there—"

"I need no help from you," I answered haughtily, my head held high.

"You're a stubborn woman," he said as he rose and walked toward the door in long sure strides. As I moved to show him to the door, he stopped, suddenly and unexpectedly, squarely in my path, so that I was forced to stop, too, and tilt my head up to look at him. We remained there, unmoving, facing one another, standing only inches apart, as though we were momentarily paralyzed by some unseen force. I felt stifled by his closeness, overcome with it, yet I was unable to free myself, to move or take my eyes from his face.

Suddenly, before I could move, his arms reached out to encircle me. I gasped, tried too late to break away, found my arms pinioned by his. Roughly, harshly, he brought his lips down on mine. It was done with deliberate insolence, as though he would pay me back in this manner for my taunts and my refusal to take seriously his demands that I leave, would show me how weak and powerless I was against him, against his superior strength. I tried to twist my head away, but his lips came down on mine, imprisoned them as his arms imprisoned the rest of my body. I struggled, futilely, to break free before he could guess the power he held over me, know that he had discovered my vulnerability, my one weakness where he was concerned. But even as I tried to break loose, I felt my lips weaken under his onslaught, my body relax in his arms.

Perhaps this was what he was waiting for. As suddenly and unexpectedly as his arms had reached out and grabbed me, he released me.

The minute I was free, I sputtered indignantly, "How— How dare you?"

But my outrage was too late. He looked down at me with a small knowing smile that added to my inner fury. Again, as on his previous visit, he let his eyes travel boldly over my body, even more insultingly this time than they had on the occasion that had so incensed Felipe. I did not want to meet his gaze, knowing he could not help but be aware of the feelings he had stirred in me, yet I forced myself to raise my eyes to meet his stare, defiantly and contemptuously.

"Get out of here this minute," I demanded, careful to keep my voice even so that he might not guess how much he had upset me. But there was no need for me to say the words, for even as I spoke them, he turned and opened the door and was gone.

After he had left, I upbraided myself. How could I? What madness had possessed me that I had even for a moment found myself responding to him, returning his insolent, insulting kiss? I remembered that Felipe had compared the way Thorne had looked at me to the way men looked at the whores in San Antonio de Bexar, and I thought of my unwilling response to his closeness and wondered if I was really any better than the women of the street, after all. I clenched my fists in ineffectual anger at the shame of it as I heard him ride away. How I hated him! From the first moment I saw him, I had detested him for his arrogance, his bland self-assurance. Now he had forced me to recognize something cheap and tawdry that had heretofore been deeply buried within myself, and for that I despised him even more. I couldn't have stopped what he did, since he was much bigger and stronger than I, but I could have, should have, shown that I was able to resist him. In the future, instead of measuring me as an opponent of some moral strength and stature, he would be laughing at me, at the unbelievable ease with which he had forced a response from me. I raised one hand to my lips, touched them, half-expecting them to feel different in some way.

I, Serena Williams Varga, who had always considered myself so well controlled, so competent at masking my thoughts and keeping my emotions within bounds, had responded to him with the ease of a woman of the streets. I began to wonder if I had ever really known myself at all.

That evening Felipe returned from Nacogdoches, his face shining with joy. He came into the cabin and dropped two dress-lengths of cloth on the table, laid a scissors on top of them. "I thought it's about time you had a few dresses, Mother. There's another length in my other saddle bag, and some lace and some plain domestic Mrs. Bryant said would be good for shifts and petticoats. Or pantaloons,

38

if you want them." He smiled at me. "It was Mrs. Bryant who suggested what to buy. I don't know much about ladies' clothes."

"You bought all this, for me?" I fingered the cloth, a soft green domestic, and the other length of a pale lilac. "How thoughtful! But you should have bought something for yourself."

"Buckskins are fine for me," he demurred. "If you have some material left over, maybe you can make me a shirt for summer." He went outside, returned with some red wool and the white domestic and lace, and some thread and needles. "I wish they were better," he said, pulling away in embarrassment when I kissed his cheek. "They had some satin ribbons and some expensive pink silk material—"

"What would I do, wearing satin ribbons and pink silk material here?" I asked, laughing. "Can't you just see me out hunting in a fancy ball gown? No, Felipe, you couldn't have chosen better, or pleased me more, not with all the fancy silks and satins in the world." My heart swelled with pride as I thought of his unselfishness. With the first money he had ever known since Esteban's death, he had thought not of what it would buy for himself, but for me.

Obviously embarrassed by my gratitude, he said, "I'll put my horse away. I've got lots to tell you." When he returned a while later, he was frowning. "I see that Stewart man was here again."

I nodded, knowing he had seen the prints outside, wondered briefly if my shame were equally visible, if he could possibly guess what had happened. I knew he could not, but the memory of Thorne Stewart's kiss set my lips to burning.

"I hope you sent him packing."

"He wants us to leave. He seemed especially anxious to see us go, offered his coachman and a wagon to take us wherever we chose, even to San Antonio de Bexar."

"Oh? Maybe—I wonder if what I found out today had something to do with his being so anxious?"

"And what was that?"

"Well, I got to talking to the man who bought the horses, like he said he would, and he was telling me that Edwards has troubles."

"I suppose that's good for us, then. What kind of troubles?"

"There was an election for *alcalde* in Nacogdoches, and Edwards thought he had it all set that his son-in-law would win. But there were more votes for another man, and Edwards has been upset about that, says it will undermine his authority and open the door to a lot of forged titles. My friend said that Edwards wrote to Saucedo in San Antonio de Bexar, expecting him to back him up, and I guess he didn't."

"Is someone there forging titles?"

Felipe nodded. "Edwards claims somebody is, and my friend seemed to agree it was likely."

"You may be right. That might be what was worrying Thorne Stewart enough to try to get us out of here quickly. He knows we have no proof of our claim, and he's afraid we'll have a title forged."

Felipe put his hand on my arm. "I never thought of that! Mother, why don't we? I don't know how much it costs, but I can find out. I have a little money left, and we can always sell some more mustangs."

I looked at him in surprise, shocked that he should even consider such a suggestion. "Our claim is valid. We have no need of a forged title!"

"Why not? Isn't it better than none at all? It isn't as if we were being dishonest, as if it hadn't really belonged to *Papá*—"

"No!" I said emphatically. "It would only make it appear that we really had no claim at all. Such things are bound to be discovered sooner or later."

"But what else can we do?" His voice showed his impatience with me. "We have no proof—"

"It exists somewhere," I insisted, knowing I must never

40

permit myself to doubt the truth of my words. "We'll find it."

"Where? And when? We've found none in Nacogdoches or in San Antonio . . ."

"We'll try Saltillo, since the states of Texas and Coahuila share it as a state capital."

"When? Let's go soon—"

"Why not?" I said, smiling to myself. "How about tomorrow?" After what had happened earlier that day, Thorne Stewart would know that by leaving I had defied him, denied the response of my lips, my body, to his. He would know we had not gone for good. He would see our belongings unmoved, and he would know we would return. Let him puzzle over our sudden absence and worry about where we had gone and when we would return!

"But what if he comes in and destroys our things or burns our cabin down?" Obviously, Felipe's thoughts had also been turned toward Thorne and his reaction to our sudden departure.

"We'll chance that. I don't think we need worry. To a man of his nature, such an unearned victory would be hollow. He'll leave our things just as they are, I am certain of that."

I smiled at Thorne's probable confusion at finding us gone, finding his adversaries had suddenly disappeared without explanation just as he was spoiling for a fight with us. Let him fight shadows for a while, as I had for eight long years. As badly as he wanted us gone, I knew he would not have a minute's peace till our return.

I smiled at Felipe. "Choose the four best mustangs for the journey. On our way home, we can stop and do some hunting. We're no need to rush back from Saltillo."

# Chapter II

## HAYDEN EDWARDS'S COLONY—
## Summer 1826

It was the first part of June when we returned from Saltillo, where we had found no more satisfaction than we had by stopping en route at San Antonio de Bexar to talk again with the officials there. The records of anything done in the three hundred years of Spanish rule seemed simply to have vanished. If anyone in Texas or Coahuila had the least idea of where to locate any of them, they were unwilling to admit it. We were sent from one place to another, and occasionally our hope sparked briefly, but each time it was extinguished with the words, "I can find no record . . ." In San Antonio de Bexar, they said, "You might try Saltillo," and in Saltillo they said, "You might try in the national capital." But we had gone as far as we dared, so, disappointed, we returned to our small cabin, empty-handed except for the dried meat and hides we brought back with us.

Our miniscule cabin and the three others similar to it came into view. They were small and insignificant structures, but they were our home, and they were all part of something much larger, which I knew I must do everything in my power to hold intact for Felipe's sake. Somehow, some day, we must find proof of the existence of the Varga grant, even if we had to go to far away Mexico to do it. Then we would be able to force Thorne Stewart to move, and to keep others like him from encroaching on our land.

But a more pressing concern soon took precedence over these thoughts, for first and foremost was the ever-present problem of survival. We would have enough dried meat to last for some time, but most of that should be saved for winter. I knew we could shoot enough game to assure us a supply of fresh meat, but we would need more than that. I had only a little corn left from the previous fall, and we had planted none that spring. As we rode by my garden, I saw a few spindly plants all but choked by weeds, but there, too, it was too late to plant any more that season.

As my eyes fell on all this, I sighed. "I don't know how we'll manage this winter. I suppose this was not the right time for us to leave."

"Don't worry, Mother," Felipe said, and I was touched by the protectiveness of his manner. "I've been thinking that maybe in the next few days, after you get settled, I can go out to find some mustangs. With the Americans so eager to buy them, we can sell them the horses and buy what we need. Besides, I'm sure I can get some sort of work in Nacogdoches. The man who bought the two mustangs said I shouldn't have any trouble at all finding a job."

"Working for some American, no doubt. In their need for labor and for mounts, they seem to be serving a purpose for us, after all," I said as we dismounted and tied our horses in front of the cabin. I was amused at the thought of Thorne Stewart's irritation if he knew we benefited, however indirectly, from the presence of his compatriots. "Maybe Mr. Stewart needs some mustangs or someone to help him around his farm."

Felipe did not share my amusement at the thought and frowned at the mention of Thorne Stewart. "I wouldn't work for him if he paid me ten times what anyone else might. And I'd sell him only winded horses."

We went inside. As I had predicted, nothing had been touched. We had been gone for four months, and our trip had shown no tangible results as far as obtaining any proof of the Varga grant was concerned. But it had served to strengthen us rather than to defeat us, to reinforce our shared hatred of Thorne Stewart as the embodiment of those who would dare to encroach upon Felipe's land and try to deny us our right to remain on it. Also, for me, time had served another purpose, for the shameful memory of the way I had reacted to Thorne's kiss had dimmed considerably. The man was my archenemy. It would be traitorous to Felipe and to the memory of the good man who had been my husband ever to permit such a thing to happen again. But even as I tried to strengthen my resolve to overcome what I knew to be an unreasonable awareness of Thorne's virility, I began to remember with renewed clarity the way I had felt drawn to him, helplessly, as a moth seems to be drawn toward its destruction in a flickering candle flame.

A few days after our arrival, Felipe left in search of wild mustangs, and returned two weeks later after a successful hunt. He turned the string of horses loose in our corral, and the following day went into Nacogdoches, returning late that night to tell me excitedly that he had found a job working in a small store that had just been built.

"If you can saddle-break the mustangs for me, I can start day after tomorrow," he said, and when I agreed, he scowled and added, "It's that Stewart man who worries me. Since he hasn't been around lately, I thought he might have left. But he's still there. I passed by his place today and saw the girl and her brother out front. I hate to leave you here alone."

I smiled at his concern, his assumption that I needed him to protect me. Maybe I did. "Don't worry about me. I'll be fine, and if Thorne Stewart shows up, I'll send him packing in short order." I spoke with far more certainty than I felt.

"But if he threatens you—"

"Threats can't harm me." It was not Thorne's threats that I feared, or his physical strength, but my own weakness. No one could offer me protection from that.

Felipe moved to Nacogdoches, returning late on Saturday night with a package of food sent to me by his employer. He did not have long at home, for he had to leave again on Sunday noon. This was to become a pattern, and he never came empty-handed. Always, there was some small gift from the man and wife who employed him—a bit of cheese, a measure of rice, some wheat flour.

One day when Felipe had been gone over two weeks, I rode into Nacogdoches to see him, and to thank Mr. and Mrs. Bryant for the gifts they had sent. The Bryants were a pleasant couple, and they doted on Felipe, who was also adored by their four small girls. He slept in a shed built onto the back of the store, and took his meals with the family.

I was surprised at how much Nacogdoches had grown since I had last seen it; the Bryant store was by no means the only structure that had been built since we had left. From the Bryants, I learned that there was still continued confusion over land titles in Edwards's colony. I listened with satisfaction to their account of the growing number of disputes, hoping the Americans might become mired in their own confusion and be forced to give up in despair and leave us in peace. I derived the most satisfaction of all from envisioning a crestfallen Thorne Stewart leaving his cabin forever.

In the past year, Felipe had been growing in jumps and spurts, and I even imagined I could see changes in him from one week to the next. His legs had become so long and gangly that he seemed to be walking on stilts, but even in that period, when his legs seemed to have surged ahead of the growth of his body, he had not lost the fluid grace with which he had come to move in recent years. His movements had begun to show a promise of added power. Watching him with maternal pride, I was reminded of the way a puma bounds from one spot to another with great forceful leaps, and yet scarcely seems to touch his feet on the ground.

I spent the first part of the summer lazily. Even though I had to train Felipe's mustangs to the saddle, I considered it to be something which was better not rushed. It was the first summer since Esteban's death that I had not had a sizable garden to tend and a field of corn to hoe. I looked after the few volunteer plants in my garden, hunted, and gathered what foodstuffs the earth had to offer. In my spare hours, I stitched the fabrics Felipe had brought me into dresses and shifts and petticoats. Still I found I had time to spare, and I often filled idle hours by taking a book to a quiet spot to read, though there was not one of our books from which I could not have quoted whole passages by memory.

One day in mid-July, I rode again into Nacogdoches, and on my return, I couldn't resist the urge to swing by the Stewart place to see what work had been done there. A large area had been cleared to one side of the cabin, and I presumed that Thorne Stewart had sold some of the lumber or given it away, for he surely hadn't needed it all for the buildings he had added near his own cabin: several smaller cabins, similar in size and shape to mine; a covered shelter for his animals; and the start of a large building, undoubtedly a barn. He had fenced a small corral. I was irritated by the appearance of solidity and permanence he had created there, yet I consoled myself with the thought that one day all of it would belong to Felipe. Never, for one minute, would I let myself doubt that this was so. Satisfied at that thought, I turned toward home.

The next day, I went out riding, taking with me the book Felipe had given me the previous day. He knew how highly I prized books, and with his first wages, he had bought me a volume of Lord Byron's poems. I had reprimanded him gently for spending his money on such a luxury, but I was touched by his unselfishness and thoughtfulness, and he knew I was pleased with his gift.

I looked forward to reading the book slowly, savoring each word, making a sort of fetish of the reading of it, so that I would not go through it too quickly. There was a place where the creek widened to form a small quiet pond, which had a grassy bank to one side. Esteban and I had frequently carried a lunch to the spot, and it was there I headed. When I reached the place, I hobbled my horse, and settled myself on the bank, my book in my lap and my

47

rifle on the grass nearby. Eagerly, I opened the book and started reading. I had not read far when I realized there were horses approaching. Annoyed at the interruption, I laid my book aside and reached for my rifle. Real danger, I knew, was apt to approach stealthily, and whoever was coming was making no secret of their presence. I sat motionless, listening, and then I heard the voice I recognized as belonging to the Stewart girl shouting, "Come on, Will, it's this way!" I hoped they might not see me, might ride right on past, but instead they burst into sight not thirty feet away.

"It's you!" Cassie said accusingly as she rode up to me and jumped down. "You're still on our land! Why haven't you left?" She stopped to glower at me, then continued, "Besides, this is a very special place I found all by myself, and I want to show it to my brother. You shouldn't be here!"

My annoyance at the interruption turned to amusement, and I smiled at her childish indignation, the seriousness of her tone. Behind her, the boy who had come with her was also dismounting. Felipe had told me Thorne had a son, and I saw that he bore a striking resemblance to his father. He was quite a bit larger than the girl, and it surprised me later to learn that he was two years her junior.

My eyes returned to Cassie, and I realized she was still glaring at me with as much malevolence as she could muster. I remembered the day she had come to our cabin with her father and his uncle, and she had remained behind to return Felipe's taunts. Her nature would be volatile, like Felipe's. Obviously, she was genuinely upset at finding me there. I forgot my annoyance at the interruption and smiled at the two children. After all, my quarrel was with their father, not with them; they were young, and it was certainly not their fault he had brought them to Texas and had settled on the Varga grant.

"So you've found this spot, too," I said. "It is lovely, isn't it?"

Her face softened a little as she saw I was not going to

argue with her. "Yes, but . . ." Her objection drifted off uncertainly, and I sensed that she had lost heart for the argument, yet was hesitant to give in so quickly to the enemy.

"If you sit very quietly, sometimes you can see some small fish in the pool."

"Cassie can't be still," the boy commented, coming forward, "but I can."

"I can be if I want to!" she said quickly, but I knew she had only spoken so because she had felt compelled to defend herself against a possible slight. I was certain the boy had been right. She would never sit still; she had her father's impatience. The boy's movements were slow, his words quiet, his voice even. He would be more even-tempered than the girl, I thought, and I doubted if he possessed any of his father's irritating arrogance or haughty abruptness of manner, for all that he looked so startlingly like him.

Cassie's eyes fell on my book. "You can't read, can you?" she blurted out in such obvious astonishment that I could not take offense at the rudeness of her question.

I answered lightly, "It would be rather foolish of me to carry a book around if I couldn't, don't you think?"

She dropped to the ground beside me, leaned over to look at my book. "Poems!" She wrinkled her nose in disgust. "Can many Indians read?"

"Some," I answered. "I'm only half Indian, and I learned to read in a schoolroom, just as I imagine you did. How did you know of my Indian blood?"

"Your son, Felipe, told me."

"Did he?" I asked, pleased with such proof that he did not consider his Comanche blood a taint or try to hide it. Esteban had wanted him to be constantly reminded of his background so that he would take pride in every part of his heritage, and gather strength from each component of it.

"Mama brought books with us—school books, so we could do lessons." Cassie made another wry face. "She says we can't grow up as ignorant as redskins." She looked at me and gasped as her fingers flew to cover her lips. "I didn't mean—"

"That's all right," I assured her. "I'm certain you meant no offense. But you know, you may consider Indians igno- rant as far as white man's learning is concerned, but they have their own kind of learning. They have lived off the land for many generations, and there are things they know that white people don't, and would do well to copy from them. Some things they have already copied."

"Like what?"

"Many things." I indicated her moccasins and mine, then my buckskin dress. "Using hides to make clothing and covering. Drying meat." I pushed myself to my feet, got out three pieces of jerky from my saddlebag, and offered one to each of them, keeping the third strip for myself.

They both bit into theirs, and Cassie said, "We have jerky, too. Papa bought some from somebody at first, but then he had an Indian squaw come right to our cabin to teach Sukie how to dry it." She giggled. "Mama almost fainted when he brought her home."

It was the first reference I had heard to the woman who was Thorne's wife and the mother of these children, and I wondered what sort of woman she was. I had not even thought of her as a person before, but Cassie's mention of her made her seem suddenly real, as though she had just that instant materialized out of nothing. How had he dared kiss me, deliberately stir sensual feelings in me, while his wife was waiting for him back in their cabin?

"Your jerky is better than what Sukie makes," Will con- tributed, "Papa says you can't make an Indian out of a black cook."

"The Indians have handed down their knowledge from one generation to another." I smiled at him. "I should think it would be easier for them to make better jerky than someone who just started trying."

"What else can they do better?" Will asked.

"They know how to live off the land and not use up the things that give them life. They don't waste anything. White

50

men come into virgin land and think only of their needs that day, that year. They use things carelessly and wastefully, not thinking about the many years to follow."

"That's not so!" Cassie said, bristling. How quick she was to take offense at any slight, real or imagined!

"She's right, Cassie," Will disagreed. "Remember Uncle Todd told us how during the first few years in Austin's colony, so many people came and didn't bring enough with them to eat till they could get settled and raise some crops, and how they killed off most of the game, and it was hard for anybody to find any? And you know it's true that Indians can ride horses better. Remember the one that tried to take Mama? He didn't even have a saddle."

Cassie apparently saw the futility of denying his words. "Can you ride without a saddle?" she asked me.

I shook my head. "I never learned. But my son can."

"Gosh, can he?" Will's eyes opened wide in awe. "That's great! I wish I could do that!"

"I don't like him," Cassie reprimanded her brother, shooting him a disapproving look for the disloyalty of his misplaced admiration. "He called us names." Then, seeming to realize that the very act of talking to me could be considered an act of disloyalty to her father, she stood up suddenly and said coolly, "Come on, Will, we'd better go home."

"I'd like to stay a while. Maybe we can see some fish if we watch."

"We can do that another day. Come on. We have to go tell Papa. He doesn't know they're back." She shot me a significant glance.

"Oh, all right." Slowly and none too agilely, the boy pushed himself to his feet. He started walking toward his horse, then turned to explain to me, "She never wants to stop any place for very long."

I nodded my understanding. "Good-bye, children," I called after them as they rode away.

"Good-bye, ma'am," the boy called back, but the girl didn't answer. I knew she would be certain to rush to her

51

father with the news of our return. I also knew that he would lose no time in coming to call. In spite of my resolve that nothing would happen between us, my pulse quickened at the thought of seeing him again.

The next morning, I decided to hurry from the cabin, determined to remain away all day, so that he would not find me home if he called. But before I could make my escape, I heard him approach, and I knew I was trapped. Panic seized me as I remembered our last meeting, remembered, too, how determined I had been not to weaken in his presence, not to give in to the inexplicable physical attraction he held for me. But when I knew I was about to see him again, knew the moment was upon me, my heart began to thump wildly. I caught my breath as I heard his footsteps approaching and jumped nervously as he pounded on the door.

The way he banged on it—demandingly, imperiously, as though I would not dare deny him entrance—reminded me that he was trying, in that same arrogant manner, to rob my son of his land, and I forced to the back of my mind my foolish fears of a moment before. I would meet bravado with bravado. I would show no girlish giddiness or womanly vapors in his presence.

Resolutely, I walked to the door, opened it only part way, placing myself in the opening to forestall any move he made to enter. "Yes?" I said questioningly, pulling myself up tall. "Have you come to threaten us further?" I hoped that, with the door only partially opened, he would assume Felipe was inside.

He ignored the deliberate belligerence of my words. "You were gone a long time."

"That is no concern of yours."

"I saw your son in Nacogdoches yesterday, saw him working for Abner Bryant. And the children said they talked to you yesterday, too."

So he knew, then, that Felipe was not at home. I felt suddenly exposed, as though I had built sham defenses that pretended to a strength they did not possess, and that he had seen them, assessed them, and quickly reduced them to nothing. Still, I stood firm, blocking his way into the cabin. I would keep him from entering, to make certain that no such thing as had occurred last time he had come would happen again.

But he seemed to have no intention of coming inside, asked, "I came to ask you to go riding with me. I want to show you something."

"Go riding with you?" I looked at him in surprise, taken aback by the unexpectedness of his suggestion. "I have no reason to ride with you, Mr. Stewart. And now, if you will excuse me, I'm very busy."

"It's something you should see," he persisted.

I hesitated, disarmed by his change of manner. I had been prepared to meet hostility with hostility, demands with counter-demands, but he was showing no hostility, making no demands. If nothing else, going with him to see whatever he had to show me would give me a welcome excuse not to ask him inside. "Well, all right," I agreed reluctantly, wondering at my own foolishness, "if it won't take too long."

The only horses Felipe and I owned at that time were the mustangs, and though I had chosen the largest of them, I was particularly aware that morning of my own smallness as well as that of my mount, for Thorne, seated on the large horse he always rode, towered far above me. But, for the first time since we met, I did not feel he was trying to take advantage of his size, trying to use it against me for the purpose of intimidating me. He had saddled my horse for me, and he seemed almost friendly, making casual comments as we rode. We might have been any neighbors on good terms, out on a pleasant morning ride. We headed south, in the opposite direction from his cabin, and at last he signaled me to a halt near the edge of some trees. He pointed through the trees to the activity beyond. There were a number of men—ten or twenty, at least—erecting a cabin, and off to one side, some women were busying themselves around the cooking fires. Scattered about both groups were a number of children.

"Are we still on your land?" Thorne asked.

I looked at him, surprised by the wording of his question. Did it imply that he believed me, believed what I had told him about the Varga grant? "Our land goes much farther south."

"I thought it did, and I wanted to show you this. These people are putting up a cabin for one of the families. You see, I am not the only one. If I were to leave, there would only be others, like these."

I bristled defensively. "Is that why you're showing me this? To try to frighten me?" I glared at him angrily. The respite from quarreling had been as brief as it had been unexpected. Again, we were adversaries.

He shook his head impatiently. "I'm only trying to point out what should be as clear to you as spring water. It will serve no purpose for you to fight me." His eyes held mine, as though they would convey a message beyond his words, and I felt the pull of his gaze and was weakened in spite of my resolve. It was as though I were helpless to keep from being dragged into the center of a whirlpool, from which I would be unable to free myself. Had he been speaking just then only of the land, or was he referring to us as well? I had thought I would feel vulnerable, feel susceptible to whatever strange compelling attraction existed between us only when we were close enough to touch, but I felt it strongly at that moment, and there was a full horse's length between us. I knew I must break away quickly, before I was completely overpowered by the desire to feel the strength of his arms around me, the arrogant demand of his kisses on my lips. I wheeled my stallion around, dug my heels into his sides sharply, and rode off. I did not look back to see if he followed, though I did not doubt that he did.

He soon caught up with me, and we returned to my cabin in silence. I wanted to dismount by myself, avoid any contact with him, but he was there ahead of me, had

54

jumped off his horse, was waiting. Purposely, pointedly, I pulled my horse to a halt some distance away from him, but he covered the ground in a few long strides and reached up to help me. He was standing so close that it was impossible to avoid his arms. As I slid from the saddle, his hands closed around my waist. Nor did they release me when my feet touched the ground. I tensed, tried to pull away from him, but his hands held me fast.

"You must learn there are some things you cannot fight, Serena," he said, leaning down to kiss me. This time, his kiss was not rough and demanding, as it had been that other day months before, but gentle at first, building to a deliberate sensuousness that nourished the inexplicable desire I felt for him. But I had been forewarned by my own weakness a short while before, so I braced myself against that weakness. With conscious effort, ignoring the feelings he so easily awakened within me, I kept myself tense and unyielding. It took every shred of resistance I could muster to deny my feelings, but I did not give in to them, did not let my lips answer his or my body relax in his grip.

At last, when he realized I was not responding as I had before, he released me, drew back and looked at me quizzically. "You really are made of ice, aren't you?"

Apparently, he had had no doubts of his ability to stir me, had been certain I would melt in his arms. I shot him a look of triumph as I brushed quickly past him and walked to the door.

"I suggest you save your advances for your wife. Perhaps you will find her more receptive to them than I am. Good day, Mr. Stewart."

As I closed the door, I remembered the look of frank puzzlement on his face, knew it should have filled me with smug satisfaction. But it didn't. Trembling, I leaned heavily against the door, for I knew, if he did not, how difficult it had been to steel myself against him when my whole body was quivering with desire, knew how perilously close I had come to answering his kiss, matching his sensuousness with my own. I had pretended to a victory I had not earned, had no right to claim. I knew that I would be helpless against another such onslaught, for every time we met, the pull between us seemed to be increased in its intensity. I had been gone four months, had not seen him for well over another month beyond that, and I had hoped that time and distance would erase any foolish feelings I had for him, but it hadn't helped at all. I was still the same woman who had been unable to keep from kissing him back that day months before, and the desire to respond to him again had not been weakened by absence or by the passage of time. It had only become stronger.

Why, why must he be so persistent? Why did he continue to come to see me, long after there was any reason for him to come? We had said everything we had to say to each other about the land in our first few meetings. Why couldn't he leave me alone? I could only hope my refusal to show him how much he stirred me would discourage any future calls, any future advances, for I doubted if I had the strength to deny him any longer the closer physical contact for which we both yearned.

I had misjudged Thorne to think that he might have been fooled by my refusal to respond to his kiss that day, and it was only a few days later that he found me by the little pond where the children had come upon me earlier in the week.

"When I found you weren't home, I thought you might be here. Cassie said you told her it was one of your favorite spots." He dismounted, carefully hobbled his horse, and came over to me.

I put down my book. "Why have you come here? We have nothing further to say to each other. I will not leave, so there's no sense in you continuing to make your foolish demands."

He dropped to the ground beside me, close to me. Far too close. "I haven't said anything about you leaving, have I? We have more important matters to settle between us."

My heart raced as I looked up at him, painfully aware of his nearness. "I don't understand," I lied.

"Don't deny it, Serena. You know very well what I mean. This."

One arm reached out to encircle me, pull me toward him, as the other rested on my shoulder, and he brought his lips down on mine. Helplessly, I felt myself being pulled into the whirlpool of emotions and desires long denied, and I knew that this time, there would be no escape. Dizzy from his lingering kiss, shaken by the force of it, I cried out in my powerlessness, but my cry was quickly silenced by his lips as they again covered mine. When, briefly, he took his lips from mine and drew back, I made no attempt to cry out.

As my lips had given way under his, so did my body respond instantly to his caresses. His hand moved down my back, my leg. He leaned over me, slowly pushing my head down until it rested on the ground. I made no protest. Gone was all will to resist him. I slid my arms around his neck, pulled him toward me as my lips sought his eagerly, my action admitting to myself and to him that I hungered for him, for his kisses, for his touch as much as he hungered for me. Gone for the moment was all shame, all self-censure at what I was doing. Though I knew this man was my enemy, that he was married, it didn't matter any more. Nothing mattered, except that we were together, and I was filled with a burning, searing desire for him. This passion, this yearning had been building within me since the day we had first met, and now it was entirely beyond my control. I could only yield to it and to the man who sparked it.

His hand moved under my dress, up my leg, traveled intimately over my inner thigh, pushed aside my shift. I gasped, knowing I should surely die of it if he left me then, unfulfilled.

"Oh, please," I murmured, but there was no need to say more, for he shared my urgency. I waited in an agony of longing, caught my breath sharply as he flung himself upon me a moment later without further preamble.

Abruptly, quickly, impatiently, we sought and found gratification. When we had finished, his body relaxed over mine and we continued to lie there, too spent with passion to move or to speak. I lay back weakly, feeling as though I had been caught up in the tumultuous violence of a raging tornado and finally released and flung back to earth, exhausted and bewildered.

I remained on the grassy bank of the pond long after he had gone. My pride was in tatters. In my years in Natchitoches, I had borne in silence the overt signs of the senseless prejudice most of the people had shown against me because my father had been a Comanche. Through it all, I had always carried myself proudly, held my head high. And then Esteban had found me, and his acceptance of me as I was and his love for me had nurtured and strengthened my pride, while yet tempering it with humility.

But now Thorne Stewart had ripped that pride from me, had degraded me in my own eyes as well as his, shown me that I had no more control over my actions than a bitch in heat. My pride, which had been at once both a shield against hurt and a badge of honor, had been destroyed in only a few minutes, and by a man, I realized, I scarcely knew.

I sat there quietly, idly watching the bubbles rising to the surface of the pond and spreading in ever-enlarging circles. I felt that I had been drained of all my energy, as much by the realization of how easily I had yielded to him as by the act itself. He had not forced me. I had surrendered to him, willingly and wantonly. If I had loved him or felt any affection for him, my submission might have been understandable. But I felt nothing but loathing for him. He knew this, and because he knew it—knew my body would betray me—his victory over me was even greater.

In a few days, Felipe would come home for his brief weekly visit. How could I face him, how could I hide from him the knowledge of what I had done, how readily I had betrayed him? With my pride stripped from me, surely my shame was a visible thing, something that hung about me like a pall, for all the world to see and to point at derisively as they jeered cruelly at my humiliation.

I didn't move until darkness had fallen. Then, with a heavy sigh, I picked up my book and my rifle and went home.

Felipe returned to the cabin, as usual, late the following Saturday night. He must have suspected something was amiss, for several times I caught him looking at me warily, and once he asked me if I felt well. I assured him there was nothing wrong with me, but I avoided his eyes as I spoke. I had made some wheat bread for him, made the top dark and crusty as he liked it, and had spitted and cooked one of our hens. I had made a hearty stew as well, and as he looked at all the food I had prepared, he laughed, said teasingly, "I think I'll have to stay home at least a couple of extra days to finish all this."

"You know your appetite has increased tenfold lately," I answered. "I'm sure you'll manage to get most of it eaten before you leave tomorrow noon." I did not tell him the real reason I had felt compelled to make so much food for him. It had been a sort of self-imposed penance, as though I must demonstrate to myself as well as to him that I loved him and that I regretted my disloyalty to us both.

When he left the following afternoon, he gladly accepted the remainder of the chicken and bread. I stood in the doorway, watching till he was out of sight, then turned back into the cabin and shut the door, alone once more with my shame and guilt and with the secret I had been so afraid he might somehow guess.

A week after my encounter with Thorne on the bank of the pond, he came to the cabin. I had just become able, for whole hours at a time, to push from my mind the humiliating memory of our last meeting. I had convinced myself that such a thing would never happen again, that my body's overwhelming desire for him, having been placated, would no longer trouble me.

But at the sound of his approach, as soon as I knew he was near, I could see the folly of that notion. In a state of near-panic, I reasoned that if I could only keep him outside, prevent him from entering the cabin, I would be safe from his advances and from the demands of my own treacherous body as well. Perhaps such reasoning would have been justified if I had simply slid the bolt on the door into place, but, illogically, I stepped outside, putting myself on the same side of the door as he.

"Why have you come?" I asked, watching him as he looped the reins around the hitching post with a maddening coolness.

He looked up, seemed about to answer, then changed his mind, returning his attention to what he was doing. When he seemed satisfied that the reins were firmly secured to the rail, he took several long strides toward me, stopping only a few feet away. His eyes, once he had started toward me, never left my face.

Disconcerted by his silence and the steadiness of his look and the implacability I read on his features, I knew I had been foolish to come outside. But it was too late to escape into the cabin. I took a step backwards, felt my heel bump the door. I could back no farther away from him unless I opened the door, an action he would be bound to interpret as an invitation to follow. He stood where he was, continued to watch me. Silently, I damned him for prolonging the moment, for I knew he sensed my building uneasiness. He made no move to come any closer or to reach out to touch me. He didn't have to touch me in order to elicit a response, and I damned him for knowing that, too. As my resolve drained from me, it was replaced by the anticipation of feeling his arms close about me, his warm kisses on my lips.

I could no longer stand there, motionless, like a startled doe. There was no retreating into the cabin, not now. It was too late for that. I had no choice but to attack in a desperate attempt to wrest control of the moment from him.

"Have you come to force yourself on me again?" I hoped the bravado of my foolish words masked the feelings I was unable to hold in check much longer. I felt my cheeks flush warmly, felt the pounding of my heart.

"Force myself on you?" he asked quietly. He shook his head slightly, and we both knew his answer was not a denial of my question, but of the lie it had implied. Still holding me in his bold stare, he took another step toward me.

"No!" I gasped, moving to back away from him. Again, my foot struck the closed door, firm, unyielding. And again, I was reminded that I had no place to go.

"Go away!" I said, but the words came out sounding like a weak plea rather than the demand I had intended. "Leave me alone," I added desperately, not even caring any more if I was begging. Never before in my life had I ever begged anyone for anything.

"Are you sure that's what you want?" He put one hand on my shoulder and bent his head down to kiss me, softly, lingeringly. And though I kept my hands clenched at my sides, I could not keep my lips from yielding.

"Why do you persist in denying what we both know is true?" he asked, his words little more than a whisper. He slipped his hand off my shoulder to reach behind me and open the door, then he scooped me into his arms.

"Put me down!" I demanded. "How dare you push your way into my home like this?"

His arms held me fast as he carried me inside, and he kicked the door shut with his foot.

"I dare," he said, still not raising his voice above a whisper, "because I'm far too busy to spend all day every day waiting for you to come to the little pond. And besides, a bed will afford us more comfort than the grass."

I started to protest, but I lacked the strength. Suddenly, I was weary of fighting a battle I knew I could not win, and I let myself go limp, resting my head against the broad expanse of his chest. I told myself that I would relax like that only for a moment, only long enough to gather my strength, so that I could resume the constant battle between us.

His lips brushed my forehead as he felt me relax. "That's better."

With an unexpected gentleness, he put me down on one of the beds. I willed myself to jump up, run from the cabin, but instead I heard myself utter a low sensuous moan as he sat down on the edge of the bed and started slowly unbuttoning my bodice. At each button his fingers lingered, and he pushed my loose shift out of the way to brush the flesh beneath it. Occasionally, he stopped to lean over and kiss me. When he had finished with the last button, he smiled. "Let's get rid of this dress. Can you raise yourself up a little? I think this other thing will slip right over your feet with your dress, won't it?"

I nodded, and, as obedient as a well-disciplined child who knows the futility of resisting orders, I did as he bade me do. But I did nothing beyond what he requested, lest my actions divulge to him how eagerly my body would greet his. As his hands slid caressingly over my flesh, I closed my eyes, hoping to lessen the effect he was having on me. But that only made me yet more aware of every movement of his hands, and I squirmed uneasily as they moved upward, over my breasts, staying there to circle them.

Of what use was it to pretend to indifference any longer? I opened my eyes, found him looking at me with a softness I had never seen there before. When he saw me looking at him, he leaned down to brush my temple with his lips, then turned to remove his clothing, and when he lay down beside me, I felt the warmth of his flesh as he pressed himself against the full length of my body. With a shiver of anticipation, I dropped all pretense of passiveness and moved into his arms, pressing myself against him, willing my flesh to join with his.

Still, he didn't rush, then or later. His lips, his fingers tantalized my face, my neck, my shoulders, my breasts. His hands moved lower, and he led my hands to explore his body, which I did shyly at first, then with increasing boldness, until he gave a soft sound of pleasure and moved his body over mine. Still, there was yet more pleasure to be wrung from denying our urgency a while longer. Not until we thrust toward each other in a final climactic frenzy did he abandon his easy gentle manner.

"You see," he said a moment later, "what joy we can bring to each other?"

I nodded. Later—tomorrow, the days after—I would try to deny it to him, and to myself most of all. But at that moment, I was caught up in the spell he had woven about us, and I could only agree.

Nor could I deny the quiet pleasure of continuing to lie there, nestled in his arms. In a little while, a pleasant languidness crept over me and I fell asleep, my head resting on his chest.

When I awoke some time later, he was gone; except for my nakedness, it might all have been an erotic dream. But it had not been a dream. I had responded to him that day just as I had when he had found me by the pond, and I would respond again and again, every time I let him get near me. The only way I could hope to prevent it was by keeping the cabin door always closed and locked between us, and by avoiding the little pond.

On the following Sunday night, I was awakened from a sound sleep by an urgent pounding on the door.

*Felipe,* I thought sleepily at first, wondering why he would have returned. He had left to go back to Nacogdoches earlier than usual that day because he had sensed a coming change in the weather. I got out of bed, walked to the door, and would have unthinkingly slid back the bolt if Thorne's voice hadn't stopped me.

"Serena, let me in!"

My indignation at his insistent demand jolted me into wakefulness. He apparently assumed that he could call at any hour of the day or night and gain admission to my cabin.

"Certainly not!" I replied through the door. Twice, I had foolishly allowed him the opportunity to persuade me to yield to him. I would not give him that opportunity again. I rested my hand on the thick door that separated us, as though to assure myself of its solidity, its strength.

His tone changed from demanding to importuning. "Please, Serena. It's raining. I'm getting wet."

I listened, noted for the first time the light patter of rain. I found a perverse pleasure in hearing his supplication. At our last meeting, it had been I who had done the pleading, and he had not listened. Now it was my turn to ignore his plea.

"There are three other cabins nearby, and they will keep you equally dry." I smiled as I pictured his discomfort, heard him mumble something unintelligible in answer. I stifled a laugh. I was beginning to enjoy the situation. "What are you doing out at this hour, anyway?"

"I've been hunting. I wanted to be out first thing in the morning, so I planned on sleeping out. But I didn't plan on this damned weather. I wasn't far away, so I came here, seeking shelter. And now you keep me out here while you ask a lot of fool questions!"

I did not remind him that I had asked only one. "You can seek shelter elsewhere. You're welcome to use any of the other cabins you choose."

"They have no fireplaces. My clothes are dripping wet, and have to be dried. I have no others with me."

"It's too warm to start a fire in here."

"It's much cooler now that the rain has begun, I assure you, and I am getting thoroughly chilled standing out here." As though to give credence to his statement, he sneezed, and just at that moment the rain, which had been coming down steadily but lightly, started falling in earnest. He renewed his pounding on the door with such vigor that I backed away in surprise.

"For God's sake, let me in! There are no eaves, and I'm getting drenched!"

I put my hand on the latch, hearing the beating of the rain, undecided as to what I should do, knowing the inevitable result if I let him in. Unless I extracted a promise from him. I did not think he would fail to keep his word, once he had given it.

"Will you stay away from me if I do?"

"Yes! Yes! Only open the damned door!" he shouted.

I slid back the bolt and heard him stumble into the cabin

in a headlong rush as the door flew open. I could not help but laugh, for it was obvious from the way he tumbled into the cabin that he had been pressing himself against the door in an effort to stay as dry as possible, and that my sudden releasing of the bolt had taken him by surprise.

I couldn't see him in the dark, but there was something ludicrous in knowing that the man who had never seemed for a moment to doubt his ability to dominate me was standing in the middle of my cabin, shivering and dripping wet. I laughed again, visualizing the picture he must make.

My renewed laughter did nothing to soothe his irritation. "You didn't have to keep me standing out there half the night. That's hardly proper frontier hospitality." His voice was gruff, and I heard him knock over one of the stools as he groped his way toward the cold hearth. He swore under his breath. "Where's the flint? Come here. You'd better light the fire. I'm soaked. There are sheets of water pouring off me and they'd put out any spark."

He continued his grumbling as I busied myself starting the fire. "Nobody else in the whole state of Texas would have denied anyone entrance on such a night, or kept them standing out in such foul weather, asking a lot of fool questions."

The flint sparked and the tinder caught. I fanned the tiny blaze and added a few more handfuls of moss. "It was scarcely my fault you were out in such weather. Anyone with a grain of sense would have seen it was apt to rain this evening. Felipe left early to reach Nacogdoches before the storm hit." I added a few pieces of kindling, another handful of moss, then carefully piled on some larger pieces of firewood. "And besides, you can hardly call this middle-of-the-night demand for shelter a routine call and expect what you call proper frontier hospitality." The fire started to glow, and I rose to my feet and faced him.

He stripped off his wet shirt, then admitted ruefully, "No, I guess you couldn't say this was a routine call, at that." He took a step toward me.

"Stay back!" I said warily. "You promised."

65

"So I did." He grinned, his mood improving. He picked up the stool he had kicked over, moved it to the fire and draped his shirt over it. Then he started to remove his pants, saw my look of surprise and shrugged. "I can scarcely dry them by the fire without removing them, can I? If my nakedness will offend you, fetch me a towel to drape around myself."

Uneasy, I did as he directed. He wrapped himself in the towel and sat down on one of the beds, motioning me to the other. "Sit over there. I want to talk to you."

I was beginning to distrust myself again, in spite of the promise I had extracted from him. "Well, I have no desire to talk to you," I said uneasily. "I just want you to go away, leave me alone——"

"That's exactly what I want to talk to you about." He waited until I sat down before he continued, "Since the other day, I've been doing a lot of thinking. You're here all alone. Your Spanish protector is gone——"

"Esteban was my husband!" I reminded him indignantly. So he still didn't believe that I had been truly married!

"Your husband, then," he agreed, shrugging carelessly, but the doubt still lingered on his face.

"We were married in Natchitoches by a Catholic priest. You can check the records there."

"That doesn't matter. What does matter is that you're alone now, with no man to protect you, or to satisfy your needs——"

"I have lived without such protection and also without such satisfaction for eight years." I raised my chin defiantly.

"Will you stop interrupting? I'm trying to say something to you, and you won't be still long enough to let me say it!" He frowned his annoyance, and when I lapsed into silence, he continued, "I have been married for fourteen years, and for all but the first few of those, my marriage has existed in name only. I have not bedded my wife in a long time."

"Why are you telling me this?" I asked, my own irritation growing. "Why should your personal life be of interest to me, or affect me? What does it matter to me whether or not your marriage is successful?" But in spite of my protests, I understood that he was trying to justify to me—and perhaps to himself as well—his pursuit of me. Oddly, I was relieved to learn that I had not deprived his unknown wife of the attentions that were her due.

"It makes a lot of difference to both of us, in the situation in which we find ourselves. I hope you will see that. I am reminding you, my dear, that you are a free woman and telling you that I am also free, in a manner of speaking, for I have no ties of any emotional sort to Angela, nor do I feel any disloyalty to her for what has happened between you and me. It is only as the parents of our children that we share any bond at all."

I started to interrupt, but he held up his hand, and I again listened in silence.

"I cannot satisfy my physical needs with my wife, and I am a man, after all." His voice dropped lower. "And you, my dear, are very much a woman. Why, in our mutual need, should we not turn to each other?"

"You seem to forget, a woman exposes herself to problems that a man does not. It's scarcely an equal exchange." I was surprised to find myself considering his suggestion. Why had I even listened? Why was I starting to discuss it with him now, as though I might possibly agree?

"You mean the danger of conceiving? I know that's a risk, I won't deny that. But there are some ways to prevent it, I understand."

I nodded. My mother, in her wisdom, had discussed such a matter with me, though it was not until that instant that I had ever given it any thought. Had she, perhaps, foreseen for me some such alliance as Thorne was suggesting? Had she realized how improbable it would be for a halfbreed to find a man willing to marry her? In that, I had been unbelievably lucky. Esteban had found me and made his honorable proposal of marriage, showered me with devotion and kindness. How likely was the possibility of any such thing ever happening to me again? I had not even given the matter any thought until that moment. Certainly, it was a remote possibility, at best. I could hear again Uncle's twanging voice, when he had been talking with Aunt Sophie the day after my mother's death. "*A man don't look to a half-breed when he's choosing a wife.*" It was true. Thorne was asking me to commit myself to him. If I did, there would no longer be any girlish reticence, any pretense at fighting the desire aroused by his very presence, the desire I was so helpless to combat. To satisfy that desire, was I willing to give up the respectability Esteban had conferred on me when he had shared with me his good name?

Respectability. What, after all, did it mean to me now? While Esteban lived, it had meant everything, but what had it done for me in the years since his death? It had gained me nothing, like a shabby cloak that cannot keep out the cold. Looking back over the last eight years, I realized how lonely I had been with only Felipe for company, how much had been missing from my life.

As I considered Thorne's words, I saw he was watching me, waiting for me to say something. In the flickering light of the flames, everything seemed unreal, and the absurdity of the situation suddenly struck me. What was I, Serena Varga, doing here in my cabin, talking with an almost naked man, calmly considering the possibility of becoming his mistress? I stood up, walked to the window, opened the shutters. I stood there, letting the cool rain-washed breeze blow over me, and when I turned, Thorne was standing behind me.

"There's something else I have not yet mentioned," he said as our eyes again met. "And that is the feeling that comes over us every time we're near each other."

Instinctively, I started to deny it. "I don't know what—"

"Don't pretend, Serena. Be honest with yourself, if not with me. We both felt it the very first time we met, as though something was drawing us together, in spite of ourselves, in spite of knowing we were adversaries. I've become obsessed with you, with wanting you, needing you. I find myself looking for the flimsiest excuses to come here.

Can you deny that you have felt the same about me?" His eyes seemed to bore through me. "Can you?"

"We are enemies—"

"You mean because of the land?" He raised his eyebrows. "The way things are going in Nacogdoches, we may both come up losers. Who knows? We may even become allies to ward off other claimants, before it's all over." He smiled at the thought.

He was right. If there were not already other claims to conflict with Thorne's, others besides our legitimate one, there soon would be. And he had shown me that there were others building on the Varga grant, besides him. There was no longer any reason for me to single him out as the object of my struggle to hold Felipe's land.

Felipe! I had been thinking only of myself. I had not thought of him. How would such an arrangement as Thorne was proposing affect my son?

"What is there to prevent us from admitting openly to our feelings"—Thorne prodded gently—"and doing something about it?"

"But Felipe—!"

"—Need never know," he finished. "I certainly have no intention of telling him. And neither, I think, do you. What happens between us only concerns you and me. It is of no concern to him."

"One day, he'll find out."

"Possibly. Would that be so terrible?"

"He would hate me, lose all respect for me."

"Tell me, why have you stayed here since your husband's death? Why have you stubbornly refused to move away, even though you must have known it was dangerous to remain?"

"There was no place else to go."

"That's not true. There were many other places you could have gone, safer places. What was the real reason you stayed? And why did you just make that long hazardous trip to Saltillo?"

"How did you know?"

"Oh, yes, I knew where you had been. Why did you undertake such a wildly foolish journey?"

"It was not foolish!" I objected. "I was looking for proof of Esteban's ownership, so that Felipe—"

"Felipe," he interrupted, nodding, and it seemed he had just been waiting for me to say his name again. "And you stayed here all through the dangerous times, alone with a child, at a time when all authority and law and order had vanished, all for Felipe, as though you could protect his rights to the land by sitting on it as a mother hen sits on her nest. And that trip to Saltillo, that was for Felipe, too. How long have you been alone?"

"I have been widowed for eight years."

"Eight years! And I'll bet that during that time you have thought of nothing but Felipe, of his upbringing, his right to the land you claim belonged to his father."

"It did belong to Esteban, and to his father and his grandfather. It is up to me to see that it passes to his son, to Felipe. I—"

He held up his hand to stop me. "For eight years, then, you have been thinking only of your son. Don't you think it's time now you thought of yourself, considered your own life, your own pleasure?"

"And yours, of course," I added wryly.

"Of course. I have never pretended to seek only your pleasure in the relationship I propose. And you quite obviously would enjoy it as much as I would. I am asking you to admit to the feelings we share. I am getting weary of this constant battle between us. Why not be honest with yourself, admit you want me as much as I want you?"

"Let me think a minute," I said, turning away from him again, mulling over his words. What he said was true. For eight years, I had lived, breathed, existed only for Felipe, for the day I could tell him, "This is your heritage, your land, which I have held for you until you were old enough to claim it yourself. I have seen to it that you grew up bright as well as strong, with enough learning so that no man can rightfully call you an ignorant backwoodsman,

70

with enough pride in what you are so no man would dare to malign your blood." I had nurtured him, made a home for him until he was able to lead his own life. Now he was fifteen, and wasn't he already leading his own life, completely apart from mine?

What did I have to look forward to besides endless hours of loneliness, until I grew old and ugly and finally died? I was thirty-two years old. What could I hope for? Surely not for marriage. That I had already admitted to myself. Even if, miraculously, another such man as Esteban should appear and offer me an honorable proposal, what then? Would my body cry out for his as it did for Thorne's? I knew it was disloyal to Esteban's memory for me to admit it, but with him I had never felt the press of urgent desire, the soaring pinnacle of release I had experienced the two times I had lain with Thorne.

No, not even if there were, somewhere in the world, a man who might yet find me and want to marry me, it would be unlikely that he would excite me as Thorne did. As Thorne had reminded me, I had existed the last eight years only for Felipe. Now it was time to think of myself.

Slowly, I turned back to him, raised my eyes to his.

He must have read my answer there, for a slow smile lit his face. "Now may I have your permission to kiss you, please?"

He looked so foolish, so boyish standing there, hesitating, that I had to smile.

"Yes." I took a step toward him, and already the exultation I felt was overcoming any remaining concern about the scruples of the arrangement he had proposed.

He let go of the towel and held out his arms to me as it dropped to the floor.

And so, like two horse traders both satisfied with the bargain they have struck, we moved together as I agreed to become Thorne Stewart's mistress. Nothing had ever been said of love.

# Chapter III

## HAYDEN EDWARDS'S COLONY--
## August 1826

Thorne and I moved easily into our new relationship. Surprisingly, in the light of how few words we had exchanged during our earlier meetings, we found many things to talk about, and we both derived a great deal of pleasure from quiet conversations. I soon came to realize that our talking was as important to Thorne as our physical contact, for his marriage obviously lacked far more than an outlet for his normal male needs.

We usually saw each other every few days, and though the sexual attraction between us had not lessened, we did not, after those first few times we lay together, move so impatiently toward a sexual union. Our agreement had been reached; we were certain of each other. There was no longer the need to press so urgently for the gratification of our desires, for we both knew that such gratification would come in the natural course of events. Sometimes we didn't lie together at all during Thorne's visits with me, for there were days when it was clear that his primary need was to have someone to talk with, someone to listen to his problems with a sympathetic ear. Frequently, our conversations might lead nowhere in particular. They could be about some impersonal subject, or the events within Edward's colony, or even some of Thorne's concerns about his family, or my worries about Felipe working too hard and sleeping too little. Somtimes, Thorne told me of his youth and I listened with interest, eager to hear all about his life before we met. As we talked, we might be sitting or lying next to each other on one of the beds, and perhaps he would reach out for my hand and enclose it in one of his or pull me toward him till my head rested on his shoulder. Often, we sat at the table, talking over a cup of coffee.

During the time I was a widow, coffee had been unobtainable. First, there had been no place to buy it closer than Natchitoches. If I had had the money I would still never have gone there, not for any reason. Even while Esteban lived, I had always declined his offer to take me with him on his occasional shopping trips to Natchitoches, for I had no desire to return to the place where I had spent so many unhappy years. With the coming of the Americans to Texas, coffee would have been available closer at hand, but Felipe told me it was very expensive, so it was an extravagance I didn't even consider. During my years as Esteban's wife, I had acquired a taste for the dark bitter liquid, a taste I gladly renewed with Thorne. When he had awakened the morning after we agreed on our arrangement, and found I had none, he had said nothing, but the next time he came, he had brought a five-pound sack.

"Five pounds!" I exclaimed as he put the large sack in the corner. "Why, that must have cost a fortune."

"Five dollars," he answered with a grin. "One-twentieth of what I offered you to leave. Now I offer it as a bribe to make you stay."

"It will take some time to drink all that."

"I intend to be here to help you as much as I can. I've brought you a mill and a coffee pot as well."

Thorne made some other changes, too. He brought some sheets for the beds, and some blankets, far softer and nicer than the buffalo hides we had always used. One day, he complained about the size of the stools. "I feel," he said, "as though I'm trying to balance myself on the head of a nail."

About a week after he made that statement, he brought two chairs he said he had bought from a man who was returning to the East.

"But how will I explain these to Felipe?" I asked, looking at them in alarm. The coffee and the coffee pot and mill, the blankets and sheets were all more readily concealed, but how could I possibly get two chairs up into our small loft?

"That, my dear," he said, "is something you must figure out."

I nodded, knowing he understood that I was thinking further ahead than the day I would tell Felipe about the chairs, for we both knew it was only a matter of time before I must tell him about us. This I was not anxious to do, for before I would be ready to face any problems that might arise when I told him, I needed more time to adjust to the idea myself.

*Like a bride,* I thought, *adjusting to her marriage.* And then I was shocked that such a thought had entered my mind. Still, as the weeks passed, it did seem more like a second marriage to me than an illicit affair, an illusion that Thorne's bringing of the various items for the cabin had done nothing to dispel.

If Thorne derived more from our arrangement than he had originally expected, so, too, did I. For eight years, I had had only a child for company. Just as Felipe had reached an age where he was able to offer me real companionship on an adult level, he had left. But even then, he had not had a wide range of experiences in his limited lifetime, and of course those he had had paralleled mine, so our subject matter was necessarily limited. Thorne could keep me enthralled by talking about almost anything—his stories of life in the East, back in Georgia, from which he, his family, and his Uncle Todd had originally come; his telling of his struggles to get a shipping company started in Savannah in the face of his half-brother's unrelenting opposition; and his recounting of his family's voyage to New Orleans and of the hurricane that had almost sent their small ship to the bottom of the Gulf. He seemed to enjoy talking about anything and everything that popped into his head, and I realized that he was almost as starved for adult conversation as I. Every word he spoke, every tale he unfolded, gave me a little more insight into the man I had agreed to take willingly to my bed, and into the people who surrounded him. Seeing these people through his conversations, I began to admire some and dislike others. I pitied his wife, partly for her pathetic insecurity, partly for Thorne's open disgust and disdain for her. But I still knew I would be unable to keep from disliking her in the unlikely event that we should ever meet. I realized from the things he told me that he was overindulgent to his daughter and inexplicably hostile toward his son, whom I felt called upon to defend whenever he said something deprecating about him.

"I took Will hunting with me yesterday," he told me one morning over our second cup of coffee, "and would you believe that he had a rabbit in his sights and refused to pull the trigger? He said he couldn't bring himself to kill the poor thing. Bah! Where does he think the meat he's been eating comes from?"

I jumped to Will's defense. "Remember that he's town-bred, Thorne," I reminded him. "He's not like Felipe, who has known that our very existence has depended on the game we could bring home. Will probably hasn't given much thought to where his food comes from."

Seeming not to hear me, he went on, "Then I made him take aim again, at another rabbit, told him he wasn't going home till he shot something. He raised his rifle and took aim and fired. Then when the rabbit scurried away unharmed, he looked up at me and said, 'I missed it.' The way he looked at me, the defiant way he said it, I knew he had missed it deliberately and he wanted me to know it. But I already knew. I saw him jerk his rifle up the last minute. He has a good eye, can shoot a hole through a piece of cloth tacked to a tree well enough when he's a lot farther away from it than he was from that rabbit!" He shook his head. "I wish to God Cassie had been the boy! She's got spunk, and she'd not shirk from shooting something. In fact, she's been after me to take her out hunting.

76

I've a notion to do it and leave her brother behind, with all his girlish qualms. He's got a damned animal hospital behind our cabin, brings home every starving cat and stray pup he can find, and if he sees a bird with a broken wing, he puts a splint on it and hand-feeds it till he figures it can fly."

"How old is Will?" All Thorne said about him only made me feel more drawn to the quiet, compassionate boy.

"Let's see. He's eleven now, I think."

"He's still a child. He might outgrow his reluctance to shoot game."

"I doubt that. He says he'd rather draw a picture of an animal than kill one. And Todd, who has always been so sensible and even bought the children their rifles, actually encouraged him in this foolishness, bought him a portfolio of drawing paper and supplies, with sheets to spare."

"You have to let him be himself, Thorne. You can't make him want to do certain things just because they're what you like to do." I knew his uncle understood this, as Thorne obviously did not, or he never would have bought the drawing paper. I was just as certain that I would like Todd, the man I had met so briefly and with whom I had not exchanged a word, as I was that I would not care a bit for Angela.

"He can enjoy the things a man should enjoy and not go prissing about with a drawing pad and a piece of charcoal or a pen in his hand."

"Is he good? Does he have any real talent?"

He looked at me in surprise, and I realized it had never occurred to him to wonder. "How should I know?" he asked gruffly.

And so his children began to emerge for me as individuals—Will, quiet and sensitive and introspective, and Cassie, willful and headstrong and as impatient as her father, but with a real interest in people, an outgoing nature and the ability to charm.

"I would like to have a chance to know your children," I said, and I realized it was as much because they represented a part of Thorne, a part of that other life he led, as because I was becoming interested in them as individuals. Day by day, I was growing more attached to him and found I was more than a little jealous of anything that kept him away overlong, and jealous, too, of the portion of his life I would never be able to share.

"You'll probably run into them occasionally around here," he said. He pushed his chair back and stood up, walking around the table, as I also stood and turned to move into his arms. "Right now," he said as his lips brushed my hair, "it's the children's father who craves your attention."

"No more than I crave his," I answered, standing on my toes to bring my lips closer to his, thrilling as always to the feel of his arms closing around me.

It was late in September before I told Felipe about the chairs. We had always used one of the empty cabins for storage, and for weeks I had carried the chairs there, taking the chance that Felipe's brief weekly visits would not allow him much time to look around. I always made certain that I had enough of everything I needed on hand, so he had no reason to go into the storage cabin to fetch supplies for me. And though Thorne grumbled at my foolishness, he yielded to my wishes and left his horse in the woods nearby instead of riding up to the door. Every Saturday morning, I carefully erased all signs of his footprints near the cabin.

On the last Saturday of September, I decided it was time to accustom Felipe to the idea that Thorne and I were no longer enemies. As I had started to pick up one of the chairs and carry it from our cabin, I changed my mind and resolutely set it down again. It was cowardly of me to keep putting off admitting to my son that Thorne came here as a friend; perhaps more cowardly still not to tell him that he came as far more than that. But for that shocking news, he must first be prepared.

That evening when Felipe came home, the chairs were in place on either side of the table. His eyes fell on them at once.

"Where did you get those?" he asked in surprise, moving to test one of them as I went to dish up some of the soup I had kept hot for him.

"From Mr. Stewart," I said, hoping I succeeded in keeping my tone light. "He's really not so bad. He's stopped fighting us and has decided to be a good neighbor. He knew someone who was leaving and selling these. He had seen that we had none, so he told me about them, offered to bring them here for me." I looked over my shoulder at Felipe, saw that he was momentarily stunned into silence, and took advantage of the chance to add hurriedly, "I paid for them from your mustang money. They weren't much. I hope you don't mind." It was the first time I had ever lied to Felipe. But it was a necessary lie, I reasoned, pretending to be unaware of his shock as I finished stirring the soup and ladled some into a bowl for him.

"Thorne Stewart?" Felipe said at last, his voice rising in disbelief. "He brought chairs, for you?"

"He's not really as bad as we thought, dear. In fact, he can be quite nice when he's not glowering at us and telling us to get off what he considers his property." I set the soup in front of him. "Would you rather have tortillas or bread?"

"Either," he answered distractedly. "You don't mean you're actually friendly with the man?" he persisted. "Not after the way I saw him look at you that time, and what he said about me—"

"Those things were done in anger," I answered, bringing him some tortillas. Then I pulled out the other chair and sat opposite him. "Eat your soup while it's hot."

He picked up his spoon. "But he still . . ." He shook his head and left the thought unfinished, then took a spoonful of soup.

I took advantage of the chance to press on as he continued to spoon the soup into his mouth hungrily. "I know you count him as our enemy, Felipe, and so did I, at first. But there are others now, all around us. Someone has put up a cabin about fifteen hundred *varas* to our south, and

79

Thorne says there are one or two more I haven't seen to the west."

Felipe put down his spoon with a clatter. "Thieves!" he said disgustedly. "All of them!"

"I know, but we really can't blame them for the mix-up. It's no more their fault than ours. Time will show we have right on our side. But meanwhile, I can't very well go around picking fights with all of them or tearing down their cabins, can I?"

"You don't have to get so friendly with them," Felipe said as he returned to eating his soup, and I couldn't help but be amused by the way his hunger had overcome his indignation.

"I met the Stewart boy one day, too," I continued, anxious to change the subject, "and saw the girl again. The children found me by that little pond on the south fork of the creek. The boy is very quiet, completely different from his sister."

He nodded. "I know. I've seen him in the store a couple of times. He and Cassie come in every couple of weeks with their father. She's always trying to start an argument with me, and the boy tries to calm her." He smiled. "Last week when they were in, I gave the boy a piece of candy and didn't give her one, and that really made her mad. She didn't say anything about it, but she shot me a look that had more poison in it than a water moccasin's bite."

"Next time, you must give her one, too. She has a quick temper, I know, but you're scarcely the one to cast the first stone at her for that fault, are you? Besides, she's still a child, and you're almost grown."

He looked up, and I could tell from his expression that a rebuttal was shaping itself on his lips. But instead, he smiled sheepishly. "I suppose you're right. I guess I haven't shown much patience with her. As you say, she's still a little girl."

Our conversation drifted to other things, and I was relieved that he had accepted with so little protest the news of my friendship with Thorne. It was at least a start. Yet I was forced to look ahead with continued concern. Getting Felipe to accept the fact that I had developed a casual friendship with the man we had considered our principal enemy was a long way from having him accept the idea of my far more intimate relationship with Thorne.

The next day, Felipe left a little earlier than usual for Nacogdoches, for he was leading into town two mustangs I had saddle-broken within the past few months. The sale of the mustangs and the wages he had been earning had brought us a steadily growing pile of silver coins, safely tucked away in a hiding place by the hearth, and though I counted most of it as Felipe's, its presence gave me a feeling of security.

Thorne's visits continued, giving purpose to my days, direction to my life. Each morning, I found I began anxiously looking outside for some sign of him long before he would be likely to arrive. And if I missed seeing him for three or four days, I became depressed, enveloped in a gloom of my own making, and I wondered how I could have lived for so long without him and how I could have accepted without question the dull monotony of my days.

I was in the corral working with another of the mustangs one morning a few weeks later when I saw Thorne approaching. Happily, I waved and stopped what I was doing, climbing over the wooden rail fence to go toward him, wishing he had not caught me wearing a buckskin dress. Felipe had augmented his original gift of three dress lengths with others, and the only time I wore buckskin any more was when I was out riding or was working, as I was that morning, with the horses. Looking back from later years, I can see that my preference for cotton or woolen clothing at that time stemmed largely from my desire to deny my Indian background—for the first time in my life. I didn't know how Thorne felt about it and was reluctant to remind him in case it somehow degraded me in his eyes. It was not that Thorne ever indicated that he disapproved of my buckskin clothing, or even thought anything about it.

81

Whenever I chanced to be wearing it, as I was that day, he seemed not to notice or to care.

I moved into his arms. Usually he greeted me by lifting me off my feet and spinning me in a little half circle, but that morning, he just put his arms around me quietly and held me close to him.

"My dear," he said.

As attuned as I had become to his moods, I knew instantly that something was wrong. I drew back, looked at him anxiously. "Thorne, what's the matter?" I searched his face, desperately afraid that whatever was troubling him might have something to do with us. "Angela didn't find out—?"

"No, nothing like that. How could she? It's just that I received some terrible news from San Felipe a little while ago."

"Your uncle?" I asked anxiously, knowing how close he was to him. And yet I couldn't help but be relieved that whatever was troubling him was not anything that threatened our relationship.

"Todd's all right. It's his wife. She died in childbirth."

"Oh, no! Not Rebecca!" I said, remembering her name and all the good things Thorne had told me about her. Oddly, I felt as though I had known her and had lost a friend. "Oh, Thorne, I'm so sorry. Will you be going to San Felipe?"

He shook his head. "There's no reason to go. Todd's gone. He wrote the note a few days after they buried her. It said so little, and yet so much. He said he had left, that he was already on his way, and that he couldn't face anybody just yet. He said just as soon as he felt he was ready to see people again, to talk, he'd come here." Tears filled Thorne's eyes and ran down his cheeks. I reached up and brushed at them, as though by doing so I could stop them from flowing and alleviate his sadness.

"What about the baby? Who's caring for it?"

"There is no baby." He put his arms around my shoulder as I slipped my arm around his waist and we started walking slowly toward the cabin. "It's so terrible for him, Serena. He lost his first wife and baby the same way. I always suspected that was why he didn't marry again for so long after she died—because he was afraid it might happen again. And now it has." He sighed heavily. "They had so little time together, and they were so close. Rebecca was exactly right for Todd. It made me feel happy just seeing them together." We went inside and he pushed the door closed behind us.

"Come," I said, motioning to the chair that I had come to think of as his and feeling very close to him because he had come to me to share his sorrow. "Sit down, my dear, and I'll make us a pot of coffee."

Over our coffee, he continued to talk about Rebecca and Todd, recounting again many things he had already told me, such as his surprise at learning that Todd—who had been the first to come to Texas—had married a widow named Rebecca, who had immediately captivated him and the children, and even Angela when they met her in New Orleans. I let him talk on, feeling it gave him some comfort, that this was one of the times he needed someone to listen. "And now this," he finished with a shake of his head. "Because of you, I can imagine how Todd feels."

"Because of me?"

He nodded, his eyes holding mine. "Because I can guess how I would feel if I ever lost you. I never knew before how important a woman could become to me. You have become very dear to me." He reached across the table and covered my hand with his own. "Don't ever leave me, Serena. I need you."

I smiled softly. "No less than I need you." Though his words were not exactly a declaration of love, they were enough for then and confirmed his growing affection for me. We rose from the table and he moved toward me with a new gentleness; I knew that our relationship had changed subtly, taken on a new meaning for him. And though it had been borne of the sad reminder he had received that day that nothing in this world is permanent, I could not help but revel in it.

A few days later, I came upon Cassie and Will by the pond where they had found me three months earlier. I was only a few feet away when Cassie happened to look over her shoulder and see me there. To my surprise, she gave me a wide smile.

"Hello," she said. "I'm glad you've come. I hope you'll talk to me. Will's so interested in his old drawing that he won't say hardly anything."

"I can't think what I'm doing if I keep talking all the time, Cassie," he protested. Then he, too, smiled at me. "Hello, Mrs. Varga."

"Hello, children," I said, dropping to the ground between them and laying my rifle down near me. "Have you seen any fish yet today?"

"Well, no," Cassie admitted as Will returned to his drawing. "I guess what you said about having to be quiet is right, and I've been skipping stones across the water. Or trying to. They always seem to sink instead of skip." She smiled again. "I get bored if I sit still too long.

"I saw Felipe in Nacogdoches the other day. I guess he's not so bad, after all. Papa says we shouldn't be mad at him and you about the land, that it's not your fault. Felipe gave Will and me each a piece of candy."

"He's a fine boy, and I'm proud of him. As proud as your father must be of you and Will."

Will looked up, his eyes wide open in surprise. "Papa's not proud of me," he said quietly, as though he felt compelled to correct my error.

"Of course he is," I said quickly. "Anyone would be proud and happy to have such a well-mannered son as you."

"Not Papa," he said firmly, then bent his head again over his work.

"I'm sure that's not true," I insisted, my heart full of compassion for him. "You must be mistaken."

He didn't answer, seemingly lost in concentration.

"May I see your drawing when you finish? I'd like to."

He shrugged, not looking up. "All right. If you like it, I'll give it to you."

"That would be nice," I said, touched by his offer. "I'm certain I'll like it."

When I turned my attention back to Cassie, I saw she was studying my clothes. "You don't look like an Indian today. You're wearing a real dress."

"It's very old. For a long time, it was the only one I had, besides the buckskin ones I made myself."

She wrinkled her forehead. "Why didn't you buy some material and have some more made?"

I smiled at her lack of worldliness, at her bland assumption that things were available in stores and therefore could readily be bought by anyone. "For a long time, there were no stores anywhere near. And besides, I had no money. Do you remember the big cabin you passed on your way to the little cabin where you visited me?" She nodded, and I continued. "When that cabin burned down, my dresses all burned with it. So I had to make dresses of skins."

"Are you very poor?" she asked, her head cocked to one side. If asked differently, the question could have been insolent, but she clearly had just begun to grasp the idea that the essence of poverty was the inability to buy dresses when one needed them. Thorne had said he had barely made a living when he was in business with his uncle, so apparently his family had not lived on too high a plane. But still, it was higher than mine—high enough so that Cassie had never before considered the possibility of anyone being too poor to buy clothing.

"I suppose you could say I am poor, by your standards."

"Did you have lots of dresses before the fire? Was that the same fire your husband died in?"

I nodded. "Yes, the same fire. And I had many dresses. He was very good to me."

"And after he died, didn't you have any money?"

I smiled. "I'm sure he had some, but he never told me

where it was. I think he hid it too well. Or perhaps one of the peons found it and stole it."

"And you've been poor ever since?"

"That's right."

"If Papa died, I wonder if we would be poor."

"I don't know, Cassie. I suppose you might be, at least a little," I answered, upset at the sudden thought that Thorne could be swept away from me as quickly and unexpectedly as Esteban had been. It was something I had not considered, and an unreasoning fear swept over me. How could I live without him? Suddenly, I realized how he had felt the day he received Todd's note about Rebecca's death and it occurred to him that he could lose me.

"Then I'll tell him to be very, very careful," she said after a minute. "I should miss him very much, and I shouldn't want to be poor."

*No less would I miss him, my dear,* I thought, *no less would I.*

Will finished his picture and showed it to me, and I looked at it in surprise. The forms and shapes were far from perfect, but there was a certain quality that shone from the drawing, a certainty of line, a sureness of purpose. Each mark of the charcoal was firm and definite, as though Will had known beyond a doubt exactly where he wanted to place it. It was a picture of the pond and the trees beyond it. On the near bank was a rabbit, its ears raised alertly, and with a few deft strokes he had caught the animal's attitude of alarm.

"Why, Will, this is excellent! And the rabbit is perfect. I can tell he's frightened and about to run away. Did you really see him there?"

"No, he'd have gone when he heard us coming. I just pretended. Rabbits are fun to draw."

"Did you say I may have this?"

"If you want it." He lowered his head and kicked at a clump of grass. "You can throw it away if you don't like it."

"Of course I like it, and I shall treasure it. Why would I want to throw away such a lovely picture?"

"Papa does. Mama likes to keep the ones I give her, but she hides them from Papa. He doesn't like for me to draw."

"You're quite talented," I said, feeling compelled to encourage him even though I knew I was being disloyal to Thorne in doing so. I tried to picture Angela—known to me by name only, so her figure, her features were of my own imagining—furtively hiding her son's drawings from Thorne. The thought angered me. Why should she have to hide them? Why should Thorne deny the aptitude that brought Will so much innocent pleasure? Even if his talent proved to be only mediocre, what harm was there in it? "I hope you won't stop," I added.

"I won't," he said matter-of-factly as he was getting his notebook in order and preparing to leave. "I wouldn't, not even to please Papa."

"Maybe when he realizes how well you draw, he'll stop being displeased," I suggested, feeling a surge of tenderness for this misunderstood child. I determined to talk to Thorne, make him see that he mustn't stifle what could possibly grow to be an exceptional talent.

He shook his head. "He doesn't even look. Whenever I give him a picture, he just crumples it up and throws it in the fire without looking at it."

"I can't draw anywhere near as good as Will can," Cassie said. "And he's two years younger than I am." Then she added irrelevantly, "I can run faster, though."

"Everyone has something he or she does best," I said, following the direction of her thoughts.

She nodded. "Will can shoot almost as good as I can, but only when we're aiming at a target. He won't kill animals or birds. Papa's going to take me out hunting with him sometime soon instead of Will. He's promised he would. Will doesn't like to hunt." She stood up and brushed the grass from her riding skirt. "Well, it's been nice talking to you, Mrs. Varga. We have to go now. Mama will be worried. She always is if we're gone too long. Papa says she's afraid to go out to the necessary house, and if she had her way, that's all the farther we'd go."

"Good-bye, children. It's been nice meeting you again. And thank you, Will, for the drawing."

"I'm glad you like it." He smiled shyly. "If you fold it, it'll smudge. It's best to roll it real easy." He turned to follow Cassie toward their horses a short distance away.

"I promise you I'll be very careful with it," I answered solemnly, thinking how diverse were the personalities of these two children. And yet, in spite of this difference, I could sense that there was a closeness between them, that they felt a deep affection for each other.

When Thorne came to see me the next day, I told him about meeting them.

"Cassie gets prettier every time I see her," I said. "She's quite a chatterer, isn't she?" I paused, then continued, "And Will is such a sweet child. Please don't be too harsh with him, Thorne."

I realized as soon as I had spoken that I had chosen my words poorly. Thorne, seated on the edge of the bed, looked up and mimicked, *"Such a sweet child!* A fine thing for a boy to be! By the time a boy is eleven, he shouldn't be sweet. Sweetness is for babies and little girls. A boy of eleven should be getting into deviltry, falling out of trees, smoking corn silk behind the barn. He should even be showing a little plain cussed meanness. But not Will. He's not doing any of these things. Instead, he prisses about with his drawing portfolio under his arm and tends to his sick animals! A man likes to think he's sired a real boy, a boy who will grow into a man he can be proud of. But Will?" He looked squarely at me. "I'll be ashamed of him till the day I die!"

"Oh, Thorne, what a terrible thing to say!" I had started toward the corner, where I had placed the drawing I had rolled up carefully the previous day, but his words made me hesitate, and I wondered if this was the wrong time to show it to him. But what better time would there ever be? I was to determined to help Will—to get Thorne to accept

88

him as he was and to be proud of him. After all, what good would it do to delay my start? I picked up the drawing, carefully unrolled it as I sat down beside Thorne. "Look at this," I said. "Will gave it to me. Look at the rabbit—"

His glance brushed the drawing without really fastening on it. Then he turned his head away, as a child might do in pique. "Childish scrawlings!" he scoffed.

"They're not just childish scrawlings," I said, my anger building at his stubborn refusal to look, to listen. "You didn't even look. If you had, you would see that there are signs of what could be a real developing talent there. The rabbit—"

He interrupted me, his voice cold. "Since when," he asked cuttingly, "has a backwoods half-breed become a connoisseur of art?"

I recoiled at the unexpected blow dealt me by his words. I had long been accustomed to being called a half-breed, had hardened myself against it from the time I was six, and had thought the taunt could no longer upset me. But hearing it so unexpectedly from Thorne's lips and in such a derisive tone of voice hurt me deeply. After the first shock of the sting inflicted by his cruel words had passed, all I felt was a quiet fury. I forgot how much the man beside me had come to mean to me, forgot how I thrilled to the mere touch of his hand, forgot everything but what he had just said.

Carefully, deliberately, I rerolled the drawing, forcing my tense fingers to hold it lightly, even in the white heat of my anger remembering Will's admonition to keep from smudging the charcoal. Slowly, I rose to my feet, walked back to the corner, put the drawing away, and then turned to face Thorne.

"Get out," I said quietly, inwardly shaking with rage. "Get out of here and don't ever come back." I walked to the door, held it open.

He stood up, looking penitent, and started toward me. "Serena, I—"

"Get out," I repeated, and when he tried to rest his hand

on my shoulder in a gesture of contrition and affection, I shrugged it aside. "You are a cold-hearted arrogant man. You can't even find it in your heart to love your own son, just because he dares to be different than you would like him to be. I can't see why I was ever drawn to you."

"What I said just now, about you. I didn't mean . . . I never think of you as—"

I brushed aside his words as I had brushed aside his hand. "Get out," I repeated. "I despise you."

He looked at me for a minute, and when I returned his look unswervingly, showed no signs of wavering, he shrugged and said, "If that's what you want."

He turned and left, not seeming at all like the arrogant man I had accused him of being as he walked slowly from the cabin, his shoulders rounded, his head bowed. Watching him go, I felt, through my fury, the urge to go after him and put my arms around him.

He didn't turn to look back. I'm sure if he had, I would have weakened, called to him, told him I hadn't meant what I said, that I had only been striking out at him for the hurt he had inflicted on Will and the insult he had hurled at me. But he kept walking slowly, toward the woods and the horse he had left there, and I watched him till he was out of sight. I was still standing in the open doorway when I heard the hoofbeats fade away into nothing.

Only then did I close the door.

I walked to the table, sat down heavily in one of the chairs, and lay my head in my arms on the table top. My fury faded, and I was overwhelmed by a sense of loss. What I had said to him about himself was true. He was arrogant, and he was heartless to reject Will, who obviously was crying out for the approval Thorne denied him. And I did hate him for the way he had lashed out so unfairly at me, so deliberately trying to inflict hurt because I had dared defy him.

I also loved him, and I knew there would be no joy in my life unless he returned.

My pride and my wrath had combined and made me tell

him to leave and never come back. And he, too, was proud. In the light of what I had said, I did not think he would be apt to return.

I lowered my head to the table, resting it on my arms, and stayed like that for what could have been minutes or hours, wishing I had learned how to cry. But the denial of tears was rooted too deeply in my nature, and even though there was no one to see, I was unable to seek the comfort of their release.

One day followed another, and Thorne did not return. As the week wore on, and still there was no sign of him, I began to despair. It was just as I had feared. He was taking me at my word, would never come back. I longed for the sight of him, for the feel of his arms around me. I would have forgotten my pride, sent him a note begging him to come, if there had been any practical way to do so. But there was nothing I could do, except wait and watch. And hope against hope that he would come. I stayed close to the cabin for fear he might come when I was away and leave before I could see him.

After both of us had endured two weeks of misery and uncertainty, he came back to me. I heard him coming, quickly smoothed my gown, brushed my fingers over my hair to push any stray wisps into place, and went to the door, threw it open just as he rode to a stop.

"Thorne!" I ran into his arms as soon as he dismounted, didn't wait for him to apologize, didn't care any more about my pride. Hadn't he, too, forgotten his pride in order to come back to me? "Thorne! Oh, Thorne!" I seemed unable to say anything else.

His arms held me so tightly I couldn't breathe, but I didn't care, wanted him to hold me even closer, crush me to him. "Serena, my love," he whispered, his mouth close to my ear. "I've been so miserable. I couldn't stay away any longer." He released me, held me away from him. "I love you, Serena. I don't think I realized it till you sent me away. I know I hurt you terribly. Can you forgive me?"

I was filled with tenderness and love, knowing what it

must have cost such a proud man to return to me after I had sent him away, and to utter such humble words. "I already have. And I love you, too, more than you can know." I slipped from his arms, took him by the hand, savoring the joy of the moment. "If you'll come inside, I'll show you how very much I love you."

"You're shameless," he teased. "You haven't even given me a chance to tether my horse."

"He won't wander far," I said, still holding his hand. "And I'll always be shameless where you're concerned."

We spent much of that day making love, as though we could never be done with showing how much we cared for each other. Later, looking back, I felt certain that that had been the day on which our child was conceived.

I was not sorry to realize I was carrying Thorne's child. In fact, the thought of it exulted me, as though the growing seed within me were positive proof of his love for me. I knew that later, once my pregnancy could no longer be disguised, I must not go far from my cabin. I knew that soon I would be forced to tell Felipe about Thorne and me, and also that I would have to take pains to avoid Cassie and Will.

But all that was some time away, and the knowledge of my pregnancy gave me a secret pleasure. Selfishly, I wanted the baby, hoped I might carry it to term and that it would live, so I would have the child with me always, a living reminder of Thorne every hour of every day, living proof of our love. But I dare not let my hopes soar too high, for I knew there was something within me that produced babies incapable of clinging to the thin thread of life in those first precarious days after their birth. They seemed healthy enough at first, but soon inexplicably weakened and died. Felipe, my firstborn, had been the only exception. I welcomed the idea of the baby, but I knew from my childbearing history that it was not apt to survive for long, so that even as I began to make plans for the arrival of the baby, I also began to prepare myself for the eventual loss of the child as well. But, as always, I hoped that this time, it would be different.

Except for knowing that I must eventually tell Felipe, and knowing equally well that I must at all costs keep Thorne's children from finding out lest they begin to realize what was going on between us, I was not concerned about how other people would accept this child. Who, after all, would know of its existence? I was living in complete isolation, had set my course on a life that, except for an occasional encounter with Will and Cassie, involved only Thorne and Felipe. I did not meet other people, did not need to, so there was no need to concern myself about their acceptance or rejection of my pregnancy. But Felipe's reaction concerned me deeply. When the day came, as it would soon, when he must be told, how would he accept the news?

I was also concerned about how Thorne would feel about having me bear him an illegitimate child. Strictly speaking, I had not been born out of wedlock, had never thought of myself as illegitimate. But the white man's world had looked at the matter differently and disallowed my mother's status as my father's wife; more than once I had heard myself referred to as a bastard child. I knew that the child I carried, should it live, would also some day have to face such taunts. But, I reasoned, surely something could be done, when the child was old enough to make his own life, to enable him to lose his identity in the anonymity of frontier life. Who, after all, really knew which of the men milling around in Nacogdoches and elsewhere in Texas were bastards and which legitimate? Our son, if he lived, would manage.

Our son. I had already given identity to this unborn child, barely started in my womb. I had accepted the fact that I would have it and that it would be a boy. But what if it were a girl? A girl born out of wedlock would have more problems, would not be able so easily to rid herself of the label *bastard child*, not be as free to put distance between herself and those who must know her background. If this

93

baby should survive, it would be better, far better, if it were a boy.

If it should survive. Thinking of the four tiny graves nearby, I did not consider it likely.

But Thorne had led a more conventional life than I and might be upset at the thought of having sired a child he could not openly claim. And so I put off telling him, long after I was certain I had conceived.

In November, Thorne's visits came unexpectedly to a halt. I did not see him for ten days, and after the first three or four days had passed with no sign of him, I could not help remembering the quarrel that had separated us once before. I began thinking back over the last time we had been together; I searched frantically for some clue, some explanation of his failure to visit me. Had I unwittingly said something to turn him against me? I could think of nothing. What, then, if he had simply tired of me, found somebody else? Or what if he was ill? And—the unthinkable thought—what if he never came back?

Finally, when I heard the long-awaited sounds of his arrival, I went outside to greet him. As he swept me off my feet, kissed me hungrily, I knew that nothing had changed between us.

"I can't stay more than a minute, sweetheart," he said, backing away from me to look at me, holding both my hands in his, "but I knew you'd be anxious, so I stole away on the excuse of looking for a stray horse."

"But it's been so long! Why?"

"Todd's here. He came last week, the day after I saw you last, and he's been with me almost every minute. You know I can't very well tell him, 'Now, look here, Todd, I simply must go visit Serena today, so I'll leave you to your own resources.' "

"Will he be staying long?" I hated myself for it, but I was jealous of Thorne's uncle, just as I knew I would always be jealous of anyone or anything that kept us apart. I wanted Todd to go away, so that things between Thorne and me could continue as they had been.

"I don't know. We want him to stay with us, of course."

"Do you think he might?" I asked in alarm, knowing how his presence must affect us. If the past ten days were an example, I would hardly ever see Thorne.

"I doubt it. We've tried to get him to come live with us before, but he wouldn't." He kissed me lightly. "I must go. I have to get back." He turned and started to mount.

"Thorne," I called, not wanting him to leave just yet.

He stopped, looked at me questioningly.

"Can't you come in? I have some coffee made." Couldn't he guess how desperate I was to have him spend some time with me, assure me that nothing—not the arrival of his uncle or anything else—could change the way we felt about each other?

"I really can't. As I told you, I just sneaked away for a little while, and Todd will wonder where I've gone."

"Just for a minute?" I pleaded. "I want to talk to you."

"Talk?" He grinned and raised his eyebrows.

"Please?" I looked up at him, not even blinking, trying to will him to understand how much I needed his assurance at that moment. I had decided I would tell him of the child if I could get him to come inside with me. Perhaps I wanted him to know that now I had a stronger claim on him than I had had before, that there was yet another reason for him to be committed to me.

"Well," he said, relenting, "I suppose . . . but just for a minute."

I did not tell him about the child that day after all. Nor did we drink any coffee, for once we were inside, we fell hungrily into each other's arms, knowing we must satisfy the desire that still sparked between us as strongly as it had on the occasion of our first meeting.

Later, as I watched him getting ready to leave, I said, "You can't imagine how much I've missed you."

"No less than I've missed you, my sweet," he said, but I knew it was not so. He had other things to do, other people around him, his family to care for and look after. And now his uncle was here, as well. My life was different, had be-

95

come focused almost entirely on him, on the time we had together. And that morning, we had had so little time! Our lovemaking had been satisfying, but it had been rushed, quickly done. There had been no time for quiet moments, no opportunity to tell him I was going to bear his child. It was not something I wanted to blurt out suddenly. I needed time to prepare him for the news, let him see how happy I was about it, so that he might understand and share my happiness.

"Vixen," he said, smiling down at me as we walked outside together. "Now I'll have to make up a fine tale to explain my long absence." He kissed my forehead, unhitched his horse, and mounted. "By the way, Todd was asking about you. You made quite an impression on him. He's concerned about you, and about Felipe. He says he's going to come see you one day, has something he wants to talk to you about."

"What might that be?"

"I've no idea." He frowned. "I think I'll let him come alone."

"That would be best," I said, following his thinking. Anyone who saw us together could not help but guess how we felt about each other.

He blew me a kiss. "Good-bye, my love. I don't know when I can get away again."

"Don't let it be too long. Please."

I watched him ride away, feeling lonely and not a little sorry for myself. Would this be the way it would be, as more and more things pressed for Thorne's time, more people demanded his attention? He had already confided to me that he hoped to get involved in Texas politics as soon as he had his place fixed up as he wanted it. That would be yet another claim on his time. Would I have to content myself with what few moments he could spare for me, always wondering when I would see him again, how many days or weeks would elapse before he returned to me? *Don't be foolish,* I chided myself. *He loves you, and you knew from the start that he could not offer you a full-time commitment. And this is only temporary, while his uncle is visiting.*

But what if Todd weren't just visiting? What if he did decide to stay? How could I bear it, how could I avoid being jealous of the man whose eyes had held such compassion for me in our brief meeting almost a year earlier? Selfishly, because his presence was bound to continue to interfere with my own life, I hoped that he would not remain long.

I was unaware of it at the time, but events were taking place that, within a few short weeks, would change things between Thorne and me far more than had the arrival of his uncle.

# Chapter IV

## HAYDEN EDWARDS'S COLONY—
## November 1826

Todd Stewart called on me a few days later, and it was all I could do to remember that he was supposed to be virtually a stranger to me, for Thorne had talked about him so often that I felt I knew him well. He looked older and moved more slowly than he had the other time I had seen him, as though his recent suffering had aged his body as much as it had saddened his heart. I had expected to feel some hostility toward him, knowing his arrival had made it impossible for Thorne to come to me, but my resentment quickly dissolved in his affable presence. I did not think anyone, however hostile, could fail to like this soft-spoken amiable man, who seemed to view the whole world with compassion. Though his status had been that of a quasi enemy during our first meeting, this time there was no mistaking his friendly intent, his sincere interest in Felipe, and his desire to see justice done in the matter of our claim to the land, even though his own nephew might be hurt in the process.

As soon as we had dispensed with the preliminaries of meeting again and I had offered him a cup of coffee, he came to the point of his visit.

"*Señora* Varga," he said, looking at me seriously across the small table that separated us, "I don't know if you're fully aware of what has been going on in Nacogdoches these last months concerning all the claims and counter-claims to various parcels of land. It seems things are in a pretty jumbled mess."

I nodded. "I know. I've been there. I talked to Mr. Edwards some months ago, hoping he might have some record of the Varga grant, but he apparently knew nothing about it. My son lives there now, and he tells me matters are getting worse all the time as far as land claims are concerned."

"I don't want to say all the blame rests on Hayden Edwards, but it does seem that he—well, he lacks Austin's talent for administration. I must admit, he did have quite a problem here, but still, it seems he's mishandled it. I understand that he left for a while, putting his brother in charge, and that the brother wrote a letter to Governor Blanco, trying to get the whole mess straightened out. I hope, for everybody's sake, that he is successful. As things stand now, nobody is sure who owns what, or if anybody really owns anything at all."

"I'm sure our grant—"

"Oh, yes," he interrupted, but in such a quiet way that it seemed no interruption at all. "You're sure in your heart, I can tell that. I never did doubt the truth of what you told us about your husband's claim to vast acreage."

"Twenty-five million square *varas*," I reminded him.

"But the unfortunate truth remains: you have no proof."

"Somewhere there must be a record of the Varga grant," I insisted. "It is only a matter of finding it."

He nodded. "But meanwhile, you and your son must live."

"We have lived from this land for many years—"

"That's not exactly what I mean. Perhaps my wording was wrong. What I should have said is that you must prepare yourselves to live without this land, just in case you're unable to find proof of your husband's right to it, his right to pass it on to his son."

"There can be no question," I protested. "In time, we will find proof." It was what I believed, what I had to believe.

"I would like to hope you are right, even though your grant overlaps the land assigned to Thorne, and he is my nephew, as dear to me as if he were my own son. Your courage, your determination and faith in the future are commendable qualities, but unfortunately, they aren't going to change a thing, any more than my hating to see Thorne lose his land would alter the outcome any.

"That's what I want to talk to you about. Just in case things should go against you, and you lose this land you have guarded so zealously, what will your son do with his life?"

"We won't lose our land. We can't!"

"But what if you should? I know your boy is working for Abner Bryant. Would he go on working for him? Bryant is a good man, a good employer, but I talked with Felipe quite a while when I was in the store the other day, and I don't think he's really too well suited for such a job, or too happy there. Am I right?"

I hesitated before I answered. Felipe had never complained, never said anything about the long hours he must spend inside each day. But I knew without his having to say anything that he would never be happy with an indoor job. "He's not used to being confined. My son has a very restless nature, Mr. Stewart. Mr. Bryant understands this and has agreed to let him take some days off next month without pay to go out and try to find some mustangs. He's looking forward to it."

"*Señora* Varga, I have a notion I'd like to have your boy work for me, and that he might prefer the job I have in mind over working for Abner Bryant."

"On your farm?" As soon as I said it, I realized I had made a slip, that I was not supposed to have any idea that Todd Stewart had a farm. Still, he had mentioned Austin's colony, and anyway, it was a natural enough supposition. All Americans got grants of land, whether or not they worked them. That was, after all, why they had come to Texas.

"No, not on my farm. I have a place near San Felipe, but I don't intend to go back there to live. I'd like to see Thorne take it over one day soon. My nephew and I have a

101

coach, a big one, big enough to carry six passengers and some merchandise as well. When we bought it, we were thinking of getting some young fellows to drive it for us, carry passengers back and forth, say, from San Felipe to Bexar, take it back to Natchitoches occasionally to pick up merchandise. Felipe would be a big help. I heard him talking Spanish to one of Abner's customers. That would be a boon to me, to have him with me in Bexar."

"You intend to set up a stagecoach line?"

He smiled, but his smile looked tired and wan. "Hardly that ambitious, at least not at first. One coach doesn't make a stagecoach line. It would be a very loosely run sort of thing, unscheduled."

"And you want Felipe to be one of the boys to drive it? He's never handled a coach before." *And he's so young,* I was thinking, *so young to be gone from his home, to be far from his mother!*

"He's handled horses all his life, hasn't he? The harnessing can be learned by anyone in an hour. Besides, I'll be with him. I intend to go with the coach myself. There is no longer anything to keep me in San Felipe. My wife died two months ago."

"I'm so sorry—"

With a wave of his hand, he indicated that he didn't care to prolong his discussion of such a painful subject. "I just wanted you to know that I'll be with him, if that would make you feel any better about letting him go. I know he's very young to leave home, but I wish you would consider permitting it. It will be good for me as well, for it will be setting my own life in a new direction, as well as his."

I thought over his words. Felipe, at fifteen, seemed so young to travel so far from me, from his home. But after all, I scarcely saw him since he had started working six days a week in Nacogdoches. Our circumstances had forced him to assume the role of man of the family at far too early an age. That Felipe would profit from close association with Todd Stewart, I had no doubt. He would probably, in time, come to look on him as a replacement for the father he had lost. For Felipe's sake, I had no qualms about giving my permission for him to go with the kindly compassionate man who sat across the table from me. But as a mother, I could not help but fear the parting for the wrench it would be. How empty my life would be about to become if it weren't for Thorne, and for his child I carried!

"What does Felipe think of your idea?" I asked at last, for, after all, it was his life we were discussing.

"I haven't mentioned it to him. I wanted to talk to you first. I realize you might not want him to leave you so soon. Of course, there's nothing to stop you from moving to San Felipe or Bexar to be near him. As far as your presence here is concerned, I can't believe that whether you go or stay will alter the status of your Varga grant any. In fact, if you want to consider Austin's colony as a place to live, I could offer you my old cabin there, about three miles out of San Felipe."

"I won't leave here," I said, thinking not of the Varga grant, but of Thorne.

"That is for you to decide, of course. But what do you think of my proposal for your son?"

"I have taught Felipe to think for himself. Young as he is, I consider him capable of deciding on his future. He would be the one to accept or refuse your offer. I think he will accept, and willingly."

"I admire your good sense, Señora. I figured you'd leave it to him, but I thought it best to tell you about it before I mentioned it to him."

"What about your nephew? You said you own the coach together. Have you mentioned your idea to him?" I wondered how Thorne would feel about having Felipe directly involved in an enterprise in which he shared. From what I could glean from both Thorne and Felipe recently, it seemed their original hostility had altered only to a cool tolerance, no more. I had begged Thorne to try, on his occasional visits to the store, to do all he could to make Felipe like him. I knew when I asked it of him that he was unlikely to comply, for I sensed that he had never quite forgiven Felipe's original belligerence toward him. I was irritated with Thorne for not putting himself out more to do as I asked, for he must have known how important it was to me to have Felipe accept him. And yet, at the same time, I knew that what I was asking went against his nature.

"I told Thorne yesterday what I had in mind. As you might have guessed, he isn't overly fond of your boy, but he has no objection to what I propose." He frowned. "There is something else, one thing that I want you and your son to consider, and that is that this venture could fail. I have not been much of a success as a businessman in the past. I've done well enough here in Texas, managing my farm and bringing in a few things to sell to the folks I know. But that's nothing to go on, really. Before that, I—well, I hadn't a very commendable record. In fact, I was quite a dismal failure in my last business venture."

I remembered what Thorne had told me about their efforts to keep their small company going in the face of his half-brother's resolve to be rid of them. Certainly, Todd was deprecating himself overmuch. I smiled at him. "Aren't all you Americans who have come to Texas failures, in a way? If you had been terribly prosperous at home, I doubt you would have left."

He laughed at my audacity, and it was good to see the sadness in his eyes lessen for a few moments. "I must confess I never thought of it that way before."

As he stood to leave, I asked him when he and Felipe would be leaving, for I had no doubts that Felipe would elect to go with him, and eagerly.

"I think it would be only fair if Felipe gave Abner a few weeks' notice, don't you? Presuming, of course, that he's as interested in my proposition as you seem to think he'll be. That would be around the first of December." Hat in hand, he walked toward the door.

"That seems so soon," I commented, walking with him. And yet, that was two and a half weeks away, two and a half weeks in which I would be unlikely to see Thorne, and

104

I knew that, in that respect, the time would seem endless.

He offered me his hand in farewell. I took it, felt the warmth of his handshake, saw again the sincerity in his eyes. "Mr. Stewart," I said, "no mother is anxious to see her son go far from her, especially one as young as Felipe. But I want you to know that I'm glad he'll be with you. I feel certain he will be in good hands."

"Those are kind words, Señora Varga. I'll do my level best to justify your faith in me." He started out the door, turned, asked, "Would you mind if I came to see you again before I leave? I've enjoyed the ride over here, as well as the company, and you do make a fine cup of coffee. Besides, there are times when I can sense that Thorne would prefer to have me out from under his feet for a few hours."

"Come whenever you like," I said sincerely, wanting to know better this man to whom I was entrusting my son. I didn't know whether to feel amused or frustrated at the thought that Todd's absence was unlikely to afford Thorne the opportunity for which we both wished. "It would be best if you mentioned to your nephew that you are coming here," I added. "He may consider that you are consorting with the enemy."

"He realizes now that the problem about the land is not your fault any more than it is his, and I don't think he bears you malice for your dispute. Good-bye, Señora." He bowed his head to me and left.

As soon as Felipe walked in the door the following Saturday night, I could sense his excitement.

"Guess what, Mother?" he said as he deposited a few small packages on the table, small gifts of food from the Bryants.

"You are going to drive a stagecoach with Mr. Todd Stewart," I answered with a smile.

He hugged me exuberantly. "Isn't that great? Just think, I'll be sitting on top of a stagecoach, handling a team of fast horses!"

"It might be wet up there when it rains," I reminded him teasingly. "You won't have Mr. Bryant's store to run into."

"I won't mind. Besides, Mr. Todd has thought of that. He told me there's a new kind of coat all the sailors wear now. It's made of a special material and keeps the rain out. A mackintosh, I think he called it. And he said he has big-brimmed hats for us, made out of the same stuff."

I smiled at his enthusiasm. "I'm happy for you, if that's what you want to do. Todd Stewart seems an exceptionally good man."

"He's great. Nothing like his nephew."

"Haven't you made peace with Thorne Stewart, Felipe?" I tried to keep my voice light. He mustn't guess, yet, how important it was to me to have them accept one another, if not as friends, then at least on some neutral ground midway between enmity and friendship. "I told you he no longer bears us any malice. He's become quite a pleasant neighbor, in fact."

"I don't like the man," he said flatly, and to that statement, uttered with such finality, I could think of no answer. Since Todd's visit, I had wondered if it might not be wise to tell Felipe about Thorne and me, and of the child I carried, before he left. But now his tone of voice, more than the words themselves, made me decide to wait.

What was I waiting for? I posed the question to myself, was forced to admit the truth: Felipe was leaving, and I would be alone, and the baby, even if it were carried to term, was not likely to survive for more than a few days. With Felipe gone, perhaps there would be no need to tell him about Thorne and me, after all. I knew he would be shocked if he knew, and angry. And after his anger had cooled, what then? Would he have lost all respect for me? Would he look on me with loathing, consider me no better than the *putas* in San Antonio de Bexar? The decision I had reached was perhaps more a failure to reach any decision at all. It was cowardly of me, but I did not intend to say anything to him; I reasoned that he was too young to understand. I did not know that events in Nacogdoches were rushing headlong toward a climax that was to change my life, and that I would soon be forced to tell him what I dreaded having him know, to blurt it out, directly and bluntly and without a chance to prepare him for the news.

Todd came to call on me twice the following week, and the more I knew him, the more I liked him, the more convinced I was that Felipe would be in good hands. For all of Felipe's independence, he was still young and could be easily influenced by those with whom he came in contact. And what better influence could there be than Todd Stewart, who had been like a father to the man I loved? From Todd's conversation, it was plain to see that he was becoming increasingly fond of Felipe, and this, too, was reassuring, as was his air of quiet authority.

I saw Thorne only one time during that week, and that was a hurried visit, and again I forestalled telling him I carried his child. Soon, I reasoned, Felipe and Todd would leave, and things would again be as they had been between us. And one day soon, when we were not pressed for time, I would tell him my news.

But things in life seldom work out precisely as we plan. A few days before Felipe and Todd were to leave, Thorne came riding into the clearing, and I could tell at once that he was in a state of agitation. I went to meet him as I always did. As he enclosed me in his arms, he told me the news that was to shatter our peaceful existence, change our lives completely.

"Governor Blanco has ordered the Edwards brothers expelled from Texas!" he said.

For a moment, it didn't occur to me that the news would be of much importance to us, and I couldn't at first understand his agitation. What difference to us was the fate of the Edwards brothers?

"Good," I said, smiling. "The Edwardses have nurtured nothing but confusion. I'm glad they're going."

He backed off, looked at me. "You don't understand, Serena. How can any of us be sure of our claims any more, claims that they've issued? Todd says I have no choice but to leave, and he's right."

"Leave?" I was dumbstruck at the thought, could only

107

repeat, "Leave?" and look at him, shaking my head in denial of what he was saying. He had become my whole life, except for Felipe. How could he talk of leaving? My stomach twisted into a hard knot at the thought.

"But surely things will work out," I protested, when at last I had found my voice. "Once Hayden Edwards is out, there's no need for you to leave," I insisted with blind stubbornness, not seeing, not wanting to see that he should leave. I started to say more, but my words dwindled off to nothing as I saw him standing there, looking at me sadly, shaking his head.

"I can't take that chance," he said. "Every tree I cut, every seed I plant, I'd be wondering if I was doing it for myself or somebody else—"

"But nothing has really changed. You've always known you might lose your land. The Varga grant—"

"Sweetheart," he said with a touch of exasperation creeping into his voice, "I never gave a damn for the Varga grant."

The old fury, the conditioned response to any doubting of the validity of the Varga grant, came without conscious thought. "The King of Spain, Carlos III—"

He held my shoulders, shook them gently. "Will you stop telling me about Carlos III and your precious Varga grant? I'm telling you, it doesn't matter any more. And something else, something else I didn't tell you about. I didn't see any reason to worry you, but there are other claims now, overlapping parts of mine. Sweetheart, I know when I'm licked. I won't stay, I won't fight it. It's not worth it. There's too much other land for the taking, better land. I'd have packed up and gone weeks ago, if it hadn't been for not wanting to leave you." He hesitated. "And there's more to it than that, too."

"But where will you go?" I asked, the significance of his words finally taking hold. Clearly, he had already decided he was leaving and I was forced to accept the knowledge that nothing I could say would make him change his mind. "And what about us?" I added, my voice dropping to a whisper, for it was a question I knew I must ask, and yet I feared it had no answer.

"We'll work something out," he said.

Just as I had feared, he had given me no answer at all. He put his arms around me as we walked toward the cabin, and for the first time in months, I failed to find comfort in his touch.

Still too shocked by his news for clear thought, I busied myself preparing a pot of coffee. As I moved about the cabin and finally put the coffee on the fire to brew, he told me his plans. He would move his family to Todd's place in Austin's colony and they would live there.

"That won't keep me from getting a grant of my own somewhere else, to hold for later. But Todd has a house started on Rebecca's place, and he says he never intends to live there again or farm it himself, so he's offered it to me to live on now. As he says, it will eventually be mine, anyway."

Austin's colony! So far away!

"I still don't understand why you must leave here." Ironically, I remembered that less than a year before, I had been demanding that he leave. Now, I would beg him to stay if I thought it would do any good, even if it meant losing some of the Varga land. "Those other claims you mentioned are fraudulent, surely, and will be proved such. Why—?"

"I told you, there's more to it than just some more fraudulent claims. The Edwards brothers are going to fight. They've written to Austin for his support, and they're going to try to recruit a force to hold this colony, defy the order for them to leave."

"It sounds like they're declaring war!" I looked at him in alarm. The idea was absurd, but frightening. "What about Austin? Will he support them?" I set the cups on the table, the china cups and saucers Felipe had brought me.

"Todd says not. He says Austin's far too smart to put his head in Hayden Edwards's noose. Nor can I afford to put mine in it, either, and that's exactly what I'd be doing if I

109

stayed. If I were to remain here, it would in effect be siding with the Edwards brothers, and unless they're successful—which isn't very likely—everyone with them would be sure to be expelled from Mexico. I can't take the chance of being mistaken for one of the rebels. Now do you see why I have no choice?"

I sat down heavily, noting that the coffee was boiling over, and not caring. I was only dimly aware of Thorne jumping up to grab the coffee pot from the fire.

"I'm going to have a baby," I said bluntly, my words all but drowned out by the hissing of the coffee splashing on the hot coals. How differently I had envisioned breaking the news to him—quietly, happily, in a moment of tenderness and closeness! But his news had changed all that, changed everything. I had wrestled only briefly with my pride. A proud woman would never have used her unborn child to hold the man she loved, if she knew he chose to leave her. But almost from the first, my feelings for Thorne had overridden my pride, and now I only hoped that the news I had blurted out would keep him from leaving me, from forgetting about me. I had not even waited to see if he had, in these suddenly changed plans for his future, included some plans for me. Perhaps I was just a little afraid to find out that he hadn't.

Thorne had his back to me as I told him my news, so I could not immediately tell the effect of my words on him. When at last he turned around, I could see he was shaken. He set the pot on the table, sank to his chair, and reached out to cover my hand with his, in a gesture that had become familiar to us both.

He smiled wanly at me. "That does complicate matters, doesn't it?"

I nodded my agreement. I did not remind him that, of the five children I had borne, only Felipe had survived more than a week. I wanted him to take me with him, even if it was for the sake of his child and not for love of me, and just then, I did not want him to realize the probability of losing our child at its birth.

I slipped my hand from under his, picked up the coffee pot and filled our cups. "I just want you to know I'm not sorry, Thorne. We didn't want this to happen, but I'm not sorry it did. No matter what your feelings are about this child, I'm glad I'm going to bear it."

As I set the coffee pot on the table again, he caught my hand, held it tightly. "Sweetheart, I'm not sorry! You mustn't think that! It's just that it's a big surprise, especially coming right now, when things are so confused. And a—a natural child . . . you must understand, it's a shock. . . ."

"A not altogether pleasant one, I take it," I said wryly, disappointed at his reaction. I lowered my eyes, focused them unseeingly on the little clouds of steam rising from our cups. I pushed back my chair and stood up. "I forgot the milk and sugar—"

"The devil take the milk and sugar! It's you I care about." Thorne stood up suddenly, his knees bumping the table as he did so, spilling coffee everywhere. He came to me, enveloped me in his arms, cradled my head in one of his big hands. "Did you think I could leave you behind? Is that why you told me about the baby now?"

I looked up at him, nodded. "Oh, Thorne, don't leave me here alone! I would feel that my life was over if I thought I'd never see you again."

He held my face in his hands, leaned down and brushed my lips with his in a gesture of infinite tenderness, then said huskily, "I couldn't leave you. I love you, Serena. Don't ever forget that or doubt it for a minute."

I reached up to put my arms around his neck, offered my lips eagerly to his. This kiss was no less gentle than the one before it, for all the pent-up desire of which it spoke.

"Oh, Serena, my dear." His glance darted toward the bed, then back to me. "But I suppose we mustn't, or it might harm the babe—"

Surprised, I looked at him. "What are you talking about? There's no reason to build a cocoon around me yet."

111

He shook his head. "But Angela . . . she always said I shouldn't. . . ."

I smiled. "I gather that Angela was quite adept at devising ways to keep you out of her bed. I suppose I'm shameless, for I'll never stop wanting you in mine."

That day we gave ourselves to each other more completely, more irrevocably than we ever had in the past, as though with our bodies we could pledge endless devotion to each other. The future was pushed aside for a short time, and only the present had meaning.

After our empassioned lovemaking, I lay, pleasantly wearied, in Thorne's arms. Only then did we remember the future and return to the problem of what we were to do.

"Todd has an empty cabin," he said. "It's the one that was his before he and Rebecca were married and he moved into hers. It's not far away, only half a mile or so from Rebecca's place, where I'll be taking my family."

"I would like being so close to you. But didn't you tell me once it was on the Bexar Road? Wouldn't it be better if we could find some place more secluded, some place far from any road, like this?"

"You're right, but I'm at a disadvantage, not knowing the area well. We'll have to ask Todd for his help."

"Tell your uncle about us?" I asked, startled at the thought.

"We have no choice. We'll need his help to find some place for you, some place not too far from me." His arms tightened around me.

"But surely he'll disapprove, try to talk you out of taking me with you."

"Don't worry. He'll understand. He knows what my marriage is like."

"Are you certain?" I asked uneasily, pulling away to look at him.

He tightened his arms around me, kissed my forehead. "You just let me worry about it. I'll talk to him. We'll work things out. He'll help me think of something when I tell him I'll not leave you."

I settled back in his arms with a sigh, wishing his assurances had set me more at ease.

The next day, he returned with Todd. I waited in the doorway as they approached, not knowing what to do, how to act, wondering how much Todd knew. Thorne solved the problem for me, leaned down and kissed me as he entered, and put his arm around my shoulder possessively. So that was my cue. Todd knew about us. He had already told him. We would proceed from there.

Todd greeted me somewhat less cordially than he had on his other visits, and as the three of us stood near the door, it somehow reminded me of the day they had come to see me the first time, after Felipe's encounter with Cassie. That had been the beginning of things between Thorne and me. What lay before us now? Was this to be another beginning, or the end of everything? In spite of Thorne's assurances that he would not leave me, I was afraid. The solemnity on both their faces did nothing to allay my fears.

Thorne gave my shoulder a final squeeze, then walked over to sit down on the edge of one of the beds, motioned his uncle to one of the chairs.

"Coffee?" I asked, and when they both shook their heads, I settled myself uneasily in the remaining chair, feeling somehow that I was on trial.

Thorne cleared his throat nervously. "Todd thinks it would be foolish for me to take you to Austin's colony with me."

I didn't answer. What could I say? I had feared that very thing, dreaded hearing those very words. I didn't take my eyes off Thorne, waited for him to continue, feeling sorry for him because I knew the words had been almost as hard for him to say as they were for me to hear. Finally, he lost his look of strained solemnity and burst out, addressing himself to Todd, "Hell and damnation, Todd! I can't leave her alone! She's going to have my child!"

"That is the main reason you must leave her," Todd answered quietly. He turned his gaze on me. "Serena—I may call you that now?—you will see the sense of it. He wants

113

to bring you to San Felipe, let you live in my old cabin—"

"The same one you offered me a few weeks ago so I could see Felipe more often," I reminded him.

"But that was under quite a different set of circumstances. Surely you can see that it is quite out of the question now." His voice softened. "My dear, I am not condemning you and Thorne. You must live your lives as you see fit, and I've no right to interfere, to either condemn or condone. I am willing to help you all I can, but I will not help you to hurt innocent people. And if I should give my permission to let you stay in my old cabin, that is exactly what will happen. It is in full view of the Bexar Road, which is becoming increasingly busy. It is hardly comparable to the seclusion in which you live here, and it would only be a matter of time before everyone in the colony realized what was going on. How would that affect Cassie and Will? And Angela? Pathetic as she is, she does have feelings, and she is, after all, Thorne's wife." He paused. "If you won't consider them and their feelings, think of the child you carry. There is no way possible for that child to remain anonymous, to escape the taint of bastardy if you follow Thorne. I grant you that the child will probably still have to contend with that, but this way, he would have no chance at all to escape it. It would be too obvious, too easy for any logical mind to follow."

"So you're suggesting that I stay out of Thorne's life," I said dully.

"I'm not suggesting that at all, nor, as I said, would I consider it my place to suggest it. That is between the two of you. But Thorne has asked my help, asked if I know of any place in Austin's colony where you could be close to him and still remain secluded and unknown. And I must tell you that, to my knowledge, there is no such place, at least none that is accessible. Austin's colony is successful, full of people. And people, unfortunately, tend to have an insatiable curiosity about other people."

I looked at Thorne, putting to him the unspoken question, *Is this true, or does he just want to keep us apart?*

114

He nodded. "Todd would tell us if he knew of any place suitable for you to stay within a reasonable distance of where I'll be. There just is no such place."

I turned back to Todd, for, oddly enough, this seemed to have become a matter between us, rather than between Thorne and me. "What do you suggest, then? That I stay here?"

He shook his head. "That's not practical, either, with things about to get in such a stew here. I propose that I take you to the crossing of the Colorado on the Bexar Road, in Green DeWitt's colony. He came about the same time Edwards did, and he's doing well. I'll say you're recently bereaved, my brother's widow, and I'll build you a cabin just off the road a way. Felipe and I can use it for a stopping place, keep a change of horses there."

"DeWitt's colony," I repeated. I remembered hearing, vaguely, of the new colony. "But the Colorado River— why, that's two or three days' ride from San Felipe, at least!"

They didn't correct me, and I knew it was that far, or farther.

Thorne leaned toward me. "I'll be there to see you, sweetheart, as often as I can. We're going to get another coach, just as soon as I'm able to get away to New Orleans to buy it. And I'll drive it myself, be coming through there regularly."

*Through.* My mind caught the significance of the word. He would pass through briefly, pass through my life from time to time, but he would never again be as much a part of it as he had been. "How often do you think that would be?"

"Every month or two," Thorne said, and though he tried to say the words lightly, I knew the thought of the long separations, the hurried visits made him as miserable as it did me. But what other course of action was there? It was better than staying here alone where I would never be apt to see him at all.

"What choice do I have?" I asked dully. Then, suddenly,

I remembered Felipe. All this couldn't be done without his knowledge. And if the coach he and Todd drove were to stop there, he would have to know about my pregnancy, as well. "Felipe!" I said, looking from one to the other. "He doesn't know."

"He'll have to be told," Thorne said.

"You'll need his cooperation," Todd reminded me, "to back up your story of widowhood. It might or might not be believed, but in DeWitt's colony, away from Thorne, there's at least a chance that it will be. Of course, it's possible people will think you're my woman, bearing my child, but I thought if I built myself a cabin somewhere else, several miles away from yours, it would help to stop any such talk."

I nodded. This, then, was the solution Thorne had promised me the day before. It was, as I had known it would be, far from satisfactory. But, for the time being, it was the only solution we had.

"When do you want to leave?" I asked.

"Day after tomorrow. Can you be ready that soon?"

I nodded. "Day after tomorrow."

They stood up to go, started toward the door. Was Thorne to leave me like this, then, so casually, so quickly?

"Thorne, when will you be leaving?" How could my inquiry have sounded so matter-of-fact, when my whole life was falling apart?

"The day after you do, if I can get ready in time."

"This is the last time I'll see you before I go, then?" It was more statement than question.

He hesitated. "Yes."

Todd had reached the door, looked at us. "I'll be outside."

As Todd closed the door behind himself, Thorne swept me into his arms. "I'll be thinking of you every minute," he said, between our desperate kisses. "It won't be long till I come to you, I promise. I'll manage somehow."

"Make it soon," I urged, but without conviction, remembering that he had promised, too, to take me with him. It wasn't him I blamed, or Todd. All this was nothing any of us could have foreseen or expected, or controlled. What, after all, would we have done differently? I had no regrets about giving myself to Thorne, about what we had come to mean to each other, and I hoped he had none. I thought how my life always seemed to change directions suddenly, unexpectedly: first, when I had been wrenched away from my Indian village, again when Esteban had suddenly appeared and taken me away with him as his wife, yet another time when he had died, horribly and suddenly, in the fire. And then, when I had thought life held nothing more for me than continued loneliness, Thorne had appeared and changed all that. And now we must leave each other, not knowing what the future had in store.

"I love you, Thorne. Even if we should never meet again, I'll always go on loving you."

"Sweetheart, don't talk like that! I told you, I'll come to you just as soon as I can."

"I know," I said. "I know."

"Good-bye, sweetheart."

"Good-bye, my darling."

He turned and was gone. He stopped once to turn in his saddle and wave.

As I watched him go, I wished, again, that I had learned how to cry.

# Part Two—Todd

# Chapter I

## SAVANNAH, GEORGIA—
## Winter 1811-1812

Angela was all wrong for Thorne. The good Lord knows, I tried to stop him from marrying her. But he was so taken by her air of innocence and a sort of fragile prettiness that he missed seeing what was as plain to me as the sun in the sky—that a pathetically weak creature lived inside that attractive young body.

Angela's facial features and other physical properties were arranged appealingly enough, there was no denying that. She had soft doelike eyes that seemed enormous in her tiny, rounded face. Her nose and mouth were shaped well, and her bosom was firm and her waist small, no larger than Thorne's handspan. But it was her hair that was breathtaking. It was the color of flax and had a lustrous sheen, so that even indoors it seemed to be shining in the sunlight. She always wore soft blues to set off her hair, and soft curly wisps were pulled down over her forehead, underneath a wide, blue satin band. With the Grecian dresses then in vogue, the effect was one of purity and innocence. The hair styles and fashions were peculiarly suited to her, as they were to few others. She was of average height, but seemed smaller.

Thorne, smitten by her frailty and flattered by the way she hung on his every word, hovered protectively over her, oblivious to the fact that her childish innocence was based as much on shallowness of character as on lack of worldliness. I tried to warn him, but his infatuation had deafened his ears as well as dimmed his eyes, and he was as unheeding to my words as he was blind to her faults. I, who knew him better than any other living soul, knew he worshipped strength and held weakness in deep contempt. How could he possibly find happiness with a wife who was the living example of everything he abhorred?

Yet I knew it was I who was to blame for his susceptibility to her physical charms, and the ease with which he was taken in by her mother's plans. She threw her seventeen-year-old daughter in his path. Oddly enough, that formidable widow—a woman almost as large and as big-boned as Thorne and I—had first set her sights on me as a potential husband for her daughter, a prospect I regarded with amused detachment. I had been a widower for many years, and as soon as I realized what she was about, I quickly eased myself away from both mother and daughter.

But I hadn't thought to warn Thorne, who had had virtually no experience with women. To my horror, I realized that the widow's eyes had fallen on him. It was for his inexperience with women that I had to accept blame. I had selfishly kept him with me in the backcountry long after he should have been sent someplace where he could be with people his own age. He was twenty-one that fall when we came to Savannah together, after I had sold the plantation, and until then the few eligible females he had ever come to know were of unappealing looks, unmarried sisters or cousins of some of the folks out our way. Too late, I realized Thorne had been trapped. If the girl had even half-way suited him, he'd have had my blessing.

Thorne was my nephew, the orphaned son of my only brother, Grant, and at the time Thorne and I came to Savannah that fall of 1811, he had been with me for eleven years. Grant had died when Thorne was nine, and the boy had continued to live with his mother until her death a year later. She had been Grant's second wife, an empty-headed frivolous woman, and before her death she signed away Thorne's birthright to his half brother, Thaddeus, who was fifteen years Thorne's senior, and every bit as grasping and greedy and unscrupulous as my brother Grant had been.

Grant and I had started out in business together some years earlier. We were as different as day and night, and had never been close. Our partnership came about only because Grant knew I had done particularly well at the gaming tables. He set about convincing me that I should put my winnings with his small savings so that we could buy an all-but-defunct company, the chief asset of which was a small barnacle-encrusted ship. My heart was always a gambler's, and Grant's idea appealed to me, sounded every bit as exciting as a game of chance. So we bought the company and had the barnacles scraped off the hull of our small ship and loaded her with goods and sent her to France. My luck held, and we prospered a bit. I was pleased, but even when we had put aside some profits, Grant was still dissatisfied. He said we were too vulnerable, too much at the mercy of fate.

"Only one small ship!" he said with a worried frown one day. "Where would we be if something happened to it? We must get one more, at least."

Grant insisted on borrowing heavily to purchase another ship. Within a year, we had it paid for and were again making a profit. It would have suited me to remain the size we were, but Grant was a man with a burr under his saddle, and again he persuaded me to use our savings on a third ship, and then a fourth. For all that Grant never touched a deck of cards, he was more of a gambler than I. His timing was perfect, his business decisions infallible. I could never fault his judgement, but his lack of scruples began to eat at me. I have never had a stomach for any man willing to sacrifice some of his humanity in order to get what he wants. Grant became utterly ruthless in his dealings with others, and I objected vigorously to this; but so drunk with his own power had he become that he waved my objections aside impatiently, and began to act without consulting me. It was inevitable that our differences would finally erupt into a bitter argument about his methods, and when in the heat of our quarrel, he offered to buy me out, I was only too willing to agree. I was surprised at my relief on knowing that I would no longer have to concern myself with Grant's actions. The price he named was unfair, but I put up no opposition. Money itself was never important to me as long as I had enough of it to do as I wanted. I had been blessed with good card sense, and whenever I felt the need for more cash, there would always be another game somewhere, another chance to strike it rich.

By the time Grant and I dissolved our partnership, I wanted to get away from Savannah, out into the open spaces where the air is fresh and pure, and you can go for miles without seeing a house. To this day I cannot understand why every townsman must build his house right on top of the next one, so that a man can hardly sneeze within his own walls without the whole town wondering if he's catching cold.

I saw Grant about once or twice a year after that, stopping in to see him whenever I was in Savannah. We bore one another no particular animosity for the way we had parted; we had both derived our own sort of satisfaction from the break, just as I think we had known from the start that a partnership of two such different people could never last.

Whenever I stopped to see Grant at his warehouse-office, I noticed that his oldest son, Thaddeus, was usually there. He had apparently taken an exceptional interest in the business at an early age, and this pleased Grant. Seeing the boy around the place whenever I came by made me that much more satisfied with my decision to remove myself when I did, for young as he was, his eyes gleamed with the same acquisitiveness as his father's. I could never dislike a child, but I found myself unable to feel any real affection for him. It was different with Thorne, Grant's younger son. He was a more open child, and even though I saw him infrequently, he always greeted me with heartwarming pleasure and affection. Though his mother was flighty, she was not unkind. I think she would have been a good step-mother to Thaddeus if he had let her, but Thaddeus met her overtures with open disdain. He seemed to delight in pointing out her shortcomings in front of Grant and in ridiculing her stupidity. I don't know why Grant tolerated such behavior from him.

Thaddeus seemed to derive even more pleasure from inflicting small cruelties on his younger brother. Once, I happened to enter a room just as he was coercing Thorne into buying his silence over some small matter, something that would have brought Grant's disapproval down on Thorne. I forget what prompted the demand—a broken piece of bric-a-brac, a rule disobeyed, a chore forgotten—but I never forgot the hard gleam of triumph shining from Thaddeus's eyes as the younger boy tearfully handed over a precious hoarded coin. Thorne was only six at the time, and Thaddeus, twenty-one and about to marry, certainly had no need of the pittance he had wrung from his little brother. I expected Thaddeus to be visibly shamed when he saw me standing in the doorway and knew I had overheard his petty blackmail. But the opposite was true, for as he walked past me, he tossed the coin into the air and caught it, smirking as he did so. The flaunting of his triumph had been as unnecessary as the original cruelty. Later, when I told Grant I had seen Thaddeus taking Thorne's money away from him, he amazed me by nodding his head in approval.

"A good lesson for him. Only fools are weak, and let themselves be used by those who are strong. Perhaps the boy will learn from the experience."

I doubted if this was the first or the last of such "lessons" taught Thorne by Thaddeus. Such bullying was bound to have a pronounced effect on the boy's character, and by the time Thorne came to live with me, he had no sympathy for weakness. Strength had become a god, to be worshipped for its own sake. This was true in all things. Even when he was choosing a puppy for his own, he studied all of them carefully and picked the most aggressive of the litter. And until I gave him a firm setdown, I found he was

125

bullying the weaker of the house slaves. In his respect for strength and his disdain for weakness, he had become almost as cruel as Thaddeus. I didn't care for this callousness in his nature and would have changed it had I been able, but it was as though he had hardened himself against being hurt by aligning himself always on the side of the strong. Though I came to love him like a son, I was not blind to this trait, which seemed to increase as he grew older.

Grant died in 1799, and his wife followed him a year later. As soon as I heard of her death, I jumped on a horse and rode hell-for-leather into Savannah, determined to take the boy to live with me. Thaddeus and the prudish woman he had married, as sour and unsmiling as he, were visibly relieved to hand the boy over to my care. With his mother dead scarcely a week, they had already begun preparations to send him away to school.

By that time Thaddeus and Eulalie had a son of their own, though I couldn't for the life of me imagine either of those two stiff-necked people unbending enough to perform the necessary preliminaries for such an event. But perform it they must have, for Eulalie had presented Thaddeus with a son a year after their marriage.

Thorne recovered quickly from the grief and confusion of having his life change directions several times in the course of a few days, and before long it seemed he was as truly my son as if he had sprung from my own loins. He was not shy, and we soon became far closer than most fathers and sons. He filled a void in my life left years earlier by the loss of both my young wife and the son she had tried to give me. We were constant companions, except for the hours that he spent in the schoolroom.

It did not take me long to realize it would be a mistake to show any overindulgence in my treatment of Thorne. He would have loved and respected me the less for it. And so I indulged him some, but I didn't spoil him, and he felt the heavy hand of my discipline on many occasions. He submitted to it without protest because he always knew he could depend on fairness from me, and his punishment was never more nor less than he deserved.

I never even considered sending him away to school. Instead, I hired a tutor, who stayed with us till Thorne was sixteen. I knew that was selfish of me, that certainly his education would have been more complete and his childhood more normal if he had gone away to be with other boys his own age. But once the boy was established in my life, I could not bear sending him off for most of the year. He became the joy of my life, and I was grateful to the Providence that had sent him to me. I kept him with me as long as I could, continually finding excuses to put off the day he would leave. Not until he fell prey to Angela's frail attractiveness and her mother's scheming did I realize I had wronged him by keeping him so long isolated from the mainstream of life.

Thorne and I had come into Savannah in the fall of 1811, and asked Thaddeus for cabin space aboard any of his ships going to Europe. It was risky to travel then, we knew, for the British were blockading our ports and impressing our men into their navy, but it was a risk we were willing to take. Our plans were vague. I had sold the plantation, having tired of it long before. The joy of gambling on that piece of backcountry, the challenge of pitting myself against the elements to make something productive out of nothing—these were past. I would never have remained on it as long as I did if it hadn't been for Thorne, and once he was of age, I decided I would go with him to Europe, take him on his Grand Tour, and then we would come back, go somewhere west, Kentucky or Tennessee, maybe. My plans were vague. As I had done so often in the past, I would let the future guide me where it would.

When we had asked Thaddeus for cabin space aboard one of his merchantmen, I had expected him to offer it to us free, if grudgingly. But the acquisitiveness which had been apparent even when he was a small child was still very much a part of his character, and he named a price that was just short of outrageous. Still, his captains were

127

canny and had all evaded the British up to that time, so we accepted. Thaddeus promised us two berths on the first ship to France, so we settled down to wait.

It was while we were waiting that Thorne met Angela. We were staying with Thaddeus. He had at least shown us that courtesy, and Eulalie seemed to feel compelled to include us in most of her dinner parties. I suspect she did so more to keep people from criticizing her than from any genuine desire to entertain us. Their house was not a comfortable one, and I would have been well pleased if a ship had been available the day after our arrival. But as Fate would have it, we did not find a ship immediately, and before a vessel was available, Thorne became interested in Angela. When, two months after our arrival in Savannah, the first ship was ready to depart for France, Thorne refused to board her. It was then that I began to fear that he might be hopelessly smitten with Angela.

"Just a year," I pleaded with him. "Just come with me for a year. I've never been to Europe myself, you know, and I'm anxious to see the sights, too." I was certain that if I could only get him away from Angela for a time, he would see her in proper perspective when he returned.

He shook his head. "I'm sorry, Todd, but I'm enjoying myself here. I just haven't had my fill of Savannah yet. Couldn't we wait a bit longer?"

And so the first ship sailed without us. And the second. When the third was about to leave, five months after our arrival, Thorne said the words I had been dreading to hear.

"Why don't you go without me?"

"Without you?" I looked at him, trying to hide my alarm, then said with a forced casualness, "Why, there's no need for that. If you want to wait for the next ship, I suppose we can, though I'm getting mighty tired of Thaddeus and Eulalie's grudging hospitality, and I imagine you are, too. I think perhaps we've overstayed our welcome. . . ."

He set his jaw stubbornly. "Then I'll find other lodgings."

"No need to, if we just get on board the *Carolina Miss*."

"I'm not going, Todd. I . . . I'm sorry."

"Come, now, we've been planning this for two years!"

Again, the stubborn set of his jaw. "Sometimes plans change. You've often told me yourself it's best not to make plans too far in advance."

I disliked having my own words come back at me in that manner, especially when I knew what he had in mind. I hesitated, then decided I might be able to turn those same words around in the other direction, in hopes of keeping him from making the foolish mistake of speaking for Angela.

"That's right," I agreed, getting my pipe out of my pocket and sprinkling some tobacco in it, then tamping it down carefully. I did this with a deliberate slowness. I have often used this ritual of pipe filling to give myself a chance to think things through, to forestall uttering any hasty words which might be regretted later. "By the same token," I said as I tamped the last of the tobacco in place, "it's best not to commit yourself to anything too far in the future without giving it plenty of thought." I stood up and walked to the fireplace, carefully chose a piece of tinder, and put it into the banked coals till it caught. I lit my pipe.

"You mean Angela?" Thorne raised his eyebrows. Before I could answer, he continued, "I already have given the matter lots of thought, all I need give it. I am going to speak to her mother tomorrow."

"You surely aren't thinking of marrying her?" I asked with deliberate incredulity, looking at him over the top of my pipe.

He did not flinch as our eyes met. "Yes, I am."

Though I had thought I was prepared for this, I found that having him affirm my fears was more of a shock than I had anticipated. I felt as though the wind had been knocked suddenly from my sails.

I tried to hide my agitation, walked back to my chair slowly and sat down, puffed several times on my pipe, aware all the while of Thorne's eyes upon me. Until then, I had not come out and said anything derogatory about Angela, fearing such words would drive them closer together. But now it had to be warfare, open and declared, not so much between me and Angela as between me and her old tyrant of a mother. I was as determined to show her daughter as the spineless young woman she was as the termagant was to show her in the best light possible. But I hadn't counted on the extent of Thorne's stubbornness.

"You've only known her four months," I reminded him. "Don't you think you're being a bit hasty?"

"She needs me," he countered. "And what's so hasty about it? Four months is a long time, long enough to know I want to marry her and care for her—"

"She's weak, Thorne—"

"That's why she needs me to take care of her, protect her."

"Let somebody else protect her!" I said in exasperation, putting my pipe down with a clatter. I could no longer pretend to a coolness I did not feel. "At least make your Grand Tour before you speak for her. If you still want to marry her when we return, then so be it, and have my blessings. But give yourself a chance to think it over."

I might as well have pleaded with the walls. "She will probably have married someone else by the time we get back," he said. "Her mother has told her she must marry this year. I won't chance losing her. I've decided. I'm going to speak for her tomorrow when I go to her house for tea."

In despair, I suggested, "Then get betrothed before we leave, if you must, but come with me to Europe. The *Carolina Miss* won't be sailing for two or three days, so you'll have ample time to say your good-byes."

"I'm not going to say good-bye to Angela," he insisted. "I want to marry her, as soon as she'll have me."

*That will be the instant decorum will allow, if her mother has her way*, I thought to myself, *and not a minute longer*. Angela's mother would certainly not give him time for second thoughts once he committed himself to taking her weakling daughter off her hands. Couldn't he see that foolishness about her mother insisting she marry within the year was a lie fabricated especially for his benefit, designed to push him into marriage?

"Please reconsider, Thorne," I begged. "Angela is everything you've ever despised and rejected. She's completely without character. And she's spineless. You can see that from the way she refuses to stand up to her overbearing mother. She doesn't have a single original thought of her own—"

Thorne shot out of his chair. "Stop it!" he protested angrily. "I'll hear no one run down the woman I love, not even you. I'm going to marry her, with or without your blessings, and that's all there is to it!"

As I watched him stomp out of the room, I felt overwhelmed by the realization that, somehow, I must have failed him. Otherwise he would not be throwing away his young life by marrying a woman like Angela. It was all my fault for not having prepared him better against the possibility of meeting someone like Angela's determined mother.

I could not dissuade him, and Thorne and Angela were married in April. When I saw it was impossible to keep him from marrying her, I offered them a prolonged honeymoon in Europe, hoping that Angela might gain a little in stature if she could get away from her mother for a while. But Angela told Thorne she didn't want to go.

"I shouldn't go that far away when Mama's so sickly," she said. "She wants me close by, in case anything should happen to her."

When Thorne reported those words to me, it was all I could do to keep from laughing aloud. The old widow was strong as an ox, probably strong enough to outlive us all. But I was instantly sobered by the realization that she had outmaneuvered me, that she had no intention of letting her daughter get out from under her jurisdiction, not even for a long honeymoon.

In the end, Thorne took his bride to a place up the coast, then returned a month later to begin working for Thaddeus.

I didn't like the looks of that any better than I had liked

his marriage to Angela. The sum Thaddeus offered him was far too low, certainly, when by rights a share of the business should have belonged to him, as Grant had intended it should. His salary was scarcely enough to support a family properly. I bought him a house, so at least he'd not have to worry about a roof over their heads, nor would he have to consider moving in with Angela's mother.

"You must come live with us," he said as soon as they had returned from their brief honeymoon and set up housekeeping.

"That's something I'll never do," I said, then added pointedly, "I gave you the house so you and Angela could live alone."

"I realize that, and I appreciate it. But there's no comparison between Angela's mother and you. You know I . . . we . . . would enjoy having you with us."

"Still," I demurred, "I'd not place upon your marriage the burden of having an extra person in your household." I did not add that I thought making a success of marriage with Angela was enough of a challenge in itself, without the pressure of having another person in the house. "Besides, I plan to go to France on the next ship."

Thorne looked concerned. "You're still going? Do you think that's wise? The British are getting bolder by the day, attacking more and more of our ships. It's gotten intolerable—and unsafe."

"I'll take my chances. I doubt if I'm young enough to be of much interest to them if they're looking for ablebodied seamen to impress into His Majesty's service. And I'm getting tired of Savannah. The older I get, the less I care for town life."

That was only part of the truth. Thorne and Angela had come back from their honeymoon early in May of 1812, and it hurt me to see the trapped look I sometimes caught on his face. He must have realized the mistake he had made, God help him, for Angela was unable to make the smallest decision without consulting him—unless, of course, she was acting on direct instructions from her mother. Her utter dependence on others, primarily now on Thorne, which had so flattered him in the days of their courtship, had already begun to irritate him. He was no longer able to hide his annoyance at her indecisive manner. That despairing look on his face was more than I could bear.

There was another reason I preferred to leave Savannah. I had had a pleasant liaison with a widow about ten years my junior, and she had begun to speak of marriage, so that what had been a comfortable accommodation of our individual needs had become, for me, distinctly uncomfortable. She was not the kind of woman I would have considered marrying, and as it was impossible to avoid her if I remained in town, the best thing to do was to leave. So when the next of Thaddeus's ships was ready to leave for France, I was on board.

I hadn't been on the Continent long when word reached me that our Congress had declared war on England. The blockade of our ports began in earnest, making it impossible for me to return to America, so I had no choice but to remain in Europe. I roamed around the Continent aimlessly and, after six months, had looked my fill at monuments and castles and other antiquities, had admired the majesty of the Alps all I cared to, and had begun to wait only for the day I could go home. It didn't matter that I no longer had a real home to return to, for to me the openness, the vastness of America was what beckoned. Long before I was able to leave Europe, I had sickened of its dirty crowded cities and longed to feast my eyes once more on virgin land, walk again through endless acres of hushed uninhabited forests. Even the smallest of the European towns teemed with people, and it seemed impossible to get away even for a few moments from the odor of unwashed bodies and the stench of garbage. And always, inescapably there was the strict class consciousness of their society, the worshipping of any title, no matter the character of the man behind it. I can truly say that the time I spent in Europe made me appreciate more fully the wonder that was America.

It was May of 1815 when I returned to America, after an absence of three years. Perhaps I am overly sentimental, but I was shaken at the thrill of again setting foot in my native land. I bought a horse and set out on the long ride south.

On reaching Savannah, I rode directly to Thorne's house, where I was greeted by Angela. She did not at first recognize me, though there are few others with pure white hair like mine. My arrival seemed to throw her into a quandary, and she kept me standing in the entry hall till I at last suggested that we step into the parlor.

"Oh, yes, of course," she said, flustered, but obviously relieved to have been directed toward a course of action. She led the way into the parlor. "Thorne may be home any minute, or it could be hours before he comes. I never know when to expect him. He works so late every day, you know." Having completed what was, for her, a long speech, she motioned me to a chair, perched herself stiffly on the edge of the sofa, then smiled nervously and began twisting a strand of hair around her fingers. We sat in silence for a moment. She seemed to be searching for something to say to me. I had expected that she would offer me refreshments, for the day was damp and I had ridden far, and I could have done with a cup of hot tea or a glass of brandy. But that normal welcoming gesture apparently never occurred to her.

When it was obvious that she was not even going to inquire after my horse, I suggested she see to having someone take him around to the stables and give him feed and a rubdown. I fought down my irritation at her complete lack of initiative, at her failure to offer the most obvious amenities.

My simple request seemed to throw her into a new dilemma. "Thorne told Daniel to wash the buggy this afternoon, and he's probably doing that right now. But I suppose I can stop him and tell him to take your horse around back." She rose, then hesitated a minute. "Maybe it would be better if Sukie asked him. I'll see if she will." She started out of the room, then paused as though compelled to offer some sort of explanation. "Mama is out just now." With a little ineffectual wave of her hands, she turned and left. I couldn't help feeling sorry for her, so fraught with indecision was her every movement.

She returned a few minutes later, and once more seated herself opposite me. She cleared her throat, again reached up abstractedly to wind a strand of hair endlessly around her finger. Her hair, I noted, had lost its flaxen sheen and faded into a nondescript color. I had not realized until then how much her attractiveness had been dependent on her hair. Without its brilliance, a light seemed to have gone out in her face as well, and I realized that her features, except for her eyes, were really very ordinary. And her eyes, because they were so devoid of animation, were not really pretty at all, for all their large oval shape. Her movements were sharp and quivering, like those of a frightened bird, and her voice, which I had remembered as timid, had taken on a whining note. I pitied her, but I could not keep aversion from mixing with my pity.

"Is Cassie awake?" I asked, finally. "I would like to see her if she is."

My request seemed to please her. It was plain she was ill at ease at the thought of having to make conversation with me till Thorne arrived. She jumped up and pulled the bell cord. "I'll have Calla bring the children."

"Children?" I looked at her inquiringly. I know of only one.

"Cassandra and Williamson Todd."

"I'm afraid my information is a bit outdated. I didn't know there were two. The last letter I had from Thorne was written when Cassie was six months old. Let's see, she'd be over two by now, wouldn't she? And how old is the boy?" I was pleased that the child had been given my name for one of his.

"Oh, he's still in the cradle, just two months old."

"If he's sleeping, you mustn't disturb him on my account. I can always see him tomorrow."

"Yes, I suppose that might be better. He hasn't been very healthy. And Mama does so hate for me to interfere with his schedule."

I winced inwardly at Angela's second reminder that her mother lived under their roof. The old harridan had outwitted me in all ways; not only had Thorne tied himself to her pitiable daughter, but she now lived with them in the house I had bought for them. But I had to admit that if Angela's ineptitude at entertaining guests was any example of her other housewifely abilities, it was probably the lesser of possible evils to have her mother live under their roof.

Cassie stole my heart the moment I laid eyes on her. She had Angela's enormous eyes but she did not look at me vacuously. There was an active curiosity in her eyes, a sparkle of life that her mother's eyes lacked. Nor did she show any hesitancy or shyness when she approached me. I wondered later if I had sighed audibly with relief as I studied the child. I hadn't realized how much I had feared she would be a small copy of her mother, complete with Angela's timidity. But except for her eyes and the soft waviness of her hair, she was Thorne's child through and through.

I called her name and held out my arms toward her, and at once a smile lit her face. She pulled her hand from her young mammy's to run and throw herself into my arms. Few two-year-olds will approach a total stranger so fearlessly.

I sat her on my lap, and when she had finished investigating the buttons on my coat, I produced from my pocket the present I had brought her, a gold locket from Toledo. She examined it, and when I indicated where it would go, she wanted me to put it on her. I obliged by fastening it around her neck, and she was content for a while longer to remain sitting on my lap, playing with the pocket watch I had bought in Switzerland. I continued to attempt to make polite conversation with Angela until Thorne came home.

At the first sound of her father's arrival, Cassie slid from my lap and ran to greet him. "Papa!" she cried excitedly. "Look, Papa! A locket." She stumbled over the new word.

He scooped her up into his arms as she displayed her new locket. "Now where did you get such a pretty new bauble, Duchess?" His frame filled the doorway to the parlor as he hesitated a minute, then called, "Todd! You're back! It's about time!" He put the child down and strode over to give me a bear hug. My eyes misted as we embraced, and I noted when we backed away to assess the changes three years had wrought in each other that Thorne was also shaken. "It's great to see you again," he said warmly.

Thorne and I had much to talk over after our long separation, and we stayed up far into the night. He was thoroughly disgusted with working for Thaddeus, who was currently trying to set his son, seventeen-year-old Beauford, over him. I agreed such a situation was intolerable, and before we retired in the small hours of the morning, we had decided to start our own firm in competition with his half brother. It was my suggestion, and I knew I lacked sufficient capital to do it right, but I reminded Thorne that his father and I had started with even less.

Perhaps what I really wanted was an excuse to stay in Savannah awhile, near Thorne and his children. I loved the youngsters and never ceased to be amazed at how different they were. Will was a far less energetic child than Cassie, easily amused, and so placid and slow to object to anything he didn't like that at first I feared that he might be another Angela. But as he became a little older, I realized his apparent acquiescence was misleading. In his own quiet way, his stubbornness and determination were more than a match for Cassie's. In appearance, Will was exactly what Thorne had been at his age. It bothered me that he seemed to find Will's quietness and subdued nature irritating, and he made no secret of the fact that Cassie was his favorite by far.

As far as Thorne's and my venture into shipping was concerned, neither of us had Grant's or Thaddeus's genius for making money, and though we managed, literally, to just barely stay afloat, our company was never more than a step or two ahead of its creditors. After the war, the economy of the whole country was in bad shape, so perhaps it was poor timing more than anything else that made success elude us. Besides that, we were competing directly with Thaddeus, and small and insignificant though we were, he never missed an opportunity to undercut us. Thorne was a hard worker and had gained valuable experience working for Thaddeus, but between us we managed only to keep going. By the spring of 1817, I felt compelled to do something about the stagnant character of our venture, right or wrong.

"I'm going west, Thorne," I told him one day as we were sitting in the small office we shared. "I'm going to New Orleans."

Thorne looked at me, his eyebrows raised. "Leave Savannah?"

"I've no attachment to the place, besides my attachment to you and the children. I hate to miss seeing them grow, but I feel we must expand or go under, get out from under Thaddeus's thumb."

"I think you're right. I've thought of the same thing, but of course, it wouldn't be easy for me to leave." He paused and gave a derisive little laugh. "You won't miss any grandnieces or grandnephews, I can promise you that. At least not legitimate ones."

"I see," I said. "I'm sorry."

"I'd like to have more children, sons to be proud of. Will—somehow I just can't feel close to him. Maybe it's because he was such a weak little thing when he was born, and Angela and her mother were always fussing over him, and the old biddy yelled that I was being too rough with him if I just chucked him under the chin. I would like to try again, have another son, one I can feel belongs to me instead of to them." He sighed heavily. "But it's not likely. Angela has developed an aversion to me in bed, though she scarcely ever tolerated my advances. I suppose it has as much to do with the terror she feels at the thought of getting pregnant again as it has to do with me. She did have a hard time with Will. Well, whatever the reason, I'm not going to push my attentions on her." He gave a sharp, nervous laugh. "I wouldn't force her, Todd, not even if she is my wife. If I so much as get near her, she freezes with fright. I haven't touched her in over a year. For all that, she doesn't inspire much desire in me any more. She has killed any affection I once felt for her. But I would like another son."

I sought for something to say. Though I had long suspected what he had just told me, his revelation deepened my disgust for Angela. Many women didn't want more children, but were willing to take some chances for the sake of their husbands. Surely very few denied their husbands the marriage bed completely after less than four years of marriage and only two children. I brought out my pipe and started filling it to cover the silence between us. After I had lit it, I pointed out that Angela did seem to love the children and was good to them. I could not bring myself to say she was a good mother, for she hadn't the strength of character to be good at anything, but I felt compelled to offer Thorne some consolation. After all, he was married to her, and there was nothing he could do about that.

"Yes," he agreed with finality. "She does love the children." After a moment's silence, he said abruptly, "Let's get back to what we were talking about. It's true Thaddeus will never get over resenting our intrusion here. God knows, we're not his only competition, and certainly have never been a threat to him, but he still seems determined to put us out of business."

I nodded. "The way things are going, in another year we'll have to admit he's succeeded. Now that my capital's gone, there just isn't enough for both of us to live on. You stay here and try to keep your head above water, and I'll see what I can do in New Orleans."

"I guess it's the only way, but, God, I'll miss you! We all will."

139

Events moved along quickly, and in a few weeks, I was preparing to sail on one of our two rickety old ships. Thorne had brought the children down to see me off, and they had come on board to see my quarters.

"It's such a little bed!" Cassie said with her usual bright-eyed alertness. Will, a sturdy child at two, busied himself walking around and looking silently at everything. I was glad that, for them, the whole episode of my departure was merely a lark, an excuse to visit one of the ships. They did not realize, as Thorne and I did, that it might be a long time before we saw each other again. The future, that of our lives as well as our business venture, had never been as unfathomable.

Up on deck again, I said with forced joviality, "Who knows? We may soon find it's best to move our whole operation to New Orleans."

Thorne nodded. "Let me know. I can get packed and loaded onto one of our tubs in a week's time. I wish I could go with you now."

"We've been over all that. You can't pack a family around with no certainty about the future. It's best that I go first."

I called Will over to me and gave him a final hug. For all that he was an exceptionally self-sufficient child, seeming perfectly content to be ignored and allowed to amuse himself for hours on end, he was not lacking in affection. Without realizing the significance of the long solemn hug I gave him, he returned it without question. In a way, I felt that I was deserting Will. Even at the age of two, he sensed that his father did not really care for him. I put him down and picked up Cassie.

I blinked back the tears as I felt Cassie's arms encircle my neck as Will's had done. She, I knew, was closer to realizing the meaning of our parting than Will was. "I'll send you both something from New Orleans," I promised as I put her down, "to make sure you don't forget your Uncle Todd."

The captain came by and told Thorne he would have to

go ashore. Thorne nodded and he and I shook hands and looked at each other for a long moment.

"I'll write as soon as I arrive," I said, avoiding the saying of a final good-bye.

Thorne, too, seemed to feel the same superstitious reluctance to say the word that sounded so final. "Good luck. I'll be looking for your letter."

I nodded solemnly, and reluctantly, we let our hands drop.

I watched as Thorne and the children left the ship. They turned to wave as we got under way. I didn't know if it was the failing light or the mistiness of my eyes that kept me from seeing them well, but at last I could see them no more, and turned to go below. I would not set eyes on them again for nine years.

# Chapter II

## NEW ORLEANS, LOUISIANA—
## Fall 1821

As a gambler, I know there are times when luck can run against a man with an uncanny disregard for the odds, and I guess you could say that is what happened to my attempt to build up our fortunes by moving to New Orleans. There were times when things looked hopeful, but the hopes never quite materialized. For everything that went right, three things went wrong, and it was all I could do to eke out enough for my own sustenance, picking up a bit of cargo space here and there on other vessels. Not even at the card tables could I seem to reverse my fortunes. So my life, in the four years I lived in New Orleans, was simple at best, and I was never able to write Thorne and tell him to pick up his family and come join me, as I had optimistically hoped to do.

Back in Savannah, Thaddeus continued his spiteful harassment of Thorne, and though we didn't lose our two small ships, neither could Thorne replace them or acquire any more. The ships were old, and our captains, because we were unable to pay them much, were inferior. We were trapped by our own mediocrity.

It was in the fall of 1821 that I happened to see an advertisement for colonists to go to Texas, west of the Mexican border. I made inquiries, was intrigued by what I found out, and soon was writing a letter to Thorne to tell him that I had decided to leave New Orleans.

"My fellow colonists will all be Americans," I wrote, "so

it isn't as if I were going into a foreign country all by my-self. As you know, Mexico has just recently gained her freedom from Spain, after a struggle that has flared up a number of times in recent years. There are many in our country who dispute the right first of Spain and now of Mexico to own Texas, and who knows but what Mexico will ultimately be persuaded to sell Texas to the United States? I think that hope is in the back of the minds of all of us who have agreed to go; only time will tell if the hope is fulfilled.

"There is a great deal of enthusiasm for the venture among those I have met. I hope to find some opportunity for the transportation of freight there, either overland or by way of the Brazos or Red Rivers, which I understand are both navigable fairly far inland."

Ostensibly, that was my excuse for going, and I did hope I might uncover some such opportunities there, but the truth of the matter was that it was the adventure of it that appealed to me. I had had my fill and more of the day-to-day monotony of going to an office, and I longed to get out into the backcountry again. Once before I had risen to the challenge of pushing back a wilderness, but I had been years younger then. It seemed, in a way, a chance to renew my youth to try to extend myself again. At the age of forty-nine, I was anxious to find out if I was still capable of meeting such a challenge, this time on a totally untested frontier.

Stephen F. Austin, the young man who was to head our enterprise, had a single purpose, and that was to take over the work of his father, who had sickened and died the previous June after he had returned from Texas with permission to bring in a group of settlers. When he knew he was dying and would never see the fulfillment of his dream, he had asked his son to see to it for him. If the younger Austin seemed unduly serious for a man in his late twenties, it was probably because he carried a tremendous amount of responsibility on his shoulders. For all his youth, he carried it well. He was intelligent, quiet and methodical, and given

144

more to working out the many tedious details of getting a company of people together than to mouthing extravagant claims about the place to which we were going. He was handsome, with an abundance of dark wavy hair, which he wore brushed back off his high forehead. He had deep-set eyes, and a lower lip that jutted out just enough to give him a purposeful, determined expression.

"It's good land," he told a group of us one day, "but it's up to each man what he makes of it. It should grow cotton or corn or sugarcane, but it will only be as good as the work a man is willing to put into it."

For all of Austin's quietness and youth and understated claims, his subtle quiet enthusiasm was contagious, and his promise of nearly free land was a lure too strong to resist. Few of those who listened to him failed to sign up as colonists.

Basically, Austin's plan was for every man to get six hundred and forty acres—a square mile—with half again as much if he had a wife, a fourth again as much for each child, and an eighth for each slave. The land would cost a bit an acre, or roughly the cost of surveying it. In August, Austin had been to San Antonio de Bexar to check the details and make certain his right to colonize in his father's name remained valid.

Austin and some of the men went by ship to Natchitoches; others of us traveled overland and met him there. I went in the company of several congenial men and am glad I had the pleasure of that leisurely journey, for it is one of my happiest memories of travel in our country, so open and generous was the hospitality we found on our way. We had to travel slowly because we had several heavily laden wagons, one of them mine. I had stretched myself to purchase a number of things beyond what I estimated to be my own needs: barrels of flour, an assortment of tools, dried meat, bolts of domestic and needles and thread I thought the ladies would want after we were settled. Impulsively, I had even thrown in a bolt of a new type of striped satin material that the womenfolk of New Orleans fancied for their best dresses.

We traveled up one of the bayous, and the row of big plantations stretched endlessly ahead of us, for where one stopped the next began. Sometimes the houses were visible at the end of the avenues leading off our road, and sometimes the avenues, with their rows of trees on each side, curved away out of sight. Every evening, as darkness started to descend, we would wend our way through one of the long tree-lined drives to the house at its end, always assured we would find hospitality there. Some of the accommodations offered us were simple, and the fare was adequate but not elaborate. Sometimes we slept in barns. At other houses, we were treated as honored guests, fed elegant meals accompanied by the finest wines and served in formal candlelit dining rooms, and our rooms were the ultimate in comfort and luxury. But whether the hospitality was simple or elaborate, it was never grudging, and this, above all else, endeared the people to me. To some of my hosts, I recounted my previous experience in creating and running a plantation such as they were doing. They were always interested and plied me with questions. We often sat up into the night, comparing methods of planting and discussing problems.

There was to be one big difference in the way I proposed doing things in Texas. I had brought no slaves, nor did I intend to buy any again. I planned to use whatever free labor I could find in Mexico, and if this meant the difference between being a planter and a simple farmer, then that was just the way it would have to be. I had had my fill of owning others, for it went against my nature to be the cause, however indirectly, of any man not owning his own soul. Granted that I had been a far better master than most, I still would not willingly become a master again. When I had sold my plantation, I freed all my slaves and gave them enough money for passage back to Africa, where a colony of freedmen had begun at a place on the west coast called Liberia.

"But my dear fellow," said one of my hosts when I told him that I would never own another slave, "how can you possibly hope to succeed in planting cotton if you have no slave labor? It is the very essence of profitable cotton growing. *Mon dieu,* what you propose to do is impossible, I fear."

"If it is, then I suppose I'll have to find something else to plant besides cotton," I said firmly, and I meant it.

At the head of the bayou, we entered the piney woods, and everything seemed more hushed as we made our way through the dappled sunshine beneath the tall sparsely topped trees. Then we paralleled the Red River for a distance, until at last we approached the town of Natchitoches on another plantation-lined road.

Natchitoches was an old town, its heritage as well as its mixed population proclaimed by the polyglot mixture of its architecture and the babble of the various languages spoken there. Its French background was predominant, but the town had been strongly influenced by the Spaniards as well. Some of its inhabitants had drifted over from various parts of the United States and its territories, others had fled from Mexico, and there were even a few Indians in evidence on the streets. Later, this town would acquire a bustling busyness, situated as it was at the doorway to Texas; but on the day I first saw it, it could have been likened to an older person just awakening from a long sleep. And awaken it did during those days we were there, for our numbers grew daily as we and others joined Austin's group and made our final preparations to go to Texas.

From Natchitoches, we proceeded to Cantonment Jessup, which was only twenty-five miles from the Sabine River and Texas. It was a lonely outpost for the two companies of men stationed there, and they welcomed the diversion our arrival offered in the monotony of their lives.

We continued on, along the road that had been known as the Camino Real, and were pleasantly surprised to find it in passably good condition. We were able to make it to the Sabine without having to stop for repairs. Across the

Sabine was Texas, and the road continued on. We passed through Nacogdoches, a town that had been deserted for most of the previous eight years.

Our band of colonists reached the Brazos River—sometimes still occasionally called by its Indian name of Tonkanhono—in December, and we settled to the west of it, along with a number of other families who had heard of Austin's colonization and had reached the site of the colony ahead of the main body of settlers.

It didn't take long for those of us in Austin's first families to separate ourselves into two distinct groups; those who owned slaves and those who did not. With Austin's help, we all selected our land as soon as possible and quickly set about seeing to our needs. The first and most urgent of these was shelter, for the winter winds of Texas can be harsh and bone-chilling.

My own land was a little to the north and a few miles to the west of the crossing on the Brazos, and it was at that crossing that the town of San Felipe later came into being. My claim shared a common border on the northeast corner with the land of a man I had disliked on sight. I have met lots of people in my lifetime, good and bad, and I can never remember being so instantly repelled by anyone before or since as I was by that man. He called himself Samuel Butler, and with his four house slaves and ten field hands, he had already established himself on one of the choicest pieces of property before the arrival of the main group. By what right he had done this I don't know, but nobody seemed to challenge his claim. His land touched at one point on the river, which gave him a coveted steamboat landing.

Sam Butler was a florid-faced man I guessed to be about five years younger than I. I suppose it was partly his clothes that irritated me, for they were ill-suited to a man who had come to do the honest back-breaking work of settling a new land. He always wore tight-fitting breeches of a fine white wool, a bright-colored vest, a cutaway coat, and a high-crowned hat. He was a big man with a large stom-

148

ach, and I suspected he wore a corset to nip in his nonexistent waist in an attempt to conform as closely as possible to the small-waisted fashions of the day. Even if his shape had been suited to the mode, such outfits as he wore belonged in the drawing room, not on the frontier.

His wife was young and pretty, and I would say she was only just old enough to have borne a nine-year-old son, who I understood was hers from a previous marriage. It seemed to me that the wife and the stepson, as well as his retinue of slaves, were a mere veneer—an attempt to hide the uncouth man who lurked under the peacock clothes. And though I could not have told on what I specifically based such a surmise, I had the feeling that Sam Butler was no stranger to the western side of the Sabine. The speed with which he had grabbed some of the best land before the rest of us knew what we were about had certainly done nothing to dispel this suspicion.

For some years, the boundaries between the United States and Mexico were disputed and ill defined, and much of Texas, particularly the eastern portion, had been a lawless area, which no one could—or dared—try to govern. It would not have surprised me to find that Sam Butler had belonged to one of the unscrupulous bands of renegades who were virtually the only ones who had dared to inhabit the place during the previous eight years. Obviously, the man had money, and I'd have wagered everything I owned that he hadn't come by it honestly.

There were others with whom I found it far easier to become friends. My neighbors directly to the west were Josiah and Rebecca White, who had come from Arkansas. A childless couple, they were accustomed to the hard life of the frontier, and their quiet determination was an inspiration to everyone who knew them. It just happened that neither Josiah nor I chose to center our cabins on our land, so we built them closer to one another than they would otherwise have been, an accidental happenstance I never regretted.

The first cabins we put up were simple structures, with

no windows, and rifle holes between the logs. These openings were stuffed with rags except when we were called on to defend ourselves against marauding Indians. Austin suggested this type of building for its relative invulnerability, as the Karankawa Indians along the lower river had been stirred up not long before. Austin's fears were justified, but fortunately the Karankawas never attacked any of us with any sizable force, for they were water-borne nomads, and generally traveled in one- or two-family groups. It was not until some time after our arrival that I learned they had another characteristic—the unsavory habit of eating their captives at special feasts.

We helped one another erect the original structures, and with many hands to help, they were quickly finished. There was no question of waiting for the green wood to dry. No sooner was the felling and trimming of the trees finished than we started shaping and notching the logs and mixing the mud with which we would fill in the chinks. Our need was too urgent to brook any delay. On claims where there was little or no timber close by, people fashioned crude structures of mud and staked hides over them for roofs. More habitable dwellings were built later, at our leisure, and then most folks used the original structures as barns or tool sheds or other auxiliary outbuildings.

Each time we got together to put up one of our first crude homes, the women cooked while the men worked. There was an ample supply of game when we first arrived, and the womenfolk roasted wild fowls and baked unleavened bread in hastily contrived ovens to keep our bellies full as we did the heavy work. Even the children were set to helping, stripping the logs of the smaller branches and mixing and carrying mud for mortar. We all worked hard from sunup till sundown, and though the work was exhausting, none of us minded. The food was good, and the feeling of comradeship was close among most of us in Austin's Three Hundred, as that first group later became known.

There was one senseless event that first winter, which

occurred when some of the men from our colony—Sam Butler among them—decided to go to Galveston Isle to Lafitte's deserted town of Campeachy to look for the treasure it was rumored the pirate had left there. We had all heard the rumor, of course, and most of us just joked and laughed about it, but there were those among us who really believed the treasure was there, and they lived in mortal fear that somebody else would get to it before they did. And so a group of our men left to search for Lafitte's gold. They didn't find it, and only ended up making it worse for all of us by stirring up the Karankawas again—or the Kronks, as we came to call them. Apparently, the Indians had been having one of their feasts, with singing and dancing, at a place called Three Trees on Galveston Isle. Instead of turning around and coming back home, our men attacked them and even carried off one of their boys. Luckily, none of our men lost their lives, but as they hadn't had enough strength to mount a proper attack, their action had been foolhardy and served no purpose at all.

After that, we all settled down for a lot of hard work. I had intended to barter the things I had brought for what I needed, or to sell them for profit, but things didn't work out that way, at least as far as the foodstuffs and hoes and shovels and axes were concerned, for some of the things Austin had shipped from New Orleans by way of the Brazos never arrived, so of course I felt duty-bound to do what I could to help matters. The extra food I had brought was used to keep us all from starving and the spare tools to help us all get our first crops into the ground quickly. Most of us planted only food that year, but some, like Samuel Butler, put in a cotton crop the very first season.

Around the first of March, Austin left with some others for San Antonio de Bexar—more commonly called by the shortened name of Bexar—to report to the authorities there concerning the establishment of his colony. But when he arrived in Bexar, he found he would have to proceed to the capital at Mexico City, a long, arduous, and dangerous journey. But Austin was a man who did whatever needed doing, no matter how difficult it might be, and he set out with two other men for Mexico City. There they found the government, freed from Spanish domination less than a year before, in a state of turmoil, so Austin could only wait until the fledgling government sorted itself out before he could hope to get official confirmation and approval for his colony. It was not until January of 1823 that a colonization bill was passed, and Austin, feeling that at last the safety of all our claims was insured, was free to return to us.

We were told that other Americans were in Mexico City at the time Austin was there, and they, too, were pressing for the right to bring colonists into Texas. Among them was a man named Hayden Edwards, and it was said that he entertained Mexican officials quite lavishly in an attempt to win their approval of him as an *empresario*. Later, in 1825, he was given permission to set up a colony in the area around Nacogdoches, but it was not until that time that any man besides Austin was granted the right to bring in settlers. Still, that didn't seem to deter any individual Americans from coming to Texas, and many of them stopped and settled in likely looking places before they got as far as Austin's colony.

Hunger was no stranger to us our first few years in Texas, though once we could depend on our own crops, we were no longer as dependent on game as we had been. It was a good thing that this was so, for as our numbers grew, game became increasingly difficult to find, and we often returned from hunting trips empty-handed. I suppose such a dropping-off in the supply of game must always be looked upon as a natural result of the encroachment of civilization, for not only had we killed the wild fowls and animals for food too rapidly, but as we cleared and tilled more land, the remaining wildlife retreated ever deeper into the wilderness.

The Kronks were not the only hostiles to give us trouble, and when Indian harassment became intolerable during those first years, we were forced to move into crude, hastily erected stockades, which were made from long posts merely upended and stuck into the ground. When we had to take refuge inside these makeshift fortifications, food was apt to be in short supply, and hunting parties had to go forth cautiously, always with more men than we needed to hunt, for while some searched for game, others protected them. The children ran to greet us on our return, and if they saw us carrying a deer or a number of large birds, their faces would light up with smiles, and they would run to report the good news to the others. But if we returned empty-handed, their expressions would change from expectation to disappointment, and their eyes would look up at us in silent reproach.

We were often plagued with a shortage of food. As more and more people arrived, it put a strain on us to feed the newcomers. Some folks had apparently picked up and come to Texas with no more preparation or forethought about what they would do or how they would exist when they arrived than if they had been going on a Sunday picnic. Many of them brought no axes with which to fell trees, no plows with which to till the land, and no food to fill the bellies of their hungry children while they got settled and waited for their first crops to mature.

I usually went once or twice a winter to Natchitoches or New Orleans to buy a wagonload of things I figured folks would be sure to need. Mostly, I brought foodstuffs and farming implements, but I never failed to put in a number of bolts of domestic and wool. The men had mostly taken to dressing in buckskins, at least in the winter months, but the ladies usually preferred their cloth garments, and as soon as they had money to spare, they bought the fabrics for dresses. But it was food and farming tools that were most urgently needed by the new arrivals. More often than not, they had no money to buy these things, which threw them too much on the charity of those of us who were fairly well established. I'll be as Christian as the next man, but we had all come to Texas with the hope of making our fortunes, and a man who does nothing but dispense charity soon ends up with nothing for himself. Yet I could scarcely demand cash when so few people had it, so I bartered with those who couldn't pay; a shovel for so many bushels of corn a year later, an axe and some other tools for part interest in a bale of cotton, or so much molasses. The system worked passably well, though of course in any group of people you will find those who never pay their debts.

There always seemed to be more work to be done in those first years than there were hours in the day to do it. We finally got around to erecting proper cabins to replace the ones we built so hastily when we arrived, and by then we were less rushed, able to let the logs dry out properly. Most of these second cabins had two sections, each about fifteen feet square—some more, some less—separated by a dogtrot of roughly the same dimensions in between, which was completely open at the front and had a door cut into the closed rear wall. The doors of both sections opened onto the dogtrot, and in each section there was a window front and back, with a chimney on the far side of at least one of the sections. A ladder from the center led to a storage loft. The dogtrot served many purposes: we could hang our meat up to dry, or the womenfolk could string lines across and hang their washing out of the weather on rainy days, and it was always a pleasant airy place to sit on the warmer evenings and smoke a pipe or two before going to bed. Some folks preferred simple one-room cabins, and built them of various sizes and shapes. In the construction of these cabins, as in the erection of the first crude dwellings we built in the winter of '21–'22, we all helped each other with the final raising. A man might fell his own trees and saw his own beams and cut his own shakes, but when it came to hoisting the logs into place and putting up the heavy roof beams, there was no substitute for the combined labor of many strong backs and husky arms.

The slave-owners among us had no need for such community help. Some of the slaveless folks looked on these slave-owners with open envy, but for myself, I never once regretted my decision to avoid enforced labor, and wouldn't have wanted it even if I had had the money to buy some strong bucks. I never lacked help at any time I really needed it, for folks remembered that I had dispensed without question the food and tools I had brought with me that first year. My biggest problem seemed not that I failed to receive enough help when something required more than my own labor, but actually that I often had a surfeit of aid proffered, and it was embarrassing at times to decide whose help I must accept and whose decline.

As we labored on our land, Austin, with his boundless drive and energy, was busy doing enough to keep ten men busy. He gathered data for a proper map of Texas, for existing maps were poorly drawn and highly inaccurate; he composed a code of criminal law for our colony; he settled any disputes between the people; and he worked toward getting our own cotton gin and a sawmill built, though these didn't come into being till 1825. He established his local government at the townsite of San Felipe, where we had originally crossed the Brazos. For local government, he set up an *ayuntamiento,* a group of the colonists, but mostly he assumed the responsibility of maintaining order himself. Among all the other things Austin did, he continued to bring more colonists to Texas. The longer I knew him, the more my admiration for the man grew. For all his youth, he was a truly great man.

After the first few years, things had quieted down enough so that some of us could go off on hunts to find the wild mustangs the Spaniards had so obligingly left for us. They were small, and at times I felt downright cruel placing my big frame on even the largest of these undersized animals, but they seemed not to mind. They had amazing strength and never appeared to tire. Occasionally we rounded up bunches of these and brought them back to the colony, where they fetched a fair price, once they were saddle-broken. I became interested in crossbreeding some of the mustangs with the larger saddle horses we had brought with us. The resultant animals made exceptionally good mounts, selling at a premium over the full-blooded mustangs.

In some places, there were wild cows for the catching, too, and after the supply of game in our colony was much exhausted, we began to domesticate these animals and to depend on them for meat as well as milk.

My friendship with the Whites continued to deepen. In such a community of families as ours, a bachelor or widower is often left to feel that he doesn't quite belong, but the Whites made certain that I never felt left out. They were both in their mid-thirties, and, unblessed with children, said they could certainly afford to adopt me unofficially as a brother, and that is exactly what they did. Josiah and I helped each other whenever we could, and we even worked parts of our two farms together. At the end of a long day of our combined labor, I frequently shared one of Rebecca's good meals with them. They invited me to supper at least twice a week, and I came to love them both as dearly as a true brother and sister during those first three years. They were both fair-skinned, with blue eyes and dark brown hair. But their resemblance to one another ended with their similar coloring, for Rebecca had a round, full face, and her hair was softly waved, while Josiah's face was lean and austere, and his hair was straight as a string and swept back severely off his high forehead. But any who thought his appearance stern soon found it belied his nature, for he was a soft-spoken, pleasant man, always courteous and helpful to everyone. It was plain to anyone who saw Rebecca and Josiah together that they were devoted to each other. In all things but one, they seemed contented with their lives, and that one was their childlessness.

"Seventeen years married," Josiah said to me one night when we were smoking a final pipe together before I took my leave. We were sitting on stools we had carried out to the dogtrot. It was very early spring, and the air still had a touch of wintry sharpness to it, just enough to be refreshing. Rebecca had already excused herself and gone to bed. Josiah sighed, then continued, "We hoped and prayed for young ones, but we've long since given up. Some things we want are denied us, and we must accept it as God's will. It's a deep sorrow for both of us, but it's most wearing on Rebecca. Have you ever watched her face when she holds someone's little one? It fair tears me up, the way she looks. I can just feel her thinking, 'Why couldn't this child have been ours?' Many's the time she's apologized to me for not giving me children." He hesitated. "Imagine! As though she could help it! But it's a pity. She'd make such a good mother. It's a downright shame there are no children for her—for us—to love."

I felt compelled to say something—yet what was there to say? I had not missed that look on Rebecca's face, nor the eagerness with which she always offered to mind other people's children. And I had seen Josiah, too, as he watched other men's sons working beside their fathers. It was not envy I saw there, for Josiah was too big a man for such a petty emotion, but sometimes he could not keep a certain wistful expression from crossing his face. I felt it was vastly unfair that a family was denied to two such good people, who would have so loved and cherished children.

"It's hard to figure things out sometimes, Josiah," I said at length, "like why one man prospers and another doesn't. Look at poor hard-working Tom Elkins and the bad luck he's had these two years with losing crops, while the very ground seems to turn to gold for an out-and-out bastard like Sam Butler. Why does the good Lord bless some folks with more young ones than they want and deny them to good people like you and Rebecca, who would give them the best home children could wish for? It's more than I can understand. But at least you have each other, and you're both in good health. That's something to be thankful for."

"Yes," he agreed. "That's something to be thankful for."

That conversation came back to me two weeks later when Josiah stopped plowing early one day because he didn't feel well. He was apologetic about wanting to quit early. He had had a bad cough and a cold for days, but it was unlike him to give in to illness. I had known him to keep working till he all but dropped from exhaustion; he was not given to coddling himself. For this reason I was concerned and went over to his cabin that evening to check on him.

"He's dozing, but his head is burning up," Rebecca said as she met me at the door. "I've never seen a fever come upon him so suddenly." She turned her candid blue eyes up to me and said, "I'm worried about him, Todd."

"I'm sure he'll be all right," I said, with all the false heartiness I could muster, knowing it would only add to her concern if I agreed with her. "By morning, he'll probably be banging on my cabin door to roust me out at sunup to make up for the work we left unfinished today."

"I hope so . . . I do hope so. He's had that cough for days, and you know he won't take care of himself."

"A good night's sleep and your ministrations will fix him up."

"You're probably right." She tried to smile reassuringly at me, but couldn't quite do it. Rebecca was not beautiful, but her nature was so sweet that a sort of goodness shone through. The longer I knew her, the prettier she seemed. Her features were good, and pleasingly arranged. She was well filled-out, but not to the point of excessive plumpness. I had often thought that if she were to wear the fripperies worn by townswomen, she would have been exceedingly attractive. But she made no attempt to enhance her appearance and wore her wavy hair pulled back and caught in a bun; and she clothed herself with almost puritanical simplicity, always in gray homespun. Her one good dress was of a lightweight wool, but it, too, was gray.

She looked exhausted with worry that evening. "You look as if you could do with some sleep," I offered. "Why don't you go in the other room and turn in? Let me sit up with Josiah." I looked over at the bed, where Josiah was beginning to mutter with delirium and toss and turn about, and I hoped that Rebecca couldn't guess my concern.

"I couldn't sleep, not when I'm so worried about him. I

know you're worried, too, and you're welcome to stay if you like."

"I'll do that, if you don't mind."

"I'll get some fresh wet cloths. Sponging him may help to break the fever. If we can get his temperature down, I think he'll be all right."

Josiah worsened that night, while we sat around doing useless things like putting wet cloths on his fevered head. The cloths immediately took on the heat of his body and needed constant changing. This kept Rebecca occupied, and for that I was grateful. I thought her ministrations might keep her too busy to worry about Josiah.

Finally, with the first glow of morning light, I jumped up resolutely. "I'm going to get Doc Graham."

I thought she'd protest, for she and Josiah had boasted once that neither of them had ever needed a doctor in their lives. But she nodded. "Please hurry. I thought a night of rest would help him, but he's been so restless—and he's worse the last hour or so, don't you think? It seems harder for him to breathe."

I literally flew into San Felipe on the fastest horse Josiah owned, and dragged the doctor away from his breakfast before he had a chance to take the first bite. Rebecca and I watched tensely as he examined Josiah. He leaned his head down to put his ear to Josiah's chest, and looked at us solemnly as he rose. With a discouraging shake of his head, he said that Josiah's lungs were congested, and it was just a matter of waiting to see what happened. He told us to make him as comfortable as possible and get good nourishment into him to help his body fight off the affliction.

But even Josiah's work-hardened body wasn't up to the job of fighting off the illness, and after the doctor left, Rebecca and I watched helplessly as his breathing became increasingly labored. The doctor returned that afternoon, and told me privately that he didn't hold out much hope. On the morning of the next day, just after dawn, Josiah coughed feebly and died.

"Josiah, don't leave me!" Rebecca gasped as she looked

at his still body. "You mustn't!" Then she turned to look up at me, as though willing me to tell her that he hadn't died. When I could only look at her helplessly and shake my head slowly from side to side, she lay down her head and burst into tears.

I bent over Josiah and closed his eyes gently, my own so blurred with tears that I could scarcely see what I was doing. I reached below the covers and straightened him out and put his hands up to cross them on his chest. "Goodbye, my dear friend," I whispered as I leaned over and kissed his forehead. I started to pull the covers over his head, but Rebecca stopped me.

"No, not yet," she said. "Leave his face uncovered. I would like to be alone with him for a few minutes, if you don't mind, while you do . . . whatever must be done."

"You should sleep. I'll build you a small fire in the other section of the cabin, if you'd like."

The tears ran silently down her cheeks. "No," she said, her face contorted with grief, "I don't want to leave Josiah, not just yet. I need just a little more time, to be able to accept the reality of . . . of what has happened." I left them alone.

We buried Josiah the next day, a day of sparkling spring sunshine, and Rebecca invited Father Muldoon to say a few prayers over his grave. Like all of us who were Protestants, the Whites had taken the oath to become Catholics in order to come to Mexico as colonists and get their grants of land, and they read their Bible only in the privacy of their own home. Few Protestant colonists actually converted to Catholicism, but there would have been fewer still if it hadn't been for Father Muldoon. He regarded Austin's families as his special flock, and only the most narrowminded failed to welcome the friendly Irish cleric into their homes as a personal friend if not as their religious advisor. Nor did he seem perturbed that he made few converts. He was friend and confessor to all, Catholic and Protestant alike, and it was his special friendship with Josiah that prompted Rebecca to ask him to officiate at the simple graveside service.

"Josiah always said the Catholics have the same God we do," Rebecca had explained sensibly, "and I know this is the way he would want it." She paused. "Do you think Father Muldoon would be offended if we read the Twenty-third Psalm and sang one of Josiah's favorite hymns? That psalm was always our favorite, and I'd like for you to read it, if you would, unless you think Father Muldoon would be offended. I'm not sure if the Catholic Bible is much like ours, if they have that psalm—"

"I don't think it matters. No, I'm sure Father Muldoon wouldn't be offended. The only thing that would offend him would be if he were not allowed to come and pay his last respects."

"That's what I thought, too." She seemed relieved by my reply. She had shown remarkable stamina, pulling herself out of her devastating grief to make arrangements for Josiah's burial. She even picked out the spot where she thought he would have liked to be buried. My respect for her grew as I saw her courage.

There was no longer anything more I could do to help Josiah, God rest his soul, but I was much concerned about Rebecca, about what she would do next. She had no family of her own, and I knew her well enough to know that she would never present herself to any of Josiah's family as a burden. But I forebore asking about her plans for the future. Until after the burial, I figured she had enough on her mind.

It turned out that some of the good folks in the colony had already talked it over and decided among themselves that Rebecca would go to stay with the Duncans, a generous family, and I blessed those who had made that decision. The Duncans had eight children, and I knew that by staying with them, Rebecca—whose nature it was to jump in and help wherever help was needed—would be kept too busy to brood overmuch about Josiah's death.

Life for me was almost unbearably dreary that spring and summer. I worked alone all day, missing the compan-

161

ionship I had so enjoyed, the easy friendliness I had always found in the Whites's cabin, the pleasure of smoking a leisurely pipe with Josiah. I was painfully aware of the emptiness of their cabin. It seemed that a bright and cheering light had gone out of my life forever.

I stopped in at the Duncans's from time to time to see Rebecca, see how she was making out. She seemed to me to be as contented as was possible under the circumstances, but apparently the strain of being in someone else's house had begun to wear on her. She had been there three months when I stopped by one day and she asked me to take her out for a breath of air. It was a summer evening, and after we had walked away from the cabin a short distance, she turned to me, and said,

"I'm going home, Todd. Home to my own place."

I stopped walking and turned to look at her. "You can't stay there alone!"

"I can and I will. That cabin was our home, Josiah's and mine, and it's still mine. The Duncans couldn't have been kinder, but . . . well, I'm surrounded day and night by people, until I feel that I have been swallowed by them, that I have lost my identity in theirs. And besides, Elizabeth's ways are not mine, so it's just as hard for her to have me there as it is for me to be there." Her voice took on a pleading note. "Oh, please, Todd. I'm ready to go back now. The Duncans have been so good; I don't mean they haven't. I needed them these past months, needed to be kept busy from morning till night, so that I fell in bed each night too exhausted not to sleep. But I don't need that any more, and I want to go home. Will you come by and take me tomorrow, please?"

"Are you sure this is what you want?"

"I'm certain."

"But a woman alone . . ." I shook my head slowly.

She had been waiting for my objection. "Men are often gone on hunting trips for three or four nights at a time, and their women are left alone. So what's really the difference? I know I can't plow much land by myself, and I don't intend to try, but I can put in a nice big garden next year, and maybe get a few cows and sell cream and butter. And I'm a passably good seamstress, too. Some women can't sew, or just don't have the knack. Mostly, I just want to live on what I can do. I appreciate the Duncans' charity more than I can ever tell them. But I can't live forever on others. You won't try to talk me out of it, will you?"

"I would if I thought it would do any good. Josiah told me how stubborn you can be."

"Oh, thank you!" She smiled at me, and it occurred to me that few women have such an open and sweet smile. A dimple always appeared, surprisingly, in one cheek, spreading the smile over her whole face and giving it a slightly lopsided, impish quality. I nodded, said approvingly, "It's nice to see you smile again."

"Josiah would hate it if he thought I didn't." She slipped her arm through mine. "Now, if you don't mind, I would like that walk you promised me."

"Of course."

As we walked, I was aware of the pleasant feeling of having her arm on mine. My relationships with women in the years since the death of my young wife had always been based on urgent physical need for relief. The sort of women with whom I had had liaisons were not the kind with whom one went walking about. With them, it was always a short visit, usually made under cover of darkness, to satisfy a bodily urge, strongly felt and quickly appeased. I had forgotten the quiet pleasure of being alone with a woman I respected and admired and liked.

We walked for well over an hour, enjoying the beauty of the evening and the tranquility of the soft night sounds, reluctant to return to the friendly noise and confusion that always prevailed at the Duncan cabin. It was one of the most pleasant hours I ever spent. We talked, she and I, about the same things Josiah and I might have discussed. I told her how the crops were coming, and reminded her that she had a good stand of corn and that Josiah and I had prepared two of their fields for cotton before he died. "I went ahead and planted them, of course."

"Todd!" I felt rather than saw that sweet impish smile turned toward me. "How very thoughtful you are! And I'm glad I shall be back in time to help pick it."

I knew better than to protest. I had seen her too often out in the fields helping Josiah. "We'll do it together."

She didn't refuse my help, as I was afraid she would. "Thank you," she said simply. "I'll need a money crop this year, especially since it's far too late to get my garden in. I'm sure it has long since gone to weeds."

"Not as much as you might think. I've weeded it some, though not as well as you would have done. I didn't plant it carefully, just threw out a few seeds here and there. Some nice volunteer tomatoes came up. They're getting good blossoms, even have some small tomatoes already."

"Then it's time I came home to nurse them along."

When I returned her to the Duncans's and left to return to my own place, I found myself humming happily. Rebecca was coming home, and I was glad.

I picked her up the next afternoon and took her to her cabin. Beforehand, though, to brighten things up, I picked some flowers and put them in a pewter tankard in the middle of the table.

She noticed them as soon as she entered. "Todd, how very sweet of you! It looks as if I am expected."

I carried in her things and helped her get a small fire started. Josiah had chopped plenty of cordwood the previous winter. The evening was warm, and Rebecca certainly needed no fire for warmth, but I knew she always loved to have a cup of tea, and besides, I didn't want to leave her alone in a dark cheerless cabin.

"Are you sure you'll be all right?" I asked as I started to leave.

"Of course."

She gave a slight wave of her hand, as though she would brush away my unnecessary concern. "I'm back home and I'm . . . well, I can't say I'm happy, because I feel that I

164

can never be truly happy again, without my beloved Josiah. When two people have no children, they get very close to one another. At least Josiah and I did. He was not only my husband, but all the children we never had as well. You do understand, don't you?" She didn't wait for me to answer. "But I have come to accept his passing now as the Lord's will, and I think I can find a measure of contentment in being back here, where we had our home together."

"Of course I understand." I smiled at her. "Well, then, Josiah and I were sort of business partners, so I hope you'll let the arrangement continue. Your Alfie is a better plow-horse than any I have. All mine are strictly for riding, and one of my oxen is ailing. So I hope you'll continue to let me use Alfie, and in return I'll handle your fields as well as mine."

"Todd, you're very transparent! You and I both know there will be little further need for a plow-horse this season, and you're trying to use your need for him as an excuse to help me. Well, I'm not a bit too proud to accept the help of a very dear friend, and I'll take it gladly. And I thank you—for both of us."

Embarrassed at the ease with which she had seen through my ruse, I took my leave of her, but not before she had extracted a promise from me to come to dinner the next noon.

"I can cook, and that's something you can't do, at least not very well. So if you're going to help me in my fields, then you must plan on taking your dinner here every noon."

I hesitated, was on the point of refusing when she said pleadingly, "I need to feel useful, Todd. You'll be doing me a favor. And Josiah and I always did enjoy your company. I suppose it wouldn't be seemly for you to take the evening meal with me, now that I'm alone here, but during the day . . ." Her eyes sparkled. "Remember, we adopted you unofficially as our brother. Surely you wouldn't refuse to break bread with your sister?"

I laughed. "When you put it that way, how could I? But

you must let me supply the meat for the table. I can still find some game, and I have a few smoked hams back at my place."

She nodded her agreement at the arrangement, which turned out to be good for both of us. For over seventeen years, she had been making a home for Josiah, and my coming every day gave her an excuse to keep some semblance of a normal day's routine, breathed an added breath of life into her silent, lonely cabin, gave her someone to talk to. And for me, the good meals were certainly a boon. I never did know a woman who could make a simple venison stew taste one-half so good as Rebecca could, and her biscuits were as light and airy as cotton bolls.

I had agreed, some time before Rebecca came back, to go mustang hunting with a group of men from the colony as soon as the harvest was completed that year. The Indians, I had heard tell, could shoot an arrow at a certain point right through the withers and stop a horse dead in his tracks without really hurting him at all, but I never did know a white man who had that knack, so we found it worked best for us to try to spook them into someplace that slowed them down, like a tree island, where they had to pick their way through thick underbrush. On the far side of the hummock, other men waited to lasso them when they came out.

I hesitated to leave, once Rebecca had moved back into her cabin, but I was already committed long before, and didn't feel I could back down, since our method depended on having plenty of men, and we were already down to the minimum number. Apologetically, I told Rebecca about it one day at dinner.

"I'm afraid I'll have to be going away in a few days," I said just as we finished eating. "I hate to go, but I've promised to join a group of the men to go hunt mustangs."

She looked at me in surprise. "Why do you say you hate to go? I thought you always enjoyed the break in routine those hunts gave you."

"But with you back here, and no near neighbors but me—"

She pursed her lips in exasperation. "Todd Stewart, if you ever once refuse to leave for a few days because of me, I'll never forgive you!"

"But if something should happen—? What if you should need help?"

"What if I should? Chances are the time I'd be needing help most, you'd not be apt to be close enough around to do any good, anyway, so I don't see any point in your turning down a chance to get away for a few days." She sighed, shaking her head at me. "Really, I have two good rifles, and I'm quite capable of caring for myself. Now you just go on your hunt, and don't you spend one minute of your time worrying about me."

I couldn't keep from smiling. "If you treat any marauding Indians half as angrily as you're dealing with me now, then I can see it would be a complete waste of time to worry about you." She laughed, and the dimple jumped into place. "I'm sorry if I sounded so mean, but really, Todd, do go and enjoy yourself. If I were a man, I'd go with you."

And so I went, but not without misgivings. I knew Rebecca had been staying alone every night, but I had always made some excuse first thing every morning to swing close enough to her cabin to see if there was a stirring of life about. I couldn't see the doors because they opened onto the middle of the dogtrot, but I knew Rebecca liked her cup of tea or two during the morning, and there was usually evidence of a small fire someplace for her kettle, indoors or out. When I saw a thin curl of smoke, or saw her out washing or hanging clothes on the line, I would go on with my work, assured that she was safe. If she ever noticed me making this morning check, she never commented on it.

We were gone a full week that time, as we had to go quite a distance in search of as many animals as we wanted. I was concerned about Rebecca, and after the first two or three days, found it hard to hide my impatience to return home. Still, it would not have been fair to the others if I had broken off early and left, so I stayed with them until everyone was satisfied that we had caught enough horses.

We approached from the west, so that we passed Rebecca's place before we came to mine. As we drew close to her cabin, I noticed that there were several horses tethered to the rail at the front of her dogtrot. Vaguely alarmed at the unusualness of her having early afternoon callers, I stared at the cabin, determined that I would return there as soon as I had my horses safely corralled. I was leading the five that comprised my share, but as we came abreast of the cabin, I recognized the doctor's buggy pulled up along the far side.

Alarmed, I gasped, "Something's wrong! Something's happened to Rebecca! I knew I shouldn't have left her here alone!"

I threw the rope with which I was leading my mustang to the man nearest to me, and didn't look back to see if he caught it. "Drop them off at my corral," I shouted over my shoulder as I spurred my mount, my heart thumping wildly at the thought of all the terrible things that could have happened to Rebecca.

I jumped from my horse and pushed open the door. How could I ever forgive myself for leaving if something had happened to her?

Doc Graham looked up in surprise as I came bursting into the cabin. "Hello there, Todd," he said with maddening calm. On the bed lay Rebecca, her eyes closed and her face white and still.

"My God!" I gasped. For one horrible moment, it was not Rebecca I saw there, but Josiah, his face quiet in death, for it was on that very bed that he had died. "No! Not her, too!" I cried out in alarm, and I heard my voice break into a sob as I rushed to kneel by her side.

There were two other men in the room, and one of them came up behind me and put his hand on my shoulder.

"She's all right, Todd. She just had a bad scare. She'll come out of it all right."

"Thank God!" I said fervently, looked up at the face of one of our neighbors, grateful to him for saying what I had not dared hope to hear. "What happened? What frightened her so? She's not a woman given to the vapors. And she looks so pale."

Doc Graham stood up and started to put things back into his black bag. "It's more than the vapors. She got a Kronk arrow through her shoulder and lost quite a bit of blood. But those arrows are so blooming long and heavy, it apparently fell out under its own weight. It tore the flesh going out, but at least it made a nice clean open wound of it. It should heal well, if she can be kept quiet long enough to let it mend."

I looked at him, a shiver of fear running through me. "A Kronk arrow?" I asked in disbelief.

He nodded. "She must have been hanging out clothes this morning early when the Kronk came by. There may have been two of them. There's another arrow wedged in a chink in the side wall. She had the good sense to run and shut herself in the cabin. I guess she got a shot or two at him—or them—out the front window. Jeb says both rifles had been fired. That must have hurt like hell, getting that kick on her shoulder each time she fired! I guess with both rifles going, it made it seem like there was somebody else inside the cabin, and she scared the Kronk—or Kronks—off. Before she passed out, she had the presence of mind to hang a bloody cloth out the window. Smart woman, that. Jeb happened by soon after and saw it. By the time he found her, she had passed out right there, near the window, still sitting backwards, astride the chair. Lucky for her, when she fainted she fell forward and the chair back pressed itself onto her shoulder to help stem the blood. Lucky, too, that Jeb came along so soon after and had the good sense to see the bleeding had stopped and let her be while he fetched help. He rode down to Wilhelm Schmidt's place and sent him for me."

169

I looked for the first time at the plump German across the room and nodded my thanks. Schmidt's cabin was to the west, on the opposite side of the road. Next to me, they were Rebecca's closest neighbors.

"My oldest girl, I go now undt send her to stay mit Frau Vhite. She iss à good nurse, my Lena."

"That's very kind of you." The Schmidts were one of several hard-working German families in our colony, and they had gained the respect of all of us for their willingness to pitch in and help others when the need arose.

"If you have no objection, Wilhelm, I'll sleep in the other part of the cabin, just in case that Kronk should return."

He nodded briskly. "A good idea, Herr Todd."

I sat next to the bed all evening, hoping to be there when Rebecca opened her eyes. They said she had regained consciousness briefly when the doctor started dressing her wound. He had given her some laudanum then as a sedative, and its effects had not yet worn off. I watched her as she lay there sleeping, thinking how vulnerable she was to such an attack, how close she had come to an unspeakably horrible end. It was not pretty, the way the Kronks ate their victims. I'd heard they sliced off the flesh while the victim still lived, and made a great show of cooking it and relishing it as they ate it. I shuddered, put my face in my hands. My God, how could I have borne it if she had been carried off to roast over a Kronk fire?

I raised my head, looked at her again, her face so relaxed and peaceful in sleep. Her breathing was slow and easy, unlabored, and I knew I need not fear for her life, not this time. But there was always the possibility of another time, another attack, when she might not be so lucky. I knew too well how that soft relaxed look on her face could change to a look of stubborn determination when she set her mind on something. And I knew she had stubbornly set her mind on living in her own cabin, and would not listen to arguments to the contrary. The idea of having her continue to live there was unthinkable. She couldn't stay on alone. She must go someplace where she had more protection.

The next morning I was up early and was there when she opened her eyes. The Kronk had not returned, nor had I expected him to. They usually traveled in dugouts, two families together, going wherever their hunting took them. The one who had attacked Rebecca was probably far from the cabin by that time. But there was always another day, another Kronk. A shiver passed through me at the thought.

Rebecca smiled when she saw me sitting there. "Todd, how nice. You're back," she said, as casually as though nothing of any consequence had happened while I was gone. But her voice was weak, and I saw her wince as she tried to move, and her other hand moved instinctively to her injured shoulder. "The Kronk . . ." she said, remembering.

"He iss gone. You frightened him avay. You must lie still," Lena's voice said authoritatively over my shoulder. "I vill get some mush and feed you." The girl was only sixteen, but she bustled about the cabin with the efficiency and sureness of a much older woman. She was a pretty girl, and her golden blond hair was caught into one long plait down the center of her back.

"I don't want to be a burden—"

"Don't talk foolish," Lena said curtly. "You must get vell, and I vill help you, as you vould help me." She pulled a stool alongside my chair and sat on it, holding a spoonful of gruel toward Rebecca. "Now eat," she commanded.

And Rebecca, with a half-smile playing about her face, obediently opened her mouth and let herself be fed.

I continued to stay in the other section of Rebecca's cabin, for I was determined not to leave the two of them there alone. It would have been almost as bad as it was before, when Rebecca had been alone in the cabin, for she was weak, and would be of no help to Lena in an emergency. Besides, the doctor had ordered Rebecca to stay in bed at least four or five days, and I was determined to see that she obeyed his instructions.

By the morning of the second day, I decided she was well enough to discuss her future. I was anxious about what she would do and wanted to be assured that she would listen to reason and act sensibly. I began by telling her that the incident had proved beyond any doubt that she could no longer remain in that cabin alone, that she absolutely must move in with somebody—the Duncans, the Schmidts, or someone. Many people would be glad to have her in their home, I said, for she was cheerful and helpful and much liked in the colony. I catalogued for her all the reasons she must not stay by herself: she might get ill suddenly in the middle of the night, with no one to know, or to help her; she might fall and break a leg and be unable to move and summon help; and, of course, there was always a chance of another Indian attack, if not by a Kronk then by some strays from one of the other tribes.

She listened to me in silence, and when I had finished, she said in a firm quiet voice, "I won't leave, Todd."

I had not been taken in by the docile manner in which she had heard me out, and I was prepared for the argument that I had known was coming just as sure as I knew the sun would be rising in the east the next morning.

"You must," I said, trying to match her firmness with my own. "I won't hear of you staying here alone any longer. If I have to, I'll come and drag you out, carry you away over my shoulder."

She laughed and said teasingly, "I would only walk right back here as soon as you put me down."

In spite of the lightness of her words, I knew she meant them. I frowned, said sternly, "You can't. You mustn't, Rebecca. Be reasonable. Can't you see the danger?"

Her face grew serious. "Danger? Of course I can see it. There has always been danger here for all of us. If I had been afraid to face up to that fact, Josiah would never have brought me here. And I'd lots rather face danger here in my own home than in someone else's. I positively refuse to move in with anyone. I will not exist on anybody's charity, as kind as people might be."

"You are the stubbornnest woman I ever did see! You absolutely cannot stay here. I won't hear of it. I won't let you."

"I'm afraid not even you can stop me, Todd," she said quietly. I was not fooled by her soft voice, for I knew too well that look of grim determination on her face. She was a strong-minded woman. I remembered that Josiah had remarked once that if she ever set her mind on something, there was no way he had ever been able to talk her around.

But I could be stubborn, too, and was determined that this time she would listen to someone else. She must do as I told her.

She seemed just as resolved to have things her way as I was to have them mine. As we argued on, I became increasingly angry with her for being so unreasonable. We talked around in circles, with me saying, "You will!" and her insisting, "I won't!"

Finally, when it was clear that there was no way on God's green earth I was going to convince her that she must leave her cabin, short of burning it to the ground, I said in utter exasperation, "Then if you won't leave your cabin, by God, you'll marry me so I can move in with you!"

Her eyes opened into round O's at the shock of my words, and for the first time since I had known her, she seemed unable to say anything.

Truth to tell, I was every bit as shocked as she was. Rebecca was a desirable woman, no getting around that, and a comfortable kind of woman to be around, too. If we had both been free and I had just met her in the normal way of things, I might very easily have considered asking her to marry me. But Josiah had been my very dear friend, and I had deliberately avoided any such thoughts about her while he lived. Ordinarily, there was no way I would have insulted his memory or the friendship that had existed between us by proposing marriage to his widow a scant five months after his death.

"I know it's a shocking idea, with Josiah gone such a

173

short time," I apologized. Then I asked reasonably, "But how else am I going to look after you if we don't get married?" I looked around, satisfied myself that Lena was not in the cabin, then continued, "You needn't be afraid that I . . . that I'll touch you, or bother you. It's just that you're such a gosh-darn stubborn woman, and if you won't move out, then I think I should move in. And of course, I couldn't do that unless we were married." When she didn't answer, I went on, "It isn't as if you had some folks you could go to. You're all alone, and need me to look after you—"

"You . . . you would marry me, just to look after me?" Her face had not lost its surprised look. "Oh, Todd! I don't know what to say. For me to ask you to give up your freedom, after all these years . . ."

"It's the only practical thing to do," I insisted. "And you didn't ask me to give up anything. It was all my idea." Since I had blurted out my unexpected proposal, I, too, had considered the prospect of changing my ingrained bachelor ways, and I was surprised to find that it didn't frighten me at all. It was true I had been married before, but that was years earlier, and since my wife had died in childbirth when we were married only a little over a year, I had had scant chance to become accustomed to being a married man, and was little used to thinking in terms of "we" instead of "I". It had been different raising Thorne, not the same as having a wife to care for, and I was afraid that in the nineteen years since the death of my wife I had developed into a very selfish person, thinking only of my own comfort and concern.

"It wouldn't be easy for you, Rebecca," I said. "I'm fifty-three, and set in my ways. But I want to look after you, and keep you safe." It was true. Far from being appalled at the thought of taking on the responsibility of a wife at my age, I found the idea of looking after Rebecca filled me with a tenderness I had forgotten I could feel, and the prospect of having her be totally dependent on me made me feel more a man than I had for a long time.

"But it's so soon—"

"I know that, but it's the only solution, unless you'll move out. You needn't be afraid that I'll ask anything of you. I only want to take care of you, watch after you, as Josiah would have done."

"People will talk. . . ."

"Only the few who have nothing more important to do. Let them. Most folks will see the sense of it, and understand. You do see that it's the only way, don't you? You will agree, won't you?" Anxiously, I watched her, waiting for her answer.

She smiled softly. "Yes, Todd, I'll agree. And . . . thank you. It's the nicest compliment I've ever had."

I returned her smile, surprised to find how relieved I was at her answer, for I had been certain she would turn me down. I was sitting on a chair next to her bed, and knew that if I stayed there another minute, I would be unable to keep from leaning over and kissing her.

*My God,* I thought, as I jumped from the chair, *I must keep myself from thinking things like that!* She would need time, lots of it, six or seven more months at the very least, to get over Josiah's death. And there I was already, unable to keep from thinking how desirable she was!

"We'll ask Lena to stay here through the rest of the week," I said, starting toward the door. "I'll begin moving my things into the other section of your cabin. Or would you rather sleep in that half, and let me stay here?"

"Whichever you prefer."

"Then it might be best with you in here. Come winter, we'll have the fire going in the daytime in here, and just for myself, I wouldn't bother with a fire at night in the other section. I didn't even put in a fireplace in the second half of my own place." I turned to look at her. "If you'd rather, we can live in my cabin."

"No, I love my own, and I don't want to leave it. Both the fireplaces draw well, and this section is floored, which yours isn't. Then there's my garden, too. . . ."

I nodded, not surprised at her answer. After all, it was

her refusal to leave her own cabin that had started the whole thing. "I'll bring over anything I think might be useful to you. When you're better, you can come to my place and see if there's anything else you might want."

"That would be nice," she agreed.

"If Lena stays till Saturday, I could ask Father Muldoon to come by that afternoon. You certainly aren't in any condition to go anywhere else, so the wedding must be here. I hope you don't mind getting married by a Catholic priest, but we did promise to be Catholics in order to get our land, and I wouldn't want to leave any doubt as to the legality of our marriage."

"Oh, no, of course not. We couldn't chance anyone thinking it was not all legally correct. You would have my reputation in shreds."

I saw the faintest hint of a smile cross her face. Again, as before, I was overwhelmed with a feeling of tenderness for her as she lay with her dark hair spread out over the pillow.

I turned and opened the door. "I'll go talk to Lena, see if she can stay till Saturday."

As I went outside and called to Lena, I realized I was a very happy man.

# Chapter III

## AUSTIN'S COLONY—September 1825

Rebecca and I were married the following Saturday afternoon, with only Wilhelm and Marie Schmidt as witnesses. Rebecca and Marie had gone into the other section of the cabin and somehow managed to get Rebecca into her best dress in spite of her sore and bandaged shoulder.

Events had moved so fast that I had not even thought about trying to find a wedding ring, but Rebecca still wore the gold band Josiah had given her, and she quietly slipped it from her finger and handed it to me before the ceremony.

It was a sober, solemn affair. There was none of the festive air of a normal wedding, where there would have been fiddlers and dancing and a barrel of whiskey for the gentlemen and fruit punch for the ladies. There were only the four of us and Father Muldoon. The memory of Josiah's death was still too fresh on all our minds for any pretense at gaiety. After the quiet ceremony, we sat at the table and ate the good fresh-baked bread and venison *sauerbraten* Marie had brought. Afterwards, when Rebecca and I were alone, it seemed strange to know that I would not be leaving, too.

It seemed stranger still after the evening chores were done. It was getting dark by the time I had milked the cows, looked after all of the stock, and returned to the cabin. Rebecca was seated near one of the windows, using what little daylight remained to do some mending. Before

Marie left, Rebecca had changed into one of the black mourning dresses she had made when Josiah died. Father Muldoon had brought me a few old, torn copies of United States newspapers, and I picked up the top one and pulled a straight-backed chair over to the other window, deliberately avoiding seating myself in the rocker that had been Josiah's. He had made two, one for himself and a slightly smaller one for Rebecca, and I felt it would have been presumptuous of me to sit in the chair that had been so especially his.

"I'm afraid I'm out of candles," Rebecca said, looking up and smiling softly at me as I settled on my chair. "There's an oil lamp on the mantel, if you'd like some more light."

"The light coming in the window will hold me. How about you? Can I light the lamp for you?" Wilhelm had mentioned butchering a steer a few days earlier. I made a note to ask him if he'd sell me some tallow for candles.

Rebecca shook her head and returned to her mending, and I unfolded my newspaper. When the last of the daylight had all but faded from the sky, Rebecca folded the garment she was mending and put it on top of the sewing box next to her chair, and I laid aside my paper. Even in the best of light, the newspapers would have been hard to read, for they had been handled so much that the print was worn off in places, and some pages were torn, others completely missing. Nevertheless, I had been pleased to get them. I wondered if we would ever have our own newspaper in Texas. I filled my pipe, then pushed myself to my feet and went to the fire, choosing a piece of tinder and inserting it deep into the bank of ashes and coals until at last it caught.

"I guess I'll go out for a smoke and then turn in." I held the flame to the bowl of my pipe and puffed.

"You can smoke in here if you like, Todd. You needn't go outside. This is your home now."

"Thank you, but until the first real norther blows in, I'll enjoy being outside."

She nodded. "Good night, then."

"Good night. I'll be up early, so don't you go lifting any kettles in the morning. I'll come in and hang them over the fire for you."

"They're not heavy when they're empty," she protested.

"Heavy enough. Doc Graham said not to do anything that strains your shoulder for at least a month."

"All right, I'll wait for you."

Satisfied at having extracted that promise from her, I went outside and smoked my pipe. The air was pleasant, at that perfect balance between hot and cold, and I walked up and down in front of the cabin, pausing occasionally to take in the small night sounds all around me: the chirping of the crickets, the soft soughing of the breeze through the trees, an occasional quick rustling through the grass as some small nocturnal creature scurried from one place to another. I thought with pity of the people who lived in the cities and larger towns, for they had no opportunity for such quiet moments in which to listen to the very pulsing of the earth itself.

I thought of Thorne and his family back in Savannah. Lordy, but he would be surprised to hear of my marriage! I chuckled inwardly as I imagined him reading the letter I would write giving him the news. Again, I planned to urge him to come to Texas, for it made no sense for him to be back in Savannah, constantly fighting the futile battle to keep Thaddeus from ruining him completely. In another place, at another time, Thorne and I might have made a go of it. With Thaddeus managing in many devious under-handed ways to stop us, we had never really had a chance.

Thorne had always hedged in his answers to my exhortations to pack up and come join me. I was convinced there was a rare opportunity for him in Texas. It would not be easy for him to pick up and go, I knew, especially when Angela's mother could be depended on to fight him at every turn, but I could tell from his letters that he was heartily sick of trying to get the business to produce more than a scanty support for his family and that he would like to come. He had ridden with me through the fields often

179

when he was a boy, heard me give orders, saw the results, so he would have no problem in getting the ground to produce a suitable cotton crop for him. And besides the land itself, there were countless ways a man could make money in a newly settled area like Texas. The occasional trips I made to New Orleans for merchandise were rewarding beyond all expectations. With two of us, we could increase the scale of that operation manyfold, make it into a continuing thriving business. They said the road to Bexar was fairly passable all the way, and I had long been mulling over the idea of running an unscheduled stage between Bexar and Natchitoches, and selling things along the way. There was certainly a developing need for such a means of transportation, for I'd heard there was another colony setting up to our west, and that some Americans were even moving into the old Spanish mission town of Bexar itself. If I bought a coach, I had always planned on driving it myself; now, of course, I wouldn't leave Rebecca, would try to get a few young boys to drive it. But it was still only a dream, a vague notion in the back of my mind, to be taken out and considered now and then, and then tucked away for a while.

I knocked the ashes from my pipe and went into my half of Josiah's cabin. I had been sleeping there almost a week before our marriage, and Rebecca in the other section, so I was accustomed to being there. But on that particular night, I was acutely aware that Rebecca was alone in the other part, just across the dogtrot. Before I drifted off to sleep, a picture flashed through my mind of her lying on the bed with her lovely hair spread out in soft waves on her pillow. *Remember Josiah,* I admonished myself sternly, and eventually fell into a troubled sleep.

We settled into a routine that could have been exceedingly awkward if Rebecca hadn't worked so hard at making certain it would not be. When, on the second evening after our marriage, I began to walk toward the chair I had used the previous night, she suggested I sit in the other rocker.

"You'll be far more comfortable," she said in a matter-of-fact voice.

And so, from that time forth, I sat in Josiah's rocker, and after the first few days, I got over my uneasiness about it. As Rebecca had said, it was much more comfortable than the straight-backed chair.

I wrote the letter to Thorne a week later, telling him of my marriage. He never received it. Before it could reach him, he had already left Savannah for New Orleans.

The letter from him conveying this startling news was brought to me by a stranger passing our way. By this method we received—and sent—all our mail. It constantly irritated all of us that we had no mail service in Texas, that as many or more of our letters were lost as were eventually delivered. The Mexicans used all their energy for constant political battles. The lack of established mail service was of no concern to them.

Thorne wrote that Angela's mother had died that summer of apoplexy, and that he was selling his house and would use the proceeds to come to Texas with his family. His letter reached me in mid-October, and he asked me to meet them in New Orleans around the end of November, a scant six weeks away. I would have gone gladly, but for Rebecca. How could I leave her alone in the cabin? I had married her so she would not be alone.

There was only one solution, awkward though it might be: I would have to take her with me.

I expected her to balk at the idea, but her face brightened at the prospect. "Oh, Todd, how lovely that would be! Are you sure I won't be in your way, that I won't slow you up?"

I shrugged. "We don't have to rush. I thought we might ride a couple of mustangs and take a third one along to carry blankets and food and a few cooking pots. Then we can sell them in New Orleans. I'd like to pick up an overland coach and some big horses while we're there."

"A coach?" She raised her eyebrows. "You mean a proper carriage, as I've heard the rich people use in towns? I

181

hardly think we need such elegant transportation here." She smiled at the absurdity of the notion, then added mischievously, "Besides, not even Sam Butler has one yet."

I laughed at her reference to Sam Butler. He had fancied up a buggy with bright blue paint and golden scrolls, then dressed one of his darkies in red and gold livery and had him drive them around in the ridiculous contraption. "It wouldn't be for us. I agree we're not quite ready for that yet. But I've been thinking about getting a large coach for some time now. There's need for some means of transportation between our towns, something besides horseback, for those unable to ride. The old Camino Real isn't really half-bad, except when there's too much rain. I'm sure I could get some young men to drive a coach on it for me."

She nodded. "It's true," she agreed. "I guess we are civilized enough now to need transportation between one point and another. I'm glad you won't expect me to ride in it around here, though. I'd feel terribly out of place."

I began to look forward to taking Rebecca to New Orleans, showing her the city, introducing her to my friends there. A few days later, when I was sorting out the things I had brought over from my cabin, I ran across the bolt of blue-striped satin I had brought with me in my first wagonload. It had always seemed a bit too elaborate for our ladies in the colony, so I had not yet shown it to anyone. I brought it into the main part of the cabin and laid it on the table.

"Why don't you make yourself a new dress out of this?" I suggested. "You'll need something special for New Orleans."

Rebecca had been kneading dough on a small worktable Josiah had made for her, and she looked over her shoulder at me, then looked at the bolt of fabric I had put on the table.

"Oh!" she gasped, and came over to the table without stopping to wipe the flour from her hands.

"Oh, Todd!" she exclaimed. "How beautiful! Where did you get it?" She hastily wiped her hands on her apron.

"May I touch it?" she asked in awe as she stared in open-mouthed fascination.

I laughed. "I don't know how you're going to make yourself a dress if you don't." Then I answered her first question. "I brought it with me in '21. It was a whim, and I thought maybe the womenfolk here would be ready for it if I waited awhile, till they got settled enough to think of such things."

She had unrolled some of it as I talked, and was running her fingers over its satiny stripes, as though she must touch them to believe they were truly there.

"It's so lovely!" Then she looked up, startled. "Oh, but what am I thinking? I couldn't wear that color yet, with Josiah gone not much over six months." She sighed, and it was clearly a sigh of regret. She began to back slowly away from the table, as though she would remove herself from temptation.

"Rebecca, do you think Josiah would really mind?"

She looked surprised at my question, but after considering it for a minute, she said, "No, I really don't believe he would. But it seems sort of irreverent to his memory for me to wear anything so fantastically beautiful so soon—"

I shook my head. "It's not that soon. I never did hold with wearing mourning overlong. Beyond a reasonable time, it always seems sort of a put-on, a show for the world to see. And you don't need that. You know in your heart how much you cared for Josiah, how much you miss him, and that's what really counts." I could sense the battle going on inside her as I talked. She had stepped well away from the table, but she was looking at the fabric, her eyes fastened on it as though she was afraid it would suddenly disappear if she dared to take her eyes off it for a minute.

"I suppose . . ." She took a step closer.

"Anyway," I added, "you're not going to New Orleans as Josiah's widow, but as my wife."

She looked up at me, and I knew I had convinced her, for though she said nothing, she returned to the table and held a length of the material up to her chin.

"It's your color," I said approvingly. "I thought it would be." I was amazed at how it brought out the blueness of her eyes.

"But it's not very heavy," she said in one final protest, "and dresses made of such a fabric as this have to be short-sleeved and low-necked. Won't I catch cold if I wear it in New Orleans in November?"

I laughed. "That's a hazard most ladies seem willing to accept. If you want a warm outfit, I have some tartan wool in there that I bought last year. Maybe you'd like to make yourself a riding habit and a traveling suit of that."

"But you brought it here to sell!"

I shrugged. "I'll never miss a few lengths. And in New Orleans you'll need some proper clothes."

She draped the blue fabric over the table lovingly, as though a quick, disrespectful motion might cause it to disintegrate. I smiled, thinking how unexpected her reaction had been. I had been afraid she would insist that her gray wool and her black mourning dresses would do very well. But instead, she was obviously thrilled at the prospect of new outfits. The satin was far less practical than anything she would ever have thought to own, and her eyes were shining with happiness.

"You shouldn't be so good to me!" she said, coming around to my side of the table and putting her arms around my neck to give me a hug.

That was even more unexpected than her willingness to accept the fabrics. I started to put my arms around her in return, but I stopped, knowing I dared not trust myself. I dropped my hands to my sides, and stood there rather foolishly as she unwound her arms from my neck. She hesitated for a moment, her arms resting on my shoulders, and it was all I could do to keep myself from closing my arms around her and bending down to kiss her. The past weeks had not been easy for me, being constantly around Rebecca, knowing she was my wife, yet knowing, too, that I must give her her full year of mourning for Josiah.

"I'll get to work on the patterns this afternoon," she said

as she turned back to her kneading. "I think I'll do the traveling costume first. But right now, I had better finish with my bread."

I was particularly anxious to see what she would do with the blue material, and was pleased with the results. She fashioned it into a simple dress with a nipped-in waistline and a fitted skirt that came to fullness at the hem. She had crocheted some fine white lace, and this she used profusely around the neckline, on the short puffed sleeves, and on the hem of the skirt. She and Marie fashioned cloth flowers of a deeper blue out of an old silk dress of Marie's, and Rebecca stitched several of them onto each sleeve and the rest onto the hem of the skirt between the looped rows of lace. It was not an excessively fancy dress, as such dresses go, but its simplicity suited Rebecca, and when she held it up to show it to me, I told her it was perfect, and for her it was. I did not realize till we reached New Orleans that it was up-to-the-minute in stylishness.

From the tartan plaid she fashioned a split riding skirt and a plain skirt, and made a short jacket to match both. This, too, looked right for her, but certainly not as good as the evening dress.

It was a crisp November day when we started out for New Orleans, and I noted that she wore her buckskin riding clothes instead of her new ones. "You're not wearing your new habit?" I asked.

"Certainly not," she answered. "I wouldn't want to get it wet, or wear it out. It's in my saddlebags. I'll put it on when we get to New Orleans."

I laughed. "If you wear it out, you can always make another."

"There will be no need to do that. This one will last me for years, if I take proper care of it."

"And I have no doubt you will," I said, amused at her innate frugality.

I had always felt sorry for ladies who liked to ride, for they looked so insecure and uncomfortable perched precariously on their sidesaddles, but Rebecca didn't seem to mind, and she sat her horse well. She was even more apt to urge her mount to a faster pace than I was. At such times, I would quickly catch up with her, and trailing the third horse behind us, we would ride side by side until we felt the horses were tiring, and then we would rein in, laughing like children.

But most of the time, we went at an easy pace, talking as we went. I loved my farm—our farm, now that Rebecca's and mine were joined—but it was a pleasant change and a release from the constant press of chores to leave it for a while, if only to remind ourselves what a special place it was, and how glad we were that we had gone with Austin. It was a move that I had never regretted, not for one minute, but that didn't keep me from enjoying my occasional return to civilization. As we neared New Orleans, Rebecca plied me with questions about it. I don't think she had ever had the chance for anything as frivolous as a vacation in her life.

We camped out every night. It was not a particularly good time of year for it, and would have been much cozier and more comfortable inside someone's cabin or plantation house. But if we had thrown ourselves on the hospitality of others, we would certainly have been offered a single bed to share. The third mustang carried all the things we needed to exist independently of others, and every night as the fire burned low, I made a point of filling and lighting my pipe and walking away from the fire into the darkness. When I was out of sight of our campsite, I would sit down and wait till I was sure Rebecca had had enough time to get settled for the night. Then I would return and make up my own bedroll on the far side of the fire and go to sleep. Rebecca was an earlier riser than I, and in the morning, she would always have the fire started and her blankets neatly folded before I awakened. Fortunately, good weather held most of the time. Only once did I have to fashion a lean-to of pine boughs to keep us dry. That night, though we slept with our backs to each other, there was little space between us, and I was painfully aware of Rebecca's proximity, and could not keep from my mind her desirability as a woman, could not keep my body from reacting to her nearness, yearning to possess her.

Always before, on my previous visits to New Orleans, I had returned to Monique, a woman I knew who was only too willing to satisfy my desires, but I knew that this time, I could not insult Rebecca by doing so. It was paradoxical: I couldn't go to another woman for satisfaction because I had a wife, and yet common decency demanded that I not touch her for some time to come.

Rebecca was fascinated with New Orleans. I took a two-room suite for us, and when she heard how much it cost, she gasped, "Todd, that's a fortune! Can we afford such luxury? With the price of cotton dropping all the time—"

I smiled at her concern. "We can afford it," I assured her, although that was not wholly the truth. If Thorne and I were to buy the sort of large conveyance I had in mind, and the horses to pull such a vehicle, we would certainly need every penny we had. And I didn't know how much, if anything, Thorne would have to spare. Still, with Rebecca walking around the suite looking at everything with wide-eyed wonder and unconcealed delight, I was not sorry I had chosen one of the better hotels. And there were always the gaming tables. I had done quite well the previous year on my trip to New Orleans, and hoped this visit would bring similar good fortune. As far as getting a suite instead of a single room was concerned, our peculiar situation demanded it, for we needed two separate rooms.

During the time we waited for Thorne, I showed Rebecca the sights, took her out to dine, and introduced her to the friends I had made during the time I had lived there. The wife of one of my friends took a particular liking to her, and came to the hotel often to pick her up and take her out riding, or out for tea, or to see the shops. I insisted Rebecca take some money to buy herself things, which she did, but only stintingly, and even then her purchases were all excessively practical: a bolt of domestic in the dull gray she always wore, some white domestic for collars and trim, needles and thread, yarn, and a pair of black leather slippers. I insisted she also buy a pair of blue satin ones as well, to wear with her blue dress. It was only under protest that I could get her to do so. I bought her a small blue satin reticule to match, and you'd have thought I was presenting her with a diamond necklace, she was so thrilled with it.

My luck at the gaming tables was unspectacular but steady, and gradually I began to breathe easier about having enough money to carry out my plans. The weather was chilly, and Rebecca's cloak was an old one, so I insisted she have a redingote made for herself. She objected to what she considered such an extravagance, but when I told her I would order it myself if she didn't, she at last capitulated and had her new friend take her to her dressmaker. "Imagine," she said, "me having someone else make something for me, as if I couldn't do it myself!"

"You haven't time to make it yourself. You need it now. And the dressmaker has promised it in two days' time."

Several nights later, we were invited to a dinner party, and Rebecca asked if I thought it would be all right if she wore her striped satin dress.

"Certainly," I said, and she clapped her hands, as delighted as a child who has been given a stick of candy.

She went into the bedroom to dress. I changed to an evening coat, a cutaway, and put on my gray- and white-striped trousers, then sat on the couch reading a newspaper I had bought that day. It was a luxury to read the news while it was still current, and from a paper on which the print was still a dark black against the paper's contrasting whiteness.

Rebecca was in the bedroom a long time. I had already pulled out my watch twice and looked at it anxiously before she finally emerged, wearing her blue dress, with her hair swept upward and a cluster of soft curls falling toward the nape of her neck. The front of her hair was plain, except for a few curls drawn to one side over her forehead.

The effect was stunning. She certainly didn't look like the woman who had labored beside Josiah in the fields.

"That was worth waiting for," I said, staring at her admiringly. "You're positively lovely."

She laughed. "Do I look all right? Beth showed me how to fix my hair this way. And, see? I'm wearing my satin slippers. You were right. They do look ever so much better with this dress than the black leather." She frowned slightly. "I do have a problem, though. When Marie and I were designing this dress, I wasn't thinking about the difficulty of fastening the buttons by myself. I can't reach the top ones. Would you do them for me?" She turned her back as she spoke, and I saw her dress was gaping open at the top.

Clumsily, I slid the tiny satin buttons into the loops. I was overpowered by an awareness of Rebecca's soft femininity, and of the scent of the French perfume I had bought her. At last I finished, my fingers trembling, and said in relief, "There." Then I turned quickly and walked across the room to get her redingote.

At the dinner party, I could not keep my eyes from her, or get over my awe at how striking she looked. I looked around the room, decided she was probably the only woman there who was not tightly corseted. As a matter of fact, I was probably one of the few men who wore no corset. The small waist was much in vogue, for men as well as women. I thanked the good Lord that I had no paunch to try to hide, for I could never have subjected myself to the torture of having my waist drawn in tightly by whalebone and laces. Nor did I feel that Rebecca looked unfashionable without corseting, for the hard work she had done all her life had made her flesh firm and solid. Nor did her bosom need to be pushed up for emphasis. Several times, when she caught me watching her, she smiled. She seemed to be having a wonderful time.

When we returned to our suite late that night, she removed her redingote and hung it on the clothes-hook.

"That was such a lovely evening, Todd. Thank you!"

189

"You were the belle of the party," I said, amused by her exuberance.

She laughed, and her laughter had never been so gay, so provocative. "I felt like a princess. This dress—it's so lovely. My parents were very poor, and Josiah and I never had much in the way of worldly goods, either. I feel . . . oh, I feel almost beautiful in such an enchanting dress!" She danced and twirled over to me, where she stopped and turned her back to me. "I hate to take it off, but I must. I'll need your help again with the buttons."

I put my hands on her shoulders. "You are beautiful."

I don't know what came over me next, but when I had unbuttoned the top buttons, I didn't stop. Feeling compelled to continue, I kept slipping the little blue satin balls from the loops till none remained fastened. I heard my own breathing, heavy and tense, and tried to hold my breath, knowing Rebecca must hear it, too, but I couldn't. As I unbuttoned the final buttons and the dress fell away from her shoulders, I couldn't keep my hands from moving caressingly over her smooth white shoulders. I caught my breath at the softness of her skin, and kept moving my hands down, over her arms, pushing the sleeves of her dress before them till the dress fell with a soft swish to the floor.

Rebecca stood there, not turning, started to protest, "Todd, I—"

"Hush," I said softly, turning her toward me and wrapping my arms around her as I crushed my lips down on hers. All the pent-up desire and frustration of the past few months, all the thoughts I had not dared let myself think, came tumbling in on me. I was out of control, no longer responsible for what I was doing. I led her into the bedroom, to the bed.

"Todd, no. Not yet. Josiah . . ."

I paid no heed to her words, seemed to hear them from far away. Quickly, impatiently, I shed my own clothes and lay down, pulling her down beside me, half covering her body with my own. I gave her no chance to object further,

190

for at each small sound from her, I covered her lips with mine, smothering her protests before she could give them voice. I cupped my hand over one of her breasts, as soft and lovely as I had known it would be, then moved my hand down to lift her petticoats out of the way, caressing her buttocks.

When at last I moved over her, I felt her recoil at the shock. But I paid no more heed to that than I had to her words. Nothing could stop me. I knew only that she was desirable and that I must have her. My movements held nothing of the gentle concern I always felt for Rebecca. I could think only of my own urgent desire, was driven by it, momentarily enslaved by it. I knew I was being too brisk, too demanding in my own overpowering need for her.

"Forgive me! Forgive me!" I heard myself saying the words over and over, until they had lost all meaning.

When I had finished, I waited for the feeling of relaxation, of satisfaction that I knew should follow. But such feelings were denied me that night. In their place, I felt a sickening disgust with myself, a revulsion at the crudity of my actions. As sanity returned, I wondered how I could have behaved so brutally.

"Rebecca, oh, Rebecca! My God, what have I done? I'm sorry, so sorry!" I tried to think of something more to say, some way to explain my actions, but I couldn't.

She raised her hand to my head, stroked my hair. "It's all right, Todd. It's all right."

But it wasn't. As I pushed myself from the bed, I saw there were tears glistening on her cheeks. I went into the other room to sleep in my habitual place on the couch. I had promised Rebecca that this would not happen, and she had believed me, put her trust in me. And I had betrayed that trust.

Never had I hated myself so much.

The next morning, Rebecca made a gallant effort to pretend that nothing had happened. She came out of the bedroom wearing her tartan plaid costume and, with a smile on her face, wished me a pleasant good morning. I looked

191

away from her, shame burning deeply inside me, and couldn't even bring myself to return her smile.

Things were different between us after that. We still spoke politely to each other, but there was a strain, a tension that had never been there before. And it was all my fault. Until then, I had been enjoying watching her delightfully naïve reactions to New Orleans and all its pleasures, but my brutish actions had ruined everything. Certainly, they had taken the edge off her pleasure.

That night after dinner, I took her up to our suite and said I would be up much later. She merely nodded when I told her, said, "Good night, Todd," and walked into the bedroom. I went to the card game to which I had committed myself, but my thoughts were not on the cards that night, and I lost, though not heavily, for I have the sense to bet cautiously when the cards are running against me or when I find myself unable to concentrate properly. I excused myself as soon as possible and set out for the house of Monique, the woman who had obliged my sexual needs during the years I had lived in New Orleans. She had been left fairly well-off by her deceased husband, and had no intention of sharing his money with a new husband. Yet she was a frankly sensuous woman, and had never objected whenever I wanted to stay the night with her. I hadn't deluded myself into thinking I was her only lover. She went to bed with men because she needed them, and that night I needed her to rid myself of my desire for Rebecca. My disgust with what I had done the night before all but overwhelmed me, and I was determined I would not let it happen again.

Monique was at home alone and welcomed me warmly. It wasn't long before we were in bed together. We coupled, and it was just that, for there was no love, no tenderness on either side. We were human animals, and like animals, we relieved our physical needs. I left soon afterward, and as I walked through the brisk night air in search of a hack, I knew I was no more satisfied than I had been before I lay with Monique. I entered our suite quietly and settled down on the couch. The bedroom door was closed, and I wondered if it was locked, too. I shut my eyes, wondering if I hated myself more for forcing myself on Rebecca or for sneaking around like a thief in the night to satisfy my lust. I knew it would be the last time I would visit Monique.

A few days later, Thorne arrived with his family and his four house slaves. I had hired a boy to stay down at the docks to watch for Thorne's ship, and as soon as the boy heard it was coming up the river, he ran to get me, so I was there when it docked.

The children were the first ones off and ran to meet me as soon as the gangplank was in place. Cassie easily outdistanced Will, for all that he was taller than she, and threw herself into my arms.

"Why, it can't be Cassie!" I said in mock disbelief. I don't know why it is we older people have a hard time realizing that children grow up, but it was a shock to me to see how Will and Cassie had changed. Thorne had sent me several silhouettes of them, but these had given no indication of their size, and seeing them in the flesh, I was amazed at how they had grown.

"Let me look at you," I said, backing off a little from Cassie. "Why, you're almost a young lady now!"

"I'm twelve and a half," she answered, and I noted that already the bodice of her dress was pushed out into two little swells where her breasts were starting to form. Her shining brown hair glinted red in the sunshine, her eyes were a deep green, and her mouth full, promising to become sensuous. She was on her way to becoming a very pretty young lady.

"And Will," I said, turning to him. "You've changed quite a bit, too, since I saw you last." His resemblance to Thorne had grown more startling with the years. He had the same round full face, the same dark brown hair and brown eyes. He was large for a boy of ten, as Thorne had been, and my mind went back twenty-five years, to the boy I had taken to live with me. It could almost have been the same child standing before me now.

I hugged Will, and he returned my hug, but he was a more restrained child, and there was none of the spontaneity with which Cassie had thrown her arms around me. I wondered suddenly if he considered himself too big to be hugged, but as I released him and offered him my hand, I saw that, in his subdued way, he was as happy to see me as Cassie was in her exuberance.

By that time, Thorne had come off the ship with Angela. He had changed little, except to add some weight.

"That's what comes of sitting at a desk all these years," he laughed when I commented on it. "Todd, you don't know how much I'm looking forward to getting settled in Texas. I've had more than enough of dingy, dark warehouses and drab offices. I can hardly wait to get someplace where I can look for miles in any direction and not see a living soul."

I turned to Angela, knowing it had been wrong of me to leave her till last. She stood behind Thorne, hiding in his shadow like a pathetic, frightened animal. Her hair had become even more faded in the years since I had seen her, and it had darkened considerably, too, so that it had become even duller and more colorless than I remembered. Her expression was as lifeless as her hair. She was overly thin, and her dress hung limply from her shoulders.

"Angela," I said, offering her my hand, "I trust you had a pleasant journey."

"Hardly that," she said in her toneless voice. "We were on the edge of a hurricane, and it's a wonder we ever got through it. And the rolling was so terrible, I couldn't keep a thing on my stomach."

"I'm sorry," I said, then added in a deliberately cheerful tone, "Well, that's all behind you now. I hope the rest of your journey will be more enjoyable."

"Enjoyable? Hardly that. I hear there are Indians . . ." She shuddered.

I searched for something further to say to her, something pleasant that she couldn't nullify, but I could think of nothing. Even if I had pointed out the clearness of the blue sky

194

overhead, she probably would have complained about the rain that was sure to follow. I felt sorrier than ever for Thorne.

Thorne no longer tried to hide his contempt for her and addressed her cuttingly. "Must you be so terrified of everything and anything, even before you know what it is? First you were worried about pirates, and then when we hit the edge of the hurricane, you lived in mortal fear of capsizing and sinking, and now it's Indians!" He looked at her in open disgust. "You're out of Georgia for the first time in your life, in the fascinating city of New Orleans. Will you please try to enjoy it, or at least have the courtesy to pretend you do, for all our sakes?"

Angela seemed on the verge of tears. To cover the awkwardness of the moment, I turned to greet the servants. They had been standing silently behind Thorne and his family.

Then I turned again to Thorne, motioning to the portmanteaus near them. "Are these all your things?"

Thorne nodded. "For now. Until they unload the hold."

"Come along then. I've hired three hacks, which ought to hold all of us."

Thorne and I rode in one of the hacks, Angela and the children in another, and the servants in a third.

"There's something I must tell you before we get back to the hotel," I said as we started moving. "I'm married. You'll meet my wife—"

"Married!" Thorne whooped in surprise. "I thought you were a confirmed bachelor. Who is the lady who finally caught your eye?"

I shook my head in denial. "It wasn't like that at all. I wrote you about my friend Josiah, about his death. Did you get that letter?" Thorne nodded and I continued, "Well, Rebecca . . . his wife . . . insisted on coming back to live in her cabin a few months after he died. One day last September she got a Kronk arrow through her shoulder, but she insisted on staying in her cabin, even though it was dangerous for her to live there. She'd have done it, too.

She's the stubbornest, most determined woman I've ever met, and I knew that nothing would make her move, so I married her so I could move in. It was much too soon after Josiah's death for her to marry. I knew that, but what else could I do?"

"I can tell you right now I'm going to like your Rebecca," he said when I had finished, and I knew without him telling me that he was comparing her with Angela.

"I'll leave it to you to tell Angela and the children. I wanted her to come down to the dock with me, but she thought it might be best if I had a chance to talk with you first."

"I'm glad you did. I might have thought she was your kept woman if I'd met her without previous warning." He grinned, offering me his hand. "Congratulations. How long have you been married?"

"A little over two months. It was last March that Josiah died."

He whistled. "She wasn't a widow long then, was she?"

"Not long enough for propriety. But it was the only solution. I couldn't let her stay on there alone, and there was no way I could get her out of her cabin when she was so set on staying in it."

He nodded his understanding. "I'm sure frontier life makes compromises necessary many times. I hope you're happy and haven't regretted your hastiness, as I have constantly regretted mine."

"No regrets," I said, then added silently, *except for my own boorishness in leaping upon her a few nights ago.*

Thorne and Rebecca took to each other instantly, as I had known they would. In fact, I never knew anyone who didn't take to Rebecca. She was strong willed and had a nature as positive as Angela's was negative, but she was never overbearing, as strong women often are. Even Angela seemed to perk up in her company, and by the next day Rebecca was helping her take in a few of her dresses and making a list of items she should be certain to have for housekeeping on the frontier.

Cassie and Will adored Rebecca openly, and while Thorne and I saw to the purchase of a coach and two wagons for overland travel, Rebecca took Angela and the children around to show them the sights that had so enthralled her. Angela livened up a bit, and surprised all of us by demonstrating her not inconsiderable ability to converse in French. We were in a shop one day, and the French shopkeeper obviously couldn't make out my atrociously bad French. Angela came forward and timidly translated what I was trying to say, and when we all praised her for it, she said blushingly that she used to do quite well in French when she was in school. "I started teaching the children a little on board ship, whenever I felt good enough to be on deck."

"Teaching and school!" Cassie said exasperatedly. "That's all you ever think about, Mama. Aunt Rebecca, do you know she brought school books all this way and wants to give us lessons when we get settled?"

"A sound idea," Rebecca said. "You don't want to be ignorant. My own schooling was stopped far too soon, and that's something I've always regretted."

Cassie, obviously disappointed at not finding an ally in her new great-aunt, made a face. "What good will book learning do me? I want to learn to shoot Indians!"

Angela gasped, and her face grew suddenly pale. "Don't be absurd, Cassandra. A proper young lady doesn't do such things. You must learn how to embroider and to pour tea gracefully. These are the things that matter."

I caught Rebecca's eye, and she smiled and winked at me. I thanked the good Lord she had learned to shoot a rifle instead of learning to embroider and pour tea.

Thorne said, "Angela can't seem to get it through her head that the things that counted for so much back in Savannah might not be so important in Texas."

"But shooting—" Angela protested, shuddering.

"—Is necessary, Angela," Thorne finished, impatiently. "I doubt if you'll ever learn to fire a rifle. You'd certainly faint dead away if there ever came a time you'd have to use

197

it. But before we leave New Orleans, I intend to buy one for each of the children, and will teach them to use them as soon as possible. This will be for their own protection and, incidentally, for yours as well."

A few days after their ship had docked, Thorne and I went down to see to the unloading of his household goods. There was one conspicuously large wooden crate marked *fragile*.

"What in the name of heaven is that?"

Thorne laughed. "Angela's mother's piecrust table and her silver tea service. I had them crated together in hopes the whole thing would get lost. But it seems that I wasn't that fortunate. You remember the things, don't you?"

"How could I forget them?" They had always been in the parlor, in front of the fireplace, and every afternoon, Angela's mother had to make a fetish of serving tea in the formal manner. I tried to picture the table all set for tea in a dirt-floored cabin, and couldn't do it. "Well, it will certainly be unique in Texas, at least in our part."

"I'm sure of that. I've never seen Angela so set on anything as she was on bringing that. I was almost proud of her for sticking to the notion and not letting me dissuade her. I do believe she'd have stayed behind if I hadn't finally agreed to bring it."

"I hope the rest of your things are better suited to frontier life," I said with a chuckle. "We'll have those wagons full if all these things belong to you. I've bought quite a few things to take back to sell, too . . . things like axes and knives and needles and thread. I've bought lots of domestic . . . it sells for seventy-five cents a yard. And coffee . . . we must bring some of that. Would you believe it fetches a dollar a pound? Merchandising is profitable business, Thorne, and if we can hire some young boys, particularly in winter when they're not so sorely needed at home, we can set up a sort of a traveling store and still have room for passengers as well. I've turned a tidy profit on anything I've brought in, without even budging from my own cabin. You'll probably set up to the west a way, since the land around my place is all allotted, so you could cover the ground around there and I'd continue to sell to those in and near San Felipe."

Thorne frowned. "I'm not certain I want to get my grant from Austin. There might be something better elsewhere. I was talking to a man in the hotel lobby yesterday. He was telling me about a colony just getting started around Nacogdoches. A man named Edwards is the *empresario* there. It's a new colony, and I feel it would be better if I could get in on one just beginning. Edwards only went there the end of October, I understand."

I nodded. "I hear there are a couple of new colonies being established on the Guadalupe, too. Check them all out, but I can't recommend Austin highly enough. He got his second grant last spring. He's proved himself an expert organizer, and he's good at governing. He's set up a sort of governing body, an *ayuntamiento* it's called, and . . . well, there are never any conflicts over claim boundaries in his colonies, and he's just, and quick to settle any disputes that arise. I'd be a little hesitant about the Nacogdoches area, if I were you. It used to be quite a sizable town back in the days of the Spaniards, and they even had a garrison stationed there. The residents mostly all fled back in 1813, but I've heard some of those original inhabitants have moved back in the last few years. And there are others already there, too. A number of the people who crossed the Sabine heading for Austin's colony stopped before they got as far as the Brazos, lots of them around Nacogdoches. There could be conflicts over land."

"With squatters?" Thorne looked amused.

"I guess that's all they are, but don't forget the others, who have more legitimate claims to some of the land. And even the squatters can't be expected to give up easily what they've taken for their own. Anyway, they're bound to cause confusion."

"I'm sure it will be quickly straightened out. After all, Edwards is the duly appointed *empresario* for that area, and his word will be law."

"I hope so."

In the end, he decided to go to Edwards's colony. I continued to have misgivings about it, but I didn't interfere. It was his life, his decision, and I realized I could well be wrong.

A week after Thorne's arrival, we were ready to leave. I told him I had enough camping gear for all of us, so there would be no need to ask hospitality of the people on the way.

"But couldn't we stay at the plantations as long as we're near them? I remember you wrote how you had gone up that first time, stopping each night at one house or another, and I sort of promised Angela we would do the same. She's so afraid of the frontier, I thought it might help a bit if she sees the planters' big homes, knows that someday I intend to build one just as grand as the best of them. Besides that, it's winter, remember, and hardly a good time for the women and children to be sleeping on the ground."

"I know, but . . ." I broke off, unable to think of any viable excuse for insisting on camping out. I had assumed we would return in the same manner Rebecca and I had come. If we stopped at homes, Rebecca and I would be expected to share a room.

"Angela's going to be a poor enough traveler and hard enough to live with," Thorne continued, "without making her endure undue discomfort. And Will looks robust, but he catches cold at the slightest chill. I really don't see why you would want to subject Rebecca to the rigors of camping, either."

Reluctantly, I agreed to do as he wanted, but warned him that sooner or later, Angela must learn to accustom herself to the roughness of the frontier.

"She'll never get accustomed to it. She's conceded that New Orleans isn't so bad, but I'd hardly call it the frontier."

I shrugged and said no more. There was really nothing to be said in Angela's defense. We both knew she would not adapt well to the change Thorne was forcing on her. It was no secret that she had been begging Thorne to settle in New Orleans instead of going on to Texas.

Thorne and I bought two good saddle horses, which we planned to ride most of the way. His coachman, Daniel, was capable of handling the carriage, and the three female house servants could manage the two wagons between them. Angela had never learned to ride, so she would go inside the coach, with Rebecca to keep her company. The children were supposed to go in the coach, too, but the way things turned out, they spent most of their time up on top of the coach on the box, alongside Daniel.

"I know you don't think much of me bringing slaves," Todd said once. "I know how you feel about owning them, but with Angela, I need them."

I said nothing. Again, that was Thorne's affair, and it was not up to me to play the part of his conscience. I could understand his reluctance to do without them. I could not envision Angela bustling efficiently around a cabin to finish the many household chores any more than he could.

I had told Rebecca the night before we left that we would be stopping at homes along the way, and she had nodded silently. She knew as well as I that this would present an awkward situation, forcing us to share a room.

"I'll sleep on the floor, of course," I added.

Another silent nod acknowledged my words. She continued with her packing.

At our first stop, we were greeted cordially, as I had known we would be, for the owner was one of the planters with whom I had developed quite a friendship, having stayed with him and accepted his hospitality several times before. That night, after the ladies and children had retired, Thorne and I visited in our host's study, sipping some of the French brandy I had brought him. We talked into the small hours of the morning, and when I finally went upstairs, I opened the door to our room quietly, not wanting to awaken Rebecca. To my surprise, she was sitting up in bed, knitting by the light of a candelabrum on a table near the bed.

"I thought you'd be asleep."

"I've been waiting for you."

"You shouldn't have. It's late. I'll just take my pillow on the floor and throw a coverlet over me—"

"That's not necessary."

I looked at her, startled at her words, and she continued, "Stop being so foolish, Todd, and come to bed."

I remembered the night we had spent under the lean-to, remembered how aware I was of her body near mine, how it took all my willpower to keep from touching her. And I remembered too well the night I had not been able to stop myself in New Orleans. It would be impossible to lie in the same bed with her and not cross that invisible but very real line between my side of the bed and hers.

"I . . . I can't."

"And why can't you?" she persisted.

"My God, Rebecca, do I have to spell it out? You know what happened the night of the dinner party. You can't imagine how much I've hated myself since. I was out of my mind with wanting you—"

"That was as much my fault as yours. I should have suggested sooner that we share a bed, but I felt that in some way I would be disloyal to Josiah's memory if I did. I'll admit I was confused and shaken by what happened, but I know now I shouldn't have been. Do you still want me as much as you did that night?"

I blinked at the bluntness of her question. "You know I do."

"Then why don't you come to bed?"

"But, Josiah. . . . It wouldn't be right. I intended to give you at least a year."

"We are man and wife, Todd. You have been a good husband, but the more you have done for me, the more I have felt like the mistletoe that clings to the trees: decorative, perhaps, but useless to its host, a parasite that takes everything but gives nothing in return. I love you, and I want to be a proper wife to you, starting now. I don't want to be just cared for and pampered. I want to be loved and held, to feel you need me as I need you. Will you deny me the pleasure it will give me to be a true wife to you?"

"But Josiah—"

"Do you think that because I love you, I loved Josiah any less, or hold his memory any less dear?" She wrapped her knitting around the needles, laid it carefully on the small bedside table. "I've been Josiah's widow long enough. I think it's time I started being your wife. Now please, let's have no more foolishness about you sleeping on the floor," she said with finality as she settled herself under the covers.

Before I snuffed out the last candle, I took one final look at her lying there, with her hair spread out on her pillow, making a frame for her dear face.

I walked around to the other side of the bed, sat on the edge to take off my shoes. "Rebecca?"

"Yes, Todd?"

"I love you very much." I removed the last of my clothes and slid between the sheets. I started to reach for her, stopped. "I usually sleep without a nightshirt. Does that shock you or offend you? I would have had some made in New Orleans, if I had thought—"

"I'm not shocked, nor offended, nor is it a surprise to me. Remember," she said, and I could hear the subdued laughter in her voice, "I have been doing your laundry since September."

"I had forgotten that." I reached toward her, found she was facing me, lying almost in the center of the bed. I laughed. "Why, Mrs. Stewart, I do believe you're on my side of the bed."

"I intended to be, Mr. Stewart. I am a very forward woman."

This time there was no question of her response. She was completely lacking in artifice and would never have pretended to emotion she didn't feel, so when she clung to me and gave a soft moan of pleasure as her body tensed against mine, my own pleasure was increased tenfold.

Never had I thought it possible to feel such an overwhelming tenderness and love for anyone as I felt for Rebecca that night. Perhaps having lacked true sexual love for so many years made me appreciate it more. Whatever the reason, I knew I loved Rebecca more than I thought it was possible for a man to love a woman.

"My dear wife," I said as I drifted off to sleep with her cradled in my arms. "My dearest Rebecca."

# Chapter IV

## TEXAS—Winter 1825-1826

Our trip was marred by one unpleasant incident involving Angela. The second day after we had crossed into Texas, it chanced that Thorne and I had ridden ahead of the coach and wagons. It was early morning, and I did not find out till later what had happened. Will's stomach was upset from something he had eaten the previous night, and the women, seeing he was about to be sick, had signaled Daniel to stop the coach. Then, since the coach and the wagons were all stopped anyway, the ladies decided to take advantage of the opportunity to go into some nearby bushes. Thorne and I were out of sight around a bend in the road and had no idea they were not following right behind us. We were not aware of any trouble till Angela's piercing scream rent the air.

"Oh, my God! That's Angela!" Thorne and I wheeled our horses around and raced back down the road. My heart gave a fearful lurch as we passed the coach, thundering down the road toward us, empty, one door swinging open and Daniel up on the box, wide-eyed with fright, frenziedly whipping the horses on to yet greater speed.

*Rebecca!* I thought, driving my heels sharply into my horse in a frantic effort to make him go faster, reaching for my rifle as I rode.

When I rounded the bend, I saw the wagons and a confusion of moving figures off to one side of the road. I saw an unsaddled pinto barely visible on the other side of the figures, and my mouth went dry with apprehension. Before I reached the place, one figure separated itself from the others and leaped onto the pinto. The horse surged ahead, and the man leaned down over his neck, his bare torso gleaming in the sun, seeming more a part of the horse than merely its rider. An Indian, he had to be. No white man ever rode like that.

Anxiously, my eyes darted from one figure to another. Were there any more? Were Thorne and I riding incautiously into a trap, so we would be helpless to save the others? But I saw with relief that there were only the figures I recognized, and I cried out Rebecca's name as my eyes picked her out from the others. When I reached her, I reined in sharply, and jumped off my horse before he stopped. Still clutching my rifle, I ran to her.

"Everything's all right," she assured me as she moved into my arms. "He's gone now. He must have been a stray from a war party."

I held her close. "My God, I thought you might be . . . I thought something might have happened to you!"

"I'm all right. It was Angela he was after. She always goes further into the bushes than the rest of us, for privacy. Come, she's over here. Cassie kept him from carrying her away."

Thorne had come up right behind me, and Rebecca led us quickly to where Angela lay on her back, her head turned to one side, sobbing wildly. Will and the three female servants were standing nearby, and Cassie was kneeling over her mother, saying reassuringly, "It's all right now, Mama. The Indian's gone." Cassie looked up and saw Thorne and told him proudly, "I bit him, Papa. He tried to take Mama away on his horse, but I grabbed his leg and hung on, and I bit him on his heel as hard as I could. He kicked my eye with his other foot, but I wouldn't turn loose till he let Mama go. I guess he got scared when he saw you and Uncle Todd coming. As soon as he threw Mama down, I let go of his leg." She made a wry face. "Ugh! He tasted terrible!" She spat on the ground.

Thorne and I heard her matter-of-fact explanation in amazement, then he said, "I'm proud of you, Duchess. You saved your mother." He patted her on the shoulder and bent over her solicitously. "Let me see your eye. Does it hurt?"

"A little. It's starting to hurt more now. You'd better see about Mama first. I hope she's all right. He threw her down hard."

"I'm sure she's fine, thanks to you." He knelt down by Angela and asked her if she felt any pain anywhere. She looked up at him blankly, as though she could see right through him, hadn't heard him. She opened her mouth to speak, but all that emerged was another of the deep wracking sobs of hysteria.

"I doubt if she's injured—just shaken up a bit," I said. Then I turned to Angela and said softly, "It's all over now. You're safe. He's gone."

She continued to lie there, sobbing convulsively, her whole body shuddering. She seemed beyond hearing any of us, beyond thinking, beyond reason with the terror that had gripped her.

Thorne put his hand on her shoulder, shook her, said gruffly, "Come, Angela. It's all right. You heard what Todd said. If you're not hurt, get up." When she didn't answer, he continued impatiently, "You've cried enough. After all, nothing happened to you."

"She's had quite a shock," I said, appalled at his heartless words, feeling compelled to defend her on this occasion from his unreasonable disgust. "Let her cry a little, get it out of her system. That was a very close call. And we were much to blame. We should never have ridden so far ahead of the coach."

"The coach!" Thorne said, looking down the road. "Daniel ran away, took the coach. I'll blister his hide—"

"He was frightened out of his mind," I said, remembering the horror on his face as he had passed us. "He didn't know what he was doing. Don't be too hard on him. I'll go bring him back." I stood up, relieved that everyone was all right, and still with us. Disaster had been averted, however narrowly, and for that I was thankful. As I moved toward my horse, I saw there would be no need for me to go in search of the coach, for it had just come into view around the bend of the road ahead. A few minutes later, a sheepish Daniel alighted from the box.

Thorne's callousness was not limited to Angela. Before we continued on our way, he addressed Will accusingly, "Where were you? Why didn't you try to save your mother?"

"I did, Papa. I ran, but—"

"He tripped," Cassie finished. "He tried to run to Mama. He would have been there ahead of me, but he fell." It was not the first time I had seen her jump to her brother's defense.

"Cassie should have been the boy," Thorne said bitterly, and I thought it a cutting and cruel thing to say in front of Will.

The episode made quite a heroine of Cassie. Somehow, news of what she had done had traveled ahead of us, so folks we met along the way were apt to remark, "So, you're the brave little girl who saved her mama!" She basked in the praise that fell to her, even wore her black eye proudly.

For all that Cassie looked so feminine, Thorne had been right in saying she should have been a boy. She was virtually fearless, perhaps made more so by Thorne's constant efforts to see that she grew up as little like Angela as possible. He lavished praise and affection on her, but I often thought he could have spared a little of both for Will.

It seemed a source of constant irritation to Thorne that Will was not a coordinated child. Thorne made no secret of the fact that he thought a boy who did not excel in matters physical was no boy at all. Will loved to sketch, and to read. His sketches, for all that he was only ten, had a certain promise to them. I had seen this, and had bought him a sketching portfolio and some pens. Thorne had not been pleased with my gift, and had mumbled something about drawing being a prissy way for a boy to spend his time.

It was not that Will was actually timid or fearful, in the manner of Angela. The only thing he seemed to fear was his father's displeasure, and the more he tried to avoid it, the more he seemed to incur it. Since he was unable to approach Cassie in physical prowess, he generally avoided pointing up that shortcoming by refusing to compete with her in Thorne's presence. When Angela had needed help, Will had not hesitated to run to her. He had been ahead of Cassie when he tripped; yet I was certain Thorne wouldn't remember that, but only that he hadn't reached her at all.

It was Will's misfortune that he looked so much like his father, for I think it was this striking physical resemblance that caused much of Thorne's impatience and lack of understanding as far as his son was concerned; he looked like him, was built like him, and he could not comprehend how he could then fail to be like him in other respects. I have noted that few fathers can bear for their sons not to have the same interests and aptitudes they themselves have, and Will's amazing resemblance to Thorne merely seemed to accentuate Thorne's irritation with him. It was as though he looked in a mirror, wanting, expecting to see himself, and the distortion he saw instead confused and upset him.

We were delayed in our journey for three days, as Angela was not fit to travel until she had rested. I truly believe she had come close to actually dying of her fright, and her body was slow to recover from the shock. Her reluctance to go on immediately was certainly understandable to everyone but Thorne. His impatience with her grew, and even Rebecca, slow to criticize anyone, commented to me that she thought he was far too harsh with her.

The rest of our trip was without incident. Thorne and I had previously decided to go first to Rebecca's place and leave Angela and the children with her there, with the house slaves staying down the road in my cabin, so that they could come over each day and work. I smiled at the thought of Rebecca having four servants to do her bidding, and was willing to give odds that she would have them sitting around while she did the work herself. I intended to ask

Wilhelm to let one of his boys come over and stay with them. I wanted two people in the cabin who knew how to handle a rifle well.

We crossed the Brazos on the ferry at the town of San Felipe de Austin, which had officially come into being two years earlier and was the heart of Austin's colony. The town seemed larger every time I saw it. We had a sawmill by that time, and I noted there were already a few houses of sawed boards in the town. I decided right then that I would build a real house for Rebecca at my first opportunity.

As we rode on and approached our land, I felt a sense of belonging and couldn't suppress a surge of pride. This was ours, Rebecca's and mine. She and Josiah and I had claimed it, worked on it, made it our own. Several years before, Josiah and I had set out cuttings of *bois d'arc* trees some of the settlers had brought with them, and they were doing well, growing along the boundaries of some of our fields. At the base of a few of their leafless branches clung bunches of mistletoe. We passed my cabin, and I pointed it out to the servants, so they would know where it was and could return to it that night. It wasn't much farther to Rebecca's place, and as we rode into the yard and tethered our horses in front of the cabin, I had a sense of homecoming, a feeling that this was where I had always belonged, and where I would stay.

Near the cabin and a little to one side, so that it threw shade on part of the roof, stood one of the prettiest live oak trees I have ever seen, and Cassie lost no time in climbing high into its leafy branches. She tried to coax Will to join her. He seemed to consider the idea for a minute, but when he saw Thorne was watching him, he shrugged and said, "Not now. Later maybe. First, I want to see inside Uncle Todd and Aunt Rebecca's cabin."

The day after our arrival, I took the children with me to look at the horses and invited them each to choose a mustang from among those that were saddle-broken. Cassie immediately spied a coal-black mare and claimed her.

"I'll call him Cinder," she said delightedly.

I chuckled. "You'd better make that Cinderella, honey," I said. "That's a mare you've chosen."

"I'll still call her Cinder for short," she said unshakably. "Can I ride her right now, please?"

"After a while. I have another surprise for you. I bought you and Will each saddles in New Orleans, for your very own. We'll try them out after dinner."

Will seemed to have more trouble choosing a horse. He scanned them all, a slight frown puckering his young brow. "I saw one in that other field that we passed. I liked him best. I think I'd like to have that one."

"The horses in that other field aren't gentled yet. If you tried to put a saddle on one of them, he'd throw it right off on the ground."

"But these horses had to learn to let you put saddles on them, didn't they?" He looked up at me earnestly.

"Yes, but—"

"Then why can't he learn, too?"

"He can, but it will take time."

"I'll wait. While you and Papa are gone to pick out our land, I'll come talk to him every day."

"You show me which one," I said, capitulating, "and we'll see what we can do about saddle-breaking him."

Will's happiness shone from his eyes as he slipped his hand in mine and led me back to the other field. The horse he had selected was a two-year-old crossbreed. "That one. Can I have him? Please, Uncle Todd? I'm afraid I might hurt one of those smaller ones, especially if I grow any bigger."

I smiled. "The mustangs can carry more weight than you might think. But you're a big boy and growing fast, so I think your choice is a good one. We'll see if we can't find another horse for you to ride while you're getting this one saddle-broken."

Will looked up at me in frank adoration, and it struck me that he was starved for approval of anything he did,

211

and was totally unaccustomed to hearing any words of praise from his father.

Later that day, Cassie could not hide her disappointment on seeing that I had bought her a sidesaddle. Actually, I had debated for some time before I had decided that it might be best if she were made more aware of the limitations of being a girl.

"Can't I ride astride, like Papa does?" she asked. "I know in Savannah I had to use a sidesaddle. Mama said it was the only ladylike way to ride, but I thought that here—"

"Well, now," I said cajolingly, "your Aunt Rebecca rides a sidesaddle, and I just don't think she'd care to ride any other way. Of course, it takes more skill than riding astride, and if you think you aren't able—"

My words had the desired effect. "Of course I'm able," she bristled. "Put that saddle on Cinder and I'll show you."

I had been surprised and pleased to learn that Thorne had taught both children to ride back in Savannah, and soon discovered that it was the one thing in which Will surpassed Cassie. No one, seeing him mounted, would guess that he was lacking in coordination, for he sat the saddle well and seemed to move as one with the horse. He had a firm, gentle way with horses that his sister, in her constant impetuosity, lacked.

We waited until after Christmas to leave for Nacogdoches. It was a merry time with all of us together, and I was glad for the presence of Thorne and his family, for Rebecca's sake. Still, at times, she would suddenly grow unnaturally quiet, and I knew she was remembering the previous Christmas, and the sixteen before that, when Josiah had been with her. But with a cabin full of people, she had scant time for sad reminiscences, and her thoughts were soon drawn back to the present.

The day before Christmas, Cassie and Will returned from a visit to the Schmidt cabin, talking excitedly about their custom of cutting a small pine tree and decorating it with strings of colored berries and popped corn. Nothing would do but that we must have one, too.

It was dark before we had the tree in place on Christmas Eve, its branches drooping under the weight of the decorations the children strung on it. Rebecca had even lent them a few pieces of the inexpensive stamped jewelry that Josiah had given her. We set the tree to one side of the fireplace, and after supper, we all gathered there and sang Christmas songs, humming the words we didn't remember. Even Angela seemed to relax under the mellow feeling of peace and contentment we all shared. *My family,* I thought as I looked at Rebecca and then at the others, and I counted myself a lucky man to have them all with me.

Cassie kept pleading with Thorne to let her go to Nacogdoches with us. I don't think he would have agreed if Angela hadn't been so frightened and appalled at the idea. Perversely, he decided to take Cassie along.

"No, Thorne! Please!" Anegla protested. "You won't be able to stay with her every minute, and you know she's far too bold for her own good. What if some Indians . . . ?" She shuddered, unable to finish the thought.

Thorne laughed. "Then God help the Indians," he said. "She certainly dispatched the one who grabbed you quickly enough. Will can come, too, if he'd like."

"I'd rather stay here and work on gentling my horse," Will said, and Thorne, obviously displeased at having his bounty refused, said testily, "As you wish."

Cassie rode her mustang to Nacogdoches. The mare's legs were short, and Cassie had to work constantly to keep up with us, but she never complained or asked us to wait for her.

"Come on, Cinder," she urged, prodding with her heels whenever the mare began to lag. "We have to get to Nacogdoches."

I passed through Nacogdoches once or twice a year, and each time it seemed a little more alive than it had the time before. When I had first passed through with the group of Austin's original colonists, the previously deserted town had barely begun to come back to life. But when Thorne and Cassie and I arrived in January of 1826, the town was bustling with activity. Even the shabbiest of the residences, the smallest of the shacks in the town, showed signs of occupancy, as Hayden Edwards's colony formed around its hub. Many of the buildings sported hastily added lean-tos, and everywhere there were signs of new arrivals. I thought of the older residents, the ones who had fled in terror in 1813 and had begun to return eight years later, rebuilding their lives on the ashes of what they had left behind. And now Edwards was superimposing his colony on top of what they had been reconstructing, and I wished again I had been able to convince Thorne to settle almost anyplace but there. There was the matter of the squatters, too, as I had reminded Thorne when he had first begun to show an interest in Edwards's colony. Their presence would surely help confuse the issue of land ownership still further. Even though some of them had no legal rights, they were there, and they couldn't be totally ignored.

Apparently Hayden Edwards, the *empresario* for the colony beginning there, was aware of possible problems revolving around previous ownership, for we learned that he had arrived in October, and in November he had issued a decree stating that anyone with a prior claim to the land must present his claim for consideration immediately, or lose all rights to it.

"You see?" Thorne said complacently when he heard about it. "That should settle your concern about any previous ownership, then," and I wondered that he was so easily satisfied. But it was the place he had chosen to settle, and he discussed possible claims with the man, and each day we rode out to look over one place or another. He felt it would be advantageous to be on the old road to Bexar, and at length he found a parcel of land he liked some miles west of town. The site he selected for his cabin was at the edge of a grove of pine trees, not far from a creek.

"Running water right close by," I commented approvingly. "Angela will like that."

214

"Angela won't like that, or anything else," he said bitterly. "There will be no pleasing her. I've known that ever since I left home. She'll be terrified of everything every minute of every day she lives here. But there is no sense in trying to make her happy, because it is impossible. Still, this does seem the right place for a cabin. We can put the necessary house to the other side, away from the creek."

There was ample timber on his land—too much, I thought, for the claim to be good for farming—and Thorne and I went to work felling the pines, sawing them to the proper lengths, and dragging them to the site he had chosen for the cabin. From the creek, Cassie helped us gather stones for the chimney.

Cassie soon grew bored with staying close to the cabin site and begged Thorne to let her go farther afield.

"I want to explore your land, Papa. May I, please? I'd like to take Cinder on a long ride, take my lunch with me."

"All right," he agreed. "Just don't go beyond the south fork of the creek. Even I haven't been farther than that yet."

A little while later, we watched her ride off, her pockets stuffed with jerky and hardtack.

"I really don't like her going off all alone like that until I know more about what to expect around here," Thorne admitted as we returned to our work. "But I'll not have her cowering in a corner like her mother."

"I don't think you have to worry about that one being afraid of anything," I said. "My only concern is that she's a bit too fearless."

The day had been bright and the weather unseasonably warm when Cassie left, but by late afternoon, a norther had blown in and brought with it chilling winds and clouds that obscured all traces of the sun. Thorne didn't express his anxiety, but I noted that, as the afternoon wore on, he kept looking in the direction which Cassie had taken, as I did, and I knew he shared my concern for her. When at last the little black horse and its rider did appear down the road, his relief was plain to see.

Cassie was shivering with the cold when she dismounted, for she had taken no wrap with her. "I got lost, Papa," she explained as we bundled her into a blanket and quickly built a fire by which she could warm herself. "When the sun went in, I couldn't tell which way I'd come from. I . . . I finally found my way," she finished lamely, and I couldn't rid myself of the feeling that she was holding something back from us.

A few days later, I discovered that my suspicions had been right, for Cassie came to me privately and said, "Uncle Todd, I have to tell Papa something, but I'm afraid to tell him. Do you remember the day I went riding alone, and I was so late getting back?"

"And a very cold and shivering little girl you were," I agreed, sitting down on the floor of pine needles and motioning for her to sit beside me.

A furrow creased her brow as she dropped to the ground. "I met a boy that day—"

"An American boy?"

"Well, not exactly. I mean, he said his mother was half American and half Comanche, and his father was Spanish."

"Where did you meet him?" I urged gently.

"That's the trouble. I met him the other side of the south fork of the creek, where Papa told me not to go. But Cinder was thirsty and wanted a drink, and then she just seemed to keep going."

"So you disobeyed your father and crossed the south fork and met a boy."

"Well, I didn't exactly meet him. He sort of found me. I'd left Cinder and was chasing a rabbit to see if I could find where his home was, and then I saw the sun was gone, and didn't know which way I'd come—" She looked up at me, her large expressive eyes pleading for understanding.

"I started calling Cinder," she continued, "and then this voice right behind me—this boy—said I'd scared away every bit of game within ten million *varas*. I didn't even know anyone was there till he said that. He was very angry with me." Her lower lip trembled as she told me about it. "But it wasn't my fault. I was lost, and I hoped Cinder would hear me call and whicker. Anyway, I told him it was Papa's land, and I guessed I had the right to scare away the game if I wanted to."

"Did this boy say who he was or where he came from?"

She nodded. "That's why I must tell Papa about him. But I'm afraid to tell him, because I did disobey him and go past the south fork, and he'll be mad at me when he finds out. The boy said his name was Fel-eep-pay, or something like that, and that he and his mother lived not far away on what I thought was Papa's land and that it really his. Oh, Uncle Todd, this is Papa's land, isn't it? I like it here, and I think Papa likes it, too, and we want to stay. I couldn't bear it if this boy was right and if we'd have to leave, like he said. But how can I ever tell Papa about him?"

"Sometimes we have to tell things on ourselves we'd rather not tell, and I'd say that's the way things stand with you right now. You know you did something wrong, but you must let your father know about this boy. You wouldn't want us to do all the work of putting up a cabin if it really is somebody else's land, would you?"

She shook her head violently. "That's something else he said. He knew you and Papa were getting ready to put up a cabin, and he said you should just keep on, because it was on his land and pretty soon it would be his cabin!" Two large tears ran down her cheeks. "Uncle Todd, that's not true, is it? It can't be true! This is Papa's land, isn't it?" She put her face in her hands and cried, and I put my arm around her to comfort her.

"I guess that's something we'd better find out," I said as I patted her shoulder. "Let's go together and tell your father what you just told me."

Thorne listened in silence till Cassie had finished, and he didn't even bother to reproach her, as she had feared, for going beyond the limits he had set for her, for he seemed too preoccupied with the import of what she was telling him to concern himself with her disobedience.

"A breed and her bastard whelp!" he said disdainfully. "I'm sure they're just squatters. They must be. If they had any valid right to the property, they'd have come forward and registered it in November when Edwards called for all such claims, and he would have told me about it. I guess we had better go see them, tell them to leave." He asked Cassie, "Can you take us to this boy's cabin? Do you know where he lives?"

"I'm not sure," she said. "I think I can find the place where I got off Cinder, and he said his cabin was just west of there."

"Good. Then we'll go in the morning. I'll not put up with having squatters on my land."

"What's a squatter?" Cassie asked me.

"Somebody who just claims land by right of settling on it."

She shook her head. "Then I don't think that's what this boy and his mother are. He said his great-grandfather got a grant from the King of Spain for twenty-five million square *varas*—"

"The King of Spain!" Thorne scoffed. "A likely thing for a breed to have. Well, we'll soon make them move on."

Early the next morning, we followed Cassie, who led us to the other side of the north fork and on across the south fork. At length, she stopped. "Right in here is where I left Cinder," she said. "He told me he lived a little to the west."

"That's this way," Thorne said, taking the lead.

We came first to the burned-out remains of a fairly large cabin. Only its chimney stood intact, stark and naked against the sky. "A good-sized place," Thorne commented. "I wonder who lived here?"

We came to a second clearing, and there stood four small cabins, simple one-room affairs, not a quarter of the size of the foundation we had passed a short while before. As we approached, a figure silently materialized at the doorway of one of them. I don't know when she came there; one minute, I looked and there was only the closed

218

door of the cabin, and next time I happened to glance at it, there she was, a tiny figure framed in the doorway, her hand resting easily on a rifle butt. She was so small that at first I mistook her for a child, but then I noted the fullness of her bosom, the braids twisted around her head into a sort of a crown, the adult features of her face. I guessed her to be somewhere between twenty and thirty-five, and I could not have pinned it down more accurately than that, for she had about her a timeless look, as though her sharp features had always been the same and would remain so. She stood unflinchingly, defiantly, watching us carefully as we drew closer.

"She looks like a queen," Cassie said in a hushed whisper, and I knew her thoughts paralleled my own.

"Mr. Stewart?" She looked straight at Thorne as we dismounted. "I have been expecting you. Won't you come in, please?"

Once we were inside the small cabin, which was barely big enough to hold two small beds and a crude wooden table and a few stools, she motioned for us to sit where we would. Thorne had not said a word, and I knew he was as surprised and awed as I. Whatever we had expected to find, it was not this tiny woman who had about her an air of regal dignity.

"I am Serena Varga," she said as we seated ourselves. Her complexion was more olive than red, and if she were indeed a half-breed as Cassie had indicated, the only sign of it was her high cheekbones, which gave her face a carefully sculptured look. She was not a beautiful woman, but her appearance was striking. Her dress was faded and obviously had been patched a number of times, but it was clean. The cabin was neatly kept, and a big kettle of something that smelled mouth-watering good simmered over the fire.

"Mr. Stewart," she continued after we had settled ourselves, Thorne and I on the edge of one of the beds, and Cassie on a stool, "I will not waste words. I am afraid you will have to move. The place you have cleared for your cabin is on our land."

"Your land!" Thorne sputtered, obviously taken aback at the audacity of her statement, and not a little irked at having been preempted in his own demands. "You think because you and your boy have been living on a piece of property that makes it indisputably yours?" He didn't wait for an answer. "No, madam, I fear it is you who are on *my* land."

As they argued on, saying essentially the same thing over and over again, I noticed that Serena Varga never raised her voice in anger, and I couldn't help but admire her self-control, the quiet confidence with which she spoke. Certainly no ordinary half-breed was she. I could tell that Thorne, too, sensed her superiority.

As Thorne's anger increased, so did the volume of his voice. "What right can you possibly have to think you own my land? Hayden Edwards issued a call for any previous claims to be registered several months ago. If you indeed thought you had any sort of a valid claim, you should have come forth and said so then—"

"I take no orders from your Mr. Edwards. Felipe and I heard of no such call. Nor would it have mattered if we had. The authority of the Spanish crown is indisputable. This land was given to my husband's grandfather by King Carlos III. In time, the records will be straightened out." She never looked away from him as she spoke, and she talked with the self-assurance of one who never doubts for a minute that he, or she, is right.

Thorne scoffed at her. "I doubt if any such Spanish records are left intact, and furthermore, I don't think they would show any such grant if they were." His eyes blazed at her as he spoke. "Madam, I have come many hundreds of miles, have brought my family on a long and hazardous journey to reach this place, and make my claim upon it, with the aid and blessing of the Mexican government and the help of Hayden Edwards, who is the officially appointed *empresario* here. You are on my land, and since you have no way of validating any vague claim you might

220

think you have to it, I suggest you and your son leave peacefully before I am compelled to use force."

Thorne's words, obviously intended to intimidate the woman, did not have that effect at all. She rose to her feet, still did not look away from him as she spoke. "Mr. Stewart, I have stayed here with my son, have lived in this peon's cabin for eight years since my husband's death. We have refused to leave, in spite of hardship and deprivation. We have remained through invasions of lawless hordes, through near-starvation, illness—and many other trials. We have stayed, determined to see the day that our claim is recognized. Do you think foolish threats of violence can frighten me away now?"

Thorne stood up, towering over her. "Consider yourself warned, woman. Now, I am asking you to leave. Later, I will resort to force if I must."

Thorne walked to the door, and I nodded to Cassie and we followed. As we started to mount our horses, a boy of about fourteen came around the corner of the cabin. He was dark, tall and lean, with a certain sine about him. His cheekbones were not as high as those of his mother, but his features had something of the same well-carved look, the same hint of strength to them. He was clad in buckskins, which where too short in the legs as well as the sleeves, as though he had suddenly grown away from them, in the manner of boys that age. He had a dead rabbit in one hand, and in the other he clutched a rifle, which he held so naturally and effortlessly it might have been an extension of his arm. He shot angry glances first at Cassie, then at Thorne and me.

"Thieves!" he shouted accusingly at us. "Land-grabbing Yankees!"

Thorne and I were too surprised at his sudden appearance and the fury of his attack on us to do anything but look at him in frank astonishment, but Cassie was not.

"We aren't thieves!" she shouted back at him as she swung herself onto her mustang. "It's our land, not yours! You're lying if you say it belongs to you!"

As we rode off, he shouted some epithets at us in Spanish.

"Churlish boy," Thorne said. "He certainly could stand to learn some manners. I'll have to get them out of here as soon as I can."

"Just how do you propose to do that? In spite of your threats, I can't see you picking them up bodily and moving them somewhere else. And do you really think it would make any difference, even if you did?" We rode away, side by side. I had gone there prepared to hear lies, claims with no substance to them, prepared to find some dirty unkempt squatters. I had not expected to find such a woman, or to believe her story, but there was something compelling in her manner, her self-assurance, her sincerity, so that I believed her in spite of myself. "If they are merely squatters as you seem to think," I said, "then they have no real claim. But I somehow have the feeling that there really was a grant from Carlos III. Maybe it's best to see what you can find out about it. If their claim is valid, it follows that yours is worthless."

"Valid!" he scoffed. "Do you think it's really likely for a breed to own twenty-five million square *varas*? As far as her having a husband is concerned, I'd have to see proof of that before I'd believe it, too. I doubt if there was any such thing as a formal marriage. Spanish landowners don't go about marrying half-breeds."

We glanced behind us and saw Cassie was not following. As we paused, she came riding up, her face streaked with tears. She reined in only after she had passed us, pulling in her mare so sharply she threw back her head and paced around in a circle.

"I threw a piece of hardtack at him!" she said. "He called us names in Spanish, I know he did, and I threw it! It was all I had. I wish it had been a rock and I had hit him! I wish I had never met him! I wish—!"

"Hush, child," I soothed. "Wishing never solved anything, not anything at all."

After that unpleasant episode, I suggested repeatedly to

Thorne that he change his mind, go someplace else. There was Austin's second grant, and there were several other new colonies starting up around the Guadalupe. But Thorne would not listen; in fact, he was more determined than ever to stay where he was. "I won't let a woman not half my size and a boy I could whip with one hand tied behind me scare me off the land that is rightfully mine!" he said.

"But why not go someplace without such problems, and probably get better farmland in the bargain?"

"I'm staying," he said, and I knew that, to him, leaving would be an admission of weakness, a sign that he had let that tiny woman in the peon's cabin get the better of him, and knowing Thorne, I resigned myself to the knowledge that he would stay and fight. But I wondered if he had not underestimated the strength of his opponent.

We were there over a month, stopping our work from time to time in order to help with other cabin raisings. When we were at last ready for Thorne's cabin to be raised, we had the help of others as well. The cabin was built on a similar pattern to Rebecca's and mine, but larger.

I found myself impatient to return to Rebecca, and now that Thorne was ready to move his family to his own place, I was looking forward to having our cabin to ourselves once again, to enjoying a comfortable existence together. I was looking forward to Rebecca's companionship, to savoring fully the depth and solidity of the love that had grown between us.

It was well into February when we returned, and as I hugged Rebecca to me I knew I was happier than I had ever thought possible.

"I'll never leave you again," I promised. "Not ever!"

As she looked up at me, her face was shining with happiness. "I've missed you, too," she said simply. But her expression said far more.

Thorne and his family left a few days later, taking with them the two wagons we had bought in New Orleans. Perched on one of them was the crate containing the mahogany table and silver tea service that had been Angela's mother's. Remembering the dirt-floored cabin we had just built at the edge of a stand of pines, I couldn't keep from chuckling. "I don't think Angela's mother would approve one bit of the place her tea service is going."

Rebecca nodded. I had told her back in New Orleans about the tea service. "Poor Angela," she said with a sad smile. "She doesn't belong here. I think Thorne is going to regret bringing her."

"People like Angela make their own private hells, no matter where they go," I mused. "They're always unhappy, too swamped by their own fears and uncertainties to see what there is about life to be enjoyed. I don't think it really matters one iota where they are. Angela has always been afraid of life itself, even back in Savannah. And Thorne has his own future to think of, and that of his children."

"I suppose," she agreed, "and yet it does seem sort of brutal to expose someone like her to life out here, where there are so many truly frightful things to fear."

When we could see them no longer, I put my arm around Rebecca's shoulder, and we walked back into the cabin.

"It's so quiet," Rebecca said, leaning her head toward me as we entered, "with only the two of us." As I closed the door, she turned and put her arms around my neck. "Oh, Todd, I've been bursting to tell you, but I wanted to wait until we were alone. I . . . I'm breeding, I'm sure of it! Oh, isn't that wonderful?" Her face seemed suffused with light as she said the words that nearly knocked my legs out from under me.

"Breeding?" I repeated dumbly, unable to hide the shock I felt at such news. "But I always thought . . . you and Josiah—"

"It isn't always the woman's fault, Todd," she said softly. "But I'm glad it never occurred to Josiah to think it might be him." Her hands moved to my face, and she held my chin, looked up and asked, "Aren't you as thrilled as I am? Aren't you glad?"

"Of course," I said, trying to sound convincing. "When will it be?" My mind went back thirty years, to another place, another woman whose belly had swollen with the seed I had put there, the seed that brought her to her death.

"In September. Oh, Todd, thank you! You've given me so much happiness, and now you've given me a child as well. I've wanted one so desperately for such a long time, and I had despaired of ever being able to have one. Thank you, my dearest Todd." Her hands reached to the back of my head, and she pulled my face down to hers. We kissed, and I held her to me, hoping she didn't sense the desperation with which I clutched her, glad she couldn't see the moistness in my eyes. I was unable to blink back the tears forming. Abruptly, I pulled away from her, said, "I've been neglecting the stock since I came back. I must go see to the horses."

Quickly, I turned and left. I didn't stop till I was out of sight of the cabin. Then, when I was sure Rebecca could no longer see me, I sat down against a tree, put my head in my hands, and cried like a baby.

Next day I rode into San Felipe and talked to Doc Graham, told him my concern. "Rebecca's thirty-six," I reminded him. "Isn't that too late to be having her first child?"

He tried to brush away my fears. "She may have a harder time, Todd, but don't look so concerned. It's quite a common consequence, you know." He smiled, and I knew I was not the first, nor would I be the last, to be reminded of that.

I couldn't share his humor, just nodded soberly. "Rebecca—"

"—Is in the best of health," he finished, "and I see no reason for you to be so gloomy at the prospect of becoming a father. Most men would be whooping with joy."

I tried to smile. "Rebecca is very happy about it."

He looked at me seriously. "Then why don't you try to be happy, too? There's nothing you can do about it now,

225

my friend. Try not to be afraid, and if you can't help yourself, then by all means hide your fears from Rebecca. It won't do to get her upset, too."

"You're right, of course. Thanks, Doc." I turned to leave. "And when she tells you, try to act surprised, will you?"

He smiled reassuringly. "I always do."

It was impossible not to share Rebecca's enthusiasm during the next months, her blind faith that all would go well. As one month followed another and her stomach began to grow and she looked forward yet more eagerly to the coming of the child, and remained in robust health, I pushed my worries to the back of my mind, trying not to remember that other girl who had been my child-wife so many years before, and her agonizing screams as the child she had carried to term refused to be born. But she had been tiny and frail and in delicate health, and wasn't Rebecca in the best of health, with a broad-hipped figure that surely was created for childbearing? I tried to console myself with such thoughts, but was not wholly successful.

Rebecca insisted on working in her garden that summer. "It will be good for me. You can't expect me to sit in the house all day long. I've made the child so many clothes I'll have to change him six times a day to use them all, and if I just sit and rock while I wait, I'll die of boredom."

I drew the line at letting her help me in the fields, and even that she protested. "You would think I might melt in the sun," she complained. But I think she secretly enjoyed my concern for and coddling of her, and she did as I asked.

It was not until her last month that she began to show any signs of poor health. Her hands and her face grew puffy, her legs and ankles swelled, and she no longer complained about boredom, but sat around much of the time with an unaccustomed lassitude.

"You mustn't worry," she assured me one day. I had returned to the cabin for dinner to find her lying on the bed, and though I hadn't realized it, my face must have mirrored my concern. "This often happens toward the end of a pregnancy. It only means we won't have long to wait now." She smiled and slowly got to her feet and started serving the food.

I moved behind her, my arms encircling her and the child I could feel moving restlessly in her womb. I leaned down to kiss her cheek. She looked up at me over her shoulder, the serenity that had become a part of her the last months shining through the pallor of her face. I wished heartily that the coming ordeal was past, that she held the child she wanted so badly in her arms, and that she was again in her usual brimming health.

She smiled, seeming to sense my thoughts. "It shouldn't be more than a few weeks. Maybe a little more. They say sometimes first babies are late."

I couldn't keep my anxiety from growing as the time approached, could no longer keep from my mind the memories that returned unbidden to crowd in on me, memories that were no longer as painful as they had once been, but poignant, and, worst of all, a reminder that things could go wrong this time, as they had so long ago in the past.

I have never been a deeply religious man, but during those last weeks of Rebecca's pregnancy, I stopped twenty times a day to repeat the same fervent prayer. *Dear God, don't let anything happen to her!*

One morning in early September, I awoke to find her already awake and watching me. It was unusual for her to remain in bed once she was awake, for as soon as she opened her eyes, she usually got up to start the fire for breakfast. I smiled at her, leaning on one elbow, and bent over to kiss her.

"What a lazy slug-a-bed you are this morning! Let me start the fire."

She returned my smile, ran her hand over my forehead, pushing the hair from my eyes. Then she shook her head. "You best not bother to start up the fire. I think it's time to send for Marie."

My heart lurched. "You're having pains?"

She nodded.

227

"Why didn't you tell me? How long—? Are they close together?" I didn't wait for any answers, threw back the covers, scrambled out of bed.

She smiled at my concern. "No, they're not close yet. They're not even very hard. But you made me promise to send for Marie as soon as they started, remember?"

"But you didn't. You should have waked me—"

I dressed in a matter of seconds. Rebecca watched me all the while, showing her amusement at my concern.

"Are you sure you'll be all right till I get back?" I asked as I moved toward the door.

"Certainly. As I just told you, the pains are still very light, and it's a long time between them."

I opened the door, returned to kiss her quickly. "I'll hurry."

"I'm sure you will," she said with her impish grin.

When I reached the Schmidt cabin, I did something I had not told her I was going to do. I sent one of their younger boys into San Felipe for Doc Graham. I had suggested the possibility to Rebecca once, and she had told me that would be foolish, that Marie was an experienced midwife and there would be no need for the doctor to come and waste his time sitting around waiting for the baby to be born, when Marie could handle things alone.

"I hope you don't mind," I said apologetically to Marie. "It's not that I doubt your ability, but it will make me feel better to have both of you there."

She shrugged, smiled. "It makes no matter. Everything vill be fine, you vill see, Herr Todd," she said, gathering her things. I had put Rebecca's saddle on a second horse, and I helped Marie mount, then we rode back to our cabin. It was all I could do to curb my impatience, for Marie was plump, and an inexperienced rider, and I had to slow my pace to hers. I wanted to ride on ahead, return to Rebecca quickly, but I knew it was Marie she needed, not me, so I swallowed my impatience and rode alongside her.

When we entered the cabin, I noted instantly that Rebecc's face was no longer as relaxed as it had been, saw that her hands were clenched into fists. I moved quickly to her, took her hand in mind, kissed the palm of it. "Is it bad? We came as quickly as we could."

"The pains are harder, and closer." There were drops of perspiration on her forehead, and I picked up a towel and gently wiped her brow.

Marie lost no time in establishing her authority over the proceedings. "Now, Herr Todd, if you vill make a fire outside and put a kettle of vater to boil—a large kettle—I vill see vhat is happening here."

Realizing I had been dismissed, I reluctantly went, did as I had been told as quickly as possible, then returned.

The waiting began. Through the interminable hours of the morning, as Rebecca's pains grew worse, we waited.

*Oh God,* I thought, *why couldn't this be one of those fast births I've heard about, where the woman has a few sharp pains and then expels the baby, and it's all over? If it had been like that, it would all be over with by now. And where is Doc Graham? What's taking him so long?*

From time to time, Marie sent me out of the cabin while she examined Rebecca, and by early afternoon I noted that she was looking for the doctor as anxiously as I. Something was wrong, I sensed it in her attitude. My heart gave a shudder of fear and remained leaden in my breast. *If anything should happen to Rebecca . . .* I refused to finish the thought.

"You sent Gunter. He iss little, but dependable," Marie said at last in answer to my unasked question. "The doctor must haff been busy."

I nodded. Of course, Doc Graham had other patients too, I reasoned, other calls to make. He couldn't be expected to sit in his cabin waiting for a summons from me. And he knew Marie was capable, had delivered many babies in her lifetime.

Marie sent me outside again, and a few minutes later she stepped outside herself. "I vish the doctor vould get here," she said. It was the first time she had hinted openly at her fears.

229

"Is something the matter?" I asked, waiting for her answer. I seemed unable to let out my breath until she told me. "What is it? What's wrong?" I heard my own voice demanding anxiously, and I knew what her answer would be before she gave it. I had heard essentially the same answer, had lived through that very moment once before. The first time, I hadn't known what the answer would be. This time, I did.

"Dhe baby iss not coming out like it should. I cannot get it turned."

I stared at Marie in horror, trying to will her to take back her words, to tell me she could have made a mistake, she could be wrong. I shook my head in denial of what I had heard. It couldn't be! It mustn't be!

"No!" I cried. "Not Rebecca!"

Memories of the past crowded in on me, as past and present and future merged into one jumbled series of events. "*It is a breech birth,*" another voice was saying, a voice from out of the past. "*I can't get the baby turned. . . . I must cut open the womb. . . . No other way, no other hope. . . . Sorry, so sorry.*"

I remembered the doctor who had uttered all those terrible words. His face had been lost to me for much of the last thirty years, but now it returned to me in all its clarity, as though it had been only yesterday that I had seen him. And as I stood, mesmerized by the horror of my thoughts, his figure faded and Doc Graham was there, standing in front of me, talking with Marie in hushed tones, telling me before he went into the cabin that I should remain outside a few minutes while he examined Rebecca.

And then he was outside again, his face as somber as that other face out of the past, his voice as grave. I heard his words as though they were only fragments of sound, and I had to catch them, piece them together in order to know what he was saying. "Caught in the womb, sideways. . . . Most unusual. . . . Baby can't be turned. . . . Slight chance . . . right itself."

At last I could listen no more. "Do something!" I

begged. "For the love of God, do something! Don't let me lose her! I don't care about the baby, only Rebecca—"

He backed away from me, and I realized he had had to struggle to break loose, for I had been holding him by the shoulders, shaking him. "If the baby won't come, there's only one thing we can do. Cut into her womb and take it."

"No!" I cried out in a great choking sob of despair, and Doc Graham's voice faded into that other voice, his face merged with that of the other doctor, became the same face, telling me that he could try to take the child, but that my wife might be apt to die of hemorrhage when he had cut open her womb. Desperately, I said, "There must be another way, something else you can do!"

He shook his head helplessly. "I'm trying. Marie, too, she's tried. We'll have to wait as long as we can, and hope."

"Oh, God!" Then I heard Rebecca cry out, bolted toward the door, was stopped by Doc Graham's hand gripping my arm.

"Don't let her see how upset you are," he reminded me. "I suggest you go splash some water on your face before you go in to her."

For the next two days, I refused to leave Rebecca's side. She clung to my hand, and when the pain became too intense, she squeezed my fingers until they were bruised. I only wished that by squeezing them harder, she could transfer some of her agony to me. Even in her torment, she often smiled at me, and reminded me over and over again that it didn't matter how much discomfort she suffered, it would be worth it when we had our own child. And again and again, she thanked me for giving her this child. Thanked me, when she should have despised me for it, as I despised myself!

"This will all be worthwhile," she reminded me again with an attempt at a smile just at twilight of the second day. "I'm sure the baby will come soon now."

But the night wore on, and still there was no baby. There was only Rebecca's continued agony, and at last she grew too weak for speech, too pain-racked to smile. Doc Graham and Marie hovered about her anxiously, but they were as helpless to force the baby to come as I.

"I don't want to operate, except as a last resort," the doctor said on the morning of the third day. "I keep hoping . . ." His voice drifted off into nothing, and I knew that he had despaired of a natural birth and what he hoped for was nothing short of a miracle. Whenever I could bear to take my eyes off Rebecca for a moment and look at him and Marie, it showed in their faces: their hopelessness and fear, their helplessness and defeat. Finally, on the afternoon of the third day, he said, "I must operate before the light fails. I don't think she can survive another night. There's always the chance the womb might rupture—"

Despair enveloped me at his words. Again, past and present were fused into one, and it was the other doctor saying essentially the same words, adding, as he was adding, that it was the only chance, explaining as he measured out some laudanum and forced it through her lips that he hadn't given her any of it sooner because he wanted her help to expel the baby if it ever got started right. "But the baby won't come naturally, and she's grown too weak to help us now if it did. I must try to take the baby abdominally. . . ."

Rebecca's eyes opened for a moment as he held up her head, held the laudanum to her lips. Her eyes never left my face as she let him pour it into her mouth, and she tried to smile at me as she lay back on the pillow, tried to say something.

"Don't try to talk, my dearest," I said, forcing the words past the lump in my throat.

No sound emerged, but her lips formed the words, "I love you." Her eyes closed again.

"We must wait a little while for that to take effect," Doc Graham was saying. "Marie has gone for Lena and Wilhelm. I don't want to ask you to help hold her. I think it will be better if you wait outside."

I nodded dumbly, felt Rebecca's hand slacken in mine as the drug took effect. I hadn't even realized that Marie had left. Occasionally, through the drug, Rebecca stirred uneasily, and her hand seemed to tighten a little in mine.

"My poor dear Rebecca," I said, brushing a stray wisp of hair from her forehead, wondering if she could still hear me. "I want to bring you only happiness, and instead I've caused you so much suffering."

Wilhelm and Lena and one of Wilhelm's older sons returned with Marie, and they all soon forgot me in the bustle of preparation. The table was cleared for the surgery to come, and a sheet was put on it. Wilhelm came over to carry Rebecca to the table, and he put his hand on my shoulder. "Dhis is dhe only vay," he said softly. I nodded dumbly and looked up at him.

"Let me carry her," I said, and I knew as I gathered her limp perspiring body in my arms that it was the last time I would ever hold her. Gently, I placed her on the table, watched as they tied her arms and legs to the table legs. Doc Graham assembled his instruments, had Marie take them outside and pour boiling water over them. She returned and Doc Graham nodded to me and motioned with his head toward the door. I leaned down, kissed Rebecca on the forehead, and left her to the inadequacies of man.

I sat on the ground just outside in the dogtrot, twisting my empty pipe in my hands. I heard a sharp scream that I knew must have come from Rebecca, and I tensed, breaking the stem of my pipe in two. I tried to keep from picturing what was going on inside the cabin, but I couldn't. I could see all too clearly the knife blade cutting into her smooth flesh, the blood gushing forth, her precious blood. . . .

Turning away from the door, I leaned over and retched, but I did not vomit, for I had eaten nothing for two days. I sat there, listening anxiously, straining to hear the sounds from within. I heard the murmur of muted voices, the bustle of activity. There were no more screams, and I assumed that Rebecca, having been awakened by the tearing of the knife through her flesh, had, mercifully, lapsed into unconsciousness. I sat there, my heart heavy, waiting without

233

hope, knowing the inevitability of what I was waiting for, yet praying that I was wrong.

And then it came. The voices within the cabin were raised in alarm, the sound of the footsteps clattering across the boards became more urgent, the bustle of activity accelerated to a fevered pitch. Some excited outcries. More hurried footsteps.

And then, silence.

They didn't have to tell me. I knew. My seed, my murderous seed, had killed my beloved Rebecca, just as it had killed my young bride so many years before.

I heard the cabin door open, heard Marie say, "I'm sorry, Herr Todd."

And then Doc Graham's voice: "The bleeding. I couldn't stop the bleeding."

And again Marie: "The baby—"

I turned and looked at them through my bitterness and profound sorrow. "I don't care about the baby!" I cared only about Rebecca, and she was gone. "I never wanted the baby!"

"The child iss dead, too," Marie finished, as though she had been waiting patiently for me to finish my outburst. She nodded her understanding and patted my shoulder when I said, "I could never have loved the child that cost Rebecca her life!"

I pushed myself to my feet, aware, through my numbness, that I was weary and alone. No matter where I was, or how many people there were around me, I knew I would always be alone, always be lonely, from that moment on, for the rest of my life. There would never be anyone after Rebecca. I would have gone into the cabin then, but Marie put out her hand. "Vait until ve get it cleaned up, Herr Todd."

I nodded, walked away from the cabin. I was aware of sad eyes fixed upon my back till I heard the gentle closing of the door.

The sun was low, would be gone in a few minutes, leaving only the darkness. Rebecca had been like the sun to me, had been the very embodiment of warmth and vitality. I had basked in her glow, but for such a short time. How, in that time, could she have come to mean so much to me? I only knew that I must have spent much of my life unconsciously searching for her. And then, just when I had found her, I had lost her again. She was gone now. Her laughter, her sweet lopsided smile, the joy that shone from her . . . all this was gone, to be no more. I walked slowly, letting my feet lead me where they would, until I stood by the stone that marked the head of Josiah's grave.

"She's with you again, my dear friend," I said softly, trying to find some comfort in the thought as my tears fell on his grave. Then grief overwhelmed me, washed over me like a giant wave, and I dropped to my knees and, leaning over Josiah's grave, gave full vent to my sorrow.

We buried Rebecca by Josiah's side the next afternoon, and buried the baby in an unmarked grave nearby. I remembered that Rebecca had asked me to read aloud the Twenty-third Psalm at Josiah's burial, and I read it again. My voice choked on the words, and several times I had to pause, but I continued on until I had read it all the way through. This time, it was for Rebecca.

Later, after everyone had left, I returned alone to the graves. I had ordered a double headstone, with Josiah's name on one half and, on the other, *Rebecca, beloved wife of Josiah*. There would be no mention of me. She had belonged to Josiah, and he to her, for the better part of seventeen years. She had shared my life for only a scant year. And yet, in that time, she had brought me more happiness than most folks find in a lifetime.

I turned away and walked slowly to the cabin. As I opened the door and looked inside, I saw it as though I were seeing it for the first time. I recoiled as I noticed the bloodstains on the table and the floor beneath it, the stains Marie and Lena had tried in vain to scrub away. Rebecca's blood.

I looked at the bed, empty now, the bed Rebecca and I had shared, where she had shown such a surprisingly passionate response to my lovemaking, and where, at the end, she had known such agony.

And her rocker, the rocker Josiah had made for her, in which she would never sit again, leaning sideways toward the firelight with her mending.

The cabin and everything in it magnified her absence. She was gone, would never return. I closed the door and walked away. There, a short distance from the cabin, was the start of the house of sawed boards I had promised her, with piles of lumber stacked nearby. It had just begun to take the shape we had planned: a cozy parlor with its own fireplace and three large windows that would open onto the deep porch that went the length of the front, our bedroom, and next to it the nursery. The kitchen ran along the back on one side of the house. The summer cookhouse was to be separate, connected to the house proper by a short covered walkway. I had promised Rebecca that we would be in our house by Christmas.

I turned away, walking aimlessly around the yard. Everywhere I went, everything I saw brought fresh painful memories of things we had done or plans we had made. I walked by Rebecca's garden, recalling the things she had planned to plant there the following spring. I passed the clothesline, and I could see her when she was hanging up the washing, her skirt billowing out behind her in the breeze.

Every memory cut into me like a knife blade, with a stab so sharp it was almost physical. And, suddenly, I knew I could no longer remain there, in the place I had loved so well.

I went to the corral, chose one of the biggest and strongest saddle horses, and saddled him. Hastily, I returned to the cabin and packed my saddlebags. As I closed the door for the last time, I knew I was closing another door, too, a door to a part of my life which was too beautiful to look back upon yet without unbearable pain. One day—later, perhaps—I would be able to look back and remember the joy it had given me without feeling the sharp sting of fresh sorrow. With time and distance I would build a bridge, over which I might some day return. But for the moment, I lacked the strength to stay among all the reminders.

Last of all, I walked over to the two graves, the one weathered, the other fresh. I said my farewells to those who could no longer hear my laments, could no longer see my tears.

# Part Three—Felipe

# Chapter I

## HAYDEN EDWARDS'S COLONY—1826

I resented the presence of the Americans in Texas from the day I saw the first of them come riding into Nacogdoches. I had always thought of the land as belonging particularly to me, ever since I could remember—not just the Varga grant, but everything I could see, or reach, or imagine. Maybe it was my Comanche blood asserting itself, but I couldn't accept the limitations of man-made boundaries; I wanted to go where I chose, do as I wished. It wasn't that I didn't recognize ownership, because that would have kept me from considering the Varga grant mine. But that still didn't stop me from feeling that the land—all the land— was there for my benefit, to be used but never misused, so that I could take from it each day enough to fill our needs, yet leave the rest for another day.

From as early as I could remember until the fall of 1821, there was nobody else present to claim any part of the land over which I roamed so freely. I was told that until I was two years old, we had had some neighbors, though most of them were a half-day's ride away, in the town of Nacogdoches. But after the savage slaughter at the Battle of the Medina not far north of San Antonio de Bexar in 1813, everyone around us disappeared across the Sabine, and everything was quiet. Even the Spanish troops who had been stationed in Nacogdoches withdrew farther into Mexico. Of all the residents in our vicinity, we alone stayed, with our peons. The Indians were still all over Texas, of course, different tribes in various parts: Creeks, Cherokees, Chata-hootchies, Wacos, Tarankawas, and Kronks in the east, Li-pan Apaches over south and west, and sometimes, from out of the northwest, other Apache tribes as well. The powerful Comanches were also to our west, though sometimes they raided one of the other weaker tribes nearby. But none of them ever bothered us, or even came near us, except for one old Comanche who came to live with us.

The land, it seemed, existed solely for us, for our benefit. My father died when I was seven, and our peons left then. But still my mother and I stayed on alone. I took over the hunting chore soon after my father's death, though for the first few years I was so small that the kick of the rifle al-most blew me off my feet, and left my right shoulder con-stantly bruised. But I was accurate even then, and managed to find meat enough to fill our table.

For a few years, there were again three of us, for the man I called my Comanche grandfather came to live with us. He fostered my feeling of possessiveness about the land, showed me how to use wisely what the earth provided. We used to go out hunting or sometimes just walking together, and I can still remember the heady feeling that it was all ours: the trees that shaded us from the summer sun, the water we drank from the streams, the deer and buffalo we killed for meat and hides, the mustangs we caught and tamed, the herbs we picked, the wood we gathered, the soil that grew the corn we planted. I knew that, when I was grown, I would limit my interests more to the boundaries of the Varga grant. I would get peons to farm it, as my father and grandfather and great-grandfather had done before me. But that would be later, at some time in the vague future, and in those early years there was no reason to confine either my thoughts or my wanderings to any specific boundaries.

Late in 1821, after my Comanche grandfather had died and we had buried him in a tree as he had asked us to do, the first change came. The Spanish had put down a revolt in 1813, and had fought off other attempts to gain independence, but finally they had been forced to leave Mexico. As news of this reached those who had left eight years before, they felt free to return at last. Still, we were not much aware of their presence. We were not conscious of any change in our lives, just because we had suddenly become citizens of the independent Republic of Mexico.

It was about this same time that the Americans began coming to Texas. We had had some Americans around before, off and on—mostly either adventurers or criminals—but they were not the kind who came to stay. They had ridden into Texas, pillaged or robbed or tried to stir up unsuccessful revolutions against the Spanish and then had ridden out as quickly and as unexpectedly as they had come. But in late 1821 came the first of those who intended to stay. Unlike the Americans who had preceded them, these weren't just rough men on fast horses, but whole families. They usually came in wagons, bringing with them all their possessions. At first, most of them were just passing through Nacogdoches, briefly, on their way to the new colony of Americans started by Stephen Austin. They came by way of Nacogdoches because the Camino Real, the Old Spanish Road, passed through there, and it was by far the best way to bring in wagons.

If they'd kept going along that road for another eighty-five miles or so, they'd have reached the northeast corner of the land assigned to Austin to give to his colonists, and if they'd continued on it still farther, they'd have been traveling along the northern limits of his colony, heading toward San Antonio de Bexar. But nobody much wanted to settle up that way for some years to come. It was pretty dangerous territory as far as the possibility of Indian raids was concerned, and so isolated from Austin's main settlement that there would have been no protection from that quarter. Austin and his first settlers turned toward the Gulf, and most of them settled down south a way along the Brazos River, about halfway between the Camino Real and the coast.

As time went on, a few of the Americans, for one reason

243

or another, simply stopped traveling when they got around Nacogdoches. My mother seemed unconcerned about these people settling all around us, but I resented it from the first. Still, there was nothing I could do about it. At least, I reasoned, there weren't many of them, and nobody had settled on the Varga grant itself.

It was late in 1825 when a large group of American colonists came with their newly appointed *empresario* to our area. I seethed with resentment as I watched them getting ready to stay, and then saw yet more of them coming in, with their wagons full of children and household belongings. I watched them unroll their rough maps—I saw some of them, and there was not one among them that was even reasonably accurate—and take the covers off their wagons and start unloading their belongings and building their cabins. They didn't even seem to know about any previous claims to the land. The first of this group came in October, and others followed, until it seemed they were all around us, and the peaceful woods through which I'd walked with my Comanche grandfather resounded with the dull thud of their hatchets and the screeching whine of their saws and the staccato crack of their rifles.

Filled with righteous indignation, I watched them, wondering at their brashness for daring to fell our trees and build their cabins on our land and shoot our game. They continued to arrive, their eyes always searching for likely pieces of land, much as turkey vultures circle overhead looking for a carcass to pick clean. My resentment grew. It was our state of Texas, our Republic of Mexico they were filling. They were grabbing our land and shattering our peaceful existence. Why had they come? Why hadn't they stayed in their own country? Surely there was still plenty of land not yet claimed back there. Why, then, must they come and lay claim to what was ours? Why didn't they go back where they belonged? Silently, I watched them, willing them to fail, to return across the Sabine and leave us in peace.

But they didn't. They continued to come, and they

stayed and built their cabins and cleared fields for planting.

It was not until I saw that someone was getting ready to build on the Varga grant itself that I became really alarmed. I was out riding one day and happened to see two men starting to put up a cabin on the north edge of our property. I watched them for a few minutes as they dragged some logs toward the area they had cleared for the cabin. I saw that the trees they had felled nearby were all cut into uniform lengths. I turned away and raced home, my fury building. Enraged at their audacity, I could hardly wait to tell my mother what I had seen. I don't know what I expected her to do, but I felt certain she would think of something, some way to make them stop. It was enough to have the Americans swarming all over our area, but on the Varga grant itself—that was too much!

It's not enough to say that my mother had never been an excitable woman. Never, in my whole life, did I see her cry or hear her so much as raise her voice. I didn't doubt that she felt things just as deeply as other people did, but she always kept her feelings well hidden. Not even on that horrible day when my father died did she become hysterical. I was the one who was screaming, trying to break away from her, to run after my father and pull him back from the fire. I know now that it must have taken all her strength to restrain me, for she is a tiny woman and I was a large, healthy, active child of seven, and I was crazed with grief, which undoubtedly gave me added strength. Only when I stopped struggling and started crying, when I had realized at last, as she had from the start, that it would do no good to run after my father, did she release her strong hold on me. Then she put her arms around me and tried to comfort me, telling me that from that day forward, I would have to be the man of the family and look after her. And all the while she was trying to console me and lessen my grief, her own heart must have been unbearably heavy, for she and my father had been close, and they had loved each other well. But even on that day, she shed no tears.

Nor did she show any agitation that day eight years after

245

my father's death when I burst into our cabin to tell her about the two men who were getting ready to build a cabin on our land. She just smiled softly and said, "Why so excited, Felipe? Perhaps they will build a better cabin than this one we are in, and when the old records are found and our ownership is finally established, we will move into it."

Upset as I was, I had to smile at the suggestion that they were building the new cabin not for themselves, but for us. Still, I protested, they were cutting down our trees.

"Clearing the land for us," she corrected me calmly. Then she added, "I hope they remove the stumps as well. Now do stop wasting your time watching them, and see what you can find for our supper."

Thus diverted, I did as she suggested. But my irritation remained, festering as though it were a gigantic sliver embedded in my flesh, spreading hatred of the Americans through my body like a poison.

This hatred was provoked into surfacing a few days later when I was out hunting. I always moved as softly as possible, putting my feet down noiselessly as my Comanche grandfather had shown me, in order to avoid spooking the game or alerting any possible enemies to my presence. Irritated, I heard other sounds, knew I was not alone in the woods, and hoped I might find something for our supper quickly, before all the wildlife was frightened into hiding. Whoever was there was certainly making no effort to be quiet, and my irritation grew as I heard the frequent cracking of twigs and the crunching of dried winter grass being trampled heavily underfoot. The sounds came first from one side, then moved around behind me to come from the opposite direction, growing closer. Just as I saw a rabbit and was raising my rifle to take aim, the animal's ears shot up alertly and it bounded out of sight. The sounds that had frightened it away came nearer, and soon a little girl came running into view. I remembered having seen her with the two men who were building the cabin on our land. She didn't see me, stopped not ten feet in front of me and called out, "Cinder! Where are you! Stay where you are! I'll find you!" There was the beginning of panic in her voice.

Exasperated at her untimely appearance and at the way she had been stomping along so noisily, I lowered my rifle in disgust. "Not before you scare off every bit of game within ten million *varas,* you won't."

She whirled around to look at me, her mouth open in surprise. After she recovered from the shock, she seemed relieved. "My horse is lost," she explained, smiling tentatively at me.

Her smile was a pretty one and made her whole face prettier, but I was in no mood to smile back at her. "It's not your horse that's lost," I said gruffly. "It's you."

Her smile quickly disappeared. "I'm not either lost!" she snapped defiantly. She hesitated indecisively for a minute, then stepped off uncertainly to her right.

"Not that way," I said, after she had taken a few steps. "You just came from there."

She faced me, her hands on her hips. "I suppose you think you know where Cinder is!" she challenged.

"I have a pretty good idea. But of course you don't need me to help you if you aren't lost." I turned and started to walk away, knowing she would call me back.

"No, wait," she said quickly. "If you could just start me off in the right direction . . ."

I turned, saw her lower lip tremble and knew I couldn't leave her there. She would panic and probably never find her way back to her horse. "All right. Come on, then. I suppose I'll have to take you to him. If I didn't, you'd only get lost again." I started toward the direction in which I had first heard her approaching, deliberately walking fast so that she had to run to catch up.

"Not so fast!" she complained breathlessly. "Who are you, anyway, and what are you doing on my father's land?"

"Felipe Varga." I stopped abruptly and turned, and she almost ran into me. "And this is not your father's land. It's part of the Varga grant."

247

"Feh-lee-pay," she repeated my name slowly. "That's a funny name. And this is, too, my father's land."

"Maybe I'd think your name is funny, too." I scowled at her. "You'd better stop arguing with me or I'll let you find your horse by yourself." I started walking again. "Who are you?"

"My name's Cassie. Cassie Stewart. And my father is Thorne Stewart. My Uncle Todd is here, too, helping Papa build us a cabin."

"I know. I watched them. I saw you there, too."

We walked on in silence, till I heard her horse stomping restlessly off to one side, and led her there. "Here's your mare, though it's a wonder she hasn't run clear away. Don't you know enough to hobble her?"

"Cinder's my own special horse. She wouldn't run away. And I'm sure I could have found her by myself."

In spite of my irritation, I couldn't help but be amused at her stubborn refusal to admit she had ever been lost. "But not till next week," I teased.

She ignored my taunt. "Is your name Mex'can?"

"It's Spanish."

"You don't sound Spanish. How come you're talking English as good as I do?"

"My father was Spanish, and my mother half American and half Comanche. I talk Spanish and English, and some Comanche, too."

"Comanche!" Her eyes opened wide, and she backed away from me. "That's Indian!"

"Of course it is, the greatest of the Indian nations. Don't worry. I won't scalp you. My grandmother was taken captive. She and my mother were rescued, though, when my mother was six."

My words seemed to reassure her. "My mother was almost captured by an Indian, but I saved her."

"You?"

"I bit him, on the back of his ankle." She made a face. "He tasted terrible." Shrugging, she added, "You don't have to believe me."

"Oh, but I do!" I said, bursting out laughing at the thought of this bold little girl getting her teeth around the back of an Indian buck's ankle. "I'll bet he was surprised."

"Surprised enough to drop Mama. Papa says I'm a hero-ine."

"I suppose you are. Not many little girls get the best of an Indian buck."

"I'm not little," she protested. "I'm twelve, going on thirteen. How old are you?"

"Fourteen," I said, couldn't resist adding, "going on fifteen."

"Where do you live?"

"West of here. That way." I motioned. "Not far."

"In a cabin?"

"A little one. It used to be one of our peons' cabins. My mother and I moved into it when our big cabin burned down. My father died in the fire."

"Oh, I'm sorry." Abruptly, she switched from sympathy back to belligerence. "You shouldn't be spying on people, you know. You have no right." She walked over to her mare and mounted.

"I have the right to spy on anybody who comes and builds on our land, or goes tromping through our woods."

"They're not yours. And I'm going to tell Papa I caught you hunting on his property!"

Irritated, I said, "Vargas have owned this and been hunting here since before your father was even born! This land isn't his. It's mine. It was given to my great-grandfather a long time ago by King Carlos III of Spain."

She glowered at me. "That's a lie! Papa says Mr. Edwards made a rule that everybody who had an old claim had to say so last November. And we didn't get here and get our land till a week ago, so it can't be yours. If you thought it was, you should have said so sooner!"

"My mother and I never heard of that rule, or of a Mr. Edwards," I retorted. "And even if we had, we don't have to file a claim for what's been ours for years and years, just because some Yankee says we do. You Yankees make me sick! You come to our country without a by-your-leave and grab all our land, without even caring if it already belongs to somebody else. Why don't you all go home and leave us alone?"

She looked at me with her eyes wide open in surprise at my outburst. "But—but you said you were part American!"

"Only part. I was born here, and that makes me Mexican. And I don't go to other people's countries to steal their land!"

She pointed her chin up in the air and looked at me haughtily. "Neither do we. Papa says the Mexicans invited us to come."

"Well, I'm Mexican, and I didn't invite you! You'll find out soon enough who this land belongs to when you have to get off of it. Now go back to your father and your uncle and tell them to work hard building that cabin, because it's on our land, and pretty soon my mother and I will be living in it!" I had run out of patience with this rude little girl, who hadn't even bothered to thank me for leading her back to her horse, and I didn't want to stand there any longer listening to her foolish prattle about her father owning our land. I gave the little black mare a swat on the rump that startled her, making her lurch forward.

"Keep going that way till you get to the Camino Real," I called after the departing horse and rider. "Otherwise you'll get lost again, and next time I won't help you!"

If she answered, her words were carried away on the wind. I glared after her, sensing that our encounter had been just the bare beginning of my troubles with her and her father. Then I turned and started off toward home. I was unlikely to find any meat for our table that day, and I was only too willing to blame Cassie Stewart for it.

It wasn't long before she returned with her father and her uncle. They came to our cabin, and though I wasn't home when they arrived, I returned in time to speed them on their way with some choice Spanish curse-words.

Thorne Stewart didn't return again for a month, and I

might have hoped he had left the area for good, except that I saw that he and the other man had finished building the cabin on our land. Apparently he had gone to fetch the rest of his family. The next time he came to our cabin, he was alone. I was glad I happened to be home that day, because I didn't like the way he looked at my mother at all, as though in his mind he had ripped off all her clothes and was looking at her naked. He brought a paper he claimed was signed by Hayden Edwards, the man he said had the right to give away all the land in and around Nacogdoches. As if anyone had the right to give away what had been ours for three generations and more! He told my mother the paper he had ordered us off our land, and when he waved it in front of her threateningly, I grabbed it from him and threw it on the fire before he could stop me, to show him what we thought of him and any papers he brought. He was furious, and I was glad. We sent him packing.

I suppose his threats really must have worried my mother because, a few days later, we went into Nacogdoches and she talked with Hayden Edwards. She tried to get our claim registered with him and to set him straight on the mistake he had already made by giving some of it to the Stewart man. We should have known better than to expect a fair hearing from a Yankee. Edwards quickly dashed my mother's hopes that he would want to see justice done. Soon after that, we went to San Antonio de Bexar to try to get the record straightened out there, but everyone demanded proof, just as Edwards had done. We wouldn't have had to be there at all if we'd had any proof. We went on to Saltillo in search of that proof, but we failed to turn up any record of the grant we knew had been given to my great-grandfather.

Shortly after our return, I started to work in Nacogdoches, and was home after that only for half a day each weekend, so I wasn't able to protect my mother in case Thorne Stewart came to threaten her again. I knew she would stand up to his bullying well enough, but when I remembered the way I had seen him look at her, I couldn't help but feel uneasy.

I resented the presence of the Americans, but I had to admit that individually some of them were nice enough, like the man I worked for, Abner Bryant, and his plump pleasant wife. They took to looking after me, and even insisted I take my meals with them. Each Saturday afternoon, when I left to go home, they always gave me some small gift of foodstuffs to take to Mother. I liked the Bryants. I worked hard for them, knowing it would not be for more than a few years. When I had saved enough to buy some seeds and bring in a few peons, I intended to turn my efforts toward working our land.

The first time Thorne Stewart came into the store after I started working there, I walked away, refusing to help him. Mr. Bryant saw this and quietly took over and sold him the things he wanted. After he had left, Mr. Bryant called me over to him and explained that he couldn't afford to have me insult his customers and that, even if I disliked some of them, I must remain civil.

"But he's a thief!" I protested. "He's trying to steal our land! And he threatened my mother. How can I be civil to such a man?"

"If you cannot be, then you can no longer work for me," he said firmly. He softened the harshness of his words by adding with a sympathetic smile, "Just try to think of him as my customer, not as a man you despise. A merchant who sells only to people he likes is soon out of business, Felipe."

"All right, Mr. Bryant, I'll try," I promised. "I don't want you to lose customers on my account."

After that, I was civil but cool toward Thorne Stewart. He usually came in every two or three weeks with Cassie, the girl I had met in the woods, and his son, Will. Cassie was too ready to pick a fight, reminded me too much of her father, but Will was a quiet, friendly sort and unexpectedly shy. After he got to know me, he started asking intelligent questions about things in the store and what they were for. Except for a strong physical resemblance to his father, he didn't seem to belong to the same family as the other two.

I began to suspect that Thorne Stewart came to our cabin to threaten my mother more than she told me, for I noted that she had taken care to brush away any imprints around the cabin. I couldn't imagine who else would have been calling that she wouldn't have wanted me to know about. At the time, I assumed she kept his visits from me because she didn't want to worry me, and I was surprised when she told me he had brought her some chairs. She mentioned it casually enough, and said that he was not such a bad neighbor as we had supposed. Looking back, I think I refused to acknowledge the suspicion that began to take root in my mind. I didn't want to believe it, so I just accepted what she said and asked no questions.

It was in November of the year the Stewarts arrived that everything seemed to happen at once. Todd Stewart came to visit them, and he told me he wanted me to go with him to help drive a coach between San Felipe and San Antonio de Bexar, maybe going as far as Natchitoches now and then. He had come into the store a few times and talked to me before he told me what he had in mind. By that time, I knew he was not at all like his nephew. I liked him. What he suggested appealed to me, for I had never become accustomed to staying under a roof all day long, and though I liked the Bryants, the work in the store was not to my liking. I yearned to be outside. I was used to the feel of the sun beating down on me, the wind whipping past me, used to seeing the change of the seasons all around me. I gladly accepted Todd's offer and told Mr. Bryant I would be leaving in a few weeks. I hated to leave my mother without anyone to look after her, but she knew well enough how to take care of herself and didn't seem upset at the thought of staying there alone. She reminded me that I had been gone most of the time anyway while I was working in Nacogdoches. Todd offered to let her live in his old cabin near the town of San Felipe so she could see me more often, but she didn't want to leave her home.

Trouble had been brewing in the area ever since Hayden Edwards had come to Nacogdoches as *empresario*, and it was just at this time that it erupted.

There was such confusion over old claims, new claims, and forged titles, that nobody knew who was supposed to own what. Hayden Edwards's brother wrote and complained to Governor Blanco, expecting him to support them. But he gave them short shrift and ordered them expelled from Texas. This set them on their ears and got all the other Americans pretty upset, too. A lot of them began to pack their belongings to move someplace else, saying they'd find a spot where they could get a piece of land that wasn't claimed by three or four other people. I couldn't help but gloat as I watched them get ready to leave. This was what I'd hoped for from the first day I'd seen them— that they would go, leave us in peace—and it seemed that was exactly what most of them intended to do. I had heard some talk about gathering a force together and fighting, but most people seemed to figure it was better to just leave peaceably, go someplace else instead.

I said my final good-byes to the Bryants, who were also planning to go, and went home feeling pleased about the way things had turned against the Americans. I hoped Thorne Stewart was one of those who planned to leave. Then my mother could move into his cabin, which was much bigger and better than ours. I smiled as I recalled her words about the cabin he and Todd were building. She had been right, after all.

I was in high spirits when I arrived home that afternoon. I would stay home only a few more nights, and then Todd and I were to leave. My mother was working on some new buckskins and a new pair of moccasins as a surprise for me, fancy ones with beading on them. I knew, because she had been stitching on them when I had come home the week before, and though she had quickly pushed them out of sight, I had seen them and knew she would give them to me before I left.

"Mother, I'm home!" I called out as I rode up, though I knew it was unnecessary to yell, since she would have heard me approaching. I expected her to come outside to greet me as she always did, and was surprised when the door remained closed. I dismounted, tied up my horse, called again, wondering at the unaccustomed silence. I looked around, toward the corral, thinking she might have gone there, but there was no sign of her.

Puzzled, I removed my saddle bags and rifle and carried them inside. I was even more puzzled when I saw my mother in the cabin, in the midst of getting her own things together, as though she were going somewhere, too. As I entered, she looked up, and came to kiss my cheek.

After she greeted me, I walked to my bed, put my saddle bags down on it, saw the new buckskins laid out there and thanked her for them. Then I motioned to the things she had spread out on her bed. "What's all this?" I asked. "Have you decided to come with us, go live in Todd's old cabin after all?"

"No," she said quietly. She stopped folding the dress in her hands and looked up. "I'm going someplace else."

"Someplace else?"

She put the dress down on top of some others. "Sit down, Felipe," she said, motioning me to one of the chairs. "I must talk to you."

I sat down, and she sat in the chair opposite me. I remembered, as we settled ourselves on the chairs, that Thorne Stewart had been the one who had brought them to her, and I wondered why I remembered this at that particular time.

It turned out it was one of those rare intuitive flashes we sometimes have. I listened in surprise, then in disbelief, as she told me she had been seeing Thorne regularly, that she loved him, and that he was leaving and so would she, to go someplace where she could see him occasionally. Last of

255

all, she told me the shocking news that she was to bear his child.

I listened, shaking my head in denial of what she was saying. For all that Thorne Stewart's name had flashed through my mind a moment before, I couldn't believe what she was telling me. I had been able to tolerate the idea of a cool and discreet friendship between the man I hated and my mother, but what she was telling me was too monstrous to be creditable.

"It's not true!" I insisted. "It can't be!"

"It's true, Felipe. That's why I'm leaving here. You and Todd will take me to the place where the Bexar Road crosses the Guadalupe, and build me a cabin in a new colony that's started there. Thorne will get a second coach and drive it himself, so I'll see him every time he crosses the Guadalupe. It won't be much, but it will be all I'll have."

"You can't mean it!" I said. "You can't be serious!" I jumped from my chair, heard it fall with a dull thud to the dirt floor behind me.

"You can't change anything by refusing to believe it, Felipe. You don't need me any more. You're starting to lead your own life now. I've let you decide what you want to do, and I intend to lead my life as I choose. I'm sorry if you don't approve of the way I have chosen, but that is the way it is."

Horrified, I looked at her as though I were looking at a stranger. This woman had been intimate with a man who was my enemy, and who I had thought was hers as well, a man who already had a wife and a family. Who was she, this woman who had just told me such startling news? Could she be the same woman I had always known as my mother, and thought to be virtuous, her character above reproach?

I thought of my father, in his grave nine years, and I was suddenly angry on his behalf, indignant for him, because she had besmirched his memory. How could she have done such a thing?

"How could you?" I asked, angry tears stinging my eyes.

"How could you be so faithless to my father's memory? He was so good to you, to us!" I paced up and down, gesticulating pointlessly, wildly.

She didn't raise her voice. "Your father was very dear to me. I will always remember him for the kind and considerate husband he was. But he has been gone a long time, Felipe, and ghosts make poor companions." Her voice dropped so low that I could scarcely hear her words. "It's been very lonely, living with memories, and having nothing, no one else. I know I will always have you. Even when you are gone from home, as you will be now, I hope we will remain close, but that is not the same as having someone to love me as a woman wants to be loved. I'm sorry if that upsets you. I didn't want to tell you like this, but—"

"You're sorry it upsets me!" I repeated. "Is that all you can say? You have dirtied my father's name, lowered yourself to the level of a *puta*—!"

She stood up saying firmly, "That will be quite enough. I had hoped you would understand what I've been trying to tell you: that my relationship with Thorne has brought me much happiness. And I hoped that, knowing this, you might find it in your heart to be happy for me. But I see I was wrong. Nevertheless, I must ask for your help, whether you care to bestow your approval on me or not."

"You want help?" I scoffed, heading toward the door, feeling the need to get out of the cabin, away from my mother and the terrible things she was telling me, insisting I must accept. "Why are you asking me for help? Ask your lover! See if he can help you!" I slammed out the door and quickly untied my horse and mounted. I felt the blood pounding wildly in my temples, was only vaguely aware of my mother standing in the doorway, calling after me to come back. I paid no attention to her, but flicked the reins sharply across the horse's neck and rode away.

Thorne Stewart! My hatred, my rage, fixed itself on him, on his image. He was the one who had brought my mother down to the level of the cheapest whore, brought dishonor to my father's name. Unthinkingly, I found I was heading

257

for his place. I didn't know what I would do when I got there. I only knew I must confront him with the enormity of what he had done, make him sorry for the terrible shame he had inflicted on my mother. I wanted to pummel him with my fists, kick him in the groin until he cried for mercy, put my hands around his throat and squeeze the very breath out of him.

It was getting dark as I approached the Stewart place, and I saw that luck was with me, for Thorne was just going into his newly built barn, and he was alone. I rode up, dismounted, ran after him.

"You filthy bastard!" I shouted, not caring who heard me.

He looked at me, then turned and disappeared inside the barn.

I ran after him. "How dare you dishonor my mother?"

He walked over to the side wall of the barn, turned to look at me disdainfully. "I assume your mother has told you about us." His coolness, his open contempt added fuel to my fury, and I lunged for him.

So blinded had I been by my own rage that I hadn't noticed the rifle leaning against the wall by his side. Too late, I realized he had been sidling over to it, stalling me until he could reach it. Suddenly, he grabbed it, raised it, pointed it menacingly at me.

"Stay back," he commanded, his voice still maddeningly calm. "It's loaded. It will do your mother no good to have you shot."

I looked into the muzzle of the gun, then at his eyes just above it, and I was certain he would not hesitate to use it. "You bastard!" I said again. "You'd like an excuse to shoot me, wouldn't you?"

He made no move to lower the rifle, kept it trained on me. "The only reason I would hesitate would be because it would upset your mother if anything were to happen to either of us. And, contrary to what you seem to think, I would do nothing to hurt her." He kept moving toward me, forcing me to back out of the barn, toward my horse.

258

"Now, I suggest you get on your horse and go home, and accept something which it is out of your power to change."

I wished I had had my own rifle handy, to counter the threat of his. But mine was back at the cabin, and I was helpless against him.

He motioned toward his cabin. "I want you to go quietly, without alarming my family. Letting them find out about this could only help create a scandal, and your mother would be the first to be hurt. With Todd's help, and yours, she will go to Green DeWitt's colony, and will pretend to be the widow of Todd's brother. Now stop acting like a spoiled child and get back on that horse and start riding home. Your mother needs you."

Tasting the bitter gall of defeat, knowing that, for the moment, I was beaten, I mounted, searching for something to say, something I could do, some way to get the best of him before I left, something that would bring to him the agony of mind he had brought to me.

As I swung into the saddle, a sudden thought occurred to me. From out of nowhere, a quotation popped into my mind, something I had read somewhere at some time in the past.

*An eye for an eye, a tooth for a tooth . . .*

As I settled myself into the saddle, I looked straight into his eyes, smiling with perverse pleasure—a smile I knew had twisted my mouth into an unpleasant grimace—as I anticipated his reaction to what I was about to say.

"You're right," I said. "I can't change what's happened, and telling your family what a bastard you are might hurt my mother more than it does you. Right now you've got a rifle pointed at me and you've got the best of me. But I'd like to remind you of one thing. You have a daughter, and she will be grown in three or four years' time. And you won't always be around with a rifle to protect *her* honor."

My threat found its mark, I noted with satisfaction. Even in the gathering twilight, I could see his lips turn white as they pressed together tightly. He stared at me, shocked at last into silence as he absorbed my words.

When he spoke, his voice was raspy and hoarse, barely audible.

"Get out! Get out of here before I forget I love your mother and shoot your balls off. And if I ever find you around Cassie, that's just what I'll do!"

I wheeled my horse around and rode away, savoring the look of stupefaction I had seen on his face.

Let him worry about that every day for the next three or four years!

# Chapter II

## ON THE BEXAR ROAD—
### December 1826

It was hard for me to reconcile myself to what my mother had done, and what she had become: Thorne Stewart's kept woman. She had degraded herself, insulted my father's memory, tarnished the good name he had given her. I had been too enraged the afternoon she told me about it to think clearly, but in the days that followed, when my temper had cooled, I began to think more reasonably about it. If she had renounced Thorne even then, I could have regained my respect for her. But she was firm in her determination to move to DeWitt's colony just so she could see Thorne every month or two, and it was obvious that nothing I could say would make her change her mind. The blame for what had happened must fall squarely on Thorne, of course, but I still felt that my mother should have sent him away before things got to the point they obviously had. I was being torn by my own conflicting emotions: I felt I should turn away from my mother because of what she had done, but I couldn't do it. Yet neither could I find it in my heart to give even a grudging sort of approval to her affair with Thorne.

It was Todd who helped me resign myself to the situation. Hesitantly, I tried to explain to him how I felt, expecting him to jump immediately to Thorne's defense. But he spoke instead of my mother.

The two of us were sitting huddled close to a fire on our way to Green DeWitt's colony. We had just eaten and my mother had gone to a nearby creek to wash the cooking utensils.

"She never deserted you when you were young, did she?" he asked. The answer was obvious, for his statement needed no words to confirm it, so he went on. "Well, I think that now she needs you, needs you very badly, more than she ever has before in her life, except maybe when your father died. She doesn't expect your approval of what she has done, but it would be cruel beyond measure if you were to withdraw your love from her now."

Idly, I picked up a twig, tossed it on the fire, watched it catch and flame briefly. "Do you approve of what they've done?"

He shifted his weight, turned his other side toward the fire. "Approve? I don't feel it's up to you and me to approve or disapprove. We're affected only incidentally. This is something between your mother and Thorne, and we've no right to sit in judgment of them. Whether they're right or wrong is something for the good Lord to decide, not us. They've made their decisions, and I can understand how they made them while I still neither condone nor condemn either of them. Who are we to say we might not have acted the same way in their place? I think we must accept what's happened and go on from there, helping those we love without questioning whether they are right or wrong. It's your understanding your mother needs, not your approval."

"But she's insulted my father's good name—"

"Your father is long dead, Felipe, and your mother must have had a very lonely life these past nine years. Women like to be cherished and loved, like to know somebody needs them. And unselfish women like your mother have so much love to give. To them, it's as important to lavish this love on someone as it is to receive love in return." I started to protest, but he held up his hand to stop me. "Oh, I know what you're going to say: that your father had loved her and that you love her, and she still has you to love in return. But that's not enough, my boy. She no longer has your father, and the love between a mother and a son can't replace physical love between a man and a woman. Thorne has given her this other kind of love."

"But he already has a wife!" I protested bitterly. "His interest in my mother is dishonorable!"

"You've never met Angela, have you?"

"No, but what does that matter?"

"It's just that if you had met her, you might understand better how all this came about. Angela's life is dominated by fear. She's afraid of anything and everything. And she hasn't been a wife to Thorne in years. I'm telling you this only because I think it might help you see how Thorne and your mother came to be drawn to each other. Your mother had no one, and Thorne saw in her the kind of woman he should have married. They both had a need—"

"Physical!" I scoffed.

"Yes, physical, of course. But deeper than that, a need to love and be loved. Whatever you might think of Thorne, don't doubt for a minute that he feels a strong affection for your mother. He takes his obligation toward her very seriously."

Out of the darkness, my mother returned to the small circle of light around our fire, and our conversation came to an abrupt end.

We rolled ourselves into our blankets and settled in for the night, but before I gave myself over to sleep, I went over Todd's words and had to admit he was right: it wasn't up to me to pass judgment on my mother's actions. And much of my misery had stemmed from trying to do that very thing. My mother didn't expect me to approve, only to accept things the way they were.

But whether or not I judged my mother, the fact remained that Thorne had dishonored her, caused her deep shame, for it was his bastard she was to bear. And for that I could never forgive him.

I slept then, my mind more at rest than it had been since the day I had found out about my mother and Thorne.

We built a house of adobe bricks for Mother on a little

creek that ran into the Guadalupe River, at a place not far off the Bexar Road. Todd checked first with Green DeWitt and questioned a number of his settlers. Only when he had satisfied himself that the colony was well managed, that there was scant chance of another fiasco such as the one that had occurred in Nacogdoches, did he see about acquiring a small piece of property on which to build her a house. On the back of the house, with a separate entrance but with a door connecting it to the house itself, were two separate rooms with a smaller room separating them, and in these rooms we planned to house and feed the coach passengers we hoped to begin carrying. The road was little more than two parallel ruts, but Todd felt that if we used heavy reinforced wheels and axles, we could manage to pull the coach overland.

A little way down from my mother's new place, where later the town of Gonzales was to come into being, right on the east bank of the river at the crossing, we began to work on a log cabin for Todd. "Just to keep folks from surmising the wrong thing about your mother and me, and gossiping about it," he said. "You and I can work on it a little every chance we get."

It was late February when we left my mother in her adobe house to go to San Felipe and pick up Todd's coach. She came outside to watch us leave.

"I wish I were going with you," she said wistfully.

Todd's voice was sympathetic. "Any messages you want delivered?"

She shook her head. "Only that I'm fine."

"I'll tell him."

She stood outside and waved to us, and as I looked back at her silhouette, I realized that her pregnancy was becoming obvious. For the first time, I thought of the child she carried as a person, and of the problems he would have to face if the truth were ever known, or guessed. But then, he probably wouldn't survive long enough after birth for it to matter. None of my brothers or sisters had.

As we approached the cabin Todd had left some months

before, in which Thorne and his family were living by this time, I told Todd that I thought it would be best if I stayed away, ate and slept somewhere else.

"Nonense! You'll be far more comfortable inside."

"But Thorne and I—"

"You let me take care of Thorne. By this time, he might even have finished the house I started building before . . ." He paused, and I knew he was unable to complete the sentence. My mother had told me about his wife's death. "At any rate," he began again when he had recovered himself, "even if he hasn't finished it, there's no need for you to stay elsewhere. We're business partners now, you and Thorne and I, and I intend for us to stay at his place whenever we return to San Felipe. Besides, he'll be gone from home a fair amount once we get the second coach going, and Angela will be glad to have us around when he's not there."

"But—"

"I won't listen to any objections, not from you or Thorne. Whatever words you two had are best forgotten, and I know you wouldn't be so foolish or cruel as to tell Angela or the children about Thorne and your mother."

"No, but still—"

"Then that's the end of it. You'll be staying there with me."

As we approached the cabin in which he had lived with his wife, he became unnaturally silent, and I knew he must be thinking of her tragic death.

"There's less timber around here than there is on my land," I commented, hoping to start a conversation that might take his mind away from his sorrowful thoughts.

But he was in no mood for small talk, and he answered, with an unaccustomed brevity, "Better farm land," and then withdrew inside himself again.

I was glad to see Cassie and Will running out to greet him as we rode into the yard. It was impossible for him to continue to be morose with Cassie's excited chatter and Will's subdued happiness at seeing him again. As he hugged them both and answered all the questions they fired at him, Thorne came out of the cabin. Our eyes met, and we glared our hatred of each other. I knew, from the way he looked at me, that he had not forgotten my threat. I had not intended that he should, and I felt a surge of satisfaction, knowing it would continue to worry him.

Todd looked up, saw the rancor neither of us tried to hide, and told the children he wanted to talk to their father a minute. He sent Cassie into the house with his saddlebags and rifle and asked Will to take his horse to the corral. Then he turned to me. "Felipe, you go with Will to get your horse settled, too."

I knew I was being dismissed, and as I turned away, I saw that Todd had already started speaking earnestly to Thorne. I wondered what they would say to each other. Whatever it was, I hoped Thorne wouldn't tell Todd of the threat I had made the day I found out about him and my mother.

I never did know what they said, but I don't think Thorne told him, and from that day on, it was always taken for granted that I would stay at the Stewart place whenever Todd and I came.

During those visits, Thorne and I maintained a truce of sorts, but we spoke to each other only when it couldn't be avoided.

I had always thought it odd that Angela Stewart had never come into Abner Bryant's store with her husband as most of the other women did, but as soon as I met her, I knew it had to do with what Todd had been trying to tell me about her. She stayed inside her cabin all the time because she was scared to death to set foot outside of it. She pulled the walls and roof about her in the same way a caterpillar spins his cocoon around himself to shut out the world. Her frailty made her seem smaller than she really was, so that the first time I saw her, I would have guessed her to be about my mother's size. But later, when I stood next to her, I realized she was at least half a head taller than Mother. I wondered if she had always been so thin, or

266

if fear of frontier living had eaten the very flesh from her bones. Todd had told me Thorne was thirty-six, and his wife was apt to be younger, but Angela Stewart looked years older than her husband.

The house Todd had mentioned was not yet finished, so the family was still living in the cabin, which was better furnished than most. One piece of furniture particularly caught my attention, and I couldn't resist walking over to it to look at it closely. It was a small table of dark wood, smooth and shining, and on it was a tray, which held a teapot, creamer, and sugar bowl, all of silver. It was beautiful, but I could scarcely keep from laughing aloud when I saw it there in the cabin. It could not have looked more out of place sitting in the middle of a prairie.

"That was my grandmother's," Cassie said, walking over to me when she saw my attention had been caught by the odd piece of furniture and the items it held. "The grown-ups always used to have tea every afternoon before she died. Mama said she wouldn't come to Texas without it."

"It's pretty," I said, touching the smooth wood, fingering the design on the silver teapot.

"We used to keep it in the parlor. Papa says it looks ridiculous here." She giggled. "It looked even sillier in our other cabin. We just had a dirt floor there."

"Cassie, you and Will should go wash up for supper now." Even when she gave a command, Angela Stewart's voice was weak and wavering. I hadn't realized until she spoke that she must have been right behind us and heard what Cassie said.

"I'll tell Will, Mama," Cassie said, and after she had run outside, Angela Stewart stepped forward and stroked the table, as someone might run a hand over the silky fur of a pet dog. When she spoke, I didn't know if she was talking to me, or to herself. "It will look far better in the new parlor, of course."

"I'm sure it will," I said, suddenly feeling sorry for her, knowing her own husband and daughter laughed at her openly, knowing, too, that she was as much a misfit in the

267

cabin as the table and tea service she had insisted on bringing with her.

That night at supper, Thorne told us what had happened at Nacogdoches after we had all left. The Edwards brothers had recruited about two hundred men, and they had taken possession of the old stone fort and proclaimed a new republic, which they christened Freedonia. They hoped people would come running to join them from all over Texas, but none did. They wanted to fight, but no one came forward to contest their claim. Disappointed, ignored by both friend and foe, they began to drift away one by one, till by the end of January, there remained no more self-proclaimed Freedonians in Nacogdoches; every one of them had either gone back across the Sabine or lost themselves in the anonymity of one of the other colonies.

"I've written off my place up there," Thorne said as he finished telling us of the Freedonians. "You were right all the time, Todd. It was a mistake to go to Edwards's colony in the first place."

I heard his words with a feeling of smug satisfaction, pictured his vacant cabin on the Varga property. It would be ours now, and when I returned there some day, I would probably move into it. But the edge was taken off the pleasure I would have felt at the thought by the knowledge that Thorne had destroyed my mother's honor. The structures he had left on the Varga grant for my use seemed a poor exchange.

It was the next day that I met Jeremy Butler, and we became friends almost instantly. He was a year younger than I was, and at that time, a good head shorter. Later, he was to grow even taller than I was, but at the time we met, the difference in our ages put him a year behind me in growth. His cheeks and the bridge of his nose were liberally dotted with freckles, and he had straight sandy-colored hair. He lived on one of the other farms nearby, and alternate weeks Angela Stewart and his mother took turns at having school lessons for him and Cassie and Will. The first morning I was there, it was Angela's turn to have them. Promptly at seven-thirty, Jeremy came into the cabin, put a pile of books on the table, and said politely, "Good morning, ma'am," and then seated himself at the table to begin his lessons. My first impression of him was that his behavior was too perfect, his attitude too submissive, and certainly, judging by his clothes, I thought him too much a dandy.

Mrs. Stewart said helplessly, "Now where have Cassie and Will gone? They know they should be here. Would you get them, Jeremy?"

"Yes, ma'am." He went outside, came back with the two Stewart children.

"Lessons!" Cassie said in disgust as she dropped onto her chair and noisily flipped open one of the books in front of her. No one could accuse her of excessively good behavior. Will sat down quietly, opened his book without comment.

I spent the morning helping Todd and Thorne work on the new house. We had just stopped for dinner when Jeremy stepped outside the cabin, about to leave. He walked over to me, put out his hand. "I saw you inside there before, but I didn't have a chance to talk to you. I'm Jeremy Butler. I guess you're the one who's driving with Todd."

"Felipe Varga." We shook hands, and I motioned to the pile of books he was carrying. "You must do a lot of studying."

"I have to." He shrugged. "My pa's got it in his mind that I'm going to be a lawyer, so I have to study hard. He has me bring my work home every day to make sure I'm keeping up."

"Do you want to be a lawyer?"

"Might as well. What's the difference? I've got to be something, and Pa says a good overseer can take care of the land, so there's no need for me to be just a planter. A lawyer's as good as anything else I can think of." Again, he shrugged indifferently, then said, "If you've got time, why don't you ride over to my place this afternoon? Todd can tell you how to get there. It's easier to come across the fields than to go the long way around."

"I'll see if Todd wants me to help him this afternoon. If he doesn't, I'll come over."

"Right after dinner?"

I nodded. "If I can get away."

He mounted and rode away, and I watched him, saw to my surprise that he sat his horse naturally. Frowning, I wondered why he wore such prissy clothes. Somehow, they didn't fit him, didn't go with the way he walked, the way he rode.

Todd said he planned to spend the afternoon sorting through some of his things he'd stored in the half of his cabin we used, and he wouldn't need me for that. He told me how to get to the Butlers's house, said it was the largest in the colony, and that they'd sent off to the East for all the furnishings for it, from the big carved bedsteads down to the bric-a-brac. Still, I wasn't prepared to find anything so fancy. The house was two stories high, made of sawed boards, and had columns the full height of the house itself, forming a verandah across the front, clear from one end to the other. I felt overpowered by the size of the place. A servant answered my knock, and when I said I had come to see Jeremy, she led me to a room that was like nothing I had ever seen before. On the floor was a big patterned carpet, mostly in shades of reds and wines. It was almost as big as the room itself, and so soft to walk on I felt like I was stepping on a cloud. The furniture was all polished wood and velvet and satin. I sat on an upholstered settee, couldn't resist bouncing on it a little, testing its unaccustomed springiness.

My eyes traveled around the room. There were several tables of the same dark wood as the one in the Stewart cabin, another settee just like the one on which I sat, and a number of other chairs with padded seats and backs. There were damask draperies at the big glass windows, and I wondered why they'd gone to all the expense and trouble of putting in so much glass and then had covered most of it with the dark heavy fabric, cutting out most of the light. In one corner of the room was an enormous odd-shaped stringed instrument. I walked over to examine it and plinked at one of the strings.

"That's a harp," Jeremy said as he came into the room. "Nobody here plays it. It's just for show. Pa says all houses must have either a harp or a pianoforte, so he ordered a harp. He says Ma should at least look like she can play it, anyway."

I liked his frankness. I had begun to feel uncomfortable, as though I had no right to be in this place. Jeremy's words set me at ease, and I was grateful. I matched his frankness with my own. "I've never been inside a house like this before." I noticed that he was dressed in buckskins, more weathered and worn than my own. The change in clothing had transformed him, erased all signs of the dandy I had thought him to be.

He saw me looking at his clothes and guessed what I was thinking. "Pa makes me wear those fancy clothes to school every morning, even when we have it here. I feel like a pansy when I put them on."

I grinned. "I thought you might be, when I first saw you in them," I said, and we both laughed.

Just as we were about to leave, a man I assumed to be Jeremy's father came into the room, and Jeremy introduced us. He didn't have to tell me he was afraid of him. It was apparent from the way he talked, the tone of his voice, his deferential manner.

I didn't like the looks of the man at all. He was big and rough looking, a heavy-set man with a ruddy complexion. His clothes, like the ones Jeremy had worn that morning, were too stylish, too fancy, and they suited him not at all. He didn't smile or even give me a pleasant look as he acknowledged the introduction with a curt nod of his head. It seemed to me he studied me carefully for a minute, and then decided that I was not worth his time. He said nothing to me, and turned abruptly and started out of the room. At the doorway he stopped and said gruffly to Jeremy, "Be sure you're not late for supper again. You know I won't tolerate tardiness."

"I'll be on time, sir," Jeremy said.

When the man had left, Jeremy explained, "He's not my real pa. He married my mother six years ago, before we came here. My real pa died when I was seven."

"So did mine."

"He was different, much nicer. He never beat me."

"Does he?" I motioned to the door to indicate the man who had just left.

He nodded. "He's always glad to find an excuse. I got a beating just last night for being five minutes late to dinner."

"I guess I was lucky my mother never got married again." What Jeremy had just told me explained a lot of things: why he wore the fancy clothes to school without questioning the sense of it, why he accepted his stepfather's plans for his future, why he had acted so timid just then. His stepfather was a bully. Still, it did seem he shouldn't always give in to him so easily. I was to learn it was a mark of Jeremy's character to always follow the course that offered the least resistance. "Doesn't your mother ever try to keep him from beating you?"

"It wouldn't do any good, once he's got his mind set on it. She used to try to get him to quit, but that only made him lay it on harder, so she stopped saying anything. She says I have to remember that he's very good to us."

I didn't see how his mother could figure that beating Jeremy was being good to him, but I held my tongue.

"Let's get out of the house," Jeremy said. "Would you like to go down to the river? I'll show you a good fishing spot. I know it's a bad time of day for fishing, but we could try anyway. I'll get a couple of poles. Come on. I'll show you my map, too."

"Map of what?" I asked as I followed him out the door. "You'll see."

Away from the house, Jeremy seemed to become at once more sure of himself, might have been an entirely different person from the one who had groveled in the presence of his stepfather. As we walked to the river, I followed him, watching how he set his feet down. His steps were slow and deliberate, and should have been heavy, but somehow they were just as quiet as my own. He led me to a place where the river had undercut a small bluff a few feet above the level of the water.

We fished a little while but caught only one fish, so small we threw it back. Jeremy told me he and his mother came from Tennessee, from a small settlement in the hills.

"I knew you couldn't be town-bred," I said. "You don't walk heavy-footed like townsmen do."

He nodded his acknowledgment of what I said as we wordlessly put our fishing poles aside. As Jeremy had pointed out before we left the house, neither the hour nor the day was right for catching anything.

"I'll show you the map now," Jeremy said, looking behind him, as if he expected someone to materialize out of the air to look over his shoulder. With an air of mystery, he pulled out a worn piece of paper that was heavily creased where it had been folded and unfolded many times. He smoothed it out, spread it on the grass between us. "Do you know what this is?" he asked in a conspiratorial whisper.

I looked at it for a minute, then shook my head. "Nope. What is it?"

"It's a treasure map."

"Treasure? What kind of treasure?"

"Just treasure. Gold and silver, probably. Maybe some jewels, too. Whatever Lafitte left behind on Galveston Isle."

I studied the map for a minute. "What are those squares?"

"Houses. This is Lafitte's town of Campeachy. It's deserted now."

"The Kronks still use the island, don't they?"

"I think they mostly use the other end for hunting."

"I thought some men from here went looking for Lafitte's treasure once and never found it."

"That's right. Pa went with them, but they didn't have this map. Nobody else has one like it. Pa doesn't know I have it, either, or he'd probably take it from me and go himself. I got it from a man who was passing through here once. He was one of Lafitte's men, and he even helped him bury this treasure, so he ought to remember where they put it. He told me it was in a wooden casket about this big." He showed me the rough dimensions with his hands.

"Why'd he give you the map?" I asked suspiciously. "Why didn't he go back and get the treasure himself if he knew just where it was?" Though I was belittling the map, I couldn't help but be excited at the thought that it just might prove to be authentic, the guide to a real treasure.

"He couldn't go back. He had a bad leg, and anyhow, he was too old."

"That still doesn't explain why he gave it to you," I persisted, forcing myself to remain skeptical. "Why didn't he give it to one of his friends, get him to split it with him?" I voiced my doubts mostly because I wanted to rid myself of them, wanted Jeremy to talk me out of them. All the while, I was thinking of what I could do if I suddenly found myself in possession of a large fortune. I guess that's what always makes people go hunting for treasures, even though they know there's not much chance they're really there.

Jeremy looked at me disgustedly, started to fold the map. "If you're going to act like that, I'm sorry I showed it to you. I've never shown it to anybody before."

"Wait! Don't put it away yet. I was just asking. I didn't say I thought the treasure couldn't be there."

"It's there, all right." He hesitated a minute, then opened the map again, laid it on the ground.

"Are you going to look for it? I'd like to go with you, if you are."

"Me? Pa'd wear me out for sure if I did!"

"Then what good is the map going to do you?"

"I was thinking maybe you could go, and we could split, like you said the man who gave me the map should have done."

I considered the idea for a minute. Even if there was a treasure, it wasn't likely that this map would lead anyone to it. Still, there was just that chance that I was wrong, that Lafitte really had buried a casket, and that it was just where this map showed it. "I've never been down to the coast. I've always wanted to see it. I suppose it wouldn't hurt to try to find any treasure that might be there when I go."

Jeremy's eyes were bright. "We split fifty-fifty?"

"If there's anything to split."

"There is. When do you think you can go?"

I shrugged. "Not now. Todd and I will be leaving in a few days. Some other time. I'll need at least a couple of weeks."

He folded the map, put it back in his pocket. "I'll keep this till you're ready."

That was the beginning of our friendship. Jeremy would never have shown me his map if he hadn't been as sure as I was that we would become good friends.

The next morning, I woke up early and went outside, getting dressed and picking up my rifle and powder horn quietly, then easing noiselessly out the door, even though I knew it wasn't too likely Todd would wake up. He was a heavy sleeper and seldom got up early. I stopped to load my rifle, then walked through one of the fields, cutting across toward some trees, not really heading anywhere. Near the edge of a creek, there were a couple of big cottonwoods, and I sat down, leaning against the trunk of one of them. If I was lucky, I might be able to bring Mrs. Stewart something for her table. My eyes moved over the ground, over the trees upwind as I looked for any small movement to alert me. Off to my right, there was some noise, but it was too much commotion for a small animal to make, even too much for a deer. Carefully, I raised my rifle, pointed it toward the sound, and waited. Through the tree trunks I saw a flash of red, and then another. I lowered my rifle. It was Cassie, skipping through the trees, her red cape lining showing each time she took another hop, her fishing pole dragging noisily behind her. I shook my head at her carelessness. I could just as well have been an Indian. Still, I couldn't help but be amused as I watched her settling herself near the edge of the creek, inexpertly putting a worm on the hook, then throwing the line in the water with a noisy splash.

"Go catch me a big fish for Uncle Todd!"

I wasn't twenty feet from her, and she hadn't even noticed me.

"You'll never catch a fish that way," I said.

Startled, she turned, then said accusingly, "You're always sneaking up on people! What are you doing here anyway?"

I laughed at her surprise. "Protecting you, I guess. Where's your rifle? Don't you know you should never go out without it?"

"I'm fishing, not shooting."

"A fishing pole isn't going to help you stop a stray Indian. And anyway, you aren't likely to catch any fish here. Especially not the way you put that worm on. If a fish hasn't gotten it, the current has probably carried it clean away by now."

"I suppose you know how to put it on better," she said belligerently.

"I'll show you how, if you'll stop being so ill-tempered."

She withdrew her line from the water, saw the hook was empty.

"You could put the next one on, if you really want to," she said grudgingly.

"It won't do any good to try to fish here. The current's too swift. Fish like still water." I stood up. "Come on. I'll help you find a better place. And while we're walking, see if you can't put your feet down easier. You sounded like a whole band of marauding Indians when you were coming."

She giggled. "Did I? I'll bet you were scared."

"It's healthy to be scared of any noise, till you find out who's making it." I took the pole from her. "Here, let me carry that. You just concentrate on seeing how quietly you can walk. Watch me, and try to do just like I do."

276

"I don't think I can. I've watched you before. You move like a ship with a steady wind in her sails."

"Well, you move like a ship that's just about to sink to the bottom of the sea," I countered, laughing at the comparison. "Don't stomp your feet down so hard. And always keep looking around."

We went upstream, where I found a little better spot for her to fish, but I told her I doubted if the small creek held anything big enough to bother catching anyway.

"Now let me have a worm," I said as we settled ourselves on the bank. "I'll show you how to thread it on the hook so it won't get away."

She watched me, said admiringly, "You know a lot of things, don't you? Can you teach me some more?"

"Anybody who likes to go out alone like you do should learn to read signs."

"Show me how!" she begged eagerly, and so I began that morning to show her how to look for evidence of animals or people having passed by ahead of her, showed her how to look for broken twigs, footprints, to judge the age of animal droppings. Each morning she came out early, before time for her school work, and if she found I wasn't up yet, she tapped lightly on the door to wake me. Her belligerence was gone, and she was an eager, attentive pupil, so I actually enjoyed teaching her. I couldn't help but be flattered by the way she hung on every word I said, and began to be easier in my mind about her safety, because she at least learned during those few weeks to have an awareness of the possibility of danger. By the time Todd and I left, she was moving much more easily. Since her skirts always brushed the grass and underbrush as she walked, it was impossible for her to be completely silent, but at least she had improved. And I noted with satisfaction that she never forgot to carry her rifle.

On our first trip to San Antonio de Bexar, we carried only two passengers, an old man and his daughter who had fled from there to Natchitoches in 1813. They had managed to get back as far as San Felipe, but lack of transpor-

277

tation had stopped them there, since the old man was too shaky to sit a horse. They were pleased to learn of Todd's coach, and our trip went well. In San Antonio de Bexar, we found an American widow and her two children, who wanted to go back East.

We always stopped overnight at my mother's place. She seemed contented in her little house and had put in a small garden, which was beginning to flourish by the time we came through the second time.

When we reached Todd's old place again, we found that Thorne had completed the house enough to move his family into it. It was not fancy on the outside, but was comfortable enough inside. It had a small parlor, a large kitchen for cooking and eating, and three bedrooms. Behind the house, connected to it by a covered walkway, was the summer kitchen, where the food could be cooked in warm weather without making the house uncomfortably warm. The main house was a squat boxlike building, single story, with an extension of the roof across the front to form a verandah, much in the same manner as the Butler house, only smaller, and with no claim to pretentiousness. The table and tea service had a place near the fireplace in the parlor, and I had to admit it gave the room a sort of permanent look.

After our arrival, Thorne announced that he was ready to go to New Orleans for the other coach, and Todd decided to go with him, which left me free for about the next six weeks. First, I decided, I would go to Galveston Isle and look for Jeremy's treasure, and then I would go back to stay with my mother for a while, see what I could do to make her house more livable, and be there with her when her baby was born.

On the afternoon after we arrived, Cassie wanted me to go riding with her, but I told her I couldn't, that I was going to Jeremy's. It had become a habit for me to spend the afternoons with him when I was there.

"Can I come, too?" she begged, as she often did. "Will's

going to be busy taking care of his animals, and I have nothing to do."

"You can't come," I said. "Not this time. Jeremy and I have something private to talk about."

"What?"

"If I told you, it wouldn't be private," I said, regretting having said as much as I had, because her eyes got bigger at the hint of a secret.

"Please? I won't tell anyone."

Annoyed at her persistence, I said firmly, "I know you won't, because you aren't going to know what it is. Just because you can twist your father around your little finger with your begging doesn't mean it will work on me!" I turned and walked away from her, toward the corral and was relieved to notice she didn't follow me. When I looked back, I saw she was standing in the doorway, pouting. It was easy to see she was used to getting her own way.

That afternoon, at the place near the river where Jeremy had first shown me the map, he and I studied it in earnest. "I suppose Lafitte's red house is pretty weathered by now," I said, pointing to it on the map, "but it will be easy to tell it from the others anyway."

"The box ought to be buried about sixty feet from the corner. He said twenty paces."

A twig snapped behind us, and Jeremy stopped talking. Without moving our heads, we both checked the position of our rifles. Then we began talking again, as though we hadn't heard anything, but we were alert, listening. Whoever it was was coming closer. When the footsteps couldn't have been more than three or four feet away, we grabbed our rifles and jumped to our feet at the same instant, whirling to point the barrels at the intruder.

Cassie, motionless as a startled fawn, eyed us in alarm. "Don't shoot! It's only me!"

Jeremy and I looked at each other, and burst out laughing as we lowered our rifles.

Cassie frowned. "A fine joke! What if you'd killed me?" Then she added petulantly, "I was only trying to surprise you," which I knew wasn't the whole truth, since she'd been so determined to find out what secret I'd referred to earlier.

"Surprise us?" I said. "You came crashing through the brush like a wounded buffalo. I thought I'd taught you to walk quietly."

"I was walking just like you told me," she said, pushing her lower lip out further. I saw her eyes dart to Jeremy's map, still lying on the ground where we had left it.

"What's this?" she asked, reaching down suddenly and snatching it from the ground before Jeremy could get to it.

"It's mine!" he protested. He grabbed at it, but she jerked her hand away.

"You'll tear it!" she taunted.

"Give it back to him, Cassie. It's his," I said.

She backed away from him, toward the river. "This is the secret you told me about, isn't it? I won't give it back till he promises to let me see it and tell me all about it. I'll let it blow into the water!" When Jeremy didn't agree, she said, "I heard you talk about treasure. It's a treasure map, isn't it?"

"You might as well tell her, Jeremy," I said. "She heard us talking anyway. She won't tell."

Reluctantly, Jeremy agreed, and Cassie listened in awe-struck silence. Not until he finished and had refolded the map did she speak. "And you two are going to look for it?"

Jeremy said, "Felipe is. I'm not."

"How will you get there?" she asked, her eyes shining as she turned her face toward me.

"That's what we were trying to decide when you came bursting into the middle of things." I frowned at her. "I told you Jeremy and I had something private to talk about. Now he's told you about the map, so why don't you be a good girl and go home and leave us alone?"

She shook her head stubbornly and sat down on the ground. "I want to hear all about it. Besides, I don't want to go home. There's nothing to do there. Will's busy with his animal hospital, Mama's in bed with one of her sick headaches, and Papa and Uncle Todd are getting ready to go to New Orleans early tomorrow morning. I'd rather stay here."

Jeremy and I looked at each other helplessly. We both knew just how stubborn she could be.

"You'll have to be quiet, then," Jeremy said resignedly, "and swear you won't tell a soul."

She smiled triumphantly. "I won't say a word. And I told you I can keep a secret."

Jeremy and I dropped to the ground and started talking about the best way to get to Galveston Isle. Jeremy knew the country to the south, at least by hearsay, while I knew little or nothing about it, so I was anxious to hear his suggestions.

"There's a trace on both sides of the river," he said, "but the east side is lower, and it's probably pretty boggy over there now. I think you'd better follow the one on this side."

"Where can I cross?"

Jeremy shrugged. "Lots of places. There's a crossing at the old fort, down at the bend. It'll probably be better to keep going all the way to the coast, if you can. Down along the coast, there's a spit of land that juts out toward Galveston Isle. I think it's high enough to travel the length of it. Watch out for that saw grass near the coast, though. I've heard it can cut a horse's legs worse than a knife." He took the map out of his pocket, handed it to me.

True to her word, Cassie hadn't said a thing, but as we stood up she seemed to consider her promise fulfilled and asked, "When are you going?"

"Tomorrow."

"Before or after Papa and Uncle Todd leave?"

"After. Why?"

"Because I want to go with you!" she said unexpectedly. "And if they leave before we do, there'll be no one to miss me, or to send after me."

Jeremy pointed at her and laughed derisively. "You?"

Cassie shot him an angry glance. "Why not? Anyway, it's Felipe I'm asking, not you."

"You know I couldn't take you. It's Kronk country, much too dangerous for a little girl."

"It's just as dangerous for you as for me. And I wish you'd stop calling me a little girl! I'm fourteen now. Oh, please, Felipe! I won't slow you up any. I have this new buckskin riding outfit Uncle Todd had made for me in Bexar. The skirt's split, and I can use Will's saddle and ride astride. See? I'll keep up, honest! Oh, please?"

"Don't be foolish! Your mother would never let you go, and your father would be mad enough to horsewhip us both—"

"Nobody will know till it's too late to stop me! Papa and Uncle Todd will be leaving early, so Papa won't even know I'm gone till it's all over and I'm back again. And Mama won't have school tomorrow. She'll still be in bed with her sick headache, so she won't miss me till dinnertime. And even then she won't have anybody to send after me.

"See? It's as if it was all planned specially. There couldn't be a better time for us to get away. This will be the most exciting thing I've ever done. I just have to go with you! Please—?"

"No!" I shouted my refusal. "Now will you stop talking such nonsense? You're not going with me!"

Jeremy couldn't resist firing another barb at her. There always seemed to be a current of hostility between them, and when I brought her with me sometimes to see him, he resented her presence and made her as miserable as possible. He didn't seem to mind Will being around him, but he always reacted unfavorably to Cassie's presence. "You'd get scared at the first little noise you heard, and come high-tailing it home crying!" he jeered at her.

"I would not!" Tears spilled from her eyes. "At least I'm not scared of my papa, like you are!"

"See? You're crying already!"

"Cut it out, you two," I said. "Come on, Cassie, get your horse and I'll ride home with you." This time, I was in-clined to share Jeremy's feelings about Cassie. We had been in high spirits, laughing and joking about how rich we'd be, and with me looking forward to the adventure of it, and Cassie had come along and put a damper on our enthusiasm.

All the way back to the Stewart place, Cassie kept begging me to take her. As we approached their yard, I turned to her and said firmly, "For once and for all, you can't come with me. Now quit pestering! And remember, not a word about this to anyone, not even Will. You promised to keep it a secret." I had said nothing about my plans to Todd, feeling he might not approve and think it foolish and unnecessarily dangerous to go. Time enough to tell him after it was all over.

"I won't tell anyone," Cassie answered dejectedly, wiping a tear from her cheek with the back of her hand.

I left the following day, about an hour behind Todd and Thorne. It was a warm spring morning, and the sky was clear and blue overhead, a good day to start on an interesting venture. I rode along at an easy pace, knowing there was no rush, enjoying seeing country that was new to me. On my third morning out, I began to have the uneasy feeling that I was being followed. There was nothing I could specifically put my finger on, but the feeling persisted. In the early afternoon, I saw a storm approaching, so I stopped in a sheltered spot and fashioned a hasty lean-to, took refuge under it while the storm spent its fury. After it was over, I left my makeshift camp on foot, walking away from the river, then waited till whoever had been following me had had plenty of time to find my camp. I returned, approaching cautiously, expecting whoever it was to be lying in wait there. I edged forward, noted that some things I had purposely left in specifically noted places had been moved. Only when I was certain that whoever had been there was gone did I move past my camp toward the river. I made my way to the edge of the water, saw a place where a dugout had been beached not long before, since the storm. There was two sets of footprints, big ones. Two Kronks, then, following me by water, since they knew I was heading downriver. But why, then, had they left? If they were after me, why hadn't they waited for me to return to my camp?

There was only one answer: they had given up following me because they had found someone else instead. There was no one ahead of me, I was sure of that. Whoever it was the Kronks were after had to be behind me. I left again, circling well away from the river, heading back north.

I heard a horse whicker softly, and followed the direction of the sound, back toward the water. It was Cassie's Cinder, her legs cruelly cut by the sharp grasses.

Cassie! I remembered how she had pleaded with me to take her along. I should have known my refusal wouldn't be the end of it. She had been following me for two and a half days.

And now two Kronks were following her.

She had propped her rifle against the trunk of a tree nearby, where she had apparently taken shelter from the rain. Her water bag was gone. She had probably gone to the river to fill it. And the Kronks would be there, waiting for her.

I picked up her rifle, checked it, saw with relief that she had managed to keep it dry. Muzzle loaders were useless if they got wet. I made certain that both rifles were loaded, ready to fire, then slung hers over my shoulder and carried my own in my hand. Two Kronks. Two rifles. Two shots. I couldn't afford to miss. Forcing myself to stem my anxiety and move cautiously, I worked my way toward the river, glad the recent rain had soaked the ground, making it easier to move silently toward the trap that even then might have already closed in on Cassie. I only hoped I wasn't too late.

But she had not headed directly toward the river; she was just moving toward it when I saw her. I stopped, wanting to call out to her, but knowing I mustn't dare. I eased toward the water till I had the Indians' dugout clearly in my view, then carefully took cover, leaning Cassie's rifle against a tree, ready to be grabbed quickly. I raised my own rifle to my shoulder and waited.

I didn't have to wait long. Cassie, walking incautiously toward the river, reached the water's edge, spied the dugout, and gave a little yelp of pleasure. She ran to it, peered inside, and froze there, and I knew she had just realized that the Kronks who owned it were probably not far away.

From where I stood, I could see one of the Kronks, heard the other one to the other side of the dugout. It was my good fortune that their attention was fastened on Cassie.

The one who hadn't been in view stepped out of hiding, stood in front of Cassie. I heard her gasp, saw her arms spin and stop in mid-air, like a bird poised for flight and yet unable to flap its wings and leave the ground. The Kronk was tall and muscular, and I knew just the very size of him would be enough to paralyze her with fear. The sun had come out, and its light glinted on his grease-coated shoulders. In his hand was a bow almost as tall as he was. I wanted to shoot, but Cassie stood directly between me and him. My hand twitched at the trigger as I waited my chance. Before I dared fire, both of them had to be in clear view, and Cassie must be out of the way. I couldn't afford to miss. Neither of them must get away.

Finally, Cassie lifted one foot from the mud, put it behind her, instinctively trying to back away from the Kronk who confronted her. She had not yet seen the other one. She took one step backwards, then two, then another, in a sort of macabre dance-step, but for each step she took, the Kronk took a larger one, slowly closing the distance between them.

The other Kronk stepped out of the undergrowth, said something to the first one, and Cassie gasped as her eyes darted toward him. The two started to converge on her, speaking to each other in low guttural monosyllables that sounded more like animal grunts than human speech.

The Kronks were closing in on her, but she was still between me and the farthest one from me, in my line of fire. I heard her breath coming in deep choking sobs. Another few seconds would be too late. If they grabbed her, they could use her for protection, and I wouldn't dare shoot.

I aimed for the one nearest me, and as I pulled the trigger I yelled, "Get down, Cassie!" hoping she could hear my shouted command over the report of the rifle, hoping she wouldn't be too frightened to obey if she did hear me.

The first Kronk crumpled to the ground, and I grabbed Cassie's rifle, raised it quickly and sighted. Cassie had flung herself down in the mud. The other Kronk, momentarily stunned by the suddenness of what had happened, stood immobile. I aimed at his chest and pulled the trigger just as he lunged toward his dugout.

He toppled to the ground and lay there writhing. I figured he had been mortally hurt, but I could take no chances, so I unsheathed my hunting knife and ran to throw myself on him and plunge the knife into his throat again and again. Only when I was certain that the last breath of life had left his body did I get up.

I walked to the other Kronk, kicked his lifeless body to reassure myself that there could be no response. Then I went to Cassie, lifted her to her feet.

"It's all right. You can get up now." I turned her to face me, held her up. Her legs seemed unable to support her. Her face and arms were covered with mud.

"F—F—Felipe!" she said, seeming scarcely able to pronounce my name. She was crying and laughing all at once. She threw her arms around me so hard she almost choked me.

"You left your rifle back there," I said, trying to sound gruff. "Haven't I told you never to be out of arm's reach of it?"

Still clutching me tightly, sobbing wildly, she nodded. I looked down at the top of her head, saw that her hair was covered with mud, too. I knew I should be angry with her, reprimand her for following me, but I couldn't. Her body, pressed against mine, was trembling like a leaf in the wind. She had been terrified. I couldn't bring myself to berate her, not then. Instead, I said softly, "You fool little girl.

You almost got yourself killed." I put my arms around her to comfort her, patted her shoulders gently. "Hush now, Cassie. It's all right. There were only two of them. I got them both."

"H-H-How did you—?"

"How did I find you?"

She bobbed her head up and down, and I told her what had happened, knowing that more than anything she just wanted to hear the soothing sound of my voice after her fright. "I hate to admit it," I finished, "but it was really a lucky thing you left your rifle back there, after all. Otherwise, I'd have had to try to take the second one with just my knife."

Her sobs were letting up a little, and I reached in my pocket, pulled out a piece of jerky. "Here, eat this. It'll do you good."

She loosed her hold on me, started to take the jerky. Then she drew her hand back, shook her head. "I—I couldn't." Her breathing was still uneven, but less convulsive than it had been. "My mouth . . . dry . . ."

"Eat it," I insisted. "It'll make you feel better." I led her over to a tree. "Sit down here and rest a minute, till your legs stop trembling. I'll get you some water." It was muddy where she sat, but I didn't think it mattered, she was so covered with mud anyway.

I found a gourd in the bottom of the dugout, scooped some water into it, took it to her. "Drink this."

She took it eagerly, choked once on a sob, then drank deeply. Gradually, her sobs diminished.

"I—I only w-w-wanted to go w-w-with you." She turned her eyes up to me, and in her mud-covered face, they looked even bigger than usual, and they begged me not to be angry with her.

"I know," I said reassuringly. "It's all right. It's all over now. I'm going to take you home."

"B-B-But what about the treasure?"

I shrugged. "I guess we'll just have to leave it for Jeremy to find some day. I never did really believe there was any

287

treasure, anyway. The man who drew the map probably made it all up." I took the gourd from her. "Are you all right now? We can ride a little way before dark." I put both rifles over my shoulder, gave her my hand, pulled her to her feet.

As we started away from the river, she stopped, looked back. "When I think what—"

"Don't think," I said. I pointed to the bow on the ground near the taller of the Kronks. "Want a Kronk bow for a souvenir?"

She shook her head violently. "No!"

I laughed at the force of her reply. "Then let's get started home."

# Chapter III

## AUSTIN'S COLONY—May 1827

We returned to the Stewart place to find it in an uproar. Two of their slaves, reflecting their mistress's distrust of the Texas frontier, had apparently been planning to run away as soon as Thorne had left. Angela Stewart, never strong, had fallen in a swoon when she discovered Cassie gone as well as the two Negro women. She was bedridden when we returned and was to remain so for the rest of her life.

When she saw her mother lying on the bed looking pale and sickly, Cassie burst instantly into tears. "Oh, Mama, what have I done to you?" she asked contritely, dropping to her knees by the bed.

I thought Angela could have consoled her, told her it was not her fault, but she said nothing. I even fancied I saw a slight smile on Angela's face as she stroked Cassie's bowed head, and the thought crossed my mind that she might have snatched—consciously or unconsciously—at Cassie's escapade as an excuse to withdraw even further from the life that terrorized her. Enclosed in her bedroom, remaining in her bed, she could spin a still smaller cocoon about herself and pretend the world she so feared was not even there. I may have been wrong in what I surmised. The doctor had come from San Felipe, was there when I brought Cassie home, and said it was Angela's weak heart that had caused her to take to her bed.

With two of the house slaves gone—Sam Butler had tried to catch the runaways, but failed—and Angela's withdrawal still further into herself, Cassie's life changed over-night. Selfishly, Thorne did not alter his plans to drive the other coach, and he was gone from home for increasingly longer periods, until he scarcely spent any time there at all. Cassie found herself saddled with the responsibility of maintaining their home and caring for her invalid mother as well.

The school lessons Cassie had so detested stopped abruptly for her. Priscilla continued tutoring Will and Jeremy for another year, until Sam decided to send Jeremy to New Orleans to study. Will was still passionately interested in drawing, and Priscilla, whose enthusiasm for art matched his but whose innate talent lagged far behind, had a basic knowledge in the use of oil paints, so she taught him to work in that medium. Will's concern for all living creatures led naturally to him taking over the care of the horses and the few cows the family kept. Most of the Stewart farm was in pasture, as Thorne had continued to develop the horse-breeding farm started by Todd. In spite of Thorne's long absences, the business grew, for, young as Will was, he had much more of a feel for the raising and training of horses than did his father. People from all over the state bought their riding horses from them. The unused portion of his land Thorne leased to Sam Butler for cotton.

Sukie, the slave who had been cook for Angela's mother before she belonged to Thorne and Angela, continued to make their meals, but she was useless outside the kitchen. She was an enormous woman and moved around only with difficulty, so the other work in the house was left for Cassie. Daniel, too, was slowed with age. His work had always been outside and, to the limit of his ability, he helped with the horses and saw to the milking of the cows.

In a way, the change was good for Cassie, but I always had the feeling that she had had to grow up a little too fast, too suddenly. She changed from the spoiled headstrong girl she had been to a sensible, responsible young lady. She took her work seriously. I think she considered it a penance of sorts, for I felt she never stopped blaming herself for her mother's illness.

With the way thing were when we returned, I didn't feel I could leave the Stewart house until Todd and Thorne came back from New Orleans, so I sent a letter to my mother by a passing rider, telling her that I would be delayed, and why. I learned later that she never received my message; it was not unusual in those days for letters to be lost, since their delivery depended entirely on the reliability of the chance carrier.

It was July before Thorne and Todd returned with their new coach, so I was unable to be with my mother when she had Thorne Stewart's son late in June.

Thorne lost no time in blaming me for Cassie's wild escapade. "If you hadn't lured her off on a crazy notion of finding lost treasure, none of this would have happened!" he said, glowering at me darkly.

Todd jumped immediately to my defense. "See here, Thorne," he said in his slow easy manner, "Felipe was hardly to blame if Cassie took it in her head to follow him. She told you he refused to take her."

"Still, she wouldn't have gone if it hadn't been for him. And to Karankawa country, of all places! I'd like to whale the tar out of him!"

We were standing in the parlor shortly after Todd and Thorne arrived, after they had been in, briefly, to see Angela. I glared at Thorne angrily. "I've stayed here till you came home, feeling somebody should be with Cassie and Will, all the while I should have been with my mother while she's bearing your bas—"

"That's enough!" he shouted. "I'll have no such talk in this house! You filthy-tongued young jackal, I should—"

Again, Todd intervened. This time there was no mistaking the fact that he was clearly out of patience with Thorne. "You might at least thank Felipe for what he's done. From what I understand from Cassie's tale, he risked his life to save hers. And he's stayed here till we came, all

291

the while knowing he should be with his mother. A fine lot of thanks he's getting for all that!"

"If it hadn't been for him, Cassie never would have—"

"If it hadn't been for him," Todd reminded him quietly, "your daughter would have been subjected to a horrible, terrifying death, tied to a Kronk stake as they sliced off pieces of her flesh and roasted it and ate it in front of her. I think you're the most ungrateful man I've ever seen in my life. If that's the way I raised you to be, then God help me, for somehow I've failed." He turned and walked out of the room.

I shot Thorne a final glance, half-angry, half-triumphant, and followed Todd, knowing Thorne would cut out his tongue before he would ever thank me for what I had done.

Todd and I left two days later for Gonzales, this time on horseback, for we were both anxious about my mother. She ran out to meet us, and I knew from the way she hugged me extra tight that she had been as concerned about me as I had been about her.

"You said you'd be back in a few weeks," she said.

"Didn't you get my letter?"

She shook her head. "I know you can take care of yourself, but I couldn't help worrying a little."

I backed away from her, saw her shape was back to normal. "What about the baby?" I was afraid to ask, knowing how anxious she had been for this baby to live. I waited, expecting her to tell me that it had not. But instead, she smiled.

"He's two weeks old, and thriving. Oh, Felipe, I think this child is going to make it! At first, I was afraid to hope. He's small, but he's so healthy, and growing already, and he's shown no sign of failing, like the others."

I nodded, not certain quite how to accept her news. It certainly would have been less complicated for all concerned if the child had died. Still, seeing the soft look of happiness on my mother's face, I couldn't help but be glad for her, since she had wanted the child so much.

Todd, who had stood back during all this, came forward now. "When can we see this fine boy?"

"Right this minute. He was just beginning to stir when you came."

She had named the boy Andrew, chose it because of Thorne's admiration for Andrew Jackson, who had come so close to being elected president of the United States back in 1824. I'd heard of the man—heard, too, that he was strongly in favor of westward expansion of the United States. Westward expansion meant Texas, of course. How could their country expand westward when Texas was a part of Mexico? I'd heard a number of the Americans say it had been a mistake for the United States to have ceded Texas to Spain back in 1819 when they signed a treaty settling the disputed boundaries, and that it should rightfully belong to the United States. I'd heard talk several times since then that the United States was trying to buy Texas from Mexico, but the talk had died down when Jackson had failed to be elected. Taking all that into consideration, it seemed an odd name for my mother to choose.

I followed her into the house, not at all sure how I would feel about the baby. He was my mother's child, my half-brother, but he had been sired by Thorne Stewart, the man I detested above all others.

I found my answer as soon as I saw him, so helplessly trusting and dependent on an adult world. "He's so little," I said, laughing, when Mother picked him up and held him out for our inspection. How could I continue a grudge against his father on this helpless little baby? On that day, I christened him Tico—little one—and that's what I always called him.

Tico thrived, and my mother seemed happier than I had ever known her to be. Thorne came to see her, bringing coach passengers to stay the night, who were housed and fed in the rooms attached to the back of her house. Todd and I stopped with her for the night, too, with our passengers, but at different times, so we were never there when

293

Thorne was, and the part of my mother's life that he shared remained apart from the portion that involved us. It was almost as if she led two different lives. After that first day, I no longer even thought of Tico as belonging to Thorne. He had a special place in my affections. As soon as he could toddle, he would always come running out to greet me whenever I came into the yard.

I spent much of that summer with Todd in the newly established town of Gonzales, working with him on finishing his cabin so that he would have a permanent home there. Several times, he mentioned to me his intention of continuing only for a few years on the coach.

Though Thorne and I seldom saw each other, our lives had come to interlock. He was at my mother's much of the time when I was not, and the Stewart place near San Felipe became as familiar to me as my mother's home. When Todd and I were there, we did many of the chores that needed doing, and even sometimes finished things that Thorne had started. The same was apt to be true at my mother's Gonzales place: I finished a fence he had begun, he painted some shelves I had built, and we worked alternately on the barn.

Back near San Felipe, all the frivolity had gone out of Cassie's life. Angela Stewart was a demanding invalid, not an easy person to care for, and seldom half an hour went by without her summoning Cassie with the bell that had been put at her bedside for that purpose. It was usually some small chore she wanted done—a blanket added, some fresh water brought, a window opened or closed—but these small demands were piled one on top of the other endlessly, and Cassie began to show the strain. Whenever I arrived, I always went first to pay my respects to Angela, and felt compelled to inquire after her health. Then I had to listen impatiently to her recitation of the complaints and symptoms around which her life had come to revolve.

Cassie always tried hard not to be out of patience with her mother's querulous demands, and I knew she would never stop being plagued with guilt, feeling that if she hadn't run away to follow me, her mother would not be ill. I tried to reason with her, convince her it wasn't her fault, that in all likelihood her mother's heart would have acted up anyway, sooner or later. But she wouldn't listen to me. She never showed any resentment directly to her mother, but whenever the bedside bell rang, her hands clenched into tight fists and her whole body tensed before she ran to see what Angela wanted.

Cassie grew more serious as the months ran one into the other and became first one year, then two. More and more responsibility was piled upon her, for Thorne had become active in the affairs of the colony, and his place on the *ayuntamiento,* the governing body that met in San Felipe, claimed yet more of his time. Our coaches carried either passengers or merchandise or freight, sometimes all three, and gradually things fell into a pattern, so that Todd and I carried most of the passengers and Thorne usually had only merchandise or freight. I was not unaware of the reason for this: he was able to prolong his visits with my mother if he had no people waiting to continue on their journey.

Todd made no secret to me of his concern for Cassie, his feeling that Thorne was not being fair to her or Will in leaving them alone most of the time. Cassie seldom got out of the house, except to go to church meetings occasionally when Todd was there to take her. Cassie loved to go because it gave her a chance to get out of the house. I always stayed behind to look after Angela, a fact which she resented when she realized I was the only one in the house to answer her summons. Cassie told me later that she was always in a sulky mood for several days afterward when this happened. But I didn't mind if Angela was a bit curt with me on those occasions. It was worth it to see Cassie so sparkling and vital when she returned, as if she had been changed back into the vibrant girl she had once been. Just getting out and having a chance to be around other people brought the color back to her cheeks and a sparkle to her eyes.

Will, who was by his very nature as well satisfied with

his own company as with anyone else's, didn't seem concerned about the dullness or the loneliness of the lives that he and Cassie lived. For him, animals and drawing were enough. About the only visitors they ever had besides travelers asking hospitality of them were the Butlers. Priscilla came to call on Angela every week, and whenever Thorne was home, the Butlers were invited for dinner one night.

To Cassie, the dullness of their lives did matter, as it didn't to Will, and I began to bring her little gifts, wanting to bring a little interest, a little foolishness and frivolity into her drab life. Sometimes I picked up Indian trinkets for her. The Comanches came and went as they pleased in San Antonio de Bexar, and occasionally I was able to bargain with them for a tomahawk or a pair of moccasins. They were always surprised when I spoke their tongue, and pleased enough to bargain with me. The residents knew they were responsible for the occasional disappearance of young girls from the outer edges of the town, but nobody dared stop them from coming and going as they pleased. The Comanches commanded the plains and were too formidable an enemy to take on.

But it seemed nothing could keep the settlers out of Texas, or frighten them into leaving once they were there, and they kept coming in from the United States. Most of them came on their own by that time, just settling in whatever colony they took a fancy to, or in no colony at all. The *empresarios* no longer had to make any effort to lure people to Texas. Word had gotten back that there was land to be had in Texas, and the Americans came across the Sabine in a steady never-ending stream. They were moving west, and it bothered them not at all that Mexico stood in their path.

The Americans spread out, even began to claim some of the coastal land, the last stronghold of the Kronks, who seemed to finally just fade away. They had never been united, getting together only on special occasions. They were heard from less and less frequently, until finally they were mentioned only by the earlier settlers as an all-but-forgotten horror of the past. In the northeastern part of the state, the Indians, except for strays, didn't harass the colonists overmuch. And Austin's punitive attack against several of the tribes who were giving his settlers problems seemed to have settled them down considerably. Still, Indian troubles flared up like brush fires from time to time in various parts of Texas as the white settlers encroached more and more on the Indians' territory.

During those years, we didn't lack for passengers for our coach, or for people clamoring for merchandise. There was nothing that wouldn't sell. Todd and Thorne grew comfortably well off, and I kept adding to the savings my mother kept for me.

As time went on, my friendship with Todd grew apace, along with my admiration and respect for him. There are not many men I would describe as "good", but Todd deserved to be called just that, not only for what he did for me, but for the interest he took in anyone who needed help. There was no meanness or pettiness in him, and he always seemed to understand what I was trying to say to him. I felt that I could talk to him as I had never been able to talk to anyone before, even about subjects that should have been difficult between us, like my feelings about Thorne and my mother, and my wish that the Americans had not come to Texas. We often joked about the latter subject, with him calling me a stubborn Creole, and me calling him a land-grabbing American, but the lightness with which we treated the matter didn't make it any less important to me, and Todd knew and appreciated this fact.

I was secretly pleased when I began to hear rumors that the government of Mexico was no longer going to be so lenient toward the American colonists. Things began to change after Bustamente became president in 1829. Maybe it was a natural reaction to the election of Andrew Jackson as president of the United States the previous year, because Jackson certainly made no secret of the fact that he wanted his country to reach from coast to coast, and cared not one whit that Mexico stood squarely in the path of his expansionist dreams. Later in the year that Jackson took office as president, we began to hear rumors that Sam Houston was going to head an expeditionary force to take Texas.

The Mexican government under Bustamente apparently grew as alarmed as I did at the possible aim of the United States toward Texas, and in April of 1830, passed the Exclusion Act. I remember well the day I heard about it, because it was one of the few times that we were at the Stewarts' at the same time Thorne was there. The night the news reached us, there were eight of us around the supper table. Sam and Priscilla were there with Jeremy, who was home from his studies for a few months.

"It's outrageous," Thorne said, his face red with anger. Seeing him so upset gave me a satisfaction of sorts, especially when I learned what had caused his irritation. "This will virtually stop immigration!" he continued. "Can you imagine such ingratitude from the Mexicans, after all we've done for their country?"

It was on the end of my tongue to ask him just what he had done for my country, besides making himself a pretty good living off it and taking a lot of the land in it for his own, but I said nothing.

Sam Butler said, in effect, the same thing, but he said it in a way that was more palatable to Thorne than my words would have been.

"Why should it bother us if they keep too many more Americans from coming in?" Sam asked with a careless shrug of his shoulder. "They'll still permit filling of existing grants. And anyway, we're here."

Thorne shook his finger at him. "The more Americans, the better the chance they'll sell us Texas," he said. "It should have been ours by rights, anyway. Surely, Sam, you'd prefer to live under the flag of the United States! This idiotic government changes from one day to the next, and they're still denying us the separate statehood they promised us in the Constitution of 1824. Imagine, as big as we've grown, still sharing the government of the state of Coahuila. Why, it's like the tail wagging the dog!"

Sam shifted his weight, squirmed a little, and I wondered if the corseting everybody knew he wore was uncomfortably tight. "Let me ask you this, Thorne. You haven't paid a penny in taxes or customs duties since you came here, have you? And did you ever have it half so good back in Savannah? From what you've told me, you weren't doing so well. Nor was Todd. And I make no secret of the fact that I've prospered here. I'm living in a big house, have furnished it luxuriously, and I own ten times as many slaves as I did when I came." Sam Butler, I had noticed before, never missed a chance to brag. "I think you worry too much about this Exclusion Act. Look at the slavery issue, the laws they've passed to prohibit it. But I've brought in all I've wanted. The law hasn't stopped me, hasn't even slowed me down. I suspect this new law will be just as poorly enforced as the others they've made."

"But they seem serious this time," Thorne objected. "What if they really do enforce this fool Exclusion Act? It can cut off further expansion completely. That's what they've intended for it to do, and if it does, a fine chance we'll ever have then of getting them to sell Texas, or even getting the separate statehood they seem to have forgotten they promised us. I'm telling you, if they're serious about this, and enforce it, it's going to brew trouble, and the only way we can settle things will be by force. It will happen sooner or later, and they've nobody to blame but themselves."

Until that moment, Todd had not said anything, but at last he spoke. "Just a minute there, Thorne." Everyone turned to listen to him, and he paused while he helped himself to another biscuit, put some molasses on his plate to dribble over the insides of the biscuit. He often made some excuse or other to pause before he said anything. In another person, it could have been an annoying habit, but everyone sort of accepted the habit as a part of Todd, and it seemed to make people more anxious to hear what he had to say when he finally got around to speaking. "I'm not sure I agree with what you're saying. The government invited us here. Invited, mind you. Nobody forced us to come, and even though we all hoped some day to maybe see Texas belong to the United States, the Mexicans never gave us any encouragement along that line. We all had high expectations a couple of years ago when we heard rumors that there was an attempt afoot to try to buy Texas from Mexico, but that came to nothing. Now, with Andy Jackson in office, we have more to back up our hopes than we've ever had before, and you know that I hope as strongly as you do that it will eventually come to pass. But it's one thing to wish for a legal sale of Texas to the United States, and quite another to talk of the use of force, of armed rebellion—"

"I wasn't saying it's likely to happen any time soon," Thorne said, backing down a little. "I just said that the Mexicans might be asking for trouble with this new law, and that armed rebellion is a possibility, that's all." There was no doubt in my mind that Thorne Stewart would do all he could to see that the possibility materialized.

Later that evening, while the Butlers and Thorne and Todd continued their political discussion in the parlor, Cassie and Jeremy and I went outside to sit on the verandah steps.

"It's been a long time since the three of us have been together," I commented as we sat down. It was a clear late spring evening, and the moon was bright, throwing shadows that were almost as strong as those thrown by sunlight. Cassie sat between us, and I studied her. She had always been a pretty child, and now, just turned seventeen, she had fulfilled the promise of something that was not exactly beauty, but even better. Although she had become much more subdued in the past three years, there remained about her a hint of irrepressible vitality, the vivaciousness that was an important part of her prettiness. Her hair was parted in the middle after the current fashion, and was a rich brown that glinted in the moonlight. She didn't have time to twist it into the long tight curls that were in style, but I thought it looked much nicer the way it was, falling softly and naturally to her shoulders. Her eyes were a soft green color, rimmed with long dark lashes and topped with brows curved in a soft upward arch. Her mouth, always expressive, was soft and full. Yes, I decided, she was really a very pretty girl.

Jeremy, too, had changed a lot from the freckle-faced boy I had met three years before. He was almost six feet tall, though he still hadn't filled out to his weight. He was wearing striped pants, a tailed coat, and a white vest. His cravat of striped silk was wound around and tied in a complicated bowknot just below his high-standing collar. He didn't seem to rebel against the gentlemanly clothes as he had when we first met. He was even trying to grow a mustache, but all there was to it was a bit of fuzz over his upper lip.

We sat silently for a few minutes, a deep comradeship among the three of us, a closeness of childhood shared and adulthood almost achieved.

It was Cassie who broke the silence, and for the first time it occurred to me that her voice was no longer sharp or petulant, but soft and just a little bit husky, with a quiet strength to it.

"You know, Felipe," she said, "I got to thinking when they were talking at the table about the Mexicans, they were talking as though that was somebody completely apart from any of us, somebody we didn't even know, a lot of strangers down in Mexico City or Monclova. And all of a sudden, I realized it was really you, that you're a Mexican, as much as those people in the state and national capitals. And I couldn't help but wonder how you must have felt about what they were saying." She laughed. "I'll never forget how upset you were that day you found me on your land."

"I still remember it, too. You were a terribly spoiled little girl, and I wanted to shake you, the way you went on about that being your father's land." I smiled at the memory, then became serious again. "But I never pretended I liked the idea of having Americans swarming all over Texas." Yet, as I spoke, I thought of the Americans I

301

knew, those who were my friends. I had a few Mexican friends, but none who were close. I thought of Jeremy and Cassie and Will, of Todd, of the Bryants back in Nacogdoches, of Johnny Gorham in Gonzales. It certainly wasn't their presence I resented. Mostly, it was the overwhelming numbers of the Americans I objected to; except for Thorne Stewart and Sam Butler, there were few individuals I personally disliked. But as for allowing thousands upon thousands more faceless strangers to come across the Sabine, eyeing the Varga grant and every other piece of good farm land in Texas—yes, to this I did object.

"Has anything ever been settled about the Varga grant yet?" Jeremy asked.

"No. Todd has been helping me. We've been after one of the officials in San Antonio de Bexar, and I've written at least a hundred letters in the last couple of years, or anyway, that's how many it seems." I shrugged in disgust. "Just as I begin to think I'm getting somewhere with one man, he's out of office and somebody else is in, and I have to start all over. In '28, when they changed the state capital from Saltillo to Monclova, that set me back again. Nothing is settled yet, but some day they'll get everything straight."

"I hope so," Jeremy said. "When I'm a lawyer, maybe I can help you. You'll be my first case."

"Would you take a Mexican client?" I asked jokingly.

"No matter what Cassie says, you're not exactly a Mexican, any more than I'm exactly an American any more. It's funny, but I feel like a foreigner in New Orleans. I guess we're all Texans." Some years later, I was to remember his words again, the words he uttered so carelessly and half in jest.

All this while, the voices from the living room were coming through the open windows, and suddenly, over the sound of Thorne's voice was the ring of Angela Stewart's bedside bell. Instantly, Cassie jumped up and headed toward the door. The endless demands upon her, her unthinking and spontaneous response to the summons, like a dog who has been well trained to come when his master whistles, angered me. "Your father's in there," I said. "Can't he answer it this time?"

She stopped, her hand on the door handle. "Papa doesn't even hear it. He's really only a visitor here these days." She opened the door and went inside. There had been so much wistfulness in her voice that I felt a sudden compassion for her. More and more, Thorne spent his time away from his home, and I saw increasing evidence that his stays with my mother had lengthened, as though the little adobe house outside Gonzales and not this place in Austin's colony were his real home. And even when he was around the San Felipe area, Cassie said he often stayed in town because of his *ayuntamiento* meetings. I was angry for Cassie's sake, because he had forced her to take on the responsibility that should have been his.

"Cassie doesn't have an easy life now," I said when she had gone.

"I guess taking care of her mother must keep her pretty busy, at that." From the offhand tone of Jeremy's voice, I knew he had not really thought much about it, about how things had changed for Cassie, how little joy she had in her life.

"It's not just her mother," I said, feeling compelled to enlighten him, make him share my indignation. "She has to keep the house clean, and do the mending, and supervise the candle dipping and soap making. She even has to churn the butter sometimes, when Sukie's got a shoulder misery. It's a cinch Thorne doesn't try to make things any easier for her. He's always promising to bring her a maid to help, and he never does. Listen to him now, tirading against the government! Cassie's right, he didn't even hear the bell. He hasn't missed a lick in his carrying on since the bell rang."

"I guess Cassie does have it kind of rough, all right. But she'll make a lot better wife now than she would have the way she was going before her mother got sick, trying to prove she could outride and outshoot every boy in Texas."

"I suppose," I agreed. "But it still isn't right for her to have to work so hard."

The thought of her becoming a wife surprised me. It had never occurred to me to think of her as being grown up enough to marry anyone.

"We'll probably get married in about four years, after I finish my studies. I'm going to Harvard next year."

I looked at him sharply. "You and Cassie, marry each other?"

"Of course. I thought you knew that. Pa and Mr. Stewart have been planning on it for years."

"Do you still do everything your father tells you to do?" I asked, suddenly irritated with him, with his customary bland acceptance of whatever his stepfather proposed. "Surely he doesn't beat you any more," I added sarcastically.

"Hardly. But why shouldn't I do what he wants, in this case? Cassie's pretty enough, and she's settled down these last few years."

"What does she think of the idea?"

He laughed. "I honestly don't know. I've never asked her. I suppose she takes it for granted, just like I do. But I'm not even eighteen yet, and four years is a long time away. In the meantime, there's nothing says I can't have some fun first with other girls."

"I suppose not," I said, catching his meaning.

"Have you ever been with a woman? You know . . ."

"I guess I've been too busy." That was not strictly the truth. When we were in San Antonio de Bexar, Todd often left me alone, and I knew he was off gaming, and that there was a woman with whom he sometimes spent the night. I had thought about trying it out, had even walked down to La Villita a couple of times, past the houses where the women sat in the yards in their negligees and called out to the men to get them to come inside. I got as far as approaching one of them once. She hadn't looked too bad at a distance, but when I got close to her I saw she was filthy, and old, and there had been big sores on her face. I shuddered and turned away, feeling that somehow I had escaped from something that would have been too disgusting to bear.

"I've had girls—women, really, I guess you'd say, since mostly they're older," Jeremy continued. "I tried it first a couple of years ago. One of my friends had a fancy woman, and he had her bring a friend for me."

"And her friend let you?"

"Of course. It was all set up ahead of time." He waved his hand carelessly. "I've been back to her some, but I've found others I like better. You ought to try it, get yourself a woman. The older ones are best, about thirty or so."

"I might," I said noncommittally, realizing I felt no envy for him, but only disgust at what he was telling me, and I wondered if the women he had known weren't every bit as repulsive as the one from whom I had run in La Villita. I didn't tell him what I was thinking, fearing that he might laugh at me, but I knew that I had to feel something special for a girl, or a woman, something besides just a desire to be relieved of discomfort, before I would want to do anything with her.

The voices from the parlor moved to the small vestibule, and Jeremy's mother and stepfather came outside, ready to leave.

"Come on over tomorrow," Jeremy said as he stood up. "We'll go riding."

I nodded, looking again at his clothes, thinking how little he looked like a boy who had come from the hills of Tennessee. On Sam Butler, the same kind of clothes looked all wrong; on Jeremy, they had begun to look right. I thought of how parallel our early lives had been, the same in all the things that mattered, but how we had been beginning even then to go different directions. We would have little in common when we each got a little farther down the separate roads on which we traveled.

Jeremy followed my gaze, tried to guess my thoughts, came close. "Don't worry. I still have some buckskins. I won't go riding like this."

I laughed. He was the same Jeremy again, after all, the

same freckle-faced boy who had been my first real friend. "I'm glad. My horse might shy and try to throw me if he saw you like that."

Priscilla Butler wished me a pleasant good night, but, as always, her husband did not bother to address me. Since that day long ago when he had first met me and studied me briefly, and decided I was not worth his note, he seldom spoke directly to me, not even to exchange the normal courtesies. I don't think he actually felt any malice toward me; it was just that he would have gained nothing by being pleasant to me, and Sam Butler was a man who never did anything unless he stood to gain by it. He probably would have been shocked to know that I considered him a loud-mouthed braggart and a sadistic bully, and cared not at all that he did not speak to me.

The Butlers climbed into their open buggy—by that time, they had a proper one with a hood over it, such as townspeople used—and their liveried coachman clicked to the horses and flicked the reins and they left.

As always, Todd and I slept in the original cabin he had lived in with his wife, the cabin the Stewarts had occupied till the house was finished. The first time I had seen it, there had been a stain on the floor under the table. Cassie had noticed me looking at it, told me it was the blood of Todd's wife, who had died on that very table. Next time we came, the place was covered with a rag rug Cassie had braided out of old clothing, so that Todd wouldn't see the stain and be reminded of his wife's death and be sad. I had been touched by such thoughtfulness on Cassie's part, especially since I knew that the quiet pursuits like rug braiding bored her. It had truly been a labor of love for her uncle. The rug stayed there even after the Stewarts moved out of the cabin into the house. Todd seldom mentioned his wife any more, but I noted that every time we visited, fresh flowers appeared on the two graves a short distance from the house. If it was the wrong time of year for fresh flowers, there would always be a small bouquet of dried plants on each grave.

306

I had trouble falling asleep that night, because I couldn't get out of my mind what Jeremy had told me about him and Cassie. I suppose it was a logical thing for the two of them to marry, but the thought had never occurred to me before, and Jeremy's matter-of-fact acceptance of the idea irritated and upset me. I couldn't help but wonder how Cassie felt about it, if she accepted it as casually and unquestioningly as Jeremy did. There certainly wasn't anything notably special about the way they acted when they were together. Their old hostility had eased up, but there was no extra warmth in their glances at one another, no special smiles exchanged, not that I had seen.

Next day, I kept watching for an opportunity to ask her, but she was always busy, never alone. The next afternoon, I went to Jeremy's and didn't return till suppertime. Early the following morning, Todd and I left, so I never got to question her about it.

We didn't get back to the Stewart place for the rest of the summer, and all that while I puzzled over what Jeremy had told me, oddly disturbed by the news, yet not sure just why it upset me. I couldn't get Cassie out of my mind, and in San Antonio de Bexar I bought her four narrow bangle bracelets of silver. They were not good ones, had no stones in them, but they suited her and I thought she would like them.

We were in Gonzales a month that summer. Tico was three years old and wanted to go with me whenever I left the house. I took him along most of the time, putting him in front of me on my saddle. Mother smiled and said my father used to take me around with him in the same manner.

It was Todd's unquestioned respectability that gained limited access for my mother and Tico in the town of Gonzales. Mother pretty well kept to herself, didn't seem to want or need other women friends. Her place was far enough out of the town so that she didn't have to concern herself much with the ladies there. As Tico grew, I realized why Todd had taken the precaution of inventing a dead brother as my mother's supposed husband, for Tico looked a great deal like Todd and Thorne and Will. I always wondered if the people of Gonzales didn't suspect the truth of the matter, for though Thorne always kept his coach out of sight inside the barn we had built back in the summer of 1827, there must have been those who knew of the amount of time he spent with my mother. But if the town of Gonzales did not openly chastise my mother for her illicit relationship with Thorne, neither did they extend their acceptance further to offer her any sort of friendship. She went into the town to shop occasionally, where she was greeted politely but not overly cordially. I thought it was a good thing that she didn't seem to need, or miss, having friends, and I was more than ever glad she had Tico.

The people of Gonzales seemed to accept me with less reservation. Through Todd, I had met most of the folks and had become friendly with a few of the young men my age. One in particular, Johnny Gorham, whose parents had come with Green DeWitt's first colonists in 1825, became my very good friend. It was he who, during that summer of 1830, asked me which side I would be on if it ever came to a fight between the Texans and the government of Mexico.

"What are you, Felipe? A Texan or a Mexican? If it ever came to choosing one side or the other, which one would you be on?"

We were sitting on the ground, leaning against a tree, and had just ended a contest of marksmanship between us by declaring it a draw.

"I don't know," I answered truthfully, surprised at the question. I remembered Jeremy's statement that we were all neither Mexicans nor Americans any more, but Texans. "I've never really thought about it much. My great-grandfather, my grandfather, my father—they were all in the army part of their lives."

"But that was the Spanish army, wasn't it—when Mexico was a part of Spain?"

"I know, but all of them were Creoles, except my great-grandfather, who came over from Spain. They were of pure

Spanish blood, but weren't born in Spain. My great-grandfather and my grandfather married Creole ladies, so my people have been here for four generations, counting me. Technically, I'm not really a Creole at all, because my blood is mixed."

Johnny pushed his unruly blond hair out of his eyes, said laughingly, "I suppose that makes you Mexican, then. I hope you won't take up a rifle against us. I sure wouldn't want you shooting for the side I wasn't on."

I pointed to the target we had made on the tree trunk, its center perforated with the bullets from both our rifles. "I could say the same." I stood up, made uneasy by talk of fighting. The first time I had heard it mentioned had been by Thorne, and coming from him, it had not surprised me. But this was Johnny, my friend, who had brought up the subject. Was it really in the back of the minds of all the Americans who had come to Texas?

"It's all a lot of foolishness, to even talk of fighting," I said. "All the Mexican government did was pass a law saying not so many Americans can come in and that the ones who are here will have to start paying customs duties. After all, there are about twenty thousand of you now. Don't you think that's enough of you Yankees for us Creoles to put up with?"

He laughed, swung Tico up on his shoulder, then stooped to pick up his rifle. "You natives just better remember that we Americans don't take too well to laws we don't like. Look what we did to our English oppressors!"

"We aren't oppressing anybody," I said, not sure he was joking, unable to keep the irritation out of my voice. "All we're doing is trying to keep all the rest of the Americans from coming to Texas. The way things have been going, your country would soon be empty, and all the Americans would be here instead."

It soon became apparent that the government intended to put teeth into the ordinance setting up the payment of customs duties. At the start, the Americans had been promised the right to bring things in duty-free for seven

309

years, and that time limit had more than expired. Customs houses were set up, and detachments of troops were sent to Anahuac, Velasco, Nacogdoches, San Antonio de Bexar, and La Bahia, which had been renamed Goliad. There was another detachment sent to Fort Teran on the Neches. Americans complained about the troops, for the common soldiers were chosen from among the peasants, and many, it was said, were even recruited in the jails. But the officers were, for the most part, high-class Creoles, and even some Americans who had gone to Mexico earlier were among them. Most notable of those was Elias P. Bean, an adventurer who had spent quite a few years in Mexican jails under the Spanish and had stayed on in Mexico after independence.

The Americans grumbled about the soldiers, and about the collection of duties on goods brought in, but I felt a deep sort of satisfaction every time we came to a town where the troops were stationed. Not even to Todd did I explain how I felt about the presence of the Mexican soldiers in Texas. It was a deeply personal sort of feeling, as though they had been sent there specifically to keep the Americans from getting too brash and taking away my land, my rights. Let the Americans talk of war. Mexico, too, had men who could fight.

The customs houses didn't collect a fraction of the amount they should have, for it became a game for the Americans to circumvent them. The coastline was long, and it was impossible to guard it all. And all along the eastern edge of the state, contraband traces began to crisscross the older routes. It was on these traces that the stream of Americans also continued to flow into Texas. The Exclusion Act slowed them very little, if at all; it had not dammed the stream, but only diverted it.

The next time we were at the Stewart place, I gave Cassie the bracelets I had bought for her. She was sweeping the parlor floor when I brought them to her. I had gone into the room as she worked, sat in the large stuffed chair that I knew was supposed to be the specific and private property of Thorne, and I watched her, smiling in anticipation of her pleasure at receiving the unexpected surprise I had for her.

She looked up, returned my smile. "You look like the rat that stole the cheese," she said.

"And you look like the goodwife who chased him out of the kitchen with her broom," I countered. Such foolish light talk had become a habit with us, for I took it as a personal challenge to make her forget the heavy responsibilities and hard work that had become her lot, and see how often I could make a smile light her face and bring that sparkle into her eyes.

I was rewarded with another laugh, and I reached in my shirt pocket for the bracelets. "I do believe you're even prettier than the Comanche squaw I stole these from," I said, holding them in the open palm of my hand. "I think they'll look much better on you."

"Oh!" She dropped her broom to the floor and ran over to peer at the bracelets. "Oh, Felipe, are they for me? Oh, I love them! They're so—so gay! Could I try them on?" She took them from my hand without waiting for any answers, slid them over her hand, moved her arm to make them slide up and down. "They even feel gay! Oh, Felipe, thank you!"

"They do suit you. It was worth all the clawing and kicking I had to take to get them off that squaw's arm." I grinned, glad that the gift had pleased her so much. I tried to imagine Jeremy bringing her foolish little presents like that after they were married, and I couldn't do it. Jeremy, for all that he was a good friend, would be a dull husband. Suddenly I asked, "Cassie, are you going to marry Jeremy?"

She stopped shaking her arm to make the bracelets jangle and looked at me in surprise. "What makes you ask that?"

"Jeremy said that Sam Butler and your father had sort of agreed that you and he—"

"Well, I haven't agreed!" she said emphatically. "This is the first I've heard about it. Nobody has consulted me."

311

Relieved that she hadn't known about it and hadn't accepted it, I still persisted, "But would you?"

"Marry Jeremy?" She shook her head. "I don't think he and I would be suited. He would expect me to be—well, he would expect a sort of blind obedience, and I don't think I could be that kind of wife, not to anybody."

I smiled, strangely relieved. "I can't imagine you that way, either." I stood up. "I'd better go see Todd. He wanted me to ride into San Felipe, see if anyone's shown up there to go to San Antonio de Bexar or Gonzales."

It was early in 1831 that Todd suddenly announced that he would not be going with me on the coach any more. We were in Gonzales at the time, sitting just outside the door of the one-room cabin we had built for him.

"Why not?" I asked in surprise. I had all but forgotten that he had told me four years earlier when we had started with the coach that he did not intend to ride with it for more than a few years.

"For one thing, I think you're old enough and capable enough to handle things every bit as well as I can. For another, I'll soon be fifty-nine years old, and sitting up there on the box, the winter winds just seem to blow clean through to my very bones. I might take the notion to go with you once or twice more some time later in the spring, when the weather gets milder, but as long as there's a chance of a norther dropping the temperature twenty and thirty degrees, and whipping those cold winds around me, I'm going to stay home by my own fireside."

I thought a minute. "I suppose Johnny Gorham might be willing to ride with me. He'll be getting his own place in a year or so, but I think he might agree to go with me a couple of times before he starts farming."

"A good idea," Todd agreed. "Why don't you ask him?"

"I will," I said, glad the matter was so easily settled. I had something else to say to Todd, something I had been thinking about for some time, but I didn't know just how to begin.

312

Todd, who knew me so well, prodded gently, "What's troubling you, boy? Can you tell me about it?"

"It's about avoiding the customs houses, bringing in contraband." I looked at Todd, saw him nod. "I just don't want to take part in—in open defiance of the Mexican troops. It goes against me. Please don't ask me to bring in things illegally any more."

I waited, watched him light his pipe, knew he wanted time to consider my words before he answered. Only once had I gone with him to Natchitoches since the establishment of the customs houses, and we had returned to Texas that time on the contraband traces, avoiding the main roads and thus the troops stationed there and the payment of duties. Though I had said nothing at the time, it had bothered me and been eating at me ever since.

Todd puffed on his pipe to get it started. "Well," he said, "I expect you might feel a little differently about such matters than the rest of us do. But I don't really understand. We continued to sell merchandise here after the state declared it illegal for foreigners to sell anything, and you didn't object to us using your name so we could continue."

"That was different. It was a law, I know, but it was just a foolish state law, passed just to help somebody who was maybe a friend of the legislators. Nobody even tried to see it was enforced. Anyway, you pay me well, and I really am a part of your business, so it wasn't actually a lie, using my name. But this business of avoiding the customs is different. You Americans knew after your original exemption was up you'd have to start paying customs. It's as though by going around the customs houses, you're defying the army, laughing at the way you can fool them so easily, and—well, it makes me uncomfortable. It's as though you think the Mexican army is just pretending to be soldiers, as though you're mocking what they stand for!"

"I guess I see," he said, giving me a long searching look. "I suppose the friends you've made among the officers at Bexar have been talking to you, too."

"How did you know?" I asked, surprised. Todd and I

313

had always gone our separate ways when we reached San Antonio de Bexar, and I had always assumed he knew nothing about where I went, whom I saw, except what I told him.

Todd smiled. "I wasn't all that busy with my own affairs in Bexar that I couldn't keep tabs on you." He became more serious again. "In fact, I've been getting concerned about you lately, Felipe, about the way you seem to be sort of—well, the only word I can think of is belligerent. Maybe anti-American is more accurate. I see you leaning more and more that way, ever since the Exclusion Act was passed and the Mexican soldiers were stationed around in Texas. It's almost as if you've turned against the Americans. After all, you've lived among us long enough now, and except for some of the young Mexican officers and maybe a few more casual acquaintances, your friends are all American."

"That doesn't make me any less a Mexican!" I bristled defensively.

"You're a Texan, Felipe, and that's not the same at all. You're one of us, whether you admit it or not. Oh, I know there's that business about your land, and that you feel we came in and tried to take it away from you, but the truth of the matter, and you know it, is that the Mexicans don't recognize your claim any more than the Americans do."

"They will! The Varga grant is mine!" I interrupted him defiantly, shocked at the thought that he might have any doubts about my getting clear title to the land I had inherited from my father. Todd had always helped me, encouraged me to try to push for recognition of my claim.

"I know it's rightfully yours," he said soothingly, "and nobody hopes more than I do that you'll be successful in establishing that fact. But that's no reason to cast your lot with the Mexicans against the Texans."

"What else am I to do?" I asked angrily. It was one of the few times I had ever felt out of patience with Todd. "Am I to side with the Americans, join them in making a mockery out of the government's attempt to enforce the

314

law in Texas? Am I to side with them in flaunting their contempt for the law?"

Todd looked at me sadly, shaking his head. "Maybe I'm asking too much of you, Felipe, but I wish you would promise me you won't take sides, not yet anyway."

"That's impossible!"

"Perhaps you're right," he mused, puffing on his pipe. "Perhaps it is." He sighed heavily, and I thought the sigh made him sound very old.

*Almost fifty-nine,* I thought. *He's no longer young.* The thought saddened me, and I felt suddenly contrite for having said things that worried him, upset him. He had been like a father to me the past four years. Surely I owed him what peace of mind I could give him.

"I'll try not to take sides," I said hesitantly. Not for anyone else would I have said that. "At least, not till it's forced on me. But please don't ask me to bring in contraband any more."

"Thorne will have to see to it himself."

I nodded my acceptance, but I knew what his statement implied. Thorne would not be apt to forgive my refusal to defy the soldiers at the customs houses.

# Chapter IV

## THE BEXAR ROAD—1831

Johnny agreed to go with me to San Felipe once, until I had time to find somebody else, but as things turned out, he continued to go with me for over a year and took over after I left, but we didn't know all that when we set out the first time from Gonzales.

He was a good traveling companion. He was cheerful and outgoing, and when we reached the Stewarts's, his presence served to lessen a little bit Cassie and Will's disappointment on finding that Todd had not come with me.

Johnny was enthusiastic about everything life had to offer, and instantly accepted Will's invitation to see the stables. He listened with sincere interest as Will pointed out the various crossbreeds, and I knew he had won Will over completely when Will offered to show him his special pets and the menagerie of sick and injured animals. He couldn't get over the wonder of the Stewart house, which was far better than anything yet built in Gonzales, and he repeatedly ran his hand over the walls, saying, "Sawed boards! Imagine that!" He and Cassie took to each other at once as well, and he constantly went out of his way to amuse her. Even Angela liked him and seemed to brighten a little in his presence. He listened patiently to her whining talk, encouraged her to say more. He was the kind of person nobody could dislike, and most people, male and female alike, responded to his open friendliness immediately.

We left the coach in San Felipe to have it repaired, and

made several trips into the town to see how the repairs were progressing. Both coaches had been reinforced with metal and wood wherever possible before they ever left New Orleans, but they were constantly being weakened and torn apart as they bounced and twisted their way over the rutted roads. At the beginning, many people said Todd and Thorne were out of their minds to start trying to take coaches overland, and we had certainly had our trials those first few years.

On our second ride into the town, Johnny asked if I would mind stopping with him to see a family friend. "Lemuel Parker. I hardly remember him, but Pa heard he's in San Felipe, and asked me to stop in and pay my respects."

"I know Lem, but I'm not sure which house is his. We'll ask around."

We not only found Lemuel Parker's house that day, but Johnny also found Lem's youngest stepdaughter. Lem had come to Texas as a widower six years earlier, and soon after his arrival, he married a widow and acquired not only a wife, but three stepdaughters as well. Two of the girls had since married and gone, but the youngest, Eliza, was still living at home.

Patience Parker greeted us at the door. She was a large woman, somewhere in her forties, with a figure that was not so much fat as stately. She was tall. Her eyes were almost on a level with ours. Her hair was gray as granite, her skin coarse, her hands big-knuckled and work-roughened. I learned later that most of her life had been spent on a farm, where she had worked side by side with her first husband at the heavy chores, as though she could atone in that manner for her failure to present him with sons to share his work. But Lemuel was a townsman, and such work was not called for. Lem owned and operated a livery stable and several small stores, and Patience directed all her considerable energy into her home and her garden. It was obvious that she took great delight in welcoming and pampering guests. She lost no time in leading us into the kitchen, where the air was heavy with the aroma of freshly baked

318

cake. She insisted we sit in the two most comfortable chairs, brought us each a glass of ale and set the pitcher down between us. Then she proceeded to put before us slices of thick-crusted bread still slightly warm from the oven, and an array of cheeses and meats and pickled vegetables it would have taken ten men to consume. Then, apparently having satisfied herself that we could survive for a few minutes without her ministrations, she excused herself, explaining that she must run next door to find her daughter and send her to find Lem. Patience returned a few minutes later from her errand, set a few more heavily laden plates before us, and then settled herself with her knitting until Lemuel and his stepdaughter came home.

Lemuel Parker was as small and slight as his wife was tall and big-boned, and somehow this seemed not incongruous, but right, as though their two extreme statures balanced one another. The same could be said of their personalities. Lem was pleasant enough, but his nature was so tempered with timidity that, if it hadn't been for his wife's enthusiasm for guests, he might not have been able to emerge at all as an individual. It was as though Patience's volubility reflected on him, and enabled him to be something he was not, while his quiet manner tended to keep Patience's personality from overwhelming guests. When seen separately, they didn't appear to match. But when placed together, they formed a perfect whole.

Eliza was a further surprise to us both. She was a tall slim girl, but not as tall as her mother. Her hair was that rarely seen golden-red shade, which contrasted richly with her milk-white skin. Her lips were red, her cheeks pink, and her eyes blue-green. When she smiled she exposed perfect teeth, startling in their whiteness. She was a study in pleasing color contrasts, and this even extended to her clothing. On that day, she was wearing a dress of bright lime green and darker green. I realized later that she always wore vivid colors which, on someone else, probably would have looked cheap and gaudy. But on Eliza, the brightness seemed natural, an extension of her own rich coloring. I could not begin to picture her in gray. She moved gracefully, effortlessly, about the kitchen, helping her mother. It was a surprise to learn that she was only fifteen. She looked and acted much older.

"Of course you'll stay for dinner," Patience said, handing Eliza five plates to set upon the table before we had a chance to refuse.

"If you're certain it won't be too much trouble," Johnny replied quickly, looking at me hopefully, his eyes begging me to join in his acceptance, which I did willingly.

"It's no trouble at all," Eliza answered, looking at Johnny and smiling. From that moment on, Lemuel, Patience, and I might not have even been in the room for all that Eliza and Johnny knew or cared. Johnny continued to talk with Lem, answering questions about his family, inquiring politely in return about Lem's life since the two older men had last seen each other. But no matter who he was addressing, or what he was saying, his words, his glances were all centered on Eliza, and whenever there was a lull in the conversation, they looked at each other and smiled.

We left about three in the afternoon, amid Patience's exhortations to come see them again soon, to stay with them next time we brought the coach to San Felipe.

"For myself, I'll be happy to, ma'am," Johnny said enthusiastically, then turned to me and asked when we were coming back again.

Surprised at his sudden change of mind, but well aware of what had prompted it, I answered, "In about six weeks, maybe two months or more. It's never definite. If the roads are too bad, we can't run for awhile."

"Well, you just come whenever you can, and mind you, we'll be disappointed if you don't both stay with us."

Johnny renewed his promise to accept their hospitality. I thanked Patience, said I usually stayed with the Stewarts, but that I would remember her offer if I ever needed a place to stay. The truth of the matter was that though I wanted to continue to stay at the Stewart place, I was certain that Thorne would object to my continued use of the cabin on his property now that Todd would no longer be with me. I realized that it had only been because of Todd that Thorne had tolerated my presence. I had already decided to talk with Angela the next day, to resolve the matter before we left. It was on her indecisiveness that I was banking. In this, as in anything else, I didn't think she would have the strength of character to form a definite opinion one way or the other. I hoped that she would at least fail to take a negative stand in the matter, and I intended to use this failure as an excuse to continue staying there, at least until the time Thorne heard about it and left instructions that I was no longer to be welcomed. This, I was certain, was only a matter of time, for Angela would not dare to defy his orders.

On the ride back to the Stewarts's, Johnny talked of little else but Eliza. "What a beauty! And the way she moves, so gracefully, she seems to float across the floor, did you notice? You know enough people around San Felipe. Could you find out if she's spoken for? Not that it makes any difference if I find out she is. I'm going to marry her, one way or the other."

"Marry her?" I repeated in surprise. "But you only just met her!"

"What does that matter? I intend to get to know her a whole lot better before I propose, of course, but that's a mere formality. Once I get my own place, I'll be anxious to settle down. I'll be twenty-one in December, and I expect to apply for my own land then." He grinned. "I've considered the idea of settling down, but until today, it's never seemed so inviting."

"You certainly lost no time in making up your mind."

"No reason to. Of course, it's different with you. You and Cassie have known each other for a long time—"

"Cassie?" I looked at him, frankly puzzled at the turn his talk had taken.

He seemed as surprised by my reaction as I had been by the words that caused it. "Don't tell me the thought of marrying her has never entered your head!"

321

"Actually, it never has, her or anybody, not yet—"

He shook his head in disbelief. "Well, I can tell you, it sure Lord has occurred to her. It's plain enough to tell how she feels every time she looks at you."

"You're imagining things," I scoffed. "My visits help to break up the dull routine of her days, that's all. She doesn't have an easy time of it, taking care of her mother. Sometimes it seems to me that Angela is still punishing her for frightening her that time she ran off." I told Johnny about the time Cassie had followed me, and how we had returned to find Angela bedridden. "Cassie feels she's responsible for her mother's state, and Angela takes advantage of that to practically enslave her," I finished. "Cassie wouldn't leave her, I don't think, not to marry anybody. I guess she's sort of promised to Jeremy Butler, or at least her father and his seem to think it's all settled."

"Does she want to marry this Jeremy?"

"I guess not. A while back she said she didn't."

"Well, then? You said she never gets out to meet anybody. I'd say that clears the road for you."

"Not with Thorne standing in the middle of it, it doesn't," I answered, surprised to realize I was actually discussing the possibility of marrying Cassie. "Thorne and I—well, we don't get along. I think he'd almost rather see his daughter dead than give his permission for her to marry me. I doubt that I'll even be welcome to stay in his house now that Todd has stopped coming."

He nodded his understanding. "Because of him and your mother, I suppose."

Too shocked to answer—not only by his words, but also by the casual manner in which he had said them—I made no reply. He had mentioned it so offhandedly, as if it were common knowledge. Was it? How many other people knew?

We rode in silence most of the way back to the Stewart place, and after a while, my thoughts returned to what he had said about Cassie. I had never really stopped thinking of her as the foolish and fearless young child who had so craved excitement and so feared to be left out of an adventure that she had determinedly set out to follow me through Kronk country. I suspected that the adventurous spirit that had driven her to such foolhardy action was still there. But now it was controlled, contained, and the foolish child had become a sensible young woman—far too solemn, far too sensible for a girl of seventeen, I thought. Still, I had a feeling that, given a chance, the spirit of recklessness, the yearning for adventure that had driven her then would again assert itself, that it was subdued only temporarily, held captive by her guilty feelings about her mother's illness and her need to atone for what she felt she had done. I didn't see that anything short of Angela's death would set her free, and callously, for Cassie's sake, I couldn't help but hope that Angela's life would not be prolonged for many more years. I didn't think it likely; each time I came, Angela seemed a little paler, her arms appeared yet more frail and fleshless than they had the time before, and her voice sounded weaker and yet more whining. Still, it was hard to tell. Sometimes, people like that cling stubbornly to the thin thread of life endlessly, for years and years.

It was odd that it took Johnny's words to make me see Cassie in a different light, awaken me to her obvious charms. Until that day, I had never even considered the idea of marrying, except in an abstract manner. What, after all, could I offer a wife? I had written endless letters to an endless number of people in my desperate attempt to obtain official confirmation of my right to inherit the property which had been handed down from one generation of Vargas to another. But my efforts to date had produced no effect, and I knew I must take more drastic action if I were ever to get anything done. Though I had mentioned it to no one but my officer friends in San Antonio de Bexar, I had been giving serious thought to the possibility of going into the Mexican army when I reached twenty-one, which would be just over a year away.

If the matter of the Varga grant had been settled, I doubt if I would have considered the idea of entering the army. I

323

had been saving almost everything I had earned, and if the matter of my land had been resolved, I might well have thought of settling down some time in the near future. Once I was settled and had things going, I would probably have thought about taking a wife.

I did not confide these thoughts to Johnny. What would the revelation that I was considering becoming an officer in the Mexican army do, what effect would it have on my friendship with Johnny? Or Jeremy? Or Todd? Or Cassie? I felt as though I were walking on the top of a wall that was becoming progressively higher and higher, knowing that before it became too high I must jump to the ground one way or the other. I remembered my conversation with Todd a few weeks earlier, and how he had asked me not to choose sides, at least for the time being. How long would I be able to keep that promise?

But that decision was still almost a year away, and there was a more immediate problem facing me. The following evening, I went in to talk to Angela about the matter of my continuing to stay at the Stewart place. As always, I inquired about her health before I spoke of anything else. And also as always, my queries produced a boring accounting of the day's discomforts and displeasures.

I listened as she told me of her lack of appetite, the chill of the air creeping in around the cracks in the window frame. She seemed to enjoy the opportunity to focus her attention on her declining health. It gave her something close at hand to hold her attention, so that she could forget the larger fears she had been unable to face. Surely she must have known long ago that she had lost her husband, but by continuing to think only in terms of the trivialities that made up her own limited life, she had no need to face this unpleasant fact. She leaned now not on her husband's strength, but on her daughter's. Like a parasite that saps the strength of the host on which it feeds, her demands upon Cassie's vitality were endless.

As soon as Angela paused in her complaints, I took the opportunity to turn the subject away. I reminded her that

324

Todd would seldom be coming any more, asked if she preferred that I stay elsewhere.

"But why?" she asked querulously. "You're such a help fixing things about the house. Thorne is never home long enough to make any repairs any more, and Daniel—well, he always needed Thorne to prod him. Will does try, but he just lacks the knack. Cassie tells me we really do need you, Felipe, to keep things going around here."

"I'm happy to help all I can," I said, pleasantly surprised—and just a little astounded—at her answer.

"I know that Thorne and you have never gotten on well, and that he might object if he knew. So we just won't tell him."

I couldn't believe I had heard her right, but I nodded, stood up. "Then I'll be happy to continue to stay here, ma'am," I said. "And now I'm sure you'd like to rest. I don't want to tire you." Quickly, before she could call me back and say she had changed her mind, I hurried from the room.

In the parlor, Cassie and Will were seated on the braided rug near the fire, watching Johnny, seated across from them, shuffle a deck of cards. Johnny loved card games, and had brought the deck with him. Unlike Todd, who gambled heavily at times, Johnny played only for fun. Will and Cassie had never seen playing cards before he came, and they were enthralled with them. Each evening, the four of us sat on the rug in the parlor, playing one or another of the endless varieties of easily learned card games Johnny suggested. At first, Cassie had not played, insisting that she must use the evenings to keep up with her mending and sewing. But finally she could not stand being left out. She had put aside her sewing basket and had joined us. In those few short days, she had become the most avid cardplayer of us all.

As I entered the room, Cassie jumped up, came over to put her hand on my arm. "What did she say?" she asked anxiously. I raised my eyebrows at her questioningly, wondering how she had known what it was I had spoken about to Angela. She told me that Johnny had told her about it that morning. "This afternoon, I sort of told her all the reasons we had to have you stay here . . ."

I laughed. "So that's where she got all those ideas about how much good my visits do! Was it your idea for her not to tell your father, too?"

She blushed, lowered her eyes. "Well, I did suggest that it might be best if we just didn't mention it to him." She looked up at me, and a smile broke over her face. "She agreed, then? Oh, Felipe, I'm so glad! It would be unbearably dull around here without your visits! It would be terrible if you couldn't come here any more!" She threw her arms around my neck.

Surprised at the suddenness of her action, I was even more surprised to find myself overcome with the desire to keep her just where she was. As I put my arms around her and held her for a minute, my eyes caught Johnny's over her shoulder. He was looking at me with a knowing grin and a scarcely perceptible nod of his head, as though he were saying, *See, what did I tell you?*

I grinned back at him. I couldn't deny I was enjoying the moment.

As Cassie and I took our places on the floor, a frown darkened her face. "Just what is it between you and Papa, anyway?" She picked up her cards and sorted them.

"Does everyone have ten cards?" Johnny asked.

"What game are we playing?" Will asked, after we had all ascertained that we had ten cards in our hands.

"It's a new game," Johnny said. "I'll have to explain the rules."

Cassie was not to be denied, persisted, "Is it because he blames you for that time I ran away and followed you? But that was so long ago, and it wasn't your fault!"

"It's nothing you can change," I answered tersely, seeing that she was not going to be put off by my ignoring her questions.

"But why, then—?"

"You start, Cassie," Johnny said, and then went into an

326

explanation of the game. I shot him a grateful glance as Cassie turned her attention to what he was saying and became engrossed in the game. She had apparently never suspected that the reason for Thorne's prolonged absences from his home and the reason for our hatred of each other were one and the same.

After that, I stayed alone in the cabin on the Stewart place whenever we brought the coach to San Felipe, and Johnny stayed in town with the Parkers. He soon found that there were already a number of contenders for Eliza's hand, and he also discovered that Patience would not allow Eliza to choose among them until she approached her eighteenth birthday, which would not be until September of 1833. But even though there would be no officially announced commitment for some time, it was clear that Eliza had already made her choice.

"I've half a notion to carry her off come December next," Johnny complained one day as we were taking the coach toward Gonzales some months after they met. "What if someone else comes along when I'm not here, sweeps her off her feet—?"

"It appears to me you've already done the sweeping," I said with a laugh. "I can't see you have any problem, besides waiting for her longer than you'd like to."

In the spring of that year, I had brought Cassie a deck of cards, and it had become our regular habit to play cards in the evenings. Will didn't always join us, for he often preferred to work on one or another of his drawings. He had begun to use some of the oil paints Priscilla Butler had given him, but those he worked with only in the daylight, and he still seemed to prefer pen and ink and charcoal sketchings to working in color. One summer evening, he sat silently sketching as Cassie and I played cards, and after we had finished, he handed us two pen and ink drawings of ourselves. The likenesses were good enough, but he had caught more than that: he had trapped on the paper our laughter, our pleasure. There was such an economy of line that I would have thought he had done the drawings in

327

only minutes had I not known they had taken him the better part of the evening to complete.

My interest in the drawings pleased Cassie as well as Will, and she told him to get his animal sketches to show me. When he left the room, she said, "Animals are what he does best, and I've encouraged him to keep the best of his drawings separate. He doesn't show them much, because of Papa."

"Your father objects?"

"He thinks only dotty old spinsters paint and draw, or so he says."

"But Will is good! He should encourage him!"

"I know. To Will, his animals and his drawings—well, these two things mean everything to him. They're not just hobbies, they're his whole life, and I know he wouldn't be happy without either."

"How about girls? Magda Schmidt seems to be over here quite a bit, and she and Will always seem to have their heads together about something."

"About their animals," Cassie said, laughing. "It's her interest in horses and animals that interests Will. She has her own menagerie and is always coming here to ask Will what to do about one or another of her pets."

Will returned with his portfolio, and I looked through it with interest. In the sketches he had made of us, he had caught the essence of our foolish laughter more faithfully than the actual forms of our faces. In his other drawings, this was even more true. He had put into his picture the shakiness of a newborn colt trying his knobby little legs for the first time, the placidity of a cow lying lazily in the shade, the alertness of a bird poised for flight. There was no facet of animal or bird life he had omitted: on one drawing, he even had the vultures lighting on the carcass of a dead puma and preparing to feed off its entrails. I could even sense in that picture the revulsion with which he had faithfully recorded what he saw, and I knew without being told that it had taken a lot of effort on his part to keep himself from turning away. But he had not turned away, and had caught in his drawing the callousness of the natural world: one thing feeding upon another, and that upon yet another, until the cycle came around full circle, endlessly on and on.

When I had finished looking at the drawings and commenting on them, Will separated two from the others and made them into a roll.

"Would you take these to your mother for me?"

"My mother?" I questioned, surprised, as I took them from him. I knew that he and Cassie had met her once or twice, and they always inquired politely after her health, but in all the time I'd been going between the two houses, I had never carried any personal messages back and forth.

Will nodded, smiling. "I gave her a picture of a rabbit once, because she said she liked it. Maybe she'll like these. Anyway, it would please me if she took them."

"Can Felipe and I keep the drawings you made of us?" Cassie asked.

"If you want them," he agreed. Then he gathered up his remaining drawings and said good night.

When he had left the room, Cassie said, "You know, I always ask you how your mother is, and you always say she's fine, and that's the end of it. But how is she, really? Does she like Gonzales? Is she happy there? I always felt— well, that she belonged sort of specially to the place you had in Nacogdoches."

"She did belong there."

"I know, but I mean that it seemed she was a part of the place. When I saw her the first time, I was reminded of a picture I had seen once of a queen, and that's the way I always thought of her, as if the land around there was her kingdom. I'll bet she misses it."

"She keeps herself busy," I evaded.

"Does she still read poems? I remember that day I went to show Will the pond I'd found on Papa's land." She caught my eye and grinned. "On your land," she amended hastily. "She was there, sitting on the ground near the pond, and she was reading a book of poems. I still remember, it was by Lord Byron."

"I gave her that book. I wanted to buy her something special out of my first wages, and I knew a book would please her most, but there weren't many of them to choose from in Nacogdoches."

"I was surprised to find her reading, because you'd said she was half Comanche, and I didn't think Indians ever knew how to read. And there she was, reading poetry! I was certainly surprised."

I laughed. "Mother reads anything she can get her hands on."

"I don't imagine she has so much time for reading in Gonzales."

I looked at her sharply. How much did she know, or guess? "What makes you say that?" I heard the harshness in my own voice.

"Now that Gonzales is getting so big, I imagine she has lots of friends. I hear there are about five hundred people there now."

Relieved at her answer, I said, "She's not right in town."

"Uncle Todd said you and he fixed up a place for the coach passengers behind her house, so they could stay there overnight."

I nodded. "We've got some other places we can stop along the road, too." I hoped my reply would lead her thoughts away from Gonzales, away from my mother. I did not want her to know that the thing that most occupied my mother's time was caring for her father's bastard and, much of the time, for her father as well.

But her thoughts remained on Gonzales, circling around dangerous ground. "I suppose Papa stays there when he goes through Gonzales."

"I suppose." I tried to sound casual, unconcerned.

"You suppose? Don't you know?"

"I'm not home much. How do I know if he stops when I'm not there?" I couldn't keep the irritability out of my voice.

330

She sighed exasperatedly. "You don't have to get angry, just because I asked you about Papa and you don't like him." She started gathering up the playing cards still scattered on the floor and I helped her, relieved that she had placed her own interpretation on my irritation.

I had come to feel very protective where Cassie was concerned. Originally, my reason for not wanting her to find out about Thorne and my mother, about Tico, had been because I had wanted to protect my mother from the shame that would fall on her for being the mother of Thorne's bastard child. *But now,* I thought as I helped Cassie gather the cards, *I would be more concerned about the effect the news would have on Cassie.* Five years before, when I had gone to work in Nacogdoches, I had considered myself grown, the head of the family that consisted only of the two of us, and I had felt, pompously, that my mother needed my care, my protection. Perhaps that was what had angered me and upset me as much as anything when she had told me about her and Thorne, and the child she was to bear him, for she had made it plain that she had never needed or wanted me to protect her from him, and I felt rebuffed and hurt.

Now it was Cassie whom I felt I must protect as much as I could, must shield from the truth as much as it was in my power to do so. Even though I despised Thorne, I could not bring myself to destroy Cassie's love for him, her loyalty to him in the face of his desertion of her and Will and her mother. I sensed her need to retain her faith in her father.

Feeling very tender toward her, I stood up, offered her my hand to pull her to her feet, watched her as she laid the drawings and the cards on the table, next to the silver tea service. There was no fire that night, for it was August and there had been no need of one. She picked up the candelabrum from the hearth, and I saw the sparkle of the light on her bracelets as she blew out the candles, one by one. I heard the scrape of metal across the stone as she put the candelabrum back in place. My arms reached out for her, found her. I took her face in my hands, kissed her lips softly, easily.

"Good night, little love. Sleep well."

"Good night, Felipe," she whispered, and there was something special about the way she spoke my name. We lingered there, knowing the moment was important to us, neither of us anxious for it to end.

But time and Angela intruded, and the harsh jangling of Angela's bell ended the moment abruptly. With a sigh of reluctance, we drew apart.

The next morning, Will's sketch of me was missing from the table. I smiled, took the sketch of Cassie and rolled it up with the other two sketches Will had given me, knowing that there was one of them I would not give to my mother.

After that, Cassie and I always found brief moments for quick stolen kisses and short embraces, and for a time, that was enough. I brought Cassie silver earrings to match the bracelets she always wore. She was delighted with the new present, and didn't seem to even care that Will was in the room as she threw her arms around me and kissed me.

In January of 1832, Todd made one final trip to San Felipe. He had been to Bexar a month earlier, and when he returned, said he had arranged for me to pick up a middle-aged Mexican serving woman named Esperanza.

When I returned with her to Gonzales, he said, "Good. Now we'll take her to San Felipe to take care of Angela."

"We?" I questioned, surprised.

He nodded. It was the first time he had mentioned his intention of going with Johnny and me that trip. The weather was cold and bitter, and I remembered he had specifically said he did not want to travel in the winter.

"Cassie will be nineteen in May," he said. "If Thorne won't see to her welfare, and would use her as though she were one of his slaves, then it's up to me to do something about it. If I haven't been misled, Esperanza's the best worker in all of Bexar, and I hope I've offered her high enough wages to entice her to stay, and to put up with Angela's incessant demands. I have high hopes of it all working out well. That's why I'm going with you. I'm determined to see that it does work, and to make Cassie understand that I am ordering her out of the house."

"You'll never get her to leave her mother for more than five minutes at a time," I said dubiously.

"She'll leave her," he answered with a tightening of his lips.

Cassie and Will were amazed to see that Todd was with us, and delighted. When they had finished greeting him, Todd brought Esperanza forward and told Cassie why he had brought her. "If she agrees to stay, I'll have Felipe bring her daughter next trip."

"It will certainly be nice, having someone to help." Cassie smiled at Esperanza and received a smile in return. That began a relationship that worked well from the start. Cassie spoke only a few words of Spanish, and Esperanza's English was limited to five or six words, but somehow they managed from the first to communicate perfectly, as though no language barrier existed.

"We're going to get you out of this house, young lady," Todd said sternly to Cassie, "starting tomorrow morning."

"Tomorrow? Oh, no, I couldn't! Mama—"

"—Can get used to Esperanza," Todd finished emphatically.

"But Esperanza can't speak any English, can she? And Mama doesn't know a word of Spanish. I couldn't leave her, not so soon. Maybe in a few weeks—"

"You'll be surprised how fast Angela will learn, if she wants something badly enough," Todd said acidly.

After he let us off at the Stewart place, Johnny had, as usual, taken the coach on to San Felipe, and Todd insisted that, the next day, Cassie go with me to visit the Parkers. "It's all arranged," he said when Cassie continued to protest. "Johnny will tell the Parkers you're coming. I think that Patience's Eliza is near enough your age, and I hope you'll be friends."

Cassie was still objecting next morning, but Todd silenced her and said firmly, "You'll go. Right now, why don't

333

you run into your room and see what I had Esperanza put on your bed? I had Will send me the measurements of some of your clothes, so they ought to fit."

Unable to resist the promise of a present, Cassie ran into her room, and Todd chuckled when he heard her gasp of delight. A few minutes later, she came out, wearing a buckskin riding outfit, much like the ones he had ordered made for her when she was younger, the skirt split so that it was really wide-legged trousers, but that fact was cleverly disguised by the fullness of the legs and a deep pleat in the back and the front. The new buckskin was bright butternut yellow, and the contrast made Cassie's hair look even darker and richer than usual. On the jacket and the skirt, there was green beading, and I wondered if Todd had had my mother add that, because the pattern was one I recognized as especially hers.

Cassie came out and twirled for our benefit. "It's perfect!" she said.

"If there's ever any need for you to move fast, you can jump astride a horse and ride hell-for-leather," Todd said approvingly, as he watched her.

"But you're the one who talked me into riding a side-saddle!"

"There are times when you might need to hurry, and there's nothing wrong with riding astride at such times."

"Last week, some folks who stopped here were telling about a couple of riders who were found out west—"

He nodded, knew she understood. "You'll be safe enough on your sidesaddle today, with Felipe to take care of you."

She laughed. "I'm sure of that. He's the one who taught me to watch where I was going. The only trouble is that I haven't gone anywhere in so long I'm not sure I remember my lessons."

"Then he'll just have to start today, teaching you again." He leaned down and kissed her cheek. "Have a nice day, my dear. I've had Will saddle your horses."

334

"But I can't leave right now! I haven't shown Esperanza—"

"She'll figure out what she has to know, never you worry. She was the best maid in Bexar. I stole her right away from a general's wife! Now get going, you two. I'll tell your mother you've gone, Cassie, don't go in there now or you'd never get away. I told Johnny you'd be there by midmorning, and you don't want to keep Patience Parker waiting."

Cassie threw her arms around Todd and buried her face in his shoulder. "Uncle Todd, you're so good to me!" She turned and ran out the door so eagerly it was hard to realize that a few minutes earlier she had been insisting she couldn't leave Angela.

Cassie had tied her hair back away from her face with a bright green ribbon. She looked more carefree and more radiantly happy than I had ever seen her.

We talked little as we rode, but it was not an uncomfortable silence. I sensed that Cassie preferred not to talk, that she was busy filling her eyes and ears with the sights and sounds she had missed. Once, she had taken them for granted, but now they held her enthralled. She was taking in everything, in much the same manner as a starving man clutches hungrily at food. Occasionally, she would comment on something, or merely point to it wordlessly: a tree that had grown much taller than she remembered it, a new fence, a barn that had been raised since she'd passed by. Just outside of San Felipe, a tin peddler passed us, leading a pack horse loaded down with a clanging array of everything metallic that was light enough for him to carry: pewter dishes, needles, pins, scissors, forks and spoons, mirrors, and even a few small cooking pots and their lids. Cassie paused after he passed us, and motioned for me to be silent and listen. The swaying movement of the animal formed the rhythmic basis of a metallic symphony, and the breeze that blew through the assorted wares added to the melody. As the peddler moved out of earshot, Cassie smiled wordlessly and we continued on our way.

335

Patience had outdone herself preparing for our visit, had baked meat pies and spitted three hens, which Johnny was conscientiously turning over the fire for her. She hugged Cassie to her warmly, as though she were greeting one of her own daughters instead of a young girl she had never seen before. Eliza's greeting lacked the force of her mother's, but it was none the less warm, and later, when Lem came home for dinner, he, too, made Cassie feel she was welcome. I could sense that she was basking in the warmth of their hospitality and friendliness.

It was plain to see that Cassie enjoyed every minute of that day, and when Patience interrupted the card game we were playing that afternoon to tell us that she had prepared a snack for us to eat before we started back, Cassie said with obvious disappointment, "Is it that late already? I didn't realize it was almost time to leave."

"I'm afraid you must leave soon, if you're to get home before dark, my dear." Patience rested her hand momentarily on Cassie's shoulder and smiled. "But we won't let you go without a promise to come see us again soon, you know."

Cassie looked up at Patience and smiled, and seeing the two of them together, it struck me that Cassie's whole life would have been different, and so much better, if she had had a mother like Patience. It was not that I doubted Cassie's love for Angela, but pity had to be too much a part of her devotion. And, in recent years, guilt must have colored her feelings for her mother as well. The love Angela gave in return, though undoubtedly sincere in her own mind, was warped and selfish, and it asked, demanded everything, giving nothing in return. Patience's love was expansive and giving and asked for nothing in return.

"You know I'll be back, just as soon as I can manage to get away," Cassie answered. I hoped that, with Esperanza's help, she would manage often. Cassie chatted and laughed happily as we rode back, but as we neared the Stewart place, she stopped chattering, and her laughter died away. She slowed her horse to a walk and said wistfully, "I wish we

336

could just keep going, all the way to Gonzales, and then to Bexar. I suppose Gonzales is about like San Felipe used to be, but Bexar seems so far away, so unreal. Tell me about it, Felipe."

I had described it all to her before, but I knew she wanted to hear me tell about it again, so I did. I told her of the narrow streets and adobe buildings, some of them painted white, a few painted bright and even gaudy colors, most of them just the color of the earth from which they were made. I told her of the different missions, the one with the rose window supposedly carved by a disappointed lover, the Alamo with its church roof gone, its walls partially caved in. And I described the way I had seen the Indians swaggering through the streets on many occasions. "The American School there is getting lots bigger, I hear," I said, thinking that might be of special interest to her. "Quite a few Americans live there now, but somehow they just haven't been able to change the place much. It's still an old Spanish mission town, as different from San Felipe as day is from night."

"Will you take me there someday?"

"If you want to go, if you wouldn't be afraid some Comanche might lift your scalp."

"I wouldn't be afraid, not with you."

The Stewart house came into view, and Cassie halted her horse. "I hate to go home, because I don't want this day to end. It's been—well, it's been almost magical to me."

"The magic is inside you," I said, pulling my horse alongside of hers and reaching out for her hand.

Her fingers responded as my hand closed around hers. "But you're all a part of it—you and Johnny and Eliza, and the Parkers, and Uncle Todd. Today I feel I'm somebody special, somebody quite apart from the girl who was scrubbing the hearth when you came yesterday."

"Both those girls are special to me."

She smiled. "I remember reading a story once, long ago, about a girl who was changed magically from a ragged creature into a beautiful girl in a lovely ball gown. She was

337

whisked away to a castle, and she had a wonderful time, until suddenly the magic ended, and she found herself again in rags. I feel that's what happened to me today. I've felt so carefree, so special, and I almost forgot about how things were yesterday, and the day before, and the day before that. But now I can see the house, and I know I must go back, where things will be like they were before the magic. And I'm a little reluctant to return." She smiled again, this time her smile tinged with sadness. "I'm afraid I'll look down and find Uncle Todd's lovely new riding outfit has disappeared and left only one of my work dresses instead."

"You have Esperanza now," I reminded her. "Things won't ever be as bad as they were before."

"Yes, and she's going to be wonderful, I can tell that already. But in a few days, you'll be leaving again—you and Uncle Todd and Johnny—and when you go, the magic will be gone with you. It's never less than five or six weeks before you come back. And I don't think Uncle Todd will ever come here again."

I didn't deny her words about Todd, for I had seen the supreme effort this trip had cost him. No, he would never be back. "He's getting old."

She nodded. "I know, and it's sad. He's the only uncle I've ever had, besides Uncle Thaddeus. Uncle Todd is the one who made the magic, because he brought Esperanza, and brought me this lovely riding outfit and pushed me out of the house. I'll never stop being grateful to him. And you—well, I haven't told you all of the story. There was a prince, too."

"A prince?" I laughed. "I'm not—"

"At the end of the story, he found the girl and took her away with him."

She looked up at me, and as our eyes met and held, it seemed as though we were looking into each other's hearts. More and more, we understood each other, our growing commitment to one another. But as always between us was

338

the image of Thorne, as real as though he was physically separating us, keeping us apart.

"And what about the dragon? Surely there's a dragon who is determined to keep the prince from carrying her away?" I tried to make my question sound light and foolish, but I couldn't keep the bitterness from edging into my words, my voice.

She bit her lower lip absently, as she did whenever she was upset. "You mean Papa?"

"Who else?"

"But there isn't any dragon in the story I read," she protested, and her words sounded like a desperate plea. "Maybe you're wrong, maybe if you'd only try to like Papa, you'd find he doesn't really hate you at all."

I smiled at her, not wanting to say more, spoiling for her a day that had been so perfect. Already, I had said too much. I released her hand. "We'd better get back."

She sighed. "I suppose. Only promise you'll try . . ."

She didn't finish the sentence, and I smiled again, to soften the denial made by my silence. Slowly, hesitantly, we walked our horses back to the Stewart place.

# Chapter V

## THE BEXAR ROAD—January 1832

By the time we left three days later, it was clear that the arrival of Esperanza was going to make a big difference in Cassie's life. For the first few days, Angela had behaved sulkily and peevishly if Esperanza answered her summons or brought her food in place of Cassie, but she soon came to accept the presence of the stocky peasant woman, and she even began to eat better for her. Two days after Cassie and I rode into Bexar, I happened to be there when Esperanza returned Angela's lunch tray to the kitchen. The soup bowl and the plate on it were both empty. Often before, I had noticed the food tray returning from the invalid's room virtually untouched; never had I seen it come back with the food all gone.

"Mrs. Stewart was hungry today," I commented in Spanish, indicating the empty dishes.

Esperanza shook her head and laughed. "She said she was not hungry, not even a little bit, and pushed her tray aside, but I told her I would not rub her back tonight if she did not finish her food." She hesitated a minute, then added, "When she wants something, I also make her say the word for it in Spanish before I will give it to her." She looked up at me questioningly, as though she was not quite certain she should have revealed so much.

I laughed, hugged her. "Esperanza, you're a tyrant!"

Surprised, she smiled broadly as I released her. "I make it easier for *Señorita* Cassie, is it not so? She is very young, and it is not right that she should stay always in the house because of her mother."

"You make it much easier for her," I agreed readily. "You aren't sorry you came, are you? You won't leave, will you?" I had been afraid, at first, that she might find Angela too difficult, might regret having come, but my fears had eased when I saw the way she settled easily and efficiently into her new work. Still, I was anxious to hear her confirm my hopes.

"But of course I will stay," she answered with an air of certainty, as if to assure me that the idea of leaving had never crossed her mind.

"Next time I come back, I will bring your daughter."

"That will be nice, *Señor* Felipe," she answered with an enthusiastic nod of her head. "I will like that very much."

I turned to leave and she resumed her work, singing happily in her low husky voice as she bustled busily about the kitchen. She always attacked her work vigorously, as though disorder and dirt were her personal enemies. Several times I had heard Cassie suggest that she rest a while, but she always said that she would just finish what she was doing, and rest later. But after she finished one job, she immediately began on another. Smiling to myself, I wondered whether there would be enough work remaining to keep Esperanza's daughter occupied. Certainly, Cassie's life was going to be much more pleasant.

The following morning, Johnny came riding out with the news that four people wanted to leave San Felipe for San Antonio de Bexar the following day. Our schedule was determined strictly by demand, and the coach had already been declared fit for another journey, so we arranged to leave early the next morning.

Cassie and Will came outside to see us off. They were disappointed to have Todd's visit cut so short, and they both looked solemn as they said good-bye to him.

Todd had said his other final farewells the previous afternoon. After Johnny had returned to San Felipe, I had seen Todd dig up some small evergreens and carry the plants toward the two graves a little way from the house. Later, when he returned, he looked so woeful and his steps were so slow and heavy that I wanted to say something to cheer him. I wished I could have promised to look after the graves for him, but I couldn't make such a promise, for I knew I might not be able to fulfill it. When I reached San Antonio de Bexar, I would talk with my army officer friends and make my decision on whether or not to go to Mexico City. It was likely I would go, and if I did, I would probably remain there and enlist in the army, if I could get a commission. In that case, my next trip to San Felipe with the coach would be my last one.

It was four days later when we reached Gonzales. I spent the night with Todd, as I always did when I found that Thorne was staying at my mother's.

"We didn't expect you back so soon," my mother said when she came out to greet us, as though that explained Thorne's presence, and excused it. We arrived late in the afternoon, and Tico ran out to greet me with his usual puckish enthusiasm. I picked him up and swung him around and gave him a piece of sugarcane I had brought for him. I heard stirrings inside the house, and knew Thorne was in there. I did not go in, nor did he come out.

Since Thorne was spending so much of his time in Gonzales, it was inevitable that he and I would occasionally be there at the same time, but I had not so much as caught a glimpse of him for over a year. Whenever I arrived at my mother's, I quickly looked for signs of his presence, and if I knew that he was in the house, I left without going inside. If it happened that he arrived when I was staying at home, I quickly disappeared at the first sound of his approach. I didn't want to see him swaggering around inside her house, acting as though he owned it, and her and Tico as well. I remembered that often when I was little, I would close my eyes or look the other way to shut out the sight of some unpleasantness that it was beyond my power to change. I still recalled vividly the time when I had run out of the house behind my father before I realized he was carrying the dead baby to which my mother had given birth only a few days earlier. My father had been preoccupied with his own thoughts and hadn't been aware of my running behind him. He went out to the barn and laid the tiny body down on some straw, and when I saw it, so still and lifeless, I burst into tears, more for the finality and cruelty of death itself than for the brother I had never known. My father had turned as soon as he heard my sobs, and knelt to put his arms around me.

"Poor little Felipe! You would have liked a little brother, wouldn't you?" He pulled my head down on his shoulder, and I felt a deep sob shake him. "You had better go back in the house for now, with your mother."

"I think she's asleep," I said, sniffling. "Anyway, I want to stay with you and help you." As distasteful and repellent to me as was the starkness of my first glimpse of human death, I sensed my father's deep grief, and I wanted to stay with him and comfort him, even as I was comforted by him. He was so strong and sure, and I was frightened by the realization that anything in the world could be terrible enough to make him cry. My eyes fell again on the tiny corpse, which had had that power, and I was shaken anew by the sight, and burst into fresh tears. "I want to help you," I insisted again, clamping my eyelids down tightly to shut out the fearful sight, surprised at how much it helped not to look at it.

"Of course you do," he said, patting my shoulder. "He was your brother."

I clung desperately to him for a minute longer, my need for his reassuring nearness only slightly more overpowering than my revulsion at the sight of death, and my desire to turn away and run from it.

He sent me to the other side of the barn on an errand, and when I returned, the baby was wrapped in several layers of cloth, and had become only a bundle. It was no longer a human shape, no longer so terrible. Even though I knew the contents of the cloth bundle, not having to look at the still tiny face and the unmoving limbs made it easier to accept, and I soon forced myself to think of other things until, as I helped my father build the small coffin and bury it, I could almost forget what was inside.

Maybe it was childish of me to react in the same manner to Thorne's presence in my mother's house. I knew he came regularly, knew he spent much more of his time there than he did with his family, and yet I chose not to be a witness to his presence, felt that in that manner I could ignore my mother's role as his mistress as much as it was possible to do so.

It was late that night by the time Todd and I had settled down to go to sleep. I had put some quilts on the floor for myself, for he had only one bed in his cabin. Though I had been up since before dawn and would be on my way again early the next day, still I was unable to sleep. I tossed and turned, thinking of the future. Sleep would not come. Finally, I got up and dressed, then walked quietly outside, closing the door softly behind me.

The night air was crisp and cold, but there was no wind, so it was not unpleasant. Just outside the cabin door, I sat on the bench that Todd called his smoking bench, which he and I had made long before. In only five or six hours, Johnny and I would resume our trip to San Antonio de Bexar, and when we arrived, I would have to make the long-deferred decision about my future, would have to decide which way to go, on which side of that high wall I must jump to earth. I could no longer delay choosing sides.

In all likelihood, if I went to Mexico City, I would stay and would join the army. The matter of the Varga grant would probably not be something that could be settled overnight in my favor, not even if I was lucky enough to reach the proper authorities at once. It was apt to drag on for many months, perhaps even for years. If I could not immediately find someone who would approve my claim, then surely the best thing for me to do was to join the army as I waited—and strived—for that approval.

But my action would go much deeper than that. It would be more than just something to do with myself as I remained in the national capital and made friends, sought out the right people. By joining the army, I would be showing that I had chosen to defend the Mexican flag against those who would defy it.

Yes, if I did go to Mexico City, it was bound to lead to the irreversible decision, the long-delayed jump from the wall. Once that jump was made, the irritation and indecision that had troubled me almost since the day I saw the first Americans coming into Nacogdoches would be resolved. I would no longer be passively accepting their presence, the possibility that they would somehow manage to get Texas away from Mexico and into their own precious union.

I felt that the time was drawing near when everyone would have to make a similar decision, for I realized that all Americans didn't think in terms of taking Texas away from Mexico. There were those who would not have hesitated a minute to snatch Texas by force if they had thought there was any possibility of success, but there were still a number of others who were appalled at the idea of such perfidy. And in the middle, only caring about their day-to-day living, were others, committed to neither one course of action nor the other, because it simply hadn't occurred to them to think about it. But the day was coming when everyone, even the most passive of the Americans, would have to choose one side or the other.

The activists had jumped on the high-handed actions of certain Mexican army officers in Texas, and each complaint they uttered, each expression of indignation contributed a little more height to the wall developing between the two factions; on one side, there were those who accepted Mexico's right to impose her rule on all who lived within her borders, and, on the other, those who were willing to concede to Mexico only a passive role in governing them. The latter claimed the right to resist any restraints on their actions or the enforcement of any laws they personally disliked, and many of them would have welcomed even the feeblest excuse to take up arms, if they had thought there was any chance of winning against the whole of Mexico. Obviously, it must be the Mexican army that would stop them, put down any attempted insurrection. If I were to become a part of that army, would it shock my American friends? Most of all, I wondered, what would Cassie think of it?

I knew well enough by then that I wanted to ask Cassie to share whatever future I chose, but I felt I must settle things in my own mind before I spoke to her. If I became a Mexican army officer, would she see the sense of it, understand my pride in making that commitment? Jeremy had said that night the three of us sat on the porch steps at the Stewarts that we were all Texans. That was true only in a general sense, for I knew I was different. Unlike most of the other Texans, I had been there all my life, and my only loyalty was to the land that had nurtured me. That land was Mexico. That it had changed from the flag of the Spain of my father's people, when that country had become too weak to hold onto her New World possessions, to its own independent flag was unimportant. It was still my native land, still deserved my undiluted loyalty. This was not true of those Texans who had come from the United States, for their loyalties were halved at best.

Would Cassie understand all this? If I were to join the army, would she continue to feel the same about me as I thought she did then? All her life, she had been exposed to Thorne's belligerently anti-Mexican sentiments. Would she mirror those feelings? Would she feel, as he certainly did, that the Mexican army was to be derided, its officers ridiculed? Would she feel hurt, feel that if I went to Mexico City for a time and joined the army I would be denying her my first loyalty?

I heard the door beside me close. So engrossed had I been in my own thoughts that I hadn't heard it open. It was a cloudless night, and the moon was three-quarters full, so I could see Todd clearly as he walked over to a bush and broke off the end of a branch. Then he sat down next to me and took out his knife to trim the green twig to his satisfaction. Slowly, he removed his pipe from his pocket and began to push the twig into the stem, moving it back and forth. He often cleaned his pipe in that manner in idle moments, when there was no convenient fire from which he could catch a light for his beloved smoke.

"I couldn't sleep, either," he said at last. "Old age is my reason. Would you care to tell me yours?"

"I just couldn't sleep, that's all."

"Couldn't sleep," he repeated. "Mmmmm. In thirty, forty years, you might be troubled by some sleeplessness without having a specific reason for it, but right now I find it hard to believe that you're still awake unless there's something bothering you. If it is, it might help if you talk about it a little, instead of letting it stay inside you and eat on your stomach like a sour apple. Since Thorne came between you and your mother, you aren't as close to her, I know, so maybe you feel you can't talk to her any more."

I smiled, thinking how often he had listened sympathetically to my problems, large and small, real and imagined, over the past five years.

I hesitated, wondering where to begin and he asked, "Is it because of finding Thorne at your mother's today? Is that why you're upset?"

"No. I won't pretend that doesn't bother me, but that's not why I couldn't sleep. It's something else, something I have to make up my mind about. Do you remember—about a year ago, you asked me not to choose one side or the other, not to decide yet if I was on the side of the Mexicans or the Texans? I put off deciding, like you suggested, but I don't think I can put it off any longer. In fact, the way things are going, I think it might not be long before all of you Americans will have to make up your minds, too."

He made a small sound that sounded like, "Umhmm," and waited for me to continue.

"The way I see it, it's not necessarily just Mexicans on one side and Americans on the other. It's the authority of government that's in question. Who has the right to govern us? That's the real issue. Some of the Texans—and I hope

348

it's most of them, but I've no way of really knowing—accept the fact that they're in Mexico, and the Mexican government has the right to run its states however it wants to. But some of the Americans, like Thorne, won't accept Mexican rule. They never intended to accept it. Sure, they agreed to it when they came. They mouthed all the proper words and signed anything they had to sign, agreeing to become Catholics and Mexican citizens and obey Mexican laws. But they only did it to get their hands on some land, and they never for a minute had any intention of doing any of the things they promised."

"That's true enough," Todd drawled in his deep resonant voice. Much of the comfort I always derived from talking with him came as much from the smooth serenity of his voice as from what he said. "It's true many colonists didn't keep their promises to the Mexican government, but you mustn't forget, Felipe, that Mexico made promises to the colonists that haven't been kept, either. The Constitution of 1824 promised us we could have our own state government when we got big enough. We have upwards of twenty thousand Texans, and yet we're still tied to the state of Coahuila, whose population is far below ours and whose problems are in no way similar to our own. Nor is there a sign that anything's being done to change matters. You have to remember that we Americans are a touchy lot when it comes to the subject of states' rights and representative government—perhaps unreasonably so, but that's just the way it is. I suppose we got that way a couple of generations back. But it's not just us. In recent years, people all over the world have started clamoring for governments in which they have some sort of representation. Look at the way the Mexicans threw out the Spaniards, so that they could govern themselves! The common people have no way short of revolution to change things they find unpalatable, unless they have a voice in their own government."

"If the Americans weren't willing to accept the way things are here, they should have stayed home," I said testily.

"Maybe. But they didn't. They're here. They've worked hard clearing the land for their farms and building their cabins and houses and barns. This is their home now."

"But it was Mexico before it was their home, and they knew it was when they came here! Sure, this is a new country and we have problems. So did the United States at first. But we'll get things straightened out one of these days. And, in the meantime, that doesn't give anybody the right to disobey our laws."

"You mean like avoiding paying customs duties? I'll agree that's certainly one law the folks are eager to see changed. There's a good example of what I mean when I say that we Americans want representation in our government. If we had had fair representation and the law was made, we'd probably have been willing to accept it and obey it until such time as we were able to work to change it. But the way it is now, there's no hope of getting it changed, so we merely circumvent it."

I noted that he called himself an American, not a Texan. "But some of the Americans don't want to just change a few laws they don't like," I insisted. I knew I didn't have to tell him I was thinking primarily of Thorne. "They want to take Texas away from Mexico, by force if they have to, and they won't be satisfied till they do. You've told me yourself that the United States has been trying to buy it."

"That's true, and it's no secret. There are many who feel we made a terrible mistake back when we were settling borders with Spain. In effect, our government ceded Texas to Spain in return for the Spanish Floridas. It was a foolish thing to have done, to give away so much good land for a lot of swampland, especially when everyone knew that Spain was too weak to hold onto any of it much longer."

"Just because some Americans think their government shouldn't have agreed to let Spanish Mexico have Texas doesn't mean they have the right—now—to come and steal it away from us," I said indignantly. "It's ours, whether they like it or not!"

"Steal is a strong word, Felipe. We know the United

350

States has been trying off and on to buy Texas ever since they let it go. But what would be wrong with that, if it is all done legally and properly, to the satisfaction of both governments?"

"There's more than one way to steal a country," I said, and after I had spoken, I realized I had at last given voice to my inner conviction. The Americans were trying to steal Texas, and I suspected that had always been their intention. Bit by bit, they had been nibbling away at the state for ten years, establishing colonies, staking claims, until eventually they would have enough land to feel they could justify claiming the whole of Texas. For that reason, I was more obsessed than ever with the need to establish the validity of the Varga grant. As we sat there talking, I felt suddenly that there was a more urgent need than I had thought to get my ownership recognized before it was too late and they took that, too.

There were those in the national capital who had realized the danger of allowing the Americans to continue to come to Texas, or the Exclusion Act would never have been designed and passed. And if those who controlled the allotting of the land felt alarmed, wouldn't they look on me with suspicion? It was true I had been born in Texas and lived there all my life. Still, they might consider me in the same class with the American immigrants. But if I wore the uniform of an officer in their army, they would know I was one of them.

And I was. It didn't particularly worry me that most of the common soldiers were ignorant and poorly trained. It was still the Mexican army, my army, and it was all there was to stop the Americans from revolting against Mexico the way they had revolted against England. It was not only so I could show the land officials I was one of them that I wanted to join the army. I felt very strongly about the need for a good army, which would act as a deterrent to any ideas the Americans might have about repeating what they had done to England. I wanted to do everything in my power to improve that army, to help make it strong enough to do the job.

While these thoughts were tumbling around in my head, Todd was mulling over the meaning of my outburst and putting his own interpretation to it. "So that's it," he said. "Now at least we've reached the heart of the matter. You're afraid the United States will try to take over by force, by way of the people within. Well, I guess you're not the only one that's occurred to, and I can see in a way that your fears might be justified. But I feel that as long as we get our own state government, we'll manage to calm down the hotheads and get along just fine as a part of Mexico."

"But this government you want might not come soon enough to suit some people. What then? Does that give them the right to defy our laws?"

"Of course not. But I guess we can all see that there could be trouble ahead if things aren't worked out some way to satisfy everybody. You know, I heard something this afternoon that sounds encouraging. Have you ever heard of a General Antonio Lopez de Santa Anna?"

I started at the name. "General Santa Anna? Yes, I've heard of him. One of my friends at the Alamo has an uncle who's on the general's staff. He's offered to give me a letter to his uncle. He thinks he can use his influence to get me a commission, and a place on the general's staff. Why? What did you hear about him?"

"It seems the garrison at Vera Cruz pronounced in early January—you know, they issued one of those unofficial public statements—"

"A *pronunciamiento*."

"Yes, that was it. Anyway, it came out lambasting some of Bustamente's ministers, and in favor of the Constitution of 1824. This General Santa Anna was named as its champion. He might be just the man we need to put it all together, get us our separate statehood. I hope so." He paused, then went on, "Now let's back up a bit and you tell me what you were just talking about a minute ago, about knowing somebody who has an uncle."

352

"I'm going to Mexico City the next time I get back from San Felipe. Unless I can get something positive on the Varga grant as soon as I get down there, I'm going to join the army." There it was, the decision, the commitment. The agony of trying to decide was over: I had chosen, and put my choice into words. I waited for Todd's reaction. When he didn't say anything, I added defensively, "It's my country!"

"I know."

Another period of silence followed, and I felt called upon to justify my decision to Todd. "If I stay in Mexico City, it will be easy to keep in touch with the land officials, and I can probably get my ownership all straightened out before too many months. You know I've accomplished nothing yet, for all my letters and inquiries."

"I know about that. But it's not just because of the land that you're going to do this, is it?"

"No," I admitted. "I guess I'm ready to take sides now. I've waited a year since you asked me to put off choosing, and now I've made my choice. Do you disapprove of it?" I asked the question belligerently, then was ashamed of my attitude. This was Todd Stewart, the man who had befriended me, been like a father to me.

He reached over, patted my knee. "No, I don't disapprove, and I think I can even understand why you have chosen this way of expressing what you feel. Patriotism, if it's sincere and tempered with reason, is never misplaced. But it will make a gulf between you and a lot of the people you know, a lot of your friends."

"I realize that. That's what has made the decision so hard for me." I noted that I had unthinkingly put the making of my decision in the past tense, without consciously intending to do so.

"It's not always the easiest course of action to do what we feel is right. It's usually a lot more natural to take the easiest path. If I didn't think you felt very strongly about this, I'd try to dissuade you."

"I appreciate your understanding."

"You know I'll always be your friend."

"I never doubted that."

"What about Cassie? How do you think she'll accept this?"

"I don't know." I shrugged, pretending to a lack of concern I didn't feel. How *would* Cassie accept this?

"Don't you care? I thought I sensed some strong feelings between you two. She was certainly excited that day you took her to San Felipe."

"Cassie's just lonesome out there by herself so much, that's all, and glad to get out. She'd be excited about going anywhere with anybody." I didn't like not being truthful with Todd, but some instinctive caution intervened, kept me from admitting to him my true feelings about Cassie. He was, after all, Thorne's uncle, and his first loyalty would be to him. And if, through Todd, Thorne should discover how I felt about Cassie, and the way I suspected she felt about me, he would do everything in his power to stand between us, even to marrying her to someone else before I returned—Jeremy, for instance. The deliberate lie to Todd bothered me, but I felt I could not afford to tell him the truth. Todd couldn't tell Thorne what he didn't know.

If Todd was aware of the lack of truthfulness in my answer, he made no comment about it. He stood up, returned his pipe to his pocket, tossed the twig down to the ground. "Now I think we had both better get some sleep—you especially. You'll have to get up in just a few hours."

I stood up, pushed the door open for him. "Thanks for your ear."

"Any time," he said as he walked slowly back into the cabin. "Any time."

A little while later, just before I drifted off to sleep, a thought crossed my mind. Thorne Stewart was vociferously opposed to the presence of the Mexican army in Texas. It would give me no small amount of satisfaction to align myself so decisively with the other side.

When Johnny and I reached San Antonio de Bexar, everyone was talking about General Santa Anna and the Vera Cruz *pronunciamiento,* and for the first time it occurred to me that the timing of Santa Anna's overnight rise to popularity with the Texans might well work out to be personally favorable to me. No longer would my joining of the Mexican army be considered so drastic a move when I made it known that I expected to be on the staff of the very man the Texans all over San Antonio de Bexar were proclaiming as their hero. It began to look as though I could have things both ways at once: do what I felt I must do, yet avoid the disapproval of my friends while doing it. Such *pronunciamientos* as had been issued by the Vera Cruz garrison in early January were not uncommon whenever there was widespread dissatisfaction with an existing government. It was a sort of testing for possible insurrection, to see if popular support could be obtained for whatever movement or man it backed. Then, if it seemed the *pronunciamiento* was well received and widely hailed, the instigators allowed the movement to advance. Of course, the large percentage of these declarations failed to gain popular support and never came to anything at all. But this one seemed to have attracted a sizable following among Mexicans and Texans alike. If I could enlist in the army under none other than General Antonio Lopez de Santa Anna, wouldn't I be considered by my Texan friends to be aligning myself with their friends, not their foes? If the feelings of the Americans living in San Antonio de Bexar were any indication of the sentiments of the rest of the people of Texas, I had nothing to worry about, for they were loud and enthusiastic in proclaiming Santa Anna as their benefactor.

Nor did I really object to the *pronunciamiento* coming out, in effect, for separate statehood for Texas. I had to admit that it was absolutely necessary to appease the Texans by giving them their own state government. As Todd had pointed out, the Americans had already established themselves, and they were not likely to abandon the land they had cleared and planted or the houses they had built on our side of the Sabine. If separate statehood was what it would take to quiet them down, then it was certainly better to give them that than to risk open revolt.

We were on our way out of San Antonio de Bexar when I told Johnny of my plans, told him of the letter I would carry to one of Santa Anna's close aides. I had expected him to be impressed by the mention of the popular general's name and the significance of going almost directly to the man who was being so widely hailed.

"But what if this *pronunciamiento* doesn't come to anything?" he asked skeptically. "You've told me yourself these things don't always mean much. Just because some people decide to protest something doesn't mean everybody in Mexico is going to jump up and down and shout, 'Hurrah, hurrah!' for the man behind the movement."

"The Americans here in Bexar seem to be shouting loud enough," I reminded him, disappointed by his response.

"I suppose so, but what does the rest of Mexico care about separate statehood for Texas?"

"You don't understand," I said impatiently. "They didn't pronounce just for that, but for the whole Constitution of 1824, and against Bustamente's government."

"I still don't see that's any reason for you to be running off to join the Mexican army. Anyway, even if you do think this Santa Anna is on the Texans' side, what makes you think you'll be working under him? They'll send you wherever they want to."

"If a general wants a man on his staff, I imagine he's got enough say to keep him there," I argued. "My friend at the Alamo, the one who wrote the letter, said he was sure Santa Anna would welcome someone who knew so much about Texas and who understood how the Texans think."

Johnny's voice dropped so low I could scarcely hear him over the pounding of the horses' hoofs and the rattling of the coach. "Do you understand us, Felipe?" he asked quietly, turning to look at me. "I thought you did, thought you were one of us. But now you've told me what you plan to do, I'm not so sure."

356

His eyes remained fixed on my face, as though he was trying to read something there. It made me uncomfortable, and I averted my gaze uneasily, looked down the road ahead. His reaction had not been at all what I had anticipated.

"This will be my last trip. I know Todd would like for you to take over the coach route, if you're willing."

Johnny seemed as relieved as I was to change the subject. "You don't think anything could keep me from going to San Felipe, do you?" he asked lightly. "I'll be going regularly, with or without a coach. I'd walk if I had to."

I grinned. "I'm sure Todd would lots rather you'd take the coach."

We didn't discuss my plans again.

Would Cassie feel as he did? As we neared the Stewart place, I worried increasingly about how she would receive my news.

I jumped down and opened the door for Esperanza's daughter, Lupe, and helped her alight as Johnny swung her belongings down from the carrier on top of the coach. Esperanza came rushing around front to meet us, a big smile on her face. Mother and daughter embraced as though it had been years since they had seen each other, instead of only a few months. A moment later, Cassie came running out to greet us.

There's nothing that makes a person appreciate someone he's fond of more than knowing he won't be seeing that someone again for a long time. As I opened my arms and waited for Cassie to run into them, I was struck anew by her prettiness, her vivacity, as though I were seeing her for the first time. There was nothing of the child in her any more. She was almost eighteen, an adult, and very dear to me. As she threw her arms around my neck, I clasped her to me so tightly that she gasped, "Felipe, I can't breathe!"

I released her. "Sorry. It's just that I'm so glad to see you again."

"I've missed you, too."

There had never been anything of the coquette in Cassie.

357

Her directness, the straightforward admission—this was part of what I loved about her.

"I'll get my things down," I said, turning back toward the coach, "so Johnny can take our passengers on into San Felipe."

Her hand on my arm stopped me. "No, wait. There's something I have to tell you." Her smooth forehead wrinkled into a frown. "It's Papa. He found out you've been staying here. I think Daniel accidentally let something slip. Papa's forbidden me to let you use the cabin any more. He said some terrible things about you. I suppose you can stay with the Parkers." She looked very unhappy.

"Not this trip." It was not the time to tell her that this would be my last visit for many months to come. "San Felipe's much too far away from you. He didn't say I couldn't camp in the woods, did he?"

Her face brightened immediately. "No, he didn't."

"He didn't forbid you to bring me something to eat now and then, did he?" I continued.

"He only said you couldn't stay in the cabin." She smiled conspiratorially. "With Esperanza and Lupe here, I'm sure I can manage to slip away from Mama."

"You don't mind?" We both knew I was asking her to defy Thorne.

"Mind? Oh, Felipe, I'd hate it, knowing you were in San Felipe when you should be here with us!"

"Remember that place where you were trying to fish right after you moved here? The one where you lost your worm?"

She nodded.

"That's where you'll find me. I'll get back on the coach now, so Daniel and any of the others will think I'm going into San Felipe. Then they won't have to lie to your father. I'll meet you at that spot in the morning."

"But what about your supper tonight? You'll be hungry."

"I've got plenty of jerky and hardtack in my bag, and some dried corn. I'll manage."

"If you're sure . . . " She looked at me uncertainly, and I was pleased by her concern.

"I'll be fine. If you can't get away in the morning, just come whenever you can. Don't worry about me. I've lived off the land for more than a couple of days at a time."

"I'll be there early." She smiled.

"Till tomorrow, then."

"Till tomorrow."

Cassie walked over to the coach to greet Johnny. As they talked, I heard the jangle of Angela's bell. "Give my regards to the Parkers," Cassie said, and turned and ran into the house.

As I climbed up beside Johnny again, he looked at me questioningly. "You're not staying here?"

I shook my head. "Thorne's orders. Don't look so surprised. I'm amazed I've been getting away with staying here for this long. You can leave me off down the road a way, out of sight. Thorne didn't forbid Cassie to let me stay in the woods north of the house. He lived on the Varga grant for a year or so. I guess I can camp in his woods awhile."

"Why don't you come with me to the Parkers? They've invited you often enough."

"I know, but remember this is the last time I'll be here for a long time. I want to be near Cassie. I have some things to settle with her before I go."

"It seems to me you'd better settle a few things with her father first," he commented wryly. He flicked the reins and the coach started to roll toward the road.

"Settle things with Thorne?" I gave a short bitter laugh. "There's no point in even trying."

As soon as we were out of sight of the Stewart cabin, I had Johnny stop the coach. I swung down, asked Johnny to throw down my things and a blanket. "Get word to Cassie when you're ready to go. And remember, I'm in no rush at all to leave. Maybe Davey Stokes ought to give the coach a thorough going-over this time."

359

Johnny nodded and we exchanged grins. "I imagine he'll need at least a week to get it in really good shape."

"Or even longer." I caught the blanket and waved him off. Then I picked up my things and made my way toward the trees.

The next morning, I got busy fashioning a watertight lean-to for myself. We were well into spring by then, and the air had been balmy for several weeks, but winter was not quite over, and changes could still come suddenly. If I were to stay there as long as two weeks, I would need to make myself fairly comfortable. As I paused in my work, I heard Cassie softly calling my name. I was partially hidden by some underbrush and the trunk of a big cottonwood, so she didn't see me as soon as I saw her. She found my burned-out fire, set a hamper down by it, and called again.

I was in no hurry to answer. She was wearing a sprigged muslin dress of white and gold tones, and she had a white shawl thrown around her shoulders against the early morning chill. She looked so fresh and bright-eyed and vital standing there looking around for me that I wanted to watch her for a minute before I answered.

When I saw her eyes were nearing the place I stood, I said, "Here I am!"

With a little cry of joy, she ran to me, straight into my outstretched arms. She raised her face to mine. "I came as soon as I woke up. It must be early. Esperanza isn't even up yet."

"I spent the whole night watching for the dawn, knowing you would come to me this morning if you could. And then, when finally it was light, I started to worry that you might not be able to get away."

As I talked, I looked down at her upturned face, anticipating the moment I would kiss those soft full lips. It was odd how long it had taken us to pass through all the stages of knowing each other and yet not really knowing each other, to this stage. It had happened much as a bud will not open until it is ready. That was the way it was with our love.

360

Something I had long anticipated had suddenly unfolded before my eyes.

"I wanted to come last night, but I couldn't get away."

"All that matters is that you're here now."

Slowly, I brought my face close to hers. She tightened her arms around my neck and reached to meet me.

"I love you very much," I whispered.

"And I've loved you for a long, long time, for almost as long as I can remember."

We kissed until we were both gasping for air. Laughing with the heady joy of the moment, we drew apart, but only a little.

"I seem to recall a time when you didn't think too much of me," I reminded her.

"That was years ago, before I really knew you." She laughed again, and it struck me that her laughter was as pure and melodious as the musical tones of perfectly cast bells. She added, "You were rather hateful the first few times we met. Remember?"

"I never threw a piece of hardtack at you."

"It fell short, and when I saw you pick it up and start to eat it, I was so furious I wanted to run and snatch it from your hand." She pulled away, took my hand to lead me to the food hamper she had brought. "Come, you must be hungry. I had to bring you last night's biscuits. I didn't want to wait till Sukie baked fresh ones this morning. But I brought you some honey, and there's a big slab of cheese." She opened the hamper, spread out the cloth, then sat on the ground beside it. She brought out the food. "I was lucky no one was up. I brought you all sorts of things— plates, and knives and forks, even a few pans. I can sneak smaller parcels out under my cloak each time I come." She smiled up at me and motioned for me to sit beside her.

I dropped to the ground, leaned over to kiss her again. "I'd rather have more of your kisses than the food."

"There's no reason why you shouldn't have plenty of both."

I had intended to tell her of my plans as soon as we were

together, but I didn't, not that day, nor the next, nor the day after that. I rationalized about delaying, told myself it was because Cassie was so happy that I didn't want to spoil her happiness by telling her I was going away. But the fact was, I was afraid. What if she were angry, turned away from me?

Yet, I couldn't put it off indefinitely. So, on the fourth day, I told her.

She always managed to get away to see me early in the morning, and again in the middle of the afternoon, while Angela slept. That afternoon, she arrived much later than usual, and she was breathless from running.

"Mama just fell asleep," she explained. "She's in one of her bad moods, and she's been calling for me every few minutes. I wanted to leave, but I knew I mustn't do anything to let her suspect you're here."

"Do you think she'd tell your father? Remember, she helped keep our secret for over a year."

"That was before Papa found out you'd been staying with us all along. He was so terribly angry, and he does rant and rave so when he gets mad. I know he doesn't always mean everything he says when he's like that, but his anger terrifies Mama. He stomped around and yelled at her and said he held her responsible. She was so upset she cried for hours on end, and would hardly eat a thing for three days."

I had pulled her into my embrace while she talked. "I can feel your heart pounding. Were you afraid I'd be gone if you didn't hurry?"

"I'm always afraid of that." As she raised her face for my kiss, I saw the worry wrinkles creasing her brow. I smoothed them away with my kisses, and for a few minutes we didn't speak.

I led Cassie over to sit on what I called my settee—some Spanish moss I had spread over a patch of smooth ground on the near side of the big cottonwood. She asked, "Oh, Felipe, what are we going to do? With the way things are between you and Papa . . . " She stopped, bit her lower lip as a few tears rolled down her cheeks.

I knew this was the time I must tell her of my plans. "Sit here beside me. I must tell you something about my future, because it must be your future, too."

We sat close together, and I put my arm around her protectively, as though by that gesture I could ward off the shock and surprise of my next words. I started by reminding her about the Varga grant, my need to establish ownership of the twenty-five million square *varas*. "That is an important part of our future," I said emphatically. "It's useless to write any more letters. They never reach the right people, and I'm not even sure most of them reach anyone at all. I must go to Mexico City myself."

She looked up at me in alarm. "When?" she asked, and the word came out in a whisper, as though she were afraid to voice it aloud.

"In a few weeks. I'll leave as soon as I take the coach back to Gonzales."

She looked stricken. "But how long will that take? How long till I see you again?"

"It may be quite a while," I hedged.

"How long?" she persisted. "How long does it take to get to Mexico City and back? Oh, Felipe, that will take months, and the road is so dangerous. I hear there are Comanches all over that country!"

"Don't worry. They may be my cousins," I reminded her lightly.

I could not divert her thoughts so easily. "How long will you be gone?" she asked again.

"I don't know. These things take time. I will probably have to stay awhile." I hesitated, then blurted out the rest. "If I can't get something settled right away about the Varga grant, I'm going to join the Mexican army."

She pulled away from my encircling arm, turned to look at me, her face clearly registering shock. "What?"

I plunged headlong into my explanation. "I've been thinking it over a long time, Cassie, and it's not a decision

363

I've made lightly. Of course, if I can settle the matter of the Varga grant right away, get title to my land without delay, I'll bring some peons back and start farming as soon as I can."

"But if you don't get title right away, you'll join the army," she said flatly, all the animation drained from her voice.

"Not just as a common soldier. I have a letter to an aide of General Santa Anna. He's the man behind the Vera Cruz *pronunciamento*. All the Americans in San Antonio de Bexar think he's the best friend the Texans ever had, since he's in favor of the Constitution of 1824, and it promises Texas separate statehood. I'm sure I can get on Santa Anna's staff."

My careful explanation, my deliberate portrayal of Santa Anna as a hero to the Texans, seemed to wash over her without penetrating. "You, in the Mexican army!" she said, her eyes wide in disbelief.

"Just think how it will help my position on the Varga grant if I join! If I'm right there, in the national capital, I can keep in contact with the land officials there, make them see—"

"I don't care about the Varga grant!" she said vehemently. "I only care about you!" She burst into tears, put her face in her hands.

I reached for her, tried to pull her into my arms to soothe her, but she pulled away from me, her shoulders shaking with sobs. Every time I tried to touch her, she shook my hands off. Never had I felt so helpless, so ineffectual. Deeply moved by her tears, I knew I had only to say that I would come right back and they would stop.

But this I couldn't do. "It's for our future," I said, knowing I must somehow make her understand, see the reasoning behind my decision. "If I'm in the army, the officials at the land ministry will probably be much more willing to listen to me, to honor my claim. They'll think of me as a Mexican, not as a Texan. Don't you see? Once my ownership of the land is established, I'll come back for you. If it's impossible for me to come back, then I'll send someone for you. But I'm almost certain I can get sent back to Texas any time I ask. It's not a very popular assignment among the officers I know. Except for San Antonio de Bexar, where there are a number of Creoles living, the Mexican officers aren't welcomed into the homes of the Texans, and they don't like Texas assignments." I paused, and still she continued to sob, her shoulders shaking. "Please, Cassie, tell me you understand," I begged.

She looked up at me, her dear sweet face streaked with tears. "How can I tell you that when I don't? I only know that you say you love me, yet you're telling me that you're going to leave me, and you aren't coming back!"

"I do love you! You must never doubt that, not even for a minute. And of course I'm coming back."

"If you loved me, you wouldn't want to stay gone so long, you wouldn't be talking of joining the Mexican army! I can see why you feel you must go to the capital, but why can't you turn right around and return after you've talked to the right people about your land?"

"It won't be that easy. You just don't know how confused all this can get. Every time a different president comes in power, he sweeps away everything his predecessor has done and starts over, so anyone who is trying to get something done must start over, too. My mother and I tried for eight years to get some kind of proof—"

"If you weren't successful after eight years, then what makes you think you can succeed now? Why can't you just forget about the Varga grant? There's other land, lots of it!"

"It's not the same. The Varga grant is mine. It belongs to me by rights, and I intend to see that it is recognized as mine."

"Don't be so stubborn! If you feel you must go to Mexico City, then go, but why can't you return to Texas right away? Then you can continue on the coach, so we'll be able to see each other every few months."

"You're talking around in circles, and you're not even

365

listening to me. I just told you why I can't come right back, unless I just happen to be lucky enough to get my claim recognized within the first few weeks, and that I don't expect to do. It will take lots of time and constant attention to accomplish anything. If I continued on the coach, how could I build a future for us? I need something permanent, a place to build us a home, and then I want to stay there with you. I don't want to have to leave you."

She would not be diverted by talk of permanence. "You don't really love me, or you'd promise to hurry back to me. You'd want to!"

"You know I love you. That has nothing to do with it."

"It has everything to do with it. If you loved me, you'd forget this foolishness about the army, and you wouldn't be talking about staying away so long! You'd come back to me as soon as you'd argued for your claim."

"It's not that simple at all," I said in exasperation. "You're being unreasonable!"

She pushed herself to her feet. "And you're being pigheaded! Go to Mexico City, then! And stay there! Stay there for ten years, for all I care, because I don't intend to wait for you to get back!" She turned and started running, still sobbing.

"I just might do that, if that's all you care about me!" But I retorted in the heat of anger, knowing even as I said the words that I didn't mean them. I wanted to follow Cassie, take her in my arms, kiss away her tears. But I knew that if I did, I would end up promising not to go into the army. So I watched her go, and listened for her to return. But she didn't return, and when her sobs had faded to nothing and the woods were again quiet and lonely, I leaned back against the cottonwood, feeling utterly defeated and miserable.

Finally, I stood up and began to gather firewood, though I already had an ample two-days' supply under my lean-to. When I had finished I noticed that Cassie had left her cloak behind. The food she had brought that afternoon lay where she had dropped it, along with her cloak. I picked up the food packet, found some slices of Sukie's golden-crusted bread, generously buttered. Absently, I bit some off and chewed it, then spat it out in disgust. I knew it was as good as ever, but that day it tasted like sawdust.

I spent a miserable night, dozing lightly, tossing and turning on my mattress of Spanish moss, and as soon as the sun showed itself through the trees, I got up, feeling as though I had not slept at all.

I busied myself starting a fire. The mornings were cool, and a few cups of hot chocolate always warmed me considerably. Cassie had brought me chocolate and sugar, and I still had milk left from the evening before. I used my flint to start the first little pile of moss burning, then added bits of twigs and finally the larger pieces of wood. I sat near the small fire, poking at it idly, waiting for it to die down before hanging the pot of milk over it. I was still without appetite, even though I had eaten very little the previous evening. I kept looking up every few seconds, hoping to see Cassie running toward me, wondering if she would ever come again.

And then, when I saw her, I blinked, not sure whether she were real or drawn from my imagination.

But she was real, and she called out my name as she ran. I stood up, ran toward her. We flung ourselves into each other's arms, each murmuring apologies.

"There's only one solution," I said after we had kissed the desperate kisses of near-loss averted and reunion confirmed. "You must come away with me. I know it's a dangerous journey, but I'll take care of you. It's the only way."

"If only I could!" she said with a wistful sigh. "But you know I can't leave Mama. She needs me."

"She has Esperanza to care for her, and now Lupe as well."

"That's not the same. They're good with her, but I'm her daughter, and she needs me, especially with Papa gone so much."

"Then your father can damn well stay home," I retorted.

"Don't be angry with Papa, Felipe. He can't stay home.

367

He has to travel constantly to move goods from one place to another. You know that."

*Not as constantly as he would have you believe,* I thought bitterly. Still, I knew that I could not be the one to tell her that her father cared more for his mistress than his wife, more for his bastard son than for his legitimate children. Some day she might find out, but it would not be from me. Instead, I said, "Will is here."

She shook her head. "Will and Mama aren't that close any more. It just isn't the same with a son as with a daughter. Besides, Mama's so modest, she'd be uncomfortable having him do things for her. Anyway, it's my fault she's like this. If I hadn't run off to follow you that time—"

"When are you going to stop blaming yourself for what happened to your mother? You know she would have taken to her bed sooner or later anyway. It just happened to be when you left that time, that's all." I didn't add that I had long suspected that Angela had chosen that specific time in order to tie Cassie to her. By that time she must have known she had already lost her husband.

Cassie shook her head stubbornly. "It's my fault. I know it is."

"Cassie, Cassie," I said gently, "are you going to give up your whole life for your mother? What if she goes on like this for years? I don't want to wait until we're both old and gray before we marry. Come with me now, come with me to Mexico City. Then we can be together."

"You know that's what I want, but I can't do it. It would be different if we could settle somewhere with Mama. You wouldn't mind having her with us, would you?"

"She's your father's responsibility," I reminded her.

"But Papa can't take care of her. He's always gone. Besides, even when he is home, he's too impatient with her. It would be best if she went with me when I leave home."

"Come with me now. Esperanza and Lupe are very capable."

"Oh, Felipe, you know I want to go with you, more than

368

anything in the world. But I must look after Mama myself."

I sighed heavily. Again, as on the previous afternoon, our conversation had gone full circle, without solving anything at all.

I looked at my fire, saw it was reduced to coals. "Come," I said. "Let's have a cup of chocolate together."

"Let me fix our breakfast." She knelt on the ground and poured the fresh milk she had brought into the pot.

After we had eaten, we walked hand in hand through the woods, stopping where we would to look more closely at the signs of spring all around us, making our way to the creek, turning toward each other at the same instant to embrace, to kiss. Several hours later, when we returned and sat down by the cottonwood, Cassie leaned back against the trunk, closing her eyes.

"Let's plan our house," she said. "How many children shall we have? We'll have to build a place big enough for them all."

"At least six." I lay down with my head in her lap and looked up at her.

She opened her eyes, smiled down at me. "Boys or girls?"

"The first one should be a boy, so he can inherit the Varga grant. The rest can all be girls, if you'd like. Just as long as they all look like you."

We talked on, playing the foolish pretend game, and nothing more was said about the painful separation soon to come. We talked only of happy things, of the time when we would be together again.

The days sped by, and on the afternoon of the tenth day, Cassie came running toward my small camp, urgently calling my name.

"Cassie, love, what's the matter?" I encircled her trembling body with my arms, felt her heart racing. "What is it?"

Her cheeks were wet with tears. "Johnny was just here."

"Nothing has happened to Eliza, has it? Or Mr. or Mrs. Parker?"

"N-no," she stammered. "It's not that. It's just that—Oh, Felipe, he said there are three people in San Felipe who want to go to Gonzales, and that they're in a terrible rush. They want to leave tomorrow morning early."

So this was it, the parting we had both dreaded. I tightened my arms around her.

"Don't go! Please don't!"

I kissed her cheek, tasted the salt of her tears. "You know I must leave. I always do."

"But this time it's different! You're not coming back!"

"What kind of a foolish idea is this?" I asked, my voice tender with concern. "I've told you I'll be back."

"But you won't be! You're going to Mexico City, and you'll join the army, and I'll never see you again!" She burst into fresh tears and clung to me.

"What nonsense!" I chided gently. "You know nothing could keep me away from you, not a minute longer than is absolutely necessary."

"You won't come back," she insisted stubbornly. "I know it! I just know it!"

I put my hand under her chin and raised her face to mine, kissed her lips softly, lingeringly. "I promise I will. I can't tell you just when that will be, but don't ever doubt it for a minute."

"I'm so afraid." Her voice was reduced to a whisper.

"What? The girl who was brave enough to go into Kronk country alone is afraid?"

"I'm afraid I'll lose you!"

"You couldn't if you tried. Come, let's sit down, so I can hold you."

With our arms around each other, we started walking toward the cottonwood.

"Please, Felipe, don't go into the army! Papa has told me all the Mexican soldiers are stupid and horrid!"

"Your father would say that," I commented, trying to keep the bitterness out of my voice. "Do you think I'm

370

stupid and horrid?" I sat down, drew her down beside me.

"Of course not, but you're different." She moved easily into my arms.

"Nothing about me is going to change just because I put on a Mexican uniform."

"There will be girls in Mexico City, and they'll see how handsome you are in your uniform, and you'll forget all about me," she said irrationally.

I laughed at her foolish fears. "I'll fight them all off, and tell them I've left my heart with a pretty girl on the Bexar Road." I tried to keep my voice light and teasing to hide my own fears. What would happen to her after I left? If Thorne somehow found out about us, would he force her to marry Jeremy without delay? Surely, I reasoned, nobody could make Cassie do anything she didn't want to do—not even Thorne. I wanted to believe that, but I could not rid myself of a nagging fear that somehow he would interfere, manage to make her do as he wanted. The previous ten days had been happy ones, marred only by our one quarrel. Since that time, I had avoided saying anything that would intrude on the perfection of that happiness. Now I felt it was time to face unpleasant realities. Most of all, I must make Cassie see the danger of letting Thorne know about us.

"You must promise me something, little love. I want you to promise not to tell your father about us. Let him think I mean nothing to you, that I'm no more than a friend."

She looked at me in surprise. "But if I tell him how we both feel, tell him how very much I love you, I can talk him 'round, and by the time you get back, he'll be ready to give us the biggest wedding Texas has ever seen."

"It would never happen like that. You mustn't dream impossible dreams. Believe me when I say that the only way will be for me to return for you and carry you away in secret. Later, after we're married, you can tell your father."

"But why should we have to run away? Oh, I know Papa doesn't like you very well at all, and I know you don't like

371

him any better, but surely, for my sake, you two can forget your differences and stop your foolish quarreling."

"Not even for you could we do that."

"You don't want to try!" she said accusingly.

"Only because it's impossible." I kissed her.

She would not be diverted from her line of thought. "Tell me what it is that has made you such enemies. Was it because Papa tried to take your land away from you back in Nacogdoches? That's all far in the past. He doesn't care about that any more, now that he has this place."

I shook my head. "It's nothing you can change."

"That's what you always say! How can I help you if you won't tell me what's caused you to hate each other so?"

"It's just a fact you must accept, Cassie. If you'll take my word for it that it's something you are helpless to change, then you'll save yourself a lot of worry. Just promise me you'll wait for me."

"You know I will."

"If your father finds out about us, he'll do everything he can to drive us apart, to make you forget me. But you mustn't let him."

"No one could make me forget you, or keep me from loving you. Not even Papa."

"He'll try." I stood up. "I want to give you something to keep till I get back." I walked over to my bag and reached inside it for a small package. Then I sat down beside her again and handed it to her. "This is for you to keep, so you'll remember you've promised to marry me."

"I've no intention of forgetting," she said as she opened the small box. "Oh! A gold wedding band! Oh, Felipe!" She threw her arms around me and put her head on my chest and cried.

"What's the matter?" I asked solicitously, holding her close.

"Nothing!" she said through her tears. "Nothing's the matter. It's just that I'm so happy!" She raised her face and I could see that she was smiling.

"That's a fool reason to cry," I said with pretended gruffness, almost too choked with my own emotion to speak. "Come, let's see if it fits. I had to guess about the size. We can have it adjusted later."

"Here. You put it on for me," she said, handing me the ring and extending her finger.

It slipped on easily. "It's a little large." I started to remove it.

"No, don't!" She pulled her hand away, made a fist to keep the ring from slipping off. "Let me wear it for a little while. I want to pretend it's there for always."

"It will be, as soon as I can manage. I promise to come for you as quick as I can. The minute I get confirmation of the Varga grant, I'll start trying to get back to you. That should be no more than a year and a half from now, at most."

"A year and a half! What if you still don't know anything for sure after all that time?"

"If I haven't accomplished anything by a year from the day I get there, I swear to you I'll come back anyway."

She threw herself into my arms. "Oh, Felipe, you must! If you don't I'll die!"

"There's something else for you in the box, something you can wear now. Look under the cotton." Still holding her close with one arm around her shoulder I picked up the box, held it for her.

"Something else?" Eagerly, she lifted the cotton, looked at the small gold locket and chain in the bottom of the box. "A locket, in the shape of a heart! Oh, Felipe, it's lovely!"

"Here, let me put it on for you." I fastened it around her neck, then leaned over and kissed her softly. "I told you I was leaving my heart here with you. Now you have it. Take good care of it. There's a lock of my hair inside, too."

"Oh, I will take good care of it, I will! And you must promise to hurry back and claim it."

"You know I will." Though I didn't voice my fears, I thought of all the uncertainties between this day and the one on which I would come back to claim her, and I was afraid. I was even on the point of changing my mind about

373

going to Mexico City, but reason intervened. What, after all, could I offer her now? What kind of life? I had nothing, no place to take her. I must see first that the Varga grant was acknowledged as mine, for it was there we would make our life together.

We exchanged few words the rest of the afternoon. A new desperation overtook us both, and we clung together longer, kissed more passionately, more hungrily. During those ten days that we had been having our secret meetings in the woods, I had been guarding Cassie's honor—guarding it from myself, for I was at once the predator who would ravish her and the protector who would prevent it. Until that day, that afternoon, I had been conscientiously forcing myself to break up our embraces when I felt they were becoming too ardent. Constantly, I fought down the ache of desire, the longing to continue our kisses and caresses to their natural end.

But on that last day, during what we thought were our last few hours together, the ardor of our embraces increased. We slipped down lower, and lower, until we were lying on the ground, wrapped in each other's arms, our lips seeking one another's insatiably. I moved my hands over Cassie's supple young body, feeling the full swell of her breasts, the tautness of her stomach. I drew her closer as our kisses became more intense. I reached for the hem of her skirt with one hand, pushed aside her petticoats, and moved my hand over the smooth skin of her calf, then higher, to the softer flesh of her thigh. My other hand pushed against the small of her back, crushing her to me, knowing she could feel the hard maleness of my desire against her.

It was as though the protector had been watching, waiting for things to progress as far as they dared. Another minute—less, even—and there would be no stopping. Reluctantly, I relaxed my hold on her, withdrew my hand from her thigh, slowly pushed myself away from her, gently untwined her arms from around my neck.

She opened her eyes wide, looked at me. I kissed her

374

tenderly and smiled. "I love you, and I want you," I said, "but we must wait." She could not know the amount of self-control it had taken to stop. "I think I had better see you to the edge of the woods now. It's getting late."

She nodded. "Mama will be calling, wondering where I am. I told Esperanza to tell her I had a bad headache and was napping. But by now she will be getting impatient." As she talked, she reached behind her neck, undid the clasp on the chain and removed the wedding ring from her finger, slipping the ring onto the chain before she fastened it again. Then she slipped both locket and ring inside her bodice, and smiled at me.

"I'll wear them always."

"Keep them out of your father's sight," I admonished, and she nodded.

We stood up and reluctantly moved in the direction of the house. All too soon we reached the edge of the woods. I drew her into my arms for one last embrace. We kissed one last kiss of hope, of promise, of vows affirmed.

"Good-bye, my dearest love. Next time I come back, I'll put that ring on your finger, where it belongs."

"Don't say good-bye! It sounds so—so final." She burst into tears. "Oh, Felipe, I'm sorry to cry like this, but I can't help it. I have the most terrible feeling that something will happen to keep us from marrying."

"We won't let anything happen," I said firmly. I didn't want her to know I shared her fears.

"It's almost twelve hours till you go. I don't want to leave you yet!"

"Nor do I want you to go, but you must. Your mother will be calling for you."

"Then I'll come back to you tonight, after everyone is in bed."

"You mustn't do that! Someone might find out you were missing, and you'd have the place in an uproar. Then your father would be bound to find out about us. If he does, he'll be sure to do something drastic to keep us apart."

"Nobody will ever miss me. I'll wait till I'm sure everybody is asleep, then I'll slip out of my window. You won't be leaving till a little before dawn. Why shouldn't we spend part of that time together?"

"You know very well why."

"But we've had so little time."

"I know." I held her tight. "When I come back, we'll have a whole lifetime to catch up."

"Oh, Felipe, my dear love, I'm so afraid I'll lose you." She clung to me, leaned her head on my chest. Then, with a sob, she pushed herself away from me and turned and ran toward her house.

I felt the sting of tears in my eyes as I watched her go. Then I faced the opposite direction to return dejectedly to my camp.

I bedded down early that night, because I knew I must get up before dawn in order to reach the place Johnny would pick me up. He would be starting from San Felipe while it was still dark, and I didn't want to keep him waiting.

I didn't know how long I had been asleep when I awoke, suddenly tense, listening. Some noise over and above the usual night sounds had awakened me. From somewhere off in the distance came the rumble of thunder, but I knew that was not what I had heard. Slowly, careful not to make any noise, I picked up my rifle and got to my feet.

Then I heard Cassie saying my name softly. I dropped the rifle, ran toward the sound of her voice.

"Cassie, where are you?"

"Here."

I followed the direction of the sound, and a few seconds later, she threw herself into my arms.

"What are you doing out here? I told you it was too risky for you to come!" I wrapped my arms around her, realized she was wearing only a thin nightgown and wrapper. As I held her, I was aware of every curve of her firm young body.

"Don't be angry with me. I had to come." A norther had blown in as I slept, dropping the temperature drast-

376

ically. Cassie was trembling with the cold, and her teeth chattered as she spoke.

"You should have dressed warmer," I said, trying to be angry. "You're about to freeze."

"I meant to wear my cloak, but I forgot."

"Come, let me wrap my blanket around you. I hate to chance a fire, but I'd better make one. You'll have lung fever for sure if you don't get warm right away. What ever possessed you to come out here now, and not even dressed?" I got the blanket out of my lean-to, shook it out and wrapped it around her.

"But this is your only blanket, isn't it?" she protested. "And you're cold, too."

"Not half as cold as you are. I'll get a fire going, and we can both get close to it. We'll just have to hope that nobody happens to see it. Then you can tell me what possessed you to come running out like this in the middle of the night. And after you've told me, I intend to take you straight home." Several times, as I was starting the fire, building it up, I heard again the rolling roar of thunder. It was getting closer.

When at last I was satisfied that the fire needed no more attention, I said, "Now, come sit nearer, so you'll warm up."

She scooted toward the heat and I sat beside her. "I told you not to come tonight."

"I know. I guess I won't make an obedient wife, will I?"

I leaned over, kissed her. "I never expected you to. You're too stubborn."

"Now you're going to catch cold. We'll have to share your blanket." She unwrapped one shoulder, moved the blanket around to make room for me, and wrapped the far end of it around my shoulder.

I hesitated.

"I don't want you getting lung fever, either."

She looked so serious that I laughed and moved close to her, wrapping the edge of the blanket around me, feeling the welcome warmth of her body beside me. Desire rose in me

377

as I became acutely aware of the thinness of the gown and wrapper she wore. "As soon as you're warm, I intend to take you home. That will have to be soon. It's going to rain before long."

"I won't go. I'm staying here until you have to leave. Then you can drop me off on your way. Please, Felipe, put your arm around me and hold me close."

With one hand, I was holding the corner of the blanket. I slipped my other arm around her shoulder, drew her closer still, kissed her. "Oh, Cassie, love! I must take you home in just a minute. Don't you see? It's impossible for you to stay here all night! I love you too much, and I wouldn't trust myself."

"I trust you."

"You shouldn't. Don't you understand what I'm telling you? I'm almost crazy with wanting you. You shouldn't have come here like this, in the middle of the night, and with almost nothing on."

"Do you want me, Felipe?" she asked softly.

"Do you have to ask? You know I do." I felt the heat pulsing through my loins, tried to move a little farther away from her, but was stopped by the limitations of the blanket.

"Felipe?" Her voice was questioning, shy.

"Yes, my foolish little love?"

"I'm wearing your wedding ring on my finger. See?"

She dropped her corner of the blanket in order to hold her hand out toward the firelight, and the blanket slipped from her shoulders. I picked up the corner, put it around her shoulder again. My hand brushed against her breast, and I let it linger there, cupped my hands over it. Her wrapper had gaped open and through the thin fabric of her gown, I felt the nipple of her breast grow taut at my touch. Hurriedly, I withdrew my hand, as though it had been singed. "Hold the corner of the blanket around you."

She did as I told her. After a moment's silence, she asked, "Don't you want to know why I'm wearing your ring?"

"I already know. For the same reason I gave it to you. To remind you that you belong to me."

"That's only part of it. I'm wearing it for the same reason I came here tonight." She hesitated. "I don't want to just say I belong to you. I want to really belong to you, Felipe, to be truly yours before you leave. I want to feel that we're married. Now, tonight."

"You can't be serious!"

She looked up at me, the glow from the fire lighting half of her face, leaving the other half in darkness. Never had she looked so soft and feminine and desirable. And never had I craved her as much as I did at that moment.

"I was never more serious in my life."

"You don't know what you're saying! I'm going to take you home right this minute." I dropped my corner of the blanket, started to get to my feet, but she reached over and put her hand on my arm.

"I'm not leaving," she said determinedly.

"You must!"

"I won't! Oh, Felipe, don't you want me? I thought you'd be pleased—"

"Of course I want you! I've never wanted you more than I do right at this moment, but God knows, one of us must have some sense!"

"We'll have a year and a half to be sensible! Oh, Felipe, why do you make me shame myself like this, begging you to take me? I'm offering myself to you, and instead of being glad, you haggle about it, as though I were a tin peddler trying to sell you some inferior needles—"

"Only because you seem to have lost your reason, Cassie. And I'm trying to retain mine. What if something would happen—?" I leaned toward her, kissed her pouting lips gently.

"I don't think it would. Esperanza talks to me about all sorts of things. I asked her some questions this afternoon, after I got back to the house, and from what she says, I don't think it's the right time of the moon for me to conceive."

379

I smiled at the thought of Cassie extracting such detailed information from Esperanza. It was a wonder they managed to communicate at all when they had no more than ten words in common, but they seemed to have no trouble. "It sounds as though you've given this considerable thought."

"I knew you'd object, so that's why I found out. I thought you'd want me, and be so glad when I came to you. I never expected you to argue with me about it, or try to send me home! I never thought you would be so sensible—"

I smiled at her. "I never would have thought I'd be so sensible, either. It's just that I love you so very much that I want no harm to come to you, least of all from me. Don't you see? I'm only trying to protect you."

"Protect me? Oh, Felipe, I love you with all my heart, and I want to belong to you now, tonight, before you go. I can't explain the way I feel exactly, not even to you. But I want to have a tie between us, a stronger bond than we have now, a bond so strong that nothing will be able to prevent us from getting married. If we belong to each other now, tonight, I don't think anything in the world can separate us. Maybe it's foolish to feel that way, but I'm so sure, and I feel so strongly that this is right—"

"So strongly that you'd be willing to give yourself to me now?" I asked, deeply touched by what she had told me. The blanket had slipped from our shoulders, and we made no move to pick it up. Reluctantly, I stood up, knowing I must take her home at once, while I was still able to reason.

The thunder boomed again, loud, close.

"Come along, my dear foolish love. We're not going to carry this conversation any further. I'm taking you home right now. We'll have to hurry or we'll both get soaked." I offered her my hand and picked up the blanket to wrap it around her again. I tried to sound cross with her, knew I mustn't let her suspect how much I wanted her at that moment.

"You're taking me home?" she asked petulantly. "Oh, Felipe—"

"Of course. It's what I must do, Cassie."

In the end, the weather made the decision for us, for the rain started just at that moment in a torrent of gigantic drops.

"Hurry! Into my lean-to!"

I took her by the hand, and dragging the blanket behind us, we scrambled under cover and fell, laughing, into each other's arms on the bed of Spanish moss. Her body, pressed next to mine, was warm and vital, her lips were sweet and soft.

As the storm raged all around us, we made love. The thunder boomed, and the lightning flashed, and the rain came down in sheets, and all my good intentions dissolved in the violent downpour.

It was almost dawn when the rain stopped. I gathered up my gear and we walked together to within a few hundred *varas* of the Stewart house.

"Can you get in all right?"

"Through my window. The same way I got out."

"Cassie, if Esperanza should be wrong, if anything should happen because of tonight, you must get word to Johnny at once, have him send riders after me. Wherever I am, I'll turn around and come back to you, right away. Promise?"

"Promise."

I wrapped her in one last desperate embrace. "Keep safe, my dear little love."

"And you. Oh, be careful, darling Felipe! For me." I could feel the dampness of her tears brushing against my cheek.

"I will," I promised. "And I'll hurry back, as fast as I can." I released her. "You must go."

As she turned to leave, I called after her. "Cassie?"

"Yes?"

"This was the first time for me, too."

"I'm glad you told me."

"I'm glad I waited."

"*Hasta luego*, my love," I said, remembering she didn't like the finality of the word *good-bye*. "Until we meet again."

"*Hasta luego*." Her voice came back like an echo out of the night.

In the faint half-light that precedes dawn, I watched her go.

Then I turned and made my way toward the road.

It was not until many hours later that my thoughts turned to Thorne. I should have warned her about him again. If he ever found out what had happened between Cassie and me . . .

With a cold feeling, I remembered my own words of six years ago. Like a specter, they returned to haunt me. They were the words I had uttered in the white heat of my fury when I found out my mother was to bear Thorne's bastard.

*"You have a daughter. . . . And you won't always be around with a rifle to protect her honor."*

That night, when Cassie and I had lain together, exchanging vows of eternal love, I had been overcome with tenderness and love for the girl I would one day return to make my bride. My vengeful threat had long been forgotten, and revenge on Thorne had been the farthest thing from my mind. But he would never believe that.

# Part Four—Cassie

# Chapter I

## AUSTIN'S COLONY—Spring 1832

I don't know exactly when I started loving Felipe. Maybe it was that day he rescued me from the Kronks and treated me with such gentle compassion, instead of giving me the tongue-lashing I knew full well I deserved. Or perhaps it was even earlier, on that morning he had found me skipping noisily through the woods and had taken it upon himself to teach me to be more careful, and had opened my eyes to the wonders of the world all around me. But I do know that by the time he gave me the heart-shaped locket and the gold wedding band, I had long been certain that I would marry no one else. Even though he had never actually told me in so many words how he felt about me until that last visit before he went to Mexico, I knew.

I'm sure he thought it was shameless of me to want to belong to him completely the night before he left. If it hadn't been for a sudden thundershower that drove us into his lean-to for protection, my dear idealistic Felipe would probably have sent me back to the house untouched. For my own part, it wasn't that I had been overcome with physical need. I had too recently awakened to the effect his ardent kisses could have on me to be fully aware of what the tumultuous feelings inside me really meant. I certainly didn't recognize them as physical desire. It was important that we be together as the ultimate expression of love and trust, a sacred pledge between us, a commitment no less binding than the solemn vows of marriage. The joining of

385

our flesh made us one. It was our promise to each other that, no matter what the obstacles, Felipe would belong to me and I to him from that moment forward.

Felipe's tenderness the first time he took me that night, his gentleness and hesitation in spite of the urgency that I sensed was driving him, his concern for any initial pain he might be causing me, all this endeared him to me that much more.

And there was pain, but it was quickly dimmed by the joy of realizing that his flesh was within my own, a part of me forevermore.

Joy and pain. I did not yet know how often the two existed together in the presence of love, as though they were opposite sides of the same coin. And, like a coin, when one face showed, the other was hidden from view. But I was to learn all that later. That night, after the first thrust of pain subsided, there was only the joy.

Afterward, when we clung together tightly, he said, "Oh, my little love, I'm sorry! I didn't want this to happen."

"But I did," I assured him, overwhelmed with love for him."

Outside, the cold winds blew and the storm raged, and from time to time, brilliant flashes of lightning illuminated a water-drenched world. But inside the snug shelter Felipe had built, a shelter just big enough to keep us out of the weather, there was warmth, and peace, and contentment.

We lay with our bodies entwined the rest of the night, and even as I drifted off to sleep, exhausted by the force of our emotions, I knew I was smiling for the happiness of it all. I awoke to the feel of his kisses soft upon my lips, and I looked quickly toward the end of the shelter, afraid I would see the first light of day, afraid our time together was at an end. But I saw only the darkness, and I was reassured, and drew his head down to mine to return his kisses, to renew our passion. Again, we slept. And the next time I opened my eyes, I saw Felipe looking at me tenderly, and I knew the night was over and it would soon be time to leave. He would have said so, but I quickly put my fingers to his lips.

"Not yet!" I said, "not until you've loved me again."

He smiled, pulled me closer into his embrace, murmured caressingly against my ear, "My dear sweet wanton!"

Later, he walked with me as far as he dared, and it was all I could do to tear myself away from him and return to the house. I turned back my unused bed and lay awake, and when I heard the coach rumble past, I knew he had gone. Then I felt the first stab of lonesomeness. I thought of the months that must pass before we saw each other again, and I knew I would never be more than half alive until he returned.

Often in the months that followed, I would reach inside my bodice to touch the golden wedding band he had given me. It was a reminder of his love, my assurance that I was always in his thoughts as he was constantly in mine. It was the talisman that would bring him back to me. For the few fleeting seconds that my fingers closed around the ring, it would make me feel that I was closer to him. Then I would tuck it back inside my bodice again, hidden from all the world.

I hated the secrecy on which Felipe had insisted, and felt that it was unnecessary. It seemed somehow to demean our feelings for each other, made our love seem shoddy, as though we had committed a crime by caring for each other. I would have preferred to tell everyone of the wonder and joy of our love; and I especially wanted to tell Papa, for I knew that he loved me. I was sure that, once he knew how I felt, he would not let his dislike of Felipe stand in the way of my happiness.

I did confide in Will. And Esperanza certainly guessed, for she commented that I had changed, that I looked different. And she was right: I had changed.

I had never really thought much about Felipe being Mexican until he told me that, unless the Varga grant was acknowledged at once, he intended to join the Mexican army. Perhaps once or twice before that, the thought had crossed my mind, but only fleetingly, such as on the night two years earlier when he and Jeremy and I had been sit-

387

ting on our front steps, with Papa's voice reaching us from the open windows in the parlor as he talked on and on about the terrible Exclusion Act the awful Mexicans had passed. It had suddenly occurred to me earlier that evening that it was Felipe's country, Felipe's people against whom he was ranting, and I felt suddenly ashamed for Papa's outburst. We had spoken then of Felipe being Mexican, and though he admitted that he did resent the coming of Americans into Texas, the full implication of what that might mean hadn't penetrated my mind.

I had been terribly hurt when he told me of his plans, for I saw them as meaning he was not as anxious to get back to me as I wanted him to be. I was jealous of both the Varga grant and the army, for the first was causing him to leave me, and the second threatened to prolong our separation. We quarreled bitterly, and parted in anger. But I knew Felipe's stubbornness was more than a match for my own, and so, because I couldn't bear the thought of wasting our few days together in pointless quarreling over something I couldn't change, I forgot my pride and went to him. When he begged me to run away with him, I longed to do so. But I knew I couldn't leave Mama. Even with Lupe and Esperanza always on hand, there were certain things that only I could do exactly as she liked to have them done, and she had come to depend on me. I could never forget it was all my fault that she had become so totally dependent on others.

If only Felipe had been willing to forget the Varga grant, and apply for some other section of land, then I would willingly have married him at once, and taken Mama and gone to join him as soon as he built a place for us to live. But he wouldn't even consider such a possibility, refused to discuss it. He didn't want just any land, not even if it happened to be a better piece of property than the Varga land. He was obsessed with the need to have his claim affirmed.

And he wanted to become an officer in the Mexican army, too. Because I loved him so, I had to try to accept the fact that he was pleased over the presence of the army

388

that most of us resented. In this matter, his attitude was truly Mexican.

I had always noticed certain gestures and manners of speech that set him apart from others. There was that funny little exaggerated shrug he gave that could mean any number of things: his lack of knowledge about a given subject, his indifference toward something, or just, with a slight change in the tilt of his head, the implication that what someone else was saying was so obvious that it should not have to be said at all. And there was the way he sometimes injected Spanish words or phrases into conversations, and his habit of always calling San Antonio de Bexar by its full name, instead of shortening it to Bexar and biting down hard on the X like the rest of us did. But these things, and other little gestures and mannerisms, I had not thought of before as being particularly Mexican. They were uniquely his own, like the darkness of his eyes, and the way he walked, moving in a manner that was at once both graceful and strong.

And I sometimes sensed a certain hostility about him, too —not toward me, but toward Americans in general.

In truth, I must admit that if I had been native-born, I, too, would probably have resented men like Sam Butler, and even, I suppose, like Papa. They had agreed to become Catholic and obey Mexican laws only because it was necessary in order to get their land grants, and never intended to fulfill either vow.

As far as Papa's promise to obey the Mexican laws was concerned, he had always willingly enough abided by the rulings of Austin's *ayuntamiento,* which, during those first years, were really the only laws that directly concerned us, besides the Colonization Laws which allowed us to come and claim our land. But the first time the Mexican government passed decrees of which Papa disapproved and tried to enforce some of them, then Papa refused to obey. When customs houses were established and Mexican soldiers brought in to collect customs duties, Papa had begun to circle around the collection points. Several times, he audaciously picked up goods from ships that were barely out of sight of the customs houses. He justified his actions by saying that the duties were prohibitively high. Felipe had disapproved openly of this, I know, and refused to be involved in the evasion of duties. Certainly, this added friction between them and made them even less tolerant of each other than they had been before.

It was the second week in June when Papa came home all excited with news. He had just arrived home from the west the previous afternoon and, as was his custom, had gone into San Felipe early the next morning to collect his newspapers and transact some business. He usually stayed all day, often returning after dark, but that day it was not yet noon when he came back, riding into our yard with his horse all in a lather. He jumped from the saddle even before the horse had stopped fully.

"Quick!" he shouted when he saw me at the door. "Get all the bullets you have molded. And tell Sukie I'll need plenty of hardtack and jerky, enough for a couple of weeks. Where's Will?"

"What's the matter?" I asked apprehensively, then remembered to answer his question. "He's in back of the house."

"Go get him. And here, take my patch bag and fill it— all it will hold." He threw me the little buckskin bag.

At that moment, Will walked around the far corner of the house. "You're back early." He eyed the horse. "He needs a good rubdown. I'll go do it." He ran his hand over the stallion's neck, then threw the reins over the animal's head and started leading him toward the barn.

"Wait!" Papa demanded, stopping Will in his tracks. "Let Daniel rub him down. You don't have time. I want you to come with me. Saddle the two fastest horses we own."

"Why?" Will asked. "Where are we going?"

"To Anahuac!" he answered, as though that should explain everything.

"Papa, please," I urged, "tell us what happened. Is Aus-

390

tin raising a company to go chase Indians? At Anahuac? I didn't think there were any around there—"

"It's not Indians this time. It's Mexicans! And it's not Stephen Austin who's raising the force. He's not here, and I'm glad. He'd probably be preaching about how we must stay calm, and talking about having meetings among ourselves to discuss everything, and then some more meetings with the Mexicans. He's always giving in to them, trying to mollify them. This time, it's not useless words we need, but action. We've got to show them our mettle, show them we can't be pushed around any longer."

"You mean you're going to fight?" Will asked, and I wonder if Papa noted the pained look on his face.

"Fight? Of course we are. After what happened—"

"But what did happen?" I asked again. "You still haven't said."

With a sigh of impatience, he started to tell us. "Well, nobody seems to know exactly, but I gather it was some trouble at Anahuac involving a Mexican soldier and one of our women. You know what scum of the earth those Mexican soldiers are! They get them from the jails, and then send them up here to harry us. It's insupportable!

"I understand that this was a case of—well, of a delicate situation. Whatever it was, the Texans knew they'd get no justice by reporting the matter to that idiot Bradburn, so they took things into their own hands. And then Bradburn had the gall to arrest Buck Travis and two others!" The words came tumbling out of Papa's mouth, one right behind the other, as though he knew he must stop to tell us what had happened, but begrudged every second the telling delayed him. "When a group of our men armed themselves and went to the fort to demand the release of the men, offering to exchange some Mexican soldiers they held, Bradburn agreed. He said he would release them as soon as our men turned the soldiers loose and backed away from the fort. And when they did that, assuming his word was good, the scoundrel reneged!

"Just a few hours ago, a rider arrived in San Felipe, ask-

ing all ablebodied men to come to their aid. We'll storm the
fort if we must, and kill every dirty Mexican in it, if that's
what it takes to get our men out." He said to Will, "Don't
just stand there! I just told you everything you need to
know. Get moving, get our horses saddled. You'll be coming with me, of course. How old are you now?"

"Seventeen," Will answered hesitantly.

Papa nodded. "That's old enough. We'll need all the
marksmen we can get, and you've proven yourself handy
enough with a rifle when you're not aiming at animals or
birds."

Will paled. "You mean you expect me to go with you
and—and shoot people?"

"Of course, if it's necessary," Papa snapped impatiently.
"This time, I don't think even Stephen Austin would expect
us to sit on our hands. Bradburn has been asking for this
for a long time. We'll accept his abuse no longer!"

I frowned at the disapproving tone of Papa's voice when
he mentioned Austin. When we had first moved from Nacogdoches, Papa couldn't praise Austin enough. But in the
last two years, he often hinted that Austin talked too much
and did too little.

"Now both of you," Papa finished, "go and do what I
told you, and quickly. Run!"

Will started toward the barn, and I turned to go back in
the house. I slowed my steps before I entered Mama's
room to ask her if I could rummage in her chest for one of
her old dresses. I let her assume I wanted it for cleaning
rags rather than patches for Papa's rifle. I had come to
realize that it only upset her to mention more than was
absolutely necessary about outside events. The slightest hint
of any trouble worried her for days on end, and I truly
believe she preferred not to know of anything unpleasant
that occurred beyond the scope of her vision. I did everything Papa had told me to do, and when I went out on the
porch carrying all the things he had asked for, I noted that
Will had returned with only one horse.

"You're not going?"

He shook his head. "I can't, Cassie. I don't want to kill—not birds or animals or anything. Certainly not people. I know shooting is necessary sometimes, like when someone's pointing an arrow or a rifle at you, and it's either you or them. But I don't want to point my rifle at anyone unless I'm forced to. Even if I saw an Indian with his bow drawn back ready to loose an arrow at me, I'm not really sure I'd be able to squeeze the trigger, not even if I knew it was the only way to save my own life. I can't help it. It's just the way I am, the way I feel. Do you think Papa will understand?"

I knew he would not, but as I was trying to think of some way to soften my words, Papa came around the side of the house. When he saw Will leading a single mount, he did not rage and bellow as I expected him to do. Instead, he shot Will a cold look full of disgust and loathing. He said cuttingly, "By God, I've bred a lily-livered coward. Well, stay home with the rest of the womenfolk, then." He jerked the reins from Will's hand, threw them over the horse's head, and mounted.

"Oh, Papa, do be careful," I urged, suddenly aware of the danger involved.

He stooped to pat my shoulder briefly, but the gesture was hurried, full of impatience. "Don't worry, Duchess. I can take care of myself. Anyway, those Mexicans couldn't hit a barn door with their blunderbusses!" His eyes sparkled with excitement, and I realized with a jolt that he was actually looking forward to the encounter, and would be disappointed if he missed it.

"Don't take any chances!" I called after him as he spurred his horse forward. Even though he acknowledged my admonition with a wave of his hand, I knew he had scarcely heard my words.

I watched him till he was out of sight, apprehension in my heart. Then I remembered that Will was still there, and I turned to him.

"He hates me," he said. "He thinks I'm staying home because I'm afraid."

It would not have been honest of me to try to deny Will's statement, for there had been no question of Papa's contempt. "You had to do what seemed right to you." I knew that when Will defied Papa's wishes, it was not from cowardice but from strength. And yet the kind of strength it had taken was not the kind Papa would acknowledge, or even recognize. But I understood, and along with Will, I wondered how some men could enjoy fighting to the death. I shuddered at the thought.

Papa was gone almost two months, and mingled with my deep concern for him was a nagging dread of what the future might hold. If there should be more trouble between the Texans and the Mexican army, what if Papa and Felipe should both be involved in it, pitted against each other?

Until Papa returned, I didn't understand that there were two opposing factions of the Mexican army. To my relief, I heard him praise the Mexican general, Antonio Lopez de Santa Anna. I recognized that unusual name instantly, because it was the same man Felipe had praised, the very general whose staff he had hoped to join. Papa extolling the man's virtues put things in an entirely different light. How could I worry, when Papa and Felipe were cheering for the same man?

Eagerly, I questioned Papa, and he answered me with equal eagerness, though he pointedly ignored any questions Will asked. There had been a lot of shooting, but not at Anahuac. The action had occurred instead at Fort Velasco when the Texans had tried to take a schooner past the fort. Though men had been killed and wounded on both sides, everything had turned out unexpectedly well for our side. A Colonel Mexia, sent by ship to punish our men for what could only be called open rebellion, had ended by drinking toasts with them to the health of Santa Anna!

"Thank God for Santa Anna!" Papa said fervently. "He's attracting more followers every day. He already virtually controls the army, and surely it's only a matter of time till the Bustamente government topples."

General Antonio Lopez de Santa Anna. I didn't know

then of his capacity for treachery, could not foresee that his very name would strike terror in my heart and the hearts of all Texans a scant three and a half years later. I only knew that he had miraculously appeared, like some guiding angel, just when he was most needed to heal the festering distrust between Texans and Mexicans. He had my heart-felt gratitude.

It was not until Papa came home next time six weeks later that I learned there had been another sequel to the original trouble at Anahuac. Jim Bowie, the man who designed the multi-purpose Bowie knife so prized on the frontier, had led a group of men who forced the Mexican troops stationed at Nacogdoches out of Texas because their colonel wouldn't declare himself for Santa Anna.

By the end of the summer, few Mexican soldiers remained anywhere in Texas. Most of them had either drifted quietly away of their own accord or been run out by Santa Anna's backers. We all cheered lustily for Santa Anna, the man who was uniting us with the rest of Mexico even as he saved us from our oppressors and promised us our separate statehood. How easily he deceived us all!

The Exclusion Act of 1830 hadn't stopped immigration as Papa had feared. It did stop the granting of rights to any more empresarios, but those who had existing grants were still allowed to continue bringing in people. Papa always beamed his approval on any arriving settlers.

"Every man who comes makes us that much stronger," he said one day as he came out of the house onto the porch. I was sitting in a rocker, sewing, and Will was on the steps, sketching. It was a measure of Will's assertion of independence that he no longer hid his sketch pad, but used it openly in front of Papa.

"There can no longer be any questioning our right to separate statehood," Papa continued. "Or maybe Mexico can even be convinced to sell Texas to the United States. If they won't do one or the other, then, by God, we'll just pull out and start our own government!"

395

Alarmed, I looked up at him. "But surely when Santa Anna gets in power, we'll have separate statehood."

"You never know," he said. "If they won't do as they say, then we'll fight for our rights."

"You mean war?" I shuddered at the thought.

He nodded. "We fought before, and we'll do it again, if we have to."

"Fighting is foolish," Will commented without raising his head. Since the day he had refused to go to Anahuac, he had changed. He was no longer acquiescent toward Papa, no longer seemed to be begging for his favor. I wondered if Papa had noticed.

Papa's jaw tensed. "It is necessary sometimes, when people are oppressed."

Will set his jaw in the same stubborn mannerism. Before he could answer with further open defiance, I said hastily, "It doesn't really matter, does it? There will surely be no need for war. Santa Anna will soon be in power, and he'll see that we have our rights."

"I hope so, Duchess." Papa rubbed his chin thoughtfully. "I certainly hope so."

During the months that all this was taking place, I lived for the days when Johnny would wheel the big lumbering coach into our yard and, smiling, hand down some letters for me. Since we had no mail service, Felipe had arranged with an officer friend of his in Bexar to use the official army correspondence pouch to transport our letters back and forth between Bexar and Mexico City, and Johnny was to carry them on the Bexar–San Felipe portion of their journeys. The system was utterly dependent on the two men, and it worked well until Johnny suddenly and unexpectedly stopped going on the coach. In mid-September, he brought me a hastily scrawled note that Felipe had written en route to Mexico City and entrusted to a Texan he passed going the other way. As he handed it to me, Johnny told me it was the last letter he would be able to bring me, for he planned to leave two days later from San Felipe to ride to Virginia and bring back his three small orphaned cousins.

"I'm really sorry, Cassie," Johnny said apologetically when he saw how his news distressed me. "We just got word that my uncle died, and his three little girls have no one but us to look after them. My brothers are all too young to go fetch them, so that sort of leaves it up to me." He grinned. "I can sure Lord imagine that Eliza is going to have a thing or two to say about me running off from her like this!"

I forced a smile at his attempt to treat the matter lightly. "Will anyone else take the coach to Bexar and back while you're gone?"

"There isn't anyone else. Todd said to just leave it in San Felipe till I get back."

"What about Felipe's army friend in Bexar? Does he know you won't be coming any more?"

He shook his head. "I'm truly sorry about this, Cassie, for your sake. I know how much it means to you to get those letters. I didn't know about this when I was in Bexar. I just found out when I got back to Gonzales."

"If you'll give me the name of Felipe's friend, maybe I can write him, ask him to find another way of sending Felipe's letters on to me."

"You can try." He frowned. "His name is Ramirez, Diego Ramirez, I think it is. He's a major, and he's at the Alamo. Or he was. He talked like he might not be there much longer."

"I'm sure our letters will still get through. It just might take them longer, that's all." I said the words as lightly as I could manage, knowing how few letters ever found their way to the proper recipients when entrusted to chance carriers. The face of one of the coach passengers appeared at the window, frowning impatience at the delay. "I mustn't keep you any longer," I said, starting toward the house. "Do be careful on your journey, and hurry back, for Eliza's sake."

"I will. Felipe and I will both be back here before you

and Eliza know it." With a wave and a smile, he was gone.

I went straight to my room, ignoring the persistent summons of Mama's bell, leaving it for Esperanza or Lupe to answer. Anxiously, I unfolded my letter. It was disappointingly short. He had written it while the man who would carry it waited, and he said that he was well and safe, not more than four days from the capital, and he loved me with all his heart.

I sighed, wishing Johnny had been able to make just one more trip, bring me one more letter, at least, saying that Felipe had arrived safely in Mexico City. If Felipe's friend left Bexar, how would his letters reach me? I fingered the gold chain around my neck and pulled out the wedding band, looked at it and put it to my lips.

*Patience!* I admonished myself. *You must wait.*

But the waiting wasn't easy. As September gave way to October, I thought that surely, soon, a passing rider might stop and squint for a minute at our name on the gatepost, and then turn into our yard and pull a much-weathered letter from his pocket. Even though I knew I could not possibly expect another letter for some time after Johnny left, that didn't stop me from watching anxiously every time I saw a rider approach from the west, hoping, yet not daring to hope, that he might carry a letter for me. And when the rider would continue east without even hesitating at our gate, I would turn and walk away from the window in disappointment. But it was impossible for me to stay away long, and soon my eyes would again begin to scan the road, waiting for the next rider. I even asked Will to repaint Papa's name on the gatepost sign, which he did to please me, even though we both knew it was clearly legible as it had been.

The days grew shorter, and the faded greens of late summer gave way to the golden tones of autumn. The air became crisp with the promise of winter days to come, but still no more letters arrived from Felipe.

By November, I was beside myself with anxiety, in spite of my firm resolve to accept the possibility that all our letters could get lost. Twice I had written Felipe's friend in Bexar and had no answer. If only I could get one more letter, I thought, one more letter telling me that Felipe had arrived safely in Mexico City, then I would not worry so. There was always a possibility that Felipe might have written his mother or Uncle Todd, and that their letters had managed to get through even though mine had not. When Papa came home for a few days in mid-November, I was determined to find out if he had possibly heard anything about Felipe from either of them. But I knew I must be very careful, and make my inquiries seem suitably casual.

Early on the next morning after his arrival, Papa went, as usual, into San Felipe for the day. He returned in time for supper and, afterwards, settled himself in his high-backed chair in the parlor, with a stack of *Texas Republic* newspapers by his side. He always read every word of the Harrisburg papers, then carefully refolded them into a neat pile to take to Uncle Todd.

I had ordered Lupe to make a blazing fire that night, for strong winds were blowing the chill air of a fresh norther through every crack and crevice of our house. Papa was on one side of the fire, and I was on the opposite side, mending one of Will's shirts in the welcome light of the flames. Will was lying on his stomach on the floor between us, thumbing through a book of engravings Priscilla had loaned him. It was Papa's first night at home in a month and a half, and he pored over the papers, methodically reading the old ones first. "That black mare foaled yet?" he asked Will from behind his paper.

"Last week," Will answered without looking up. "I had to turn the colt."

Papa lowered his paper. "That so? How'd you manage that?"

"I watched Owen Baines do it once at Schmidts' place. They'd called him in when one of their cows was having trouble calving. I asked him a lot of questions."

Papa nodded. "I'd have hated to lose that mare. She's

got good bloodlines, and this is only the second time she's foaled."

"I know." Will's eyes had never left the book that held his attention. His indifference to Papa's praise was not feigned. I wondered if Papa was even aware of the change that had begun that day, six months earlier, when Papa had said such cruelly cutting things to him for refusing to go to Anahuac. Until then, Will had always striven pathetically hard to earn Papa's approval, so rarely and grudgingly given to him. It had always embarrassed me because, Papa approved openly of almost everything I did—even, when I was younger, my naughtiness and disobedience. I had often sensed how much Will yearned for some of the approval and praise Papa lavished on me and denied him. Sometimes, I would point out something good that Will had done that merited Papa's attention. But Will seemed to have passed suddenly beyond caring, as though at last he had resigned himself to the fact that what he had sought after for most of his seventeen years was unattainable, and it was useless to expend any more effort to seek it.

"Did you get to Bexar this trip?" I asked Papa after he had again raised his paper.

"Umm-hmm," he answered affirmatively without lowering it.

"Are there still Mexican soldiers in the Alamo, or have they all gone south?"

"Many of them have left, I think," he answered vaguely, and I still had no clue as to whether or not Felipe's friend might have gone.

I forced myself to sit in silence for a few minutes before I asked in what I hoped was an off-hand manner, "How is everybody in Gonzales?"

"Everybody?" The paper rattled as Papa lowered it, looked at me with his eyebrows raised questioningly.

"You know—Uncle Todd and *Señora* Varga. I wish Uncle Todd would write once in a while. I miss his visits. Is he well?"

"He sends his love. He claims he can't write because of

400

his rheumatism, but he never was much of a letter writer, and I think he secretly is glad of the excuse."

"I hate to think of him getting old. He's sixty now, isn't he?"

"Yes. He says he feels good, considering. He works in the garden, walks around town every day, goes out riding occasionally."

"And *Señora* Varga—how is she?" My heart pounded apprehensively as I steered the conversation in the direction I wanted it to go.

The newspaper went up again. "Fine, I suppose," he said with finality.

"Suppose? Don't you see her when you go through Gonzales?" I was determined to keep him answering my questions, so that it would seem natural to continue until I had inquired about Felipe.

"I told you, she's fine." From behind the paper, I could hear the impatience in his voice, and I knew he was irked by my persistence, and wanted to be left alone to read.

But I couldn't stop asking questions until I had tried to find out what I longed to know. "Has she heard from Felipe since he left?" Did my inquiry sound casual enough, or did my voice betray my anxiety, the importance to me of the question I was asking?

The paper crackled as Papa dropped it into his lap, and he said exasperatedly, "I've read the same paragraph three times now, and I still don't know what it said. Ask your questions and be done with them, and then, please, let me read in peace. Now, what was it you asked?"

"I asked about Felipe," I said, lowering my eyes over my mending so he wouldn't be able to read in them how anxiously I awaited his answer. "Has Señora Varga heard from him since he got to Mexico City?"

"Why should I care?" he asked gruffly. "What that wild rapscallion does is of no interest to me. Small loss it would be if he disappeared down there forever!"

"I thought his mother might have mentioned something to you about him. I miss him coming on the coach." Then, lest he interpret that too personally, I added hastily, "I miss Johnny, too. I just wondered if Felipe had reached the capital all right." My eyes misted so that I couldn't see the place I had been stitching. I waited anxiously for Papa's answer, but I heard the crackling of the paper as he raised it again, and I knew he was not going to say any more. After a few minutes, I folded my mending and excused myself, saying I was very tired.

Dejected, I went to my room and closed the door. If Papa knew anything about Felipe, he was not going to tell me. Could his evasion have been deliberate? Did Papa suspect how we felt about each other? Had that been why he had forbidden Felipe to stay in the old cabin any more? But how could he have known when, at that time, there had been nothing to know?

I had learned nothing.

Next time Papa was home for one of his brief stays, in mid-December, he and Sam Butler sat up late one evening, talking. Priscilla had sent an apology that night, saying she wasn't feeling well, and Sam had come alone for dinner. I had instructed Lupe to serve coffee in the parlor after the meal, and I poured it for the two men and then stayed only long enough afterward to be polite before I excused myself. Sam Butler irritated me beyond measure. I had met other men as gruff and unpolished as he and liked them. It was not his crudeness that irked me. I truly believed him incapable of compassion for either man or beast, and he always talked as though he assumed his own opinion was the only one that really mattered. I had always resented the way he forced Jeremy to do his bidding. I would never have submitted to such bullying, and I was angered by the way Sam used his authority on someone who lacked the spirit to fight back. I was annoyed by his supreme egotism, his self-seeking grasping ways. I had never been adept at hiding my feelings, so I usually found some excuse to absent myself from his company as soon as it was possible. Neither of them seemed to mind that night when, a few minutes after

402

Will had gone to make certain everything outside was locked up, I excused myself and went to bed.

It must have been hours later when Mama's bell wakened me from a sound sleep. I sat up, reaching for my wrapper, assuming that Papa had already gone to bed in Uncle Todd's cabin. He did not share Mama's room when he was home, had not for a long time. As I passed the parlor door, I heard Sam and Papa still talking, and I wondered idly what they could have been discussing at such length. Perhaps they were dickering over the price of the bottomland Papa rented to Sam each year. Papa had mentioned the day before that he intended to ask Sam for twice what he had been charging him the past few years.

The next morning, I found their conversation had concerned neither politics nor land rent. Papa was up early and smiled when he came into the kitchen. That in itself was unusual, for he was usually as grumpy as a bear till he had downed his first mug of coffee.

"Good morning, Duchess," he said with unaccustomed cheeriness. He came over to kiss my cheek. "You look like a busy little goodwife this morning, bustling about the kitchen."

I smiled. Soon, surely within a year, I would truly be a wife, in my own house, my own kitchen, with Felipe across the table from me. "I'll get your coffee," I said. I filled his mug with the steaming brew and set it in front of him as he took his place at the table.

"Two eggs?"

He nodded. "And I hope those are biscuits I smell. How I do miss those when I'm gone. Nobody in the world can make them like Sukie!"

Sukie, standing in front of the fire, turned around to smile acknowledgment.

As he finished his breakfast, I poured him another mug of coffee. He motioned for me to sit down across from him.

"Sam and I had a long talk last night."

I smiled, knowing that somehow their conversation of the night before must have pleased him. "Did you get him to agree to your price for that strip of bottomland he farms?"

My guess seemed to amuse him. "It wasn't land rental we were discussing. It was you and Jeremy."

Surprised, I asked apprehensively, "Why would you have been talking about us?"

His smile broadened. "We figure on a wedding soon, as soon as Jeremy can get away next spring."

I asked incredulously, "You mean you expect me to marry Jeremy?"

"What's so startling about that? Oh, I know you probably hadn't planned on marrying quite so soon—"

"But I can't leave Mama!" I protested, "and even if I could, I—I just couldn't marry Jeremy!"

"I realize how you feel about your mother, Duchess, and I think it's admirable the way you've cared for her so well. But she has Lupe and Esperanza now, and you must consider your own future."

"But not with Jeremy! I couldn't—!"

"Of course you could," he insisted impatiently. Then he switched to a cajoling manner and said, "Why, I hear half the girls in Massachusetts are eager to marry him. He's grown into a handsome young man, and of course you know Sam adopted him officially years ago. He'll be Sam's heir."

"That means nothing to me. I don't love him!" I insisted.

"Love?" he scoffed. "What does a young girl know of love?"

I wanted to tell him, then, that I knew all about love, knew that it could bring happiness, knew that parting from a beloved person could mean great sorrow. I reached for the gold chain around my neck, then stopped to reconsider. Should I tell him about Felipe and me? I was on the verge of doing so, but some instinct warned me that it was not the right time, so I dropped my hand. "I know enough to be certain that I don't love Jeremy."

"Nonsense!" he said brusquely, dismissing my objection. "Love comes after marriage. Sam and I have been planning this for a long time."

404

I began to feel panicky at his quiet persistence. I would not have been half as alarmed if he had raged and shouted. "No one has discussed any plans with me!"

"Come now, my dear. You mustn't let foolish notions of love interfere with what is best for you. You know it's only your happiness I care about. Jeremy will make you a fine husband. Why, I'll wager he's the only man in all of Texas who's attended Harvard Law School. Sam has always insisted on giving him the best education possible. During the summer, Sam's sending him to Nacogdoches to study under a very good man there. You and he can be married in April, then have time for a honeymoon trip to New Orleans before you go to Nacogdoches. Then you can go together to Massachusetts in the fall."

"No!" I hadn't meant to shout, but my violent denial of what he proposed seemed to fill the room, reverberate from the walls. To soften the bluntness of my refusal lest he be angered by it, I added quietly, "I'm sorry if it displeases you, but I just couldn't marry Jeremy."

"What foolishness! I won't be around forever to take care of you. I'd like to see you settled. Please, my dear, for me. I want to know you're properly cared for."

*Felipe will care for me,* I wanted to say, but I did not. Later, I would convince him that my happiness lay with Felipe. But first, the problem was to make him realize that I could not marry Jeremy. "Please understand, Papa," I said, choosing my words carefully, "that I couldn't do as you ask. How could I marry a man I could never respect? Jeremy lets himself be bullied by Sam—he actually cringes when he's around him! And now he's even willing to let Sam choose a wife for him!"

"Filial obedience is nothing to be ashamed of, and as for Sam choosing you—why would Jeremy want to choose otherwise? You'd do any man credit—"

"You don't understand. Whether or not Jeremy would have chosen me of his own free will, the point is that he obviously didn't."

"What utter nonsense! You and Jeremy have been

405

friends for a long time, and you seem to get on well enough. That's all that matters."

"It isn't all that matters," I said, thinking that the only thing that did matter was that Felipe and I loved each other. Still, I knew it was best to convince Papa by logical reasoning rather than by blunt unexplained refusal, so I continued, "As a friend of Jeremy's, I can accept his weakness. But as his wife, it would be unbearable. And another thing, Jeremy has never quite approved of the way I am. He would expect me to change, become docile and meek like Priscilla."

"Sam and I thought we could make the announcement soon, at Christmastime," he continued. I wondered if he had even been listening to what I said. "We couldn't have a party here, of course, but Sam has offered to have it at Roseland. He plans to make it quite an important social affair, with an orchestra and expensive French wines. Why, your engagement party and the wedding to follow will be the biggest social events in the colony since its beginning!"

I listened, too shocked to stop him. He and Sam seemed to have planned the whole thing without even consulting me! Just the very mention of Roseland irked me. Giving his house a fancy name was just one of the many things Sam Butler did to give himself airs.

I continued to listen in stunned silence as Papa talked on about the plans—the guest list, the wedding ceremony itself. Then he returned to the subject of what a fine husband Jeremy would make. "You're a lucky girl," he said. "Sam gives him an ample allowance, and he intends to increase it generously after you're married—"

Finally, I could stand to listen no longer. "And because Sam tells him to," I said exasperatedly, "he would marry me without protest, whether he wanted to or not!

"He'd surely have no reason to go against Sam's wishes." He smiled at me. "You're a very pretty girl, Duchess."

"But can't you see, Papa? Jeremy is exactly like a trained dancing bear. When Sam tells him to jump, he'll jump. If he tells him to marry me, he'll do it. Can't you see how weak he is? He can always be depended on to do exactly what Sam tells him."

"You would do well to listen to me and obey me, as well," he answered, obviously irked by my unfavorable comparison.

"I can't marry Jeremy, Papa," I said, looking directly into his eyes. "Don't force me into a marriage I don't want." Silently, I watched him, pleading mutely for his understanding, knowing I must first convince him I couldn't marry Jeremy. Later, when he had accepted that fact, then I could tell him about Felipe and me.

He stood up, frowned. "You think about it for a few days, and we'll talk about it again." He walked from the room. I sighed in relief.

For the time being, I had won. But I knew he had not given up, that he still hoped to win my agreement.

It puzzled me that he had broached the matter so suddenly, so unexpectedly, and that he seemed in such haste to have me wed to Jeremy. It was almost as if he had known about Felipe and me, was determined to have me safely married before his return.

*Nonsense!* I told myself. *How could he possibly have found out?* Felipe had told no one, except perhaps Johnny, and I was certain that he had admonished him to silence. I had told only Will, and knew my secret was safe with him. No, I concluded, there was just no way Papa could know.

I didn't know at the time that, by an odd quirk of chance, he had been given two letters from Felipe to me, and that he had read them, and knew we planned to marry. But even if I had known, I could never have imagined the lengths to which he would go in order to prevent our marriage.

# Chapter II

## AUSTIN'S COLONY—December 1832

A few days after Papa startled me by announcing his and Sam's assumption that Jeremy and I would marry, he invited me to ride with him into San Felipe. I accepted eagerly, dressed quickly, whispered hurried instructions to Will to watch for a letter from Felipe, and then mounted a chestnut mare on whom Papa had placed the new sidesaddle he had brought me from Bexar.

When we reached the town later that morning, Papa took me to the Parkers', where I received a warm welcome. Patience wouldn't hear of Papa leaving without a midmorning "bite to eat," which consisted of as complete and varied an array of food as we served at our house for a full-course meal.

Later that morning, Eliza and Patience suggested that I should spend the night with them. "We're having a dinner party," Eliza explained, "and I'm sure the talk will be all about politics. You must stay, so I can have someone to talk to about something else!"

"A dinner party?" I protested. "I couldn't. I have only my riding clothes—"

"We can take care of that," Eliza insisted. "My sister Meg is about your size, and just a little taller than you. I'm sure one of her dresses will fit well enough if we just turn up the hem a bit. And I can loan you petticoats and slippers. Please stay! Sam Houston is coming."

"Oh?" I said questioningly, and paused, knowing from

409

the way she said his name that I was supposed to have recognized it, and feeling very backward and uninformed because I didn't. "I'm afraid you'll have to tell me who he is," I admitted apologetically.

"He's the most talked-about man in San Felipe right now," Patience said over her shoulder as she removed loaf after loaf of crusty bread from the oven. "He's just arrived from the East. They say he's Andy Jackson's man, sent here to spy out our situation, but of course nobody really knows for sure. It was Lemuel who invited him to dinner, not me. Not that I mind feeding him or any other man, but I do think it's ridiculous the way everyone is fussing over him so. You'd almost think it was the second coming of the Lord, the way some folks are acting! And it's positively shameful the way some of our women are throwing their daughters at him, even though it's common knowledge he's applied for land on Karankawa Bay as a married man!"

"Nobody knows if he's really married, Mother," Eliza said. "You know a married man gets more land than a bachelor."

"Still and all," Patience insisted firmly, "if he claims to be married, then he should be treated as such and not as an eligible bachelor."

Eliza saw my puzzlement and explained, "He was married a few years ago to a young girl, while he was governor of Tennessee. They say her family forced her to marry him. I suppose they thought it was something wonderful, for her to marry the governor of the state. Well, she went through with the marriage, all right. But then, a few days after the wedding, she left him, and nobody knows if the marriage was annulled. They say that to this day, he's never told another living soul what happened between him and his wife. Her name was Eliza, too. Anyway, he still gets fighting mad if anyone dares to say anything against her.

"There's all kinds of talk, of course. Some say she was just afraid of him because he's such a big brute of a man. Others say she was secretly in love with someone else all the time."

410

Patience surveyed the loaves she had set on the table to cool. "Ten," she said with a frown. "I think that will be enough, with biscuits and cornbread besides, don't you, Eliza?"

"Enough to feed half of San Felipe," Eliza laughed. "If Mother knew Houston was unattached, she'd probably be throwing me at his head, too, if I weren't promised," Eliza continued teasingly. I marveled at the easiness of the banter between them.

"I don't think so, my dear. The man's past actions would worry me too much. They say he developed an immense fondness for the bottle after his young bride left him. You and Cassie could slice the onions for me, dear. Would you fetch about four large ones from the root cellar?"

Eliza moved toward the back door. "When his wife left him, he resigned as governor and went to live with the Cherokees. He spent three years with them, and they called him the Big Drunk. That's what Mama's talking about."

"I wonder what he's doing in Texas," I mused after Eliza had left.

"That is precisely the same question everyone is asking. What does he want here?" Patience shrugged, then walked over to the fire to lift the lid on a large kettle and stir the contents with a long-handled wooden spoon. "My only problem at the moment is how much he and fourteen other people can eat."

I surveyed the kitchen, which was full to bursting with bread, cakes, spitted chickens ready to be roasted, savory meat pies, and gigantic kettles of soup. "Only a small portion of all the food you will set before them, at best," I said with a smile.

I helped prepare for the party and soon became caught up in the exictement. By the time Papa returned to take me home that afternoon, we had already taken up the dress and chosen the petticoats and slippers I was to wear. I begged Papa to let me stay, and he smiled.

"It seems to be all arranged, so I don't see how I can refuse."

411

"Lem has invited Sam Houston and a few others to dinner," Patience explained. "You'd be more than welcome to stay, too, Mr. Stewart. We've a spare room over the stables. It's not fancy, but the bed is good. And I'll never notice if there's one more plate around the table."

Papa protested, but his eyes were alight with interest at the mention of Houston, and he soon let himself be persuaded to stay.

It was easy to see that Sam Houston had once been a handsome man. His hair was sandy, his face round, and his jaw strong and square. His skin had the weathered look of someone who has spent much of his life outdoors, but beneath the surface there was an unhealthy flush, a puffiness. He was a big man, well over six feet. Papa towered over most men, but I noted as he stood talking to Houston that evening that he was several inches shorter than the new arrival.

I commented to Eliza on the flushed puffiness of his complexion, and she whispered knowingly, "It's the mark of a heavy drinker."

"Oh." I returned my attention to the man, who was telling of his journey into Texas. It was an ordinary story, but the man was a born storyteller, not eloquent, perhaps, but compelling. As he talked, I looked around the room from one face to another, and felt an inexplicable uneasiness at the expressions I saw. Most of the men—Papa worst of all—and a few of the women were looking at him with such open adoration that it seemed almost indecent. Only on Patience's face did Eliza and I see signs of worship withheld. She was giving him her attention, as any polite hostess would, but she did not seem to be swept along in the powerful current of his forcefulness as the others were.

Later that night, as Eliza and I were getting ready for bed, I admitted that the man made me uneasy. "Not Houston himself, exactly," I said, "but what he seems to do to people."

"I know what you mean," Eliza agreed, handing me a freshly laundered nightgown. "My stepfather and your father looked like they would have gone down on their knees to him, if he had asked it of them."

"There's something about him I don't like. He's pleasant enough, I guess, and he's certainly a glib talker, and I suppose he might have a brilliant mind, but I still feel there's something sort of—well—underhanded about him."

"Exactly," Eliza agreed as she moved the brush vigorously through her shining hair. "It's not that I feel he's actually dishonest. It's just that everything he does and says seems to have a purpose, and I suspect he's figured out long ahead of time what that purpose is."

I nodded my agreement. "I think your mother feels the same way we do. I was watching her. She wasn't all overcome with hero worship like everyone else was."

"I think you're right." Eliza put the brush down on her dresser. "Mother can spot weevily flour just from glancing at the barrel."

We laughed and blew out the candle and went to bed. I lay awake for some time after Eliza's even deep breathing told me she was asleep. I was unable to stop thinking about the hulking man from Tennessee. How easily he had held everyone's attention most of the evening! Almost against my will, even I had felt that I must hear everything he had to say. It was this compelling power of his that frightened me. In the past year, there had been far too much grumbling, far too much discontent all around us. Why had Sam Houston come, I wondered? What was he doing in Felipe's and my Texas of tall pines and quiet rivers and rippling grasses? He was a forceful man, and I didn't doubt for a moment that he would use all the considerable power he had to direct the general discontent to his own ends, to sway political thinking in the direction he wanted it to take. But what direction was that? I did not think it would be long before I found out.

As Papa and I were riding back home the following morning, I didn't mention my fears, for his admiration of the man was boundless. I noticed that he prefaced many of his remarks with phrases like "Houston says," or "Houston thinks," or "according to Houston." Papa's complete capitulation to the force of Houston's character irritated me, and I listened in silence. If only Sam Houston had possessed even a small measure of the sincerity that tempered Stephen Austin's air of authority, I might have been won over. But sincerity seemed no part of Houston's nature.

*He has no right*, I thought indignantly, *no right at all to come into our midst and pretend to be one of us, when he's not!* Austin was one of us. And, for all that he was the first one to bring settlers to Texas, and had done so much to see that his colonists prospered, he didn't set himself up above us. Listening to Papa endlessly praising the opinions and words of Sam Houston, I only wished he could spare a few words of praise for Stephen Austin, in which I would have joined him wholeheartedly.

But I had no chance that day or any other to join Papa in praise of the man who had ruled our colony with paternalistic firmness for over ten years, for the name of Stephen F. Austin had faded from his lips.

Next time I saw Sam Houston was the following April, when Papa took me with him to the convention at San Felipe. Papa had spent a surprising amount of time at home between December and April. During those months, he made frequent trips into San Felipe, and he often let me accompany him. To my relief, he had stopped trying to press me into agreeing to a hastily announced betrothal before the end of the year. But he still extolled Jeremy's virtues at every opportunity, and intimated that when Jeremy returned in the spring would be a good time to make the announcement. Consistently, I told him I could not marry Jeremy, and he just as consistently acted as though I had agreed and it was just a matter of setting the time and place. Meanwhile, time was on my side, and I watched as one month faded into another. Each month was that much closer to the day Felipe would return. He had said he would start back after he had been there a year, at the very latest, even if he had not been successful in getting his claim recognized. That would put him back the following fall or, at the latest, the winter. And when he returned, I would be waiting for him. I would not marry anyone else.

The groundwork for the San Felipe convention had been laid the previous fall, and its avowed purpose was to form a constitution for the hoped-for independent state of Texas. With Santa Anna well established in power, everyone felt that at last our pleas for separation from Coahuila were about to be heeded. Papa was elected a delegate to the convention, and so was Sam Houston, who was sent by the people of Nacogdoches, where he had begun to practice law. In just a few months, he had worked his way into the hearts—and the politics—of the people.

I left Will no reminders to watch for a letter from Felipe while I was gone, for I had stopped hoping to hear from him. No word had come from him since the previous September, when Johnny had brought me that short note. I was certain that Felipe's friend had left Bexar at about the same time, for I had received no answer to any of the several queries I had sent to him.

He had been gone a full year. Any day, he might return, and letters would never matter again. When he came back, I knew I would go away with him, and send for Mama later, if Papa refused to give us his blessings. So often in the winter months just passed, I felt closer to Papa than I had at any time in the previous eight years. I had been on the verge of telling him about Felipe and me any number of times. But always, just as I was about to speak, I would remember Felipe's warning that Papa would stop at nothing to keep us apart, and I would remain silent. Time enough to tell him when Felipe returned, and see what happened then. It would hurt Papa deeply if he denied us permission to marry and we had to run away, but not even for him would I give up Felipe.

How I envied Eliza! The path of her love was so much smoother than Felipe's and mine. She had received a few

415

letters from Johnny and expected him to return to Texas the following month.

"And the wedding is set for September, two months before I'm eighteen," she told me happily as she helped me carry my belongings to the room she and I would share over the stable. Eliza had moved out of her room for Johnny's parents, Ben and Sarah Gorham, who would arrive later that day. Papa was to stay elsewhere, with one of his friends.

Papa came in to help bring in my clothes and to greet Patience and Eliza, and of course Patience insisted he have a cup of coffee and one of her ample snacks. We were seated around the table when Patience invited him to have dinner with us that evening, and he seemed to be on the point of accepting when she mentioned that the Gorhams from Gonzales would also be there. I thought I saw something akin to alarm flicker briefly across his face before he refused, claiming a previous engagement. The expression was so fleeting I almost missed it, and I wondered afterwards if I had imagined it. And yet the Gorhams were from Gonzales, and so was Felipe. Could there possibly be something they might know, something that would give me some clue to whatever it was that stood between Papa and Felipe, had made them such bitter enemies? I had always felt that if I only knew what had caused the rift, the bitterness between them, then surely I could help mend it. I decided to ask gently prodding questions of the Gorhams at my first opportunity, to see if I could uncover any clue to the problem I had never understood. But before I did that, I would first inquire for news of Felipe. Perhaps a letter had come through to Serena or someone else in Gonzales.

My opportunity came that night at dinner. I was seated next to Sarah Gorham, a short, plump, matronly woman with an open friendly manner. She was only too happy to talk about Felipe. "An unusual boy," she said. "Of all Johnny's friends, he was my favorite. I couldn't begin to keep track of how many hundreds of bullets he and Johnny wasted trying to determine which of them could shoot the most accurately. And it was all for nothing. They came to a standoff every time."

I watched her plain round face light up with laughter, and I smiled, feeling a kinship with her. She knew Felipe, and liked him, and enjoyed talking about him. And never would I tire of listening.

She continued. "Felipe has always been a bit of a puzzle to us, you know. He's Mexican and has a Spanish name, but he's never seemed at all like any of the other Mexicans we know. He talks English with no more accent than you or I, but that doesn't make him exactly like us, either. If, God willing, we get our own separate state government here, we'll be sort of set apart from the rest of Mexico, since most of us are Americans. We wondered which way Felipe would go when that happens, but I guess he's already made his choice ahead of time. I wish him well, if that's what he wants. I understand he's a captain in the Mexican army now."

"You've heard recent news of him, then?" I asked, my heart beating wildly. I could have cried with relief. He was safe! I tried to envision how handsome and dashing he would look in his uniform. His being in the Mexican army no longer concerned me as it had at first. With Santa Anna firmly entrenched in power, I was sure we would be granted our separate statehood, so the reason for any armed conflict between us and the Mexican army no longer existed. And Santa Anna would no longer need so many men south of the Rio Bravo. Surely Felipe would soon be able to come back to me. Maybe, at that very moment, he was on his way. I hugged the thought to me, and smiled at Sarah Gorham.

"I suppose he'll be coming back to Texas soon," I prodded.

She frowned. "Oh, no, I don't think so. That's what I meant when I said it looked like he'd decided to stay with the Mexicans. A friend of ours just returned from the capital. That's how we learned Felipe was in the army. Our friend said Felipe was quite helpful to him, and introduced

417

him to all the right officials to enable him to settle his business there. He said Felipe seems to have established himself very well. He's even gotten himself engaged to some general's daughter."

"Engaged?" I gasped. I felt all the blood drain from my face in a rush. Felipe engaged to someone else? It couldn't be! There had to be some mistake! Either the Gorhams's friend had Felipe mixed up with someone else, or he had been misinformed. I shook my head. "Oh, no," I said emphatically. "That couldn't be! I think your friend made a mistake. Felipe was engaged to a—a Texas girl."

Sarah Gorham shook her head. "No, my dear," she said confidently, "there is no mistake at all. Ben's friend even met the girl, said she seemed to worship Felipe. He was engaged to a Texas girl, you say? How strange! Johnny never mentioned it to me, and he would certainly have known." She shrugged. "Well, if he was, he must have changed his mind."

Changed his mind? It couldn't be true! Pressed against my skin inside my tight-fitting bodice, I could feel the gold ring that I always wore on the locket chain. It was still there, the ring that I had always been certain would bring Felipe back to me, the ring he had said he would return to put on my finger, where it belonged. I wanted Sarah Gorham to stop talking while my mind reasoned things through, found the flaw in what she was saying. She talked on.

"Lovely girl. . . . Beautiful, he said, a very delicate dark sort of beauty. . . . And Felipe treats her so carefully, like a fragile china doll that might break. . . . No, he couldn't be intending to come back and marry a Texas girl. . . . He told our friend he'd be staying in Mexico City, since his affianced doesn't want to leave her family . . ."

*Stop!* I wanted to shout. *I don't want to hear any more about her! I don't want to know anything about Felipe's betrothed!* But Sarah had warmed to her subject, and she kept talking. I wanted to revert to childhood, put my fingers in my ears as I had when I was small, to shut out the sound of something I did not want to hear. But I was grown, a young woman, and could no longer behave like a child. So I sat mutely, not trusting myself to talk, continuing to feign interest in what Sarah Gorham was saying, and not let her guess that her words were breaking my heart.

Lem Parker, on the other side of her, drew her attention away from me, and I was grateful for the respite. I could not have listened much longer to her talk about Felipe's bride-to-be. I lowered my eyes, stared at the food on my plate, and was suddenly aware of Eliza's touch on my arm. She had stopped talking to Johnny's father on her right, and was leaning toward me, asking solicitously, "Cassie, dear, are you all right? You're positively white! Are you ill? Would you like to lie down?"

I shook my head, unable to break my stare, or to raise my eyes to look at her, or to trust my voice to speak.

Felipe wasn't coming back, not to me, not ever. Not this month or next month or next year. Never. How could I bear the heartbreak? He had left me to find it out through a chance conversation with a stranger. He should have come back to tell me himself: he owed me that much. Felipe, always so sensitive to my needs, had done this to me!

The rest of the meal was an unending nightmare. I remember being drawn into conversations in which answers were needed, and I gave them as briefly as I could, hearing the unaccustomed hollowness in my own voice. But what did it matter how my voice sounded, or if I was giving inane answers? Nothing, nothing in my whole life mattered any more.

Somehow, I struggled through until there was a scuffling of chairs and I realized the meal was over. I nodded my thanks at someone who had pulled out my chair for me, without even knowing—or caring—who it was. I left the room with the others, then detached myself from them and ran out of the house to the room over the stables that Eliza and I were to share. The tears it had taken so much effort to restrain began to pour forth, blinding me, so that I stumbled over the rough ground, tripping and bumping into things. I remembered the chain around my neck, and reached up to tug at it violently. I jerked at it again and again until finally it gave way with a snap. I heaved it away from me, it and the things it held, wishing I could as easily rid myself of my love for Felipe. I groped my way up the outside stairway to the room over the stables, flung open the door, and threw myself down on the bed to sob out my misery.

Over my sobs, I heard Eliza calling my name, heard her come into the room, felt her hand on my shoulder as she sat down on the edge of the bed. "Cassie, dear, what's the matter?"

The previous December, I had told Eliza of the ring Felipe had given me, our secret engagement. As I told her the shocking news I had just learned from Sarah Gorham, she gasped, "I don't believe it! Felipe would never do that to you!"

"That's what I thought," I answered bitterly, "but there's no mistake. Felipe is engaged to a general's daughter. Mrs. Gorham even described her to me and told me how tenderly Felipe treats her!"

I lay awake much of that night, burying my face in my damp pillow to muffle the sobs that continued to shake me. I wanted to hate Felipe for betraying the infinite trust I had in him, but it was not that easy to stop loving him. *Felipe!* my heart cried out. *Felipe, how could you have done this to me?*

But he could, and he had. Slowly, bitterness began to seep into my heart. I willed it to drive out the love even as I knew it was not that easily destroyed.

The next morning, I saw Papa, and I told him about Felipe and me, about our secret engagement, and what I had learned the previous evening. I knew how he felt about Felipe, knew he could be depended upon to join me in denouncing him. Far from being angry with me for having failed to tell him sooner, he was understanding and sympathetic. But still, he was unable to keep the satisfaction from his voice.

"My dear child!" he said. "How that terrible boy has deceived you! But I always knew he was sly and untrustworthy, and you're well rid of him. I never told you, because I didn't want to worry you, but he once made some pretty terrible threats concerning what he would do to you, in order to get back at me for some imagined slight."

"You mean he threatened to harm me?" I asked incredulously, shocked at the revelation. "Felipe? What did he threaten to do?"

"Come now, Duchess, I've said too much already. There's no need to bother your little head about it now. He's out of your life forever, and we needn't concern ourselves with his idle threats concerning your honor any more."

"Oh!" My bitterness was fed by his words as I realized with a shock what Felipe's threat must have been. I suspected, as Papa did not, that his threat had not been so idle. That night, that last night he was camped in the woods near our house, I had gone to him, offering myself to him, and he had seemed reluctant to take me. Was it possible he had just feigned reluctance, had planned all along to make good his threat, to strike at Papa through me? It seemed incredible to think so, but a part of me wanted to believe the absolute worst of him, to destroy completely and finally the love that lingered in my heart in spite of his faithlessness.

"Oh, Papa, I loved him so!" Papa held out his arms to me and I threw myself into them as I had when I was a small child, and wept on his shoulder till I could weep no more.

San Felipe throbbed with activity during the convention days. There were so many strangers in town that it had prompted Patience to remark that enough men had arrived from the East for the meeting to put the Texans in the minority. "Those who seem to be protesting the loudest about the need for freedom from tyranny are those who

421

still have the mud from the banks of the Sabine caked on their boots," she commented. She did not have to add *like Sam Houston,* but she and Eliza and I shared a quick look that was understood by the three of us. Ben Gorham and Lem Parker had already made it clear that they felt Sam Houston to be exactly the man of action we needed at the moment, so we did not voice our opinions aloud.

When Eliza and I left that afternoon to pay a call on Eliza's sister, we were stopped by a man who asked us to direct him to the meeting house. After we had told him, we realized that he was not really interested in the location of the building, but had used the inquiry only as an excuse to stop us. Embarrassed and angered, we hurried on through the rutted streets, picking our way cautiously around the puddles. I was so preoccupied with keeping my skirt out of the mud without lifting it too high that I was scarcely aware of a horse and rider approaching until a deep voice asked, "May I see you to your destination, ladies?"

Remembering the bold man who had accosted us a few minutes earlier, I looked up indignantly, ready to stare haughtily at some forward stranger. And there, smiling down at me, was Jeremy.

"Jeremy!" I gasped, surprised at the extent of my delight at seeing him. As he dismounted, I introduced him to Eliza, and then he fell into step beside us, leading his horse behind him.

"I thought you were up north. Papa said Sam didn't expect you home for another month or two."

"I left a little earlier than I should have. I couldn't stay away, not from something as important as this, even if it sets me back a term. There's too much to be learned from watching. Besides, Ma wrote that Sam Houston was in Texas now, and I wanted a chance to meet him."

"Oh, no!" I groaned. "Don't tell me you're taken with him, too?"

He looked at me belligerently. "He's an important man."

"Self-important," I scoffed. "The Cherokees named him the Big Drunk, didn't they, Eliza?"

Eliza nodded and Jeremy countered defensively. "Houston might have drunk intemperately for a while to try to forget his great personal sorrow."

"I suppose you mean his wife leaving him." Suddenly, I wanted to shock him. Jeremy, stolid and unimaginative, assumed all ladies should be patterned after his mother; soft and gentle and meek. His bland assumption that I should want to conform to that pattern had irritated me since the first day we had met, and always brought out everything perverse in my nature. Maliciously, I added, "I don't blame her. I wouldn't want that horrid brute in my bed, either."

Eliza gasped sharply, and I saw she was looking at the ground, her face a bright crimson. But it was Jeremy I had wanted to embarrass, not Eliza, and I was disappointed and annoyed when he ignored my words, failed to acknowledge them with more than a slight pursing of his lips.

He began to tell us about life in Massachusetts, and I studied him as he talked, unable to keep from comparing him with Felipe. Felipe, of the quick smile which lighted his whole face in an instant, of the equally quick temper that could darken his brow as suddenly as a thunderhead rolls across the sun and obscures it. Jeremy, lacking in spirit, too unimaginative even to appreciate the wit of others; even his anger was weak, without real force. Felipe, wearing now the flamboyant uniform of a Mexican army officer. Jeremy, dressed in stylish but somber clothing, as befitted a young lawyer. Felipe, impulsive, unpredictable. Jeremy, totally predictable and dull. But that day I found a measure of comfort in knowing that Jeremy was utterly dependable, would always do what was expected of him.

I saw him every day we stayed in San Felipe. The first time he called at the Parkers', Lem grilled him rigorously about his politics. I could see he was flattered at being asked for his opinions, and when his answers pleased Lem and Ben Gorham, he was contented to bask in their praise.

"Aren't you afraid your stepfather will object to your political opinions?" I asked him later when we were alone. I was baiting him, and I knew it. I had heard Sam and

Papa talking politics enough to know that Sam had refused to participate in the constitution-making convention, or even give it his approval.

"Pa likes to keep things just as they have been. He can't see the need for change, for action, but I can. We supported Santa Anna; now it's time we asked him for our reward for that support. Unfortunately, Pa doesn't see it that way. He thinks we should wait till Santa Anna offers us our separate statehood."

I was surprised at his answer, but said nothing. Jeremy, always submissive agreement and weak compliance, daring to cross Sam Butler? Had the years he had spent away from home wrought a drastic change in him, after all, a change I had never expected and had failed to notice before? I looked at him with a new admiration.

The next day, Jeremy rented a buggy and took me out for a ride in the countryside. We rode in silence for some time, and I could not keep my mind from returning again and again to Felipe. If he had been there, he would have brought two riding horses for us, and we would have ridden wildly, recklessly, following no roads, going where our whims led us. But it was in keeping with Jeremy's character that he had chosen to rent a buggy, with a docile horse to pull it.

It was Jeremy who broke the silence. "I heard something today that might interest you. It's about Felipe. He seems to be having quite a time in Mexico City."

My pulse quickened at just the mention of his name. "Oh?" I hoped I sounded disinterested.

"That's right. It seems he has all the Mexican girls at his feet. He's an officer in Santa Anna's army, and I hear he's even engaged to a girl down there."

My heart lurched. There it was again, the cruel confrontation of Felipe's betrayal, none the less painful than it had been the first time I had heard of it. How could he have professed to love me, and then cause me so much hurt, and heartbreak, I wondered? And how much longer would it be torture just to hear his name? Surely at some point I would become insensate, the pain too great to bear so that I would pass beyond it. I didn't answer, hoping that Jeremy would stop talking about him if I showed no interest.

But Jeremy would not be silent, and I clenched my hands together tightly in my lap, my fingernails digging into my palms, as he went on. "I guess he's turned into quite a ladies' man. He's a captain, I hear—"

I could bear it no longer and snapped, "I don't care what you hear. Just be still about him! Can't you talk about something else?"

Immediately, I regretted my outburst. I would not look up, but I could feel Jeremy staring at me, and it made me uncomfortable. He was the last one in the world I wanted to know what a fool Felipe had made of me.

"You? And Felipe?" His voice rose on a note of incredulity.

"There's nothing between us," I snapped. "Nothing at all."

He stopped the buggy under a tree. "You're a terrible liar, Cassie."

Still, I did not raise my head to look at him. I felt the tears I had tried to blink back roll down my cheeks.

He put out his hand, turned my face toward him. "You're crying." His voice was not jeering or derisive, but surprisingly soft and sympathetic. "Did you and he have an understanding? I always thought it was sort of taken for granted that you and I would get married some day."

It surprised me that there was neither censure nor derision in his voice. I looked up at him, saw he was watching me. This was a new Jeremy, a Jeremy I did not know—strangely sympathetic and understanding, ready to cushion my sorrow. I told him about the ring Felipe had given me, the ring he had said he would return to slip on my finger. "And now, this," I concluded. "Foolish, wasn't I, to believe his promises?"

Jeremy covered both my hands with one of his. "I'm truly sorry he's hurt you, Cassie, but for my own sake, I can't pretend I'd have wanted things to turn out any differently. I know I was always kind of mean and hateful to you when we were younger, but I don't feel that way any more. It just never seemed right that you cared more about riding and fishing and hunting than about sewing and cooking and other things girls are supposed to like to do. But you're grown up now, and I'd like to court you, if you'll let me."

I was strangely touched by his directness and the simplicity of his awkward request, and wondered if there were anyone less eloquent, less cut out to be a lawyer than Jeremy.

Ever since Sarah Gorham's words had exploded onto my consciousness with the sharp crack of rifle fire, I had felt that all my vitality and pride were drained from me. Jeremy's words had brought back the barest breath of the self-respect I had lost when I discovered that Felipe had discarded me. Jeremy—stodgy and uninteresting, but nevertheless dependable Jeremy, who knew that Felipe had cast me off—still wanted to court me. Perhaps I should consider marrying him, after all. Papa would be pleased, and Jeremy. Eventually, Felipe would hear of it, and know that I had not mourned overlong for him after I learned he had chosen a Mexican general's daughter instead of me.

I smiled at Jeremy. "I'm afraid I still care more about riding and fishing and hunting than about girl things. I don't think I'll ever change, but I'd be pleased to have you court me."

Encouraged by my words, he leaned over to kiss me, and I drew back ever so slightly. I had not done it consciously, but my body had reacted instinctively against Jeremy, simply because he wasn't Felipe. I quickly covered up my action by deliberately moving closer to him, relieved that he hadn't seemed to notice my momentary withdrawal. He brought his face closer and I raised my head for his kiss, put one hand on his shoulder. His kiss was slow and ardent, and I deliberately slid my arm around his neck, drawing him closer, wanting to receive his kiss, to return it. I waited for some feeling, some emotion to move me, and in desperation I let my lips part slightly under his. But there

426

was nothing, no feeling at all. As he drew away from me, I felt cheated.

Nothing at all had happened to me. I had not felt even the slightest twinge of the emotion Felipe could evoke in me merely by walking into the room. I wondered if Jeremy felt cheated, too.

"I think we had better get back," I said, pretending to a reluctance I didn't feel. "Patience said she would have tea ready for us at four-thirty."

For the rest of the time we spent in San Felipe, Jeremy courted me. Papa saw us together several times, and once when he and I were alone for a few minutes, he indicated his pleasure at my apparent interest in Jeremy's attentions and hinted broadly about heaping lavish wedding gifts on us. I said nothing. I had never thought of myself as a coquette, but I knew I was flirting with Jeremy shamelessly. It was not his interest in me that I was attempting to stir, but mine in him. I wanted myself to accept him, accept the idea of marrying him. He had shown some strength in defying Sam's wishes by refusing to remain in school till the spring term was finished, and I chose to read that as a new assertiveness, a new forcefulness to his character.

And I needed his attention, for it soothed my wounded pride, and I sought it, required it, welcomed it as a parched traveler gulps in the refreshing waters of a cool sweet spring. If I liked Jeremy better than I ever had before, and respected him for thinking for himself rather than parroting Sam's ideas, then why couldn't I learn to love him? I tried. I really tried. But every time he took my hand, and I waited for the reaction that I so desperately wanted to happen, I was disappointed. It was not Jeremy, but Felipe who filled my thoughts. *I despised Felipe, could never forgive him. . . . I loved him with all my heart, with such an intense desperation that I could forget my pride, no matter what he had done, if only he would come back to me. . . . I never wanted to see him again. . . . I imagined, ten times and more each day, that I saw him far off, found his face and as quickly lost it again in a crowd, and*

427

*my heart raced wildly as it was all I could do to keep from running toward him, shouting his name, even though I knew it was only a trick of my imagination. . . . I was happy without him. Wasn't I gay and laughing, flirting with Jeremy, who wanted to marry me? . . . I was miserable, my laughter brittle and meaningless, my gaiety forced, and I would never be a whole person again without Felipe's love.* Back and forth, like a gale-whipped sapling, my emotions were battered this way and that, and I was helpless against the onslaught. Only Jeremy, this new understanding Jeremy, stood between me and this conflict that raged about me.

One day, Jeremy insisted that Eliza and Patience and Sarah Gorham and I accompany him to the convention hall.

"You told me no women go there," I protested. "We would feel out of place."

"The arrangements are already made for the four of you," he insisted. "You're the only one who doesn't want to go. The others are anxious to see firsthand what's going on."

It was true, and so, reluctantly, I agreed to go. As we took our seats, I realized why he had insisted we come.

Sam Houston was about to speak.

I glared at Jeremy, hissed, "You tricked us!"

"For once in your life, be still and listen!" he hissed in return.

Peevishly, I settled back in my chair.

Gradually, my anger melted away as Houston's voice filled the room, reverberated from the walls. Lulled by the confidence, the sheer power of his voice, I forgot that the smell of liquor seemed to hover, like an aura, all around him. I forgot my revulsion at his exaggerated manners. I forgot all the whispered bits of gossip concerning his unsavory past. I forgot, and I listened.

Everyone else listened, too. The buzz of private conversation died away. I leaned over to look at Eliza and Pa-

428

tience and Sarah Gorham. They, too had stopped their whispering and were focusing their attention on Houston.

He was no ordinary speaker. He was a commanding presence, a master with words, a spellbinder with delivery. Grudgingly, I had to admire him as an orator, as I could not as a man. He was using his position as chairman of the Constitution Committee to enhance the power he had already begun to usurp. And because he was sensitive to the whims and desires of the people of Texas—as sensitive as a well-oiled weather vane—he was bound to succeed, to acquire yet more power over Texas matters. To what end, I wondered? Behind him, seated in his shadow, sat Stephen Austin, until then the acknowledged leader of Texas affairs. Could any man, however strong, escape from the gigantic shadow cast by Sam Houston?

When Houston finished, the room filled with murmurs of approval, and I admitted to myself that I had agreed in essence with everything he had said. He wanted only separate statehood for Texas, and a constitution for the state that would guarantee every man his rights. It was no more and no less than most Texans desired: I could find no fault with that. But how, I wondered, could a man who had arrived in Texas only a scant four months earlier, and then mysteriously disappeared from sight for much of that intervening time, really care about our problems? I could not help wondering if Sam Houston didn't see Texas as an emerging political entity filled with upwards of twenty thousand Americans, a place ripe for conquest by an ambitious man who could choose his cause with infinite care, put it into words with consummate skill, and utter it with soul-moving eloquence?

Men approached Houston eagerly, vying for the privilege of shaking his hand. Behind him, still in the big man's shadow, sat Austin. Nobody waited to shake his hand.

Jeremy helped us into the buggy, then climbed in the other side. Flicking the reins, he asked confidently, "What do you ladies think of Houston now?"

429

Only from Sarah Gorham did he get an enthusiastic answer.

"He frightens me," Patience said. "He's a master politician, experienced and—well—too crafty. What chance does Austin have to control him?"

"He's too smooth," Eliza added, and I smiled triumphantly at Jeremy, couldn't help adding a barb. "Does it shock you, Jeremy, to find that women can have opinions?" When he didn't answer, I couldn't resist another jibe to increase his discomfiture. "Females aren't supposed to think for themselves, are they? They're supposed to stay home and paint teacups and make lace doilies and learn to play the pianoforte or the harp, aren't they?" I was being deliberately cruel, and I didn't like myself for it, but seemed driven to it by a desire to test Jeremy, this new Jeremy I didn't really know. The old Jeremy, the one I knew from childhood, was weak and ineffective and narrow in his thinking. Would this new Jeremy, who had dared defy his stepfather, who seemed self-assured and assertive, stand up to my taunts and counter with taunts of his own?

His answer, when it came, was disappointing. He said sullenly, "I should never have arranged to take you into the meeting house," and then lapsed into silence. The others, seeming to sense something between Jeremy and me, were silent the rest of the way home.

I, too, retired into my own thoughts. I had tested Jeremy, and he had failed. I had challenged him, and he had backed away from the challenge. The changes I thought I had seen in him had been more imagined than real. He was still weak, easily defeated, unwilling to stand his ground. Felipe was not weak. Felipe—but Felipe was gone from me forever, and I knew I must think no more about him. And yet, how could I keep him from continuing to invade my thoughts?

Later, I felt ashamed for having exposed Jeremy's weakness to others so cruelly. That night, when he came to call, I apologized. He was waiting in the small parlor for me, and I walked in, extending both my hands. I smiled at him.

430

"I was mean to you today, Jeremy. I hope you'll forgive me. It's just that we think differently. We always have and always will."

"You'll change when you get your own home and settle down to have a family." His hand clasped mine as we walked to the sofa.

I turned to face him as we sat down. "I don't think so. I'm sorry."

"I'd be willing to chance it."

"It would be a very poor risk." I felt more warmly toward him than I ever had, but it was the same sort of warmth I felt toward Will, a gentle maternal feeling, as though I must stand between him and a hostile world. How different from the fiery passion that stirred me at the mere thought of Felipe!

He put his other hand on my shoulder. "Cassie, I want to talk to you—"

I shook my head, knowing what was to come, and wanting to spare him the blunt refusal that I knew I must make. "Please, don't—"

He would not be stopped. "I want to marry you, Cassie. Not just because Pa expects it, but because it's what I want, too." As he pulled me toward him, I turned my head away, deliberately avoiding the kiss intended for my lips, felt the moistness of his lips on my cheek.

He released me and I shook my head, wishing for some way to take the sting from my words. "I'm sorry, Jeremy. I could never be the kind of wife you want."

"It's Felipe, isn't it?" he said accusingly. "You're still in love with him. But he's left you. He's not coming back. He's found another girl!"

Here again was the old Jeremy, taunting me, ridiculing me. To my surprise, I was not irked by his taunts, but only saddened. It would have been so ideal if we could have cared for each other, and married. "Yes," I said. "Felipe has found someone else. And so must you. You and I bring out the worst in each other."

"You could change—"

"No, I don't think I could, nor could you." Unvoiced, one thought filled my mind. Felipe had loved me just as I was. Felipe had not asked me to change. And though Jeremy's taunting words were true, and Felipe was lost to me, I could not bring myself to accept Jeremy in his place.

For the balance of the evening, Jeremy seemed as intent as I was on keeping our conversation impersonal. I knew I should never have flirted with him, encouraged him. I had done it out of my own desperate need, to salve my wounded pride, and that had not been fair to him.

It was with relief that I saw him to the door later. Nothing had been said about when we would see each other again. I had bared my soul to him, and I wanted only to cloak it in private sorrow, let it mend if it would in the soothing dullness of performing routine tasks in the familiar surroundings of home. Papa had said we would leave the following day, shortly after noon.

Three men had been selected to carry the official document requesting separate statehood to the central government in Mexico City. One of these was Stephen F. Austin, and in the end, he was the only one of the three to make the trip. The flag-waving, the oratory, the cheering and glory-basking were over for the moment: the difficult job of getting Mexico to accept the constitution and grant separate statehood remained.

Alone, Austin started on the long lonely road to Mexico City to accomplish what must be done.

# Chapter III

## THE BEXAR ROAD—August 1833

*Mama is going to die.* As I rode along the road in the gathering twilight, the thought kept repeating itself over and over in my brain to the rhythm of the horse's hoofs.

It had only been a few hours before that the doctor had come. I had watched with concern as he examined Mama's emaciated body, put a tube on Mama's chest and listened, frowning. Then he looked at her throat, and when he finished, he motioned for me to follow him out of the room. He was a doctor I didn't know. Doc Graham had been out seeing cholera patients, and this man had come in his place.

"The infection in her throat has become very grave. A healthy person might recover, but your mother . . . " He shook his head slowly. "There is nothing I can do for her. Her body must fight off the infection itself, and she's frail. Her fever is high, and that rash is a bad sign. If she had more strength . . . "

Before the doctor left, he gave me a bottle of medicine we both knew would do no good. I knew, more from what he left unsaid than from what he told me, that Mama was going to die.

And when I had gone in again to see her, I realized that she knew it, too. I tried to smile. "The doctor gave me some medicine for you. It will make you better in no time." I heard how forced was the cheerfulness in my voice. "I'll get some water to sponge you off. It's terribly hot today."

433

A new chill struck Mama, and she shuddered. As I moved to straighten her bed, she suddenly reached up and grasped my hand with surprising force. I looked down into her fear-crazed eyes, and knew that the strength had been born of desperation.

"Your father," she whispered hoarsely and winced at the pain it caused her to speak. "Get him. Please. I'm afraid, alone . . . "

I brushed back a lock of the straggly colorless hair that clung damply to her forehead. "He'll be here soon. He may come home any time. Meanwhile, I'll be here to take care of you." Did my words sound as lacking in confidence to Mama's ears as they did to mine, I wondered?

She looked at me imploringly. "Please. Get him."

"I can't, Mama. I must stay here and take care of you. Will is gone . . . " I broke off, unable to continue. Her eyes bored through me, did not leave my face for a moment as they pleaded with me mutely, and the fear I saw in them was a living, breathing thing—the only vital thing about her failing body.

I shook my head in answer to the insistence she could no longer find the strength to voice. "I wouldn't know where—"

Her mouth formed the words, "Find him."

"But where? I'm not sure—"

Again, the voiceless plea. "Find him."

Torn between the quiet despair of her insistence and the grim knowledge that death was hovering over her, I stood by the bedside, trying to decide what to do. Her eyes had closed, but the lids had become so transparent that I felt she still looked at me. When she opened her eyes again, it was to stare at me beseechingly.

I leaned over and kissed her cheek. How could I refuse to do as she asked?

"All right," I said softly. "If that's what you want, I'll go look for Papa. Don't worry. I'll find him somehow."

Mama mouthed a silent, "Thank you." Then she closed her eyes and I turned and ran from the room.

434

A short time later, I started on the road to Gonzales, the beckoning ribbon of road to the west that I had yearned for so many years to follow. But on that ride, I saw nothing, was scarcely aware of the cabins and houses I passed. All I saw was the road, the endless road stretching on before me, and, as I urged my horse to travel faster, my brain, numbed by the doctor's unspoken opinion, kept repeating its message: *Mama is going to die.*

*Mama is going to die.* The doctor knew it, and Mama knew it, and I was on my way to Gonzales, or Bexar, or some place else if necessary, to find Papa.

How long would it take me to get to Gonzales, I wondered impatiently? It was straight ahead, on the banks of the Guadalupe, and I only knew that I must follow the road.

I stopped only when I needed food or water, or exhaustion overcame my mount. I knew I was ruining one of Papa's best stud stallions, but it couldn't be helped. Mama was going to die, and she needed Papa's strength. I crossed the Colorado, and still the road stretched on and on. Somewhere ahead lay Gonzales.

When at last I saw the settlement ahead, I felt completely drained of energy, for nausea and vomiting and diarrhea had plagued me for the last few hours of my journey. Several times, I had been forced to stop suddenly to be sick, and I was impatient with my body for being so weak when I desperately needed it to be strong. I supposed I had eaten something spoiled.

By the time I approached Gonzales, I was reeling dizzily in the saddle. The size of the town surprised me, for I had expected only a few cabins. Where to begin? I had to find Uncle Todd, let him find Papa, because my own strength was running out. But where was he? I rode through the deserted streets in the slanting light of early morning, wondering if I should knock on a door to ask directions. At last I saw someone outside, and he directed me to Uncle Todd's cabin. Wearily, I dismounted, all but falling from my horse. At last, Uncle Todd would take the heavy burden from me,

435

and I could lie down and rest, regain enough strength to return home. I knew I would be unable to go on to Bexar if Papa was not in Gonzales; Uncle Todd would have to find someone to send if it was necessary. A feeling of profound relief surged through me as I lifted the latch and walked in. I had reached Uncle Todd, and could hand over to him the burden of finding Papa.

"Stay where you are!" warned a voice from a corner of the dim one-room cabin. Abruptly, I stopped.

"I should have knocked. It's me—Cassie—Uncle Todd. I—"

"Don't come any closer!" Weak though his voice was, there was an alarming urgency in it. "You mustn't get near me, child. It's the cholera."

"Cholera! Oh, Uncle Todd—" Despite his warning, I started toward him.

"Don't!" His command, yet more urgent, stopped me. "Don't be alarmed," he continued in a softer voice. "I'm well over the worst of it, and recuperating. In a few weeks, I'll be as good as new. I should have had the decency to die from this at my age, but I was just too cussed stubborn. What brings you here, my dear? Is something wrong?"

I nodded. "Mama is going to die." The words had repeated themselves so often in my brain that they had ceased to have any meaning.

"The cholera?"

"No. Her throat. An infection . . . " My words tapered off to nothing. I was too weary to say more.

"You've come for your father, then."

I nodded again. Sick with exhaustion, I had come to Uncle Todd for help, and he, who had always been a pillar of strength, was sick, and old, and weaker than I was. There was nothing funny about it, but something made wild laughter want to rise in my throat even as tears of defeat and despair burned my eyes. I wanted to tell Uncle Todd more, tell him how Mama had begged me to come, and what the doctor had said, but I couldn't find the strength to utter the words.

"You'll find your father at the Posada de don Esteban. That's Serena's place. It's a full-fledged inn now. Ask the boy next door to take you there. And Cassie . . . "

"Yes?" I had turned to go, in command of myself again. The momentary hysteria had passed. I knew I couldn't give up, not after having come so far, and with Papa so near. Surely, I thought, I could push myself just a little farther. I paused, waiting for Uncle Todd to continue.

"There's no time to explain everything to you, but promise me you won't judge too harshly what you'll see."

"I promise," I answered mechanically, too benumbed to puzzle over his words.

"That's a good girl."

The Posada was built on the side of a small creek. It was a flat-roofed adobe building, with colorful flowers bobbing gaily in pretty painted boxes beneath each shuttered window. The main entrance was through a grilled gate, and led to a central courtyard. Just inside the gate was a door to a small office. My guide motioned me inside and left me.

The office was empty, and I picked up a bell and rang it. In a moment, Serena emerged from a door I had not noticed in the shadows.

"I'm Cassie. Is Papa here? Mama is dying."

She seemed to hesitate just a moment. "You're ill, child." She came around the table that separated us and put her arm around me, led me into another room, directly behind the office. I leaned on her gratefully, feeling myself sag against her, surprised at the strength of her tiny arms as they supported me.

The room to which she led me was large, kitchen and living and sleeping area all in one. Seated at a table at one end of the room was Papa. Near him sat a boy I judged to be about seven.

Papa looked at me in surprise and jumped up, nearly tipping over his chair. "Cassie!" he said angrily. "What the devil are you doing here? You shouldn't have come!"

Momentarily shocked into silence, again I felt the urge to laugh mirthlessly, as I had wanted to do back in Uncle

437

Todd's cabin. Mama was dying and I had ridden ninety miles almost without stopping to find Papa for her, and he was angry with me for coming! But I mustn't give way to laughter, or to tears. I must give Papa the grim message I had carried so far, and then I could lie down and close my eyes and rest before the return ride.

"Mama is dying," I heard myself say tonelessly. "She wants you."

"Oh." Papa fell back into his chair, as though an unseen hand had pushed him.

I summoned my strength, told of the doctor's visit and its outcome as Serena spooned porridge into a bowl, indicating it was for me. I sat down and tasted it, but my stomach rejected all thoughts of food, so I dropped the spoon. "I can't. I can't eat."

I tried to fight the wave of nausea coming over me, felt my stomach rumbling. I answered Papa's questions numbly, and for a time the significance of the scene before me did not take hold. Everything—the people I saw, the voices I heard—had an unreal quality, seemed to be getting farther and farther away. Vaguely, I realized there was something utterly domestic about the three other people in the room, a domesticity that excluded me.

Idly, I noticed the child's resemblance to Will when he was younger, and wondered who he was. The boy smiled at Serena and called her "Mama," and that was puzzling, too. No one had told me Serena had married again.

Suddenly, through the fog that enveloped my brain, I was aware for a brief moment of a sudden clarity of thought that flashed through my mind and departed again as quickly as a lightning bolt. But it had left the answer, unbelievable and undeniable. The domesticity was no chance effect.

I wished that my head would clear so I could think things through. I was wrong, I had to be. My mind was playing tricks on me because I was so exhausted. How could it be, what I was thinking? Serena? And Papa? Surely things were not as they seemed. Fuzzily, my mind circled around the truth, rejected it, then slowly, dimly accepted it. Papa lived there with Serena. That was why he was seldom at home. I looked at Papa, then at Serena, then at the child neither of them had bothered to explain. Papa was talking, but I no longer listened.

It was true. It had to be true. The boy was Papa's. And Serena's.

I couldn't stay there another minute. I must leave at once!

Summoning all my effort, I pushed my chair back and pulled myself up, leaning heavily against the table. I was vaguely aware of hearing dishes clatter to the floor.

"No!" I knew I must deny the nightmare, which surely was a concoction of my wearied brain. "It can't be!"

Papa had stopped talking, and he and Serena were watching me, seemed to be waiting for me to go on. But how could I go on, how could I put such a thought—such a ridiculous, scandalous thought—into words? When, at last, the words did come, they poured out in a rushing torrent of condemnation.

I shouted shrilly at Papa, "You've been here, instead of home with Mama when she needed you! You didn't care about making a better life for us! You lied! That's not why you were gone so much. All the time, you were here, when we needed you at home with us!" I could no longer fight the hard laughter in my throat, and it bubbled up uncontrollably. I laughed so hard that tears came to my eyes.

"Cassandra! Stop! You don't know what you're saying! Stop that laughing!"

But I couldn't stop, not for anything. I couldn't remember what it was that had seemed so funny a minute before. But it didn't matter. I knew I must laugh. And I must cry. And, I remembered vaguely, for some reason that had escaped me, I must leave.

Stumbling blindly, I found the door to the office, groped my way through it to the rectangle of light which I thought must be the courtyard. I reached toward it, tried to move my feet in that direction, but they would no longer respond. I couldn't see clearly any more. The rectangle of light had merged with other spots of light and darkness. The spots of darkness grew, ran together, covering everything. I wanted to get to the door, but where was it, where had it gone? I tried to move, staggered, fell heavily against the wall. My hands reached out to catch something, anything, for support, but they grasped only a void. I knew I was sinking down, down, down into that same void, but I couldn't help myself. Voices, senseless and garbled, filled my head. Whose voices were they? I tried to remember, but it didn't matter. I would let myself sink into the great dark void that beckoned, but only for a little while. There, maybe there would be no exhaustion, no churning choking nausea, no harsh realities, but only peace and quiet and rest. I felt someone catch me as I gave myself to the blackness.

I didn't know until I was recovering that I had had cholera. Vaguely, I remembered the uncontrollable voiding and retching that tore ceaselessly at my insides. And I remembered trying, feebly, to get up, only to fall back limply. Whenever I opened my eyes, the same gentle face was always there, looking down at me solicitously. Whose face was it? I knew it, knew the tranquility and kindness of it. Even when I lacked the strength to open my eyes, I could feel the presence of someone with infinite patience beside me. I had only to move my parched lips and there was life-giving water thrust between them. I had only to claw at the hot gown that encased me and cool cloths bathed and soothed my aching burning body. Time had stopped, and I was in a hot hell and had been there for ever and ever. The only escape from the stifling heat which held me prisoner was the occasional interlude when I opened my lips gratefully to get on my tongue the minute amounts of water placed there, or when my fiery skin was cooled, briefly, by wet cloths. But there was never enough water to quench my overpowering thirst, and as soon as the cool cloths touched my skin, they were instantly afire, and I was back in the hideous hell of thirst and heat. And I was weak, so weak. I could only lie still, fighting for one breath after another. Fighting, I knew, to hang onto the slim thread of life.

I dreamt fitfully of water, always of water, and it was never within my reach. It would disappear just as I stretched out my hand for it, prepared to gulp it thirstily. Then it would appear again, tantalizing, farther away, and I wanted to walk toward it, grasp it, but my legs and arms remained limp and useless, refused to respond to my commands. I was in hell, and there was no water in hell.

The few times I could summon the strength to open my eyes, that same face was there, sometimes bathed in such glaring blinding light that I had to close my eyes quickly. Other times, I saw it in soft flickering shadows, less harsh and easier to look upon. Sounds jumbled indistinguishably in my ears. Once, I tried to make out the words a voice was speaking, but it was too much effort, so I lapsed back into my world of unidentified sounds and darkness and scorching heat.

And then, one day, I opened my eyes and though the light was still harsh, it was no longer blinding. Carefully, slowly, I let my eyes adjust to the daylight. My eyes fell on the face that had always been there, and a voice said softly, "You've been very ill, but I think you're getting better now." Then a gentle hand lifted my head and spooned savory hot broth, strong and rich, into my mouth. My stomach made protests, but accepted it, and I realized I was hungry. The face, the voice, the hands, all belonged to someone I knew. I closed my eyes and tried to remember who it was.

Whenever I awoke, the same gentle face looked sympathetically down on me. Weakly, I tried to smile my gratitude. Whose face was it? I would think of it later.

Then a vaguely disquieting feeling took hold of me. I was as dependent as a suckling infant on the person with the gentle smile. I knew I should be grateful for the never-failing presence, so why was I aware of an inexplicable feeling of conflict whenever I tried, feebly, to return the smile? Why shouldn't I smile at this person, who was as vital to me as my life's blood?

While I puzzled over the problem, another vague thought came to me. Mama. There was something I should remember, something about Mama. What was it? Oh, yes, I remembered. Mama was dying. Dying! Then I must get back to her, at once! "Mama!" I tried to raise my head from the pillow, but a reeling dizziness enveloped me, and my head fell back heavily. And when that same soothing voice that had spoken before told me not to worry about Mama, I obeyed and closed my eyes and slept.

Then one day I awoke with a clear mind, remembering the jumbled events before my collapse. I remembered, too, why I must not smile back at the woman beside me, knew I must hate her.

I looked at Serena, saw the solicitude and tenderness there, and turned my head away abruptly, toward the wall.

"You've been here all the time." I stared at the blankness of the wall as I spoke. If I looked at Serena, I knew I wouldn't be able to hate her. And I must. It was my duty. For Mama. For myself and Will as well, but mostly for Mama.

"You needed me."

"You didn't have to stay." It was so difficult to be angry, when I so wanted to be grateful. And yet I knew I couldn't permit myself to show any gratitude. It was confusing to my awakening mind. "How long have I been here?"

"Six—no, seven days."

"A week! I must go to Mama!" I raised up, swung my feet over the edge of the bed.

Serena's hand caught me as I swayed. "Your father went to her. He left right after you told him. I promised him I would take care of you. You must rest. It takes time to regain your strength after cholera."

"Cholera!" I repeated, lying back weakly, panting from the small exertion, wondering how I could have had cholera—I, who had always been so healthy! I remembered the doctor who had come to see Mama had said it was everywhere—in Bexar, in Mexico City, Saltillo, San Felipe, everywhere—sweeping through the populace like a giant scythe, cutting down all of the weak and many of the strong.

But why, then, did Serena stay there, so close to me? "You might catch it!" I said in alarm.

She shook her head. "I already had it a few years ago. I don't think I'll be likely to have it again. I've sent Andrew away."

I lapsed into silence. Andrew must be the boy I had seen—her son, and Papa's. Her mention of him reminded me that I must not soften toward her. I saw the dark circles under her eyes, the weariness and exhaustion of her movements. Why couldn't I make myself forget the patient hands, the soft voice, the kindly presence, always there during my illness, I wondered? For the first time, I noticed the small cot on the opposite wall, and I could imagine I remembered seeing her jump from the cot to be instantly by my side whenever I moaned or called out. How could I keep the thin brittle shell of my hatred intact against the obvious signs of such selfless devotion?

She gave no sign that she sensed my hostility. She stood up, smiling. "I think you're ready for a bit of solid food. Some thin porridge, maybe."

Again, I had to let her feed me. How chafing it was to be so weak, helpless to do the simplest things for myself! I knew I must regain my strength quickly, stop being so utterly dependent on a woman I owed it to my mother to despise.

My recuperation was irritatingly slow. The first day I was able to sit up, Uncle Todd came to visit. Serena left us alone, and Uncle Todd lowered himself heavily into a chair. He was still so weak himself that I wondered how he had managed to get to Serena's, and I was shocked to see how he had aged. Time and his recent illness had so ravaged his features that he looked closer to eighty than to sixty-one. *He really is an old man now*, I thought with

443

alarm, noticing the uncertainty and slowness of his movements.

After he had settled himself in the chair, he told me that he had just received word from Papa. Mama had died the day after I left.

"I should have stayed with her!" I said bitterly through my tears. "Then she wouldn't have been all alone."

"You mustn't blame yourself. You did what she wanted you to do, what you felt you had to do."

I brushed at the tears as they rolled down my cheeks. Poor Mama! "She was so frightened!"

"Your mother was always frightened."

"She wanted Papa so desperately. And instead he was here, with her!" I hurled as much accusation into the final word as I could.

"Don't be bitter, my dear. If your mother hadn't been the way she was, none of this would have happened. She was too weak to hold your father's interest. He thought he loved her when he married her. God forgive me, that was probably all my fault. Somehow, I should have prevented their marriage. He mistook her weakness for femininity, and when he discovered it for what it was, it was too late. One of your father's worst faults is that he has no patience with weakness."

I said nothing, feeling guiltily disloyal to Mama when I acknowledged to myself that Uncle Todd was right. Certainly, Mama had been lacking in strength, moral as well as physical, and Papa never should have married her. Why, then, I wondered, had he been so anxious for me to marry Jeremy, who was physically strong enough, but whose moral fiber had certainly been weakened by Sam Butler's continual bullying? Oddly, Papa had stopped trying to persuade me since the spring convention. Maybe he had, after all, realized that Jeremy was weak.

"Your father tried to make the best of it, for the sake of you and Will," Uncle Todd continued. "But long before your mother became ill, their marriage had ceased to exist. He needed—"

"Mama was always sickly," I interrupted. "She couldn't help it. Were Papa's needs of the flesh so strong—?"

He shook his head. "Your father is certainly no monk by nature, Cassie, and it would be unfair to expect monkish behavior of him. But it was much more than a need of the flesh that attracted him to Serena. He found in her all the warmth, the affection, and the giving he had missed in his marriage. And Serena was a very lonely woman."

"It was despicable of them to carry on in such a disgraceful fashion while Mama was an invalid!" Loyalty to Mama made me blurt out the accusation with more malice than I felt.

"I'm not saying it was right, or asking you to say that it was. I'm just trying to explain to you how it came about. It happened, and there's nothing you can do to change the past. I hope you can find it in your heart to forgive them. They've tried to be discreet, and Serena stays to herself to keep down the talk. I'm the only friend she has. Most everyone in Gonzales has probably guessed that Tico must be their son, but on the surface, they accept my story that she's my brother's widow. She's had enough of condemnation. She could do with a little understanding, and coming from you, it would be especially meaningful to her. It isn't so bad for your father. People will allow a man sins they won't permit a woman."

"But he's been here, when he should have been home with Will and me, and it's her fault!" I was arguing halfheartedly, wanting Uncle Todd to convince me I was wrong. I didn't really want to hate them. As Uncle Todd said, the past was over, and could not be changed.

"They've given each other much happiness, but the suffering has been mostly all Serena's. Felipe reacted as you have, and I told him the same things I'm telling you. Serena lost much of his respect because of your father, and that nearly broke her heart."

I nodded, understanding at last. "That's why Papa and Felipe always hated each other so." There was no need to phrase my words into a question. At last I had discovered

445

what had caused the bitter enmity between them. And it must have been in revenge for what Papa had done that Felipe had issued the threat against me, the one Papa had told me about. Had Felipe ever really loved me, or merely used me to get back at Papa? The question had tormented me ever since Papa had told me of Felipe's threat. I wished there were some way to find out, to be certain.

Uncle Todd took his pipe from his pocket, glanced at the cold hearth, then took a stick from his pocket and started cleaning the inside of the stem. "Felipe and Serena were very close, and his anger when he found she was to have your father's child was understandable enough, but censure was the last thing your father wanted, especially from a young lad like Felipe, and it angered him. Your father couldn't just walk away and leave Serena, even if he had wanted to, because there was the child to consider. Deception was necessary, Cassie, and in that I helped them, so if you hate them, you must also hate me. At the time, deception seemed the kindest thing for all concerned—most especially for your mother, and you and Will. So I brought Serena here, when there were scarcely the beginnings of a town here, and said she was my brother's widow. Because of me, and because she keeps well away from other people, the story has been accepted, at least on the surface."

"And Felipe and Papa have hated each other all these years, because of that."

"I blame your father for not initiating a peace between them. Felipe accepted Andrew, and I think he would finally have come to accept the relationship between Serena and your father, once he saw how much happiness it brought his mother. But your father is a stubborn man, and never made any overtures of peace. For that matter, Felipe is stubborn, too." He shifted his position slowly. "I suppose everything has worked out for the best. I doubt if they'll see much of each other any more. It seems Felipe has settled down in the capital. Funny, but I always thought I detected something between you two. I guess it's as well I was wrong about that, because your father would never have given his permission for you two to marry. He was certainly pleased when he told us about you and Jeremy. I understand Jeremy has gone back up to Massachusetts by now to his studies, hasn't he? I don't know what there is to study for all the years Sam has set him at it. I was a little surprised you weren't married this summer. You could have gone with him. But I suppose it was because of your mother that you stayed. Now, there's nothing to stop you. When will the wedding be?"

I looked at him, asked incredulously, "Wedding? Me and Jeremy?" I remembered many of Papa's unexplained actions, and I asked suspiciously, "Where did you hear about this? Was it from Papa? When?"

Uncle Todd frowned, rubbed his fingers over the white stubble on his chin. "Let's see. Last fall, I think it was, about October or so. Close on to a year now. Serena wrote Felipe about it and, surprisingly, had an answer back before the end of the year. She showed me his letter, and it puzzled us both that we detected some bitter undertones where you were concerned. If he had hopes of marrying you, he certainly had never mentioned it to either of us. You must have given him some encouragement somewhere along the line, my dear, if you intended to or not. I suspect that the news that you were to marry Jeremy helped him decide to stay in the capital. You see, you're quite a heartbreaker. I'm sure Felipe wasn't the only one who was disappointed to find you'd decided to marry Jeremy."

So it was true, then. The faint suspicion grew to become a certainty as I absorbed the full significance of his words and all the confusing implications and facts had been fitted neatly into place. The realization of what had happened, of what Papa had done to me in the name of love, knocked the wind from my lungs as violently as though I had fallen from a dizzy height.

"Papa told you and Serena that I was engaged to Jeremy? Last fall?" I could scarcely bring myself to believe what I was asking, what I was thinking. "Uncle Todd, you said Serena had a letter from Felipe before the end of the

447

year. Tell me, how did she get that letter? How did it reach her? Please, tell me. It's important that I know."

"Your father brought it to her. He brought her all of Felipe's letters after Johnny left, apparently went out of his way to get hold of them through some army friend of Felipe's in Bexar."

"The same one Johnny used to get them from," I said with a certainty.

"Why, yes, at least at first, and then through someone else after that man left. Frankly, I was a little surprised, though it was awfully good of Thorne to get the letters for her, knowing how he felt about Felipe. But he knew Felipe's letters were important to Serena—"

"And he knew Felipe's letters were even more important to me!" I cried.

"What do you mean, child? Are you telling me that there was something between you and Felipe, after all?"

I nodded. "Yes, there was something between us, Uncle Todd. I loved him with all my heart. I've loved him ever since I can remember. We were going to be married when he came back."

He leaned forward in his chair, asked slowly and deliberately, "Are you or aren't you engaged to Jeremy?"

"I'm not, and I never have been. Don't you see? Papa did this to keep us apart. That's why he was so careful to get Serena's letters from Felipe, because he wanted to intercept mine. Somehow he must have found out about Felipe's friend in Bexar. He didn't become a courier just to bring Serena Felipe's letters, but to keep me from getting mine! And he used Serena to spread his deliberate lies about Jeremy and me, so Felipe would think I no longer cared about him." I heard my voice, and it was high-pitched, on the verge of hysteria. Papa, who pretended to love me, had done that to me! I had been ready to forgive him for his desertion of Mama and Will and me, but this newly discovered outrage was beyond my forgiveness. He had meddled, maliciously, in my life, destroyed my happiness, to satisfy his own grudge against Felipe.

448

As I sat there, absorbing the import of all I had learned, I saw Uncle Todd eyeing me with disbelief. And suddenly, another thought occurred to me, a thought that changed everything. I laughed, deliriously happy. "Uncle Todd, do you know what this means? It means that Felipe thought it was I who no longer loved him! That's why he was squiring Mexico City girls around, why he said he was never going to return to Texas. It was not because he had stopped caring for me, but because he cared so very much, and he thought I had forgotten my promise to him!" After all, hadn't I tried to do the same sort of thing when I learned he had become engaged to a Mexican general's daughter? Hadn't I tried to make myself want Jeremy, who wanted me?

I laughed again, my laughter overflowing with happiness and relief. How could I ever have doubted his love, doubted that our night together had meant as much to him as it had to me? How could I have let Papa's insinuations plant the seeds of suspicion in my mind, so that I wondered if Felipe had merely been using me to settle his grudge against Papa?

But all that was past, and no longer mattered. My mind was suddenly bursting with plans. I would send Felipe word somehow, that very day, send a personal messenger to tell him I would come to the capital myself as soon as I was able to travel.

"Uncle Todd, I must write him, right now, at once. Do you know anyone who can take a letter to Felipe, be certain it will get through? I'll go to him myself, the minute I'm strong enough to travel. I can't tell you how happy—" I broke off suddenly, for Uncle Todd was looking at me strangely. Felipe was almost like a son to him, and he should have been sharing my happiness, knowing Felipe and I loved each other, and would soon be together. "Uncle Todd, you're not listening!" I said in alarm. "You're— Uncle Todd, what's the matter?"

He was crying unashamedly. His pipe dropped from his hand and he clenched and unclenched his fists as the tears coursed down his cheeks. Then he pounded his doubled-up fist on the table near him so hard that a pottery vase clattered to the floor and shattered. He didn't even seem to notice.

"May God curse your father's conniving soul!" he said with such bitterness as I had never heard in his voice before. "I hate to tell you this, to destroy your happiness, child, but it's too late. Serena had a letter from Felipe last week. He wrote it in June.

He had been married the day before."

When Papa returned to Gonzales he faced an unending string of stinging epithets Serena and Uncle Todd flung at him furiously, berating him for his vengeful interference. I could only ask quietly, "Papa, how could you have done such a wicked thing?" and then turn from him in a bitterness that had gone beyond angry words. He bristled defensively at the reproaches and kept insisting, over and over again, that he had done it for my own good. We remained in Gonzales only a few days after he returned, and Serena and Uncle Todd parted from him in anger. I would have stayed with one of them if either had invited me to remain, but they didn't, so all I could do was go home with Papa.

"Felipe would not love lightly," I had heard Serena tell Papa one day. "Nor, I think, would Cassie. How could you possibly have been so cruel as to deliberately keep those children apart with your vicious contrived lies?"

"Cassie is my daughter," he insisted churlishly, "and I have the right to decide what is best for her."

All the way home, he kept insisting the same thing to me. "I did it for your own good." Bitterness consumed me afresh every time he uttered his remorseless explanation that explained nothing at all. I couldn't answer, for I was choked with helpless rage.

I wanted to avoid him, but ironically, after one more trip to Gonzales, he spent most of his time at home. I wondered if it was a delayed touch of remorse. Did he think that by staying home he could atone for deserting Mama, leaving her to suffer her many fears and frustrations without him?

Or was it because he was avoiding Gonzales and the open condemnation Serena and Uncle Todd would continue to heap upon him for what he had done? Whatever the reason, to my intense irritation, he left home seldom during those fall months of 1833, usually only when he was needed on *ayuntamiento* matters in San Felipe, and then only for a day or two at a time.

He tried hard during those months to win back the affection I could no longer feel for him. I met with frigid reserve his attempts to woo me with his gaiety and charm. When he saw he could not reach me, he turned to Will, but with that, he was already several years too late. Failing in his approaches to both of us, he threw himself into a busy round of activities to improve our place, bringing in new breeds of horses, chopping trees, fencing pastures, repairing and painting the barn and the house. He couldn't seem to do enough for the homestead in which he had shown little interest during most of the last seven years.

Johnny had returned from the East the first part of May, and his and Eliza's wedding date had first been set for early September. But the cholera epidemic had continued to dispense sickness and death well into the fall months, killing also good Doc Graham, who had never refused to answer a sick call. At last, the wedding, after two postponements, was scheduled for late November. I was relieved when Papa said he couldn't get away to accompany me to San Felipe, so I went in the buggy with Daniel.

I was astounded at the way San Felipe had grown since the previous spring. But the sight of the town, which by then had over two thousand residents, didn't excite me as it always had before: my unhappiness cast a pall over everything, and my spirit sagged wearily.

Eliza commented on my lassitude, blaming it on my illness and the shock of Mama's death. I didn't tell her of the bitterness that was the real reason for my gloom, for the telling would do no good. Besides, I had no desire to cast any sort of a shadow over the coming festivities. Deep in

451

my own misery, I could at least rejoice for the happiness of Johnny and Eliza.

Eliza was a lovely bride. It was the first time I had ever seen her wear white, and the effect was startling. The shimmering white satin wedding gown contrasted richly with the golden-red glow of her hair, made her cheeks look rosier, her red lips deeper still. The official ceremony, at her insistence, was performed by Father Muldoon, the much-liked Irish priest who always obligingly ignored any evidence of non-Catholic religious activity.

Patience was a staunch Presbyterian, and met Eliza's insistence on being married by Father Muldoon with her usual equanimity. A few hours before the public wedding, Patience and Lem and I witnessed a short ceremony conducted by a young Presbyterian minister newly arrived in the area. After he performed the rites, he slipped unobtrusively out the back door, the same way he had entered. When, a short while later, Johnny and Eliza were joined in holy wedlock in the eyes of the Catholic Church and the republic of Mexico, they were also wedded in Patience's Presbyterian heart.

That evening, hundreds of guests attended the informal festivities held in a large barn that had been cleared and painted for the occasion. There were four fiddlers, and they soon had everyone—except the bereaved, the pregnant, the aged, and the men who preferred to cluster around the punch bowl—hopping to their lively tunes. I sat on the sidelines, for I was too recently bereaved to participate. Bored by the giggling comparisons of first confinements of two young matrons seated on my left, I turned to my right to pretend an interest in the complaints of a gnarled old woman. Finally, Lem Parker rescued me, and took me to the other side of the barn, where he had been sitting. I soon realized I had fared little better, for after he brought me a cup of punch from the ladies' punch bowl, he soon forgot me completely as he and another man discussed matters political.

"Look how long Austin's been gone," Lem said. "And we're still tied to Coahuila."

I watched the laughing couples dance themselves to exhaustion, and squirmed uncomfortably on the hard bench.

"With the cholera shutting down the government in Mexico City we have to be patient, give them a little time.

"Hogwash!" Lem said disgustedly. "We've been patient too long. They were in a muddle long before the cholera struck. They play at politics as ineptly as a bunch of children. Santa Anna is supposed to be our friend, champion of our rights! He's slick, that one is, trying to get acclaimed as dictator and when that failed, stepping aside for Farias, as if he didn't want anything for himself!"

My attention was caught briefly by a lithe willowy youth who reminded me a little of Felipe. My heart still gave a sudden leap whenever I saw someone who bore the most remote resemblance to him. I wondered if the same thing happened to him, if he ever stopped to think of me, to wonder what I was doing? But I knew that wouldn't be so, for he must still think I had changed my mind, forgotten my promises to him. Surely, he must hate me. That, as much as the knowledge that I had lost him, ate at my heart.

"Give them time, and they'll see things our way. No matter who's in power, they'll have to—"

"They'll never—"

"Father! Mr. Roberts! Shame on you! Can't you see you're boring poor Cassie to tears?" Eliza's voice cut into my consciousness, and I protested that wasn't so, that I had been enjoying watching the dancers.

Eliza extended her hand, pulled me to my feet. "Come to the house and help me change to my traveling dress, would you? Johnny promised to stay a few minutes longer and drink a toast with some of his friends."

I smiled at the happiness that radiated from her. "Of course. I'm rather tired. I think I'll just stay back at the house after you leave."

453

The guests didn't notice us slip out. We walked down the deserted street, past the darkened houses.

A short time later, I stood on the porch and waved good-bye to Eliza and Johnny as they left in the wagon he had fitted out for their trip. But even as they returned my wave, I knew they had already forgotten me, had forgotten everybody but each other.

I watched the wagon until it was swallowed by the night, listened till the squeak of the wheels no longer echoed back to me. I had never felt so alone. My loneliness was so intense it was almost a physical ache. The music, which had seemed so gay when I was in the barn, wailed with an eerie unworldliness. Eliza and Johnny were gone, together in their private world. The music, the people in the barn, were of yet another world, and there was no place in that world for me, either. I belonged no place, to no one. For me, there was only the emptiness of the street and the deserted house, the emptiness of my life.

Unbearably depressed, steeped in self-pity, I started to lower myself to the step. But as my hand moved to smooth the back of my dress before I sat down, I stopped, suddenly seeing myself in the harsh light of critical self-appraisal.

If I stayed there alone, gave in to the feeling of utter desolation, it would be an acknowledgment of defeat, an admission that I was not strong enough to conquer my sorrow and rise above it. I would be beaten, not by what Papa did, but by my own despair, my own bitterness, until I was enslaved by it, robbed by it of my dignity and self-respect. Despair and defeat and bitterness could too easily become a way of life.

I threw back my shoulders and pulled myself erect, took a deep breath of the crisp November air, as though I could draw from it the strength I needed to carry through my new resolution. Then, forcing myself to hold my head high, knowing I had won an important battle within myself, I walked toward the sound of the wailing violins.

The next day, I returned home. Though I resented being dependent on Papa, the responsibilities of running the house formed, I knew, the only substance to my existence.

Will was gone again when I returned. "He just took that infernal pallet of his and left," Papa said in a tone of disgust.

At least, I thought, Papa no longer tried to stop Will, whose eagerness to sketch and paint took him ever farther afield. He had been dabbling with oil paints for some time, and in recent months had developed a preference for them over the pen and ink or charcoal sketching he had always favored before. The previous week, he had explained to me, haltingly, that he wanted to capture the colors as well as the forms of everything he saw. In that he would eventually succeed, I was certain, just as he had tenaciously improved his ability to sketch. No one who saw his work could doubt that he possessed an exceptional talent, as well as the persistence it took to develop it. Only I knew how much derision his persistence had earned from Papa. It was odd that Papa considered his determination a weakness rather than recognizing it as the strength it was.

At seventeen, Will had grown very independent, and Papa's derision had long since ceased to touch him. If Papa was surprised at how early Will asserted his independence, he should not have been, for his own prolonged absences had forced both of us to grow up well ahead of our years. When Papa started to stay home that fall, Will relinquished the responsibilities that had become his as quietly as he had assumed them, and accepted the extra freedom as his due.

I expected Papa to marry Serena the following summer. He never mentioned any definite plans, but everything he did about the house proclaimed the fact that he was readying it for a new mistress. He ordered a cabinetmaker in San Felipe to make a new bed and wardrobe for his bedroom. He replaced broken floorboards, and he sanded and repainted the rough doorframes. I imagined he would wait a full year of mourning after Mama's death and then quietly marry Serena.

And when Serena became mistress of the house, what would there be for me to do then? I supposed that I could marry Jeremy, but I knew that if I did, it would only be to escape from home. I could not be happy married to him, and I did not think I could make him happy, either. Papa would be delighted, and Sam as well, but I had no desire to please either of them.

Christmas was not a happy time that year of 1833. In an effort at forced gaiety, Papa brought home a Christmas tree, and when neither Will nor I showed any enthusiasm for stringing berries and popped corn to drape over its branches, he did it himself. I remembered our first Christmas in Texas, and the tree we had decorated in Uncle Todd and Aunt Rebecca's cabin, and the spontaneous joy that had touched us all as we gazed at it in wonder. By contrast, there was no happiness in our house that Christmas of 1833, and the tree that Papa brought home never became transformed into something wonderful. It remained only a tree, after all. It disappeared as we slept on Christmas night, and no mention was made of it the next day. Only a few scattered pine needles on the floor attested to the fact that it had ever been there at all.

Papa left for Gonzales a few days later, and I was not sorry to see him go. I watched idly as the coach went down the road and before long disappeared in the dust cloud of its own making. When the cloud lifted, the road was empty, as empty as my existence without Felipe. With a sigh, I turned and went into the house.

# Chapter IV

## THE BEXAR ROAD—February 1834

By the beginning of 1834, activity on the Bexar Road had increased. The previous fall, the Exclusion Act had been repealed, and new waves of settlers were coming into Texas. Many men continued to come in alone, without families. They traveled by themselves, or with one or two companions, and usually led a pack animal or two.

It seemed to me that recently activity of another sort had increased along the road, for many individual riders seemed to be passing by, as many heading east as were traveling west. These men always traveled light, and always appeared to be in a hurry, as though they carried some urgent messages. I wondered if the flurry of activity had anything to do with the news that had recently shaken us all: Austin had been arrested!

In the depths of his despair the previous October, just before the repeal of the Exclusion Act, he had written a letter pouring out his discouragement to the municipality of Bexar. He told the people that they must prepare for the central government's refusal to grant the petition for separate statehood, and said that Texas was ruined unless the people took matters in their own hands.

This damning letter had fallen into the wrong hands in Bexar and had been sent back to Mexico City. President Farias had read it and sent men to intercept Austin, who was by then on his way back to Texas, and return him to the capital as a prisoner.

Austin arrested! Stephen F. Austin, who had always shown such infinite patience in the often frustrating problem of dealing with the Mexican government, had committed his discouragement to writing, and for that he had been prevented from returning home.

One clear February day, I had taken my mending out on the porch, and was basking in the warmth of the afternoon sun. I chanced to look up and saw a rider approaching who looked so startlingly like Felipe that my heart gave a leap, as it always did when I saw someone who reminded me of him. How much longer, I wondered, would I continue to see his face in every crowd, to watch each figure coming down the road that reminded me in some way of him? But on that February day, the closer the horseman approached, the more striking seemed his resemblance to Felipe. He was not as lean, but he rode hunched forward in the way Felipe did when he was in a hurry. And that rider was certainly in a hurry, for he was traveling at breakneck speed. What important and urgent message did he carry, I wondered, as I admired his horsemanship? I laid my mending aside and watched in fascination. Like an Indian he rode, almost seeming to melt into the horse and be a part of it. The buckskins he wore were dark and shiny, closely matched the dark gloss of the horse's coat, contributing to the illusion of oneness. My heart began to thump wildly, out of control, for the closer the rider approached, the more he seemed to resemble Felipe. He reached our gate, and I expected him to ride past it.

But he didn't. He wheeled into our yard without slowing down, so the horse's hoofs slid in the dust of the road as he spun sideways.

And then the rider looked at me and shouted my name.

"Cassie!"

"Felipe!"

I jumped up, heard the clatter of the scissors as they fell from my lap. It really was Felipe, and he was calling my name!

He dismounted in a leap at the foot of the steps and opened his arms to enfold me as I fell into his embrace.

I heard myself repeating his name over and over again. I couldn't say it enough times, so sweet was the sound of it upon my lips. His arms held me close, crushing me against him. And all I could do was cling to him and say his name again and again.

His lips found mine, crushed down, silencing me with a kiss that was at once both fiercely possessive and infinitely tender. We kissed, drew apart, kissed again. Once or twice, we backed away from each other long enough to look in one another's eyes and laugh and smile like two happy children at the joy of being together again. And then our arms tightened around each other once more in another desperate embrace.

*I'm alive again!* I thought joyously. *Really alive!* Only in Felipe's presence was I truly a whole person. But as he held me tightly in his arms, the question I knew I must ask rose in my throat: *What about your wife?* But I could only think the words, for once I asked them, it would be too late, and I would have to hear the answer—the answer I dreaded. *He is another woman's husband,* I thought, *but right now that doesn't matter. He is here with me, holding me in his arms, and that is all that is important. That is all that will ever be important.*

He pulled away from me, gently cradled my chin in his hands and kissed me tenderly. "Let's go inside and talk. We have so much to tell each other."

We went into the parlor, our arms around each other. He sat down, pulled me down beside him, his arm around my shoulder, pulling me close to him.

*Now,* I thought. *Now I must ask him.* But I couldn't bring myself to phrase the simple question, *What about her?*

"She is dead, Cassie," he said somberly, as though he had heard the question I had been unable to ask. "The cholera—"

"Oh!" I shouted joyously. I couldn't help it. I leaned on

459

his shoulder, too happy even to feel any shame at not being able to hide my joy at the news. How could I pretend to be saddened, even for a minute, when it meant that he was free to marry me?

He put into words what I was thinking. "I'm free, Cassie. And I don't care what anyone says about me marrying again so soon, I'm not going to let you out of my sight until we're safely married."

"Oh!" I said, contritely, remembering. "The ring you gave me—I threw it away!"

He nodded his understanding. "I guess we both lost faith in each other. No matter. We'll find another. That one didn't fit right, anyway."

Later, he told me that Serena had ridden all the way to Mexico City to tell him in person what had happened, knowing that what she had to say could not be put in a letter his wife was apt to see. "She didn't want me to hate you," he said. "But by the time she arrived, Piedad had been gone for over a month, so we came back together." He smiled at me in the special way he had, and I felt the joy of his smile down to the very ends of my toes. "It's good she's a fast rider, or I might have left her behind in my impatience to reach you."

"I suppose she told you that I found out about her and Papa."

He nodded. "He wants her to marry him next summer, but I'm not sure she will. I guess they had a terrible quarrel when she told him she was leaving Tico—Andrew—with Todd and going to Mexico City to tell me what had happened."

"So that's why Papa has been spending so much time at home recently. Your mother was gone."

"He was there waiting for her when we came back. I didn't stop to find out if she's forgiven him for what he did to us. I didn't stop for anything." His arm tightened around my shoulder. "I couldn't."

I smiled up at him, reached up to caress his cheek. He caught my hand, put it to his lips. How could I ever have

460

doubted him, I wondered? How could I have been so easily taken in by Papa's lies? But then, how could it ever have occurred to me to suspect that Papa could be so cruel and ruthless?

It had been almost two years since Felipe had gone away. Two terrible lonely years. But why look backward, over the long distressing months that, mercifully, were in the past? We were ready to start anew, and our lives lay ahead of us. What wonderful happy lives they would be!

"Where will we live?" I asked. "Did you get them to acknowledge your right to the Varga grant?"

"Yes and no. Not formally, not yet, but they've promised to make a study. These things take time, but I've been assured I'll have clear title by the time I'm ready for it."

"Oh, Felipe, that's wonderful. I know how much that means to you!" I added teasingly, "You won't throw me off your land when I want to ride over it, will you?"

"As a Varga, you'll have every right to be there. And, my little love, I intend to see that you become a Varga in as short a time as possible."

We were married quietly in San Felipe a few days later, with only Patience and Lem Parker and Will to witness the ceremony. I didn't mind having such a small wedding. All that mattered was that Felipe and I were becoming husband and wife. It wouldn't have made any difference if there had been hundreds of other people there, or none, for I still would have seen only Felipe. He stood beside me in his Mexican officer's uniform, clinging as tightly to my hand as I clung to his, and we solemnly repeated the marriage vows.

It had been something of a shock to me to learn that he was still in the Mexican army. He had been assigned to the garrison billeted at the Alamo in Bexar, and was to report there in three weeks.

We changed into our riding clothes before we left San Felipe, then stopped at our house to receive the congratulations of the servants and to pick up the pack animals we had left there.

461

Felipe had insisted on buying two new saddle horses and two pack horses for us. The mounts were not as good as some that Papa had, but Felipe wouldn't hear of taking any of his. "We want nothing from him," he said emphatically when I protested the foolishness of buying the animals instead of taking some of Papa's. "I know he'd want us to have them," I argued, but Felipe remained adamant.

We took our leave of Will and rode on alone. Every few minutes, our eyes would meet and we would smile, or laugh, just for the sheer ecstasy of being together, of knowing we would always be together. Sometimes, when we were riding side by side, Felipe would reach out and cover my hand with his as our eyes met, and we would smile at each other, knowing words were unnecessary.

We stopped long before the sun got low in the sky, early enough to build a lean-to. It was not that we were likely to need it for protection, for the day was clear with no threat of bad weather, but we shared an unspoken desire to duplicate that other lean-to we had shared so long ago. While Felipe built it, I gathered pine boughs and moss for our bed. Then he made us a small fire and we sat in front of it, huddled close together, and spoke the lovers' words we would never tire of hearing.

Once, he called me "*mi corazón*," and my ears, unaccustomed to the Spanish endearment, found the sound jarring, but his arms tightened about me and I thought no more about it.

We lay that night on our mattress of pine boughs and Spanish moss inside the lean-to, just as we had lain almost two years before in another lean-to. It was the same, and yet it was different. Before, in our youthful optimism, we had had faith in the future, faith in the belief that nothing would keep us apart. But since that time, we had both suffered loss of that faith, in each other as well as the future, and we had tasted loneliness and disillusionment and bitterness and despair. And so on that night, our coming together had all the longing and heartbreak of those two intervening years. We were infinitely older, infinitely wiser,

462

infinitely more in need of each other than we had been before. Deliberately, we prolonged that first moment when flesh touched flesh, prolonged the kissing and caressing and whispered words of love, until finally, our yearning was so intense it could be no longer postponed. And then we came together in an ecstasy of loving and giving.

"Dear heart," I said later as I rested on his shoulder, "I think I would have soon perished of sorrow if you hadn't come back to me. But now that we're together I'm almost glad for everything that happened because it makes my happiness that much more intense."

"And mine," he agreed, pulling me closer so that our bodies were intertwined. "Don't move away from me as you sleep, beloved. I want to know every moment, waking or sleeping, that you are here with me."

We stopped in Gonzales for two days, where we stayed with Johnny and Eliza in the new cabin he had built for her in the town. Being with them seemed as though we were watching ourselves in a looking glass, for their happiness in each other seemed to be a reflection of our own.

Uncle Todd hugged us both, and there were tears in his eyes as he gave us his blessings. Serena, too, seemed to share our happiness, and I hugged her and told her I could never express my thanks for what she had done for us. Our meeting with Papa was awkward, for I knew it would take time to dim my disappointment in him, and Felipe had lost none of his bitterness over what Papa had done. For Serena's sake, and mine, they were civil to each other, and the presence of Andrew, who loved them both, helped keep the tension from erupting into open hostility. Apparently, Serena and Papa had made their peace.

It was the last night before we reached Bexar when we were huddled close to the fire for warmth against the chill winds of a fresh norther that Felipe again called me "*mi corazón.*" It irritated me as it had before to hear the Spanish endearment fall so naturally from his lips, and that time I realized why. It reminded me that I was not his first bride, that there had been another, who would be his wife

463

still if the capriciousness of the cholera had not taken her life even as it had spared my own. Had the Spanish endearment come so naturally to his lips, I wondered, from habit? I felt an unreasoning stab of jealousy at the thought.

"Did you call her that?"

Immediately, I was sorry for the unfeeling bluntness, the resentfulness of my question, and would have bitten back the words. How could I have so thoughtlessly spoiled a moment of such contentment? Deeply ashamed, afraid I had hurt Felipe, or angered him, I looked away quickly to avoid the reproach I was sure I would see in his eyes.

But when he answered, his voice held no trace of anger or reproach. "Her given name was María de la Piedad, and she was known as Piedad. She was a sweet, lovely girl, and she had a delicate sort of dark beauty. I had a deep respect for her, and I cherished her. She loved me, and what had happened between us—between you and me— had not been her fault, and I determined that I would make her as happy as I could, so that she would never guess I had chosen her because she was as little like you as any girl could be. But, God forgive me, I couldn't give her the love she deserved, and I never called her '*mi corazón*' or '*mi alma*,' because you and you alone are my heart and soul. You always were, even when I thought I should hate you for your faithlessness. And you always will be."

Overcome with shame, tears welled up in my eyes, spilled over onto my cheeks. "Oh, Felipe, forgive me! How could I have been so—?"

"Let me finish, my love. Piedad was all soft femininity, like fragile Venetian glass which may be touched only with care. You are as alive and vital and indestructible as the sun and the earth. You came here, and you adapted to the land as though you had been born to it. You've become a part of it, and because of that you are an important part of me that Piedad could never have been.

"You are all that living here has made you, and you're more of a woman because of it. You're every bit as feminine as Piedad was, but your femininity has substance and

464

strength. You're pretty, but your real beauty, to me, is in what you are, and it will still be there, even when you grow old and wrinkled. It will last forever, just as I will love you forever."

"Oh, Felipe!" I threw myself into his arms, overwhelmed by the tenderness of his words, his voice, overcome with my shame at having been jealous of the girl who had been his wife only for a few short months. "I shouldn't have—" My voice broke on a sob.

Gently, he kissed away my tears. "We had to talk about this sometime. I was only waiting for you to tell me when you were ready. Now, Piedad will never come between us again, will she?"

"Never!" I agreed readily. "No one—and nothing—will ever come between us again."

I sighed and burrowed my head into his shoulder, recoiled sharply as I was pricked by the gold braid on his officer's tunic.

"What's the matter?"

"Your tunic. Is there a needle—?"

He laughed. "No. It must have been one of the gold threads. Some of them are quite sharp. Here. I'll take it off. I was only using it as a wind block. Now we can share that blanket you have around your shoulders, as we did that night when you came to me so long ago. It will be far cozier. I wouldn't want my uniform to keep you away."

Even as he cast his tunic aside and moved into the protection of my blanket, and we both sighed contentedly, events were taking shape in Mexicó City, not far from the grave of María de la Piedad, that would make Felipe's uniform increasingly important.

The next day, we entered Bexar. I loved it from the moment I first saw it from a hill nearby, thought it had an enchanted look with its whitewashed houses sparkling in the bright sunshine. Even as we rode into the town later, and I became aware of its seamier, often squalid face, I was not disappointed. What did it matter that the houses that glistened so whitely in the sun were, on closer inspection,

465

crookedly built and mud-splattered? Or that prostitutes sat brazenly outside their doors to hail passing soldiers? Or that the narrow streets separating rows of earth-colored adobe huts were filled with filthy naked children and mangy dogs? Even the squalor held a sort of enchantment for me that day. Was it perhaps because I had longed to see the town, which Felipe always called by its full sing-song name of San Antonio de Bexar, ever since I had first heard of it? Or would the very bowels of hell have seemed enchanting to me if Felipe was by my side? Whatever the reason, I was delighted with the scenes that unfolded before my eyes as we entered the water-laced town that had come into being on the prairie over a hundred years earlier.

Felipe found a house for us a scant two blocks from the San Fernando Church, which sat, majestically as a benign monarch, between the twin plazas that were the very heart of Bexar. The house Felipe found was charming, more elaborate than most. It was made in the Spanish fashion, with an outer door, the *portal*, leading into a *zaguán*, a short entrance hall that led to the inner door. The walls of the house, almost two feet thick, were made of adobe bricks painted white. At the back, a private garden was sheltered from all the world by walls that were higher than Felipe could reach.

It was a mixed world that entered our thick-walled house. When Felipe's friends came, it was a Spanish-speaking world of clanking swords and military problems and barracks-room trivia, a world that was closed to me by my failure to understand any but the simpler Spanish words and phrases. When my friends called, they brought with them the world of the Texans. To please Felipe, I tried to make a few friends among the wives of the Alamo officers who could speak a little English, but I found most of them were mere alter egos of their husbands, vain and frivolous and lacking in depth. It was the fault of their men, I thought, remembering what Felipe had said about Piedad, for they treated their women like delicate china dolls on display, decking them in jewels and fine clothes if they could afford them, and shielding them from worldly contact. The families I came to know through Felipe kept their little girls surrounded by protecting *dueñas,* and the girls were not allowed to play beyond the thick walls and heavy doors of a few select homes, so that they, too, would grow up as their mothers had, forced from habit to turn inward on themselves and their immediate surroundings until nothing outside of their tight little realms mattered to them at all.

I felt far more kinship with the Americans I met in Bexar. Most of the men were businessmen or merchants, and their wives generally lived as they would have lived back home, accepting the local customs that pleased them and disregarding those which did not. They raised their children as much in their own tradition as possible and sent them to an English-language school. Their aloofness from most things Mexican irritated Felipe.

"You Texans aren't even teaching your children Spanish," he said one day to some of our American friends. "If you didn't cling so hard to your American ways, you might understand how things are here in Mexico."

As always, I noted, he said "you Texans," not "we," and I wondered if his stay in Mexico City had so influenced him that he no longer identified himself with us and our problems. There had been many changes in him while he was gone. Some were physical; he had filled out, so that his youthful leanness had become transformed into a sinewy graceful strength. But other changes had taken place, too, more subtle changes that seemed to have affected his attitude, made him alien to us, so that he no longer seemed to think of himself as anything but a Mexican army officer.

It pleased him when I said I would like to learn Spanish, and he immediately arranged for a tutor. I applied myself diligently, thinking that if I were able to speak it better, I would have the key to understanding the changes that had come over him. As things were, I felt shut out from a part of his life, and I was intensely jealous of anything that shut him from me.

467

Much of the Mexican aspect of Bexar delighted me. There were the ritual walks of the young people around the main plaza each Sunday evening, when a slightly lifted eyebrow or the barest hint of a smile could encourage a would-be suitor.

And there were my beggars, who knocked on our outer door with predictable regularity, knowing they would always receive a few coins from Esperanza, who had followed us to Bexar, insisting that only she could keep house for us. When I commented to her on the regularity of the beggars' calls, she shrugged and said, "They have always come to the houses on this street. This is their territory." I came to enjoy especially the visits of the oldest of them: *El Ciego,* the Blind One. If he had any name other than that, I never knew it. One day, Esperanza was out and I happened to answer his summons. As he talked, I became fascinated with his manner, his humility and deference tempered with the barest amount of arrogance. He stood at the *portal,* talking to me, and he postponed until just exactly the right moment the time when he would hold out his hand for the few small coins I placed there. Begging was to him a highly developed art, and he was its master. With a lift in my heart and a feeling that it was he who had done me the favor by accepting the coins I offered, I received his blessing, and thanked him for it. After that, I always tried to answer the door myself when he called.

There were the *aguadores,* too—the men who balanced buckets of water on shoulder-yokes, selling their liquid cargo to the householders of Bexar.

For safety's sake, Felipe said I must stay within the town except when he was with me, for Comanches roamed nearby and often abducted young women, even from the edges of the town itself. I was free to walk within the town to the houses of the new friends I had made, and I enjoyed the easy companionship of being able to visit and chat over a cup of coffee or the hot chocolate for which Felipe had developed a taste during his time in the capital, which was becoming popular with the Americans as well.

I was on such a visit to one of my friends, Rosella Quigley, when I learned of the first attempt at a revolutionary meeting in Texas. It had been set for October of 1834 and had aborted even before I heard of it, but still I found the news disquieting. Rosella had mentioned it offhandedly as another woman and I sat in her kitchen drinking coffee and chatting. After she had spoken, she was obviously uneasy. I correctly guessed the reason for her discomfiture and promised to say nothing to Felipe, assuring her that since the meeting had never actually come about, there was really nothing to tell.

But was there really nothing to tell? I wondered. Would other attempts follow, and succeed? There was an increasing amount of disquietude among the Texans, to which events in both the national and the state capitals contributed no small amount.

In May of 1834, Santa Anna had ousted Farias and dismissed the congress, declaring the need of the country was for a strongly centralized form of government, an idea with which Felipe agreed. I thought he might be as disenchanted as the rest of us when Santa Anna had refused to consider giving Texas separate statehood at that time, but he merely said that the first need of Mexico right then was for national unity under a strong leader.

"And Santa Anna is the one man strong enough to do it," he said emphatically. "We can't have a bunch of petty tyrants telling the central government what to do."

"But how can we remain a part of all that corruption in Coahuila?" I asked him later. "Why, Asa Quigley says there are two separate groups, one in Saltillo and one in Monclova, each claiming to be the one official government of our combined state!"

"That's exactly the sort of thing a strong central government will stop, *mi amor*. It would only double the troubles of the national government to create another state government at this time!"

"But it doesn't make sense to force us to continue to put up with such corruption!" I protested. I wished I could get

Felipe to share the outrage of all my American friends. The Monclova and Saltillo groups had been haggling back and forth since July, when the Saltillo group looked askance at some scandalous land acts passed in Monclova, and declared all Monclova acts null and void, retroactive to a year before. And Santa Anna was insulting us by denying us separate statehood, by insisting we remain a part of that squabbling, rotten mess!

One thing that Santa Anna had done when he took over the government was to release Austin from the Dungeon of the Inquisition, where he had been confined for three months. He did keep him imprisoned for another month, but not under such inhumane conditions. And then he had released him but continued to confine him in the capital and use him as a pawn in the game of playing for time. It was claimed that Austin must be tried, but for precisely what and by exactly whom nobody could decide. Each time a possible course of action was considered, delay and indecision followed, and then that was replaced by the consideration of yet another possibility.

Finally, in October of 1834, the same month as the abortive attempt at a revolutionary meeting in Texas, Santa Anna announced at last that he would call a meeting to consider the petition and request Austin had brought him almost a year and a half earlier from the April 1833 convention for statehood in San Felipe.

And again, there was delay. If Texas were given separate status, should it be as a state or a territory of the Republic of Mexico? The possibilities were considered, tabled, brought out to be considered again, and still nothing was done. In December, 1834, Santa Anna did make an attempt to straighten out the mess between Monclova and Saltillo, and Austin wrote to advocate patience, hoping that perhaps things might be decided favorably for us after all.

"Santa Anny'll stall us till hell freezes over!" Asa Quigley said indignantly one day when I was visiting Rosella. "He'll never give us our separation from Coahuila!"

Nor was Asa the only one who was perturbed by signs of

470

Santa Anna's duplicity. The Americans in Bexar talked of little else besides the rottenness of both state and national levels of government.

But when the Americans came to our house, they were strangely silent on the subject of politics. Felipe was always a friendly and congenial host, and was well liked by everyone. But his uniform served as a visible reminder to my friends that their conversation must remain neutral, and I noticed that the men often fell suddenly silent as he approached. It was not Felipe, I knew, that stood between him and my friends, but the uniform he wore, and I hated it.

One evening when we were having a small dinner party, Felipe was seating Rosella Quigley when his tunic happened to brush her bare arm. Rosella recoiled, placing her other hand on that arm as though to ward off any further contact. She looked at me, and our eyes met. Immediately, she dropped her hand and turned to say something to someone on the other side of her. *She hoped I didn't notice*, I thought, *but I did*.

After our guests had left, Felipe remarked, "You were strangely silent tonight, *mi alma*. Something is bothering you. What is it?" He put his arm around my waist as we walked toward our room.

I leaned my head against him, noting that the coarse wool of his tunic scratched my face. "It's nothing," I said. "I'm just a little tired."

When he closed our bedroom door behind us, he turned and took me into his embrace. As his arms tightened around me, a button on his tunic dug into my cheek. I forced myself to keep from withdrawing, angry with myself for letting it bother me so. *It's only a button*, I told myself, *just like any other button*. But that was not true, for there was a malevolence about it, as there was about the scratchy wool and the prickly gold braid, and I could not keep from despising the tunic as though it were my personal enemy.

I forced all such foolish thoughts from my mind, and raised my lips to his for a kiss that was long and lingering

471

and laden with desire. "I'm sorry to hear you're so tired tonight, my love," he said, smiling down at me. "All evening, I have been thinking how desirable you looked, and I could scarcely wait till everyone left to get you alone."

I returned his smile and turned my back to him. "If you'll undo all those buttons down the back of this dress, I'll show you how wide awake I suddenly feel."

A short time later, my dress lay in a heap on the floor and his uniform was flung carelessly over a chair as we lay together in our nakedness, our bodies igniting each other wherever they touched. We moved together in perfect harmony, and nothing mattered but the deep love we shared and the fierce passion with which we fulfilled each other. Later, we slept, still unclothed, our bodies intertwined as they had been on our wedding night. Desire had been sated and the depth of our feelings reaffirmed, and political problems seemed remote and unreal and unimportant.

But political problems were all around us, and when in January of 1835, Santa Anna declared that state militias would be limited to one man for every five hundred inhabitants, the news was greeted in Texas with a roar of indignation.

"It's us they're aimin' at, of course. Nobody but us!" Asa Quigley's bright red hair seemed aflame as he sputtered his irritation to Rosella and me. Asa was always one of the first to voice his indignation at any new affront, real or imagined, of the Mexican government. "They ain't nobody can deny Santa Anny did this just for spite!"

But deny it Felipe did. "You Texans!" he said impatiently that night at dinner when I told him that all the Americans were visibly shaken by the decree. "This won't really leave the settlements vulnerable to Indian attacks as everyone seems to fear. Nobody is going to go around trying to take rifles away from people. It's just that there can be no official organized force which might stand in opposition to the central government. You have to consider the alternative: each governor could be a petty dictator

472

with his own private army. We must have unity at all costs!" He rolled up a tortilla, bit down on it angrily.

"At the cost of freedom?" I asked incredulously. Sometimes, I felt like I didn't really know Felipe at all. It seemed almost as though an imposter who looked like him but who no longer cared about the future of Texas had returned from Mexico City in his place.

He threw the rest of the tortilla down on his plate. "Cassie, can't you Americans understand that your ideas of freedom and states' rights and all the other things you yell so loudly about just won't work here? Mexico is different. We have millions of poor illiterate *peones*, and to try to pattern our government after that of the United States would be to invite disaster. Democracy—your kind of democracy—wouldn't work here. I'll admit that Santa Anna is a disappointment to me, and I certainly don't approve of everything he does, but he is strong, the only one strong enough to keep Mexico united, and right now we need him."

"But he wasn't honest with us! We supported him, helped him, and then he broke his promises to abide by the Constitution of 1824 and give us our separate statehood!"

"The Constitution of 1824 is unimportant. It's unity that matters!"

"But it is important, just as it's important for a man to keep his word! You can't be so blind that you can't see—"

"It's you who are blind!"

I started to answer him angrily when suddenly I thought, *What are we doing? This is Felipe, whom I love with all my heart. Why are we quarreling over something we can't change, not with all the angry words we can summon?* I jumped up from my chair, and went to kneel by him. "Oh, Felipe, how can we quarrel so foolishly, when we know that what we say will resolve nothing? It's being here in Bexar, with you in the Mexican army and me with my American friends, that is tearing us apart. Couldn't we leave? Please?" I watched him, waiting, hoping for him to understand, and to agree that we couldn't remain there.

"You mean you want me to leave the army?" He stroked

473

my hair, and I felt the sensuous pleasure I always felt at his touch. Nothing had changed between us. We still loved each other with a deep devotion, with a passion that knew no bounds. If only we could escape from the controversy that seethed all about us!

"That's impossible just now. I think if I stay in the army, say, another year after this one, and have a good record, then when I go back to Mexico City to see about my land, there will be no problem."

"Why can't that be settled now as well as a year or two from now? What's taking them so long? You said they'd as good as admitted the legitimacy of your claim."

"The government doesn't act that fast, I'm afraid. They've promised to try to get hold of the old Spanish records, and that takes time. They might even have to send to Spain for confirmation. And then the matter must be referred to first this one and then that one. You know how those things go. And besides, the longer I stay and get a captain's pay—or a major's pay starting next month if the rumor I heard yesterday is true—then the better it will be when we go back to live on the Varga grant. We'll need money to get started right, the more the better. I want to build you a very special house, Cassie, maybe even bigger than the Butlers's!"

"I don't care about a big house! I'd gladly live in a sod hut, if you'd only go away with me now!"

"Not yet, *querida mía*. Just give me till the end of next year. I won't make the army a lifetime career, I promise. Now forget your worries, and think only about keeping the buttons stitched tightly on my tunic and the hilt of my sword polished to a fine gloss."

"But so much can happen before the end of next year, and I'm so afraid—"

"Afraid? What are you afraid of, my dear love?"

"Of losing you. This is driving us apart—" I lay my head in his lap.

His hands moved to stroke my shoulders. "Nothing, not anything in this world can drive us apart. Certainly not

474

anything as foolish as politics. You mustn't worry. This tempest will blow over, and soon these problems which concern you overmuch will disappear."

Soothed by his words, lulled by his caresses, I raised my head to smile at him. "I hope you're right. I'm probably just borrowing trouble."

It was not long after that when I found I was carrying the child for which Felipe had hoped so long. Each month when I had told him I had not conceived, he had tried to mask his disappointment with an intimate smile. "We must try again." But at last it had happened, and he was overjoyed at the news. He swept me into his arms. "Just think, *mi amor*, our son will be the fifth generation Varga to own the land!"

"But what if it's a girl?" I asked anxiously, knowing how obsessed he was about carrying on the ownership of the Varga grant through male descendants.

His eyes sparkled. "Then we will love her and keep trying to make a son. I see no great sacrifice in that." He held me close. "I'll be happy with a whole houseful of girls, if they're like their mother. I only ask that at some time or another, you give me one son. Whether it's this child or another doesn't matter. Oh, Cassie, you've made me so happy! How can a child conceived in so much love be anything but wonderful?"

I relaxed in his arms, savoring the quiet pleasure it gave me to be there. We were complete in our love, and now that love had produced a tiny bit of life growing within me, and the knowledge heaped yet more joy upon us. I sighed happily. We had so much. If only the world would let us be, stop intruding on our happiness!

But the world all about us was seething with turmoil, and there was no escaping from it.

In mid-March of 1835, Santa Anna again held out to Austin the hope of attaining separate statehood for Texas, and Austin wrote enthusiastically from the national capital, saying that action on the matter was currently being considered by the legislature, and that Santa Anna was said to be in favor of it, and expected to give it his support. But this proved to have no more substance than the other false hopes Santa Anna had dangled before Austin. In the end, it only served to disillusion all of us more and make us despair of ever getting the separate statehood we had needed for so long.

In late April, the corrupt state legislature of Coahuila and Texas ceased to function forever, just before it would have been shut down forcibly by General Cos, who was marching toward Monclova on orders from his brother-in-law, Santa Anna. Texas was left with a heritage of chaos and confusion of land titles that would plague us for many years to come.

By mid-May, Committees of Safety had been formed by the various municipalities to replace the outlawed militia. Also in May, Santa Anna personally led federal troops against the Zacatecas militia, which had refused to disband, declaring that they and their state would remain faithful to the Constitution of 1824. The massacre of the state troops was followed by a barbaric orgy of rape and plunder in their capital city.

Felipe stubbornly refused to believe the shocking reports of this that reached us and said, "You know how such things become exaggerated in the telling." He dismissed the whole thing with a shrug and a wave of his hand, a gesture that was thoroughly Mexican, and which was becoming increasingly irritating to me. "Santa Anna had to crush the Zacatecans in order to prevent more such flare-ups," he reasoned. "He had to do it to protect the rights of the central government. You Texans needn't be concerned as long as you pose no threat to Santa Anna's national unity."

We both knew from Serena's letters that Papa was among those who would have liked to make Texas become such a threat, but we didn't know he was actually an active member of the War Party. I was shocked to learn that from Uncle Todd when he came for an extended visit the first part of July. It was an effort for him to travel all that distance on horseback, but loneliness had apparently driven

476

him to make the effort. Serena and Papa had been married the previous August, a year after Mama's death, and had moved to the house near San Felipe. Both coaches had been sold, and Papa seemed content to remain at home with Serena and Andrew. And so, at last, Uncle Todd had given in to our frequently penned pleas to come for an extended visit with us.

He didn't mention Papa till he and I were alone. "Your father's gone to a War Party meeting in San Felipe," he said with a shake of his head. "He wanted me to come, too. I can't understand him. Most of the other rabble-rousers are newcomers to Texas. They started pouring in from the East two years ago, when they first sensed trouble coming, and now they're circling around like a bunch of vultures eyeing a sick horse."

"I remember Patience Parker talking about how many men had just come into Texas at the time of the convention for statehood two years ago last April, and about how they were loudest in their complaints about tyranny."

He nodded. "And they've been coming in ever since. They have little to lose and everything to gain. But I can't understand your father. Why would he risk losing everything he has?"

"He has always jumped at the chance to criticize or oppose the Mexicans."

"That's true enough." Uncle Todd took a few slow puffs on his pipe before he continued, "He was mixed up in that Anahuac and Velasco fracas, I remember. I guess that was really the start of it all."

"The start of what?" I asked apprehensively. "Surely you don't think all this could actually lead to war, do you?"

"War? Why, no, child," he said emphatically, "there can't possibly be a war."

My relief at his words was quickly dispelled as he continued, "If we raise a war banner, as men like your father would like to do, Santa Anna would come and squash us beneath his boots like so many annoying ants, just like he did to the Zacatecans. That's why all this war talk is so

477

insane. We're no threat to Santa Anna and his large army. But if your father and some of the others don't stop making so much noise, Santa Anna might be alarmed enough to think we are, and he'll come deal with us just like he did with the Zacatecans. There would be no war. There would only be a massacre."

"Can't someone stop them? Can't Serena talk to Papa?"

"He's only one man. There are too many others."

"Oh, Uncle Todd, I'm so afraid for Felipe to stay in the army, with all this sort of thing going on! If only he'd resign, we could move somewhere, away from all this turmoil!"

"You mean leave Texas?"

I shook my head. "Felipe would never do that."

"Then where would you go?"

I shrugged. "Anywhere. He doesn't have clear title to the Varga grant yet, but it's been promised—"

"Do you honestly think you could hide from any trouble that might be coming, on the Varga grant, or anywhere else in Texas? If men like Buck Travis and your father have their way, they'll stir up a hornet's nest and there will be no place for any of us to hide this side of the Sabine."

"Still, I'd feel better if Felipe weren't in the Mexican army."

Uncle Todd's words were disquieting, and as Felipe and I lay side by side that night, I again begged him to leave the army. I didn't mention the meeting in San Felipe. It was the first time I had held back information from Felipe deliberately; it was the first time, I realized, that I had thought of him as the enemy.

"I promised you, I'll leave the end of next year. This wouldn't be a good time for you to move around, my love. You must protect our child. Now, come into my arms, and stop worrying."

As I moved eagerly into his arms, I felt a flutter of movement inside my stomach. It was the second time that day that I had felt it.

"Oh, Felipe, I think the baby just moved! I felt something earlier, and I just felt it again!"

We both laughed delightedly at the thought of the tiny creature inside me stirring of its own accord for the first time. Felipe laid his hand gently on me in hopes of feeling the next faint movement.

We fell asleep like that, and thoughts of warmongers and Santa Anna faded from my mind. Felipe and I were together, and his child had begun to stir inside me. What else could possibly matter?

There was another meeting in San Felipe in mid-July— not a statewide meeting, yet still significant—and the advocates of peace emerged with a clear victory. But the warmongers had already made their threat, and at the end of July, General Ugartachea, the commander of the Bexar garrison who had long been liked and admired by all of us, sent out orders for the arrest of six prominent leaders of the War Party.

It was Uncle Todd who brought me the news and explained to me the frightening significance of it. He returned at midmorning from a visit with one of his friends. He looked pale as he came into the room, but I thought it was just because of the darkness inside our thick-walled, shuttered house, which was penetrated by neither heat nor light.

"You're back early," I commented, smiling at him. "Come have some chocolate with me. Esperanza is bringing it now. I'll tell her to get another cup."

Uncle Todd stood there a minute in the doorway, then started hesitantly toward one of the chairs on the other side of the low table from me. I had grown accustomed to the slowness of his movements, but there had always remained a certain sureness of purpose in them, vaguely reminiscent of his younger days. But that morning, he moved with the uncertainty of one who feels faint. Alarmed, I jumped up.

"Are you all right?" I took his arm, anxiously scanned his face.

479

"I'm fine." He let me lead him to a chair, slowly lowered himself into it. "He's done just what they wanted."

"Who? And what did he do?" I asked, puzzled. I took my seat opposite him, immeasurably relieved that his strange behavior had been caused by something other than sudden illness.

Esperanza came in with a tray, and I noted with satisfaction that she had already anticipated my request for two cups. She set the tray on the table in front of me and left. I poured the chocolate, handed one cup to Uncle Todd. He accepted it with an absent nod, and set it down untouched. He sighed deeply, and his whole body seemed to quiver.

"It's Ugartachea. I've always thought him such a sensible man. Austin trusted him, too. A clear-thinking man, never going off addlepated without stopping to figure out the consequences. It might not be his fault. Maybe the orders came from higher up, from our new military-civilian governor of Coahuila and Texas—"

"Cos?" Less than two months before, Santa Anna had appointed his brother-in-law governor of the dual state. I raised the cup of chocolate to my lips.

Uncle Todd nodded. He took out his pipe, turned it nervously in his fingers. "Whoever is behind it, the damage is done. Ugartachea sent out arrest orders for six War Party leaders."

I choked suddenly and was barely able to keep my cup from clattering to the floor. "Papa?" I asked in a whisper.

Uncle Todd shook his head. "No, thank the good Lord! His name wasn't on the list, though I can't imagine why not. Buck Travis, Zavala, and four others."

"What have they done?" I was relieved that Papa was not included, and couldn't understand Uncle Todd's concern for six men we hadn't ever met.

"They've done enough, I don't doubt, but that's not the point. I never expected Ugartachea would behave so thoughtlessly." He sighed heavily. "Well, it's done, and who knows where it will end?"

I still couldn't understand his concern. "Maybe it will do

480

some of the hotheads good, teach them a lesson if they have to stay in jail for a little while. Maybe their arrests will make Papa and some of the others stop and think before they get any more deeply involved."

"Jail?" His voice was sharp with unaccustomed impatience. "Who says they'll go to jail? This will give us Texans a cause, and people—gullible, foolish mortals that we are—will always rally around a cause.

"You don't think Ugartachea will catch any of them, do you? Why, he has about as much chance of laying his hands on those six men as he has of pulling a lightning bolt out of the sky. Every Texan will rally behind the cause of protecting those men, preventing their arrests. They'll help keep them hidden, to keep Ugartachea's hands off of them."

"But not those who want peace! Would you——?"

"You're damned right I would! War Party members, Peace Party members, or even those who, so far, have remained neutral. Not one Texan would refuse to help them now!"

The room seemed to grow a little darker. Or perhaps it was just the sudden thought that crossed my mind which made it seem so.

"No, Uncle Todd, not every Texan would be willing to help them." I set my cup on the table, looked up at him. "Felipe is under the orders of General Ugartachea."

In the silence that followed, our eyes held in unspoken agreement to what I was thinking.

Felipe could delay no longer. He must leave the Mexican army.

At once.

# Chapter V

## SAN ANTONIO DE BEXAR—Fall 1835

Felipe raised his chin defiantly. "No!" he said, "I will not request to be released from the army. I won't give in to your hysterical whims!" He paced up and down like a trapped animal, his sword clanking ominously.

Angrily, I retorted, "I suppose Uncle Todd is hysterical, too! And Austin!"

He continued to stride in front of me as I sat on the stone bench which was tucked in one corner of our cozy little walled garden. "Our own enchanted world," we had always called it. We had put in several palm trees, which had already grown higher than the wall, so that their leaves rustled in the slightest breeze. The flowering vines we had planted had thrived and filled much of the wall with their fragrant flowers, and had climbed over the top to the other side. A mosaic stone walk formed a crisscross pattern from the four corners of the garden to join at the center, where Felipe had placed a statue of a winged cupid. In the year and a half that we had lived in Bexar, we had spent countless happy hours there. But at that moment, our happiness was obscured by the bitterness of our quarrel, and it was all because of Felipe's unreasoning stubbornness.

He stopped pacing, clasping his hands behind his back. He looked not at me, but at a spot on the wall just over my head. "Austin has been ill advised by the wrong people."

Exasperated, I jabbed the needle into the small garment I had been stitching and put it aside. What else could I say, what words could I find to break through the barrier of his misplaced loyalty, to make him change his mind? I looked at him imploringly, but he was still not looking at me. I said nothing, my silence that of despair. I had long since exhausted every conceivable argument.

Stephen Austin had returned home the first of September after spending over two years in the national capital, and he had announced regretfully that he considered war our only recourse.

As Uncle Todd had foretold, the proposed arrests of War Party leaders had served to fan the flames of war. As the War Party gained support, the Mexicans were not idle, and the streets of Bexar were aswarm with newly arrived troops brought by General Cos. Felipe denied to Uncle Todd and me that reinforcements had arrived, and I remembered the information I had deliberately withheld from him. Thus the threat of war had invaded the cool tranquility of our house and disrupted the quiet intimacy of our garden and our lives, so that we no longer fully trusted each other.

In late September, a crisis arose over an obsolete cannon the Mexican government had previously given to the people of Gonzales for defense against the Indians. Alarmed at the colonists' talk of war, the Mexicans wanted it back. Uncle Todd and I became alarmed when we heard—not through Felipe—that about a hundred Mexican soldiers had left Bexar with orders to get the cannon back. The people of Gonzales, we knew, would never give it back, and Uncle Todd set out that very day to help them defend it. It tore at my heart to think of him riding into such a potentially dangerous situation, and I watched with tears in my eyes as he heaved himself up into the saddle and rode away.

Felipe, of course, was unable to understand why the Texans were making such a fuss over a worthless cannon.

"Don't you consider yourself a Texan any more, Felipe? You, of all people—"

"Of course I'm a Texan, but I'm not a disloyal one. Texas is a part of Mexico, and should remain so. My loyalty is to both."

"But nobody is trying to pull Texas away from Mexico! All we ask is that we be given our rights as a state."

"And if you don't get those 'rights' you demand, you'll use that as an excuse to break away from the republic. It's what every one of you Americans has had in mind since the day you crossed the Sabine."

"Since you've always despised all of us so for coming here," I accused, "I'm surprised you could bring yourself to marry me!"

He lowered his eyes to look at me reproachfully. "That's unfair, Cassie. My love for you has nothing to do with this."

"It has everything to do with it," I countered wearily. How I longed to drop the subject forever! But it could not be so easily disposed of, and a sudden movement of the child I carried reminded me that I must not submit to my weariness until I had convinced Felipe he must change his mind—not just for me, but for the life we had joined in creating. I had married a stubborn man, and I owed it to our unborn child to be just as stubborn as he.

I took a deep breath, continued with renewed determination. "Open your eyes, Felipe! And search your heart! Santa Anna is a tyrant and a bully! By remaining a part of his army, you're aiding him in his tyranny, and now you'll be helping him to attack our freinds: Johnny Gorham and Asa Quigley, and surely Papa. Even Uncle Todd has gone! You love him as much as I do. Would you remain a part of the army that threatens to kill him?"

I saw a flicker of concern cross his face, and knew I had touched him. But the expression was quickly replaced with that implacable look I had come to know so well in the months just past, and to despise with all my heart.

He shook his finger at me. "It is you who must open your eyes, and see that it is not Santa Anna the man that I am supporting—he is an egotist and an opportunist—but the need for a strong, united Mexico. Texas is a part of Mexico, and must continue to be. Men like your father would steal Texas from us." His voice grew quieter. "As for

485

me remaining a part of the army that has gone to attack Gonzales, don't you realize that a show of strength now is the only way to avoid something far worse? If we can discourage trouble now, it can prevent far more bloodshed later on. Our army will fire no shots unless the people of Gonzales refuse to give up the cannon."

I clenched my fists in ineffectual anger. How little Felipe knew the people among whom he had lived! Refuse to give up the cannon? Of course they would! It had become far more than just an old cannon. It was a symbol of their refusal to believe false promises and obey the senseless orders of a despotic government. Even Ugartachea must have doubted the justness of the request to give up the cannon. Why else would he have hesitated to overpower Gonzales at the start, before more Texans had arrived to help in defense of the cannon?

"Cassie, don't you see that I have no choice? If I requested my release from the army now, it would be regarded as treason. I would probably be subjected to court martial and summarily shot."

"But there must be a way," I said desperately.

"There is a way, my foolish little love." He pushed aside my needlework and sat beside me on the stone bench. He took my hands in his, but my own remained tense. I steeled myself against my desire to throw myself in his arms. "Cassie, I don't want bloodshed any more than you do, and I don't think there will be any. If there is, I pray as fervently as you do that it won't be that of anyone we love.

"It takes two strong parties to fight a war. And you Texans, for all your bluster, are not that strong. A few people have baited the central government, and now they've drawn innocent people into this foolish defiance at Gonzales. It must be quelled at once, before more innocent people are drawn into a futile war."

I sought in my memory for Uncle Todd's words the day three months earlier when he had told me about Papa being an active member of the War Party. Hadn't he said much the same thing? And yet, when I reminded him as he

486

was preparing to join the men at Gonzales that he said that Santa Anna would squash us under his boots like so many annoying ants, he answered with a sad, wise smile. "It's for a principle, my dear. For man's inherent right to defend himself against his enemies. The Mexicans say we don't need the cannon, that their army will protect us from the Indians. But there is too fine a line between a protector and a jailor."

Uncle Todd's leaving had clearly shocked Felipe, too, but he had not admitted it in so many words.

"You're a Texan, Felipe," I continued, as he sat beside me on the bench and held my hands in his. "You're much more truly a Texan than the rest of us. What did they do to you in the capital to change you so, to instill in you a blind loyalty to some idiotic ideology of a strong central government?"

"I didn't realize you considered it a crime to be loyal to one's country," he answered coldly.

"What about me?" I asked. "And our child? Aren't you forgetting your first loyalty is to us?"

He recoiled as though I had struck him, and looked at me for a long time before he answered. Then he asked in a low voice, "Do you feel you have to ask?"

I felt ashamed at his reproachful words. In my desperation, I had lashed out at him thoughtlessly, cruelly. "I'm sorry," I said contritely. "But for me, for us—you, and me and our child—can't you try to be neutral? You needn't fight on either side. Just resign, and if they won't let you do that, then let's run away!" He said nothing, and I continued, encouraged by his silence, "They'd never find us. We could slip out of Bexar so easily. And you could cover our trail, I know you could."

"No!" he said so vehemently that I knew it was no use. I could argue first one thing and then another, and still it would do no good.

"Cassie, *mi corazón*—" He let go of my hands, moved to take me into his arms. I knew he would hold me close, and I would forget about everything but us, and we would quar-

487

rel no more just then. But soon, the quarrel would continue, if not a few hours later, then the following day, and the day after that. Time was running out, and I knew I must convince him before it was too late, and yet, as his arms started to enclose me, I felt myself weakening as I always did.

As I started to move into his arms, suddenly it was not him I saw, but his tunic, the tunic of the hated army of the Republic of Mexico, the army that Santa Anna would use to crush us all.

"Don't touch me!" I pulled away, jumped to my feet. "Not while you wear that hateful uniform!"

I ran to our room, threw myself on the bed and cried. Felipe did not follow me. I did not expect that he would.

Next time we met, we stepped around the subject of war and politics with studied care, and neither of us referred to the conversation in the garden. I began to wonder if he could be right. Was it possible that a show of force at the beginning would make men like Papa realize that fighting the whole Republic of Mexico would be suicidal?

My hopes grew thinner every day, for the situation at Gonzales grew yet more serious, and more of my friends rushed to the defense of the town. Many American families were hastily packing their belongings and leaving Bexar forever.

It was difficult for me to learn what was happening at Gonzales. I was sure Felipe knew, but he shared no information with me, and the few of my American friends who still remained in Bexar no longer came to call. Esperanza went to the market every morning and brought me sketchy bits and pieces of information. But even these small garbled tidbits of news filled me with apprehension.

It was only at night, when Felipe had shed the uniform that had become the symbol of everything I hated, that the problems which loomed so large in the daylight hours seemed unimportant. What did a silly worn-out cannon at Gonzales matter when I could feel the warmth of his body as I lay contentedly clasped in his strong arms? What difference did it make if an unscrupulous Santa Anna ruled with the heavy hand of a despot as long as Felipe's lips brushed my cheek, even as he slept? What did it matter if our whole world was topsy-turvy as long as Felipe's child moved with me?

But in the harsh light of day, when Felipe put on his uniform and buckled on his sword and strode out the front door to spend yet another day in the very army that would attack those we loved, it did matter. And it made all the difference in the world.

There was one Texan who was not among the several hundred volunteers who rushed to Gonzales in answer to their call for help: Will. He came to stay with us several days after Uncle Todd left, and I wondered if he had not done so because he knew that in our house he would not be berated for his failure to go to Gonzales. When Felipe came home that night, he greeted Will heartily and asked immediately, "Did you come through Gonzales?"

Will shook his head. "I didn't want to go there. I crossed at the ford south of town. I had to skirt around the Mexican troops on this side of the river."

Felipe nodded his approval, looked at me triumphantly as he said to Will, "I'm glad you didn't get embroiled in all that foolishness."

Encouraged, Will said, "I don't understand why everybody is getting so upset. The cannon's old, and it's useless, and there aren't any cannon balls for it—"

Felipe clapped him on the back. "I'm glad that there is one Texan who can see things clearly." Again Felipe's remark, though addressed to Will, was intended primarily for me. He extended his hand to Will. "I'm happy to welcome into my home someone who has the wisdom to see a decrepit cannon for what it is, and who refuses to elevate it to the status of a pagan god, to be worshipped and defended at all costs."

I was on the point of countering with a verbal thrust, but I stopped, knowing it would change nothing, and would leave us just as we had been, each with a different set of loyalties, pulling us away from each other. Why couldn't our loyalty to one another have been enough, I wondered? Slowly, the controversy that raged all about us was eroding our happiness, eating away at it as relentlessly as a raging river at flood stage undercuts its banks.

Each morning, Will left the house and each afternoon, he returned with the most recent news of the activities at Gonzales. Someone had fashioned a banner from a white wedding dress—I wondered if it could have been Eliza's—on which had been emblazoned a picture of a cannon and the bold words, "Come and Take It." And then they had defiantly loaded the cannon with a conglomeration of nails and broken horseshoes and other bits and hunks of metal, and had actually fired it at the Mexican troops. The Mexican forces had fallen back, leaving the Texans in possession of the controversial cannon.

Nor were the warlike activities confined to the Gonzales incident. Another group of Texans had captured the *presidio* at Goliad, and, further to the east, Sam Houston had been elected commander in chief of the east Texas troops by the Committees of Safety at Nacogdoches and San Augustine. A meeting that had been set for October fifteenth at San Felipe was postponed until November, as most of the delegates had rushed instead to Gonzales.

Like sections of a gigantic puzzle, the bits and pieces of news Will brought home, augmented with those Esperanza brought from her daily trips to the market, began to fit into place. Together, they told an incredible story: we were actually waging war, a state in revolt against the republic!

On the tenth of October, Austin went to Gonzales, and was immediately elected commander in chief of the Texan force. Will brought me this startling bit of information when I was alone, and I gasped, "Even Austin!" Surely, if he had thought there remained even a remote chance of working things out, he would not have gone to Gonzales, would not have condoned the action there with his presence.

I looked up to see that Will was watching me. "You think I should go, too, don't you?"

490

"That has to be something for you to decide," I answered carefully.

"But you would go, wouldn't you, if you were in my place?"

The assuaging lie was ready on my lips. I wanted to tell him that I couldn't be sure what I would have done in his place, that I would probably be undecided. But Will and I had always been honest with each other, and I couldn't lie to him. If I had been a man, and if I had hesitated before, the news that Austin had gone would have compelled me to action. For the serious-minded Austin, the man primarily responsible for shaping the formless clay of Texas into a prosperous farm-studded, town-dotted plain, thought that the time for indecision and meek acceptance of despotism was past. His quiet reason had, for fourteen years, stilled many a discordant voice and stopped many a precipitous action.

Austin thought the time had come when we must fight. And, were I in Will's place, I would not have hesitated to take my stand beside him.

Will's eyes had never left my face. "You would have gone," he said. "I guess Papa was right about what he said so often. You should have been the boy." He turned and walked from the room.

It was near the end of October when Will brought home the most startling news of all:

There had been a skirmish at Concepción Mission.

The mission was not far from Bexar. For the Texans to snap at the heels of the giant republic with its large army was audacious enough. But to challenge them so close to Bexar, the very symbol of Mexican strength and authority within Texas, was surely madness.

In the days following, it became apparent that the Texans were eyeing Bexar itself, for more and more of them came and camped not far from town.

"It's no real threat," Felipe said with a shrug after he had admitted that the Texans had moved close to Bexar in force. "They will soon tire of this silly game, and go back home."

But apparently he changed his mind in the next few days. As had happened often during the previous days, he had come home and changed quickly into his buckskins, and when he returned I knew he had been out scouting, trying to assess the strength of the Texans. What he saw must have alarmed him, for he insisted that I must leave.

"I won't leave unless you come with me," I insisted, thinking of the danger to which he was constantly being exposed. "Please," I begged. "I don't want to go without you."

"You know I can't go," he said, putting his arms around me. "And you must, my love. It is no longer safe for you here."

"Then it's no longer safe for you, either. You must come. Please—"

"It's too late for me to leave."

"Then why didn't we leave together months ago, as I wanted to?"

He released me. "I won't be drawn into a discussion of the past," he answered brusquely. "I'm speaking of what must be done now, today. They're putting up barricades in the streets and around both plazas—"

"I'm not blind," I retorted tartly, and was immediately sorry for the senseless curtness of my reply. *What has become of us?* I wondered. *We seem always to be snapping and snarling at each other like two angry dogs. How could anything have brought us to this in less than two years? How could we have forgotten how we suffered when we were apart, when we thought we had lost each other?* "Oh, Felipe . . ." I looked at him imploringly.

He must have read the message I could find no words to convey, for he took me back into his arms and held me tightly pressed against him. When he spoke again, his voice was soft and caressing. "You must go, *mi alma*. For our child's sake as well as your own. You know I would never send you away from me if it wasn't absolutely necessary. I have found a wagon, and a horse. You must leave with Will tonight, for Gonzales."

"Gonzales?" I repeated in surprise, looking up at him.

He nodded. "It's safe enough, now that the cannon seems to have disappeared, and there's no threat of trouble. It's the closest place. I don't want you traveling farther than you must."

I choked back a sob. Leave Felipe? How could I? "I won't go, not without you. You are my life! Please, my dearest love, don't put two armies between us." I felt the tears coursing down my cheeks as I leaned against him.

And I felt, too, the dampness of his tears as they touched my forehead and ran down to mingle with my own. "Don't you see? It's because of those two armies that you must go and I must stay."

I clenched my fists, pulled away from him. No matter what we did to keep the war at bay, it was with us, a part of our lives, invading our thoughts, our words. In my frustration, I lashed out at him angrily. "You could, if you wanted to! You could slip away somehow, if you cared more about me and your child than about some high-sounding notions of centralized government and national unity! Or is it because they've dangled the Varga grant in front of you, like a carrot in front of a rabbit? Is that why you insist on staying? Did they promise you that if you stay in their army and shoot all your friends and all my family, they'll reward you by giving you clear title to your land?" The accusations seemed to pour from my throat. "You don't love me! You don't, or you'd do as I ask!"

Slowly, he released me. "And you, Cassie," he answered in a hoarse whisper, "ask far too much." His eyes berated me briefly before he turned and walked away.

Will and I left that night. I hoped, before I left, that somehow Felipe and I could tear down the barrier between us. But Felipe seemed as hesitant as I to say any more, for fear we would dissolve again into angry words and say more cruel things. Only when he took me in his arms for a farewell kiss did nothing else seem to matter but us and our

493

love for each other. We clung together with a desperation that spoke more eloquently than words of our need, our love for one another, which was at that moment both our unbearable torture and our supreme joy.

"Keep safe, my dear heart," he whispered against my ear. "Keep safe till we're together again."

"And you!" I wanted to say more, to apologize for all the terrible things I had said to him in anger, but those few choking words were all I could manage through the torrent of my tears.

"You must go now, *mi vida*." He put his hands on my arms, firmly propelled me toward the waiting wagon, and when I would have faltered, he lifted me onto the seat beside Will.

As our wagon began to move, I looked back, saw him standing in the middle of the street, arm upraised in farewell.

"Will, stop!" I cried, watching the forlorn figure grow dimmer. "Take me back! I can't leave him!"

Will silently urged the horse to a trot and Felipe's form became indistinguishable from the shadows of the night. I turned around, and as Will put his arm around me, I sobbed out my misery on his shoulder.

We reached Gonzales three days later, and found that many of the local men had gone to march on Bexar. Johnny Gorham and Uncle Todd were among them, and Eliza, four months pregnant, insisted we stay with her.

Our baby, the son for whom Felipe so longed, was stillborn a month later. The midwife quickly took the baby away before I could see him, but I had seen the way she looked at Eliza and shook her head slowly, so that even before Eliza spoke, I knew what she was going to tell me.

"Please, I want to see him," I said, and they brought me the beautiful child, his perfectly formed little body already blue and stiff and cold. I brushed at the dark down of his head and kissed his forehead before Eliza took him from my arms. I wanted to protest the unfairness of losing the small life which had become so important to Felipe and

494

me, but it had been a long labor and a difficult birth, and I was too weak to say anything, so my grief remained trapped within me.

"You and Felipe will have others, Cassie dear," Eliza said sympathetically, "lots of others."

I protested the injustice of losing our child so soon after Felipe and I had had to part from each other by striking out at anyone and anything in the next few days. I always felt contrite about my truculence later, but my contrition didn't seem to keep me from further shows of ill temper. My breasts ached with the milk meant for the baby I had held in my arms only so briefly, and I longed for Felipe to share with me the sorrow that was too heavy to bear alone. I was cross and miserable and restless, and alternately burst into tears and struck out blindly at a world that had treated me so shabbily. It was a measure of Eliza's friendship that she accepted my horrid behavior with her usual calmness and pleasantness, when, all the while, I knew she was as concerned about Johnny as I was about Felipe.

A week after I had been brought to childbed, I heard her and Will whispering outside the cabin door, and a moment later, they came inside and Eliza said, "We must tell you something, but we aren't sure how you'll feel about the news."

"What news?" I asked apprehensively.

"Word reached here last night. We've taken Bexar."

"You see?" Will said defiantly before I could say anything. "They didn't need me!" He looked at us belligerently, as though he dared us to contradict him. Poor Will! I had been so encased in my own grief that I had scarcely noticed that the struggle within him was continuing to tear at him as he wondered if what he was doing—or failing to do—was right.

"I was glad to have you here with me," I said sincerely. "I needed you." And then my mind busied itself trying to grasp the significance of the startling news. Bexar taken? Impossible! I knew the Texans had moved to a position less than a mile from the plazas a week after we had left, and every day since then I had expected to hear that they had been forced back. How could a small unorganized force, a motley group of farmers and woodsmen and wheelwrights and lawyers, have vanquished the trained troops quartered in the old Alamo? It was true that many of the Mexican soldiers were of the lowest quality, and that many of them were as afraid of the blunderbusses they carried as of enemy fire, but at least they had been formed into a disciplined army of sorts, which the Texans had not.

*There must be two powers to fight a war.* Felipe had said so. Uncle Todd had said, in effect, the same thing. We Texans a power? Absurd! Our men knew nothing of waging warfare.

And yet, they had taken Bexar.

Will had slipped out of the cabin as Eliza told me some of the details, eyeing me warily as she talked, as though she was afraid of just how I would receive the news.

I wasn't certain myself, and I heard it with mixed feelings. As a Texan, I was proud and happy at what so few men had accomplished. And yet, though I would never have voiced such a thought aloud to Eliza, to me there was something almost sacrilegious about Bexar being in our hands. It wasn't only because Felipe was there, or because it had been our home. Bexar was thoroughly Mexican in its essence, and it was the one town in Texas we Americans had never been able to truly penetrate. Some of us had lived in it, but none of us had ever been totally accepted by it, or absorbed by it. Bexar's people belonged undeniably to the old world, and they maintained an invisible barrier between themselves and those of us who were a part of the new raw world of the frontier. I remembered my nodding acquaintance with *Señora* Parras, one of my Bexar neighbors. The woman nodded, greeted me pleasantly, but always she maintained a wall of polite reserve that kept me at bay. And so the town we Texans had never been able to penetrate peacefully we had finally taken by storm. Bexar was ours, and I was not sure I was glad.

My mind had been busy with all my conflicting

thoughts, coupled with my concern for Felipe, and I realized that Eliza was still talking, and that I had not been listening. I returned my attention to what she was saying.

". . . And he said, 'Who'll go into Bexar with old Ben Milam?' and about three hundred of our men went with him. First, they took a few houses near the church, and from there the fighting was hand to hand, house to house. There were only a few Texas casualties, but one of them was old Ben himself. All the Gonzales men are all right. I'm so relieved . . ."

Casualties? My mind grasped at the word, and it brought to the surface the fear that had never left me since I had looked back and watched Felipe standing in the middle of the street, alone. My mouth went dry. "And the Mexicans? What about their casualties?" My own voice came back to me as a faint whisper.

"Just a little heavier than ours, but not bad, I understand."

Eliza had tried to soften the news of the Mexican casualties as much as possible, I knew. She continued to watch me and added, "You look so tired, Cassie. Don't you think you ought to lie down for a while?"

"I think I will," I agreed, for suddenly I felt immeasurably wearied by trying to cope with all I had just learned.

And so I lay down, but I couldn't stop thinking of Felipe, wondering about him, worrying about him. Even as I lay there, I wondered if he was gone from me. I watched Eliza bustling about across the cabin and closed my eyes on a cushion of unshed tears.

*House to house fighting.* . . . How little it meant to Eliza, secure in her own home, knowing that Johnny was safe! I wondered if they had fought in our house. I could see the garden, peaceful in its seclusion, with only the rustling palms and the runners on the flowering vines reaching above the wall. And I could see as plainly as though I were there the mosaic paths converging on the statue of cupid, the god of love: the center of our patio, the very core of our lives. What quiet contentment we could have found there in our idyllic garden, if our conflicting loyalties and the war that could not happen hadn't tugged mercilessly at us until it had torn us apart! Could that serene, sheltered spot have been the scene of bloodshed and death? *House to house fighting.* . . .

Suddenly, the scene before me changed, and the garden was no longer empty. Felipe was there, not happy and smiling, but tense, alert. He was poised, sword drawn, his eyes darting warily around the garden wall. As I looked on in helpless horror, one, then another, and yet another buckskin-clad figure climbed over the wall. More and more of them came, and I saw Papa's face among them. Felipe swung and slashed at them madly, desperately, futilely, but they kept coming, until the garden was full of them and there was no longer room for him to raise his sword. *Run, Felipe, run!* I tried to call out to him, but though my lips formed the warning, no sound came from my throat. The Texans were closing in, grabbing his arms, pinioning them. *Run, Felipe! Please run!* As before, the words I wanted so desperately for him to hear died in my throat. The men surrounded him so that I could no longer see him. Why, why hadn't he run from them, through the open door that led through the house? *Felipe, why didn't you run?*

As if in mocking echo of my desperate question, a voice shouted, "Felipe, why didn't you run?"

But it wasn't an echo after all, and the sound of my own voice awakened me from the quasi dream. As I opened my eyes, I saw Eliza was kneeling at the edge of the bed, her hand on my shoulder. There were tears in her eyes. "I guess," she said softly, as though the question had been asked of her, "it just isn't in his nature to run."

On the sixteenth of December, Uncle Todd, looking frighteningly weary, returned from Bexar. He was too old to have war foisted upon him, I thought indignantly as he paused for a moment in the doorway. He should have been allowed to spend his days puffing on his beloved pipe and visiting his many friends.

Before I could get up from my chair to run to him, he

crossed toward me in three giant strides, as though he had drawn strength from some unseen wellspring of energy. He gathered me into his arms and said, "I'm sorry, so very sorry, child, about the baby. . . ."

I leaned gratefully on his ample shoulders, and the smell of horses, gunpowder and well-worn buckskins mingled in my nostrils. I said nothing, knowing I would burst into tears if I tried to talk. What could I say, what could anyone answer that would lessen my loss, make my arms any less empty or my heart any less heavy? Only Felipe could share with me the burden, lighten its weight. But my concern for him, the fear that I might have lost him as well only added to the weight, and it was almost more than I could bear.

Anxiously, afraid to ask and yet needing to know, I drew back and looked at him. "Felipe? Do you know—?"

He nodded. "I saw him. After the fighting."

"Thank goodness!" Relief washed over me. "Is he all right?"

"We didn't talk. I thought it best for him if I said nothing. But he was all right—no bandages or anything. He just looked exhausted, like the rest of us. He was with Cos, and I didn't think it wise to remind the general of his close ties with our side."

I nodded my understanding. "Where is he? Is he a prisoner?" My hopes surged as I waited for his answer. If Felipe was in the custody of our Texans, they would probably parole him, let him go if he promised not to fight them any more.

Uncle Todd quickly squelched such hopes. "We took no prisoners. What would we have done with them? Cos agreed in writing not to fight any more against those of us trying to uphold the Constitution of 1824. He and his men were allowed to leave, to go back across the river into Coahuila."

"Across the Rio Bravo?" But that was so far away, and it separated Texas from the rest of Mexico. But far more important, it was the boundary between two conflicting worlds that had grown much farther apart than could be measured by the width and depth of a river. To the north was our world—mine, and Felipe's too—and it was a world built from a wilderness, a bustling world of determined hard-working settlers. Only in Bexar had the other world crossed the river and remained, but the victory of our men had changed even that, made it, too, belong to us. How could Felipe possibly feel he belonged in that other world across the river? The terrain was different, the people were different, and the very essence of it was different. It was a world of lonely plains and towering mountains, of spineless people who cowered, with apparent lack of concern, under first one dictator and then another. It was a world on which those who had come from Spain had tried to superimpose the pattern of their native country, force the land and the people to conform to it. It was to that world that Felipe had gone, and the barrier between us was formidable.

"Mr. Stewart, what about my Johnny? When will he be home?"

Uncle Todd turned to smile reassuringly at Eliza. "Forgive me! I meant to tell you at once. He'll be home in a few days. And Cassie, your father has decided to stay on in Bexar. As for me, war has left me wearied and I'm ready to sit by my own hearth for a while."

"You shouldn't have gone," I protested, noting the dark rings under his eyes, the month's growth of stubble on his chin. "Let the younger men do the fighting."

"Like me?" Will bristled defensively. I hadn't noticed him enter the cabin.

"You know I didn't mean that."

"It's what you said. You're just like everyone else!" He wheeled around to stomp angrily out the door, and though I called after him, he didn't seem to hear.

Uncle Todd patted my arm. "Let him go, my dear. He's waging as big a battle inside himself as any of us have fought, and it's one he must fight alone."

Most of the Gonzales men came home a few days later. They were just as dirty and ragged as Uncle Todd had been, but in their steps, their movements, there was an exultation that shone through their exhaustion.

They had won. Our Davids, with their slingshots and stones, had bested their Goliath, and they were understandably drunk with the headiness of their success. I stood by the open door, watching them return. Some were on foot, others on faltering horses as weary as their riders. A few jubilantly brandished Mexican sabers. One of the sabers looked for a moment, exactly like the one that always hung at Felipe's side, and the thought that it could be his filled me with sudden indignation. I reminded myself quickly that there were probably many similar sabers, and it was not really likely that it was Felipe's that I saw. But what if it were? The men returning from battle were my soldiers, fighting for their freedom and mine, and I had no right to begrudge them the spoils of war.

I scarcely recognized Johnny as he dismounted by the front gate and bounded up the path to rush by me with a quick greeting and sweep Eliza into his arms. He had changed since I had last seen him almost two years before. Even after he had bathed and shaved and put on clean clothes, there remained something different about him. It wasn't only the maturity that the two intervening years had added, but something beyond that, an indefinable quality I had noticed on the faces of the others passing by. Most of the Texan men, young and old alike, had, at some time in their lives, had a brush with the Indians, for they had plagued us in one way or another and in one part of the state or another from the very beginning. But from those encounters, the men had emerged relatively unscathed, secure in their acceptance of the fact that they had grown up knowing the Indians were their mortal enemies, and never doubted the necessity of killing them. But the past months of open warfare against a different type of foe had given to men and boys alike a new dimension, left an indelible mark upon their faces. Johnny's eyes, and the eyes of those who had gone with him, had looked, however briefly, on the grim reality and callous cruelty of war. In a few months, their eyes had lost any remaining innocence, and they had aged beyond time. I wondered if Felipe had changed, too.

I recovered my strength rapidly, and moved in with Uncle Todd and Will after Christmas. Eliza and Johnny protested that I would be more comfortable with them, and I had no doubt of the sincerity of their offer, but I didn't accept it. I made other excuses, but the truth of the matter was that I couldn't be around them, couldn't see their joy in each other without being reminded constantly, painfully, of my longing for Felipe.

Uncle Todd and Will made a touching effort to straighten and clean the cabin for me, but still I found it in such a state of neglect that my palms itched to set it to rights, and I soon busied myself with such chores as washing and airing quilts, and scouring the hearth, and polishing the kettle till it gleamed brightly in the firelight. I found a comfort of sorts in the physical exhaustion I courted, and worked until I was too tired to brood overlong on my problems, and fell asleep the moment I lay down wearily each night on my bed.

Uncle Todd had been too long a bachelor to feel at ease with a woman in his cabin. He would walk in with his mud-caked boots, then look abashed at the freshly swept floor and sheepishly go outside again and enter without them. Though he would never have said so, I sensed that my presence made him a little uncomfortable. He insisted I would be welcome to make his cabin my home for as long as I wanted to, but I knew I didn't belong there, any more than I had belonged at the Gorhams'.

I don't know when I first began to think of going home to Bexar. Had I confided such a desire to anyone, the statement would have been met with shocked protests. An official state of war existed by that time between the Texans and the Republic of Mexico. The November meeting of the colonists in San Felipe had produced a provisional government with a governor, a lieutenant governor, a council, and finally, a commander in chief: Sam Houston.

While the men in San Felipe were busy with their politics, others set about occupying the two fortified positions in Bexar and Goliad that had been wrested from the Mexicans. Many of the Texans who had helped storm Bexar had, like Johnny and Uncle Todd, returned to the comfort of their own homes and the warmth of their own hearths. Only a token force was felt to be needed at the Alamo, for no one thought it was in any immediate danger of being recaptured. Of course, we all knew Santa Anna wouldn't accept such an audacious blow as had been dealt to his pride by the fall of Bexar, but he was far away in the national capital, and it would be a long time before he could leave for Texas. Slowly, more of the remaining men drifted away.

Shortly after the first of the year, we heard rumors of the still further depletion of the Alamo force by a Doctor Grant for an expedition to storm Matamoros. Uncle Todd shrugged the report off as an ill-founded rumor, said that Doctor Grant had failed in November to gain any support for the absurd mission he proposed, and reasoned that he surely could not have succeeded less than two months later.

True or not, the news—or rumor—had little effect on my desire to go home. To each possible argument against that desire which Uncle Todd or Eliza or Johnny or Will would have presented, I had prepared an answer in my mind. . . . *"You had a difficult birth. You aren't strong enough yet."* . . . *"I never felt stronger in my life."* . . . *"It isn't safe in Bexar."* . . . *"When Santa Anna crosses the Rio Bravo, it won't be safe anywhere in Texas."* . . . *"Ride alone to Bexar?"* . . . *"I have ridden that far alone before."* . . . *"What will you do there?"* . . . *"I will live in my own house, and I will no longer be a charity case for my friends and my family."*

The desire grew to an obsession. I would go home, to Bexar, telling no one I was leaving, for they would try to stop me. I began to watch for an opportunity to slip quietly out of Gonzales.

The chance came on the tenth of January, when Uncle Todd and Will left to check on Serena's place, which had

503

been empty since she had married Papa. I wrote a note and left it on the table, knowing they would not return till that night to find it. With a full day's start behind me, it would be too late for them to stop me.

It was drizzling lightly as I rode into Bexar three days later. At first, nothing seemed changed. But wasn't it? I averted my eyes quickly as a gaudily clad creature came out of one of the older houses and shouted provocatively at a group of passing soldiers. Previously, she would never have dared to move from her own section of town.

As I approached the bridge over the river to the main section of Bexar, it seemed to look as it always had. But it was guarded by a bored American sentry who watched me lazily, seemed to consider challenging my right to cross, then decided to say nothing.

At first glance, as I rode down the street that led toward San Fernando Church, I didn't see the pockmarks on the houses, but then I began to notice them, and noticed, too, that some of the outer doors showed bright splinters of interior wood where an axe or a rifle butt had jabbed and pried at them.

The streets were, as always, crowded with ragged children at play, but that day, instead of looking at me with idle curiosity or friendliness as they always had, they scurried in fright into nearby doorways at my approach, and their eyes followed me warily from the protection of the interior of their houses.

Many of the houses were deserted, I realized, and here and there shutters banged forlornly in the wind-whipped drizzling rain. I caught my breath as I neared the twin plazas, saw the houses which had taken most of the brunt of the snipers' bullets. Uncle Todd had shrugged off most of my questions about the actual fighting, made it seem inconsequential. But unfolding before my eyes, was the mute evidence of a far fiercer struggle than he had admitted. The story of the battle, the story that Uncle Todd and Johnny had withheld, was written indelibly on the face of Bexar, silently attested to by a trampled bush, a broken shutter, a bullet-scarred wall.

Yes, Bexar had changed, after all, for the town, just as the men I had watched returning to Gonzales, had looked on the stark reality of battle, an experience not to be soon forgotten and never to be totally erased.

My heart beat anxiously as I turned down our street and rode toward the sixth house from the end, the house that I knew and loved so well. I approached it apprehensively, scanned the façade, saw with relief that it was unscarred. No bullets, at least, had left their marks upon the surface. Quickly, I dismounted, put my hand on the massive oak *portal*. During the day, we had always kept the outer door wide open, as was the custom. At night, Esperanza had always locked it against intruders. It gave way as I pushed against it, its hinges protesting noisily, as though I were an interloper. My footsteps resounded eerily in the empty *zaguán* as I walked to the inner door. That, too, I found unlatched, and I entered the house.

"Esperanza?" I called into the darkened room, into the silence, not really expecting an answer. Inside the *sala*, I crossed to the front window, tripping over something. I caught myself, felt for the shutters, threw them open.

"Oh, no!" I gasped in dismay as my eyes surveyed the chaos. The unscathed exterior of the house had left me unprepared for the disarray confronting me inside. Three of the four chairs which had been grouped around the low table by the window were up-ended. The velvet cushions I had made from an old ball gown of Mama's lay on the floor, feathers spilling from long slashes in the fabric. A broken china cup lay on the table, enough of it intact to show the dark stains of the rich chocolate Felipe liked so well. It was his cup, and I could picture him, lonely and depressed, sitting in his chair slowly sipping it. Had he been there, drinking his chocolate, when the Texans came, I wondered? *But he never should have been sitting there alone,* I thought indignantly. *He should have been with me, or with his Texan friends, and would have been but for his misplaced loyalty to the egotistical general, Antonio Lopez de Santa Anna.*

"Santa Anna!" I hissed angrily under my breath as my eyes scanned the wreckage, even as I knew that it had not been Santa Anna's Mexican troops who had despoiled our house, but the Texans. I blinked back angry tears, went into the large kitchen, anxiously walked over to the long oak table Felipe had bought from one of the old Bexar families when they had left. The craftsmanship, the carving on the mammoth dining set were superb, and I gazed in horror at the marred table top. Near its center, an empty skin of wine lay on its side, and from it a trail of liquid had dried into an ugly stain soaked into the wood. All along the table was evidence of a drunken orgy. A pewter mug was dented as from a violent blow. Directly in front of me, etched raw and deep into the heart of our fine table, were two clumsily gouged initials. All along the table's length were scratches, ashes, bits of debris. Chairs were tipped over, and one of them had two legs hacked off. Everywhere I looked, there was senseless destruction.

In despair, I turned and walked to the door that led to the garden, wondering why I had come. Why had I felt so drawn there that I would have walked every foot of the way from Gonzales if it had been necessary? As I opened the door that led to the garden and saw the broken remains of the statue of cupid, I knew what it was I had hoped to find, and knew it had been denied to me. I had come in search of the comforting assuagement of living among familiar things in the one place I had known so much happiness. I had come looking for reassurance that nothing had really changed at all. Instead, I found a violent testimonial to the uprooting and devastation that had occurred in Bexar, and in my life with Felipe. With each other, we could have faced anything—war, uprooting, the loss of our firstborn son—and we would have grown closer still for having shared the trials and sorrows that beset us. But we were not together, were not even on the same side of the war that had driven us apart.

506

I rubbed the back of my hand across my eyes. I had chosen to live in my own house, and the first thing I had to do was to return to it some semblance of order. I walked over to the shattered Cupid and stooped to pick up the pieces.

A few hours later, one of the maids from the Parras home next to ours knocked on our door, bearing a steaming tureen of hot soup.

"My *señora* thought you might be hungry," she said as she handed it to me, "and she wants to know if there is anything else you need tonight."

I tried to keep from showing my surprise at the unexpected gesture from the woman who had, for almost two years, restricted herself to a polite nod or a formal greeting. And when I would have expected her to shun me, she had made this gesture of friendship instead. The aroma of the vegetable-laden broth, rich with chunks of meat, made my mouth water. I stammered my thanks to be relayed to the woman, and assured the maid that I needed nothing more that night. I poured some soup into a pewter mug and drank it hungrily, fishing out the solid morsels with my fingers.

The next morning, I called on *Señora* Parras, a tiny plump woman who was always clothed in unrelieved black. I thanked her for the soup and returned her tureen.

"It is nothing." She dismissed her charitable gesture with a wave of her chubby hand. "I knew you found everything in your house very bad, and was certain you'd be hungry. Your maid told me to tell you she has gone to her people in Monclova. We thought it best to leave the house open. Otherwise, they would have broken the door down or ripped the shutters off to get in. Some of your things are here in my house for safekeeping."

"I am very grateful for all you have done and for the soup you sent." I spoke haltingly, searching for the right Spanish words, none of which I had spoken since the previous fall. "But I feel I must tell you something. Even though my husband is a major in the Mexican army, I

507

don't share his feelings. I would be happy to shoot that terrible Santa Anna with my own rifle. The people who forced the Mexican army to leave Bexar are my people. My father is with them, and I am going to find them today and offer to help them, if they need me. You have been very kind. But now that I have told you this, I am sure you will not want to offer me any further help."

She smiled softly and put her hand on my arm. "Tell me, daughter, why did you return to San Antonio de Bexar?"

I shrugged. "It was foolish, I suppose, when I had two homes offered me in Gonzales. But I felt drawn . . . "

She nodded. "That is what I thought when I saw you ride in yesterday. There is something about our town that tugs on the heart, is there not, little one? For all the threat of danger, for all the uncertainty of what you would find, you have returned, for the same reason that I have always stayed. You and I were neighbors before, but now we are far more than that. We are companions of the soul, and this is beyond the politics of the moment. Tell me what you need, tell me how I can help you, and I will."

My eyes misted as we smiled at each other across a conflict that one of us must eventually lose, but I knew as our eyes met that the results would not matter between us. At last, I thought, I have been accepted by her, not just as a neighbor in need, but as far more than that. She was a part of San Antonio de Bexar, and she had just declared that she considered me also a part of it. I wondered if she realized how much that acceptance had touched me, and raised my sagging spirit.

"Thank you. Thank you so much. For everything." I leaned down and kissed her cheek, knew she would no longer consider the gesture presumptuous.

I had not found what I sought in Bexar, but I had discovered an odd unexpected sort of comfort in returning, after all.

# Chapter VI

## SAN ANTONIO DE BEXAR—
## Mid-January 1836

It was late morning when I crossed the footbridge to the ramshackle mission and run-down fort that lay across the San Antonio River only eight hundred yards from the Church of San Fernando in the heart of Bexar. On the south side, I found a gate open and untended, and I entered. The collection of adobe buildings built into the wall opened onto a large area in the center that Felipe had called, half-jestingly, the plaza. The entrance to the mission church—much of its roof gone—was set back from this plaza on its southwest corner, leaving a gap in the rectangular enclosure.

Two unshaven men warmed themselves indolently in the morning sun, and their eyes followed me hungrily. I quickly walked past them and followed along the west wall till I came to a room with an open door. Inside were several men. One, seated at a desk, was intent upon a message he was scratching with a large quill. The other, a boy who couldn't have been over eighteen, jumped up as I entered.

He saluted smartly. "Corporal Wash Briggs, ma'am. Can I help you?"

I smiled at him, noted that his neat gray uniform was devoid of any insignia. I was reminded of a little boy playing soldier. "I'm looking for my father, Thorne Stewart."

His face lit up instantly. "Captain Stewart, ma'am? I saw him, not half an hour ago. I'll send for him right away."

From the doorway, I watched him approach the two

shabby men I had just passed, say something to them. As he wheeled around and walked back toward me, one of the men spat a stream of tobacco juice at his back in an unmistakable gesture of contempt.

He strode past me, shaking his head. "Lazy louts," he muttered. "Grant took most of the good men with him. I'll find your father myself, ma'am."

As Papa approached a short time later, I noted that he had lost weight, but the loss hadn't harmed him. His body, which had begun to grow toward flabbiness when I had seen him last two years earlier, was again hard and lean. His wide shoulders appeared broader still beneath his buckskin jacket, and his face was weathered and jowlless.

I threw myself into his arms, forgetting the strain that had kept me from feeling close to him for the last several years. I remembered only that he was my father, and that I loved him.

The young corporal brought two chairs outside for us, and we sat in front of the building and talked. Painfully, I recounted the story of the stillbirth six weeks earlier, then quickly changed the subject to the astounding Texan triumphs.

"Past victories can't help us now." With a sweeping gesture of indignation, he motioned toward several small groups of men sitting idly around the plaza. "Look at them! Most of them won't obey orders, won't do anything! And the likes of them are about all we have left since that nefarious Dr. Grant went through our ranks like a tornado, stealing our garrison, our food, our blankets, our best horses—everything!"

"Stealing them?" I recalled the young corporal's muttered remarks. How was it possible for anyone to steal a garrison?

"Grant came here with a pack of lies about loyal Mexicans across the Rio Bravo being ready to rise up against Santa Anna. He'd been trying since November to lure our men away for an attack on Matamoros, but he had no authority then. But once the council gave permission, there was no stopping him. He promised those who would follow him rich rewards, but he didn't say that it's his own land south of the river that he's concerned about! And just to protect his own selfish interests, he would divert practically a whole garrison, and leave us dangerously undermanned!"

Incredulously, I asked, "You mean he's taken men to fight south of the river? Why, that's absurd!" I remembered that Uncle Todd had refused to believe such a rumor.

Papa nodded. "It's more than that—it's disastrous! The council, that bunch of bungling idiots, is forever issuing orders that conflict with those of Houston and Governor Smith!"

"You mean the council ordered it? But isn't Houston commander in chief?"

"That's the point. If the council would restrict itself to trying to run the state and let Houston run the war, we'd be a lot better off. Grant's scheme is impractical. It would tie us in too closely with the rest of Mexico, even if there really were as many people ready to help fight Santa Anna's tyranny there as Grant claims. What we need is independence from Mexico!"

"But we're still one of the Mexican states," I protested.

"I don't think we will be for long. There's a meeting scheduled for March first, and I'm willing to bet the first order of business will be to declare our independence."

*That's what Felipe said would happen,* I thought, *and at the time, I was so sure he was wrong.*

"We had too few men here to begin with," Papa continued. "Most of the men have drifted away, back to their homes."

"They'll come back when they're needed, won't they?"

"I hope so, Duchess." He sighed heavily. "Right now, I doubt if we have more than a hundred men, including those who are sick, or still nursing wounds from the battle. Most of the men we have are adventurers from the other side of the Sabine who hurried here within the last few months. Most of them were promised land and God knows what-all, and we can't even give them tobacco money! We

511

had a rash of desertions the other day because we told the men we had no money to pay them. And there are only a few Texans among us. Most of the few men we have are useless, won't obey orders. Look at them!" His gesture took in several groups of men idling about. "How can we hope to stop Santa Anna here with a handful of such sluggards?"

As I surveyed the inactivity in the plaza, I understood his despair. There were only two figures moving, and they were walking toward us.

"Serena! And Andrew!" I jumped up and ran to greet them.

They had arrived in Bexar a week earlier, I learned. Andrew was a serious child, unrestrained in show of either affection or hatred. And Papa had filled him with hatred for anything and anyone Mexican.

This hatred manifested itself one day when I took Andrew shopping around the Plaza Mayor. We met *Señora* Parras, who spoke to Andrew in friendly tones. He remained mute and unsmiling, and I let her assume he could not understand Spanish.

"Andrew, how rude of you!" I admonished as the black-clad figure retreated down the street. "You understood every word she said. Why didn't you answer her?"

His dark eyes glowed with hatred as they followed her. "She's Mex'can!" he said emphatically. And for him, that seemed reason enough.

A few Texan residents returned to Bexar, but only to salvage some of their belongings and leave before Santa Anna's wrath vented itself on Bexar. Among those was Asa Quigley. Five days after my arrival, I passed the Quigley house and saw him busily loading things into a wagon.

"Asa," I said accusingly, "surely you're not leaving!" Obviously, that was exactly what he was doing.

"Hullo, Cassie. Yes, I'm leavin'." Seeming to think of nothing else to say, he resumed the feverish tempo of his work.

"You're not staying to defend Bexar? You, of all people!" I remembered how vociferous and militant he had always been. "Why, this is your home!"

He spat a stream of yellow tobacco juice and looked at me impatiently. "Not no more, it ain't. Rosella and the children are stayin' in Brazoria with my brother's fam'ly." He shrugged indifferently. "We might come back here some day, maybe, if it's ever safe."

"But how can it be safe, if people won't fight for it?" I couldn't let him go! Each man, each rifle mattered. "They need men desperately in the Alamo, Asa. You can't go!"

He picked up a chair, balanced it on top of the wagon, then shifted his plug of tobacco from one cheek to the other and looked at me. "How many able fightin' men in Bexar right now?"

"Less than a hundred. That's why—"

"And how many troops do you reckon old Santa Anny is goin' to bring with him when he swoops down on Bexar like a hawk on a field mouse?"

"I don't know," I lied. Once, when Felipe was trying to convince me of the futility of the Texans' revolt, he had told me that Santa Anna would bring six or seven thousand men, maybe more.

"Well, I do. It's gonna be a sight more'n a hundred, and a sight more'n a thousand. Now, I'll take on pretty high odds. I'll stand against five or six Mexicans. Them blunder-busses of theirs are no good, even if they did know how to shoot 'em. But I don't aim to go no higher than that. No sirree, I ain't no coward, but I ain't no fool, neither. I can't do nobody no good by throwin' myself in front of Santa Anny's cannons!" He put a foot on the wagon, motioned toward the house. "Anything you want in there, take it 'fore somebody else does."

"But you can't go! Papa says we must hold here at Bexar, and at Goliad, or nothing will stop Santa Anna from overrunning the settlements to the east." I watched him get into the wagon, pick up the reins. "You were anxious enough to fight once. Aren't you still a loyal Texan?"

He looked down at me. "Yes, but I'm a husband and a

513

father, too. And, like I said, I ain't no fool!" He clicked to the horses and flicked the reins.

Tense with futile anger, I watched him go. "Coward!" I flung after him. "Running away, when we need every man to stand and fight!"

If Asa heard me, he gave no sign. I walked home slowly, feeling discouraged and defeated. If only I had been able to convince him how desperate was the situation of the men in the Alamo!

The desperate situation of the men in the Alamo was not unknown back in the east. It had been communicated to Governor Smith in a letter from Colonel Neill, telling how destitute and defenseless Grant's raid on men and supplies had left them. The governor blasted the council for ordering the Matamoros expedition, and they countered by summarily "firing" him. Sam Houston, commander in chief of the Texan army, met with Jim Bowie at Goliad in mid-January, too late to stop Dr. Grant from raiding that garrison as he had the one at Bexar.

Houston ordered Bowie to Bexar, and his arrival on January nineteenth did much to bolster the sagging morale inside the Alamo. The big sandy-haired man was a born leader. The gentlemen approved of him because he was obviously well-bred, and yet the roughest of the frontiersmen felt no resentment at his polished speech and manner, because they knew he could hold his whiskey and fight like a demon. His nickname was Gentleman Jim, and under the force of his magnetism, the morale of the garrison improved. If Colonel Neill, the officer in charge, resented the fact that the men who had repeatedly ignored his orders jumped at Bowie's smallest suggestion, he swallowed his resentment as the men began to show signs of life.

The men were doubly reassured by the volunteers Bowie brought. Serena and I, helping in the hospital, noted the improved attitude of the men after Bowie's arrival.

But he had brought with him only thirty men. I remembered Felipe's prediction that Santa Anna would come with thousands. What good could a hundred and thirty do against so many? I voiced this fearful thought one night to Serena as we were returning to my house with Andrew.

"Papa said he thinks Houston told Bowie to decide whether or not we should try to hold the Alamo."

She shrugged. "I've also heard rumors that he sent orders with Bowie to blow it up and take the artillery and leave. But I think both Neill and Bowie are determined to stay."

"But we must have more men! What are they waiting for back in San Felipe?"

"The provisional state government? They're too busy placing blame and fighting petty quarrels to be of any help. No one seems to know who has any authority. How can such confusion possibly produce an organized effort to send us men?"

"If only Austin had been elected provisional governor," I said, "as he should have been!" But Austin had been with the men at Gonzales and Bexar while those back in San Felipe played with their politicizing, and Smith had been elected instead. Later, Austin had been sent to the United States to try to raise much-needed funds for our cause, something that it seemed to me others could have been more easily spared to do. We needed Austin in Texas, needed his cool thinking and his flair for organization. "Surely our government will get organized before Santa Anna comes!"

Serena didn't answer, and I took what comfort I could in assuming that her silence signified agreement.

The news from the east was more disquieting than ever. The council had empowered three different men to lead the Matamoros expedition, and had given one of them, Colonel Fannin, powers that usurped that of Houston, who had extricated himself from the confusion and bickering by requesting from the governor a furlough to parlay with the Indians until the first of March. With the state government virtually useless and the commander-in-chief of the army on extended leave, what hope was there for an organized recruitment of men to help defend Bexar against Santa Anna?

On the third of February, Buck Travis arrived with another thirty men. There was about him a conceit, a galling arrogance, and he clearly resented Bowie's control over the men. Until then, Colonel Neill had remained tacit head of the garrison, but it had been Bowie who actually commanded. Only when Travis arrived did friction begin. Travis, a colonel in the regular army, plainly considered Bowie's parallel rank in the volunteers decidedly inferior. When Neill left on February 11, he placed Travis in charge. The volunteers grumbled, claimed they had always elected their leaders before, and elected Bowie. He and Travis finally resolved their differences by agreeing that Bowie would head the volunteers and Travis the regulars, and that all major decisions they would make together.

Though no one expected Santa Anna soon, not a man doubted that he intended to return the Alamo and Bexar to Mexican hands. The demoralizing effect of that would be worth far more to him than Bexar's negligible value as a military stronghold. Our small force was equally determined to hold it for the same reason, though we knew in other parts of Texas it was considered folly. Late in January, there had been a political meeting among the men, and they had almost all agreed to defend the Alamo at all costs. The men were confident that, before the time came, Texans everywhere would rush to help.

But volunteers only trickled in. Davey Crockett, retired in defeat from Washington politics, had arrived the day that Neill left, bringing with him thirteen men, whom he called his Tennessee Mounted Volunteers. In spite of the fact that he had brought so few men, Crockett's arrival bolstered morale miraculously and was cheered lustily. What harm could possibly come to them when Davey Crockett, the renowned Indian fighter, had come to help? The men laughed appreciatively as Crockett regaled them with tales of other tight spots he had been in. He had got-

516

ten through those to joke and laugh about them, and by jingo, he'd be joking about the Alamo before long!

Meanwhile, life in the town outside the Alamo was an odd mixture of the old and new. Gone from the streets were the carriages of the wealthy, and gone, too, was the quiet, unhurried pace of life that was the very essence of Bexar. And yet the water carriers and the beggars continued on their rounds with a ridiculous calm, as though life in the old Spanish mission town was unchanged.

Inside the Alamo, the men worked unhurriedly to prepare for Santa Anna's inevitable attack, certain that help would come from the east soon. Time enough to prepare in earnest for the assault after the others arrived.

And there was Colonel Fannin, too. He had withdrawn from the Matamoros expedition, and had gone to Goliad and rallied four hundred men there. He had declared his intention of coming to our aid, and none doubted that he would respond immediately whenever he was needed.

Even I had become complacent, and was unconcerned about *Señora* Parras's grave warnings that I must be prepared to take flight at any time. I had no intention of leaving. The Alamo walls would be well defended; inside, I would be safe.

There was nothing to mark one day from another, and I didn't realize till several days later that Felipe's and my second wedding anniversary had slipped by without my noticing. Each night as I lay in my lonely bed, I longed to feel the warmth of his body against mine, ached for the feel of his arms around me. Where was he, I wondered? And when would we be together again?

Each morning, Serena and I took Andrew and went to the Alamo, did what we could to help. In my work in the kitchen and the hospital, or writing letters for the illiterate, I found a peace of sorts. Sometimes Papa returned to the house with us at the end of the day, but most nights he spent at the fort.

It was during the night of February twenty-first that the wall of complacency I had built around my own apprehensions came tumbling down with a resounding crash, for it was then that I learned with a shock that the danger we had so blandly consigned to some vague time in the future was imminent. I was roused during the night by a persistent knock at the *portal*. Puzzled, I rose from the bed, throwing a blanket around my shoulders, and shuffled through the house, feeling my way. I realized as I opened the inner door that Serena was right behind me. We stood together in the *zaguán* as I cautiously slid back the bolt and opened the door only a crack.

"It is I, *El Ciego*," came the whispered reply to my unasked question.

I swung the door open.

"You have no candle, *Señora*?"

"No."

"Good. I come to warn you to leave. It will not be safe here. Santa Anna comes. He is very near, with many soldiers."

My heart lurched. *Señora* Parras had given me warnings that were vague and general, but this was urgent, and specific. It never occurred to me to doubt El Ciego's word. The men of the town always knew everything, as though they conversed with the very wind itself. I knew I must get from him all the information I could, carry his warning to the Alamo. I poured out questions as fast as they popped into my head. "Are you certain it is *El Presidente* himself? How many men? Where are they now? How soon could they arrive?" Papa had mentioned that there had been rumors of Santa Anna's early and totally unexpected arrival, but nobody believed it was possible for him to move a whole army until later in the year.

"It is *El Presidente* himself," the beggar answered. "His personal standard has been seen, less than two days' march from here. There is no doubt. The *Señora* must go. At once."

"How many men?" I repeated.

"How many?" He shrugged. "Who knows? They are as blades of grass upon a prairie. Who can count them?" He

518

moved his head apprehensively, and a moment later I realized that his sensitive ears had picked up the sound of an approaching rider long before mine had. He stepped backwards, anxious to be away. He had risked much to warn me, I knew.

Impulsively, I pulled the blanket from my shoulders and gave it to him. "Thank you, old one. And God bless you for your kindness."

"Go with God, *Señora*." With surprising agility, he spun around and was gone.

Overwhelmed by the significance of his words, I leaned heavily against the *portal* after I had bolted it. It was incredible, what he had said. How could the Mexican troops be that close without our knowledge? Bowie had lived among the Mexicans of Bexar, had been married to the governor's daughter until cholera had claimed her life and those of their two children. He had friends among the remaining Bexar inhabitants, and some of them had been bringing him bits and pieces of information about Santa Anna's intention to recapture Bexar. One man had told him that many Mexican troops had reached the Rio Bravo, but no one thought that they could march on Bexar so soon. I'd heard Travis say that he didn't think they could attack us before the fifteenth of March, at the earliest. It was assumed that Santa Anna couldn't pull his fully laden supply wagons and heavy cannons overland without animals, and surely he would have to wait until the grass had grown enough so that he wouldn't have to haul fodder for them. By that time, the ground would surely be muddied with the spring rains, and that would make travel more difficult for him. It would be an amazing feat if he could reach Bexar even by mid-March. He could not possibly have come so soon.

It was impossible, but it was so. *El Ciego* would not have lied.

Serena and I moved back into the house. Just inside the inner door, we paused.

"You don't doubt his word, do you?" she asked.

"He wouldn't lie to me. Oh, Serena, we must go tell the men in the garrison! Santa Anna, less than two days away!" Hours, even minutes were vital.

Serena placed a restraining hand on my arm. "No, wait just a minute, please. I have seen this coming—"

I drew back in surprise. "You mean you expected Santa Anna to take us by surprise before we were ready for him?"

"There has always been that possibility."

"But men will come now. They'll rush here—"

"With the memory of what Santa Anna did to the Zacatecans so fresh in their minds?"

"Are you saying you don't think our men will come? But if they don't how can we hold the Alamo?"

She answered only indirectly. "You must do as your beggar says. You must leave."

"I won't! I'm needed here."

"Felipe will need you far worse when all this is over. I know you're confused, and angry with him now, but I also know you love him as much as you ever did—more, perhaps, because now you are more aware of his faults and love him in spite of them. He thinks he is fighting for an ideal, and he will be shocked and disillusioned when he realizes that men fight wars only for power. The ideals are only illusory, an excuse for the power-hungry to call men to arms."

"I've never doubted that Felipe and I will find each other again, but that's in the future," I said, dismissing her words impatiently. "Right now, I must go warn the men."

Her hand tightened on my arm. "You must promise me you will escape with Andrew while there is still time."

I recoiled at her words. "You talk as though you think it's hopeless!" Was she acknowledging defeat even before the battle had begun? Serena, who moved about her tasks so confidently, so cheerfully, who had never seemed for a moment to question the wisdom of the decision to hold the Alamo?

"My dear, it is utterly hopeless."

"It isn't!" I insisted, appalled at her disloyalty. "One of our riflemen is worth ten Mexicans, and more!" Even Felipe had admitted their soldiers were ineffective because they seldom sighted and fired from their shoulders.

"How many more? Twenty? Or thirty? Or perhaps even a hundred? It takes precious minutes for the best rifleman to reload. There is no substitute for sheer overpowering numbers. Barring a miracle, the men, if they stubbornly insist on staying, are doomed."

"They might not stay," I said uncertainly.

"I hope you're right, but I doubt it. Travis and Bowie both seem committed to the folly, as is your father. They think loyal Texans everywhere will rush to their aid. You and I just learned that it is too late for that, but they will still cling stubbornly to that frail hope. And your father will cling most stubbornly of all.

"That brings me to what I must say. From the time I lost Felipe's father until I met Thorne, my life was empty."

"But you seemed so strong, so independent when we first saw you!" I had never forgotten how she had looked standing in the doorway of her cabin, defiant and self-assured. To my childish eyes, she had looked so very brave.

"That was a role forced on me by circumstances. Everything has changed since then. I love your father, and I lack the strength to go on without him."

"Without him?" I said in alarm. "What foolish talk! Others will come. Nothing is going to happen to him——"

"Then nothing will happen to me if I stay with him."

"Of course not. We'll both stay. We can help inside the fort, and *Señora* Parras will care for Andrew, keep him away from the fighting."

"And what would happen to him if he should be left without any of us? No, you must take him and leave before Santa Anna comes."

"But it's you he needs!"

"Not if he has you. I love both my sons dearly, but your father is my life. I want to stay with him, and whatever happens will happen to us both."

"But I can't leave! I can help, reload for the men, and I have my own rifle, too."

Her hands reached for my shoulders. Even in the almost total blackness, I could imagine I saw her eyes pleading with me. "These things I can do, too. Please go. When I saw you here that first day, I felt you were the answer to my prayers. By then I had come to suspect that the men might decide to stay here and fight. In these past five weeks, Andrew has come to know you, and to love you. I want you to look after both my sons. Promise me you will."

I could not bring myself to answer with the brutally direct "no" that was on my lips. "I—I'll think about it," I hedged.

That seemed to satisfy her. "Thank you."

Guiltily, I turned away as soon as she released me. I had no intention of leaving, so how could I do as she asked?

Later, *El Ciego*'s words resounded in my ears as I walked swiftly through the deserted streets of Bexar in the predawn darkness. I hurried down Potrero Street, moved quickly to one side to evade a reeling drunk as I came to the footbridge to the Alamo. As I reached the gate, I was stopped by a sentry.

"I must see my father, Captain Stewart, at once," I said breathlessly.

"Could you come back in maybe three hours, ma'am?" he suggested in a maddeningly slow drawl. "Everybody's asleep—"

"This can't wait till morning. Santa Anna is coming. He's near—"

"Yes, ma'am, we've heard rumors like that for weeks now. I'll pass the word along."

"Please, we mustn't delay. This isn't just another rumor. It's true!"

The man weakened, said, "Well, I suppose I could send you to talk to Lieutenant Winthrop. He's on duty in headquarters tonight."

"Thank you," I said, brushing past him. "You needn't leave. I can find my way."

The lieutenant was an unpleasant slight-statured man with a thin line for a mouth and a gray uniform that was too new, too elaborate. One of the New Orleans Grays, I assumed, who had enlisted to help us in that city and who all wore gray uniforms without insignia. He listened to me, frowning, then asked,

"Where, may I ask, did you get this startling bit of information?"

"My blind beggar—" I knew as soon as I said the words that they were wrong.

"Ha!" His lip curled unpleasantly. "A blind beggar? Blind?"

"The beggars of Bexar know everything," I insisted. "I've known this one for two years. He risked his life to warn me. He wouldn't have lied!"

"Unless he wanted to alarm us, throw us into a panic—"

I choked back my irritation and asked him to send for Papa, emphasizing his rank as I did so. The significance wasn't lost on the junior officer.

*Papa will believe me,* I thought with relief as I waited for him.

But he didn't. He never said so, but he wouldn't waken Bowie, insisted that he would tell him after breakfast. When I protested the delay, he replied that they heard many rumors and that most of them proved to be untrue.

"We heard several days ago that many Mexican soldiers had crossed the Rio Bravo, but Bowie and Travis apparently decided it was only another ill-founded rumor. We can't get excited about each little thing we hear."

I saw the lieutenant look at me triumphantly.

"I'll walk you home," Papa offered. "You go get some sleep, and don't worry your little head about this."

"You don't have to walk me home," I answered dully. "It's getting light."

As I dragged my feet dejectedly across the footbridge, I thought, *And it's the light of another day, and Santa Anna will soon wake up and march closer to Bexar, and nobody will believe he's almost here.*

When I returned to the Alamo around midmorning, I hoped to see signs of increased activity, but I noticed with despair that nothing had changed. A few men unhurriedly hauled in dirt for breastworks, a job that had been under way for weeks and was still far from finished. Except for the mounting of most of the big guns, only minor improvements had been made in the defenses since Bowie's arrival; basically, the area was not much more easily defensible than Cos had left it. The wooden walkway the Mexicans had constructed behind a portion of the walls remained, but little had been done to augment it.

As usual, the daytime conversation of the men focused primarily on their plans for the evening. Even Serena and Papa had planned a visit with the family of one of the other Texans that night. Santa Anna, everyone seemed to feel, was very far away.

"How can you just go on as if nothing had happened?" I asked Serena. "You heard *El Ciego*!"

She had shrugged resignedly. "Thorne insists we would know if Santa Anna were really as close as your blind beggar says."

Discouraged, I took Andrew home early. We ate a light supper, and a short time later I lay down, fully clothed, beside the sleeping child. It began to rain, and the sound of it was soothing. Maybe I was being foolish, I thought, putting so much faith in the words of *El Ciego*. Perhaps Santa Anna was, as everyone seemed to believe, very far away.

I slept the deep sleep of utter exhaustion, and didn't even hear Papa and Serena come in later. I awoke when the first faint glow of dawn was beginning to show through the cracks in the shutters. Something—some unaccustomed noise—had awakened me. Ears straining, I lay unmoving, heard the creak of wagon wheels in the street outside. That was not unusual. Wagons frequently came into town in the early morning hours for the market. It had been something else. Someone was pounding on our *portal*.

524

I ran through the house, tripping over one of Papa's boots. The caller was a distraught *Señora* Parras, wearing a cloak over her nightgown, her hair falling in a disarranged mass around her shoulders. "You are too slow, daughter," she admonished as I let her into the house. "You must leave now, this moment. *El Presidente* comes and I fear for you. Look!" She walked to the window, threw back the shutters. "Everyone goes!"

I stared out the window, saw shadowy shapes, one after another, passing by, all of them hurrying, scurrying, dashing by with a sense of urgency. I heard a mother's impatient admonition answered by a sleepy-voiced childish lament. Men shouted to one another. Above the din, as though it must be heard, a voice called out, "*¡Me voy!*" and that seemed to say it all. "I go!"

*Señora* Parras nodded. "You must go too, my daughter, at once. Word has been received. Santa Anna will be here in a matter of hours. There would be those who might remember you helped the men in the Alamo."

"In only hours?" I asked incredulously. "Santa Anna is that close?" I thought of the old mission, the men inside it, so pathetically unprepared. What if they couldn't hold off Santa Anna until Fannin and the others arrived? Worse, what if no one came to their aid? I looked at *Señora* Parras, and I didn't know if it was the dim half-light or my tears that blurred my vision. "They're not ready. So few men . . ."

Her hand rested sympathetically on my shoulder. "They are fools. It is too late to worry about them. I am sorry your father is there. But you must save yourself."

"No! I'm staying!" I insisted. Of course I would not leave! Of course Fannin and hundreds of Texans from other places would rush to help us! Meanwhile, whatever force we could muster would have to hold Santa Anna at bay. We would need every man. And every woman. As soon as *Señora* Parras had left, still insisting I must go, I went to knock on Serena and Papa's bedroom door, then ran to wake Andrew.

525

Ten minutes later, we picked our way through the confusion that was Bexar to the Alamo. People, dogs, cattle, donkeys, and horses had appeared as from nowhere. The town that had seemed less than half alive was suddenly seething with life, everyone intent on the urgency of his own movements. Most of the Mexicans, afraid to be mistaken for Texan sympathizers if they remained, were leaving. For the men in the Alamo, however, there was no thought of fleeing. Grimly, they were trying belatedly to improve their defenses, for it was there they intended to stay.

I had often heard Papa complain that the men obeyed only the orders that suited them. But if the odd assortment of men refused to obey blindly any man, their stubborn insistence on a degree of independence was not without its merits. This was apparently as soon as we walked into the Alamo plaza, for all around us were small groups of men working independently and efficiently, all intent upon one common goal: to strengthen their position, prepare to hold until help arrived. The sentry who had stopped me scarcely thirty-six hours earlier was mud-spattered and unshaven, herding cows into the enclosure. A hard-bitten youth who had been involved in an ugly knifing the previous day was helping drag a corn-laden cart inside the walls. Other men rushed past us with assorted Mexican swords and rifles, which could only have been obtained by looting the deserted houses of Bexar.

Of those there were many. The streets were choked with the press of people trying to leave. Most of them didn't seem to know—or care—where they were going. They were running blindly from the danger that threatened, and as long as a road led out of Bexar, it little mattered where it went.

As I worked beside the men, I remembered Asa's parting words that day I had tried to dissuade him from leaving Bexar. He had spoken of the odds against the men who were in the Alamo, odds too high to take on. Some men had come since then: Bowie's thirty, thirty more who had come with Travis, thirteen with Crockett. But still, there

526

were so few, and what good could so few do against so many, against Santa Anna's thousands?

But that morning, none of the men stopped to worry about the odds, nor was there time for more than passing regret that we were not better prepared for an attack. As the men worked diligently, women and children began to gather in the enclosure—a few families of the Texan men, and several Mexican families who were sympathetic to the Texan cause. Still others wandered in, looking dazed and confused, and were probably there only because they had no way to flee and no place else to go. Most of them gathered in tight little clusters.

Serena and I worked beside the men, and even Andrew helped. I noted with relief that Serena had said nothing further to me about leaving. Later, I would take Andrew to *Señora* Parras, and then return to the Alamo. Who could view all the industrious activity under way and doubt that such determined men could stop Santa Anna? There was no fear, no panic; only grim resolve. The walls might be weak, but with the big guns Cos had left behind, and with our obdurate riflemen atop the walls, Santa Anna could be held at bay until help arrived. No one doubted that it would arrive soon. Santa Anna was close, and the time for delay was over; Texans would rally to the cause of defending the Alamo, just as they had rallied at Gonzales. Fannin would come from Goliad with his four hundred men, and hundreds of others would rush from the east.

Papa was confident that help would soon be on the way. I had expected him to receive the shocking news of Santa Anna's approach that morning with alarm and despair. Instead, he had only nodded and said with assurance that people would no longer hesitate once they heard that Santa Anna had come.

Shortly before noon, I found Papa, and suggested that I should take Andrew to *Señora* Parras. "She plans to stay. She has never left her house, not even back in 1812 and 1813 when there was all that trouble, nor last fall when our men took Bexar. Andrew will be safe with her."

527

He shook his head. "No, my dear. I have two horses saddled. I want all three of you to leave. I insist on it."

I was totally unprepared for such an announcement, for he had never, until that moment, suggested that I should go.

"Andrew can ride pillion with Serena," he continued as I stared at him in mute surprise.

Before my protest found its way to my lips, Serena and Andrew came up to us. Serena put her hand on Papa's arm. "Thorne has told me where to find the horses, Cassie. We can go later. There's no need to leave yet. We can still help."

Relieved, I readily agreed. Serena was right, of course. How much easier to pretend to acquiescence until it was too late to leave! She intended to stay, I knew. And so did I. The last moment, I could take Andrew to *Señora* Parras.

"There's time," Papa agreed. "This could be just another idle rumor. The lookout in the church tower will ring the bell if he sees anything—"

The words had scarcely left his lips when the church bell began to clang. At first, the sound was hardly discernible amid the clamor and shouts all around us. First one person and then another stopped talking and working to listen more closely, and gradually, the din within the walls died to a whisper and then to a sudden hush.

It was as if the moment were suspended in time and all the heartbeats in the world had, briefly, halted. There was only one sound to break the silence: the unmistakable clang of the bell, its giant metal clapper proclaiming for all to hear, *"San-ta . . . An-na's . . . coming!"* Santa Anna, no longer just somewhere on his way, but on the very edge of Bexar, within sight of the church tower! For the first time, I felt a pang of fear, as real and as searing as if I had been touched by red-hot coals.

As suddenly as the noise within the enclosure had died down, it rose up again, this time on a frenzied note. But still, over it all—Was it really clanging louder, or was it just because we were all more aware of it?—there was the bell of the Church of San Fernando less than half a mile away, resolutely proclaiming its shattering news with terrifying persistence:

*"San-ta . . . An-na's . . . com-ing!"*

As the bell tolled, I saw several people slip out of the roofless mission church, their belongings slung over their shoulders or carried in bulging bundles. They ran quickly from the enclosure without any backward glances. Others started toward the gate, hesitated, returned. It was the moment of decision: go or stay, run or fight. But as some of those who had taken refuge inside the walls on that morning reconsidered and left, I noted with satisfaction that I had not seen one of the men who comprised the garrison hesitate in what they were doing. Watching them, it made me proud. How could Santa Anna hope to defeat men with such faith in what they were doing?

I looked again at Papa, saw his face in a grim expression. "If that means what I think it does, you must leave at once. I'll go check."

"I'll go with you," Serena said. "Come, Andrew, stay with me." They turned and followed Papa.

It was about one o'clock when Papa found me again. I had assumed he had changed his mind about making us leave, and I was busy trying to soothe the hysterical children of a terror-stricken Mexican mother. I held her squalling infant in my arms.

Papa came into the church, made his way to me. "You heard?"

I nodded. Everyone knew that the man who had rung the bell had made no mistake. Two of our men had ridden out to confirm what the lookout had seen: Mexican cavalry was approaching Bexar. Time was growing short. Foraging efforts had been doubled, and more cattle had been brought into the corral.

Papa took the baby from my arms, handed it back to its surprised mother. "Come." He took me by the hand, led me from the church. "You must leave."

When the doors of the church had closed behind us, I pulled my hand free and said resolutely, "I'm not going."

"You must."

"Papa, please don't send me away! I can help. Even if I am a woman, I feel I must stay to—well, to make up for Felipe. I won't go."

He looked at me for a long time before he answered. "I'm proud of the way you feel, Duchess. But you must go. For me. And for the others."

Startled by his reply, I said nothing, and he continued quickly, "Hear me out. I'm asking you to do this for me. Serena won't go unless you do, and she and Andrew must not stay.

"But it isn't just for them that I ask you to go. It will be hazardous, with Mexican scouts to dodge, perhaps, but you know your way." He pulled a sealed message from his pocket. "If you will take this to Gonzales, we needn't spare a man. And a woman might get through where a man would not. No one would take you for a messenger."

I wavered uncertainly, my eyes on the letter in Papa's hand. It was addressed to the Committee of Safety at Gonzales, in the firm bold hand I recognized as that of Buck Travis. Grudgingly, I had to admit that a woman would stand less chance of being intercepted, as Papa had said. Serena could carry the message, but I knew, as Papa did not, that she had no intention of going. I wanted desperately to stay, to help. But who, then, would carry the letter?

Papa must have guessed my thoughts. He held the letter toward me. "It's important. Very important."

"You just want me to leave—"

"Someone must. You'll be helping more this way than if you stay."

Resignedly, I recognized the truth of his words. I took the letter, doubled it over so that it would fit in the side pocket of my skirt. I would do as he asked. Did I really have any choice?

"The horses are outside the north postern, around the corner. We'll meet you there in a few minutes."

Just after I arrived at the designated spot, Papa appeared, carrying Andrew on his shoulders. Andrew was grinning broadly, obviously unaware of the seriousness of the situation. Serena followed close behind them.

"May I use your bowie knife?" I asked, and when Papa handed it to me, I slit my skirt front and back, and the petticoats beneath it.

Papa watched me. "Petticoats make good bandages."

I nodded, stripped them off, watched as Serena did the same.

As I kissed Papa good-bye, I remembered Serena's pessimistic prediction, and I was overwhelmed with the fear that I might never see him again. Casualties among the original Alamo defenders would be high. I knew that, for all my faith in the fact that help would arrive once it was known that the time for action had come.

"Oh, Papa!" I threw my arms around him, buried my face in his shoulder. "Take care." I rubbed my hand over his bristly cheek.

He hugged Andrew, set him on one of the horses. "I want you to take care of this. It will be yours some day." Ceremoniously, he took from around his neck the spyglass which had been his father's, and he hung it around Andrew's neck. My eyes clouded. There was something so ominous, so final about the gesture. He had always treasured that spy glass.

Papa and Serena embraced warmly, then he helped her mount. "Farewell, my love," he said, his voice choked with emotion. Then he turned toward me and his face became grim. "Tell Will that unless he comes here immediately, I no longer claim him as my son."

"You can't mean that! He—"

With a wave of his hand, he dismissed my protest. "Go! Quickly! And take care of yourselves, my loved ones!" His voice caught on the words, and I choked back the sob that rose in my throat.

531

Serena touched her heels to her horse. With a final wave to Papa, I followed.

We rode in silence, making an arc to reach the Gonzales road. At the point where the road climbed a hill to the east of Bexar, we heard from behind us the boom of a cannon. Simultaneously, we reined in, wheeled our horses around. Andrew raised the spy glass to his eye.

"Look, Mama!" he yelled excitedly a minute later, handing the spy glass to Serena. "There's something red by the church tower!"

Serena raised the glass to her eye, and a shudder passed through her body.

Alarmed, I asked, "What is it?"

"Flying from the church tower." She handed me the spy glass. "A red flag. Santa Anna is flying the flag of no quarter." Serena's last words faded to a whisper.

I focused the glass on the tower, saw the patch of red that Andrew's young eyes had spotted at once. How could such a small insignificant bit of red cloth mean so much? "He's only trying to frighten us. He's—"

"Santa Anna is not a man to issue idle threats. If he wins, he will allow no surrender. He will leave no survivors."

"He won't win! We won't let him!" I lowered the glass, realized that Serena had dismounted. I watched as she kissed Andrew and put the reins in his small hands. She turned to smile at me.

"He will keep up with you. He is a good horseman."

She was going back. Protests, one after another, rose in my throat, but I left them unspoken. "You never really intended to leave, did you?" I bit my lower lip to keep from dissolving into tears. For Serena's sake, and Andrew's, I knew I must not make their parting difficult.

"I told you I wouldn't leave your father."

"Can you get back inside?"

"It will be easy on foot. Thank you, my dear, for your understanding." She squeezed my hand, and then, her head held high, her back erect, she turned and walked purposefully down the road, back toward the beleaguered fort. Once, far down the road, she turned to wave.

I sat motionless, continued to stare down at Bexar. Santa Anna had come. Had Felipe come with him? I wondered. That very moment, was it possible that only a few miles separated us? I had heard rumors that Cos would return. If that were so, Felipe would probably be with him. Felipe . . .

I felt a tug at my sleeve. Andrew had moved his horse beside mine. "Let's go, Cassie. I promised Mama I'd get you to Gonzales as fast as I could."

I smiled at him. "We'll get there, Andrew. And you're right. We must hurry. We're carrying an urgent message."

A short time later, I discovered that we were carrying nothing at all. While we were stopped to water our horses, a rider overtook us from the west. He did not bother to dismount as he let his horse drink. I recognized him as one of the men from the Alamo. Was he deserting, I wondered? But there was something about his manner that made me doubt that. Could he be a messenger, then? And if he were, why would there be two of us on the same road? It was to avoid having to spare a man that I had agreed to go, to take Travis's message to Gonzales. Nor was it likely a messenger had been sent by Travis or the ailing Bowie to the settlements beyond; surely someone from Gonzales could carry any message onward. Suspicion began to nag me.

"Sir," I said, "I'm Captain Stewart's daughter, and I've just come from the Alamo. I know you've just come from there, too. Could you tell me if you're carrying word from there, and where you're heading? Please, I must know."

He had already tugged his horse's head up roughly and was poised, heels raised, to spur the mount to a fast start. He answered impatiently, "I carry word of Santa Anna's arrival. To Gonzales." He touched the spurs to his horse and rode away.

"But the message . . . " I protested weakly to his departing figure. "I'm carrying one, too . . . "

I protested in vain, watched the rider vanish down the road. My suspicions mounted as I pulled the sealed mes-

533

sage from my pocket. Did I dare open a message addressed to someone else? But I knew I must find out the truth. I broke the seal and unfolded the paper. I looked at it, then let it fall to the ground.

I carried no message to the Committee of Safety at Gonzales. Travis's handwriting on the outside was real enough. But inside, there was no message at all. Nothing. The paper was blank. Papa had tricked me into leaving.

Andrew's small moist palm slid into mine. "Let's go, Cassie. Mama said it's a long way to Gonzales."

# Chapter VII

## GONZALES—February 29, 1836

Six days later, Eliza tossed on the bed beside me and I put out my arm to comfort her. Desperately fearful myself, how could I bring comfort to her? I said nothing. What, after all, was there to say? Johnny had gone to Bexar.

"He said he had to go." Her sob-racked voice came through the darkness.

"I know," I answered softly. If only I could offer her confident reassurances, I thought, tell her that Johnny would probably be back soon! But how could I force such a lie from my lips when we both knew that the men who had gone to help the doomed garrison at Bexar had, in all likelihood, ridden off to their deaths?

I remembered all too clearly the scene earlier that day. It would always be etched deeply in my memory. How could I ever forget that brave little band that had set out to help the men in the Alamo? Thirty-two men had gone. Thirty-two, when hundreds, thousands were needed. The small band from Gonzales had responded when they found out the shocking news that the men in the Alamo didn't know: Fannin would not be going to their aid.

Thirty-two men. Added to those who were already in the Alamo, it was as nothing before Santa Anna's thousands. It was in answer to the most recent, most desperate cry for help that the Gonzales men had set out. Johnny Gorham was among them; Will was not.

I hadn't given Will Papa's message; it seemed too cruel a

thing to do. I had told Will of the desperate plight of the men, and though he seemed to consider going, he had not gone. Remembering Serena's gloomy prediction, I could not help but feel relieved when I realized he wasn't going to go.

"This war, this fighting and killing is wrong," he had insisted. "I won't be a part of it. The men will fight their way out when they see it's hopeless. And surely Santa Anna won't harm the women." Will continued to rationalize. The war—all war—was wrong; he would not be drawn into it.

Others, like Johnny Gorham, felt that the war was right but the place was wrong, and they, too, had kept hoping the men in the Alamo would fall back, give up the idea of defending what most Texans considered a useless and poorly fortified position.

But Johnny and the others had gone at last when they found out that the men inside the crumbling mission were to be left to their inevitable fate. No one else in all of Texas was going to help them.

Fannin had been the only real hope. He had four hundred men at Goliad, including many who had backed out of the Matamoros expedition. The ninety men of that expedition who had remained with Grant and Johnson seemed to be lost somewhere southwest of Gonzales, and the aid from the east that the Alamo garrison had hoped for never materialized. The petty quarrels and bickering had gnawed at the vitals of the provisional government, until there remained only a helpless, flailing mass, issuing in its death throes conflicting and contradictory military orders, which caused any attempt at an organized military effort to break down in chaos. Sam Houston, commander in chief of Texas, had left in disgust the last part of January, and would not return until March first, when a meeting was to be held to create a new government.

And so, in the end, there had been only Fannin on whom the besieged men at Bexar could base their hopes. On February twenty-eighth, five days after Santa Anna had begun his siege of the Alamo, Fannin started moving toward Bexar. Not far from Goliad, some of his wagons had bogged down in the mire. Discouraged, he had ordered his men to turn back.

When the shocking news of Fannin's feeble feint and rapid retreat reached Gonzales, the inhabitants were horrified. No one doubted the seriousness of the difficulty he had encountered. But surely, most people insisted, he could have made it. And why had he waited so long? They did not think Fannin had the right to reason about the heavy odds, the danger of exposing his men in the open to a far superior army. He had been morally obligated to go to the aid of the distressed force, and he had failed them.

"Fannin is a fool!" Johnny Gorham had said angrily. "We can't leave the men there to die. We just can't!"

Others agreed. Time after time, they had seen the messengers returning from the east with the disheartening news that they had not been able to prod a nonexistent government to send a nonexistent relief column to the aid of the Alamo.

"Wait until we form a new government in March," the politicians advised. "Wait until after we get a real army organized," many Texans stalled. And some of them were even going on with their spring plowing and planting. But Santa Anna wasn't waiting, and the messengers who had been filled with renewed hope on each outward journey were bitter and depressed as they passed through Gonzales on their way back.

The messengers had carried a succession of increasingly desperate pleas. The Mexicans had closed in steadily, binding our men tighter and tighter inside the old mission. But there was one exit they had not found. It led to a ditch, where a swift rider could be quickly out and away. It was through this exit that the messengers left—and returned, always with the same somber, sobering news: no help.

I wondered how the men inside felt after their confident hopes of popular support were dashed again and again. Was Serena the only one who had guessed what would

537

probably happen? And Papa, who had never doubted that help would come—how would he feel, when he knew the only help that was coming was a handful of men from Gonzales?

Johnny was among them, and the tears Eliza had bravely held back as she waved good-bye to him were filling her pillow. Johnny was gone. There was nothing to do but wait.

The waiting was interminable. On March seventh, fifty more men assembled in Gonzales to set out for Bexar. Most of them were strangers from the east, but the residents gave him supplies, wished them Godspeed, and smiled to mask their growing fear and apprehension. Since word had arrived that the Gonzales men had reached the Alamo, there had been only silence. Eliza and I watched the second group ride out of town. Eliza had not been well, but she insisted on going out to see them off. "They're going to help my Johnny," she explained.

Uncle Todd, irked by a bad case of the grippe that had kept him from accompanying the Gonzales volunteers a week earlier, tried to go with the new group, but he was still too weak. Cursing, and with tears rolling down his cheeks, he had stumbled back to his cabin when he found he lacked the strength to mount his horse.

Will came by Eliza's house less than an hour after the men had left. "I'm going to catch up with them," he said, his mouth drawn into a tight, grim line. "I still don't approve, but Papa and Serena . . . I kept hoping . . . I don't know what I hoped, but I have to go." He spoke tensely, but there was none of the surliness or touchiness that had characterized his every word and action since my return. He had made up his mind, and seemed to find a relief of sorts in his decision.

I wanted to scream my protests: *No, not you, too!* It was enough that Papa was there, and Serena, and Eliza's Johnny. But Will? He was too compassionate for war. In his place, I would have gone to Bexar long ago. But Will and I did not think the same. Could he, who could not bear

538

to shoot so much as a small rabbit, take cool aim and snuff out a human life?

He gave me no chance to protest, saying quickly, "I'll have to ride fast to catch them."

"Are you sure?"

He nodded, and I hugged him and cried unashamedly. "Oh, Will, take care!"

Tears blurred my vision as I watched him ride out of sight, and I silently cursed Santa Anna. Even as I prayed fervently for a miracle that would save those in the Alamo, I also prayed that Will would be too late to share their fate if the miracle had not happened. I had seen the blood-red flag Santa Anna had flown so defiantly from the Church of San Fernando. And Serena's words about him returned to me again and again, as clearly each time as though she were beside me repeating them: *"If he wins, he will allow no surrender. He will leave no survivors."*

In Gonzales, the waiting grew more tense as no word arrived from the Alamo. The messengers no longer rode through town. The air in every house, on the very streets of the town, was heavy with the dread everyone feared to voice. And the dread fed itself on the ominous silence from the west.

From the southwest, however, news did arrive. Refugees fleeing the path of another arm of the Mexican army under General Urrea brought reports that all that remained of the Matamoros expedition had been annihilated around San Patricio—all except a fortunate few who had managed to escape and tell of it. Thus had ended the foolish attempt to carry the war south of the Río Bravo.

This news sat heavily upon our hearts as we continued to wait. Nothing had been heard from the group Will had followed, and no one else left Gonzales for the west. Colonel Neill, the man who had been in charge at Bexar when I arrived, was in Gonzales, trying to organize the men who were drifting into town from the east. Many of the volunteers came with little or no ammunition, and some even came without arms. They brought no rations, and it taxed the women of the town to feed them, but no one complained. We listened in disgust to the news from the east that many ablebodied men were holding back, waiting in Washington-on-the-Brazos until the meeting which had convened March first was over. The official delegates told the useless onlookers they were desperately needed in the west.

News of the convention's Declaration of Independence for Texas was issued on March second, and came as no surprise. Before, we had classed ourselves as a state in revolt against a tyrannical government. But since word of Santa Anna's attack on the Alamo had spread, the voices of the moderates could no longer be heard over the clamor for independence. Who could live under such a tyrannical government, which denied us fair representation? After all, wasn't it only a few generations ago that most of our ancestors had fought England for denying us the same rights? And there was the matter of religious freedom, too. Hadn't the original Americans come across the ocean for the right to worship as they chose, a right denied us in theory if not in fact?

The delegates at Washington-on-the-Brazos, spurred on by their own righteous indignation, formed a government for the newly declared independent Republic of Texas. Slowly, the wheels of this new government began to turn, to fill the void left by the collapse of the provisional state government. Houston, returned from his parley with the Indians in the east, was elected commander in chief of all the forces, and assumed command. His orders, dated March ninth from Burnham's Crossing on the Colorado, were simple and direct: Fannin and Neill would rendezvous and go to the aid of the Alamo. But his orders had come too late.

Slowly, the newly formed Republic of Texas was organizing resistance, was trying to recruit an army, both volunteers and regulars. To those of us in Gonzales, it was agonizingly slow. Houston arrived on the afternoon of March eleventh. A day earlier, his arrival would have inspired hope. But on that same day, two Mexicans arrived from the west, bringing the message we had all dreaded to hear:

The Alamo had fallen on the sixth. All its defenders were dead.

I had tried to prepare myself for just such shocking news, but there had always remained the faint hope that somehow, at the last minute, the men would escape. But they hadn't. Papa was dead. And Johnny. And Bowie. And Crockett. And Serena, too. I did not doubt that she had somehow managed to tie her fate to Papa's. All that week, while we waited, it had been over.

On the sixth, the Alamo had fallen. But Will had not left Gonzales till the seventh. I tried to find solace in the thought that he could not have arrived in time to be trapped with the others. I only hoped he had not collided with Santa Anna's massive army.

Houston claimed he didn't believe the two Mexicans, held them prisoner and branded them as spies until he could check the reliability of their news. A few people clutched desperately at the frail hope offered by his apparent doubt, refusing to believe their men were dead, not wanting to believe it. But I didn't doubt the authenticity of the news and knew that Houston was merely trying to buy more time until a force could gather, attempting to prevent a panic that might drive men away and keep others from coming.

But how could I doubt the news, when I had seen the weak walls and inadequate fortifications of the Alamo, when I knew there had been less than two hundred men to defend the large vulnerable area against Santa Anna's thousands? The wonder was that so few had held for so long, had withstood the battering of Santa Anna's overwhelming forces for twelve days. Perhaps it had been a futile show of bravado, after all, but there had been a glory in it, and even as I cried for Papa, and the others, there was pride mingled with my grief. And Andrew, who could not comprehend fully the finality of earthly parting, was proud, too.

Eliza's grief tore at my heart. For her, there was not even the consolation that Johnny had sacrificed his life for an ideal in which he believed. Papa and the original men had set themselves the task of defiantly holding the enemy's own fortress against a powerful onslaught. But Johnny had decried the foolishness of such a stand. Only compassion for his fellow man had led him to Bexar. And that compassion had cost him his life, widowed Eliza, and orphaned their unborn child.

Uncle Todd's grief was almost as heartrending as Eliza's. "Thorne was like my son." Huge tears coursed down his cheeks. "Why couldn't these frail legs have carried me there to help him? Why?"

"It wouldn't have mattered," I said, trying to find words to console him through my own sorrow. "One more against Santa Anna's thousands—"

He bowed his head, said softly, "It would have mattered. To me." He sighed heavily. "I only pray Serena is safe."

I didn't tell him I felt certain she was not.

There was so little time to mourn the dead, for we had to look to our own fates. Soon, Santa Anna would turn toward the other Texas settlements. And Gonzales stood directly in his path.

I suggested to Eliza that we should leave immediately, but she shook her head stubbornly. "You take Andrew and your uncle and go. I won't go until I'm absolutely sure about—about Bexar."

Poor Eliza, clinging with such desperation to that last hope that perhaps the two Mexicans had lied, after all! "I'll stay, too," I said, for I was anxious about Will. I wanted to wait for him, in case he came, even as I realized it was foolish to delay. The rivers were swelling under the constant rains and travel was becoming more difficult each day. Still, we waited two more days.

On the thirteenth, two of Houston's scouts returned. They had had no need to go all that distance, for they encountered on the prairie a small party of travelers who confirmed our worst fears. Mrs. Dickinson, wife of one of the

542

Alamo defenders, carried her infant daughter, and was accompanied by two Negroes, one the servant of a Mexican officer, and the other Travis's servant. One of the two scouts rode ahead into Gonzales with the news told by the weary survivors. In essence, it was the same thing the Mexican men had said. But he brought additional news: the survivors said that Santa Anna's army was again on the march, and had encamped on the Cibolo, well on our side of Bexar, two nights before!

By nine o'clock that night, Gonzales was in a frenzy of activity. Belongings were hastily thrown into carts and wagons as people prepared to run before Santa Anna. I ran to Uncle Todd's, remembered that a friend who had left Gonzales had told him he could have his oxen and cart. I opened the door of the cabin without knocking, and almost collided headlong with Will.

"Oh, Will, dear, I'm so glad you're safe!" I threw my arms around him, hugged him. When I looked up at his face, I was shocked by the misery and grief that distorted his features. "Oh, Will—" I put my hand gently on his cheek.

He pushed my hand aside roughly, broke away from me. "Don't call me, 'Will, dear!' Tell me what you really think of me. That I'm a coward! That I waited too long! That I should have gone when I first heard! They needed me—"

"It wouldn't have mattered." It was the same thing I had said to Uncle Todd. "Don't you see, it wouldn't have made any difference? You would have thrown your life away."

He didn't seem to be listening to me. He paced back and forth, and started to talk. Whatever was eating at him—the tortuous self-incrimination, the regret, the shame, the feeling that he had failed to do what he should have done without hesitation—must be heard. "I rode as fast as I could, but it wasn't fast enough. I should have gone sooner."

"You couldn't have changed anything by being there. We must leave now—"

"I'm not going with you, Cassie. I talked with the woman and Travis's slave as they were coming in to town,

543

and they told me—oh, God!" His hands sped to his face as though to block out an unbearable sight. Slowly, he lowered his hands, continued brokenly, "They—they bayoneted them. The few men who were left ran inside the buildings. But they followed them. They chased them down and bayoneted them. The wounded, too. They hacked at them. Again and again, long after they were—after there was no need. They wouldn't stop!"

"Dear God!" I sobbed. Will's words painted a macabre picture, every bit as vivid as one he might have painted with a brush, and I couldn't shake off the horror of what he was saying. I could see the men as he spoke. Papa . . . the drawling sergeant . . . the efficient young corporal . . . Crockett . . . Bowie . . . Travis. All dead, and then brutally denied even the dignity of death.

"They dragged some of the last ones out. Mrs. Dickinson said she could hear their screams—"

"Will, stop! Please!"

But he wouldn't stop. "A twelve-year-old boy. They dragged him out of the church. He hadn't done a thing. They pulled him away from his mother and killed him!"

"I don't want to hear—" I put my hands over my ears, but I couldn't shut out Will's words.

"They wouldn't stop! They wouldn't stop bayoneting them!"

I shook my head violently from side to side, trying to dispel the scenes I could envision with such horrible clarity. How could the Mexican troops have gone so berserk, have turned to such wanton senseless horror?

"Almonte's servant said Santa Anna encouraged them. He said that he'd whipped them into a frenzy of hate!" Will sank to the hearth as though his legs had suddenly given way beneath him, and he put his head in his hands and sobbed. "I'm going to kill every one of those filthy murdering bastards!" he vowed through the racking sobs that shook his shoulders convulsively. "I'm going with Houston, and I'm going to kill them!"

My own legs felt weak, too, and I sank to a chair. How

had it happened, how had our world so changed that a young man too gentle to stand the thought of harming a bird had come to lust for blood? I covered my eyes and sobbed, partly for Papa and Serena and Eliza's Johnny, who, I could only hope, had been spared those final hideous moments of terror and horror, and partly for Will, whose gentle nature had collided headlong with the stark brutality of war.

And Felipe. What of him, I wondered? Never would he have let himself be a part of such a senseless horror, I was sure. And yet, why had he insisted on staying in the army that permitted and encouraged such pointless butchery?

And that army was coming toward us, and could at that very moment be getting close. I wiped my eyes. "Uncle Todd, are Josiah's oxen and his cart still in his barn?"

He rubbed his sleeve across his eyes, nodded. "I'll get it." He threw back the quilt that covered him, and set his feet upon the floor. His voice was suddenly crisp with authority. "I don't want to hear any scolding about me being sick. I'll rest in the cart. Right now, there's work to be done, and I'm going to help do it." He stood up, staggered briefly, caught himself. "I'll bring the cart around to the Gorhams' as soon as I can. Take that food on the shelf there. And these quilts, the two lightest ones."

I obeyed, and at the door, I hesitated. "Will, won't you come with us?"

Will looked up, his face slack, all emotion drained from it. "I'll help Uncle Todd. Then I'm going with Houston."

"He's going the same way we are. He's heading east, too."

"He's running away? He's not going to fight?"

"With three hundred men?"

"Is that all he has?"

"Nobody knows. Certainly not more than four hundred, at best."

"Then he won't fight now."

I was shocked anew to hear the disappointment in Will's voice, and my eyes clouded again at the heart-breaking realization that, in a few short days, Will had so changed, become so embittered that he had become anxious to kill. I nodded, not trusting my voice to speak. Quickly, I turned away, opened the door, and went out onto the street.

"Mrs. Dickinson's here!" someone shouted. "In the army encampment."

I followed the press of people, made my way to the tight little knot of anxious relatives who surrounded the exhausted woman. She sat with her sleeping baby on her lap, talking only when necessary. Mostly, she just answered each question with a weary shake of her head. No survivors. No hope.

I edged closer, tugged on her sleeve. "Please, Mrs. Dickinson."

The young woman looked up, and I thought I saw a flicker of recognition cross her face. "Thorne Stewart? And his wife, Serena? And Johnny Gorham? What of them?"

Eyes that had seen more than they cared to remember looked at me blankly.

"Please remember," I begged.

"The men . . . dead. Serena? A few days before . . . cut her hair . . . dressed like a man. I didn't see . . . after."

Of one of the Negroes, the one who had been servant to the Mexican Colonel Almonte, I asked a different question, the question that had burned with a white-hot anguish in my mind from the moment I had seen Santa Anna's merciless signal flag in the church tower. Were Cos and the men who had fled with him back in Bexar? Had they taken part in such a hideous horrifying spectacle?

The answer was, "Yes."

Then unless he had deserted, as I had begged him to do so often, Felipe was back, closer to me. The physical miles between us had been reduced to something less than seventy. But had we ever been really farther apart? It might as well have been seven hundred miles, or seven thousand that separated us, for between us from that day forward

546

would lie the mutilated bodies of those we loved who had died in the Alamo.

I knew that Felipe could never have taken part in the brutality Will had recounted. And yet, by being identified with the men who had done such a vicious thing, could he ever separate himself from it? Wouldn't he have to take upon himself a share of the responsibility—and the blame?

Crying for the futility of the bravery that had sustained so few to hold off so many for so long, I made my way through the milling crowd, trying to remember through the chaos of my thoughts what must be done before we left.

I passed two soldiers who were prodding a yoke of oxen to pull a heavy cannon down the street. They were headed west, toward the river—toward Santa Anna. Would our pitiful little bunch of volunteers stand against him, after all?

"Where are you going? Where are you taking the cannon?" I shouted as I passed them.

"To the river!" a voice shouted in return. "We can't take it, but Santa Anna won't have it, either!"

The town was in an uproar. The arrival of the little group of refugees, the horror and finality of their words that ended all hope, their startling assurance that Santa Anna had marched twenty-four miles from Bexar the first day, two days earlier, had changed confusion to near-panic.

Deeply immersed in my thoughts, I nearly bumped into Will in the darkness.

"I've been looking for you, Cassie. I'm leaving. I'm not going with Houston."

"Then where—?"

"Someone must take a message to Fannin. I'll take it, and stay with him till he joins Houston."

"Goliad!" I gasped. "But surely Santa Anna will send a force there next. It might be under attack already!"

Will's words were brittle. "So much the better. I want to go toward the fighting, not away from it. The sooner I get my hands on some Mexicans, the better." Then his voice softened. "Don't worry. I'll get through. I don't propose to make any mistakes to keep me from having a chance at the

Mexicans. For Papa, and Johnny. And for Serena, too. You don't think she got out, do you?"

I shook my head. The time to shield Will from brutality was past. "She wanted to stay with Papa, and she did. Mrs. Dickinson told me."

"Take care of Uncle Todd." He leaned down and kissed my cheek.

"And you take care."

He turned and was lost in the darkness. Fear knotted my insides into one hard mass. Will was going to place himself under Fannin's command, and Johnny Gorham had often spoken of the man's stupidity. But still, others considered the West Point man to be the best officer material available to us.

I said a short fervent prayer that he was not the fool Johnny had thought him to be.

It was a little before midnight when we left Gonzales. Eliza took one last look around her cabin before she blew out the candle flame and closed the door. "I'll never be back. There's no reason now." Her eyes were dry, I knew, only because she could find no more tears to shed. She turned to climb into the cart.

Andrew sat between Uncle Todd and me on the small hard seat at the front. Eliza rode in back, where there was at least some softness to absorb the shock of the bouncing cart. The cart's two wheels were made of thick tree cross sections, strong and sturdy if not perfectly round. Uncle Todd had wisely thought to fill the back of the cart with hay and spread blankets and quilts over it.

"Our bed will get harder as we go," he commented wryly. There would be few tender green spring grasses for the animals to munch. The shoots had just begun to push through the dampened ground, but they were still too short to be of much use. There was consolation in the knowledge that Santa Anna would have to cope with the same problem, and perhaps he would be less equipped to cope than we.

548

We were well past the edge of town when Andrew cried, "Look! It's on fire!"

Uncle Todd's head whirled around and I heard Eliza gasp. I turned to see what had only a few short hours before been the prosperous little town of Gonzales, home to over nine hundred people, reduced to a brilliant orange glow in the night sky.

Only Uncle Todd seemed not to be shocked. He turned his attention back to the road ahead. "I heard some of the men talking. Whatever we leave behind, Santa Anna might put to use. That's why Houston ordered those two cannons dumped into the Guadalupe."

"But couldn't he have used them?" Eliza's voice was puzzled.

"He had no way to haul them. There were only two yokes of oxen left by the time all the townspeople got through." Uncle Todd added grimly, "What we can't take with us, we'll not leave for that murderous Santa Anna!"

*What we can't take with us, we'll not leave for Santa Anna.* It became our battle cry, and if the colonists along the way had not been able to harden their hearts and set fire to the homes they had come to love, to the barns they had built and the hay they had stored, then the men who comprised the newly formed Texan army, coming along behind us, destroyed these things for them. Santa Anna would find no food or shelter for his men, no hay or grain for his animals as he gave chase.

When I had first seen the bony oxen and rickety two-wheeled cart Uncle Todd had brought to Eliza's door, I could not hide my dismay. Santa Anna could be almost on our heels, and I wondered how we could hope to escape him in such a decrepit conveyance pulled by such sorry beasts. But I soon discovered that the milling mass of humanity and beasts that clogged our road moved no faster than we did, so our cart didn't lag. We rode all night without stopping, our way lighted from time to time with the orange glow of the flames that devoured cabins and barns along the road.

549

Gradually, the light of another day seeped through the overcast sky to become a dreary morning. I pulled the cart off the road to let the oxen rest at the crest of a small hill. We had been among the last to leave Gonzales, and yet as I turned to look at the road behind us, it was filled as far as I could see. Somewhere back there, out of sight, was the straggling Texan army—all, God help us, that stood between us and Santa Anna's vengeful troops.

Andrew, asleep on the seat beside me with his head on my lap, was the first to waken, and he sat up wordlessly and slipped his hand into mine. I smiled down at him, thinking how uncomplaining he had been through all the events of the last two months. "Let's stretch our legs a bit, shall we?" I suggested. We jumped down, stood together beside the cart, watching the unending stream of those who passed by. Some of the faces were pinched with exhaustion, others showed discouragement, still others registered shock and disbelief at what was happening. There were haggard, determined women shepherding flocks of sleepy-eyed, tear-stained children. There were men, too, young and old, and some of the younger ones wore belligerent expressions, as though daring anyone to question why they were not back with Houston and his pathetically small army. Some of the people walked, dragging their feet slowly and laboriously, and others were mounted on any and all sorts of animals they had been able to find: mules, donkeys, saddle horses, plow horses—anything. Still others were in carts and wagons of all sizes and shapes. Ours was not by any means the worst of those I saw.

"Where have they all come from?"

I hadn't realized Eliza had wakened until she spoke as she came to stand beside us.

I shook my head. "I thought we were about the last to leave." It was a depressing sight. The people we watched had conquered a wilderness, wrested it from the savages who had ruled it for centuries with spine-chilling terror. How was it possible that those same people had been re-duced to a nameless mass, become part of a seemingly endless stream of humanity fleeing in near-panic from one man's wrath: General Antonio Lopez de Santa Anna?

As we watched, I saw something I hadn't noticed before: there was a small countercurrent, scarcely perceptible at first, of men going the other way. Some were mounted, but most were on foot.

Eliza must have seen it at the same moment. "Look! Some men are going the other way!"

"To join Houston," I added, but even as the thought lifted my spirits, it also saddened me. *They're too late*, I thought. *They should have come sooner. Why did they wait so long?*

Suddenly, among the grim and weary men moving westward, counter to the refugee train, I saw a face I recognized.

"Jeremy!" I waved and ran toward him.

He smiled as he saw me, picked his way through the throng and dismounted. He encased the hand I extended in both of his.

"I'm so glad to see you!" I said sincerely.

"I couldn't stay away. I came as quick as I could after I got the news up north. Cassie, what about your father? Pa said he thought he was in the Alamo."

I nodded, and when he said he was sorry, I warned quickly, "Eliza's husband was there, too," before she approached with Andrew.

"And Felipe? Is he still in the Mexican army?"

"I don't know. I haven't seen him since the end of October. Uncle Todd saw him in early December, in Bexar."

"He was fighting for Mexico then?"

I nodded. "He's a major. He—he changed when he was in Mexico City."

Eliza came up to greet Jeremy and invited him to share our cold breakfast.

"I haven't eaten since yesterday morning," he said. "I'll be happy to join you."

Uncle Todd had climbed into the back of the cart shortly after we left Gonzales, and he was still sleeping. When I asked him if he wanted any breakfast, he had hardly roused to say he had no appetite. Nor did I, and I poured myself a cold mug of coffee, wishing it was fresh and warm.

"How are your folks?" I asked as I dropped to the ground beside Jeremy. It was damp and cold, but no more so than our quilts and our clothing.

He nodded. "They're well enough. Pa wasn't very glad to see I'd come, especially not after I told him I was going to join Houston."

Eliza's eyes opened wide. "Is he a Santanista then?"

"Not really. He isn't anything, doesn't want to fight anybody—not Santa Anna or the Republic of Texas, either. He wouldn't do anything to actually hurt our cause, I don't think, but he wouldn't raise a finger to help us, either. He just wants to stay out of any conflict and keep neutral. He's furious with me for going with Houston, says it might reflect on him."

"Too many Texans must think as he does," I commented. "If they didn't, they'd be here."

"I think a lot of them feel it's hopeless. Most of the men who are coming are from the southern states. People feel pretty strongly back there that Texas ought to belong to the United States, that it never should have been ceded to Mexico in return for the Floridas, which everybody says is just a worthless swampland."

"We had some New Orleans Grays at the Alamo. Even there, we had so few Texans. It seems that most of our men who were yelling for war have disappeared."

"Even a lot of those who might have come now will probably run when they hear those men we met about five hours back. They told us about the Alamo, said that Santa Anna was close behind with ten thousand men, and that he'd kill every man he found with a gun—"

"The deserters!" Eliza said, then explained to Jeremy, "About twenty men left after Mrs. Dickinson came into Gonzales last night and told about—about everything."

"Santa Anna wanted her to tell all of us how strong he

552

was," I added. "He made her watch while he paraded his men."

"I guess he knew some would panic and run when they heard," Jeremy said. "Part of the group I was traveling with did. They just turned tail and disappeared." He frowned. "Then it's all true—what they said?"

I nodded. "The Alamo fell on the sixth. I was there, with them, until the day Santa Anna came. Papa tricked me into leaving with Andrew. Serena left, too, but she went back."

After breakfast we continued on our way. By that time, the deserters had spread pandemonium in our path, so the road became even more choked with people, and the ruts became deeper still, making the road yet more difficult to travel. It was pocked with countless depressions from hoofs and feet, and ridged with the ruts formed by the passage of countless wheels. In many muddy places, these had half-hardened into hazardous pits and holes, making oxen and horses stumble, and causing wheels and axles to snap as though they were so many brittle twigs. And then the rain started, falling almost without letup, ruts turned to bogs and puddles to swamps, and travel slowed to a painful crawl. Long cherished possessions were no longer counted in terms of their value, but of their weight. As that first day wore on, the road became edged with more and more debris, for people desperately lightened bogged wagons in an effort to move them out of the muck that held them fast. Men, women, and children pushed and tugged, and whips cracked uselessly on the backs of overburdened animals. Teams were hitched double first to one wagon and then to another as people found they couldn't manage alone. Wagons moved out of one morass and into the next, through one swollen stream after another, so that we barely seemed to make any progress at all.

Eliza was not well, but she refused to submit to what she referred to as coddling. "You can't do everything yourself. I'm only pregnant, not sick," she said emphatically, and she insisted on taking her turn pulling and tugging at the oxen and sitting on the front seat of the jarring cart. When the wind blew her skirts to reveal her puffy ankles and her swollen feet, which she had stuffed into a pair of oversized moccasins found by the wayside, my concern for her grew. But I was even more concerned for Uncle Todd. He had hardly roused all day long, and that, to me, was alarming. He had taken no food all day, and only a few swallows of water.

"A day of real rest might restore him. And it would be good for Eliza, too," I said to Jeremy as he and I sat together near the cart that night. The others had gone to sleep.

"You could use some rest, too."

I shrugged. "I'm healthy enough. In three more days, we should reach the Colorado. Then in another day or two, we should be home." Home! How good that sounded! A roof to keep out the rain, a warm hearth, fresh drinking water that hadn't been muddied from the grinding of hundreds of hoofs and feet and wheels that had passed through it ahead of us. And dry clothes! The rain had soaked us all through. I inched closer to the small fire Jeremy had built with a few precious pieces of dry wood he had found. I stared into the flames, remembering the campfires Felipe and I had shared as we had traveled the other direction on the same road two years earlier. Two years ago. A lifetime ago. We had been so happy then, so confident that the future would be wonderful because we were together, would always be together. How much things had changed since then! Where was Felipe at that moment, I wondered? My longing for him was so intense it was almost too much to bear.

Jeremy's voice cut into my thoughts. "If you need help with Eliza, Ma will be there, remember. Her pa used to take her with him back in Tennessee, and she helped him birth lots of babies."

I nodded. "Eliza wants to go to her mother in San Felipe. But maybe your mother will know something to do for Uncle Todd." Once we had put the Colorado River behind us, it would not be much farther. On the other side, we would be safe. Houston was to stop at the Colorado, and had ordered Fannin to meet him there. Together, they would try to stop Santa Anna. If they could. . . . If anybody could . . .

I shuddered. "Jeremy, Houston will face Santa Anna this side of the Colorado, won't he?"

"Everybody thinks so. We're getting more men every day, and when we join Fannin's four hundred, we'll be about as strong as we'll ever be. We've got to make a stand somewhere. We can't keep running! But there's nothing we can do till we get you people safely on the other side of the Colorado."

*The other side of the Colorado.* It sounded to me like the Promised Land. I closed my eyes, tried to pretend we were there, out of the damp, cold world through which we had been traveling. It was hard to realize that we had left Gonzales less than twenty-four hours earlier. It seemed so much longer than that. *The other side of the Colorado.* I even felt certain that once we crossed the Colorado, the weather would change miraculously, and the sun would shine, warming us, drying our clothes, drying the roads . . .

My eyes flew open as Jeremy's lips brushed my cheek.

"I'm sorry, Cassie," he said as he drew away from me. "You just looked so pretty in the firelight, and so—well, sort of lost. What are you going to do when all this is over? You know how I feel about you—"

Shocked at his words, I reminded him, "I'm married to Felipe."

"But could you ever go back to him, after all this? If he was with Santa Anna, if he was part of the butchery at the Alamo—?"

"He couldn't have been! Not Felipe! Not ever!" My words were at once a protest and a fervent prayer.

"But if he was . . ."

"It's not possible," I said with a shudder, then quickly changed the subject. "Jeremy, I'm getting concerned about Uncle Todd. He just lies there with his eyes closed most of the time, and he hasn't eaten a thing all day. He's taken only a few sips of water. Some nourishing broth might help . . ."

"I'll see if I can find some." He stood up, gave me his hand. "I suppose we had both better get some rest."

Jeremy did find some broth, and brought it to us the next morning. But though Uncle Todd drank it, it failed to put new energy into his ailing body. He lay on the makeshift bed in the back of the cart all the time, his legs cramped and doubled over because there wasn't room for him to stretch out. Even talking seemed too much effort for him. I doled out the hay sparingly to the oxen, knowing that every mouthful they ate made Uncle Todd's bed that much harder. But how could he get better when the quilts that covered him were sodden, when he was tossed from side to side for hours on end? How could he gather the strength he needed to fight off his illness under such conditions?

The Texan army stopped at the Navidad for a day, and we stopped with them, hoping that perhaps one day free of the rigors of traveling might help restore Uncle Todd's strength. When we resumed our travels, we followed behind the main army, as did some other refugees. Behind us, to keep anyone from straggling or being left behind, a rear guard of sorts followed.

The road grew even worse, until scarcely a patch of it wasn't rutted or pocked with deep axle-splitting holes. The crude wheels of our cart groaned with each revolution, but they were strong, and they held in places where spoked wheels might have snapped in two. We passed countless carts and wagons pulled off the road and abandoned for want of the time or materials to make repairs. A hundred times a day, I prayed that our wheels would not break, that a sudden jolt would not snap our axle, that Uncle Todd would show some signs of improving, and that Eliza would wait till a more convenient time to have her baby. At first I tried to maintain a false cheerfulness, but I soon gave up, and found vent for my frustration in being snappish. Andrew, the only one whose spirit hadn't been dampened along with every stitch of clothing and every quilt and blanket we possessed, looked at me reproachfully once when I yelled at him senselessly, and I promised myself I would make an effort to be more patient with him. Eliza snapped right back at me when I was churlish, for she, too, seemed to find an outlet in being short-tempered.

*Across the Colorado. . . . The other side of the Colorado. . . .* It rose like a triumphant chant among us, as though it was a panacea, a solution to all our problems. *The other side of the Colorado. . . .* Eliza and I spoke of it in awed voices, and it echoed constantly in my brain. Across the Colorado was San Felipe and Patience Parker's cool confidence and bustling efficiency. Across the Colorado, Eliza could have her baby and Uncle Todd could rest and get well amid dry blankets and a warming fire.

The day of rest at the Navidad had seemed to do Uncle Todd no good at all. We reached the Colorado on the evening of the seventeenth, four days after we had left Gonzales, and he remained lethargic, was unable to stir from the back of the cart. How could he possibly mend when I had no cover to keep the rain from him, no tent to shelter him from the wind? Without the help of the men from Houston's army, who tugged and pulled every time the cart threatened to tip over and spill its human cargo, or the oxen began to founder, we would not have reached the Colorado so soon.

But we did reach it, and then, miraculously we were on the other side. We had waved good-bye to Jeremy and the others, and waved, too, to the volunteers crossing in the other direction to join Houston, to help him stop Santa Anna.

From what Jeremy had told us, things were looking much better for our cause. He said Houston didn't believe Santa Anna had as many men as Mrs. Dickinson thought, for the wily general had obviously tried to impress and awe her with a frightening show of strength, knowing she would tell others, and hoping to panic those who would fight him. But in spite of the word that had spread in front of us,

557

volunteers continued to come from the east. And Fannin, with over four hundred men in all, would surely join our men soon. The Mexicans would never cross the Colorado. The fast-forming army of the Republic of Texas would most certainly stop them.

Across the river, I turned and smiled at Eliza, ruffled Andrew's hair. We had crossed the Colorado, and a new day had dawned. With a little luck, we would be safely in San Felipe by nightfall of the next day. Not even when some stock blocked our way did I lose my temper. After all, it was probably stock our men had driven to the east side of the Colorado so Santa Anna would not find it to feed his troops. A few minutes' delay while Andrew jumped down and shooed some cows off the road didn't matter any more. Eliza, too, seemed lighter-hearted, smiling for the first time in weeks.

But our relief soon turned to alarm, for by late afternoon of that day, we realized how sick Uncle Todd had become. He didn't waken when we tried to rouse him, and his breathing was heavy and labored, his head fiery.

It was just before nightfall when I saw a woman emerge from a cabin. It was the first sign of human life we had seen all day, and I stopped the cart and ran toward her.

"Please!" I called. "Can you help us? My uncle is very sick. I wonder if you would be so kind as to let us take him inside—"

The woman's eyes were sympathetic but wary. "Why don't you take him to Doc Hamlin's place? I don't know if he's there, but maybe he could help you. It's not but half a mile or so off the road to your right at the next crossroad." She did not have to add that she did not want to chance bringing sickness into her own cabin, so there was little choice.

We found the doctor's house, but he had gone to join Houston.

"Let's bring your uncle inside," the doctor's wife said. "We'll do the best we can."

The best we could do was not enough. Uncle Todd clung

tenaciously to the thin thread of life for another week before he died. We buried him in a grove behind the house in a grave the doctor's wife and I had dug. The next morning we prepared to move on.

As Eliza climbed into the cart, the woman eyed her appraisingly. "Are you sure you want to go, my dear? Your time is near. I've helped bring many babies—"

Eliza shook her head firmly. "Thank you. You've been so kind. But I want to go home to my mother."

Before we had traveled much farther, we learned that Patience was no longer in San Felipe. We met one of the Parkers' neighbors heading toward Houston's army, and he told us that Lem and Patience had gone. "Mr. Rusk asked Lem to help out in the new government. He's our secretary of war, you know. They left last week for Harrisburg."

"Harrisburg!" Eliza and I said in unison. That was another fifty miles.

"The government's moved there from Washington-on-the-Brazos. There isn't hardly anyone left this side of the Brazos. Most folks are heading straight for the Sabine. Not many people think we have a chance of stopping Santa Anna."

*Across the Colorado. . . . The other side of the Colorado. . . .* It had been the one ray of hope in a sunless sky, the one thought that had sustained us, made us make one more effort, climb back onto the hard bone-jarring cart once more, travel one more mile. It had promised to be the answer to all our problems.

But we had left the Colorado far behind us, and we were not many miles from the Brazos. Uncle Todd was dead, and Patience was still over fifty miles away. Crossing the Colorado had solved nothing after all.

And then, even before we passed Papa's house, Eliza's labor started, and there was no choice but to keep going and try to reach the Butlers'. As we rode by Papa's house, Andrew pleaded with me to stop and let him go inside.

"I'm sorry, but there's no time now," I told him, obsessed with the fear that Eliza's baby would be born before

559

we could reach the Butler house. But there was plenty of time after all, for Eliza didn't have her son until two days later, the night of March twenty-eighth. Priscilla delivered the child with a surprising calmness and competence, and I was grateful to her. For two days, Andrew had waited patiently for the household's preoccupation with the birth to subside, and after giving the lusty infant a cursory glance, he turned to me and asked, "Please, Cassie, now can I go home?"

"Tomorrow morning," I promised, "right after breakfast. You've been very patient." I smiled at him, understanding his need to go there, to the place he had lived in contentment wtih his parents for a year and a half, until his world had fallen apart. Hadn't I been obsessed with the need to return to my own house, in Bexar?

"One of the darkies can take him," Sam offered.

"I think I should go with him," I said. Maybe I could help shield him from the disappointment he would be bound to feel when he saw, as I had in Bexar, that nothing was the same, and realized that nothing would ever be the same again.

The next morning, Andrew had been chattering excitedly as we rode, but when we approached the house and saw no stirrings of life, he lapsed into silence. We went inside, and found Sukie sitting forlornly in a rocker in the kitchen. Andrew's eyes lit up with the joy of finding something, someone familiar. He ran to her, stood by her chair as her plump arms enfolded him. "Bless you, chile! Where's yo' mammy and pappy?" She looked at me and I shook my head. Her face clouded up.

"Papa's in heaven," Andrew announced importantly, "with Colonel Bowie and lots of my other friends from the Alamo. And Mama went to heaven, too, to be with him so he wouldn't be lonesome for her. They're happy there. Cassie said so."

The tears rolled silently down Sukie's face, and I asked quickly, before I, too, dissolved in tears, "Are you alone here? Where's Daniel? And Lupe?"

"Lupe gone. An' Daniel, he went into San Felipe late yesterday, after he saw all de men passin' by. Dey our men, Miss Cassie, runnin' away from Santa Anny. Daniel—"

"Our men?" I asked sharply. "That can't be! They were stopped at the Colorado when we left them. They were going to fight Santa Anna there."

"I dunno, Miss Cassie. Daniel, he went into San F'lipe to talk to 'em. He don' like travelin' in de dark, so he say he come back dis mornin'."

Before I could ask her any more, we heard the clatter of wheels outside and an agitated Daniel burst into the kitchen door, yelling, "De Mex'kuns is comin'. We gotta go, 'cross de Sabine!"

When he had calmed down, he told us: the Texan army was in San Felipe.

"But they were to turn and fight at the Colorado!" I insisted.

"Dat's what de men done tol' me, Miss Cassie, but Gen-'rul Houston, he done changed his mind when dey tol' him 'bout de men from Goliad."

"The men from Goliad?" I repeated. Will!

He nodded. "Dey was took by de Mex'kuns. Took off to jail."

"Oh, no!" I cried in anguish. Would Will be with them, I wondered? "When?" I asked. "When were they taken?"

"I dunno. I dunno nuthin' 'cept dey was all took."

I shuddered. A chill passed through me as I remembered the red flag flying from the church tower at Bexar, and remembered, too, that Santa Anna had told Mrs. Dickinson he would kill any Texan he found with a gun. But surely, I rationalized, he would not have taken the men prisoner if he had intended to carry out his threat. Still, I grasped desperately at the hope that Will had not reached Fannin before Santa Anna had.

Four hundred men, captured! And close to two hundred at the Alamo. And the men from the Matamoros expedition who had been caught at San Patricio, about ninety of them. I remembered Uncle Todd's grim prediction: *"There would be no war. There would only be a massacre."*

"We gotta go, Miss Cassie," Daniel was saying. " 'cause now dey ain't nobody 'twixt us and de Mex'kuns at all. An' dey comin' 'cross de Colorado, columns 'n' columns of 'em, an' each column long enough to reach from here to de ribber. And de Cassahooties is goin' 't scalp us all, an'—"

"You mustn't listen to such silly rumors," I interrupted sharply, hoping my words masked my own panicky feelings. Santa Anna was coming, and there was nothing I could do to get us out of his path! "Did Houston say if they plan to turn and fight Santa Anna at the Brazos?"

Daniel raised his fear-glazed eyes heavenward. "I dunno. De men say lots o' men done run away after Gen'rul Houston cross' de Colorado. De road is so full o' folks goin' Ah had to come back on de ol' counterban' traces."

"But where is the army going?" I wondered aloud. "And how many men are left?"

"I dunno. I hear dey havin' a big hassle. Some say dey goin' up de ribber, some say dey goin' down de ribber, an' others goin' cross de ribber. Dey say dey gonna take all de boats an' ferries t'other side o' de ribber so's Santa Anny can't use 'em. We gotta hurry, Miss Cassie. We gotta leave 'fore dey take ever'thing on to de other side! We gotta get 'cross de Brazos!"

*Across the Brazos. . . .* First it had been the Colorado. Now the Brazos. When would Houston stop running?

"Please, kin we go, Miss Cassie?" Sukie and Daniel turned pleading eyes toward me, waiting for my permission to leave. I remembered the nightmarish ride from Gonzales, and I thought of these two aged Negroes. I realized suddenly that they had been old ever since I could remember, must be sixty or seventy. How could they make such a journey alone? Where would they go? Who would look after them? My eyes traveled from Daniel to Sukie and back again, and I saw the naked fear in their eyes. They wanted my permission to leave. How could I refuse it, when I would leave, too, if I could?

Later that morning, I told Sam and Priscilla what Daniel had learned, clenched my hands into tight fists behind my back when Sam said with a self-satisfied nod, "I knew it! I told your father and I told Jeremy that thirty-six thousand people were no match for eight million, but they wouldn't listen. Fools, all of them! Fools!"

"How can you talk like that? You act as if we've already lost!" I ran from the house, tears of wrath stinging my eyes. As the door closed behind me, I heard him say, "Now that's a funny way for the wife of one of Santa Anna's officers to act!"

I sat on the steps, trembling with rage. I had come to admire Priscilla during the previous days, but Sam Butler represented to me all the selfish, grasping men in the world, men who cared only for themselves and their own possessions. Our men were fighting for a cause. And Felipe, too. Even though he was wrong, he believed in what he was fighting for. But men like Sam Butler backed no cause, had no ideals. I was glad Jeremy had defied him, at last. I only wished I had been able to leave his house.

We decided to keep the news of Houston's retreat from Eliza, but two days later, one of the servants told her, and she summoned me to her room with such urgency that I was afraid something had happened to the baby.

But as I entered the room, I saw the baby was asleep in his bed. Eliza pushed herself up on one elbow. "Is it true, what Feena told me, that our men have fled, that Santa Anna is coming? She said some of the servants have already run away."

I nodded, unable to deny the truth of what she said.

"When did Houston leave San Felipe?"

"The day after little Johnny was born." I, too, had been talking to the servants, who seemed to get information from an unknown source. I had also learned that, on the same day, someone had thought Santa Anna was close and had burned most of the town.

"And Santa Anna? Where is he?" Her voice was hushed with fright.

563

"Nobody seems to know. But we'll be safe enough here." I added bitterly, "Sam has certainly done nothing to make Santa Anna think he has helped the Texan cause."

"Cassie, can't we leave? Please?" Her eyes were bright with tears, and her shoulders shook with a convulsive shudder. "Why not? I hate to burden you with little Johnny and me any more, when you've done so much for us already. But I want to go to my mother, wherever she is. Away from Santa Anna. Away from here, before he comes. Please, Cassie! I'm terrified! I've already lost my Johnny. Help me to take his son some place where it's safe."

I weighed the possibility of leaving against the wisdom of staying, knowing I was being foolish to even consider what she asked. We could not go mounted. Not only would Eliza be endangering her life if she tried to ride so soon after childbirth, but all Papa's horses were gone. In one of the far fields, Daniel had told me there were still two oxen, and there was a sturdy new wagon in the barn that Sukie and Daniel had refused to take. But if Santa Anna was close, an ox-drawn wagon would travel far too slowly to get out of his way. We would be far safer if we stayed where we were. Besides, Daniel had said that Houston's men were going to take any means of crossing the Brazos to the other side. How could we possibly get a wagon across?

"It's just not possible," I said. "I'm as anxious to leave as you, but we can't. We'd have to take a wagon, and there's no way we could cross the Brazos. Our men have taken all the ferries and boats to the other side."

I thought that would end the matter, but later that day, she broached the subject again. "I've been talking to Feena, had her ask around among the other servants. Houston has gone up to Groce's. Do you know where that is?"

I nodded. "About twenty miles north."

"They have a steamboat there, the *Yellowstone,* and a yawl. They'd help us get across. Please, Cassie! If I'm still here when Santa Anna comes, I'll die of fright!" She burst into tears.

"But it would take a couple of days to get up to

Groce's—more, maybe, because we'd have to go down to the Bexar Road, then back west to get on one of the traces that leads there. To the east, the creeks will all be too high. By the time we could get to Groce's, Houston would probably be gone."

"Then we can come back, if we have to! But at least we will have tried."

"It's too risky," I said, but in spite of my protests, my mind was busy considering the possibility. "I suppose I could go over to our place and see if the oxen are where Daniel said they are—"

Eliza smiled, "Oh, thank you! You'd better hurry. It will be dark in a little while."

Andrew and I rode double to see about the oxen and wagon. As we approached the house, I noticed a horse tethered to the hitching post by the front door. A man with an ill-fitting high-crowned hat perched on his head came out of the door, put something in the saddlebags and disappeared again into the house. So intent was he on his own actions that he apparently didn't hear or see us.

"Why, he's robbing us!" Blind fury obscured caution, and I dismounted in a leap, ran into the house. "Stay here," I commanded to Andrew. Unheeding, he followed at my heels.

I burst in the front door, heard a noise from the big bedroom. Rushing toward the sound, I saw the same man rifling through Papa's top bureau drawer. He had slipped one of Papa's silk dress shirts over a filthy buckskin jacket.

"Stop that!" I demanded. "Get out of here!"

Unperturbed, the man looked up slowly. His face and neck were blotchy and red, his eyes puffy. He was either sick or drunk, I knew. He grinned at us, a horrid mirthless grin. "You gonna stop me, Missy? You and that kid?" Then he laughed aloud, and his laugh was as malevolent as his grin. Suddenly, I realized he wasn't looking at us. I saw his eyes follow some movement behind us.

I whirled around. Another man, just as ludicrously

clothed, was only a few feet away. He held a pistol, and he was pointing it straight at me.

Gripped by terror, I pulled Andrew against my skirt. How could I have been so foolish, barged in so unthinkingly? My stupidity had endangered us both.

The realization that I had been foolish didn't lessen my rage. "Have you no shame?" My voice rocked shrilly in helpless fury. "Robbing a man who died in the Alamo? Why weren't you there, fighting alongside him, instead of coming here to plunder his home?"

The man with the gun seemed amused. "Well, naow," he twanged, "if the man what owns this here stuff is dead, he won't miss it none, will he, lovey? As for fightin' Mexicans, well, that ain't exactly what we come here for."

His companion wiped his runny nose on the sleeve of Papa's shirt. "We're just sort of passin' through, you might say." He smirked. Then he picked up a leather patch bag he had been filling, and walked toward me so that Andrew and I were caught between the two men, less than a foot away from each.

The one in the hat stepped toward me, dug the fingers of his free hand into my arm. "This ain't what we come for, neither, but I wouldn't mind—"

Repelled by his touch, sickened by his insinuations, I recoiled, pulled my arm away. "Get your filthy hands off me!" I felt Andrew's little body stiffen against mine.

He came closer, reached for me again. I clenched my fist and swung it with all my strength into his stomach. He doubled up, ended in a paroxysm of coughing.

The one with the pistol crowded in, pinning us tightly against the doorframe and said through clenched teeth, "You get smart like that, you won't get no smarter!" The stench of tobacco, the unwashed, stinking, sweating smell of him filled my nostrils till I felt surely I would suffocate.

Just as suddenly as he had closed in on us, he backed up, slapped me viciously across the face with the open palm of his free hand. "I'd like to tame that temper a mite, too, Joe, but we ain't got time."

His companion, still clutching his stomach, said between coughs, "By God, let's take time. I'll show that goddam bitch—" His hand reached for his belt buckle.

"We stayed too long already," the other man insisted.

"It won't take long. Besides, I ain't that sick—"

"She ain't worth hangin' for! If Santa Anna catches us, he'll string us up for sure for them Mexicans we kilt."

I held my breath in terror, frozen into immobility by the knowledge that killing weighed no more heavily on their conscienceless minds than swatting a fly.

They stood there, undecided, for a time that seemed endless. "You're right. She ain't worth hangin' for." The splotchy-faced one slid his belt back through the buckle. "Sure would like to teach her a lesson, though—"

"Let's go. She brought another horse. We don't have to ride double no more." They moved toward the door, and I heard their boots resounding on the porch, then the command, "You ride hers."

Not unil the sound of hoofbeats had receded into nothing did the terror that had held me motionless release me. I gasped, drinking in deep breaths of air as though I could never get enough. With the back of my hand, I tried to wipe the hurt, the stench, the feel of the brutal blow from my bruised cheek. My legs trembled crazily, buckling beneath me as I tried to take a step.

Andrew was quicker to recover. He put his hand on my trembling arm, said with bravado, "Don't worry, Cassie. I wouldn't have let them hurt you."

We reached the porch, and I yearned to sit for a minute on the step, catch my breath. But there was no time for that. Santa Anna was coming, and we were going to try to get to Groce's before he reached us.

We returned to the Butler house just before dark with the new wagon and a sturdy yoke of oxen. In the wagon, I carried the tooled sidesaddle Papa had given me so long ago, Mama's silver tea service—minus the sugar bowl, which the looters must have taken—and my grandmother's mahogany table, which had, for so many years, held the tea

567

service. They were for Priscilla, who had always admired them. On the seat beside me was an old rifle and the box containing Papa's dueling pistols. Those I would keep for myself. Until sanity returned to the world, until we reached a place where values and human decency had not turned topsy-turvy, I vowed I would never again be caught unarmed.

Sam and Priscilla tried to dissuade us from leaving. I did not dare tell them of the episode with the looters, and had cautioned Andrew not to mention it to anyone. I knew the Butlers would never let us go if they knew.

"We're leaving in the morning," I insisted, ignoring all their arguments. "If we can't get across the river at Groce's, we'll come back."

But we didn't leave in the morning. The baby cried most of the night, howling till he was put to Eliza's breast, and howling again when he was taken away. Eliza's milk had come down, and the baby should have been getting enough nourishment, but apparently he was not. Nor was there a wet nurse to be found among the servants. In desperation, we had even tried cow's milk, but the baby's delicate stomach had reacted violently and so we had had to give up. I recalled bitterly the milk that had poured from my own breasts, unused, unneeded, just four months earlier.

We were up with the baby much of that night, and at the first show of dawn, we started to get ready to leave. Eliza threw back the covers and put her legs over the side of the bed. She started to stand, sat down again quickly.

By the light of our lone candle, I thought I saw her wince. "Are you all right?"

"I'm fine. If you'll just hand me my dress. . . ."

She slipped her dress on over her head, and when she stood to step into her petticoats, she gave an involuntary cry of pain and fell back onto the bed. Before she fell, I had had a glimpse of the distended flesh of her leg, and even in the dim light, it seemed to have an unnatural whiteness to it.

She saw me looking at it. "I can still travel," she insisted.

"You know I've had swelling in my legs for months. And I've had this for a day or two already—"

"You know this isn't the same. And this time it's in only one leg. We must get Priscilla to look at it."

"Milk leg," Priscilla pronounced without hesitation a short time later. "I'll get some hot packs. You must stay in bed, stay off of it. You can't leave now."

I turned away and left the room, not wanting Eliza to see how disappointed I was. That had been our only chance, I knew. We would never be able to flee before Santa Anna's approaching army. Still, I couldn't bring myself to unpack the wagon.

I hadn't reckoned on Eliza's determination, nor on Santa Anna's delay in coming. It was almost as if Eliza commanded her leg to get better, and, by sheer force of will, had made the physical ailment give way. Six days later, she shook me awake in the gray predawn light of another overcast day.

"I'm all better," she announced. "The swelling is gone. See?" She guided my hand over her leg.

It was true. The swelling was down, and the leg had the feel and the look of living tissue once more.

I protested, but only feebly. "Are you sure?"

"Positive." Then correctly sensing that I was weakening, she hugged me. "Let's get ready right away."

We left early the morning of April seventh. Surprisingly, once Sam realized we wouldn't be dissuaded, he insisted we add another yoke of oxen to the one I had brought from Papa's place. I knew that Sam and Priscilla were right when they said it was surely madness to start out, when we had no idea where Santa Anna was or when he might be coming. We only knew that he hadn't passed anywhere nearby, and that we wanted to leave before he came.

The trace that led from the Butler place to the Bexar Road was smooth and relatively level, for it was little-used. We turned west onto the Bexar Road, away from the Brazos, in order to reach the north-south trace of which I knew. We saw no one until midmorning, when a rider approached us from the east. As I heard him coming up behind us, I looked over my shoulder and made out the outline of his high-crowned hat. My heart raced wildly with fear, and I reached for the pistol by my side, closing my fingers around it. Its mate lay under the quilt on the bed of the wagon. Eliza had silently nodded her approval when I put it there earlier.

As the man came closer, I saw with relief that it was not the man I remembered from the encounter in Papa's house, but that did little to lessen my apprehension, for he bore a frightening resemblance to the other one, and I knew even before he drew close that he was of the same breed. He rode by at high speed, and I didn't even hail him to ask for any news.

"I'm glad he didn't stop." Eliza's words echoed my thoughts and I nodded. They had a certain resemblance to each other, these furtive creatures who had come to feed on the carcass of our war-torn land. I shuddered at the bitter memory of how close Andrew and I had come to harm at the hands of the two who were robbing Papa's house.

A week ago, that had been. A whole week, and the only thing that had saved us then from the men's vicious animal instincts had been their anxiety to be gone from Santa Anna's path. Surely in that week, the Mexican leader had drawn perilously close. I took what comfort I could from the thought that the man who had just passed us was heading west. If Santa Anna were too near, wouldn't he have been fleeing east? Such creatures as he fed on decay and chaos, flourished only in a nether world where normal values did not exist. Where did such men come from, I wondered idly, and where did they disappear to again when the world was set to rights?

Still, Santa Anna could be anywhere, and the man who had just passed us might have no more idea where the Mexican army was than we did. At the thought, I flicked the whip vigorously over the backs of the animals, shouted to them. Once we had reached the Bexar Road, the pulling had become harder. I was thankful for the second yoke of healthy oxen, which should carry us to Groce's slowly but steadily.

It was not long after we had passed Papa's place that we saw a small cart approaching us. In it was an old woman, shouting unintelligibly. I had jumped down to force the oxen to skirt a dangerous water-filled hole in the road, and paid little attention to her.

She could not get past us without going into the hole herself, and she continued to yell her frantic impatience at us as I shoved and pushed against the side of one of the oxen to force him and his companions to the right. At last, when the wagon was past the hazardous hole, the woman moved her cart forward. She passed us, still shouting, and Andrew was the first to understand her words.

He came from under the protective canopy that covered Eliza and the baby. Terror-driven tears coursed down his face.

"Cassie, the Mex'cans are coming! She saw them herself!"

Over Andrew's frightened shout, I yelled to the old woman, "Where? When did you see them? How many?"

But it was too late, for she had already moved out of hearing.

"Where will we go?" Eliza asked quietly as I climbed back onto the wagon.

I flicked the whip and the wagon lurched, started to move again. But slowly—so agonizingly slowly!

"Where will we go?" Andrew repeated Eliza's question, and still I couldn't answer.

*Where will we go? . . . Where will we go?* The question pounded in my ears, echoed in my brain as though a thousand voices were asking, demanding an answer, but all I could do was urge the oxen onward. Cloying fear clung to my brain, made it impossible to reason, to think rationally. The road we needed, the road that led north to Groce's, could not be far away. Less than a mile.

"We'll try to reach our road," I said aloud, even as I

knew it was wrong to continue west, toward Santa Anna.

The words had scarcely left my lips when the same horseman who had passed us earlier that morning galloped toward us, a bulky blanket-wrapped bundle under one arm. Just ahead of us, his horse stumbled, and in the instant that the rider was thrown off-balance, his bundle slipped from his grasp and tumbled to the ground, unrolling and spreading its contents as it fell. I saw an engraved silver goblet, a gold candlestick, and various pieces of jewelry. I stared at the things, then turned my head to watch the departing horseman vanish down the road behind us.

My mouth went dry. Once Felipe and I had watched some vultures flapping their wings in panicky ascent, dropping choice morsels of a carcass from their beaks as a Mexican lion came upon them while they were gorging themselves on his half-hidden feast. The vultures, in their haste to be gone, did not contest the prize with the lion, nor concern themselves with the bits they had dropped from their beaks. They were set only on flight, on escape.

The horseman who had just raced by us had dropped a bundle of valuable plunder. He hadn't even paused to look back at it as it fell. The Mexican lion, then, must be close at hand.

My heart began to pound thunderously in my ears.

"Here come the Mex'cans! I see 'em! Two of 'em!"

It was odd, but Andrew's warning, followed by Eliza's gasp, had a calming effect on me, made me face my fears and subdue them. Ever since the night we had left Gonzales, the very thought of being caught by Santa Anna had struck terror into my heart. And just a short while before, when Andrew had finally realized what the old woman was shouting, that terror had turned to panic, had become so intense it could not have increased without choking the life from my body.

And then the thing most feared had happened. The Mexicans were near, near enough for Andrew to see. The long dreaded was the actual, the threat the reality. Suddenly, surprisingly, my mind cleared, and I began to think with a coolness I would not have thought possible a few minutes before.

There was no longer a question of staying on the Bexar Road. We must leave it at once, I knew. I remembered that we had just passed a little-used trace that entered the road at right angles from the north. It was not the one I sought, but we were within a few miles of Papa's place, and I knew the area well enough to be able to find my way indirectly to the trace that would take us far enough north to intersect another trace that led to Groce's. The one we had just passed curved after a few hundred yards, where it was sheltered from view with a dense undergrowth and some bois d'arc trees planted along the Bexar Road. If I had been thinking clearly a few minutes earlier, I never would have passed it.

It seemed to take forever to turn the wagon around, and it seemed another eternity before we reached the trace. When at last we were out of sight from the road, I halted, told Eliza I wanted to go look. Maybe Andrew had been wrong, for the Mexicans he had thought he had seen had still not passed us by the time we turned onto the trace.

But he had not been mistaken. Two riders approached, and they were wearing the uniform I knew too well. Several others were coming behind them. There was no need to watch any longer. Alone, on a good saddle horse, I could easily have outridden them.

But I was not alone. As I made my way back to the wagon, I felt a brief moment of rebellion. The yoke over the necks of our oxen was no more binding than the yoke that bound me, invisibly but just as firmly, to those in the wagon.

I sighed, shedding my rebellion. Groce's was twenty miles north, and we had committed ourselves to the folly of trying to reach it. I could only hope that we would find some means of crossing the river there.

# Chapter VIII

## GROCE'S—April 11, 1836

It took us four days to reach Groce's, for the creeks were running high, and we often had to go up- or down-stream to find a place to cross.

One of the Texans on scout duty found us about a mile from the Brazos. In answer to our anxious questions, he told us Houston and our men were still there, and that they did have the steamboat *Yellowstone* as we had heard, and a yawl besides. Relieved, Eliza and I looked at each other and smiled. We had made it.

The men were camped on some high bottomland which had been formed into an island of sorts by the river when it overflowed its banks. The light was fading by the time we had set up our own camp off to one side and I set out through the Texan camp on foot in search of Jeremy.

Was it just the approaching twilight that made all the men look so shabby, I wondered? Their faces were unshaven, their hair unkempt, their buckskins universally black and shiny from constant exposure to the weather. I saw few tents and remembered Jeremy had told us that most of the men who had come to fight had only the clothes upon their backs. Was this, I wondered, all that was left of our army? There was no way to guess how many men were scattered through the trees, but it did not seem that it could be many.

I inquired for Jeremy, and finally when one man said, "You mean Captain Jeremy Butler, ma'am?" I nodded and followed him. So Jeremy was a captain in Houston's army. I wondered what Sam would think of that.

Jeremy jumped up when he saw me coming. "Cassie, what the devil are you doing here?"

There was only one answer: "Running away from Santa Anna." I recounted briefly the events of the previous three-and-a-half weeks since we had left him and the others at Burnham's Crossing of the Colorado. He didn't act surprised when I told him about seeing the Mexicans on the Bexar Road four days earlier.

"They reached San Felipe about noon that day," he said. "They tried to cross there, but Mosely Baker stopped them. After two days, the Mexicans gave up and headed south. Wylie Martin should keep them from crossing at Thompson's Ferry. The river's high, and we've taken every boat and raft and ferry to the other side."

I thought of how few men seemed to be in the camp and wondered aloud, "Should Houston have split his forces like that? Can he afford to?"

"It wasn't exactly his idea," Jeremy answered bitterly. "There was a big argument when we reached San Felipe. Baker and Martin had already decided where they wanted to go, so Houston 'ordered' them there to prevent a mutiny."

I nodded, remembering that Daniel had mentioned that the Texans were arguing about which way to go the day he returned from San Felipe.

"On top of that," Jeremy continued, "Baker's men fired San Felipe, destroying a lot of our precious stores. We'd left them there, intending to go back for them after Mill Creek went back down." His voice was heavy with disgust. "The excuse was they thought the Mexicans were coming. I tell you, Houston isn't having an easy time of it. He keeps getting letters from Harrisburg asking why he hasn't engaged the enemy, and while he's being badgered by them, his subordinates argue with almost every command he issues. A couple of days ago, there was even a private going through our camp trying to stir up interest in a scheme to take the *Yellowstone* downstream to attack Mexicans down south!" He shook his head. "The wonder is that Houston has been able to hold as many men as he has."

"How many are there here?"

"Not many. There was a count just today. Five hundred and twenty-three."

"That's all?"

He nodded. "Then of course there are Baker's and Martin's men downriver—maybe about three hundred and fifty in all. We lost a lot at the Colorado when we heard about Fannin. Houston branded the man who told us the news as a spy, said he was just trying to cause panic—"

"It wasn't true, then? About Fannin?" I grasped desperately at the hope, even as I remembered that Houston had done the same thing to the two Mexicans who brought us word of the fall of the Alamo. And what they said had been true, after all. "Then Will—"

"Cassie, there's something I have to tell you," he said, and though I could no longer see his face clearly, there was something in his voice that alarmed me.

"Fannin was captured, then?" One hope was crushed and I grasped desperately at another. "Maybe Will didn't reach him in time. What day were the men taken?"

"The twentieth."

"Oh, then Will—"

"I'm sorry to have to tell you this, but Will was with him. Fannin surrendered near the Coleta, and the men were taken back to Goliad."

"Yes?" I asked, knowing there was more, unable to do more than whisper the word for the fear that gnawed at me. My heart boomed in my ears. My eyes were open, but they didn't see the darkened grove. They saw instead the red flag, blowing from the church tower, the red flag of no quarter . . .

He took hold of my arms, held them firmly. "Cassie, Will—all of them—were . . . a week after they were captured, the Mexicans marched them out, and—and shot them."

577

"No!" I cried. "Not Will. Not Papa and Serena and Uncle Todd and now Will!" I heard my voice rise shrilly as I denied again what he was telling me. "Not Will, too!" I felt his hands tighten on my arms and pull me toward him as I sagged weakly toward the ground.

"You're wrong!" I insisted as I collapsed, sobbing, against his shoulder. "You must be wrong! You weren't there! You don't know that Will was with him! You can't be sure!"

But he was sure. "I wish I wasn't. I wish I could offer you some hope. Only a few men got away. One of them is a friend of yours, and he was with Will. I'll bring him to see you in the morning. Maybe you'd like to talk to him, ask him some questions. Come, let me take you back to your wagon now."

I don't remember directing Jeremy to our camp, don't remember anything that happened when we reached it. I just remember that all that night, I lay awake, digging my face into the blanket on which I lay, muffling my sobs into it to keep from waking the others. The night stretched on and on, a sleepless night of tears and sobs and sorrow.

At the first light, I was up. Eliza and Andrew must eat, and I needed something to do, some activity on which to focus my mind. I found a small pile of wood that Jeremy had probably put there, made a small fire. As I blew and fanned the first faint spark into a flame, I looked up to see Jeremy approaching with another man. I stood up, vaguely recalling that he had mentioned someone who had been with Will. There was something familiar about that other figure, but his head was bent, his face obscured by a wide-brimmed Mexican *sombrero*. When he was about ten feet from me, he looked up and removed his hat.

"Asa Quigley!"

"Asa was with Fannin, Cassie," Jeremy explained. "He was with Will. That's how I was so sure. I thought you might want to talk to him."

"You, Asa? At Goliad? I thought—"

"You thought I'd high-tailed it to the Sabine? No, and I

578

guess I've got you to thank—or blame—for stoppin' me from runnin' away."

"I shouldn't have called you a coward. Forgive me. I was angry—"

"What you said sat heavy on my mind, even though I pretended not to hear. But I still didn't hold with fightin' Santa Anny at the Alamo. I knew too well how weak the place was. So I went to Goliad, 'cause I knew it was stronger.

"Well, it was stronger, all right. It was Fannin was weak, with his hemmin' and hawin'. He come there after he changed his mind about goin' to Matamoros, and he tried to get all them was goin' there to come to Goliad instead. Then he said, yes, he was goin' to Bexar if they needed him. But later, when a message come from them sayin' Santa Anny was there and they needed help bad, he hemmed and hawed some more. Should he go or shouldn't he go? Finally, he started us toward Bexar. Then when one of our wagons broke down, he changed his mind again, told us to turn around and go back. After that, he sent some men to Refugio to rescue some fam'lies there. Then he heard they was trapped there, so he sent some more. And when he got orders to fall back, he still couldn't make up his mind to obey. He couldn't make his mind up about anything at all, to go or stay, to defend Goliad or run. For four days, he acted like an ass between two stacks o' hay, and by then it was too late. We left, finally, on the nineteenth, and it was too late for three hunnerd an' fifty men."

"And Will?" I asked hoarsely.

He nodded. "Your brother was there. That's why Jeremy asked me to come tell you about it, knowin' you'd want to be sure, thinkin' you might want to know how it was." He hesitated, and I nodded.

"Go on," I said.

"Well, finally Fannin give up waitin' for them he'd sent out earlier, and we left. There was lots o' tuggin' and pullin' to get our cannons across the San Antone, and we

579

hadn't gone but about eight miles when he gives the order to stop and rest for an hour. Right there in the middle of the prairie, like we was on a church picnic, he tells us to stop and rest! Some of his officers was arguin' with him, sayin', 'We better keep goin' so's Santa Anny won't catch us.' But he sez, 'No, we're tired and we gotta rest.'

"And then we seen the Mexicans. We tried to make a dash to get to some timber by the Coleta, but we was too late. Right in the open we had to stop, with hardly more'n a blade o' grass to hide behind. We piled up saddles and blankets and anything we could find to pertect us, but it wasn't enough. We was sittin' ducks for them filthy Santanistas. There wasn't a damn tree or a bush or a rock anywhere around. Some of our cavalry had ridden on ahead to check the crossing of the Coleta, but they never come back, 'cause the Mexicans was too thick all around us. We kept firin' all the rest of that day, and even after dark, we fired where we saw the flashes of their guns. We couldn't even fire the cannons after a couple rounds, 'cause we hadn't no water to cool 'em. And we hadn't no water for the wounded, neither, and all night long they was yellin' and beggin' for it. But we hadn't a drop to give 'em."

"Was Will—"

"No, he wasn't hurt, but lots of our boys was—upwards of sixty or so. Will was right beside me, and I thought you'd want t' know, he was as brave a boy as I've seen. He's a funny kid, silentlike, don't have much to say for hisself. But when he found I was your friend, he stuck by me, and he saved my life at least once, mebbe more.

"Well, in the mornin' when the Mexicans showed themselves and we seen they was thick as bees in a honey tree, Fannin put up a white flag. 'Honorable surrender,' he called it, and he made sure it was all written down properlike, in Spanish and English, with them promisin' to send us to Copano to be put on a ship for New Orleans.

" 'Honorable surrender!' " He spat in the dirt. "We found out soon enough just how honorable them bastards was. They marched us back to Goliad and put us all inside the church, with no heat at all and us freezin', and the swill they give us not fit to slop the hogs! On Sunday that was, and then on Saturday word got started 'round that they was almost ready to put us on ships, give us our parole like we give the Mexicans at Bexar. We forgot how cold and hungry we was, and we began singin' and whoopin' and carryin' on, and even though there wasn't no room, some of the boys was dancin'. We could hardly wait to find out more about our parole.

"We found out soon enough," he said bitterly. "Next mornin', before dawn, they marched us out. 'We want to count you,' they said, and we nudged each other, and said, 'That's so's they can know how big a ship they need!'" Asa's voice shook as he continued. "They counted us, all right. Do you know how them dirty bastards counted us? With a bullet through each head!"

"Dear God, no!" I yelled in horror. "They couldn't!"

But they had.

When I could speak again, I suggested desperately, "Maybe Will escaped—"

Asa shook his head sadly. "Sorry, Cassie. More'n anything, I'd like to be able to tell you, 'Yes, he coulda got away.' I wasn't with him when they marched us out. He'd started coughing pretty bad the night before, and went off to sleep in a corner so's he wouldn't bother everyone so much. Early the next mornin', they come and marched us out, and I didn't see your brother again."

"You didn't see him?" I grasped at the faint hope. "Then maybe—"

He shook his head slowly. "It was about as easy to get away from there as it is for a dead man to get up and walk. Only six or seven of us made it, and we all come here. I had to lay there and play dead for hours, it seemed like. I was afraid to move, afraid to breathe for fear they'd notice. Listenin' to 'em bring out more. Listenin'—" He shuddered.

"But you got away!"

"Only thing saved me was the bullet creased my skull

581

and I bled like a stuck pig, so when they come with them mercy bullets . . . " His voice trailed off to nothing. "I'm sorry to have to tell you this, but it would be worse if I was to let you go on hopin'. Will was there, and like I said, he was as brave as any. You can be proud of him. But I'm sure he didn't get away. Palm Sunday, that was. Do you suppose them bastards went to church when they had done with us?"

I bit my lip, thinking of Will, who had loved all living creatures. What had it cost him to fire his rifle at the Mexicans? Will, who hated killing, and had been forced to go to war, to forget his compassion for every living thing, and kill? "Thank you, Asa," I said through the dry sobs that shook me, my eyes burning from the tears I had shed all night long. "Thank you for being Will's friend. I'm sure your friendship meant a lot to him."

I expected him to turn and go, leaving me with my grief. But he continued to stand there, nervously twisting the brim of his *sombrero* around in his fingers. "There's somethin' else . . . "

I looked at him questioningly, waiting. He ran his tongue over his lips and cleared his throat.

"What is it?" I prodded. "Is there something else you think I should know? Tell me."

He licked his lips again. "I'm glad you said that, Cassie, 'cause what I have to tell you ain't easy to say. I figured you'd want to know how it was, and all the while I been talkin', I been thinkin', 'Should I tell her what else I know?' And knowin' how you feel and all, and Jeremy said your pa was in the Alamo, and now Will—well, I think you'd want to know."

Apprehensively, I waited for him to continue. What else could he possibly know, what more could he say that would hurt any more than the shock of losing so many people dear to me in so short a time?

Asa cleared his throat again, shifted uneasily from one foot to the other. "I saw somebody else at Goliad, too. But he wasn't one of us, wasn't on our side—"

Incredulously, I asked, "Felipe?" I could scarcely bring myself to say his name. Felipe, a part of the horror, the heartless, savage murder Asa had just described? Impossible!

"No!" I said aloud, denying the thought.

"I saw him through the window the day before—on Saturday, that was."

"You could have been mistaken. Maybe it was someone who looked like him." Frantically, my mind grasped at the possibility of mistaken identity. I hadn't realized until that moment how certain I had been that Felipe had left the Mexican army, if not before the horror of the Alamo, then surely right after.

"There wasn't no mistake," Asa insisted grimly. "I saw him with my own eyes, as close to me as that tree yonder. He was talkin' with that Indian swine that was left in charge of us, that Colonel Portilla. Your husband was with him, Cassie, struttin' like a peacock in that damn fancy uniform of his! Ain't you proud of him? He was part of the whole rotten, stinkin', murderin' mess that killed three hunnerd and fifty men. And one of 'em was your brother!" Asa's voice rose shrilly, cracked.

"No!" I screamed. "Not Felipe! He couldn't have been!"

Jeremy glared at Asa, interrupted sharply, "For God's sake, Asa, stop it! I asked you to come over here to comfort Cassie, let her know you were with Will. I didn't know you'd seen Felipe. She's had enough—"

"Enough?" Asa repeated. "I'll say it was enough. If I ever see that son of a bitch again, I'll rip that goddam Mexican uniform off his back, and then I'll kill him with my own bare hands!" His hat dropped to the ground as he turned his hands palm up, clenching them into fists. "And just before I choke the life from his body, I'm gonna tell him it's for the men he helped murder at the Alamo and at Goliad!"

It couldn't be. Felipe, a part of anything as horrifying as the massacre Asa had described? A part of murdering Will? My heart denied it. Asa was wrong; he had to be. Felipe would have been repelled by Santa Anna's barbarity at the Alamo, would have realized it wasn't a united Mexico that Santa Anna wanted, but vengeance on those who had tried to deprive him of some of his power, senseless revenge and pointlessly hideous cruelty for those who had dared to defy him. Felipe could never have remained a part of that. Never.

"You're wrong," I cried. "It couldn't have been him!"

"It was him, all right," Asa answered grimly. "I've never been surer of anything in my whole life."

Asa, who had been to our house in Bexar many times, would know Felipe when he saw him. And he was sure he had seen him at Goliad the day before our men had been murdered. "Then there must be some explanation," I insisted.

"My eyes explained everything I had to know. I saw Felipe there, with Portilla, with the swine that directed the murders. They was together, and they wasn't fifteen feet from me. I'm sorry, Cassie, to have to tell you this. But I know how you feel, and I figured you'd want to know."

"There's an explanation, Asa. I know there is. I know my husband. He could not have been a party to such brutality." I looked at Jeremy, my eyes pleading with him to join with me in denying this terrible thing. "You know him, Jeremy. You know he could never have been involved in such senseless brutality."

"It's hard to imagine," Jeremy said uncertainly. "And yet . . . well, you said yourself he changed when he was in Mexico City. War does strange things to men sometimes. . . ."

Denied Jeremy's support, I faltered. Dear Felipe, so considerate and loving and tender. How could he possibly have let himself become a part of Santa Anna's vicious revenge? He couldn't, I insisted to myself. And yet Asa had seen him at Goliad the day before the massacre. There had to be an explanation for his presence. But what explanation could there possibly be? Often, when I had pleaded with him to leave the army, I had asked him if he could bring himself to shoot our friends and my family if war came. "You can't think of it that way," he had said. "In wartime, there is a chain of command, and commands must be obeyed." Had that been what had happened, then? Had it merely been one more command which had to be obeyed unreasoningly, a command to which he had been a party?

"Dear God, no!" I said aloud, looking at Jeremy, defying him to contradict me. "Nothing—not even war—could have made Felipe a part of that!"

"I hope not, for your sake," he said. "But you heard Asa. He was there. . . ."

Yes, he was there. And because there was no denying that, there remained in my mind a small kernel of doubt. "There's an explanation," I insisted, realizing that Asa had gone and that Eliza had awakened and was standing nearby with her baby in her arms. "There has to be." I said the words defiantly, but even as I defended Felipe against the suspicions of Jeremy and Eliza, I wondered again: what explanation could there possibly be? And the small doubt, the possibility that there was no explanation, lived on in my heart, a tiny seed of uncertainty that was heavy as a rock. *"Orders must be obeyed. . . ."*

We crossed the Brazos later that morning in the *Yellowstone,* but we were not the only ones, for Houston and his army were crossing, too. The Mexicans were across the Brazos. Martin had not been able to stop them. And it was almost a certainty that Santa Anna himself was leading them.

The Brazos. The *Brazos de Dios.* The Arms of God. The river that Eliza and I had so longed to cross, to be safely away from Santa Anna. The river Houston had steadfastly insisted he would never let the enemy cross.

We were on the other side. But so was Santa Anna.

We had no choice but to wait for the army, for our own protection. It took them two days to cross. They had acquired two hundred horses, and a number of wagons and oxen, and it took time to get them to the other side. And once the army started moving away from the Brazos, it was apparent they could not move as easily as they had from Gonzales. A number of the men were ailing with the common childhood diseases—chicken pox, measles, whooping cough and mumps—and the animals had to be watered and rested. Among the supplies that arrived just at the time the army was leaving Groce's were the Twin Sisters, two cannons sent to the Texans by the city of Cincinnati. The cannons had been pulled laboriously overland from Harrisburg, had arrived only—ironically—in time to return by the same route. Houston worked right along with his men, and many times, Jeremy told us, it was his shoulder that pushed and heaved the hardest to get the cannons out of the muddy Brazos bottomland.

As we made our way east, other refugees joined us. It was the flight from Gonzales all over again, with one fearsome difference, one threat mentioned only in awesome whispers, because nobody dared mention it aloud:

Indians!

Unless the Indians were to attack in overpowering numbers, we knew we would be safe as long as we stayed with the army. But if Houston should turn south to seek an encounter with Santa Anna, as Jeremy stoutly insisted he would, what, then, would become of the rest of us? On the night of the fifteenth, our refugee camp was full of the hushed exchange of frightening rumors passed from wagon to wagon. *The Indians had already attacked settlements in east Texas. . . . The dread Comanches would join the others, had begun drying meat and preparing to send their women and children away. . . . Most of the towns to the east had already been destroyed. . . . One of the tribes was lying in wait to lift our scalps at the Trinity.*

Whether from fear or lack of time, Eliza and I never discussed the rumors with each other. We had more pressing problems on our hands. Little Johnny was not gaining weight as he should have, and was constantly wailing in hunger. We gave him sugar-tits, but they did little good. We were concerned, too, about Andrew, who had a cough that was rapidly becoming worse.

That night, Andrew began to run a fever. Jeremy, too, looked concerned about him when he came to see us. Nor had we been able to find a wet nurse for the baby.

After Andrew and Johnny had fallen asleep at last, Jeremy sat down with us, said he had been talking to some of Wylie Martin's men, and told us how Santa Anna had managed to cross the Brazos. After he had been stopped by Baker at San Felipe, he went down to Thompson's Ferry and opened fire on Martin's men on the opposite bank, where they had taken the ferry. Three miles upriver, he had found a rowboat which a slave had brought back from the other side, and while he kept Martin busy at the ferry, he transported enough of his men over to mount an attack on Martin from the east side of the river. Then he forced the surprised Martin to abandon the ferry. "And that's how he got most of his troops across," Jeremy finished.

"Smart as a fox," I said without thinking. It was Felipe who had once described the wily general that way. Felipe! The very thought of him set off a confusing profusion of emotions that tugged at me mercilessly. Felipe was my husband, my dearest love, dearer to me than my life. He was gentle and understanding and compassionate, would never hurt anyone. But Felipe, the same Felipe, was also a warrior and an officer in the Mexican army. Could that Felipe possibly have remained a part of Santa Anna's army once it became clear to him that Santa Anna sought not central unity, but personal power, not victory, but revenge, not conquest over the rebellious Texans, but total extermination? *No, he couldn't have! It wasn't possible!* I insisted to myself. *But he had been at Goliad. Why? Why?* And there was no answer.

"Jeremy," Eliza asked with a frown, "will Houston fight Santa Anna? Ever?"

Her question brought me back to the present, away from my inner confusion and secret doubt. Her question was one that was on everyone's lips, echoed in everyone's mind.

Jeremy frowned his annoyance at the implication so often expressed openly—that Houston was a coward, that he would never stop running. "Of course. If the men will fight with him."

"It will have to be soon," Eliza said. "There's no place left to run."

Eliza was right. Further east were the Indians, and if they suspected the Texan army was bolting in fright, they might ally themselves with Santa Anna's army to deal us one mighty and final blow.

*Will Houston fight?*

The question was asked with increasing urgency the following morning as we continued east. Up ahead, the road forked. The right fork—little more than a trace—led to Harrisburg—and Santa Anna. The left fork led to the Sabine—and flight. We refugees would follow the left fork, the one that led almost due east. Would Houston go with us, leaving Santa Anna in undisputed possession of Texas, or would he take the road that separated from ours almost at right angles, to engage the enemy?

The previous night, Jeremy had told us that many of the refugees had been to see Houston, to beg him to stay with us and protect us from the Indians who might be lying in wait anywhere ahead. What good would independence do any of us, they asked, if we didn't live to see it?

As we approached the fork, Jeremy came to ride alongside our wagon. He had about him an air of suppressed excitement. "We'll be leaving you up ahead," he said triumphantly. "We're going south, to Harrisburg."

"Houston is going to fight!" Eliza said.

"I told you he would. He's been waiting for the right time, and the right place. There have been too many mistakes made already. One battle is all we can afford, and Houston knows it." He frowned, added, "You people won't be without protection. Martin will be going with you."

"But how can Houston spare him?" I asked in surprise. "Surely he needs every man he has!"

"Not Martin. We're well rid of him. He and Houston have had a falling out. Martin doesn't think Houston will

588

fight, so he's leaving. Baker's going with us, though. He's joined Burleson's regiment."

I reached out, took Jeremy's hand in mind. "Oh, Jeremy, take care!"

As I released his hand, he waved jauntily. "Good-bye, girls! God keep you!" He wheeled his mount around and went back to join Houston's army.

Eliza and I turned to watch him go. "Oh, Jeremy, do take care," I said again under my breath. I had taken leave of Papa and Will with that same admonition. And I would never see either of them again. Now I was taking leave of Jeremy as he was going into battle. Was any land, no matter how well-loved, worth such a tremendous cost in lives?

A short while later, we took the left fork toward the Sabine. We were one of the last wagons, and several of Martin's men were waiting a few hundred feet beyond the fork with a distraught mother and three children, one an infant in her arms. Alongside the road was a cart tipped crazily onto its side, one of the wheels gone. The donkey that had pulled the cart had already been freed from his traces and was nibbling at the grass by the side of the road. The men waved us to a stop and one of them asked us if we would take the family into our wagon.

"Of course," Eliza and I said in unison. And then my eyes took in the infant, traveled to the telltale milk stains on the woman's bodice. I smiled at her. "I think we need you every bit as much as you need us." I jumped to the ground. "While these men and I transfer your belongings to our wagon, would you consent to putting a very hungry little baby to your breast?"

Later, just before we started to move on, one of the woman's children shouted, "Look, Ma! There they go!"

We all turned to watch the men as they passed the fork. Was there really a new enthusiasm in their steps, a renewed vigor in the way they swung their arms, I wondered, or was I only imagining it?

But I wasn't the only one who noticed it.

"They look so confident," the woman said.

"Because they're no longer running away," Eliza added. "I wish them Godspeed."

Wordlessly, one of the two men with us wheeled his horse around and returned to the fork, to disappear after the men.

The road to Harrisburg. The road to Santa Anna. Dared we hope it was the road to victory? Or would it lead, as had the road to Matamoros and Bexar and Goliad, to another of Santa Anna's merciless annihilations?

I turned around to give my attention to the other road, the one we must travel. I cracked the whip and yelled at the oxen. Our wagon started with a lurch toward the Sabine.

"I'm cold, Cassie," Andrew said weakly a short while later. I looked anxiously at Eliza, who had a sated Johnny sleeping peacefully on her lap, and I climbed into the back of the wagon just as Andrew's whole body was wracked with a violent coughing spasm. He opened his eyes to look at me, and they were red and watery. There were two quilts covering his quaking body. Uselessly, I added another, then felt his head.

Alarmed, I said, "Eliza, he's burning with fever!"

If only, I thought, I could get him inside, into a soft bed, out of the cruel biting wind and the soaking rains that continued to plague us. As I watched helplessly, another coughing fit seized him, tore at his lungs and throat. He tried to sit up, fell back. "I'm cold," he complained again between chattering teeth. He opened his eyes and looked at me beseechingly, silently begging me to help him.

And all I had done was heap quilts on him—a futile gesture, when what he needed was a place out of the weather, a warm fire, a few days of rest.

I climbed back onto the seat at the front of the wagon, and as I settled myself there again, my eyes fell on a cabin in a clearing up ahead, huddled against a stand of pines. It reminded me of our first Texas home, and it looked so safe, so inviting.

I turned around to look again at Andrew. He was still

590

shivering, and his tremors seemed frighteningly convulsive. If I insisted on continuing with him, kept exposing him to the whims of the weather, he might die.

If I stopped at that cabin ahead . . .

Did I dare take Andrew from Martin's protection? What were the dangers, if I did? Santa Anna? He was supposedly far to the south, no threat to us here. Other columns of the Mexican army? Perhaps, but we had not heard anything of reprisals against women or children; it was Santa Anna the man everyone feared more than his other generals. Indians? Yes, that was a definite possibility. Even if they didn't go on the warpath as a group, they might come to steal, and would not hesitate to lift a scalp or two. Looters? There was certainly another real danger there.

I weighed one set of dangers against the other. Did I dare stop, alone with Andrew? Even as I asked myself the question I had already begun to gauge how soon we would reach the cabin ahead. Did I really dare continue, with Andrew so frighteningly ill, and getting worse rapidly? The other dangers, those we might encounter if we stayed, were only possibilities. But the danger that Andrew might die of exposure if we kept going was imminent, and real.

My mind busied itself with details. We would need fast transportation after Andrew recovered. I looked around, hailed the mounted man who had helped us transfer the other family's possessions to our wagon. As he came to jog alongside us, I asked abruptly,

"Would you trade your horse for my wagon and oxen? Please?"

The man looked startled, and Eliza and the woman we had picked up a short while before both turned to stare at me. "They're yours, as soon as these people reach safety and no longer need them," I continued. Then I turned to Eliza. "I must get Andrew out of the weather," I insisted. "If only I had been able to find some shelter for Uncle Todd, he might still be alive!"

"But there was nothing you could do. He was old, and sick—"

I brushed aside her protest. There was no time for discussion, for argument. We had almost reached the cabin. I turned again to the stunned man and begged, "Please! This child can't go on. He's too sick. He'll die—"

"But you can't stop here, alone," he protested.

"I must, with or without your horse. I killed my uncle by not believing he was sick enough to die. I'll not make the same mistake with my little brother."

"Then I'm staying with you," Eliza said resolutely.

"You can't," I reminded her. "Johnny needs his wet nurse."

"But you and Andrew can't stay here all alone!"

"Don't worry. We'll be all right. As soon as Andrew is able to travel, we'll follow."

In the end, the man left his horse, but he refused to consider the wagon and oxen his. "Call it a loan," he insisted. "You'll likely be along in a day or so, and catch us before we reach the Sabine."

As the man carried Andrew into the cabin, I hastily accepted more than a fair share of our provisions that Eliza handed down to me.

Only after the last wagon had disappeared did the enormity of what I had done overwhelm me. Surely Andrew and I had stepped out of reality into a dangerous nightmare world where other people didn't exist, never had. We were alone, in that eerie gap between civilizations, that strangely empty world so favored by the lawless and the violent.

"I'll soon have a nice warm fire going," I assured Andrew with as much confidence as I could muster. I found a cot, moved it close to the hearth for him, and set about building a fire. There was a small stack of firewood, and I piled it on generously, hoping I could find more when that was exhausted.

I brought our horse into the dirt-floored cabin that night, afraid he might be stolen if I left him outside. Once, I was awakened by the horse's restless stirring. My hand reached quickly for my rifle and I lay motionless, listening. Then I heard it, too: the faint stirring of a bush, the muted footsteps. Someone was there, just outside the cabin. Should I move, purposely make some noise, let whoever it was know that the cabin was occupied? Looters looked only for empty cabins. But if it were an Indian, scouting for a spine-chilling dawn raid, wouldn't it be better to let him think the cabin was deserted?

In the end, my own paralyzing fear made the decision for me, for I could only lie there, afraid to do more than gulp air fearfully each time my lungs were empty. Even the first patter of raindrops on the roof made me sick with terror until I recognized the sound for what it was. The footsteps had stopped, but still I couldn't sleep. A cart creaked and groaned its way eastward just before dawn, and I heard several horsemen go by a little later. It was with relief that I saw the first welcome signs of daylight in the cracks around the shutters and the edges of the door. Daylight gave no guarantee of safety, I knew, but at least danger would no longer be an invisible threat, ready to spring out of the darkness with stunning speed and frightening finality.

I circled the cabin, looking for any evidence of our nocturnal prowler, but the rain had erased any signs. Perhaps it had been only an animal, after all. I led the horse to the barn, where I found an ample supply of corn, and even neat stacks of dry firewood.

Back in the cabin, the light of day revealed red blotches on Andrew's face and neck. I had seen similar rashes among the men in Houston's army. Measles! I almost cried in relief. It was serious, but normally the disease could be expected to run its course in a matter of days. Too frequently, such childhood illnesses resulted in lasting infirmities or death, so I had no regrets at having stopped.

Later that morning, we had another visitor. Unlike our stealthy prowler the night before, he made no secret of his presence. He was a short thick-necked man, gaudily dressed. I listened to him in astonishment as he assumed I was the woman of the house, and I discovered he wanted me to sell him the land.

"It won't be worth a thing after the Santanistas take over, you know. I suppose your husband isn't here, that you're alone. He's with Houston, eh?" He didn't wait for me to answer. "Well now, if you'll just sign . . ."

Stunned, I listened to him as he continued to talk, trying to find out from me the extent of the claim, to see if I had a deed, and sign it over to him.

"I'll give you two hundred dollars, cash, if it's a sizable tract. Of course I realize—"

"Two hundred dollars!" I gasped. First, the looters had come to strip our homes of anything of value, and then men like this one came along behind, trying to steal the very land itself!

I fought down my fury and indignation, and finally convinced him that I had no more claim to the land than he did. I tried to hide my disgust as I showed him to the door. I watched him ride away, wishing I dared speed him on his way with a rifle shot just under his horse's hoofs. But Andrew and I were alone, and vulnerable, and I didn't want to chance any man's anger.

Later that day, as I fetched water from a creek nearby, I heard a twig snap, held my breath as I waited, my fingers closing reassuringly over the pistol in my pocket. Perhaps it was the nocturnal prowler returned, I thought, and lying in wait. My eyes measured the distance back to the cabin. It was too far to break and run. I'd never outdistance a fleet-footed Indian. My heart beat rapidly as I stood, motionless, scanning the opposite side of the creek, expecting a tomahawk to come sailing toward me at any moment. At length, a large white dog walked out of the underbrush, his tail wagging in an overture of friendship.

"Oh!" I let out my breath as he splashed across the creek toward me, followed me back to the cabin. I petted him and fed him and shooed him outside again, putting a pan of water near the door to encourage him to stay around.

That night, I was a little less apprehensive. Several times, the dog growled, and once he barked. Each time, I reached for my rifle until I heard again the reassuring thump of the dog's tail beating against the door.

Each night, I continued to take into the cabin the precious horse that was to carry us to safety as soon as Andrew was well enough.

Slowly, the angry red blotches on Andrew's body began to fade, and his color and appetite returned. On April twentieth, four days after we had parted from the Sabine-bound refugees, I told Andrew I thought we could leave the next day. It was the first day he was feeling better, and his temperature had at last receded. He smiled at me, accepting without question my decision to go on, just as trustingly as he had accepted my decision to stop. How nice, I mused, to be a young child during the hell of the past few months, to be unable to comprehend fully the heartbreaking world-shattering events swirling about us violently, like the waters of a wild river on a destructive rampage. How nice to be Andrew's age, to be able to put complete trust in someone, to be oblivious to the dangers lurking outside by day and by night, dangers too numerous to count and too frightening to dwell upon.

But I was only too well aware of the dangers, and of our good fortune until then. I had no desire to stay a minute longer than necessary.

The sun was shining that morning, and I opened the door to let in some of the crisp, fresh air. Several times each day, the dog had barked and run to the road to sniff at a passing figure. I went to the creek for a bucket of water, and as I was returning, I glanced toward the road, saw the lonely figure of a man. He had on a coat, and had one arm inside it, as though he carried it in a sling. He was tall and large-boned, like Will and Papa. The way he carried himself reminded me of Will, except that the man was shuffling along slowly, as though he was very tired.

It couldn't be Will, of course, for he had been a victim of murder, a terrible murder of three hundred and fifty men, in which I prayed Felipe had had no part. Surely he hadn't—had he? I could not free myself of that small persistent fear.

As the man drew closer, he reminded me even more of Will. It couldn't be, I told myself again. But the resemblance was so strong that I knew I had to get closer, see the man's face close up. He wore a hat, and with his head bent forward, it was almost impossible to see his features. He stopped, and reached to pet the dog, just as Will would have done.

I set the bucket down near the door and walked with hurried steps toward the road. The man raised his head, and I stared in utter disbelief.

"Will!" I held out my arms and raced toward him. "Oh, Will! You're alive!"

"Cassie, what—?"

I threw myself at him with such vigor that he stumbled backwards briefly. I hugged him, tears of joy running down my cheeks. I could only repeat over and over again, "I thought you were dead! I thought you were dead!"

I led him toward the cabin, still too shocked to explain anything to him. I looked at his face, noticed how gaunt it was compared with its usual round fullness. Then I looked questioningly at his arm.

His eyes followed my gaze. "I broke it. It's healing fine. But what are you doing here?"

I told him, then, about Andrew getting sick; told him, too, about Uncle Todd, and the birth of Eliza's baby.

"I had measles, too. I was pretty sick, and didn't get well as soon as I should have. That's what caused the delay. That and my arm." He walked into the cabin.

Andrew cried, "Will!" and sat up when Will came over to him, leaned down to hug him. Will sat on the edge of Andrew's cot.

"I'll get you something to eat. You look starved." I started to poke up the fire.

"Just give me anything. You don't have to heat it."

I nodded, filled a mug with some cold broth and handed it

to him. He snatched it and gulped it hungrily, held it out for a refill.

A thousand questions swirled around inside my brain as I filled the mug again, handed him several pieces of hardtack. I sat on the hearth, looked up at him. "How did you get out of Goliad? Asa said—"

"Asa?" His eyebrows shot up in surprise. "He's alive?"

I nodded. "Only he and about six others got away and joined Houston. But what about you? How did you get out?"

"Felipe."

"Felipe? Asa said he saw him—"

"He came there to try to get us all out, but all he could do was save me."

"Oh, Will!" I burst into tears, tears of profound relief. That was why Felipe had been there! Not to help carry out Santa Anna's vindictive orders as Asa had assumed, but to try to prevent them from being carried out! How could I ever have doubted him?

But I had doubted—not much, but a little. I hadn't thought it was possible for him to be a part of anything so sordid, but there had remained that small doubt that kept whispering, "maybe. . . ." And the guilty knowledge that I had not been totally certain in my heart that Felipe had not been involved would be my private cross to bear. And it would be with me always. I would never admit to anyone that I had failed to cast out that small seed of doubt, but I would have to live with that secret guilt—and atone for it—for the rest of my life. And so my tears of relief were also tears of shame.

"Where is he now?"

"He's gone to find Houston's army. A slave we met told us he'd heard Santa Anna went to Harrisburg, and that Houston went after him. We'd heard before that Houston was up at Groce's, and we tried to get there, but with me being so sick, we couldn't make it. We've been doing a lot of our traveling at night, Cassie. The Santanistas are thick a little way back. They're swarming all over the place on both sides of the Brazos. It's a wonder I haven't blundered into them since Felipe and I separated.

"Do you have any more hardtack?"

I got up, handed him some more hardtack and some strips of jerky.

"I hope I'm not eating all your food."

"There's plenty," I assured him, filling his mug before I sat down again. "When did you and Felipe separate?"

"Night before last, just this side of the Brazos."

And so Felipe had set out alone, to find Houston, to fight with his army. "But we have so little chance against Santa Anna! He has so many troops, and we have so few men left. And if he wins . . ." I shuddered. The thought refused to complete itself.

"Felipe doesn't really think we have any chance at all. We talked about a lot of things these past few weeks, Cassie. He said he'd finally been honest with himself and admitted that the promise of getting the Varga grant had blinded him to the things about Santa Anna he should have seen sooner. When he decided to switch sides, he knew he was giving up all hope of ever having his claim acknowledged. He feels that Santa Anna will crush what's left of the Texan army."

"But still he's gone to find them, to join them." I didn't have to ask why. I was afraid for Felipe, desperately afraid, for him and for all the rest of Houston's pathetic little dissension-wracked army. But I was proud, too, because they were my army. And now they were Felipe's army as well. At last, we were on the same side of the war that couldn't happen, the war that had pulled us apart. "Was he in Bexar when the Alamo fell?" I asked.

"Not during the seige. He got there when it was over. He thought Papa and Uncle Todd might have been there, and he wanted to give them a decent burial. Then when he talked to Mrs. Dickinson, he found out that Serena had been there, too, with Papa. But he was too late to bury any of them. Santa Anna had already had their bodies burned."

"Oh, no! How terrible for Felipe—!"

598

"It was already done. There was nothing he could do. He said if he hadn't been shaking so much, he'd have rushed over to the house Santa Anna was in the minute he'd found out and run him through with his sword. But when he'd calmed down, he decided he might be able to do us a lot more good by staying with the Santanistas till he learned something that might help us, or saw a chance to do something for us.

"Then he heard about Santa Anna's orders to have all of us at Goliad shot. He made up some false papers and rode to Goliad as fast as he could. But he couldn't talk Colonel Portilla out of obeying Santa Anna's orders. All he could do was save me, by pretending to want me for questioning." He shook his head. "You've no idea how heavy it's been weighing on his concience that he hadn't been able to save us all. That's why it's so important for him to get to Houston in time to join in any fight. If he'd have waited for me, he'd have missed taking part for sure. I finally insisted he go without me. I hope he makes it."

"We have so few men," I said. What would one more man matter against Santa Anna's hundreds, his thousands? But it would matter, greatly, to Felipe. He had come over to our side. Even though he didn't think we could possibly win, he wanted a chance to stand among the Texans and fight among them, to share in their glory—or their defeat. With Jeremy, and Asa—

"Asa!" I gasped, suddenly remembering his words. "Oh, Will, Asa said he'd kill Felipe! He saw him at Goliad, and thought—we've got to find Felipe, stop Asa before he—" I jumped to my feet. "I have a horse in the barn." I started toward the door.

"Do you have a saddle for him?" Will got to his feet, collapsed weakly.

"I'll go. You'd never make it. Just keep yourself and Andrew out of the way of the Santanistas. And pray, Will. Pray as you've never prayed before!"

# Chapter IX

## EAST OF THE BRAZOS—
## April 20, 1836

I was only vaguely aware of the physical discomforts during that long ride—the constant rubbing of the cinch strap on my calves as the split skirt Priscilla had given me hiked up as I rode astride, exposing my legs down to the inadequate moccasins I had forgotten, in my haste, to change for boots, the hunger that was scarcely discernible from my fear for Felipe's life.

Asa. What if I didn't find Felipe in time to warn him, in time to have somebody else explain to Asa? His temper was as fiery as his flaming red hair, and he would not stop to listen to an explanation from Felipe.

Unwilling to waste precious time going out of my way, I didn't return to the place the rough wagon road forked toward Buffalo Bayou and Harrisburg. Instead, I headed east, then cut down south as soon as I found a well-used trace. That was soon intersected by another, and yet another. Everywhere I turned, I was confronted with a maze of alternate choices. Which way should I go? Should I take the better route, the one that seemed most traveled? Or the one that seemed to point more directly in the direction I wanted to go? Each need to make a decision was a fresh agony. And after each decision, there was the nagging uncertainty, the fear that I had chosen wrong, had made an error that could delay me, and cost Felipe his life. The sun, which would have helped fix directions more clearly, was nowhere to be seen in an overcast sky. Several times, I found I had chosen wrong and had to backtrack and try another route, despairing at the delay.

I was forced to stop several times when the horse no longer responded to my urgent proddings, and I begrudged the poor animal every precious second of delay, forcing him to start again when he was only slightly renewed. I felt no remorse for driving him beyond his endurance, for my only concern was for Felipe, and the need to try to reach him before Asa did.

Daylight faded, and I rode on into the night, pulling the heavy blanket jacket that had been Papa's more tightly about me. The cold that blew out of the north even as it seemed to rise from the Gulf to the south was sharp and biting.

"Halt!" The voice boomed out of the darkness to challenge me.

I reined in. "Are you with the Texan army?" I asked breathlessly.

"I'll ask the questions, miss," my challenger said gruffly. "Who are you?"

"Cassie Varga. Cassie Stewart. Thorne Stewart's daughter, from near San Felipe," I answered him impatiently, but knew I would get no information from the man until I had satisfied him about my identity.

"Thorne Stewart, who fought with me at the seige of Bexar last winter?"

"Yes," I said relieved. "You're with the Texan army, then?"

"That's right. But I'm surprised your father isn't with us. He was always—"

"My father died in the Alamo."

"I'm sorry to hear that, truly I am."

"Thank you." I brushed aside his sympathetic words and tried to tell him about Felipe, but in my haste, the words spilled out helter-skelter. "I don't know when he would have arrived," I finished. "Probably not too long ago. He was on foot."

"Nobody like that's come in here today, or yesterday,

either. We had a few come from the east, fresh arrived in Texas, but that's all."

As relieved as I was to realize that I would have a chance to talk to Asa before Felipe's arrival, I was concerned to hear that he hadn't come in as yet. For the first time, I considered the possibility that he might not be alive. He could have collapsed from hunger, as Will had been on the point of collapse when he reached the cabin where Andrew and I had stopped. What if he had fallen by the wayside, was exposed to the bitter winds of this fresh norther? Or worse, what if he had been overtaken by the Mexicans, and recognized as a deserter?

No, I assured myself, none of those things would happen to Felipe. He knew how to care for himself, would realize the danger and move cautiously. I must go and speak to Asa, and soon Felipe would come. I had no idea what company Asa was with, so I started by inquiring for Jeremy.

"Captain Butler? No, ma'am, he's not here with us. He's with Burleson's regiment with the main army."

"This isn't the Texan army? But you said—"

"I said I was with the Texan army, and I am. But there are a couple hundred men here that had to be left behind with the baggage. Most of them are down with measles or mumps or whooping cough or—"

"But where's Houston, then?"

"Across the bayou."

"In Harrisburg?"

"Lordy, no, ma'am. There isn't any Harrisburg any more. Santa Anny'd burned it to the ground by the time we got here. Yesterday morning, he fired New Washington, too. We saw the smoke from here, just before Houston started to cross Buffalo Bayou."

"Which way was Houston going?"

"Toward Lynch's Ferry. He left under forced march to try to get there before Santa Anny did. We're sure now it's the old murdering scoundrel himself with that bunch of troops, had the good fortune to intercept one of his messengers. Houston's gone after them."

"Thank you." I flicked the reins and touched my heels to the horse, but the exhausted animal didn't respond immediately and in that instant of hesitation, the man grabbed the bridle.

"Just a minute. Where do you think you're going?"

"To find Houston. Let me go, please!" I tried to jerk the bridle free, but the man held fast.

"Why, ma'am, how do you think you're going to get across Buffalo Bayou? You can't just splash across it like you were fording some little stream. Why, with all this rain, it's swollen up till it must be three hundred feet across! And besides, there are some more Mexicans over there now, behind Houston. The last of them, with wagons and all, are lagging behind the others quite a way. We heard them across the bayou, so some of our men just sneaked up behind them and stole some of their supplies when they were slowed down fording one of the smaller bayous over there.'"

"Please don't stop me," I begged, as hot tears of frustration burned my eyes. "My husband—they'll kill him! They'll think he's a spy, and he isn't. He's gone to help them—"

The man's arm circled my waist, and he lifted me off my horse as though I were a child. Then he patted my shoulder. "Take hold of yourself, and let's see if I can't help you. I'd count it a privilege to help the daughter of a man who was killed in the Alamo. Someone's life is at stake, you say?"

"That's right," I nodded vigorously, wiped the rough wool sleeve of Papa's jacket across my eyes.

"Then why don't tell me about it, slower this time, and we'll see what we can do?"

I told him, then, and he said, "It seems to me the first thing to do is to find out if that man you mentioned—Asa somebody—is in this camp. Then if he isn't, we'll see what we can do about getting you across Buffalo Bayou. The ferry's all busted down, and this tuckered horse of yours couldn't carry a fly across. Even if he didn't sink under you, you'd get yourself a good case of lung fever, for sure.

"Let's take you to my captain over here, and while you tell him all about your problem, I'll go check to see if that man is here. Asa—?"

"Quigley," I finished.

"If he isn't here, then we'll see if we can find somebody to help row you across, and maybe we can even scare up a fresh mount. The cavalry took all the good saddle horses, but we have a few nags that'll do you a sight more good than this one."

Through my anxiety, I recognized the truth of his sympathetic words, and I followed him unprotestingly to his captain, who was lying on a cot under a crudely rigged shelter and coughing with the telltale sounds of whooping cough.

In the end, he let me go, though he named a hundred reasons why he shouldn't: I was as apt to blunder into Mexican troops as I was to find Houston. . . . I could be shot by a sentry from either side before I could identify myself. . . . There was no telling when there might be a battle, and I could stumble onto a battlefield before I knew it.

"Captain," I said at last, "all the things you say may be true, but you have no right to hold me here, and I'm going to try to find Houston's army if I have to swim across Buffalo Bayou. I've wasted enough time on useless talk." I turned and walked away, half expecting to be stopped.

Meantime, the sentry who had intercepted me had found out that Asa wasn't among the men in the base camp, and he had returned to tell me so just before I walked away. He stopped to talk to the captain for a minute, then followed me.

"He says it's all right to give you a fresh mount. I'll go do that, and then I'll see if I can find a couple of men to help get you across. You wait right here."

"Thank you," I said, "but please hurry!" I sank down on the ground, leaning against a tree, tucking my legs under me for warmth. All day, it had been overcast, and suddenly in the afternoon, the north wind had started to blow and the temperature had dropped drastically and angry clouds had begun to scud across the sky beneath the overcast. As I sat there, I looked up and saw that the clouds were beginning to break up, for a few stars were visible here and there. The next day would probably be clear, but the cold would remain. The wind was still blowing viciously, and I moved around the tree a quarter circle for more protection.

For the first time, I realized how exhausted I was. Then I remembered that I hadn't eaten since breakfast, and recalled that Will had stuffed some jerky and hardtack into my pockets. I pulled out a piece of jerky and chewed on it as I waited.

It seemed a long time before the sentry returned, leading a horse. The animal was bony and swaybacked, but at least he seemed rested.

"We'll have to go down the bayou a way. We've got a rowboat down there. Now you just stay down there while I go rustle up some men to help."

Again he left, and again, I chafed at the delay. It seemed I had been detained there for hours, when every minute, every second might be important. Finally, the man returned with two others.

As I stepped from the boat on the other side, more stars were visible, but they were already growing dim.

"Stay on the road," one of the men admonished, "at least till you get past Vince's Bayou. With the water so high, there's no way you can get across it except at the bridge, unless you go three or four miles out of your way, through sedge grass. Better stick to the road. The bridge is about five miles ahead."

"And watch out for them Mexicans," another cautioned. "They may be anywhere up ahead, and they got a bunch of stragglers at the end of their column. They'll have to cross Vince's bridge, too."

"Keep your ears open. If you hear any cannon, stay where you are."

I thanked them all hastily as I mounted and started down the road. I was grateful for their help, knew I would never have been able to manage without it, but too much precious time had been lost. Five miles to the bridge, they had said, and then only eight or nine more to Lynch's Ferry. And somewhere near there, I hoped to find Houston.

There was one bayou to cross before Vince's, and I had to pick my way carefully through it, since I couldn't see to judge its depth or width. Finally, on the other side, I spurred my horse on again. How far had I come, I wondered? How much farther to Vince's bridge? If only Felipe hadn't arrived too much sooner! . . . If only Jeremy saw him before Asa did! Whatever Jeremy believed about Felipe, whatever he thought about him being at Goliad, he would at least be fair, would give Felipe a chance to explain. . . . If only Asa—

The movement of shadowy shapes up ahead caught my eye. I reined in sharply, heard the creaking of wheels, the hum of muffled activity directly ahead of me. I stopped, sat motionless, afraid even to draw a deep breath. I remembered, too late, the admonition to watch out for the end of the Mexican column. Had they heard my incautious approach, I wondered?

Spanish phrases drifted back to me, and I heard, unmistakably, the word *"caballo."* They had heard me approach, then, had heard the hoofbeats. And there were two voices, getting louder, coming back to investigate the sound.

I wheeled my horse around, and took off at right angles to the road, hoping I could outdistance my pursuers. I was in the sedge grass, felt it whipping about, slashing at my legs. I hadn't gone a hundred yards when the animal stumbled.

I felt the tug on the reins, frantically tried to jerk the horse's head up to keep him from falling. But it was too late for that, and we were going down together in a jumble of flailing hoofs and flying arms and legs. I hit the ground, falling free of the horse, and I felt myself roll and tumble before I came to rest with a final thump. I gulped and gasped, for the blow had knocked all the air from my lungs. I heard the horse whicker some distance away, and I was thankful that he had righted himself and taken himself well away from where I lay. I lay there, fighting for breath, yet trying to make no sound. I could feel the dampness of the marshy ground on which I had landed, but as I heard the wind rustling the tops of the grass well above me, I was thankful that the place I had fallen was hidden from view.

I heard the Spanish phrases again, heard them with increasing clarity as the two pursuers must have stopped within a few yards of me. When the horse whickered again, one of the men laughed and shouted, *"¡Un caballo mas para General Cos!"* and the two men ran toward the sound. *"One more horse for General Cos!"* The column into which I had blundered, then, was that of General Cos. There was a final cry of triumph as one of the men mounted my horse and rode back to the road, amid the muffled cries of his comrades.

Heartsick, I listened to the fading hoofbeats. I wanted to stand up and scream my protests, yell out my vengeance on the man who had dared steal the horse I so desperately needed to take me to Felipe. But I could only lie there, tense with helpless fury, berating myself for being so careless.

From what my guides had told me, I knew I would not be able to leave the road before I came to Vince's Bayou, so there was nothing to do but wait until the Mexicans had moved on and crossed it first. It was getting too light for me to risk moving within sight of the Mexicans, so there was no hope of trying to move parallel to the road in an attempt to reach the bridge ahead of the front of the column. Anyway, a column that General Ços commanded would be sizable, and was probably strung out for several miles, so I would have scant chance of getting around them. There was nothing to do but lie there impatiently and hope the Mexicans would soon move on.

If only, I thought, there were some way for me to get word to Houston about Cos's approach! The Mexican general had apparently come straight from the Brazos, on the road that ran along the south side of Buffalo Bayou. What if our poor little army were to be trapped between the two Mexican detachments, between Cos and Santa Anna?

Where were the Texans now, I wondered? They had crossed over on the morning of the nineteenth, almost forty-eight hours earlier. Had they reached Lynch's Ferry ahead of Santa Anna? Or had Santa Anna reached it first, moved his men across the San Jacinto River and taken the ferry to the other side?

I lay there, listening, expecting to hear the sounds of the Mexican column as they moved forward. And then I realized: they had stopped to rest! I kept still, not daring to move, and saw the sky gradually grow lighter, but still I heard the murmur of conversation from the Mexicans. The ground under me was marshy, and the icy dampness rose up and joined with the north wind above to penetrate every inch of my being. After a while, I could no longer feel my toes or make them respond to any attempts to move them inside my moccasins. The cold had travelled up my legs, and paralyzed my fingers and arms as well, until I was aware of nothing but the numbing cold. I tried to fight off the lethargy that was overtaking me, as the same numbness that had paralyzed my legs and arms moved on into my brain. I fought to focus my thoughts on something besides the cold—anything else—but I couldn't. The cold was there, around me, inside me, like a sinister presence, a living enemy, seducing me, urging me to succumb. *Sleep!* it commanded me. *Give yourself to sleep. Don't fight it!* And, unable to stop myself, I obeyed, and let myself slip beyond the cold, beyond feeling.

When I awoke, it was full daylight, and the sun was already well up into the sky. For a minute, I lay there, confused. Then I remembered where I was, what I had been doing: I had been waiting for Mexican soldiers to move on, waiting until they had crossed over Vince's bridge ahead so I could also cross and continue on my way to Felipe.

I listened, heard nothing. Cautiously, I raised my head, looked around. I pushed myself to my feet, staggering at first as my benumbed legs seemed unable to support my weight. There was no sign of life on the road. I reached down to rub some life back into my legs. Then I made my way to the road and continued on, toward Felipe.

How much time had I wasted, I wondered? It had surely been hours, hours I could ill afford. I began to run, and after a few steps, found I was exhausted. I remembered the food in my pocket, and took out a piece of hardtack to chew on as I continued, half running, half stumbling toward Vince's bridge. I slowed to a walk only when my chest ached for want of air. Then I took it into my lungs in great gasping gulps, and forced myself to run again.

I had thought I had been close to Vince's Bayou, but it seemed a long way before, at last, I saw it ahead. I stumbled over the bridge, kept going. How much farther had the men said? Eight miles, nine miles more to Lynch's Ferry? And if I didn't find Felipe before I reached it, what then? I didn't let myself think of it.

Nine miles. *How long,* I wondered, *will it take to go nine miles like this?* I could only run a few steps at a time, and then I had to pause for breath. Finally, I could no longer elicit a response from my flagging body, and I knew I must stop and rest. Grudging the delay, yet knowing that I couldn't continue without it, I dropped to the ground, not bothering to move from the road. I would rest only a minute, try to renew myself. I put my head on my knees and closed my eyes.

When I opened my eyes again, I wasn't certain if I had slept or not. At the time, I had felt I was aware of every minute I sat there, and yet I had a feeling that I had lapsed into that state between waking and sleeping in which the mind is aware of the passage of time, but unable to make any positive movement. I looked up anxiously, toward the sun, saw that it was approaching its zenith.

The fear that I had dozed and that I might do so again if I stopped to rest was enough to make me realize that I dared not trust myself to stop again. I began walking at a pace that I knew I should be able to sustain: one foot in front of the other, one step at a time, measured and steady, each step closer to Felipe.

How many more steps to reach him? The thought that his life might at that very moment be endangered made me quicken my pace as much as I dared. I scanned the road ahead for some sign of the Mexican troops, but was relieved that they were nowhere to be seen. I walked steadily, resisting the impulse to run, occasionally taking a piece of hardtack or jerky from my pocket and chewing on it. As the sun continued to warm me, to dry my clothes, I felt strength returning. Steadiness, not speed, was what I needed, and I kept my feet moving, blotting out the sensations of pain I had felt in them since before I had reached Vince's bridge.

The sun had passed its zenith and was well on its way into the west when I saw the horsemen approaching. Panic seized me. Whose horsemen were they? There was no cover, no place to hide. Surely, they had seen me. I could only hope they were not Mexicans.

As they drew closer, it was with a surge of relief that I recognized one of them as Deaf Smith of the Texas spy company. My exhaustion suddenly forgotten, I ran toward the men, waving my arms.

They galloped right past me, obviously in a hurry.

"Please!" I shouted as they passed. "Mr. Smith! The Texan army! Where—?"

"Straight ahead! A quarter mile."

A quarter of a mile. I began to run.

The man on sentry duty remembered seeing me at Groce's. "Our men are up ahead there, all through that grove. Just be sure to keep going straight. Over southeast a way, you'd run smack-dab into Santa Anna."

Hastily, I thanked him, and again I broke into a run. After making several inquiries for Jeremy, I was finally directed to him, found him sitting under a live oak tree. He looked up, jumped to his feet.

"Cassie! You show up at the oddest times! What on earth—"

"Oh, Jeremy, you've got to help me, please! It's Felipe. Will said he was coming here, to join Houston, and I was afraid Asa—! Will's all right. Felipe saved him, and he told me—" I was babbling incoherently, but I couldn't stop. The words continued to tumble out meaninglessly. The fear that had driven me to the edge of my endurance and beyond suddenly began to choke me, made my words come out between sobs. Had I arrived in time? I kept talking, afraid to stop, afraid if I did Jeremy would shake his head sadly and tell me I was too late.

When I paused for breath, he smiled softly. "He's here, Cassie. He got in this morning. I've explained everything to Asa. At first, he didn't believe it, but now I think he does. I've got a couple of men watching him, just in case."

"You're still not sure about him, then? Oh, Jeremy, take me to him! I had better see him at once. I can tell him what Will told me, and I know he'll understand how hard Felipe tried to save them all."

"Come on." As we walked, he asked me how I got there, and I told him, told him about the horse and about the soldiers back on the other side of Vince's bridge. "They're Cos's men, I'm sure. Do you think Houston knows?"

"Everybody knows they've arrived, though I'm not sure that anybody is sure it's Cos's men. We saw them come in this morning. Houston put out the word that it was just Santa Anna walking his men around in a circle to make us think he's got reinforcements."

"But why?"

"I guess for the same reason he threw those two Mexicans in jail back at Gonzales when they told us about the fall of the Alamo, and branded Peter Kerr as a spy when he told us about Fannin's capture. I think he's afraid the men will panic and run."

"But he's the one who always runs—"

Jeremy said testily, "I don't think he'll ever be accused of that again, after today. I'm sure he means to attack. God knows, we could never find a better day for it. With our muzzle loaders, we couldn't possibly take on Santa Anna in the rain."

"Do you think we have a chance?" I asked anxiously. "With those reinforcements—"

"As good a chance as we'll ever have. We've got maybe seven, eight hundred effectives. I overheard Deaf Smith talking to Houston, and he figures with the reinforcements Santa Anna's got maybe about fifteen hundred or so."

"Deaf Smith? I passed him a while back. He was riding fast the other way."

"He's gone to burn Vince's bridge. That's another thing Houston isn't telling anybody."

"He's going to destroy it?" I gasped. "But why? What if we have to retreat?"

"I don't know what Houston's reasoning is. Probably he figures the Mexicans might get more reinforcements." He gave a wry laugh. "We got seven or eight came in this morning. Santa Anna got five hundred."

"What about Lynch's Ferry?"

"It's not there. And there's nobody likely to get across the San Jacinto River or Buffalo Bayou by swimming."

"So we're bottled up here."

He nodded and said grimly, "And so is Santa Anna."

We found Asa, and I was finally able to convince him that Felipe had been trying to help the men at Goliad. As anxious as I was to see Felipe, I was glad that I had taken the time to talk to Asa myself, because I had seen the doubt in his eyes when I started to tell him. Gradually, it was dispelled, when I told him what Will had told me.

"Now I'll take you to Felipe," Jeremy said as we walked away. "I'm glad you talked to Asa. In a battle, it would be hard to tell if a bullet came from in front or behind. . . . Come on. This way."

I shuddered. "How is he, Jeremy? Will was half-starved—"

"Felipe must have been, too, from the amount of breakfast he put away after he came in. Sherman captured a

613

flatboat yesterday, and for the first time in days, we had bread and coffee."

"Santa Anna's supplies?"

He laughed. "Probably some he'd stolen somewhere. We were only stealing them back."

"But Felipe—If there should be a fight—He must be weak—"

"You know he'd never hear of being left out. It's important to him, Cassie, more important to him than his life."

"I know," I said, trying to talk past the lump in my throat. "I know."

Jeremy stopped, motioned to a sleeping form. "There he is. You can ask him yourself what he intends to do. You'd better wake him soon. I suspect Houston's going to call us to parade any time now. There aren't many hours of daylight left."

I stood on tiptoe, kissed his cheek. "Thank you, dear Jeremy. Thank you."

Then I turned and went to the place Felipe lay, and I forgot Jeremy, forgot Asa, forgot everything and everyone else as I dropped to the ground beside my sleeping husband. He had rolled himself in a blanket, and was sleeping soundly. He was unshaven, and his face was much thinner, and pale. I sat there, watching him silently, savoring the joy of knowing that I had only to reach out and touch him, had only to wake him to have him smile at me, to hear my name on his lips. We were together again, after six months of sorrow and doubt and heartbreak.

Six months, it had been. Six long months since he had thought he was sending me away from danger by getting me out of Bexar. But we had both discovered since that day that there was no place in all of Texas free of danger. Uncle Todd had been right It had not been possible to run from it, or to hide from it. It had been in Bexar, in Gonzales, in Papa's house, in the swamps, on the roads, everywhere—waiting, like a bird of prey, to swoop down out of the sky and pounce unexpectedly in a flurry of beating wings

614

and slashing talons. Felipe and I could never escape the danger, because we ourselves were a part of it, our identities woven inextricably with that of Texas, and whatever threatened it threatened us as well.

I still had not awakened Felipe when Jeremy returned, bringing some buckskins. He dropped them on the ground near me, put a rifle, powder horn, patch bag, and a handful of bullets on top of them. "These clothes belong to a man hurt in the cavalry skirmish yesterday afternoon. They might be a little small. Houston's ordered us to parade. I'm sure he means to attack."

"I'll wake Felipe."

"He'd never forgive either of us if you didn't." He pointed up ahead to the trunk of a tree at the front of the grove. "See that tree? It's the highest one around. It's been our lookout spot. Santa Anna's over that rise yonder. You can see his camp from the upper branches. I got this for you to use." He removed a spyglass from around his neck and handed it to me. "Tell Felipe to be out in front in about five minutes." He started to walk away.

"Jeremy—"

He turned, waited.

"Thank you for everything you've done for us. We owe you so much. You let Felipe explain, kept him safe—"

He smiled. "I never should have doubted him. I should have had faith in him, like you had."

*No,* I thought, *not like I had!* But I smiled. "I knew Felipe couldn't have been a part of Goliad." Never would Felipe or anyone else suspect that I had doubted him.

When Jeremy had left, I leaned over and kissed Felipe's cheek, called his name softly. What infinite pleasure it gave me just to say his name! I repeated it again.

Suddenly, his eyes flew open. He stared at me, then looked around, as though he had forgotten, momentarily, where he was.

"Cassie!" He started to smile at me, but his smile suddenly changed to a look of horror. "What are you doing

615

here? You must go! There's probably going to be a battle soon. Santa Anna might attack—"

"He won't have a chance. Houston is going to attack him, in just a few minutes. Jeremy brought you these clothes, and a rifle." I watched him sit up, my eyes brimming with tears. We had found each other again, but we would have only a few minutes together before he would be going into the uncertainty of battle. Maybe the next few precious minutes would be all we would ever have. With a little cry, I threw myself into his arms.

Roughly, he pulled me into the circle of his arms, and the stubble on his chin scratched my forehead as he hugged me so tightly I could scarcely breathe. "Oh, Cassie, *mi alma,* has the whole world gone mad? My mother at the Alamo, and now you here, where there's sure to be a battle. Why are you here? Why have you come?" His lips brushed my forehead, my eyes, my cheeks, and our faces were damp with tears.

"I had to. I saw Will, and he told me you'd gone to find Houston. I knew Asa wouldn't let you explain. He saw you there, at Goliad."

"I tried to stop Portilla!" he cried, then poured out his anguish. "I couldn't stop him! Orders conflicting with Santa Anna's had come in from Urrea, and still I couldn't convince him to disobey Santa Anna! He must obey *El Presidente,* he insisted. I should have been able to save them all. I should have figured out a way, but I couldn't!"

"Oh, my dearest love, don't blame yourself for Santa Anna's sins! You tried. You risked your life trying. You did all you could. No one could have stopped him."

"I could have seen sooner what he was!"

"You were fighting for an ideal, for unity—"

"No, Cassie. That was only an excuse, to delude myself. I was fighting for the Varga grant, and for a return to the past. But there's no going back, and no tract of land is worth a man's soul. You can't imagine how free I feel, now that I've reconciled myself to its loss." He drew back, and for a minute we looked deeply into each other's eyes, and we smiled. There was no longer a war between us; it was all around us, but not between us. Then our arms closed tightly around each other, and our lips met.

"The battle," I whispered reluctantly. "Houston has ordered the men to parade."

The moment was over. He released me and stood up, hastily putting on the buckskins Jeremy had brought. "You must get away from here! You should never have come! You mustn't be foolish, like my mother!"

"It was what your mother wanted, Felipe. She sent Andrew with me, and she went back, to be with Papa. She wanted to be with him, just as I want to be with you."

"You must leave—"

"I can't. Vince's bridge is burned by now, I'm sure. Jeremy told me. It's one of Houston's foolish secrets."

"But where will you go?"

I pushed myself to my feet, forced a smile to my lips, knowing I mustn't let him suspect how I feared the outcome of the approaching battle. "I'll be up in that tall tree almost straight ahead." I pointed. "Jeremy gave me a spyglass and said I could see Santa Anna's camp from the upper branches. I'll be watching. And I'll be waiting for you under that tree when you come back."

He hung the powder horn over his shoulder, stuffed the bullets into his pocket. "And what if we lose? If we do, you know that none of us will come back. Santa Anna will be sure to have his best fighters here with him." He picked up the patch bag, the rifle.

I tried to sound blithely confident. "Jeremy said the odds are only about two to one. Everyone knows one Texas rifleman is worth ten Mexican soldiers. And you, my love, are a Texan. You always have been." I smiled at him, unable to hold back the tears.

We moved together in one last hasty embrace, clinging together desperately. And then he released me, and was gone.

Even as I watched him walk away, I knew he was no longer thinking of me, but of the coming battle. He

617

threaded his way through the trees, the rifle resting lightly in his hand. The buckskins Jeremy had brought for him were too short in both the sleeves and the trousers, and for a minute I was reminded of the first time I had seen him, the day he had found me trespassing on the Varga grant. He had been dressed in buckskins that he had outgrown and then, as now, he had carried a rifle in just such a way, and walked lightly through the woods ahead of me, moving easily, as I scrambled to keep up with him. Ten years ago, that had been. How much living, and loving, and learning we had done since then!

I continued to watch him, saw two other men come abreast of him. They all continued together, talking easily. He was one of us; he had been accepted without question. Another man, another rifle against Santa Anna and tyranny. As he reached the edge of the grove, he turned and waved and smiled. And then he was gone.

The woods all around me had grown still. I picked up the spyglass Jeremy had left for me and moved toward the hollow in front of the grove, where the men were forming themselves into companies. I looked in both directions for Felipe, but I couldn't pick him out from the others.

I watched the men in wonder. Could this be the same motley army I had known, the group of dissidents who had, when I had last seen them, been on the verge of revolt? It was hard to connect those grumbling, dissatisfied malcontents with the men I was watching form themselves silently and efficiently into companies. Each man seemed to know where he belonged and moved into place quickly. Perhaps Jeremy had been right when he insisted that the time up at Groce's was not wasted, that it was needed to instill discipline and order into the diverse group of men that had gathered around Houston.

My eyes traveled beyond the men, across the prairie in front of them. Santa Anna was there somewhere, just a mile or so away. Was he, too, parading his men, preparing for battle? Or was he lying in wait, his men firmly entrenched, guns loaded, cannons poised, ready to annihilate

Houston and his men, to rid themselves forever of the threat of the rebel Texans?

I saw why Jeremy had told me about the tree. The prairie rose in a slope, hiding the Santanistas from view at ground level. But the threat of his closeness was all the more fearsome for not being visible.

A voice shouted, "Trail arms!"

The command echoed down the line as it was relayed from one group to the next. There was no other sound, no voice raised in protest or complaint, no dispute of the command as the line began to move unhesitatingly, unwaveringly forward. The men walked briskly out of the little hollow onto the prairie ahead.

Behind me and to my right, the sun was already low in the sky. It was about four o'clock. One engagement only, Houston had said we could afford. This, then, would be it. Before the sun set, the outcome of the battle would be resolved. But how much would the battle itself really resolve, I wondered? Even if, by some miracle, we managed to win, how decisive would our victory be? The Mexicans had many other troops in Texas. Gaona, Filisola, Urrea—where were they, with all the men under their commands? Only if we suffered defeat would the coming battle be conclusive, for we had no more men to form into an army. There would be victory or death this day, for if Houston had thought to cut off Santa Anna's retreat, he had also cut off our own.

I watched the men march forward, closing the distance between themselves and Santa Anna's camp. On the left, some of our men disappeared into a tree island. I hung the spyglass around my neck and went to the tree Jeremy had indicated, found it had been notched and pegged for easier climbing. I pulled myself up into its limbs, as high as I dared. I worked my way out on a limb until it began to sway perilously. Carefully, I steadied myself by draping my arm over a branch just above, and raised the spyglass to my eye.

On the left, our men were just emerging from the stand

of timber. The Texas cavalry—how few mounted men we had!—was on the right flank. Between the two flanks moved the main army. The men seemed to be spread out all over the prairie. In most places, they were advancing two deep. Near the center of our line I could see the Twin Sisters, and ahead of each was a swarm of men. Even at that distance, I could detect the way they had to strain to pull the heavy cannons along. And while they pulled, others pushed.

Somewhere in that line of men who looked, even through the spyglass, not much bigger than an army of ants, was Felipe.

I saw Houston near the center of the line, riding back and forth in front of the others on his big white horse. I remembered that he had had the horse at Groce's. I thought of all the times he had been derided as a coward, and for the first time, I wondered. No cowardly general would so readily identify himself to the enemy, inviting enemy fire.

The men moved on, crested a small rise directly in front of the Mexican camp. I waited, watching, listening for the battle to begin.

Suddenly, puffs of smoke belched from the Twin Sisters, and their booming reverberations echoed over the prairie.

The battle was joined.

From that point on, it was difficult to see anything, more difficult still to guess the significance of what I could see.

I kept straining my eyes through the glass, trying to make them pierce through the haze, but it was no use, for the smoke had become thicker still. I could only listen and wonder.

And pray. For Felipe. And for Texas.

Again, I heard cannon, and then they spoke no more. Why, I wondered? The cannons were silent, but still sporadic rifle fire continued.

The strain of trying to tell what was happening combined with exhaustion to overwhelm me, and I started to lower myself to the ground. As I climbed down, I continued to hear, less frequently, the occasional crack of rifle fire. The battle, up ahead in the Mexican encampment, was surely over.

Had we won or lost? And what of Felipe?

A chill passed over me, and I realized that the sun was no longer shining on any part of the prairie. The day was ending. Soon I would know. I considered moving closer to the battle, but I was too weary, and too afraid of what I might discover. Who had won? I sank to the ground, leaning against the trunk of the tree, my eyes fastened on the direction of the battlefield, watching for some sign. Fear gnawed at me as I sat there, forever, waiting. The sun was gone and the light grew dim.

At last a column of men appeared from the timber ahead. Anxiously, I tried to see if they were Mexicans or Texans. I supposed I should run and hide, but if Santa Anna had emerged the victor, there would be no hope for Felipe or any of the others. And I was weary of running away from Santa Anna. If he had captured or killed Felipe, then I would have nothing to live for. Let him take me, too.

In the dimming light, it was difficult to distinguish one color from another. Were the men of the approaching column wearing buckskins or the uniform of Mexico? As they drew closer, I eyed them with increasing alarm. They approached, closer still, and fear became dread certainty. The men were wearing the uniform of Mexico.

A sob choked me. We had lost, irrevocably. And that meant I had lost Felipe as well. Every man who had fought for Texas was either dead or in grave danger. But even if the others did have a chance, in the unlikely event that Santa Anna would relent and spare their lives, Felipe could not hope to benefit from such clemency. He was a deserter from the Mexican army, had gone over to the enemy, and the penalty for that was death.

I should run, I knew. But without Felipe, of what value was my own life?

The column was getting close. A figure detached itself

from the double line of Mexican soldiers, and it looked as though he was dressed in buckskins, and was carrying a rifle. I frowned in puzzlement, wondering why the Mexicans had let one of our men keep his rifle.

I watched the figure approaching. He was running, and he was tall and slender, and the way he ran, the way he carried his rifle so easily—

Felipe! Only he could run like that, with his feet scarcely skimming the ground. But how could it be that he was running toward me? How would the Mexicans permit it, when they were almost to our camp?

Puzzled, I looked at the column again, noted that there was a rider alongside. Other buckskin-clad figures began to detach themselves from the file, and every one of them carried a rifle. For the first time, I noted the dejected head-down shuffle of the Mexican column, and realization swept through me, washing away despair.

"Prisoners!" I gasped aloud. The Mexicans were not coming to our camp as victors, but were being brought back by our Texans as prisoners! We had won!

Perhaps there would be other battles, and perhaps defeat lay somewhere ahead. But all that mattered was that in this battle, on this day, victory was ours.

And what mattered most of all was that Felipe was running toward me, rapidly covering the distance between us. He had passed the head of the column, and had seen me, and was waving.

"Felipe!" I cried joyously. And I repeated his name again and again and again. My weariness lifted in a rush as I effortlessly pushed myself to my feet and started to run toward him. I was not aware of my feet even touching the ground as I ran to close the gap between us.

# Epilogue

It could not have happened, but it did. Santa Anna brought approximately seventy-five hundred troops to Texas. The Texan force seldom totaled more than one-tenth of that number.

How could so few have routed so many? Mexicans and Texans alike were hampered by the difficulties of traveling over the muddy rain-soaked ground. The Mexicans had the added problem of being totally unfamiliar with the terrain, and they were further frustrated by the effectiveness of the hastily formed Texas navy, which successfully prevented them from receiving supplies by ship.

Too, the quality as well as the enthusiasm of many of the Mexican soldiers was questionable. They had short-range breech-loading guns, which had such a tremendous "kick" to them that the men hesitated to put them to their shoulders to sight. Not only were their guns ineffective, but many of the Mexican troops were Indians torn from their homes against their will, and certainly not adequately trained in warfare.

The Texans were undisciplined, and they had few professional soldiers among them, but they were composed of sharpshooters from Texas and the United States—mostly the latter—who could easily pick off a bird at two hundred yards.

The final battle, the decisive encounter which wiped out all the previous disastrous defeats suffered by the Texans, involved seven hundred and eighty-three Texans and fifteen hundred Mexicans, and lasted less than twenty minutes. In those few moments, Sam Houston, who even on that very day had been scorned and mocked by his own men as a coward for avoiding an encounter with the Mexicans, was entered into the annals of history as a hero. He had two horses shot out from under him during the battle, and suffered a bad wound in his ankle.

The Mexicans were taken totally by surprise, and many of them didn't know the Texans were upon them until they heard the shouts of "Remember the Alamo!" and "Remember Goliad!" For many of them, it was the last thing they ever heard. Long after the battle had ended, the men of the Texan army continued to extract revenge for the brutality of the Alamo and the treachery of Goliad. In their fury, the Texans resorted to using their rifles as war clubs, and many a rifle was broken over the head of some hapless Mexican soldier. The Texans relentlessly pursued the survivors, and it was only with difficulty that the officers were able, at last, to stop the carnage. The Mexicans had six hundred and thirty killed to the Texas army's eight, and seven hundred and thirty prisoners were taken. A few escaped, either by swimming Vince's Bayou or circling around the end of it.

Santa Anna was—literally—caught napping when the Texans attacked. In his haste to force the settlers from Texas, the self-styled "Napoleon of the West" had made the foolish mistake of isolating himself and the segment of his army under his personal command from the rest of his troops. It was his capture that made the Texan victory so significant. He was found near the burned-out bridge over Vince's Bayou the morning after the battle, and claimed to be a Mexican private. His own men recognized "*El Presidente*" when he was brought back to the Texan camp as a prisoner, thus ending his masquerade. It was not till some months later that Santa Anna was freed and returned to Mexico. He was not to be kept down for long by a single mistake, and he continued to dominate Mexican politics off and on for nineteen years.

Later that year, Sam Houston was elected president of the Republic of Texas. Stephen F. Austin held a subordinate post under him, and died eight months after the battle of San Jacinto.

In 1845, Texas was annexed by the United States.